GONE TOMORROW

GONE TOMORROW

Jane Gurney

BANTAM BOOKS

LONDON · NEW YORK · TORONTO · SYDNEY · AUCKLAND

GONE TOMORROW
A BANTAM BOOK : 0 553 40408 3

First publication in Great Britain

PRINTING HISTORY
Bantam edition published 1997

Set in 10/11pt Adobe Times by Kestrel Data, Exeter, Devon.

Bantam Books are published by Transworld Publishers Ltd,
61–63 Uxbridge Road, London W5 5SA,
in Australia by Transworld Publishers (Australia) Pty Ltd,
15–25 Helles Avenue, Moorebank, NSW 2170,
and in New Zealand by Transworld Publishers (NZ) Ltd,
3 William Pickering Drive, Albany, Auckland.

Reproduced, printed and bound in Great Britain by
Cox & Wyman Ltd, Reading, Berks.

Acknowledgements

So many libraries and individuals helped me with information that it's impossible to acknowledge them all individually. But I'd particularly like to thank:

Irene Poulton for her extensive knowledge about farming in Hampshire; *Aeroplane Monthly* magazine for articles about Cobham's Flying Circus; Alexine Crawford for information about her father, Colonel Strover, and the 'Every Little Helps' movement; Elfriede Windsor (née Stiefel) for memories of being a 'Kinder Transport' refugee; Win Morgan for her happy recollections of 1930s Farnham; the *Surrey Advertiser* for printing my letter about Cobham's National Aviation Day visits to Guildford, and the readers who responded; Assistant Chief Constable Tom Wood for details of sentencing policy for crimes in the 1930s; Neil Redgrove and Jack Weller, owners and restorers of a Ransome threshing machine, for their expertise; and my fellow author Gilda O'Neill for much encouragement and, occasionally, much-needed nagging to get the novel finished.

Part 1

1933

1

'*The Lord gave, and the Lord hath taken away,*' the vicar said from his pulpit. In the central aisle, the pallbearers had set the flower-strewn coffin on to its waiting trestle. Beside it, the widow sat in the front pew with her head held high, features blank.

From her expression, Louella Ramsay might have been listening to any normal Sunday service before walking home across the heath to lunch at Medlar House, instead of to the funeral service of her husband of fifteen years. Her clothing, in traditional black, had come from her own seamstresses – Louella included ladies' fashions among her range of business interests. Her suit, enviably elegant, was of fine jersey wool and her hat was low-crowned with a wide brim, accentuating her natural grace.

'*O death, where is thy sting? O grave, where is thy victory?*'

It was not apparent to the casual eye that Louella, listening to the words of Corinthians I, was experiencing sorrow; but inside she was aching and stunned, and dreadfully afraid of the feelings that would follow this frozen state in which her husband's sudden death had immersed her. She had known grief before and it had almost destroyed her.

She had married Hector Ramsay in the last year of the Great War, while still racked with sorrow and rage over the loss of her first husband, a young soldier; feelings made worse by the knowledge that Robert hadn't died by any enemy action, but by the bullets of a firing squad.

Hector had been of a different social class and, at fifty, twice her age; but gentle and kind, and that had been important at the time. Later she had come to love him – not

9

as she had loved Robert, in a way which had been part physical and part a joyful meeting of young spirits, but genuinely for all that.

She had not been very demonstrative towards Hector and probably he had never known just how much she cared for him. Now he never would. Teeth clenched, shoulders stiff, she fought back any visible signs of the regrets and the tears.

The church was naturally dark but beyond the stained-glass windows, storm clouds had been gathering while the mourners filed into the nave, and now they could hear the first rumbles of thunder. Beside the widow, Daisy Griffin, sister of Louella's first husband Robert, touched the back of her hand gently against that of her own husband and glanced up at him. Will's face was sober, but she knew that he remembered another storm breaking over this church at another, happier time, when he had come home on leave from the Western Front and told her that he loved her.

Beside Will and Daisy in the second pew, the younger Griffins sat with bowed heads and an uneasy solemnity. Hector Ramsay had been 'Uncle Hector', but only eighteen-year-old Harriet had met him more than a handful of times. To Jackie and Rob he had been little more than a source of expensive Christmas presents. To Harriet, her aunt's protégée, he had seemed amiable but shy. She wished she had known him better. She wished she had known what to say to Aunt Louella before the funeral. She wished the young man who had just come in, late, would stop looking at her.

The two rows of pews flanking the central aisle were crowded, because Hector Ramsay had lived in Blackheath for a long time and was well liked within the community. The newcomer had stalked along the side aisle to install himself in one of the few vacant spaces. It happened to be at the end of the pew opposite that in which Harriet was sitting.

Having been endowed by nature with red hair, green eyes and a broad-shouldered, slim-waisted figure, she was used to attention from young men and mostly their scrutiny did not bother her. But this one was different. He was wiry and dark-haired like Will, her father, but with an added something: a kind of hungry intensity. Almost satanic, that intensity. It made her shiver. His clothes were shabby and the gaze that he directed towards Harriet was not the normal admiration, it contained a distinct element of animosity. She focused her eyes on the back of Aunt Louella's tailored jacket and ignored him with determination.

Outside the stained-glass windows, lightning flashed, followed almost immediately by a clap of thunder, then came the steady background thrumming of rain on the leaded roof overhead. The faintly decayed damp-stonework smell of the church intensified.

'*I know that my Redeemer liveth*,' sang the choir. But all Louella Ramsay could think of was that Hector was dead and she was alone again.

By the time the congregation emerged from the church the thunderstorm was over. A string of black cars was lined up along the road outside. As Harriet climbed into the first of the official mourners' cars behind her aunt, she noticed the young man who had sat across the aisle from her in church retrieving a battered bicycle from the roadside. His dark hazel eyes met hers with the same bold stare that had bothered her before and she wondered again who he might be.

As the cortège reached the municipal cemetery two miles east of the church, the storm clouds were breaking up, revealing small patches of blue among the grey; but the wind was chilly, the grass among the graves was sodden and small puddles had collected in the mound of earth that had been excavated for today's interment.

'*Man that is born of a woman hath but a short time to live, and is full of misery. He cometh up, and is cut down, like a flower.*'

Of the two men that Louella had loved, Hector Ramsay had lived for sixty-five years, Robert Colindale for barely twenty-four. There had been no funeral service for Robert, only a hasty shovelling into a grave somewhere on the

11

Somme and a letter, barbaric in its brevity, to tell his wife what had become of him.

'*I am directed to inform you that a report has been received from the War Office to the effect that No.—, Private Robert Joseph Colindale, First Battalion, Queen's Royal West Surrey Regiment, was sentenced after being tried by court martial to suffer death by being shot, and his sentence was duly executed on 7 April 1916.*'

Those were the words of the official communication that had branded her husband a coward and sentenced his family to shame and destitution. The long-buried anguish of that first bereavement had been uncovered by the second, but even at the graveside, Louella could not allow herself to cry; although beside her Daisy, her gentle sister-in-law, was sobbing quietly into a handkerchief. All her life, Louella had survived bad times by being a fighter. She dared not give way now. Her stony, dry-eyed gaze travelled over the faces of the assembled mourners and met that of a black-haired young man with a thin, sardonic face.

Jem. The contract between them had been that he must never come near her unless she sent for him. A wave of anger swept through Louella, bringing her strength. Here was something to deal with, something on which to vent her suppressed energies. She began, even as she scattered soil on the coffin in its grave, to plan precisely what she would say to Jem Wilkins, after the funeral.

'I wish we didn't have to go,' said Daisy Griffin in the drawing room at Medlar House. It was late afternoon. The last of the mourners whose acquaintance with Hector had warranted an invitation to sherry and fruitcake had melted tactfully away, leaving only the Griffins, who had driven up from Hampshire for the occasion.

'. . . But you're needed back at the farm. I know,' said Louella. 'Don't worry. I never expected you to stay on.'

The worried crease between Daisy's eyebrows failed to clear. She absent-mindedly tucked a loose strand of her copper-coloured hair behind her ear in a familiar gesture

12

which reminded Louella suddenly and painfully of the day, more than twenty years ago, when as a young and apprehensive bride-to-be she'd first been introduced to Robert's sister.

You're very welcome in our family, Daisy had said, and in place of the expected handshake had given Louella an impulsive hug that had made her feel exactly that. Daisy hadn't changed much over the years, she was as warm and soft-hearted as ever and you'd hardly guess, to look at her unlined face, that she was the mother of Harriet, half a head taller than her, and of those two big, strapping lads. Louella suppressed a stab of envy. It was absurd that she, Louella Ramsay, with all she'd wrested from life to transform herself into a stylish lady in a grand house, should envy ordinary little Daisy, farmer's wife; and yet she always had.

'Why not come back home with us for a bit?' Daisy suggested. 'I know it's not the kind of comfort you're used to, but you'd be very welcome, you know you would.'

'It's very kind of you, but I think I need to be in my own place tonight, with my own things around me.' The Griffins meant well, Louella reminded herself, but if only they would go away! Their sympathy was becoming increasingly hard to bear. It kept inviting her to give way to the tears she had sworn she would not cry in public.

'Well, if you're sure . . . ? What about if Harry stays on for a day or two?' persisted Daisy.

Louella considered the idea. If, in order to give her sister-in-law peace of mind, she had to accept the enforced company of any of her relations at this time, she supposed it might as well be that of her niece. She and Harriet had the familiarity that Louella had once shared with Daisy but which had faded over the years as their marriages took their lives in different directions. Daisy's daughter, who came on visits to Medlar House whenever she could be spared from home, had a temper that matched her red hair and a sophistication that her mother lacked. Unlike Daisy, she wasn't shocked or hurt or infuriatingly patient when Louella exploded; she merely exploded back . . . which was a consoling thought, because at this moment the widow felt dangerously near to exploding.

'All right. Harry can stay.'

In the background, Harriet struggled to hide her dismay. Of course she must remain at Medlar House if Aunt Louella needed her. But . . . a few days ago, when the news about Hector had not yet reached the farm, she had made an arrangement for this evening about which her parents knew nothing. She hated herself for minding that the death of her uncle had upset her plans. In the midst of tragedy, it seemed shabby and despicable to be regretting the loss of a clandestine rendezvous with a young man called Gavin . . . but she couldn't help it.

'On second thoughts, no. You all have things to do, Harriet included.' Abruptly, Louella changed her mind, leaving Harriet to wonder guiltily whether her aunt had seen that spasm of reluctance on her part.

'I'd be glad to stay,' she said, wishing she could mean it.

'We don't like to leave you on your own, Lou,' protested Daisy.

'You won't be leaving me on my own,' Louella pointed out, with a visible trace of exasperation. 'I shall be attended to screaming point by a manservant, two maids, a cook, a gardener and an odd job boy. And besides,' she added, settling the question, 'like you, I have things to do.'

In the study at Medlar House, on the evening of Hector Ramsay's funeral, the black-haired young man who had made Harriet uneasy in church that afternoon faced the wrath of the widow with sulky bravado.

Jem Wilkins had been here before. The first time, eight years ago, he'd had to argue his way past Everett, who could not imagine that Madam would want anything to do with the nervously aggressive youth with the East End vowels who claimed to be related to the mistress. But Mrs Ramsay, on hearing the heated interchange taking place on her doorstep, had come into the hall to see what was going on, and after a brief discussion with the visitor had admitted him to her study.

When they emerged again, a bare fifteen minutes later, there had been nothing in the cool manner of Louella Ramsay to back up the boy's claim to be 'family'. They had not even shaken hands before he left. And yet he had come again, at irregular intervals of perhaps twice a year, and always by written invitation from Mrs Ramsay, like the one that had summoned him here this evening.

Everett had left Jem Wilkins waiting alone in the marble-tiled hall, not without some disquiet about whether it was wise to do so, while he announced the visitor. He'd made a quick inventory of the ornaments on the console table before he led Jem into the study.

'Mr Wilkins, madam.'

'Thank you, Everett. That will be all.'

Mrs Ramsay did not order sherry, as she would normally for a guest at this time of the evening. Not that this guest was the type to appreciate a glass of Amontillado – beer would be the chosen tipple of someone of his class, Everett estimated, lip curling. That suit the young man wore had seen better days, to put it mildly. Shiny with age and hard wear, it had probably come off a rag-and-bone cart and its original owner had obviously been a man of rather more generous bulk than Jem Wilkins. It hung loosely on his lean frame, trousers belted in at the waist with a scuffed old brown leather belt, over-long sleeves turned back at the wrists. Under it, the striped shirt was collarless.

Altogether, this was not the kind of caller that Everett was normally required to usher into the study at Medlar House. He was more accustomed to seeing off such riff-raff at the tradesmen's entrance, and with scant ceremony. And today of all days, with the master not cold in his grave . . . As the manservant left the room, even the set of his shoulders was eloquently disdainful.

Louella waited until Everett had closed the heavy mahogany door behind him, and for five careful seconds afterwards, before she voiced the question on her mind with controlled venom.

'What the *hell* were you doing at the funeral?'

'I saw the notice in *The Times*,' said Jem.

Louella's eyebrows lifted. '*You* read *The Times*?'

'It was wrapped round some pigs' trotters, as it happens.'

'I didn't even know you could read.'

'I picked it up,' Jem said laconically. 'Comes in useful sometimes. And seeing as how it said about your husband having turned his toes up, I thought I'd come to the service, on account of he was family. In a manner of speaking.'

'Hector was nothing to you. And you don't go to funerals for fun. You're after something. What is it?'

'You don't reckon I've come out of brotherly affection?'

'*Half*-brotherly. And no, I don't. I'm not that much of a fool.'

It was true; she wasn't, Jem Wilkins acknowledged ruefully. If he'd hoped that the newly bereaved Louella was going to be a slightly softer touch than her usual granite self, he'd have to abandon that hope. She stood behind her desk, deliberately keeping her visitor on his feet and at a distance. Behind her trim figure in the black silk *crêpe* dress – trust Lou to look smart, even in mourning – the mirror above the fireplace reflected dark hair pinned in an old-fashioned chignon and the diamond clasp on the good pearl necklace that she wore. It also reflected the cryptic twist of Jem's lips as he faced her.

'No, family feeling doesn't enter into it with you and me, does it, Lou? Never has.'

'Why should it? I hardly know you. I left home when you were small.'

'Left us to it. Got away. Smart move. I wish,' said Jem, 'that I could've done the same. Specially as it turned out so well for you.' He let his gaze travel over the antique furniture, the crystal chandelier that dangled from the moulded plaster ceiling rose, the opulent drapes at the window and the tall mahogany cupboards flanking the fireplace, with their glazed doors behind which Meissen and Derby

16

figurines testified to the current financial status of his hostess.

'We've been through this before,' said Louella coldly. 'I have neither the time nor the inclination to rake over old coals. I would remind you that our arrangement forbids you to approach me unless I send for you. You'd do well to remember that, if you want to go on profiting from our contract. However . . . I suppose it's work you want? I assume, since you were loitering in the churchyard today – in direct contravention of our agreement – that you are not yet employed elsewhere?'

Neither the time nor the inclination . . . direct contravention of our agreement . . . She might have been born a toff considering the way she'd picked up the grand manner, Jem thought, with grudging admiration. Over the years since he'd first come knocking at the door of Medlar House, she'd become noticeably harder and sharper and her language more high-flown. He favoured her with a repeat of the twisted grin, with no humour in it.

'What's the figures? Nearly three million on the dole? No, I'm not yet "employed elsewhere",' he said bitterly. 'Jobs're harder to come by than diamonds in a desert. I can survive a bit of a lean time, but I've a mother to consider as well as myself. *Our* mother,' he reminded her, pointedly.

'Well, then . . .' Louella ignored the last comment. 'As it happens, I do have a task for you.' She opened a drawer of her desk and took out an unsealed envelope. It was stuffed with folded banknotes. But when she held it out across the tooled leather surface of the desk, Jem made no move to take it. Instead, he put his hands into his pockets.

'The usual, is it?'

'Not entirely,' Louella said. She put the envelope down on the desk, confident that despite his show of indifference, Jem needed the money and would soon have to acknowledge that he did. 'This time I want you to stay in the area for a while and keep up the pressure. Use your imagination – I don't care what you do as long as it gives the man trouble. Report back to me on the after-effects. And keep your ears open. I want you to tell me what he's up to now, what his current business investments are, what his problems may be. I've included extra cash to take account of the time that will take.'

Jem thought about it. 'Won't be easy,' he said, 'finding an excuse to be about in October. Would've been better a few weeks ago in the hopping season, that's when there's work for incomers round Farnham. If I turn up there, I'll stand out. And I won't get hired.'

'I can get you farmwork,' said Louella. 'General labouring on a dairy farm, just over the border into Hampshire. I have a connection there.'

'What kind of a connection?'

'You don't need to know that.'

'Oh, but I do,' Jem said softly. 'If I'm to do your dirty work again, Lou, I want you to fill in some details this time. This Brownlowe character you've got it in for, what did he do to you?'

'That's my affair.'

'But it's me that's sticking my neck out on these little commissions, and the more I do, the higher the chances are that I'll get caught. The odd bit of fire-raising and then straight home on the train to London, that's one thing. If I'm going to be down there longer, getting my face noticed, I want to know who I'm up against. And if I'm going to be using some other tool of yours for a cover, I want to know what kind of a hold it is that you have on *him*.'

Louella faced her visitor for a long moment, eyes narrowed. Then she shrugged her shoulders and reopened the drawer in front of her, tossing the envelope of banknotes back into it.

'I'm not going into explanations. If you don't want the work, I'll find someone who does.'

Jem, the half-brother she barely remembered, from the sordid and violent family background she wanted only to forget, had no need to know the basis of her hatred for Rupert Brownlowe. In 1916, as the widow of a man shot for cowardice, when even the sparse Separation Allowance

18

for soldiers' wives was cut off, she had been pregnant, destitute and desperate. With her sister-in-law Daisy, and Daisy's baby Harriet, she had been forced to apply to the Poor Law Guardians for help and Rupert Brownlowe, in his capacity as a Guardian, had refused it.

He had told her that it would not be right to put Robert's dependents on a par with those of decent men. Louella could still remember how she had cried out at those words; had said she'd rather starve than take the charity of this cold, pitiless man. And he had said, 'As it happens, my charity is not on offer. Starve away.'

Well, she hadn't starved. She had come to London with Daisy and Harriet, and somehow they had survived; but her son, Robert's baby that was his last gift to her, had died within an hour of his birth. She'd always blamed Brownlowe for that. Danny would have survived, she told herself bitterly, if he'd been born stronger, of a well-nourished mother.

Later there had been her marriage to Hector . . . and in time, revenge. It had become an absorbing pastime, the punishing of Rupert Brownlowe with steady drips of 'misfortune' like the Chinese water torture.

When the adolescent Jem had appeared on her doorstep eight years ago with a frank demand for money, her first instinct had been to turn him away, along with the memories he represented. But then she had recognised that they could be useful to one another. If he could track her down at Medlar House, with her new surname and new social standing, he was not without intelligence and enterprise. So they'd entered into their contract: Jem would keep quiet about the connection between them and stay away from the Blackheath house except when specifically sent for. In return, she would pay him a regular amount per year and from time to time, she would give him a chance to earn extra money. And he hadn't balked at the ways in which he was required to earn it.

Louella knew enough about his childhood to understand the black side of his character; it was, after all, the life she'd escaped from herself, and it gave you little enough to survive on except cunning. From what she'd gathered about Jem's adult life, liking to settle old scores was a tendency they shared. So periodically, when she had time to spare, she gave the matter of Rupert Brownlowe her attention and Jem carried out her instructions efficiently, partly for the money she paid him and partly, she suspected, because he enjoyed inflicting damage – there was a deep well of savagery inside Jem.

Now, in the aftermath of Hector's death, Louella needed a distraction. She intended to turn the screws on Rupert Brownlowe.

Jem was still facing her on the far side of the desk, eyes black with hostility. He was going to have to back down and he hated it.

'I never said I didn't want the work. I just said I could do it better if I knew more.'

'I want Brownlowe ruined,' Louella said. 'That's all the explanation you need.'

'If you say so. You're paying.' Jem conceded the point and Louella retrieved the envelope of money from the drawer and passed it over. He counted the contents.

'Enough for you, is it?' Louella asked sarcastically.

'It'll do,' said Jem. 'Clever man, is he?'

'No, he's a fool. A self-important bigot. You'll have no trouble outwitting him.'

'Right. What about this farmer in Hampshire, then? Any harm in telling me a bit about him? His name, for a start?'

'Will Griffin.'

'You sure he'll take me on?'

Suddenly, Louella was tired of sparring. She wanted Jem out of her house, and exhaustion blurred her caution. 'Will's wife Daisy is the sister of Robert, my first husband. Daisy's daughter Harriet – well, that doesn't matter. I provided most of the capital for their farm, so if I tell Will Griffin to hire you, he'll hire you.'

'Does he know about this vendetta of yours?'

'No. It won't matter if you're careful. I'll write you a letter of introduction. How soon can you go?'

'In a day or two. I've something to take care of first,' said Jem. He watched Louella as she uncapped her inkwell and dipped a pen. 'Better tell him to take on two of us, while you're at it.'

'Two?' Louella queried sharply.

'Her name's Kitty.' Suddenly the corners of Jem's mouth curved upwards and his hazel eyes sparkled in a smile that was pure mischief, devoid of malice. 'She's my lady friend.'

The idea of Jem with a woman took Louella by surprise, though on reflection she supposed it was only natural. How old was he now? Twenty-three? When she'd left home in 1913 he'd been about three years old, a malnourished brat with a shell-shocked expression and the tracks of tears almost permanently marking his dirty face under the tousle of black hair. Not that she had wanted to remember him any more than the rest of her background. Memories like that you buried as deep as possible and all she needed to know about her half-brother was that he was discreet, reliable and ruthless. But now there came a glimpse of this other, unexpected, side to him: the appealing child. Louella could see that in his boyish moments Jem – with his lean, lithe figure, his watchful dark hazel eyes, his air of bravado and the sudden upward winging of the corners of his mouth in that smile – could be very attractive to women . . . but she pitied any woman who'd succumbed to that attraction. Because Jem was fundamentally evil. Why else would she use him? As he'd dryly pointed out, family feeling didn't enter into their dealings at all.

She signed and blotted her letter and passed the sealed envelope to Jem.

'There. And now . . .' she moved to the bell-pull beside the door and gave the woven material a sharp tug. 'I imagine you have arrangements to make.'

'You haven't asked about Mam,' said Jem.

'How is she?' Louella said, after a pause.

'Sozzled with gin, mostly, but it keeps her happy.'

'You shouldn't let her—'

'It's all that keeps her going.'

A rap at the door terminated the discussion.

'Mr Wilkins is leaving, Everett,' said Louella. 'Come back when you've shown him out, please. I would like a word with you.'

When the manservant returned a few minutes later, she was brisk and to the point.

'If you don't approve of my invited visitors, take the trouble to conceal the fact or find yourself an alternative position where you do approve. Do I make myself clear?'

'Yes, madam,' Everett said, wooden-faced. After he had gone, Louella sat on at her desk, staring unseeingly ahead. She was beginning to ask herself whether she had done an entirely wise thing in letting Jem loose on the Griffins of Welcome Farm. A photograph in a silver frame on her desk attracted her attention and, with it, the memory of today's main event forced itself back into her mind. She walked to the door and locked it. When she returned to her desk, she opened a drawer and carefully placed the photograph inside, face down. Then she laid her head on her crossed arms and for an hour, before her habit of control re-exerted itself, she forgot Jem, forgot Harriet's family and remembered only Hector, who had loved and rescued and protected her; only to leave her, without any warning.

Everett had been at Medlar House since 1924. Even during the interview that led to his appointment, he had recognized that while Hector Ramsay was a Gentleman through and through, Madam wasn't quite the thing. Oh, she spoke well enough and dressed well enough, she'd had the sense to get the right kind of coaching for that, and there was no denying she was as bright as a button, but to Everett's experienced eye it was apparent that Louella was not a Lady born and bred. He had decided to take the post anyway and in the ensuing nine years he had seldom regretted that decision, because the pay and conditions at Medlar House were more than adequate. But there were moments – and today's visit from Jem Wilkins was one of them – when the manservant felt qualms about the wisdom of remaining in the service of Mrs Ramsay.

Someone in her position couldn't afford to risk compromising that position by knowing criminal types – especially now there was no Mr Ramsay to underpin her status. This Wilkins character was a wrong 'un, you could spot it a mile off, and Madam shouldn't be having any truck with his sort. It was all very disquieting.

But as Madam had just made very plain, it wasn't his place to worry about such things. He descended the stairs to the kitchen regions and awarded himself the glass of sherry that Madam hadn't offered to her visitor, to soothe his ruffled feelings.

On the far side of the green, Jem paused to turn his coat collar up against the wind. An ambitious smile twitched at his mouth as he patted the breast pocket of his jacket, where the fat envelope containing Louella's money made a comforting bulge.

Lou had thought, when she'd packed him off to be her instrument of revenge in Hampshire, that he was still in ignorance of her motives for hounding Rupert Brownlowe. Well, she was wrong. She'd never told her half-brother what had happened to Robert Colindale, or about her pregnancy, but Jem knew. He made it his business to know such things. And it was years since, with a mixture of detective work and guesswork, he had deduced the nature of Brownlowe's 'crime' against her.

Tonight, watching Louella's face, he'd seen her eyes narrow and her mouth tighten at the memory of a long-ago confrontation leading to a loss which had not been forgotten or forgiven. For all her grand manners nowadays, she and Jem still shared the fighting spirit and the alley-cat instincts of their slum background. He admired that in her. No, Lou was no fool, except in one respect – she underestimated him. If only she'd come down off her high horse at the beginning

23

and teamed up with him, together they could have taken on the world.

Maybe one day she'd recognize the chance she'd missed. In the meantime, he quite enjoyed watching her queening it over him, deluding herself that she was the winner of their encounters. Nobody won, in the end, when they took on Jem Wilkins.

2

Evening milking at Welcome Farm had been delayed by the Griffins' late return from London, a fact emphasized by the plaintive bellowing of forty-eight cows waiting with distended udders by the field gate. Then for Daisy and Harriet there had been the cooling and churning and, finally, 'doing the dairy dishes' while Will and the boys manhandled the heavy churns on to the wooden platform by the farmyard gate to await collection by the dairy lorry.

'Supper,' said Daisy at last, easing her aching back, hands on hips, as Harriet shut the lid of the sterilizing cabinet in the whitewashed dairy behind the kitchen. 'I asked Allie to stay on for an hour or two this afternoon to make us a beef hotpot. Heaven knows what it'll taste like, but beggars can't be choosers.'

Allie Briggs, who cycled in from Bentley every day, was the home help at the farm, usually hired for mornings only because the household budget wouldn't run to paying her for afternoons as well. She was good-natured, gossipy and slapdash in her methods and Daisy, who as a young girl had been a housemaid for the Brownlowes at Maple Grange, would not normally have trusted her with the cooking. But then, Daisy's training at the Grange had left her with an abiding conviction that if silver wanted polishing or linen bleaching or indeed, if any job needed doing properly, then she was probably the best person to do it. This was a tendency Daisy's family teased her about with love, and which Allie exploited without compunction.

In the kitchen, the hotpot was simmering gently on the cooler side of the range. Daisy wrapped a tea towel round the iron handle on the lid of the pot and investigated the contents.

'Not bad,' she admitted, stirring and tasting. 'At least she remembered the salt this time. Lay the table, will you? The others'll be in as soon as they've finished watering the horses. What's the matter?' she added, because Harriet was standing with head bowed and eyes closed, fingers pressed to her temples.

'I've got a beastly headache, that's all.'

Daisy looked concerned. For Harriet, who was normally so healthy, even a headache seemed ominous. She crossed briskly to the sideboard. Her range of dried herbs for medicinal purposes was kept in a row of brown stoneware jars on the top shelf.

'Wood betany,' she decided. 'A teaspoonful infused in a cup of hot water.' With her right hand she was already setting up the teacup and spooning out the dose, while with her other hand she fished cutlery out of a drawer to lay the table herself, since Harriet wasn't well.

Harriet subsided into a chair and sipped the brew while her mother assembled crockery, salt cellar and home-made bread on the table and brought up a pat of their own pale golden butter from the cool of the larder.

'I'm sorry, Mum. I should be doing that.'

'It's done now. Any better? You do look a bit pale,' said Daisy.

'I think I'm just feeling down because of the funeral.' Harriet carried the empty medicine cup to the kitchen sink. 'I don't want any supper. I'd rather just go up to my room. I'll be all right in the morning.'

Daisy gave her a thoughtful look and for a moment Harriet had an uncomfortable feeling that her mother knew or guessed what really lay behind this headache. But nothing was said and she was able to escape to her bedroom.

Cold water in the ewer on the washstand was left over from that morning but she dared not draw attention to her plans by bringing up a jug of hot water from the kitchen. As she scrubbed the odours of the milking shed away,

26

Harriet thought wistfully of visits to Aunt Louella's London house and the luxury of bathrooms with hot-and-cold laid on. At Welcome Farm nothing had changed since the turn of the century except for Will's installation of a petrol-run generator to power the dairy equipment. It was too expensive to run household electricity by this means so the lighting was still by oil lamps and any hot water for the family was boiled on the kitchen range.

Leaving her dungarees and pullover in a heap on a chair, Harriet slipped a green woollen dress over her head and tugged it straight. It was her only decent dress that wasn't funerals-and-church-on-Sundays black, and Gavin Draycott must be sick of the sight of it by now, but she had nothing else that wasn't strictly functional and hard-wearing for farm work, and a man like Gavin couldn't be expected to take a girl out in working trousers or a hacking jacket.

The green dress had been a birthday present from Aunt Louella last spring and Louella had coupled the gift with an offer of cosmetics and instructions on how to use them, which Harriet had felt obliged to refuse because she knew Daisy would disapprove of what she called 'painting'. But a sweep of colour on her eyelids, echoing the green of the dress, would have been such a help, Harriet thought ruefully. Sometimes she wished that her mother wasn't quite so firmly wedded to the old-fashioned standards of behaviour she'd learned as a girl. In London, Louella had implied, *everybody* painted.

. . . And possibly in London everybody could slip out as the sun set to meet a young man without having to pretend to have a headache in order to do so.

Harriet told herself that she really must arrange a formal meeting between Gavin and her parents. The idea filled her with panic, because once he was introduced to her family it would be bound to come out that she'd known him for weeks, and the prospect of owning up to her deceit was daunting. But the moment would have to be faced sooner or later.

Later.

The second stair from the bottom was liable to creak and Harriet held her breath as she stepped over it, stocking-footed, shoes in her hand. There was still some daylight outside but in the kitchen along the passage the lamps were already lit and their soft light leaked from the open doorway onto the black-and-red quarry tiles of the hall. She could hear the voices of her family gathered around the table and could smell the mouth-watering aroma of the beef hotpot that she'd refused earlier. She wished she'd had the presence of mind to filch some bread and butter from the supper table, but it was too late now . . . and she knew from experience that once she was with Gavin all thought of conditions like hunger would vanish.

'I'll meet you at half past six, at the crossroads,' he had said; but it was nearly a quarter to seven when Harriet arrived, breathless, beside the yellow Austin Swallow, parked on the grass verge under the signpost.

Gavin continued to study the remains of the sunset for ten long seconds before he turned his head. His expression, in profile, was thunderous and Harriet's heart sank.

'You're late,' he said pointedly.

'I'm sorry.' Harriet pushed a slipping hairpin back into her hair, and then another. She'd squandered precious minutes in copying a sophisticated rolled hairstyle from a fashion drawing in the local paper, but then she'd had to run along the lane to make up for lost time and now the roll was threatening to descend about her shoulders.

'You're always late, actually,' Gavin said. 'I'm not used to being kept waiting by the girls I see.'

'Then maybe you'd be better suited with the ones of your sort, the ones who've got nothing better to do all day but get themselves prettied up for a date with you!' Harriet's red hair was a warning of a quick temper. Besides, her headache had not been entirely a sham. A mixture of post-funeral depression and residual qualms about deceiving her parents, coupled with the rush to get ready, had put her in a bad mood, and Gavin's casual reference to the seeing of 'girls', plural, did nothing to sweeten it.

'Certainly my *sort*, as you put it, don't have to scrape the muck of the cowshed off them before they come out,' Gavin retorted. They glared at each other.

'It isn't easy for me to get away.'

'So you keep telling me. If it's so awfully difficult, I sometimes wonder why you bother. Not to mention why *I* bother,' Gavin muttered. 'Where are you going?' he added, hastily, as Harriet turned on her heel and headed quickly back down the lane in the direction of the farm. She didn't reply but strode on, the bias-cut skirt of her dress swinging against her legs as she walked. Gavin scrambled out of the car and ran after her.

'Harriet! Hold on a minute!'

Harriet stumbled into a rut in the road and said a rude word under her breath. It was growing darker by the minute. She was a mile from home with no torch, in unsuitable shoes, and at this rate she would probably fall into a ditch. And the thought of going back and losing the evening with Gavin, after days of anticipation, was almost unbearable. But pride made her walk on.

Gavin caught up with her and seized her by the shoulders, swinging her round. His hands slipped down her arms to her wrists. She tried to pull free, face averted, but the struggle was a token gesture. She was longing for him to say something that would save the evening for them both.

'Don't go. Listen for a moment, will you? I'm sorry I upset you. Don't let's fight. Please understand. I wanted to see you so much. I've been looking forward to it all day, and then you didn't come and I was beginning to think that maybe you weren't going to . . . That's why I was so rude when you came, it was out of relief really. You're so awfully pretty,' said Gavin frankly. 'It does things to a chap, you know.'

There was no denying it, even when sulking like a schoolboy Gavin Draycott was irresistible. The mere sight of him was apt to reduce the normally resolute and capable Harriet to a jelly.

He'd had that effect from the first minute she'd set eyes on him.

She had recorded the event in her diary: *15 September 1933. Today I met a man called Gavin. I think I could fall in love with him. Perhaps I already have . . .*

It had been one of those dazzling autumn mornings, chilly out of the sunlight but with the trees along the lane past the farmhouse a singing mixture of russet and gold against the clear green of the meadows. As she was riding a black mare called Briony to the forge, Harriet had been half distracted by the beauty of the morning and half grimly geared for battle because Briony, who had been sent to Will Griffin at Welcome Farm to be schooled out of her bad habits, had a reputation for tantrums when being shod.

As anticipated, the mare, faced with the heat of the fire and the determined advance of Jeffrey the blacksmith, had recalled previous unpleasant moments at the hands of such a man in such a place, and had snorted and backed away, eyes rolling. Harriet hung on to her bridle and made soothing noises, but without success. She wished her father had been there to work his customary magic on the horse, but he had thought that this time she could manage alone. Unfortunately, Jeffrey did not share Will's faith in her. After two minutes of, *Hold up, there*, and *What's got into you, you varmint?*, in which he had still not succeeded in getting a single worn shoe off the mare, he suggested putting a twitch on Briony.

'No!' Harriet said, sharply. Briony's behaviour was undeniably irritating, but the use of a twitch seemed too harsh for her rider's taste. It subdued a restless horse by slipping a thin string noose around the tip of the animal's muzzle and then twisting the noose tightly around the gathered area of skin. This rendered the horse obedient, but opinions varied as to whether it was a benign or a cruel practice. Harriet inclined towards the latter belief.

'It don't hurt,' said Jeffrey. He rooted about in a pile of equipment on the windowsill and unearthed a piece of wood like the handle of a hammer, with a loop of string attached through a hole drilled in the top.

'No,' Harriet repeated. 'Why would it work, if it doesn't hurt? If you won't shoe her without, I'll have to take her elsewhere.'

'Well, Miss Griffin,' said Jeffrey, sweating and exasperated, 'if *you* can think of any other way to keep her in order . . . ?'

That was the trouble. Harriet couldn't. And it was all very well to threaten to take Briony elsewhere, but the next forge was miles away. Anyway, who would be more patient than Jeffrey, who shod all Will Griffin's horses and wanted to keep the custom?

While she hesitated, a car drew up by the petrol pump installed in the yard. Jeffrey, an astute businessman as well as a competent blacksmith, had recently acknowledged that the car was the transport of the future and had installed the pump in recognition of this fact. Now, glad of the distraction, he hurried out to dispense fuel. In his absence, Harriet delivered a short, despairing lecture to the recalcitrant mare.

'For heaven's sake, Briony, you *have* to be shod, so you might as well settle down and put up with it! It only takes longer if you fight. And I *know* the smell of scorched hoof isn't nice, and I *know* the hissing when he puts the hot shoe on sounds like snakes, but it isn't. So don't be so silly!'

'I gather you're having trouble,' said a male voice behind her, and turning quickly, flushing because she hadn't expected her Briony-talk to be overheard, Harriet saw a tall, fair-haired stranger standing in the doorway.

'She doesn't like the fire,' Harriet said lamely. 'And Jeffrey wants to put a twitch on her. But I don't like twitches.'

'I don't blame you.' The newcomer walked confidently to Briony's shoulder, took hold of her bridle and said calmly,

'Now, let's have no more nonsense from *you*, my girl.' At which point, to Harriet's mingled shame and gratitude, the hitherto jittery mare dropped her head and blew softly into the palm of his hand, as if to apologize for all the trouble she'd caused. She then proceeded to submit with only the lightest of protests to the whole detestable process of being shod. Harriet concluded with disgust that Briony was one of those capricious females who reserve their best behaviour for an attractive male audience.

He certainly *was* attractive. She surreptitiously studied his profile across Jeffrey's bent back while the blacksmith hammered a shoe into place and the newcomer rubbed at the mare's velvet muzzle in a reassuring way. He was in his early twenties, she estimated. With blue eyes and classic bone structure and that very fair hair, he reminded Harriet of an illustration from *Tales of the Greek Heroes*, which she had read at an impressionable age in the library at school. Theseus, that's who he looked like, perfectly capable of slaying the Minotaur and demolishing a giant or two while stealing the heart of Ariadne.

'We haven't met, have we?' the young man asked, when the last of Briony's new shoes had been fitted and Jeffrey was running a brush charged with oil over her neat hooves to finish the job. 'My name's Gavin Draycott. My family has just moved into Hallows.'

'Oh! Then we're neighbours,' said Harriet. Hallows was the grey stone Georgian house whose land adjoined that of the farm. She held out her hand. 'I'm Harriet Griffin, from Welcome Farm.' In the background, Jeffrey was giving her a sharp look – probably because her accent had suddenly become the one that she had picked up on visits to Aunt Louella but discarded at home, which her brothers called 'Harry talking posh'. Well, it was none of Jeffrey's business!

'So you're the Griffin girl.' Gavin Draycott had taken her hand, and now held it for a little longer than strictly necessary. 'I've heard about you,' he said.

'Nothing bad, I hope?'

'On the contrary.'

He smiled, and Harriet became conscious of an acceleration of the heartbeat and a weakness of the legs that was at once dismaying and exciting. She was half-relieved, half-regretful when Jeffrey interrupted the moment with a brisk

32

reminder that he was owed five shillings for the petrol.

'Well . . . I suppose I should be on my way,' Gavin said outside the forge.

'So should I.'

Neither of them moved.

'What a lovely colour your car is,' Harriet said. The coachwork of the car in question, a small two-seater with the hood folded back, was in glowing primrose yellow, with red mudguards. It gave an impression of speed and élan. 'What make is it? I know nothing about cars,' she confessed.

'Austin Swallow. Ever been in one?'

'No, never.' Will Griffin had a big black Rover for family outings and an old Austin for farmwork, which Harriet drove across the fields in the haymaking season with a board tied to its front bumper, pushing the mown and sun-dried hay into heaps ready for rick-building. The Swallow was in an entirely different category.

'They're rather fun. I could take you for a spin some time. If you'd like that.'

Harriet replied decorously that she would enjoy such an experience. Inwardly, she was turning cartwheels.

'How about tomorrow?'

'That would be nice. Will you collect me from home?'

'Better if we meet somewhere. At the crossroads, say. Might be an idea not to mention it at home,' said Gavin.

'Oh. Well, I'm not sure . . .' The norm as Harriet understood it was that when a young man asked you out he ought to call at your house, to be introduced to your parents and vetted for his trustworthiness as an escort.

'I don't like being watched when I'm getting to know someone. Do you?' said Gavin.

Harriet reminded herself that he was from London, where probably things were conducted less formally than in stuffy old Hampshire, that after all he had only suggested a 'spin', which hardly counted as 'going out', and that anyway, at this tense and tentative stage where you had just met somebody, it was better for the time being to evade the concerned scrutiny of parents and the curiosity of younger brothers.

'All right,' she said.

'Tomorrow, then, at the crossroads, at eleven o'clock?'

Harriet calculated. By eleven, she would be clear of the tasks associated with morning milking and might successfully slip away for an hour. If asked afterwards about her absence, she could always say that she had been exercising Briony . . . who must in that case be taken to the crossroads, but could be left in a neighbouring field, tied to a tree . . .

O what a tangled web we weave, When first we practise to deceive!

But surely it was worth it, for Gavin Draycott?

In the ensuing three weeks she'd been in a state of heightened physical awareness which was only just bearable between their meetings. During their snatched encounters she had learned that even Theseus wasn't perfect: he had a temper as quick as her own and flashes of arrogance, and at times he could be downright petulant. He didn't disguise the fact that he regarded his family as being a cut above that of a farmer's daughter . . . and most people would agree with him, Harriet supposed, thinking of the elegance of Hallows beside the workaday shabbiness of Welcome Farm. But it stung her pride all the same. They had sparred verbally from the first day. And yet Gavin's physical appeal was stronger now, if anything, because now she knew what it felt like to be kissed by him.

She let him lead her back towards his car. As she settled herself inside he laid an arm across her shoulders, pulled her against him and kissed her neck, burrowing his face down into the warm place where the collar of the green dress opened at the throat. It was a technique which he had already tested on Harriet and found to be highly effective. The last traces of her annoyance dissolved and she subsided helplessly against his tweed jacket. Gavin worked his way up from her neck to her mouth.

'*Now* I remember why I bother,' he said.

*   *   *

Two hours after he had left Medlar House in Blackheath, Jem Wilkins walked along a narrow, cobbled street in Bethnal Green, a few miles and a social world away from the Ramsay residence. He stopped in front of an unprepossessing building, over the door of which a board tacked to the dirty yellow brickwork announced that it was 'The Crown and Cushion, licensed to sell beer and spirits.' Jem stood still for a moment, listening to the sounds from inside the pub, as if unsure of his next move. Then he straightened his back with sudden decision and pushed open the half-glazed door with its etched pattern of lilies.

The interior was hazy with smoke, dimly lit by gas mantles and humid with the heat of sweating bodies. Someone was at the piano, playing 'Teddy Bears' Picnic', and the customers nearest the instrument were supplying the words with fervour, grinning over their beer mugs, converting what was supposed to be a kids' song into something suggestive.'*If you go down in the woods today, you're sure of a big surprise . . .*'

A young woman picked her way between the tables collecting empty glasses, her fingers threaded through the handles of half a dozen tankards. She wore a cheap cotton dress in a shade of dull green which robbed her tired features of any colour they might otherwise have had. Straight fair hair hung to her shoulders. She was the only female in the room and looked as if she would rather be anywhere else. As she passed the piano, heading for the bar, a fat man with a flushed, greasy face leaned back and leered up at her from his chair.

''Ere, luv, what abaht it, then? Fancy coming dahn the woods wiv me one of these evenings, eh?'

The girl shrank away, her distaste for the suggestion obvious. Maud, the regular barmaid in the Crown and Cushion, would have told the customer in pithy terms what to do with his trip to the woods, but she'd have grinned widely as she said it, recognizing a bit of harmless fun. This mousy little scrap of a girl had neither Maud's cocky demeanour nor her impressive cleavage, and the fat man had

35

made the comment out of pure habit, not because he expected or wanted a favourable response. But a barmaid was a barmaid, even if she did look more like a novice nun, so she'd no reason to be so hoity-toity, and to pay her back for the snub he reached out and slapped her rump as she skirted his chair. The girl gasped and the beer mugs she had been holding crashed to the ground.

The piano playing broke off abruptly as startled customers jumped sideways to avoid splintering glass. A middle-aged man who had been serving behind the bar hurried forward to inspect the damage.

'Three broken! For Chrissake, you clumsy cow! Get the dustpan and brush and clear it up.'

The girl didn't try to excuse herself. She retreated silently through a doorway behind the bar, in search of cleaning equipment as ordered. Gradually the occupants of the pub settled down again. The bartender returned to his former position and the pianist launched into a Gracie Fields song.

'*Sally, Sally . . .*' The singing became maudlin as the clientele implored Sally not to wander away from the alley.

Jem Wilkins, whose arrival had gone unnoticed in the midst of the disturbance, closed the door gently behind him and moved across the room until he was standing behind the chair of the fat man who had caused the trouble. Quite casually he hooked the forefinger of his right hand into the back of the man's shirt collar and twisted. The man spluttered into his beer and made as if to rise but Jem's left hand had descended on his shoulder, pinning him in place. Jem was lean and medium-sized, but there was an astonishing strength in those fingers. Calm-faced, he leaned forward and spoke softly in the man's ear. To bystanders the action had the appearance of a friendly greeting.

'You *ever* touch that girl again, mate, or even speak to her out of turn, and you'll find a blade in your guts up a dark alley one night. And that's a promise.'

Another tightening of the painful grip on the victim's shoulder, another little twist of his hooked finger, which brought the man to choking point, then he let it go. The fat man's baleful stare followed his assailant towards a table in the furthest corner of the room from the piano, then he turned towards one of his fellow-drinkers.

'Oo's that bloke sitting down in the corner?'

'Geezer by the name er Wilkins.'

'The little blighter just threatened me. Gissa a hand to sort 'im out, will yer?'

'Jem Wilkins? No fear! I ain't going to mess wiv 'im. 'E's got a mean streak,' the other man replied.

'So've I.'

'Garn! Yer not in the same class.'

'What's so special about 'im, then? 'E don't look that tough to me. Puff er wind'd blow 'im over.'

'You reckon? There's a few blokes round 'ere could tell you different, *and* show you the scars to prove it. Sliced 'em up a treat, 'e did. A little knick 'ere, a little knick there, blood all over the place. Right little terror wiv a knife, is Jem.'

The fat man reflected on what he had learned. His eyes met Jem Wilkins' steady gaze across the smoke-filled room and he decided that discretion was the better part of valour.

The fair-haired girl came back with the dustpan and brush and swept up broken glass. As she straightened up, she saw Jem in his corner and colour flooded her cheeks, obviously with gladness. She flicked a cautious glance towards the bartender. He was chatting with a customer while he drew a pint. She hurried towards Jem's table.

'Hullo, Kitty,' he said.

'Hullo, Jem,' she said shyly. It was plain from her speech that she wasn't a native of Bethnal Green. Her soft accent was that of a country girl from south of London. 'Did you see me drop those glasses? Wasn't it clumsy of me?'

'I saw what happened,' he said. 'I sorted the bloke out. He won't do it again in a hurry.'

'Thanks.' Kitty darted a nervous glance towards the fat man, who hastily averted his eyes. 'I'll get you a drink. What'll it be?'

'Pint of best bitter. Only don't go for a moment, I want to talk to you.'

'It'll have to be quick. We're busy tonight.'

'It'll be quick,' Jem said. 'I just wanted to say, I shan't be back in here for a while. I'm going into Hampshire to work.'

'Oh.' Kitty's spirits plummeted and it showed in her voice.

'Will you miss me, then?' he asked, smiling up at her sideways in a way that reminded her at once of the devil and of the innocence of her childhood.

'Yes,' Kitty admitted in a low voice. 'I will.'

'You could always come with me.' Deliberately, Jem took hold of her hand and played his thumb lightly over the backs of her fingers, watching her face for a reaction. Kitty trembled, partly at the sensation – she could not remember when anyone had last made any physical contact with her that wasn't a blow – and partly out of dread that the publican or one of the customers would see what he was doing.

'How about it?' Jem Wilkins said softly.

'What do you mean?'

'Well, you could run away and live in sin with me. Or you could run away and marry me. I don't mind either way. But you'll have to make up your mind to it now. I'll be gone tomorrow.'

In the background the noise continued unabated, but for Kitty it was as if she and Jem were held in a warm, vibrating cocoon of silence.

'Well?' said Jem, still holding her hand.

'All right,' said Kitty.

He had never doubted that she would come.

3

Kitty hadn't known what love could be like until she met Jem Wilkins. She'd reached the age of twenty without it. Her father, a regular soldier, had been killed in the opening days of the Great War, just one of the many that went down at Mons with the fourth battalion of the Middlesex Diehards. Kitty's sad mother had never recovered from the shock of the telegram that relayed the news. Afterwards, she had seemed to sleepwalk through life and had succumbed without a struggle to the 'flu outbreak that followed the Armistice. At six, the silent, withdrawn child that Kitty had become was uprooted from her home in a country village in Surrey and taken in by her father's brother, who kept a pub in Bethnal Green.

George Crowley was a dour man with no wife, no children and no inclination to have any. He regarded this female relation as a nuisance and at best an unpaid servant. On her arrival, he'd taken charge of the ten pounds that was supposed to come to Kitty from the sale of his dead sister-in-law's furniture, and had conveniently forgotten about it. He'd allocated her a boxroom and a grudging daily ration of food, and set her to work, before and after school, scrubbing floors and washing glasses. When she made mistakes he cuffed her, and if they were expensive mistakes he took a leather belt to her.

For the ensuing fourteen years Kitty had kept house for him in the rooms above the pub. When there was a staff shortage she served in the bar. She was not a success as a barmaid.

'Yer too perishing refined. No back-chat. No life about yer. Like a scared rabbit,' said George with disgust, as he watched the thin girl with the nervous manner creeping around. She even gave *him* the shudders, never mind the customers!

Kitty had no money and no hope. She was used to a life of hard knocks with no light in it. Despite the passing of the years, she still felt like a stranger in Bethnal Green, but she was so inured to emotional starvation that she had hardly recognized her inner craving for love until that summer of 1933, when Jem Wilkins had come into the pub on a day when there was no alternative but for Kitty to serve behind the bar.

'Pint of bitter please, love. Where's Maud?' he'd said, depositing a few coins on the counter.

'She's got the day off.' Kitty reached down a glass from the shelf behind her and pulled the handle of the pump. 'Sorry,' she added, as the brown liquid foamed into the mug, because she'd been asked the question before. Maud was chatty and effervescent, popular with the customers, and Kitty was expecting another expression of disappointment at her absence. But this customer only grinned and said, 'Why sorry? I'd say you're an improvement.' And he'd looked her up and down with his dark hazel eyes and a flame had licked through her, from the pit of her stomach to the roots of her hair, and she had been unable to drag her own eyes away from his lean, intense features.

After that, she'd lived for further encounters. She'd been shameless in inventing excuses to be in the bar. He reappeared infrequently and in between she ached for a sight of him, but reappear he did, and each time he talked to her a little more, and stood a little closer. He was different from the other customers, fine-boned where they were coarse, laconic where they were garrulous. In scraps of conversation as she brought him his drinks, Kitty began to tell him details of her life that no-one else had ever cared to know: about the home of her childhood, her dead parents, her life with Uncle George and the money he was supposed to be keeping safe for her and wouldn't give back.

Jem listened and commented sparely but with sympathy.

She knew without looking that his eyes followed her around the room as she worked, and it brought unaccustomed colour to her cheeks and a tingling awareness to her body. She told herself sternly not to be silly, he was too good-looking to want a plain girl like her, he was only being kind . . . but all the same Kitty began, guiltily, to indulge in fantasies about what it would be like to be held by Jem.

Now those fantasies were to become reality. She had never been so happy.

Jem would have found it hard to explain what it was about Kitty Crowley that particularly attracted him. Ever since puberty there'd been an abundance of women giving him the glad eye; he took it for granted and took what he wanted without much caring about the inevitable tears and recriminations when he dumped the female afterwards. But as soon as he met Kitty, he sensed that she wasn't the sort you could take behind a wall or down a dark alley and then walk away from without a backward glance. She had reserve, and quality. He was sure without needing to ask that she'd never had a man.

Was that the attraction? She certainly wasn't the prettiest girl he'd met and she was totally lacking in the art of flirtation. Maud, also of the Crown and Cushion, with her blouse buttons strained to the limit over her ample bosom and her high-piled curls, had more life and sex appeal in her, by a long way.

Only there *was* something about Kitty, a combination of scared vulnerability and dogged endurance, that rang bells with Jem. From the first time he'd seen her, so plainly miserable and out of place in the raucous atmosphere of the bar, he'd experienced a feeling that was entirely new to him: an instinctive wish to protect her. It was coupled confusingly with his usual reaction towards women, which was the exact opposite of protective. The conflict between these two emotions bothered Jem. It made him feel vaguely threatened. Sometimes, lying awake at night in the dingy little terraced house where he'd spent all his childhood and angry adolescence, he imagined what it would be like to undress her and hold her slight, small-boned body against his, to kiss her and stroke her and make her sad eyes sparkle with delight. At other times he thought he would enjoy making her cry.

'So how on earth are we going to tell them?' asked Harriet.

'I don't know,' Gavin said. The Austin Swallow was parked with the hood up in a suitably sheltered spot halfway between Bentley and Alton. Five minutes ago Gavin had admitted, rather to his own surprise, that he loved Harriet. Being a well-brought-up girl, she had assumed that the declaration was the equivalent of a proposal of marriage and now, to Gavin's secret consternation, they were tackling the vexed question of how best to break the news of their engagement to both sets of parents. The Draycotts and the Griffins were not on cordial terms.

Welcome Farm had been part of the Hallows estate until 1928, when Captain Rollinson, the previous owner, had grown tired of looking for reliable tenants in the middle of a farming slump and had put it on the market at a price that Will Griffin could afford – just – with the help of his wife's rich sister-in-law, Louella Ramsay.

In the spring of this year, five years after the Griffins moved to Welcome Farm, Captain Rollinson had died and the Draycott family came down from London and bought the big house; 'new-rich townies hankering to be country squires', according to the disparaging gossip in the Red Lion at Bentley. They had tried to buy back Welcome Farm, too, wanting to control the landscape over which their tall Georgian windows looked out. But Will wasn't selling. This had caused a certain coldness between the Griffins, who had worked hard on getting their neglected acres into shape and didn't see why they should start all over again somewhere else on the whim of the newcomers, and the Draycotts, who had made what they considered a very generous offer for an unspectacular parcel of land and were offended by the briskness with which the offer had been refused.

Mention a Draycott to Will Griffin and his face would take on a stony look. Mention a Griffin to the Draycotts and no doubt you'd get the same reaction.

'I think we should keep it to ourselves for now,' said Gavin, who didn't like confrontations.

'Oh,' Harriet said. She detached his arm from her shoulders. 'For how long?'

'Just a bit longer. Until I've got my mother prepared for the idea. If I can get her to accept it, she'll talk Father round.' Gavin was already wishing he'd had more sense than to go this far, this fast, with an unsophisticated provincial. The trouble was, she was such a passionate little thing . . . she'd stirred him up more thoroughly than any other girl he'd taken out for spins in the Swallow, though the list was a lengthy one. But the thought of his parents' likely reaction to such an entanglement made him quail.

It wasn't just that she was a Griffin. It was her whole background. The verdict of 'new-rich townies', as applied to the Draycotts when they arrived in the district, held an element of truth. For Gavin's father and mother, wealthy but not yet socially secure, a suitable match for their son would be with one of the county set, no less. In some ways Gavin himself felt attracted by this prospect – he knew that many of the rigid pre-war social divisions had perished, along with the young men who represented them, in the mud of Flanders or the Somme. He knew that he was good-looking and reasonably well educated and that in theory most county girls would take him and be thankful. But in practice he felt profoundly ill at ease with the few local young women of the 'right' class that he'd encountered so far . . . whereas with Harriet, who was of the 'wrong' class, what he felt was a complex mixture of lust for her body and admiration for her spirit. The combination was quite new to him.

Perhaps it wouldn't be so terrible being married to Harriet . . . ? If only he could think of a way of telling his mother without losing his allowance.

'So how long, exactly, do you think it will take to get your mother used to the idea of me?' Harriet asked.

'Not too long. Meanwhile, won't it be rather exciting,' Gavin improvised hastily, 'to have a secret engagement?'

'No,' said Harriet coldly. 'I think it's rather shabby, as a matter of fact. Are you ashamed of me, Gavin?'

'Of course not.' Gavin couldn't think of anything to say which wouldn't get him into further trouble, so instead he nibbled Harriet's earlobe. As a distraction, it worked beautifully.

Moving cautiously so as not to waken her uncle in the bedroom along the corridor, Kitty packed her few possessions into the shabby Gladstone bag with which she had arrived at the Crown and Cushion fourteen years ago. Shaking with apprehension and excitement, she slipped quietly downstairs at one o'clock in the morning and unlocked the side door to find Jem waiting outside among the empty barrels that were piled by the door for collection by the brewer's dray.

'Where does your uncle keep the pub takings?' he asked, taking the bag from her as she stepped out into the silent street.

'I don't know. Why?' Kitty said. She didn't know what she'd expected; perhaps a kiss, perhaps a few words of reassurance? She would have given anything for the kiss, and instead this darkly beautiful almost-stranger to whom she was entrusting her future had opened their life together with a question about money.

'He owes you ten pounds,' said Jem. 'We may as well take what's due to you. Come on, you must have some idea where he stashes it?'

Kitty tried to think. Uncle George usually did the final sweeping up and locking up in the bar after she went to bed, but a few times over the years she'd seen him climbing the stairs to his bedroom and she knew he didn't carry anything up with him. It had to be downstairs. She closed her eyes, reviewing the possibilities, and remembered a noise, heard most nights from the airless little boxroom above the scullery that was her bedroom: the clink of the iron door on the big old copper in the room below being opened and closed.

'It might be in the firebox under the copper,' she said doubtfully.

'Show me.'

'It's stealing,' she protested.

'No more'n him taking your money. Come on.' Jem's voice wasn't angry, just mildly exasperated at her lack of understanding of the situation. Depositing her bag on the doorstep, he grasped her wrist and tugged her after him into the dark interior of the pub.

'Which way now?'

Kitty knew she should argue against what he was proposing to do, but she was terrified that Uncle George might hear them if she did. She pictured him storming down the stairs to confront the intruder, perhaps brandishing the heavy steel poker from the companion set beside the fireplace in his bedroom. And what would happen then? She felt sick at the thought. Silently, she led Jem to the scullery, where moonlight from the uncurtained window cast a bright four-squared patch just where it was needed for an investigation of the small door at the base of the copper, through which the fuel was shovelled to heat the water on washdays.

Jem lifted the latch cautiously, swung the door back then crouched and groped. A moment later he straightened up, holding a canvas bag with a drawstring top. When he shook it, the contents chinked softly.

'You were right. Clever girl!' He opened the top of Kitty's Gladstone bag and pushed the money sack into it, snapping it shut again. 'Come on, let's get out of here.'

Kitty scurried after him obediently. But as they neared the corner of the street her doubts about what they had just done boiled up and spilled over.

'Oh, Jem, we shouldn't have. It's thieving. Suppose the police come after us? We could go to prison.'

'We've done no more than take what's yours.'

'We haven't even counted it,' Kitty protested, almost in

45

tears. Jem stopped dead, so unexpectedly that she bumped into his back.

'Look,' he said, quietly, 'if you want us to take the money back, we will.'

'Can we?' whispered Kitty, relief flooding through her.

'I just wanted you to have your due. Course, putting it back'll be an even bigger risk than taking it in the first place, because this time we'd have to break in. But if it matters that much to you . . .'

Kitty hesitated. She looked back over her shoulder, recognizing the accuracy of what Jem was saying. They had pulled the back door shut behind them and she had heard the Yale lock click into place. The pub door at the front was locked and bolted, with a heavy bar across it to keep out the impatient customers until opening time. She had no idea how they could gain re-entry to the building now, though she felt instinctively that Jem would manage it somehow, if he wanted to. But it would be so dangerous . . . and her uncle *did* owe her money . . .

She had seen how heavy the money bag was, and she knew that Uncle George didn't take it down to the bank every day, but let it mount up. And what if the contents did amount to a little more than the money he'd pocketed years ago? After all, she had worked for him without wages all this time. She stood there in an agony of indecision. Jem waited patiently, his expression in the pale moonlight unreadable.

'Whatever you want,' he said. 'It's you I'm interested in, not the money.'

'Honestly?'

'Straight up. Don't you believe me?' Jem deposited Kitty's bag on the pavement and put an arm round her thin figure, pulling her close. Kitty swayed against him. He dropped a swift kiss on to the crown of her head and then left a track of the same fleeting kisses over her brow and nose until he found her mouth, at which point the pressure switched suddenly from butterfly-light to demanding. Kitty's hands clung to his shoulders, her lips parted, her tongue touching against his, inexperienced but eager. *Still waters run deep*, Jem told himself, deliberately keeping his own passion in check. When he released her, he knew she would do whatever he told her.

'Don't let's waste time on the money,' he said.

'No,' Kitty said shakily. She burned her boats. 'I suppose it doesn't matter all that much. Let's go on.'

She hadn't even asked where they were going.

Jem took Kitty home to Bethnal Green. His mother, he told her, had been warned that he was bringing a girl back with him.

'What did she say to that?' Kitty asked.

'She didn't say anything. She's not much of a one for talking. She does what I tell her. I'm the breadwinner, so she has to.'

Kitty postponed thinking about what kind of welcome she would get from a prospective mother-in-law described in such unpromising terms. In fact, when they pushed open the door of the terraced house in the dirty back street, Agnes Wilkins was discovered to be in no state to offer any kind of a welcome.

'Damn,' said Jem unemotionally, looking down at his mother in the gaslight. Kitty saw an old woman slumped, eyes closed, in a chair in front of an unlit kitchen range. Her hair must once have been as black as Jem's but was now heavily streaked with yellowish-grey and all the lines of her gaunt face were dragged downwards by unhappiness. An empty bottle stood on the table a few inches away from her elbow and a glass was still clutched in the hand resting in her lap. Its spilled contents had left a fresh stain among older stains on the faded fabric of her skirt.

'Is she ill?' Kitty asked, concerned. Then as she stepped forward she caught the sweetish smell of gin on the old woman's breath.

'No, she's drunk,' Jem said, matter-of-factly. He shook the sleeper roughly by the shoulder. Mrs Wilkins' mouth fell slackly open and she began to snore.

'Should we put her to bed?' said Kitty.

'Better leave her to sleep it off. Come on.'

Rummaging in the cupboard beside the firebreast, Jem found matches and a stub of candle in a chipped enamelled candlestick. By its flickering light he led Kitty into a small, square passage behind the brick-floored kitchen and then up the narrow, uncarpeted stairs to a bedroom. The bed was unmade, the sheets and blanket still in a rumpled heap from the morning.

Kitty was taken aback by the state of the house. The living accommodation at the Crown and Cushion was shabby and, compared to the clean, comfortable cottage that she remembered from her early childhood, it had been spartan, but Jem's home was dirty beyond her experience. Downstairs, the small room had smelled of damp, rotten food and stale cigarettes. In the bedroom the reek of decay was even more overpowering. Kitty felt a pang of sympathy for Jem that he should have to live in such squalor. She thought that in the morning, when Agnes Wilkins was feeling better, she'd tactfully offer to help put the place straight.

'Can I open the window?' she asked.

'If you want.' Jem put the candlestick down on a chest of drawers beside the bed. Kitty struggled with the sash window. The wooden frame had swollen with damp and was stuck. Jem stood behind her, placing his hands on either side of hers. The nearness of him made it difficult for Kitty to breathe. With a sudden sharp exertion he forced the lower half of the window a foot upwards. Cold air flooded through the gap.

'Will that do?' he said.

'Yes, thank you.'

Jem lowered his head and just touched his lips to Kitty's neck. She quivered.

'Are you tired?' he said.

'A bit,' Kitty said.

'That's a pity.' Jem took her by the shoulders and turned her to face him. His fingers tilted her chin upwards and his eyes looked directly into hers. 'I'm not.'

Behind them a moth bumped against the streaked glass of the upper sash, dropped and fluttered through the opening, attracted by the candlelight in the room. As Jem bent his head towards Kitty's upturned face, it blundered into the flame and reeled away.

It was a distraction. Cursing, Jem swatted the insect.

'Oh, don't! Poor thing,' said Kitty, but the moth had already plummeted to the floorboards and was being ground under the heel of his boot. Kitty would have minded more, but a moment later every thought in her head was being banished by the fact of Jem kissing her.

She failed to see any connection between the moth and herself.

Kitty opened her eyes in an unfamiliar room, with a vague feeling that something was wrong. When she remembered the events of the night, she wasn't sure. She had done something which she shouldn't . . . but then it had been so sweet. The sweetest thing of all her life so far.

Beside her, his body nudging the curves of hers in the narrow bed, Jem Wilkins was still asleep. She turned her head on the pillow to look at him. Sleeping, his features relaxed, he looked so much younger than his awake and watchful self. There was a dark smear of stubble along his jaw, but one hand was curled into a fist behind his head like the gesture of a small boy. The sight of him like that seemed to dissolve her bones. She felt such a tenderness towards him that it hurt. She turned over on to her side, propped herself on one elbow and reached out a hand to stroke it experimentally across the dark triangle of hairs on his chest and down over his rib cage towards his flat stomach.

Without warning, Jem erupted. His arm flailed against hers, striking her away. Eyes still closed he said, with a terrifying force,

'*Don't touch me!*'

Kitty recoiled, her right hand nursing her left arm just above the wrist, where the blow had left a rapidly purpling bruise. Jem's eyes flew open. In one movement he reared himself up into a sitting position and glared at her.

'What are you playing at?'

'I was only being affectionate,' Kitty whispered.

'Don't you *ever* touch me like that again! Not unless I say you can.'

Scowling, Jem flopped back against the pillow and turned over, facing away from her. He dragged at the bedclothes till they covered him up to the ears and closed his eyes again, shutting her out utterly. Kitty lay down beside him, rigid and stunned. Last night, with his lips on her eyelids, her throat and all the secret places of her body that no other man had known, he had told her that he loved her. She had trusted in the truth of it. Now it seemed as if he hated her. She stared up at the cracked ceiling, too scared to ask what crime she had committed, too scared to move in case she committed some other offence.

The early morning air was chilly and Jem had all the bedcovers, but it wasn't the cold that was making Kitty shiver. It was the sinking realization that, with Uncle George's money in her Gladstone bag and that bag locked up in one of Jem's cupboards, there was no going back to the only safe place she knew.

Without words, Jem's mother dished up a breakfast of fatty bacon and fried bread onto plates that were still smeary from a previous meal. Apart from setting out an extra plate, she ignored Kitty, who sat with downcast eyes waiting for Jem to tell her what was to happen to her next. But when his food was eaten, Jem unhooked his jacket from behind the front door and announced without explanations that he would be out all morning.

'If you're wanting any dinner you'll have to give me some money,' his mother said. Jem groped in his pocket and put a few coins down on the table.

'Don't go spending all of it on booze,' he warned, 'or I'll make you sorry. Do you hear me, you daft old woman?'

Agnes Wilkins scooped the coins into her hand from the

table with a quick, furtive movement and stowed them into the pocket of her grubby cardigan.

'She was pretty once,' Jem said unexpectedly to Kitty. 'Soft and gentle and pretty. Can you believe that? And look at her now.' He gestured towards the old woman in disgust. 'That's what happens to cowards,' he said. 'They let life smash them up. And it does.'

Agnes seemed not to hear the contemptuous words. Kitty, breath suspended, nodded uncertainly. She thought that she too was a coward and that, at the moment, Jem was the most frightening thing she had ever encountered.

After he'd gone, the tense atmosphere of the dingy room seemed to lighten a little. Agnes shuffled about, clearing away the breakfast dishes. Breathing heavily, she fished an enamel basin out from a cupboard made out of an orange crate turned on its side, with a curtain rigged across the front. Most of the stacked contents of the cupboard tumbled out with the basin. Agnes stared at them vacantly, making no move to tidy them away.

'Can I help?' Kitty offered.

'Suit yourself.' Jem's mother abandoned the task to the visitor. Wavering a little in her movements, she took out a brown glass bottle from the back of the curtained cupboard, splashed some of the contents into a mug and sat at the table, chin propped on her hand.

The kettle on the range was almost empty. Kitty looked around for a tap. There wasn't one.

'Where do I get the water?' she asked Agnes.

'Water?'

'For washing up.'

'Bucket in the corner.'

Kitty glanced into the bucket. On two inches of scummy liquid a dead cockroach floated.

'Where can I find a tap?'

'Standpipe down the yard.' Agnes gestured towards the door which led into the street.

It took some time to find the standpipe, in a narrow alleyway between two terraces of houses. When Kitty brought back the bucket, swilled out to get rid of the cockroach and filled with fresh water, Agnes had not moved from her chair but already the level of liquid in the bottle at her elbow had gone down by several inches and her gaze was unfocused. She watched without interest as Kitty boiled water and washed the dishes. There was no soap, which explained the lingering grease on the plates.

'Taken up with Jem, have you?' Agnes Wilkins asked suddenly.

'Yes. I suppose I have,' Kitty said.

Agnes tipped the bottle over the mug again, but only a drop or two of gin emerged. She sighed resignedly and set the bottle down on the table with exaggerated care.

'You poor fool,' she said, and in her cloudy, pink-rimmed eyes there was genuine pity. 'He's a devil. Just like his father.'

4

In the study of his house under the Hog's Back, near
Farnham in Surrey, Louella Ramsay's enemy Rupert Brownlowe was having a pre-breakfast argument with his stepson.

'For pity's sake, Tom, you have to do *something* with
your life.'

'I *am* doing something. It just doesn't happen to fit in
with your ideas.'

'But this flying business . . . an amusement, but hardly a
settled career. You're risking your neck, squandering your
money . . .'

'Flying is perfectly safe if you know what you're doing
– which I do,' said Tom, who at twenty-three was bright,
dashing and enviably healthy. 'You don't get your licence
until you've proved yourself thoroughly competent. It's
certainly no more dangerous than fox-hunting – and a lot
more useful,' he added, with intent to offend.

Rupert had been a keen rider to hounds for most of
his adult life and though arthritis had lately curtailed his
activities in the saddle, he was still known throughout the
district for his pre-war breeding and schooling of hunters.
He reddened, searching for the right words to refute his
stepson's comment. But Tom had taken up a stance in front
of the fireplace – traditionally Rupert's own position for
dealing with recalcitrant family members or staff – and he
felt distinctly at a disadvantage. Not that he ever found it
easy to reason with Tom.

In Rupert's view, the boy should have been in the army
long ago, following in the footsteps of his father, who, before
he was gassed to death on the Somme in 1916, had been
one of the youngest captains on the Western Front. Military

service was a family tradition for the Searles and when Rupert had taken on Tom as part of the package that went with Marion Searle, war widow, he had understood that once the boy had completed his education at Malvern he would go on to Sandhurst and in due course to a commission, when he would cease to be any kind of a headache to his stepfather.

It had sounded straightforward enough. But on leaving school, Tom had blithely announced that he didn't care for the army, or for any of the other respectable occupations that Rupert had suggested. Instead he had decided to go to university. He hadn't even opted for the gentlemanly study of Literature at Oxford, as Rupert's own offspring had done, but instead had insisted on London, where there was a Faculty of Engineering.

'Good God! *Engineering!* Little better than a trade!' Rupert had protested at the time.

'But your business is engineering, of a kind,' Marion had pointed out. Behind the mildness of her tone lay an inflexible determination to see that her son got his way. And it was true that Rupert's earned income, as distinct from his inherited income, came from the ownership and management of a factory manufacturing lawn mowers.

'But I don't concern myself with the nuts and bolts,' said Rupert. 'I have designers and craftsmen for that sort of thing.'

'Tom's very bright, dear,' Marion said, gently. 'He wants to know how things work before he tells other people to make them.'

Rupert was left wondering whether she meant that he, Rupert, wasn't clever enough to comprehend the workings of a lawn-mower motor. He wanted to put her right on the matter but decided it would be undignified. If he should ever need to understand such details, he'd find it easy enough. As a gentleman, he didn't have such a need.

Tom, in contrast, was disgustingly eager to get his hands and clothes covered in oil while taking apart things that ought best to be left in one piece, and his years at university, giving bent to this peculiar obsession with machines, hadn't satisfied him. The craze for flying was the latest in a long line of activities that were expensive, dirty and dangerous. Before the flying lessons at Brookwood he'd driven racing cars.

'As you have noticed,' Tom reminded his stepfather now, 'it's *my* money I'm squandering, not yours. The money from the Searle Trust.'

It was a form of torture for Rupert, whose own finances were going through a prolonged sticky patch, that he should have to watch someone with more money than sense pouring away a solid inheritance on transitory thrills instead of leaving it in the bank or the stock exchange where it belonged – or better still, investing it in the Brownlowe lawn-mower company, which was badly in need of a cash injection to modernize the machinery and renovate the premises.

'You can't go on like this. Your mother's worried sick about you.'

'No she isn't,' said Tom, unmoved. 'Or she wouldn't be if you didn't nag her about how dangerous it's supposed to be.'

'When are you going to get yourself a proper job?' Rupert was aware of his voice rising to an uncontrolled pitch.

'I already have,' Tom said. 'That's what I came to tell you, before you started reading the riot act. Aerial photography. I start today. Must dash, I have to get to Croydon to pick up my equipment.' And Tom swung briskly out of the study, leaving his stepfather floundering. A few minutes later his car could be heard roaring off down the drive.

By the time the Great War ended, Rupert's grown-up children had flown the nest and his sister Jessie, who'd kept house for him ever since his wife died, had married a Canadian major she'd met through her war work and decamped with him to Montreal. Rupert had found himself living alone, apart from a parcel of servants, in a house that was meant for a family, and though he did not admit it to anyone, he was almost unbearably lonely. Then he'd met Marion Searle, unquestionably pretty, apparently docile, and as much in need of a home and a man to lean on as Rupert was of someone to order his domestic comforts. In deciding to propose to her, he'd barely counted her son in his calculations. In the intervening thirteen years Rupert had had plenty of opportunities to regret that oversight.

If only Marion would back him up, Rupert thought, when he tried to instill some sense into the lad . . . but in Marion's eyes Tom could do no wrong. No doubt she would be as stubbornly supportive of this latest idiocy – aerial photography indeed! – as she had of all Tom's previous crack-brained schemes for earning a livelihood.

Nevertheless, as head of the household, Rupert would have to make his reservations known. At the door of the dining room he braced himself for another fruitless discussion.

'Marion, about this business with Tom's job—'

But Marion was already rising from the table, dabbing at her lips with her napkin. 'I haven't time to talk about it now, dear. I have to catch a train. I'm going up to London.'

'Oh,' said Rupert.

'I told you, dear. Last night.'

Rupert didn't remember being told. He supposed he'd dozed in his comfortable armchair beside the drawing room fire. Marion, stitching away at her petit point, was apt to take it for granted that any information she voiced at such a time had been registered by her husband. Sometimes he suspected that she deliberately saved unpopular announcements for the moments when he nodded off.

'What is it this time?' he asked irritably. 'Another meeting of those damned Fabian women?'

'I'll be seeing Laura and the children. I'll tell you all about it this evening. I must go or I'll miss my train.'

'I might have liked to come too.'

'You didn't say so, dear,' Marion said, turning in the doorway.

'Tell Laura it's high time she came down for a visit,' Rupert called after her, without much hope.

It should have been a blessing that Marion got on so well with Laura Allingham, Rupert's married daughter. The relationship between stepmothers and stepdaughters was not always so cordial. And the war had led to an estrangement between Rupert and Laura, so that sometimes he thought that she and his grandchildren would never come near him if it wasn't for Marion. But the main reason for the friendship between Marion and Laura was that they were twin souls when it came to politics, and the politics in question were not Rupert's own.

It was thanks to Laura that Marion had joined the Fabian Feminist Group last year. For Rupert, it had been bad enough learning about Laura's connection with the Fabians, but at least he had been able to put it down to her youth and the influence of that wretched socialist husband of hers. With Marion there were no such excuses.

'I should have been more careful,' Rupert chided himself, as he sat down at the table. 'I should have enquired more deeply into her attitudes before I married her.' Well, it was too late now. A sensation of constriction in his neck and shoulder warned him that his blood pressure was climbing again. ('*Keep calm*,' that idiot of a doctor had advised him, with total disregard for the daily slings and arrows of outrageous fortune that made it impossible for someone like Rupert to do any such thing.)

'Would you like a cooked breakfast, sir?' the maid asked, bringing in a fresh pot of coffee.

'Isn't there anything ready?'

'No sir, Mrs Brownlowe and Mr Tom just had cereal and a boiled egg.'

'All right. I'll have the same.'

There had been a time when the sideboard would have carried a row of covered dishes at every breakfast, filled to the brim with bacon, scrambled eggs, mushrooms and kedgeree, regardless of the appetite of the family. That was how a gentleman should live. That was how Rupert wished wholeheartedly that he could still live, but the stark economic truth was that he couldn't afford it any more. The lawn-mower factory was doing badly and these days the home farm seemed to *eat* money instead of saving it. To add to his problems, most of this year's hay from the farm had gone up in smoke just after it was stacked, which was going to mean an expensive winter of buying in hay for the livestock.

The fire still worried him. He'd had the police round investigating and they'd found nothing suspicious, but it wasn't the first fire at Maple Grange. People had remarked that he seemed to be unlucky with fires. Lately he had wondered himself whether any one man could be that unlucky, or whether those blazes were started deliberately . . . like the arson attack that had burned down his factory in November of 1918.

He'd never really recovered from that first fire. Under-insured, he'd had to find new premises to get the lawn-mower business up and running in the aftermath of the war, and he had been struggling ever since.

The maid brought in his boiled egg.

'Thank you, Joan.'

'It's Doris, sir.'

'Eh?'

'My name's Doris, sir.'

Rupert blinked. Forgetting a name wasn't tactful, the staff liked to think they mattered to you, but it was getting increasingly difficult to remember the names of the servants these days. If this was Doris, which one was Joan? He concentrated, and remembered that Joan had left Maple Grange long ago – hadn't she married a Territorial Army man at the end of the war? Or had that been Daisy? No, Daisy was the cheerful little redhead he'd had to dismiss after she'd got herself in the family way. Pity, that. She'd been a ray of sunshine about the place . . . His memory on all points was suffering. No use denying it, he was getting old.

He sliced at the shell of the egg to reveal the yolk, nice

and runny the way he liked it. Then he put down his knife and pushed the plate away. The prospect of another solitary day had taken away his appetite.

Marion was always dashing about, leading her hectic social life and doing what he scathingly referred to as 'good works', helping with the administration of various local charities. Oh for the days, Rupert reflected bitterly, when a wife recognized that her first priority was to keep her husband comfortable. Sylvia had never given him a moment's disquiet on that score until the day she died, but there were times when it seemed that Marion was more interested in the comfort of every Tom, Dick and Harry in the neighbourhood than she was in Rupert's.

He left his breakfast uneaten and reached his coat down from the row of pegs in the boot room beside the front door, thinking that a turn round the garden might be soothing. As soon as he stepped outside he saw that Tom's departing car had left twin skid marks in the gravel of the front drive. Rupert winced. In days gone by, such incidents wouldn't have mattered because one of the gardeners would rake the drive freshly each morning. Nowadays the grounds were maintained by one gardener and a boy, whose combined efforts could barely keep the borders tidy.

He stumped round to the back of the house where the lawn, once smooth and green enough for summer tennis or croquet, was bald and patchy, yellow with moss.

'Here, Stevenson.' He called to the gardener, who was heading for the vegetable patch with a trug over his arm. 'When are you going to see to this lawn? I told you about it two days ago.'

'Yes, sir. I'll get to it as soon as I can. It's a bit difficult to keep up with everything, with only the one lad to help, sir.' Stevenson said this with an expression that could almost have been described as surly. Rupert had sacked his last gardener for adopting just such a manner when spoken to, but lately he'd had to accept that surly or not, the man was right. He couldn't achieve miracles almost single-handed.

Rupert walked on through an archway in the brick wall

beside the kitchen wing and into the stable yard. The emptiness of the place was depressing. It was more than nineteen years since the day he'd sent the pride of his stables off to the war as cavalry remounts. After the war, with only himself to mount and with his arthritis getting worse, it had hardly seemed worthwhile to start again, but still an empty stable yard brought a sense of shock. No stamping of hooves in the stalls, no comfortable smell of clean straw and warm horseflesh and saddle soap, just a cold silence and a draping of cobwebs behind the windowpanes.

He walked along the row of stalls, feeling sorry for himself. The painted nameboards were still nailed up over the hay racks: Plumbago . . . Blackie . . . Starbright, the dazzling chestnut mare for whom he'd had such high hopes when she was first foaled. He would never know what had become of Starbright . . . had she seen out the war with some cavalry detachment in Mesopotamia? He would like to think so. Better that than the fate of so many horses who went to the war: drowned in the Flanders mud or torn apart by artillery shells.

He had reached the doorway to the feed store and tack room at the far end of the row. Suddenly he stopped dead, listening intently.

Something or someone was moving in the groom's quarters overhead.

Rupert hurried outside and stood at the foot of the flight of stone stairs which led up to the rooms above the stables. 'Who's there?' he called.

The words came out hoarsely. He found that his fists were clenched at his sides and was ashamed that he should be thrown into such a panic by the prospect of confronting an intruder. Time was when he'd have seen off a wandering gipsy or vagrant without any trouble at all. This rapid heartbeat and dry mouth were further evidence that he was growing old.

'Who's there?' he repeated, in a louder voice.

The windows of the rooms above his head were dirty from long neglect, but he saw a figure cross behind the grimy glass. Then the door at the top of the steps opened and a man emerged.

Rupert let out a long breath. There was nothing menacing about this man. His age was hard to estimate – he could have been thirty or forty – but ill health was all too evident from his pale face and hollow cheeks, and the dark shadows under his eyes. His shoulders stooped and his fair hair was as lank and lifeless as used straw.

'Who are you?' Rupert demanded. 'And what do you think you're doing up there?' he added.

'Billy Marshall, sir. I'm just cleaning the rooms up a bit.' He was holding a wad of dirty rag in his left hand. His empty right hand and arm dangled by his side, the fingers curled like a claw and the hand itself turned outwards on the wrist at an unnatural angle.

'Billy Marshall,' the man repeated. 'Don't you remember me, sir? I used to be gardener's boy here before the Great War.'

The name rang no bells with Rupert and the face was equally unfamiliar. But then, the man was talking about a bygone time when gardener's boys had ranked so low in the servant hierarchy that the master of Maple Grange had hardly bothered himself with their existence.

'Yes . . . yes, I remember,' Rupert lied. 'But what are you doing here now?'

'Mrs Brownlowe said I was to come, sir. She said you'd take me on again.'

'Mrs Brownlowe? When did she tell you that?'

'Yesterday, sir, at Colonel Strover's.'

Rupert clicked his tongue against his teeth with irritation. Marion had been playing Lady Bountiful again. He remembered now that last night she'd mentioned making a visit to Colonel Strover. The colonel, a retired army officer who'd become a prominent Farnham resident, was tackling the national catastrophe of unemployment at a local level by persuading the more well-to-do people of the area to give odd jobs to the unemployed. 'A day's work, or half a day, or any work that you can find,' he urged the often reluctant householders of the district. 'Half a day's wages may not be much to you, but if you add the bits and pieces together, they can make up a living wage for a working man. Every little helps.'

Yesterday after supper Marion had started telling him about the colonel's efforts and Rupert, who already flinched at the size of the weekly wages bill for the staff at the Grange, had simply stopped listening. Or perhaps he'd fallen asleep. It seemed that what he'd missed was the news that her support for the 'Every Little Helps' organization had already progressed beyond the theoretical.

'So . . . my wife has asked you to put in a day or two here, has she?' he asked cautiously.

'No, sir. Not a day or two. Mrs Brownlowe said I could come back full time, sir. And she said I could live here, over the stables, if I cleaned the place up a bit,' said Billy Marshall.

'Did she indeed?' said Rupert, his complexion darkening. 'Well, I don't think—'

'Yes, sir, she did. I was so grateful, I nearly cried. I'll tell you, it was the best news I'd had in a long time,' said Billy, with fervour. Then he registered Rupert's lack of enthusiasm. His face fell. 'Don't say you've changed your mind, sir,' he said, on a pleading note. 'I was counting on this. My mother died in July and the landlord wants me out of the house. He let Mum have it as a favour, cheap, because she used to be the nursemaid at his place, but he wants it back for a family now she's gone. And I've no money to rent a new place because there's been no work going for a long time. There's able-bodied men enough looking for jobs, so most people don't want a man with a disability, you see.'

'I see,' Rupert agreed, thinking that he didn't want one either. Inwardly he was cursing Marion. As soon as she got back tonight, he'd have to find out exactly what she had promised and see if he could wriggle out of it somehow without blotting his copybook in the eyes of the community as represented by Colonel Strover.

'Well, good to see you again,' he said, with false

bonhomie. 'I'll leave you to get on with settling yourself in, shall I? And when you've done that . . .'

'I'll be needing a bed, sir,' Billy told him. 'There's an old bedstead up there but it's falling apart with rust, and the bedding's been half-eaten by mice.'

Rupert had been about to suggest that when this new and unwelcome employee had finished tidying up his quarters, he could find himself a rake and get started on the drive. Instead, Rupert would have to see the housekeeper and instruct her to supply Billy with some bedding. It was bound to cost money. He gritted his teeth. Damn Marion and her good works! She got the gratitude and he got the bills.

This was absolutely the last time, Harriet told herself, that she would slip away from home in secret. Today she would confront Gavin with an ultimatum. Either he agreed to meet her family and put his interest in her on an official footing, or she could not see him any more.

But what if he chose the latter option? The thought was unbearable.

Cantering Briony along the verge of the lane towards Lower Five Acres, Harriet became aware of the hum of an aeroplane engine. That was unusual enough in the Hampshire countryside, but this plane seemed to be in trouble. The engine droned, then stuttered, picked up again, coughed again . . . and finally cut out altogether.

Without warning a biplane swooped low over the trees to her right, crossed the road just ahead of her, skimmed the topmost branches of the trees on the left, and vanished from sight.

Briony did not like vast, silent birds that appeared from nowhere. She reared, snorted, snatched at the bit and bolted full tilt in the opposite direction to that taken by the plane, into the belt of unfenced woodland beside the road. Harriet sawed at the reins in a vain attempt to control the panic-stricken mare, but the first low branch scooped her cleanly out of the saddle and deposited her into a puddle.

It wasn't often that Harriet took a fall. Cursing in an

unladylike manner, she picked herself up and watched Briony crashing away through the trees.

She reviewed the damage. Nothing broken. Sundry bruises. One sleeve of her hacking jacket was badly torn. Mud and grass stained her breeches. Her black velvet hair ribbon floated on the scummy surface of the puddle and her red hair tumbled loose about her shoulders. She disentangled a twig from it, dabbed at her stinging jaw and deduced from the blood thus transferred to her fingers that a branch had whiplashed against her face.

Briony had disappeared. Presumably she would have the sense to head for home, eventually, when her fright had worn itself out. At least the fields beyond the wood belonged to Welcome Farm and the mare could not come to much harm. There remained the question of what had happened to the aeroplane.

Stiffly, Harriet picked her way back through the wood and crossed the road. The trees on the far side were only a screen. Beyond them, the biplane had come to rest in the cropped meadow. Harriet had braced herself for carnage but the machine looked undamaged. So, too, did the pilot, who was standing beside his plane, waving his arms to shoo away curious cows. She let her breath out and limped forward, aware of a clammy patch on the seat of her breeches where she had landed in the puddle and a particularly vicious bruise which was beginning to make its presence felt on her left shin. It hardly seemed fair that the cause of it all was so obviously unhurt.

His face was half-hidden by a pair of goggles and a brown leather helmet. All she could see was a straight nose, a square chin and a scowl.

'You frightened my horse,' said Harriet, by way of introduction.

'I frightened myself,' the pilot said flatly. 'Where can I find a mechanic who understands Tiger Moths?'

'I haven't the faintest idea. Why did you land on our farm?'

'Is this your farm? Because it happened to be underneath

64

my aeroplane when it obeyed that law of gravity which says that what goes up must come down. Especially when the engine cuts out.'

'I meant, what is wrong with your aeroplane?' Harriet said coldly. She was finding his brisk manner distinctly irritating. She, after all, was the one covered in mud and blood, a fact that he had so far failed to register, far less display any contrition at having been the cause of it.

'So far as I can tell, not having had the time to make a detailed diagnostic examination of the damned thing, there's probably contaminated fuel in my tank. When I get hold of the mechanic, I shall personally scrag him. Meanwhile, I'm supposed to deliver a batch of aerial photographs at Croydon by the end of this afternoon.' The pilot removed his helmet and goggles and ran a hand through his flattened brown hair. 'Where's the nearest telephone?' he demanded.

'I don't know. Bentley village, I suppose. Two miles in that direction.' Harriet pointed. 'Or there's one at Hallows.'

'Is that the white house with the outbuildings along the lane? I spotted it as I flew over.'

'No, that's Welcome Farm. We don't have a telephone. Hallows is about a mile further along, a big grey stone house.'

'I'll have to ring for help. Or I might be able to sort out the engine, but at best I'll need more fuel. Nearest garage?'

'Bentley.'

'Right. Bentley it is, then.' Belatedly, he took in her appearance. 'What happened to you?'

'I told you. You frightened my horse, zooming over the hedge the way you did. She threw me and bolted. And before you rush off to telephone, would you please help me to catch her.'

'Sorry,' he said, spreading his hands. 'I would, but there isn't time.'

'In that case,' said Harriet grimly, 'I shall leave you to your troubles and get on with tackling mine.'

'No!' The pilot stepped forward and grasped her arm.

'You can't go. You have to keep the cows off the plane. If you don't, they'll eat it!'

'Cows eat grass,' said Harriet. 'And cattle cake. And cornfields if they can get into them. Not aeroplanes.'

'It's the dope on the fabric. They love it. They'll lick it to death. I've heard of planes trampled beyond repair by a determined herd of cows. *Please* help me,' the man said, abandoning his tone of command for one of entreaty. 'I have to get these photographs to Croydon, or I'll lose my job. And I only started it this morning.'

'I can't,' she protested. 'I have things to do.'

'Come on, be a sport.'

'I can't. Really I can't. I'm supposed to be meeting someone and I'm late already.'

'Thank you,' he said, oblivious. 'You're an angel.'

'I can't,' Harriet repeated, her voice climbing. But he was already sprinting away across the field.

Daisy had been breadmaking, and had just put the dough to rise in pans in a warm corner of the kitchen by the stove, when she heard an aeroplane fly over the farmhouse. It was such an unusual occurrence that she went outside to look, and was in time to see a biplane heading north-east towards Crondall. Its engine seemed to be coughing, but she supposed that planes made noises like that nowadays. A pity it hadn't come over a bit later when Rob, her elder son, was home from school – Rob was crazy about aeroplanes.

'You wouldn't catch *me* going up in one of those things,' Daisy muttered under her breath, and then yelled 'Quiet, Skip! Quiet, Barney!' because the farm's dogs were barking furiously at the sky intruder. Peace restored, Daisy turned back to her cooking. Having skinned and cut up a rabbit, she was kneading pastry for a pie when she was interrupted by a knock at the back door.

'It's open,' she called. The door swung open and a young man stood framed in the doorway.

'Louella Ramsay said to come. Here. It's in the letter.'

Daisy's hands were still smeared with the butter and flour she had been rubbing together for the pastry, which made it difficult to accept the creased envelope he held out. She was distracted by her floury fingers, flustered by the interruption, aware that if she didn't get on with her cooking the evening meal would be delayed – and for Daisy, it was a fundamental principle of life that a good wife and mother would have the food ready and hot on the table when her menfolk came in for it.

'You'd better come in,' she said reluctantly, heading for the sink to rinse her hands. She'd thought she was inviting one stranger into her kitchen, but when she turned round again there were two of them, the man and a girl.

The man was in his twenties, with hair as dark as that of her husband and with Will's spare, strong figure. What he lacked was Will's air of decency. Daisy couldn't have explained this impression without thinking about it, but warning bells rang inside her head. It wasn't his shabby clothes – she was used to stray callers at the farm, men looking for a bit of labouring work, and nobody knew better than Daisy how impossible it was to dress smartly on an agricultural worker's wages. It wasn't his physical bulk – he was thin and wiry and not more than five feet nine or ten inches in height. And his sallow, gipsyish features by themselves wouldn't put her off, because Will had Romany blood in him so the Griffins gave more of a welcome than most of their Hampshire neighbours to the gipsies who formed part of the annual invasion of hop-pickers in Bentley every autumn. All the same, there was something disquieting about this man.

The girl was younger, pale, with straight hair the colour of butter. Obviously nervous. With the same instinct that recoiled from the man, Daisy warmed to the girl.

The letter from Louella said, *'This is to introduce Jem Wilkins and Kitty. Please can you put them up for a while? Jem has some work to do for me but he will have plenty of time to be useful on the farm. Perhaps Kitty can be of some help in the house? Jem's wages have been paid by me so all you need to do is feed them and give them somewhere to sleep. I'll explain more when I see you next.'*

It was all very well for Louella to say, '. . . All you need to do is feed them and give them somewhere to sleep.' Married for fifteen years to a man of means, her sister-in-law had no recollection, Daisy reminded herself ruefully, of the difference that two extra hungry mouths could make to a tight household budget.

'Excuse me. Please could I have some water?'

Kitty stumbled towards Daisy. Her face, already so pale, had taken on a greenish tinge. Daisy caught her arms as she crumpled. A moment later, Jem took the girl's weight from her.

'She's tired,' he said, depositing his burden in a kitchen chair.

Seated, Kitty seemed to struggle up from unknown depths. 'I'm sorry,' she said, her voice blurred. 'Sorry to be such a nuisance.'

Daisy's resistance to the newcomers dissolved in a rush of sympathy. She brought the water that had been asked for. Kitty drank it and managed a smile.

'Just you sit there,' Daisy said comfortingly, banishing her misgivings to the back of her mind along with thoughts of half-prepared rabbit-pie. 'I'll make us all a nice cup of tea.'

5

Harriet could have screamed. At least an hour had passed since she had been left to guard the fallen biplane. She was chilly and tired, her brusies were smarting and her arms ached from the energetic gestures needed to keep a score of cows away from what they seemed to regard as a particularly enticing form of salt lick.

Some time ago she had heard a car driving along the lane beyond the belt of trees. It was going a little too fast and she imagined Gavin at the wheel, furious because he had waited for her in vain. 'You're always late,' he had complained yesterday, and she wondered how much apologizing it would take to appease him this time. She would have to telephone him at Hallows and he would be angry about that as well. As he kept on telling her, his parents must not, at this stage, be alerted to their son's involvement with a mere farmer's daughter. She'd meant to tackle him on that point this afternoon, she remembered.

'Oh, to hell with the Draycotts!' she muttered under her breath. 'If I'm not good enough for your family, Gavin, it's perfectly possible that you aren't good enough for mine!'

At last she heard a shout of greeting from the gateway that gave on to the lane and a minute later the pilot of the Tiger Moth joined her, carrying a can of fuel in one hand and a jute tool bag in the other. He deposited his burdens on the grass beside his machine with evident relief and flexed his cramped fingers.

'Well done,' he said to Harriet. 'You've kept the beasts at bay. I can't thank you enough. Now if you could give me a hand with emptying out that tin bath over there, with any luck we can get this thing airborne again with the minimum of delay.'

'Oh, for Pete's sake!' fumed Harriet. 'I can't hang about here all day. I have to find my horse—'

'This won't take long.' The pilot removed his jacket and began to roll up his sleeves. 'I hope that bath'll be big enough, otherwise we'll have to tip the fuel into the ditch.'

'You can't put fuel in our ditch,' Harriet objected. 'Come to that, you can't put fuel in our bath. It's the cows' water trough.'

'No option,' said the pilot. 'I'll send someone to clean things up later. You take the other side,' he instructed her. 'Ready? Heave.' He grasped one handle of the bath and, somehow, there seemed to be no alternative but to follow suit.

'What exactly do I have to do?' Harriet asked resignedly, as they hauled the bath onto its side and the water it had contained ran away into the grass.

'Help me get this into position under the fuselage. Here. That'll do. Now I need to drain the tank into it. Then I'll have to strip down the carburettor and refill the tank.'

'So can I go now?'

'Not yet. I still need you to keep the cows off. And when I've sorted the engine out you can help me to drag the plane round and swing the prop to get her started . . . and the field's a bit on the short side, so a prayer or two on take-off might come in handy. I don't know what we'll do about the livestock, but we'll tackle that when I've got the darned thing fixed.'

At any rate, he seemed to know what he was doing, Harriet recognized with grudging respect. She admired competence in any form, and machinery had fascinated her ever since she was a small girl. This was her first chance to inspect the internal workings of an aeroplane. The pilot climbed on to a lower wing and lifted back the hinged cowling which covered the engine.

'Here, pass up that tool bag, will you.'

Harriet didn't like being ordered about, and she liked it even less when accompanied by a snapping of fingers, as if she was one of the farm dogs. She folded her arms. Belatedly, he took in her sulky expression.

'Point taken. Please, miss whatever-your-name-is, I would regard it as an enormous kindness if you could see your way to passing me that tool bag.'

'That's better,' Harriet said, swinging the heavy bag up to his outstretched hand.

'You sound just like my aged nanny. She was always trying to train me to ask for things nicely.'

'A pity she didn't succeed,' said Harriet tartly.

The pilot rummaged for a spanner. Then he raised his head and grinned. 'I like you,' he said unexpectedly. 'You're probably the first young woman I've met who's had the nerve to tell me off about my manners on first acquaintance. What's your name?'

'Harriet Griffin.'

'Pleased to meet you, Harriet Griffin. I'm Tom Searle, from Maple Grange in Seale.'

'Did you say Maple Grange?'

'That's right. Do you know it?'

'I've never been there,' said Harriet. 'But I've heard my parents talk about the house. They used to work there before the war, for a perfectly horrible man called Rupert Brownlowe, who was the owner in those days.'

'He still is,' Tom Searle said, laying down his spanner and reaching among gleaming valves to unscrew a loosened nut. 'My stepfather.'

'Oh,' said Harriet, reddening. 'I'm sorry. I didn't realize . . .'

'That's all right,' Tom told her, reassuringly. 'I don't like him much either.'

For Rob Griffin, on any normal day at the end of October the routine was that as soon as he got back from school he whistled up Skip and Barney and cycled on to bring in the cows for milking. The cows knew the way to the milking shed and if they dawdled, the dogs would hurry them up a bit while Rob pedalled behind, his mind on other things.

Today was not a normal day. It first departed from routine when, cycling down the lane towards Lower Five Acres, he encountered Briony, standing wide-eyed and steaming on the edge of Job's Wood with a dangling rein and bits of broken twig caught up in her mane and tail.

'Hullo, Briony.' He left his bicycle lying on the verge and approached the mare confidently. 'What've you done with Harry, then? Dumped her in a ditch?'

Harriet was supposed to be schooling the excitable black mare to perfect manners as a lady's hunter, a job which Rob coveted himself. When Briony came to Welcome Farm as a livery he'd pleaded hard to be given the chance of schooling her, but his father had told him that it would distract him too much from his homework. Harriet had been smug about winning the commission at the time, but Rob knew that she found Briony a handful. He left his bicycle lying on the grass verge and instead rode a chastened Briony to Lower Five Acres, which proved to contain not only twenty of his father's Shorthorn heifers, but also a fallen Tiger Moth.

'We are being watched,' Tom Searle said to Harriet, 'by a youth, a horse and two dogs.'

'My brother,' said Harriet. 'And Briony, thank goodness. She's not ours, she's a livery, so I'd have been in real trouble if she'd broken a leg. Hey, Rob! Over here! He's come to fetch in the cows for milking,' she explained to Tom. 'I hadn't realized how late it is.'

'Marvellous. So that's one less problem for take-off. I'm beginning to hope that I might, just might, get those photographs taken before dusk and so save my career as an aerial photographer from an early blight.'

Rob slid from the saddle and led Briony forward over the grass with an expression of awe on his freckled face.

'Golly!' he said simply.

'Rob, where did you find Briony?'

'Standing in the lane with her reins broken. Did you fall

off?' asked Rob, surveying his sister's grime and grazes with brotherly curiosity and no sympathy whatsoever.

'Yes, I fell off.' It hurt Harriet to admit it. She knew Rob was the better rider. He'd inherited Will's instinctive skill with horses, whereas Harriet, who would have given anything for such a gift, was merely adequate – and Rob was inclined to rub that sore point in. But for the moment he wasn't crowing. He was too interested in the aeroplane.

'Where did you come from?' he asked Tom.

'Croydon aerodrome.'

'What are you doing?'

'Mending my aeroplane so that I can get back to Croydon aerodrome.'

'Golly,' Rob repeated.

'I've just about finished, as a matter of fact. And if you'll take these cows away, I can see if I've achieved what I intended.'

'D'you mean you're going to take off?' said Rob, his voice hoarse with excitement.

'That's the general idea.'

'I'd give anything to see that.'

'Trouble is, I can't actually do it until you've removed the cows.'

'Oh,' said Rob forlornly. Harriet, who knew the passion with which her brother regarded all things aeronautical, took pity on him. Besides, she wanted to wash her face and put arnica on her bruises.

'I'll see to the cows. You can stay and watch.'

'Oh, *thanks*, Harry. You're an angel.'

'I've already told her that,' the pilot told Rob. 'A Botticelli angel, with that cloud of red hair. Or do I mean a Pre-Raphaelite?'

Rob looked blank and Harriet, who vaguely understood that she was being compared to an artist's model and didn't much want to be, put paid to any such nonsense by sticking two fingers into the corners of her mouth to produce a shrill instructive blast to the dogs. In a few minutes the heifers were filing obediently through the gate with Skip and Barney

73

nudging at their heels, while Harriet swung herself up into the saddle and followed on the black mare, swishing a hazel stick she'd broken from the hedge.

'Your sister's quite a girl,' Tom said to Rob Griffin, watching horse and rider departing.

'She's all right. A bit bossy sometimes, but she can't help it.'

'I was going to ask her if she'd like to come for a flight in my aeroplane one day, but I didn't get the chance. Will you tell her?'

'Yes. All right,' Rob said. 'I suppose . . .' He took a deep breath. At this moment, Tom seemed to him to be only slightly lower in status than a god. He marshalled his courage to ask the deity a favour. 'I suppose you wouldn't take *me* up as well?'

Tom frowned. It was one thing to offer a flight to a pretty girl with a cool manner whom he'd rather liked and to whom, besides, something was owed for her help and for the fact that he'd caused her a fall from her horse. It was another thing to hand out joy rides to air-struck schoolboys. Then he remembered how crazy about flying he'd felt at Rob's age.

'All right,' he said reluctantly. 'You too. You can telephone me to arrange it. Tom Searle at Maple Grange in Seale. And now you can start earning your flight in advance by helping me to swing the Moth round.'

Number One, Starling Cottages, sat beside the lane a hundred yards past Welcome Farmhouse on the road which led on to Hallows. Will and the boys had spent a week in the summer repairing one half of the two neglected cottages. The other half remained derelict, its roof gaping open to the sky where tiles had slipped and its blank, dirty windows with peeling paint; but Number One was neat and habitable, though sparsely furnished.

'I hope you'll be comfortable here,' Daisy said, lifting the latch on the door and leading the way into the small living room along with the last of the afternoon sunshine. The room contained only a gatelegged table with barley twist uprights standing in the middle of the herringbone brick floor, and a couple of wheelback chairs facing the fireplace.

'It looks a bit bare.' Daisy set down the basket she had been carrying on the table. 'But it should be enough to get by with. Will and I took on an extra farm hand in the summer, but we couldn't afford to keep him on once the harvest was finished. But we put in everything he needed here. I'll send one of the boys over later with some extra bits and pieces to make it a bit more homely.'

'Oh, but it's lovely!' Kitty had been carrying an armful of blankets from the farmhouse, with pillows balanced on top. She dropped them on a chair and looked round her wide-eyed. On the walk from Bentley station the quiet and emptiness of the countryside had unnerved her, but now she was getting used to it. The first sight of Starling Cottages had stirred an excitement in her that was painful in its pleasure. This was more like her imagined life as a wife to Jem: living with him in a pretty little cottage, cooking his dinners and washing his clothes and generally making him comfortable. He *had* said he would marry her, hadn't he? Even if the actual phrasing of it, 'I don't mind either way,' had been less than effusive.

'It'll do,' said Jem briefly. 'Is there a key to the front door?'

'I don't know,' Daisy said, taken aback. 'There must be one at the farmhouse, I suppose. It hasn't been locked for so long. Nobody steals things round here.'

'If you could find it,' Jem said, 'we'd be grateful. Tomorrow will do. We won't need anything else tonight. I'll come and get my instructions from the guv'nor in the morning, first thing.' He had moved to the door and somehow Daisy found herself out in the lane; dismissed as if she'd been a porter in a hotel, she thought, with a small flash of indignation, rather than the owner of the cottage and provider of work. Though strictly speaking, she supposed, it was Louella who was hiring this man – certainly the Griffins couldn't afford him. She hoped it had been all right to put the two of them into Starling Cottages – but after all, what alternative was there?

'I'll unpack,' Kitty said, when Daisy had gone. She stooped to pick up Jem's suitcase, but found her hand pushed away as he seized the handle himself.

'Leave that alone. I'll do it.'

'I wouldn't mind. It's not heavy.'

'I said, leave it alone.'

The narrow flight of stairs to an upper room was concealed behind what had looked like a cupboard door. Jem carried the suitcase and Kitty's bag upstairs, closing the door behind him. Plainly she was not to follow.

She stood in the living room listening to the sounds of Jem unpacking in the bedroom overhead. A few moments ago even the shadows had seemed friendly. Now she was scared again. She moved to investigate the basket that Daisy Griffin had left on the table. Daisy had been nice. A friendly woman, with a freckled face and untidy red hair and a glow about her that you could warm your hands at, Kitty thought, trying to hold on to the encouraging elements of the day.

The basket which Daisy had packed hastily at the farmhouse contained a cottage loaf, still with the scent of new bread about it, a pat of butter and a jar of strawberry jam with a gingham cap held on over the lid with an elastic band. There was tea and sugar and milk in screw-top jars, two generous chunks of cold pork pie, slices of bacon rashers wrapped in paper and eggs enfolded for safety in a tea cloth. Even a couple of rosy apples.

Cheered, Kitty carried the basket into the kitchen. Here there were white-painted kitchen chairs and a small rectangular table. A hod of coal stood beside the black range set into the chimney breast and there was a pile of kindling wood and newspapers on the hearth. Kitty put the food away in the larder beside the stone sink and began to lay a fire in the range, glad of something to occupy her. Jem reappeared as she put a match to the screwed-up newspaper.

'Well, this is home, for now. What do you think? Will it do?' His black mood had gone and he gave her a grin of mischief like the one that had stolen her heart on the day he first came into the Crown and Cushion.

'It's lovely,' Kitty said, feeling happy again.

'Regretting you came away with me?' he said, putting his arms round her from behind. His warm breath stirred the hair beside her ear. 'Wishing you were back with your Uncle George?'

'Oh, no,' said Kitty. It seemed cowardly, now, ever to have harboured such a feeling.

'. . . So I sent them down to Starling Cottages,' Daisy told her husband when he came back from Reading market. 'I didn't know what else to do – the poor girl wasn't well. And Louella said to put them up.'

'I suppose that's all right,' Will said, taking a metal cash box from a drawer in the sideboard. 'Lord knows, we can always use extra help.' He unlocked the box and carefully stowed away a roll of pound notes, the proceeds from the day's auction at Reading. 'Those bullocks didn't go for much today. Hardly covered the cost of feeding them till now,' he said, frowning. 'You say Louella's paid this man?'

'She said so. And his wife can help around the house, she reckoned.'

'Seems all right, then.'

'I expect so,' said Daisy. 'It's just . . . there's something about Jem Wilkins. He scared me, Will,' she admitted.

'In what way?'

'I don't know.' Daisy spread her hands. 'I'll feel better when you've met him.'

'When will that be?' Will asked, half his mind already on afternoon milking as he heard the lowing of cows plodding into the shed next door.

'Tomorrow. I told them they could come back here for their supper, but they said they'd rather settle in by themselves,' Daisy told him. '*Supper*,' she repeated on a note of anguish. 'Oh Lord! And I still haven't finished rolling out the pastry for that darned rabbit-pie!'

*   *   *

'Mum! Did you see the aeroplane?'

Rob exploded into the kitchen, eyes shining.

'I heard it go over earlier. And again a few minutes ago,' said Daisy, straightening up from the kitchen range in whose oven the rabbit-pie was now safely, if belatedly, installed. 'Shouldn't you be helping your dad with the milking?'

'Harry's doing that. I'll do one of her chores to make up. Mum, it landed, it actually *landed* in one of our fields! And the pilot talked to me. And I swung the prop so he could take off again. And he says he'll give me a flight,' Rob gabbled happily. 'Oh, *Mum*! Just wait till I tell the boys at school tomorrow. Wait till I tell Dad,' he remembered, and headed for the milking shed, leaving a cold draught behind him and an even colder sensation in his mother's stomach.

Daisy had a vivid imagination, readily able to conjure up graphic images of disaster, and all through the years since her first baby was born she'd had to battle with a tendency to be over-protective of her children. Usually it was Harriet who frightened her, jumping off haystacks at risk of neck and limbs, or taking her pony over a five-barred gate to prove that she was as good as any boy. In contrast, Rob and Jackie had seemed blessedly down-to-earth. She'd even used that phrase to describe her eldest son, she remembered ironically, until Rob developed this passion for aeroplanes. Even then she'd hoped it would limit itself to cutting out blurred photographs from newspapers to paste into a scrap-book, collecting old flying magazines and bringing home Biggles books from the library. For Rob to read about flight was one thing. Rob in an aeroplane hung thousands of feet over the Hampshire countryside was another thing entirely.

'Did Rob tell you about the aeroplane?' she asked Will, later.

'Yes, he did. I wish I'd been here to see it,' said Will. 'I'd have liked a word with the pilot! He's lucky none of the cows in Lower Five Acres was due to calve at the time,' he added, 'or there'd have been hell to pay. And twice as lucky that none of them was hit by the plane! These lads that go joy-riding over farmland, scaring the livestock, landing wherever they want to, never mind if there's a crop in whatever field they're using as a free runway . . .'

'I think he had engine trouble. Rob said he helped with the repair. The point is, Will, the pilot's offered to take him up for a flight.'

'Mmm,' said Will. 'I suppose it's the least he could do in the circumstances.'

'Do you think we should let Rob go?'

'It'd break his heart if we didn't. You know he's mad about flying.'

'It might be dangerous.'

'It won't be the last time he wants to do something that might be dangerous,' said Will. 'He's like any boy of his age, he needs a bit of adventure.' He noticed his wife's strained expression and came to stand beside her, placing a consoling arm around her shoulders. 'You can't wrap them in cotton wool, love. You have to give them their heads.'

'Even when it means risking their necks?' said Daisy sadly.

'Even then.'

'Please may I speak to Gavin Draycott?'

As dusk fell, Harriet, having borrowed Rob's bicycle without asking, was making a surreptitious call to Hallows from the telephone box in Bentley village.

'Who may I say is calling?' said the distant female voice which Harriet supposed must be a maid.

'It's Miss Griffin from Welcome Farm.'

'Just a moment. I'll enquire if he is at home.'

There was a pause. Outside the sky was growing blacker, not just with twilight but with an ominous gathering of clouds overhead. The first few drops of rain spattered against the glass, followed by one of those sudden downpours which, in this case, drove sheets of rain against the red crossbars of the telephone box, blotting out the sight of the Alton road and the fields beyond. She was going to get thoroughly soaked going home, she recognized resignedly.

'Harriet, I've told you not to telephone me here.' It was Gavin's voice, low and furious.

'But how else could I contact you?'

'You could have come to the crossroads today – as you promised.'

'I was on my way,' Harriet said. 'But an aeroplane came down with engine trouble in one of our fields.'

'Oh.' Silence, while Gavin digested this information. 'Was that the Moth I heard going over?'

'Yes. I had to stay to help. I'd have come if I could.'

'Would you?'

'Of course I would! You must know the way I feel about you.'

'Oh, Lord.' She heard him groan. 'Do you care about me, Harriet? Really?'

Harriet took a deep breath. 'I love you, Gavin. I said so yesterday and I don't pretend. Do you? If you've changed your mind—'

'I haven't. But when you didn't come, I thought *you* had. Harriet, my father's asked me to go to Newcastle for several weeks, to deal with some business for him.'

'Oh,' said Harriet blankly.

'I couldn't really refuse. I *am* supposed to be working for him – it's time I earned my keep, he says, though heaven knows he gives me such a mean little allowance . . . ' Gavin's voice took on a sharp, complaining note, as it had done in the past when talking about the money his parents allowed him. Distressed though she was that he was going away, Harriet felt a shiver of distaste at this side of his nature. 'Anyway,' he added, 'I thought it would be a good idea to go. Give me something else to think about that wasn't you.'

Harriet was silent.

'We have to talk,' he said, suddenly urgent. 'I have to see you before I leave.'

'Yes.'

'But it's raining buckets. And my car's loaded up with suitcases, ready for morning. There must be somewhere nearby that we can go,' pondered Gavin. 'A barn or something. Somewhere private, within walking distance for both of us?'

He did not offer any of the Hallows outbuildings.

'I think I know of a place,' Harriet said eventually. 'I could meet you there later. But it'll have to be much later,' she added, 'or they'll notice at home that I've gone.'

This morning she had wanted Will and Daisy to know about Gavin. She had wanted to take him home and say with pride, 'Here is the man I love. Isn't he wonderful?' But at this moment it seemed doubly important that her family shouldn't learn yet about a liaison which might well be going horribly wrong.

At Number One, Starling Cottages, Jem had been asleep, his arm across Kitty's bare shoulders in the small bedroom upstairs. Now some sound from below had woken him and, trained by a violent background, he was fully alert in an instant.

The cottage door was unlocked – 'Nobody steals things round here,' Daisy Griffin had said. And there was unmistakeably someone – or rather, more than one person – moving about downstairs. He could hear the low murmur of voices. He groped with one hand for the clothes he had left discarded on the floor beside the bed earlier that night, in the process of convincing Kitty that she had no regrets about her flight from the Crown and Cushion. Sitting cautiously upright in the dark, with Kitty still asleep beside him, he pulled on his trousers, then moved barefooted to the door, eased up the latch and slipped through onto the small square landing.

Ten steps below, the door to the front room was ajar and a lamp had been lit. Jem was used to moving stealthily. Silent as a cat, he reached the foot of the stairs and peered through the gap.

The intruders were a young man and a red-headed girl. Jem summed the man up by his clothes, his build and his haircut as upper middle class, too pretty to be dangerous, probably didn't know how to fight and if he did, would stick

to boxing by Queensberry Rules. No threat at all. The girl
had her back to him. The two of them were wound in each
other's arms in a passionate embrace. Jem's mouth twisted
cynically. A pity to break up such a tender moment. All the
same . . .

He gave the door a shove that sent it crashing back on
its hinges. That got their attention. The girl wrenched herself
from her lover's arms and spun round. He recognized her
as the one he'd watched – to her obvious discomfort – at
Hector Ramsay's funeral: Louella's niece. Her eyes were
stretched wide with shock but she wasn't screaming. In
passing, he registered that she wasn't the screaming sort and
gave her grudging credit for it. But upstairs, the crash of the
door had jerked Kitty into consciousness and she uttered a
sound which was the loudest he'd ever heard from her.

'Who the hell are you?' the man said in a choked voice.

'You're trespassing,' said the girl, on the attack.

'No,' said Jem levelly. 'You are. And I'm trying to get a
decent night's sleep, so you two lovebirds'll have to find
somewhere else for your canoodlings.'

'Now, look here,' blustered the fair young man. He turned
to his companion. 'Harriet, you said there'd be nobody here.'

'There shouldn't be.' The girl laid a hand on his arm to
silence him. 'This house belongs to my father,' she told Jem.

'True. Will Griffin owns the house and as from today,
Will Griffin has hired me.'

The girl looked at him closely. 'I've seen you before,
haven't I? At my uncle's funeral?'

'I was there.'

'What connection do you have with Hector?'

'My connection is with your aunt, Louella,' Jem told
her. He smiled, tilting his head, his eyes challenging her
resistance to the news. 'You might say we're related.'

'How?' she said sharply.

'Never mind that . . .' the young man broke in, twitching
with impatience.

'Oh, shut up for a minute, Gavin, this is important.'

To judge by his expression, the young man wasn't used

82

to being told to shut up. 'If it's that important, I'd better leave you to it,' he said, and blundered towards the front door. After a moment's hesitation the girl followed him.

'Gavin, wait a minute. I didn't mean—'

Jem grinned after the departing sounds of the man being angry; the girl, placatory. There was a movement behind him and Kitty joined him at the foot of the stairs. Her hair was tousled and her slight figure in the thin nightdress she'd pulled on upstairs was tense with apprehension.

'What's happening, Jem?'

'The daughter of the Griffin household turned up with her fancy man. I suppose nobody'd got around to telling her that we were here. They seemed a bit taken aback,' Jem said. 'So now they're having a row about it.' He crossed the room and closed the front door then returned to Kitty's side. 'Excitement over. But tomorrow,' he added thoughtfully, 'I'll have that key from Mrs Griffin. Just in case anyone else round here has got in the habit of using this place for lovers' meetings.'

He stroked a strand of Kitty's hair back from her face, noticing the shiver the gesture sent through her, enjoying his power. His hand moved to her jaw and down her neck to the top button of her nightdress, hooking a forefinger into the gap where the fabric parted beneath the button. He stroked his finger against her warm skin, deliberately rousing her. Then, just as deliberately, he switched off the message.

'Come on,' he said, turning her round and pushing her towards the stairs. 'You need your beauty sleep and so do I.'

In the lane outside Starling Cottages, Harriet caught up with Gavin. The remorseless rain beat down on both of them as she took hold of his arm. It stayed rigid under her fingers and she let him go.

'I'm sorry,' she said. 'I honestly didn't realize there'd be anyone there.'

'It's a pity you were wrong,' Gavin said, breathing hard. 'I would have liked to talk to you before I go away.'

'We can still do that.'

'Can we?' said Gavin sarcastically. Rain plastered his hair to his forehead and dripped from the end of his nose. 'We might drown in the process.'

'We could go somewhere else.' Harriet tried to think where. 'Maybe the stables at the farm?'

'Or the milking parlour, or the pig sty? No, thank you. I'd rather there was some kind of dignity to the proceedings.'

'Gavin, this isn't my fault.'

'No.' He sighed, resigned. 'But what's the use? Everything we do is beset with difficulties. We may as well face it, Harriet. You and I come from different worlds and I don't see how we can ever reconcile them.'

6

In 1919, when Will Griffin came home from four and a half years of war with the Horse Artillery, he'd had only the haziest idea of what to do next, but two things were concrete and indisputable: one, that he had a wife and a small child to support; two, that he couldn't stomach a return to his pre-war life as a groom at Maple Grange. Confront him with another employer like Rupert Brownlowe, who in Will's estimation embodied the very attitudes that had prolonged the war and cost so many lives, and he'd be in court on a charge of Grievous Bodily Harm in record time.

He was not alone in his dilemma. The country was full of discharged and disenchanted soldiers looking for a new start.

What is our task? Lloyd George had demanded in November of 1918, with ringing rhetoric. He had provided the answer: *To create a fit country for heroes to live in.* But the sheer number of men to be reabsorbed into the system was daunting. There was, however, an enormous demand for farmers – the nation's food-producing capabilities had been strained to the limit during the war years. Returning heroes whose previous employment had evaporated in their absence were offered cheap loans and grants to get themselves established as smallholders and, with grain fetching a high and government-guaranteed price, it was a tempting option.

It was with his demobilization gratuity and a government grant that Will had rented his first smallholding. He knew nothing about farming, other than what he had managed to pick up from observing the management of the Home Farm at Maple Grange; and the farm at the Grange hadn't been a thriving business, merely a convenient food source, the hobby of a man who wanted to look out on his own acres and was prepared to subsidize the farm's operations for the sake of that privilege.

Will thought he *could* learn to run a farm properly, but to start with, he preferred to stick to what he knew – and what he knew was horses. So he'd bought redundant cavalry horses and draught horses from the army and calmed them down for the different demands of civilian life. Meanwhile he moved among farmers and picked up every scrap of knowledge he could overhear and filed it all for future reference.

In 1928, in the face of dire predictions for the future of farming, when the government's fine guarantees had evaporated and profits were cut to the bone by the flood of cheap food imports, Will had made a successful bid for one hundred acres with a run-down farmhouse and outbuildings – at a giveaway price.

'You're welcome to it,' Captain Rollinson had said dryly, when the deeds for Welcome Farm were signed. 'And I wish you better luck with the place than the last tenant. He had a shooting accident, which is to say that he put a shotgun to his head behind a wall for the sake of the insurance for his wife and children. There's a lot of that kind of thing going on, these days.'

But Will had survived the lean years by a mixture of acumen and sheer hard work until, hearing rumours of government plans to set up a new marketing system which would end the cut-throat competition between farmers for sales of milk to the dairies, he'd bought a herd of Shorthorns and basic milking equipment from a bankrupt dairy farmer. It had put him further into debt with Louella Ramsay and there'd been a tense few months until the Milk Marketing Board had delivered the anticipated stabilization of prices. But the risk had been justified by the results. The Griffins weren't rich, but they were keeping their heads above water, and even paying back some of Louella's capital.

Will owed a lot to Louella. He wished he didn't. She was

a forceful, unpredictable woman, as different from her sister-in-law Daisy as chalk from cheese. Will didn't know why she had sent Jem Wilkins into Hampshire but from his experience of Louella's doings, it wasn't purely to lend a hand at Welcome Farm. So even without Daisy's misgivings, he would have been guarded in his welcome to the stranger who materialized out of the darkness at his side as he let the cows into the farmyard at five o'clock on a cold, rain-soaked morning.

'Morning, guv'nor,' said the man, his face mostly obscured by the turned-up collar of his mackintosh and the pulled-down brim of a flat cap. 'I'm Jem Wilkins. What do you want me to do?'

'Any experience with dairy cows?' Will asked, without much hope. Daisy had said the man was a Londoner.

'None.'

Will had anticipated gloomily that he'd have to spend more time showing the new worker what to do than would be saved by having the extra help. The one-word answer confirmed his fears. He sighed. 'I'll show you how we milk, then.'

'Do it by machine, do you?'

'No. Hand.' To acquire a milking machine was high on Will's list of ambitions but so far the purchase of pasteurizing and cooling equipment, and the generator to power them, had taken priority. He paused in the doorway of the shed, giving the quarters of an ambling Shorthorn a shove as she swayed past him, almost jamming him against the doorpost. 'Watch out for the cows, they'll kick if they don't like what you're doing.' He withdrew his mud-plastered hand and wiped it on his trousers. 'Not the best of weather for an introduction to this game,' he said wryly. A thought occurred to him. 'Not scared of cows, are you? Some townspeople are.'

In the lamplight, Jem grinned as he removed his hat.

'I'm not scared of anything,' he said simply. 'And you'll find I pick most jobs up quick enough. For a towny.'

* * *

Harriet woke to the sound of someone pounding a fist against her bedroom door. She groaned and rolled over in bed, burying her face in the pillow. The knocking was repeated and her brother Jackie's voice called through the door.

'Come *on*, Harry, rise and shine! You're late and Dad's furious!'

Harriet turned again and lay on her back, ungluing her eyes. She groped automatically for matches and, struggling onto one elbow, lit the candle on her bedside table. Light flared and with it, memory. The last thing she'd heard had been four chimes from the oak longcase clock that stood at the bottom of the stairs. Until then she'd lain awake, her restless mind trying to make sense of the events of the day.

Was Gavin still angry with her and had he any right to blame her for events that weren't her doing? Could the situation be rescued when he'd had time to calm down, or should she accept his judgement that the social gap between them was too wide to cross? The man from Hector's funeral . . . was he really, as he'd claimed, related to Louella and if so, what was his kinship to herself? Would he tell her parents about their midnight encounter?

Tossing and turning, she had eventually fallen into an exhausted sleep. Now the clock downstairs was chiming again and she counted automatically. Six chimes. *Six o'clock!* Appalled, Harriet flung back the blankets and struggled hastily into her clothes. No time to wash. She was indeed late for milking.

Throughout her wakeful hours she had been conscious of the sound of rain thrumming on the tiles outside her dormer window. It was still raining as, hunched under the mackintosh draped across her shoulders, Harriet picked her way among the puddles in the yard towards the milking shed. She hurried inside to the familiar sight of cows, coats matted with mud, lined up along the wall, chewing steadily at the hay strewn around their hooves. Huddled on low stools beside each cow were her father and brothers, hard at work.

Will looked up, briefly. 'We're nearly finished. What kept

you? No, tell me later. You needn't join us, you'd better go and help your mother in the dairy.'

Harriet hardly heard him. She was looking beyond him to a fourth figure, whose cheek leaned against the wet flank of a Shorthorn, his fingers stroking steadily down as milk frothed and spurted into the bucket between his feet. The dark hair, hazel eyes and twisted grin were those of the man she had last seen at Starling Cottages.

In the lamplit dairy, Daisy was washing her hands by the stone sink. Harriet began to roll up her sleeves, automatically fitting into the routines of the morning though her thoughts were scattered.

'Coming, ready or not.' Jackie staggered through from the milking shed with a brimming bucket in each hand. At ten, Jackie was skinny and undersized and in despair of ever achieving the height and strength of his elder brother. The weight of the buckets was almost beyond him, but he was fiercely determined not to admit it. He left his load in the middle of the brick floor and ran back to the shed.

Harriet shifted a stool towards the cooler with one foot. 'You pass, I'll pour,' she told her mother, climbing onto the stool. Daisy handed up a bucket and Harriet tipped it so that the white liquid ran down over the corrugated surface of the cooler into the circular pan below. Bucket followed bucket in quick succession as Rob joined Jackie to bring the milk through. It wasn't until the cooling and separating processes had been finished and Daisy and Harriet were standing together by the sink, washing the milking equipment, that conversation became possible.

'Mum . . . you know the Draycotts?'

'No,' said Daisy, heading for the door which led from the dairy into the farmhouse. 'And I don't much want to,' she added over her shoulder. 'Come on, love, let's get on with breakfast or the boys'll be late for school.'

Harriet silently followed her mother into the kitchen while her brain failed to come up with a solution to the problem of how to tell her parents about Gavin before the saturnine stranger from Starling Cottages did it for her.

The new farmhand had picked up the knack of milking with surprising speed. If his hands and wrists ached at the unaccustomed flexing involved, Jem hadn't complained. In fact, he didn't say much about anything, but this did him no harm in the eyes of Will Griffin, who was also inclined to be spare with words. The owner of Welcome Farm had to admit that Louella's envoy might yet prove to be an asset.

At nine o'clock, when Rob and Jackie had gone to school and Will was taking the newcomer on a rapid tour of the farm buildings, Daisy introduced a painfully nervous Kitty to Allie Briggs, newly arrived from Bentley on her bicycle.

'Allie, this is Kitty Wilkins. She and her husband will be helping us for a while.'

'Jem and me, we're not . . .' Kitty started to say, *We're not married*, but then her nerve failed her. Mrs Griffin was so nice, but who knew what her reaction might be to the news that the couple in Starling Cottages weren't properly united in wedlock? Kitty couldn't bear to think of eviction from the little house down the lane.

'We're not very used to country life,' she substituted, awkwardly.

'You'll soon get used to it,' said Daisy. Allie didn't say anything but eyed the newcomer with suspicion, sharpened by an awareness that she'd been a bit slack of late, a bit casual with her timekeeping and a bit too apt to indulge in gossip when she should have been rolling up her sleeves and getting stuck into the task in hand. It was not beyond the bounds of possibility that Daisy Griffin, for all she seemed so good-natured, might be planning to replace her with this timid girl.

'I'll do anything I can,' Kitty said.

'It would be useful to have an extra hand with the cows,' said Daisy, thinking aloud. 'Will's got another half dozen Shorthorns coming next week from that farm sale over at Alton.'

Kitty's eyes widened. 'Anything' had been too generous a word. She'd scrub and scour and bottle things till the crack of Doom if she had to, but deal with cows, those big, heavy, unpredictable creatures with horns and hooves? Allie saw her spasm of terror and smiled, partly out of relief. It would seem that at this stage, at any rate, the newcomer was not about to usurp her position. Allie's duties had always been strictly household.

At Medlar House Louella Ramsay, still drowsy, reached out a hand to what should have been a comforting human presence beside her. Instead, her fingers closed on the cold plumpness of an empty pillow. How long before she got used to this?

She lay on her back in the Hepplewhite four-poster which had been Hector's anniversary present to her last year. Staring up at the canopy of rose-printed linen union, she marshalled her courage for the day ahead. There would be – what? Yet more kind condolences filtering in from her husband's acquaintances, for which formal acknowledgement would be required. She'd had cards printed for that. A meeting with Hector's solicitor to discuss the details of his will and her financial situation; no surprises expected there. Mr Madigan had already intimated delicately before the funeral that Hector had left her very well provided for and after all, there was no-one else to take a share in her dead husband's inheritance. He'd been a widower when she met him and his only son had been reported missing, presumed killed, amid the carnage at Loos in 1915.

The solicitor was due at ten. What next? A trip to the workshop where her ready-to-wear ladies' fashions were made up. That was a formality – once the business was established she had appointed perfectly adequate overseers – but she had kept up the regular appearances because they gave the workforce a feeling that they were working for a real human being rather than an impersonal company. They had to be reassured by the sight of the widow, grieving but still functioning as an employer. There would be yet more genuine, clumsy condolences from the seamstresses.

Hector, why did you have to die? I can't bear it . . .

What else was there to think about?

The sardonic features of her half-brother Jem swam into mind and behind Jem, the shadowy figure of the man he had been sent to torment.

It was a long time since the pregnant Louella had gone to Rupert Brownlowe with Daisy and baby Harriet, and since he'd contemptuously dismissed their request for Poor Law assistance. Then, Rupert had been in his fifties, with greying hair and an upright figure blurred by a little too much self-indulgence at the dinner table. Too old to fight, he'd spent his Great War harrying younger men into volunteering under the Derby Scheme, in sitting on Tribunals to decide the fate of those who'd applied to be excused from active service, and in shell-making at his converted lawn-mower factory.

He must have made a bit of war profit at that factory . . . and lost it, Louella reminded herself with satisfaction. The factory had been her first act of revenge. She'd never seen the blackened shell, but the building had been blazing nicely when she'd left it in November of 1918.

Arson was an interesting pastime, but Hector Ramsay's wife could not take such a risk again. The appearance of Jem at Medlar House had been fortuitous. Thanks to Jem, there had been other fires on the Maple Grange estate: a haystack here, a barn there, a blaze in summer that had eaten up a belt of woodland dangerously close to the house. Expensive, disquieting events, spaced so that they might just be disconnected strokes of misfortune. Haystacks *could* catch fire if carelessly stacked with damp hay at their core. Barns *could* smoulder if a workman let fall the butt of a surreptitious cigarette. Jem was good at blurring the evidence.

She'd told him it was time to think up alternatives to the fires. It would be interesting to see what his ingenuity suggested.

Allie Briggs, answering a mid-morning knock at the kitchen door, found a delivery boy from a Farnham florist's shop.

He was lifting a large white cardboard box out of the wicker basket suspended below the handlebars of his bicycle.

She carried the box into the kitchen, where the trophies that Will Griffin won each autumn at ploughing matches were spread out on newspapers on the pine kitchen table. Harriet was polishing the cups with a rag dipped in her mother's home-made concoction of ammonia, powdered chalk, methylated spirit and water – Daisy still disdained proprietary cleaners in favour of the old methods she'd learned as a young housemaid at Maple Grange.

'Flowers! For you, Harry.'

Harriet put down her wad of rag and the two-handled cup on which Will Griffin's name had been engraved, for the third year in succession, last month. She lifted the lid of the box and folded back the waxed paper to reveal what seemed to be dozens of red roses.

'Long-stemmed, too. Have to be hothouse, this late. Must've cost a fortune.' Allie was impressed. So was Harriet.

You and I come from different worlds. That's what Gavin had said in the lane outside Starling Cottages, cutting short her attempts to placate him. The cold reality of his words and the finality with which he had said them had cut through her like a knife. But now these flowers. His way of saying, 'I love you', she thought, giddy with relief.

An embossed card lay among the flowers. She fished it out.

The photographs came out very well and I am still employed. I hope you'll let me take you up for a flight one day soon. Thank you again for being an angel. Tom Searle.

Sick with disappointment, Harriet stared dumbly at the card.

'What shall we do with them?' Allie asked, lifting a stem and sniffing appreciatively at the half-open bud that topped it.

The flowers weren't from Gavin and there weren't enough vases.

'Throw them away,' said Harriet.

*　　*　　*

'First off, I thought they were from her young man,' Allie told Daisy, 'and so did she. But they were from someone else, so she didn't want them.'

Harriet had taken her disappointment out on the task of mucking out Briony's stall and the box of roses, lying abandoned on the kitchen table, had attracted Daisy's notice. After a short struggle, curiosity overcame her reluctance to ask anything of Allie, whose reputation as the biggest gossip in Bentley was widely known and richly deserved.

'What young man?' she asked, filling a milking bucket with water for the roses while it was decided what to do with them.

'That Draycott lad from the big house along the road.'

'What makes you say he's Harriet's young man?'

'I've seen what I've seen,' said Allie obscurely.

'And what exactly is it that you've seen, Allie?' Daisy said, with difficult patience.

'I've seen him parked in that yellow car of his down by the crossroads at all odd hours of the day. Waiting for someone, that's obvious. And I've noticed, you must have noticed it too, how odd young Harriet's been behaving lately. Dreamy and happy one minute, snapping your head off the next. Well, I know the signs. Our Phyllis was the same, that time she took up with the plumber's son. It comes to them all, sooner or later,' said Allie wisely. 'Matter of fact, I'd say your Harriet's well overdue for falling in love.'

Daisy *had* noticed that Harriet was behaving a bit oddly but, distracted as ever by the demands of a farming day, she'd simply feared that her daughter must be sickening for something. Allie was probably right, she acknowledged reluctantly, in her assumptions that linked a yellow car and a waiting youth with eighteen-year-old Harriet, ripe and ready for romance.

She could remember her own first love so clearly, the confusion of it, the pain and the pleasure, and the longing to confide in someone . . . but Harriet hadn't said anything to her and now she wondered how many signs she had missed, how many hesitant openings she had ignored. It hurt that Allie had noticed what she had not. She terminated the conversation briskly.

'Well, roses and romance are all very well, but I've got work to do. If you haven't, Allie, you can get started on the weekly wash.'

Even thick-skinned Allie recognized a closed subject. Closed for the time being, anyway. She trudged upstairs to strip the beds. Daisy took Kitty out to the dairy to initiate her into the workings of the butter churns, in the faint hope that she could be led by degrees towards the idea of actually milking cows. At the same time, she found time to worry about what Allie had told her. Was Harriet really in love with Gavin Draycott? She fervently hoped not.

She had been concerned in the past about the effect on Harriet of her visits to her Aunt Louella, who represented a different standard of living and some different moral standards too. But Louella had hinted that she meant to make Harriet her heir. Will had said they had no right to stand in Harriet's way and that they were strong enough as a family to absorb some outside influences, and Will was always so calm and so right about such things that she had accepted his judgement. Now, if the outcome was for Harriet to get herself entangled with a Draycott, Daisy wondered if she shouldn't have stood firm and kept her daughter tied to the farm.

From the little Daisy had seen and heard of Gavin Draycott, he could spell nothing but trouble for her head-strong but inexperienced daughter.

Louella had been expecting Graham Madigan, Hector's solicitor, but the man Everett ushered into the morning room was a stranger, in his early thirties. His suit had come from a good tailor, Louella assessed automatically, and he had the tall, broad-shouldered figure to do it justice.

'Good morning, Mrs Ramsay.' He held out his hand, smiling and confident. Louella ignored it – she wasn't in the mood for strangers. Instead she glanced at the card that Everett had handed to her: *Stuart Armitage*.

'Graham sends his apologies. His gout is very severe, so I came instead.' The visitor had withdrawn his hand but his professional smile remained in place despite the snub. Brown eyes under thick brows, healthy brown hair, even teeth in a clean-shaven face. Good-looking and well aware of it, Louella summed him up.

'A telephone call would have done just as well,' she said. She was recalling snatches of conversation between Hector and his solicitor: *I have taken on a partner. Young fellow called Stuart. He seems very competent. Bit of a charmer with the ladies.*

'I don't think there was anything urgent about today's appointment.' Louella had no intention of being charmed. 'Graham just wanted to talk about my husband's estate in more depth than was possible before the funeral. We can postpone that until he's fit again.'

'Actually, he suggested I might talk to you instead. He's passing over a considerable amount of that side of his business to me these days. He's not as young as he was,' said the visitor, his smile now including Louella in the ranks of the youthful who might find advancing old age amusing.

'He's certainly not as young as *you*, Mr Armitage,' Louella said tartly, and noted with satisfaction that the remark had hit home. Stuart Armitage's face flushed and, momentarily, his air of confidence faltered. *Now why*, Louella asked herself, *should I be bothering to score points against him?* She supposed it was simply that she didn't like the idea of being 'passed over' to a junior partner without prior consultation.

Graham Madigan had dealt with Hector Ramsay's business affairs for many years and she was used to the old man's rather ponderous chivalry, his unconscious habit of stroking his bald patch while he assembled the appropriate phrases, his tweed suits which had taken on the shape of their owner, and the comfortable aura of pipe tobacco which always hung around him. She had been expecting a friendly, stress-free interview this morning. Now instead of a friend she was confronted by Stuart Armitage who was a little too clean, too uncrumpled, too *handsome*, to be trustworthy.

'I am fully qualified,' he said stiffly. 'And fully acquainted with the details of the late Mr Ramsay's estate.'

'Are you? I thought such details were meant to be confidential? Am I to understand that your firm wishes to stop dealing with my financial affairs?'

'No,' said Stuart. 'Graham just thought . . . we both thought . . . that in view of his health problems and so on, it might be appropriate if I were to deal with your affairs from now on. Naturally, if you don't like the idea, Graham will continue to advise you. To the best of his ability.'

There was a pause.

'At least try me out, Mrs Ramsay.' It was a direct appeal. Against her will, Louella felt sympathy for his situation. He had been sent out to conquer and she had proved resistant. She imagined him having to face Graham Madigan with news of his rejection.

'All right,' she said grudgingly.

He had not exaggerated when he claimed to be familiar with the details of Hector's estate. Producing a sheaf of papers from his leather briefcase, he listed the shareholdings and capital assets which were now Louella's. He added a résumé of their current values, which were reassuringly high, despite the effects of the Depression.

'You are a wealthy woman, Mrs Ramsay.'

'So it would seem.'

'And I gather that your own little business is doing well.'

'Yes,' Louella said tersely. 'It's making a very respectable profit.'

'May I have the details?'

'Is that necessary? Your partner managed my husband's portfolio, Mr Armitage, but I prefer to handle my own business affairs. I have done so for some years and with some success. I shall continue to do so. As far as my husband's holdings are concerned, I am happy for your firm to go on dealing with them for the time being, while I familiarize myself with what is involved.'

'I see,' said Stuart. He laid the sheaf of papers on her desk. 'Have I offended you, Mrs Ramsay?' he asked directly.

'No,' said Louella. 'Well, yes,' she said, on reflection. 'I don't like my very successful fashion industry being referred to as *your own little business*. I find it patronizing.'

'I'm sorry. You are quite right to take me to task on that, and I humbly beg your forgiveness.'

Louella found herself disarmed. There was genuine contrition in Stuart's brown eyes . . . and something else. Something she did not want to recognize.

'Is there anything else we need to discuss at this moment, Mr Armitage?' she said. 'I have things to attend to.'

'I suppose not. But at some stage in the not-too-distant future we need to talk about your own will.'

'I have made one. Haven't you seen it?'

'You leave a few minor bequests and the bulk of whatever you die possessed of to your niece Harriet.'

'That's right,' said Louella. 'Is there a problem?'

'Only that it doesn't take account, as such, of your recent change of circumstances; I refer to your inheritance of your late husband's estate. Most people in your situation choose to update their last will and testament.'

In Louella's beautiful bedroom the dressing table beside the bed was another expensive antique, one of many such presents from Hector over the years. The twin halves of the lid were inlaid with a marquetry shell pattern and folded back to reveal all the perfectly finished, brass-handled covers of the compartments in which she kept the cosmetics and the jewellery that her husband had given her. The mirror, only a little cloudy with age, lifted from a slot at the back on ratchets.

She faced herself in the mirror. Her hair was still black, with just a touch of grey over her ears; rather becoming, Hector had told her when he first spotted the grey. Her complexion was clear and her figure firm. She knew that Stuart Armitage had looked at her as a woman. She admitted that he had stirred something in her, and she felt ashamed.

You're a widow. Remember? The Widow Ramsay, she told herself brutally. *Hector is seven days dead and a man has only to glance at you . . .*

With a shudder of disgust she turned away from her reflected image, her hand jerking at the pearl necklace she wore. The string broke with the force of the gesture, sending pearls cascading across the floor. Louella drew a long breath, crouched and began to gather them up in the palm of her hand.

Stuart Armitage must be seven or eight years her junior, but she had seen in his eyes that he found her desirable. And this had reawakened a suppressed longing.

In 1916, when the army shot Robert Colindale for conduct that the Field General Court Martial had labelled 'cowardice', his wife had only been kept going in the months after his death by the knowledge of a new life growing inside her. In the autumn Robert's son was born and in the short hour that he lived, she had named him 'Daniel Robert'. *Danny* . . . whose small grave was kept tidy by someone whom she paid to do so, because Louella could not bear to be near the place where he was buried.

With Hector there had been no children. They had never talked about the reasons why.

I might remarry.

I could still have children.

If only that could be true . . . but if it was going to happen, it would have to happen soon. At forty, she was running out of time.

'Mr Wilkins? I want to ask you something,' said Harriet to Jem in the stable yard at midday.

'Why don't you call me Jem? Seeing as we're related.'

'That's what I wanted to ask about. You said the same thing last night. Now would you please explain what you meant.'

Jem smiled without showing his teeth and there was something mocking in those hazel eyes that left Harriet feeling prickly all over, just as she had done under his scrutiny in the church at Blackheath. She wanted to walk away, but she had to know more.

'So Lou's never mentioned me,' said Jem. 'Funny, I ain't surprised. Inclined to be forgetful, is Lou. Forgetful about where she comes from, anyway.'

'I've got work to do, Mr Wilkins, and so have you, so could you please get to the point.'

'I think you should ask her about it,' Jem said. 'Not me. If Lou hasn't told you, maybe she doesn't want you to know. And as you reminded me, we've both got work to do; so if you'll excuse me, ma'am, I'll be getting on with mine.'

The emphasis on the word '*ma'am*' was deliberate and insolent. So was the mocking way in which he touched a finger to his forehead before he turned away. Harriet stared after his departing back. She had never met anyone so rude. She felt that she should not tolerate such treatment from a man who, after all, was supposed to be working for her father. She didn't know what to do about it. She unclenched her fists.

'All right,' she called after him. 'I'll ask Aunt Louella.'

Afterwards she remembered that he knew about Gavin Draycott, and that so far he did not seem to have mentioned her midnight arrival at Starling Cottages to her parents. She supposed she ought to be grateful about that . . . but instinct told her that if Jem Wilkins was keeping any secrets, it was not out of decent reticence but because he hadn't yet worked out how best to use them.

7

By midday the rain had stopped and in the afternoon, pale sunlight filtered through gaps in the clouds overhead. Taking a bowl of potato peelings out to the pig sty at the end of the garden, Daisy found her daughter sitting on the low wall that surrounded the sty, staring moodily into the distance. She tipped the peelings over the wall and sat down beside Harriet.

'Something's up, isn't it? Are you going to tell me about it?'

Harriet didn't answer for a few seconds. Then, 'I hate that man who's come to work here,' she said, with sudden vehemence.

'I can't say I've taken to him either. But his wife's nice,' said Daisy. 'And your father says he made a very good start with the milking and might be useful to have around. Don't you think we ought to give him a chance before we make up our minds?'

'He was at Uncle Hector's funeral,' Harriet said.

'Well, after all, it was Louella who sent him here. What is it that you particularly don't like about him?'

'It's the way he looks at me,' Harriet muttered. She kicked at a stone that lay beside her shoe. 'It makes me feel nervous, that's all. And there's something else. Oh, you'll have to know sooner or later.'

'Is it something to do with those roses that came for you?'

Harriet looked startled. 'The roses? Oh, no! At least, not in the way you think . . . They were from the pilot who landed here yesterday, just to thank me for helping him. I don't know why he bothered, really. It isn't him I have to tell you about.'

'Gavin Draycott, then?' Daisy prompted gently.

'How did you know? Did that horrible Jem Wilkins tell you?'

'Jem?' It was Daisy's turn to look startled. 'No. How would he . . . ?' She broke off and started again. 'Allie said she'd seen Gavin Draycott waiting at the crossroads for someone and we just wondered if that someone was you.'

'Oh. *Allie!*' Harriet's voice was scornful. 'Is there a blade of grass that withers without Allie reporting it to someone, somewhere? Well, as it happens she's right. I have been meeting Gavin. We were – we were getting close. But that's all over now.' She stared at the ground. 'He seemed to think we couldn't go on seeing one another because our backgrounds were too different,' she said flatly.

'Oh,' said Daisy. She experienced a sudden gust of rage against the absent Gavin for having hurt Harriet's feelings – for Harriet *was* hurt, that much was obvious in spite of her determinedly matter-of-fact manner. It was part of having daughters that they must grow up and fall in love and perhaps have their hearts broken, but Daisy would have given anything to be able to spare her daughter this particular experience. She put out a hand and covered Harriet's hand, lying on top of the wall.

'He's got no sense at all, then.'

'It doesn't really matter,' Harriet lied unconvincingly. 'But I was wondering . . . do you think it would be all right if I go to stay with Aunt Louella? I think she must be lonely, for all she was so brave at Uncle Hector's funeral. And I'd like to get away, just for a while.'

Harriet's visits to Louella always meant the juggling of farm chores, and because it wasn't fair to burden the boys most of the extra tasks devolved on Daisy and Will. At least, Daisy remembered, there would be Jem Wilkins and Kitty to help fill the gap this time.

'I'm sure we could manage it,' she said.

'Madam's got over it very well, hasn't she?'

In the kitchen at Medlar House the staff were sitting down

to their morning tea when Cook make her comment.

Everett snorted, spooning two spoonfuls of sugar into his cup. 'Oh, yes. Hard as flint, she is. Doubt if she's so much as shed a tear for Sir . . . which is a shame if you ask me, because he was as decent a gent as ever drew breath, and as fond of *her* as she didn't deserve.'

'That's all *you* know,' said Rose, the housemaid. 'She comes over hard; she doesn't like to make a show of her feelings in public. But *I* know she cries into her pillows every night, and has done ever since the day he died.'

'Oh yes? Confides in you, does she, Miss Know-It-All?' Everett didn't like a subordinate member of the household laying claim to any knowledge that he didn't possess.

'Course she doesn't. Madam doesn't *confide*. Holds it in as if her life depended on it,' Rose said. 'But I'm the one that makes her bed, aren't I? And I've seen the tear stains on her pillowcase. Soaked through it is, sometimes.'

'Well, I never,' said Cook. 'Who'd have thought it? So she's got a streak of human feeling in her after all.'

Louella, grappling grimly with her streak of human feeling, was discovering that widows were accorded sympathy, but not invitations. She and Hector had enjoyed a wide circle of acquaintances, but none of the dinner-party guests or business contacts who sent black-edged cards expressing their carefully measured condolences had been close enough to Louella in the past to offer any real comfort or companionship to her now. It was taken for granted that she would stay cloistered at home for a suitable period, mourning her loss.

Six months? A year? The prospect appalled her.

Hector was gone and no amount of mourning would change that. She hated the hard knot of misery inside her that made her punch her pillows every night in the dark hour before dawn. It *must* not control her, it had to be displaced by suitable distractions, and the setting of Jem on to Rupert Brownlowe, though it had been a start, was not enough.

Into the gap crept an idea that threatened to become an

obsession. The presence of an attractive man like Stuart Armitage had reminded her that she still wanted a child.

All right. But that would mean finding another husband. She recoiled from the prospect. She'd been the driving force in her marriage, but men as tolerant and generous as Hector were rare. Suppose she made a mistake and found herself shackled to a bully or a bore?

If you don't get married, you can't have a baby.

From past experience, she knew she didn't get pregnant easily – only one miscarriage and one birth from her marriage to Robert, for all that it had been so passionate before he went to the war. Nothing with Hector. And she was older now, coming to the end of her child-bearing years. It was hopeless, not worth considering, and hence her unabated hatred for the man she held responsible for her childless condition: Rupert Brownlowe.

And yet . . . she was still attractive to men, a fact of which Stuart Armitage's manner yesterday had been a confirmation. From the look in his eyes, he'd willingly have provided her with a practical demonstration of his interest, given the slightest encouragement.

She even considered a baby fathered by Stuart. It would be good-looking, undoubtedly. Intelligent, perhaps. But the idea was preposterous, she scolded herself. Then the image of the self-assured young solicitor and his physical presence sprang suddenly to mind, forcing a sharp intake of breath. But even if she discounted the age gap between them, he was no drone. Rather, he was the kind of man who would rapidly take control over a wife's life – and her money.

Louella sat at her desk, drumming her fingers lightly on her blotting pad, eyes staring unseeingly at the Meissen figure of a Harlequin on the mantelpiece as she considered the problem. At last she sat back in her chair and stretched her arms above her head before bringing her hands down, palms flat, on the surface of the desk in front of her.

Stuart would do. Any reasonably handsome, healthy, clever man would do. She wouldn't let him become important, and she certainly wouldn't agree to a wedding ceremony, she fantasized. But she'd allow herself to be seduced with the minimum of delay if the occasion arose. If she got pregnant she'd travel abroad, to return in due course with a child. She'd claim she'd adopted an orphan, somewhere on the continent, to save it from a life of poverty. She'd have her baby, God willing, without the penalties often attached to being a wife. Tongues might wag, but she'd outface the gossips.

Mr Armitage? She rehearsed her opening gambit. *When we last spoke you mentioned that I should think further about updating my will. I'd like to discuss this with you, if I may?*

She reached for the telephone on the desk but as her hands closed round the receiver, the bell rang, making her jump.

'Aunt Louella,' said her niece Harriet, when they had been connected. 'I need your help.'

When the conversation was over, Louella hung the receiver carefully on its socket and leaned back in her chair, lips pursed.

Should she now go ahead with her planned telephone call to Stuart?

No. For the time being, at any rate, Harriet had diverted her from that particular course. The presence of her niece at Medlar House couldn't fail to inhibit the development of any emotional or physical relationship between herself and any new man.

How shocked Harriet would be if she knew what her aunt had planned to do. Indeed, the Louella of a bare two or three weeks ago would have recoiled in horror at such a scheme. So why, if she had just been saved from a gross mistake, did she feel this hollow sense of frustration?

She had read somewhere that you regret the things you don't do, rather than the things you do.

Be that as it may, for the time being, Stuart would have to wait.

'My dear Harriet, don't be so defeatist.'

Harriet sat on one side of the supper table at Medlar

House, Louella sat on the other. Louella had drunk three glasses of claret with her meal and was talking with animation. She pulsed with energy, whereas Harriet, having poured out the details of her recent romantic disappointment, was feeling rather drained.

'So his people own Hallows? What of it?' said Louella.

'I think they expect him to marry someone who's better connected.'

'Your connections aren't negligible,' Louella pointed out. 'For instance, you're related to me.'

'But I don't know how to behave in their sort of society,' Harriet said.

'That can soon be remedied.'

'I don't see how . . .'

Louella rang the silver bell beside her plate to summon the butler. 'Everett, you can clear this away. And bring us another bottle of claret, please. And a pencil and some paper.'

Harriet toyed with her half-empty wine glass while Everett carried out her aunt's instructions. She didn't want any more claret – she was light-headed enough already. Louella wrote something on the notepad that Everett had placed beside her and underlined it twice.

'Plan of attack for the storming of Gavin Draycott,' she said briskly, 'and the total disarmament of the tedious and small-minded objections of his family. We'll start with your advantages. One: you are beautiful. Two: you are intelligent. Three: you are my niece and not without prospects. Four: Gavin is attracted to you. The problems: the Draycotts' wealth is newly acquired – I have made a few preliminary enquiries. They do not require that Gavin should find himself an heiress, but they do want a daughter-in-law who can be introduced to their new friends without causing them to blush.'

By now, Harriet's complexion was scarlet. Louella made notes on her pad and raised her head again.

'Your background? Will is a freeholder, not a tenant, and he is making a success of his business, so that situation is not without hope. But not to put too fine a point on it, Harriet, to become suitable daughter-in-law material for the Draycotts, you would have to shed the aroma of the farmyard.'

'Aunt Louella!' Harriet said miserably, trying to stem the flood.

'Your dress sense must be taken in hand. You must definitely learn to paint – your face, that is. And, if you show the least aptitude for it, delicate watercolours of country scenes. Piano lessons. That's a rather long-term venture, but we can make a start. You should at least be able to recognize a Chopin Prelude when you hear one. And deportment. And elocution. *Particularly* elocution.'

'Oh,' said Harriet, crushed. 'Gavin said he loved the sound of my voice.'

'Maybe he did,' Louella told her. 'But his parents wouldn't. And that's the whole point of the exercise, isn't it? Getting past the objections of his family? They have to be able to introduce you to their friends without apologizing for you.'

'Why apologize?' Colour flared in Harriet's cheeks. 'I'm a farmer's daughter. I'm not ashamed of that. Actually, I'm darned proud of it! When I think of the way they've worked at getting the farm on its feet . . . and the way Dad studies at nights . . . after the day's work he does, anyone else would just give up and go to bed, but he stays up late reading all the farming magazines and the advice from the Ministry about crops and crop prices, and the right fertilizers and what sort of feeding a cow needs to give the most milk. The Draycotts, they just made their money with a few share deals! Then they sit in their grand house and look down their noses at people like my parents. And they don't even know the right way to take care of their brand new silver – they have to get someone like my mum, someone who's had a lifetime's training, to do it for them!'

Louella laid down her pen, waiting till Harriet paused for breath. Then, '*Aunt Louella, I need your help . . .*' she quoted. 'Remember? It isn't *me* that wants to impress these people.'

'I'm sorry.' Harriet subsided. She spread her hands helplessly. 'I don't know what's the right thing to do,' she said. 'I mean, I *am* proud of Mum and Dad, and I'd hate them to get the idea that I wasn't. And I don't want to change the way I am if it means they could get that idea. But . . . I *do* want Gavin,' she admitted. 'And sometimes I think I'd do anything and give up anything if it meant that we could get married.'

'Life is never easy,' said Louella dryly. 'You have to make choices. And stick to them. For what it's worth,' she added, 'I don't believe Will and Daisy would want to deny you anything that would make you happy, and I don't think they'd hold it against you in the long run if that meant you had to grow away from them for a while.' A thought occurred to her. 'Harry, have they ever talked to you about the time when you were born? You know it was during the war.'

'. . . And Dad was away with the Artillery? No, they don't talk about it much.'

'Haven't they said anything else?'

'What sort of thing?'

'I don't know. It's not important.' Louella changed the subject. 'Where were we? Elocution lessons.'

'Does that mean talking with plums in my mouth like those girls in the films?'

Louella smiled. 'Don't worry, it won't be as bad as you think. There's a lady called Lydia Matthews who can help you. She certainly helped me when it mattered.'

The Honourable Lydia Matthews was the widow of a young officer killed at Passchendaele in 1917, in circumstances which did him credit. He had been posthumously awarded a Military Medal. It had not taken Lydia, his grieving widow, very long to realize that citations for bravery did not pay the death duties on her husband's estate, let alone the school fees of her children.

She had met Louella Ramsay while shopping for clothes which would look sufficiently *haute couture* to pass muster in the circles in which she moved, while costing considerably less. In the course of the transaction they discovered that they had much in common.

Both of them had lost a man they loved to the war. Both were summoning all their courage to cope with a less than ideal world. They had liked each other on sight. Louella had designed some clothes exclusively for Lydia and had them made up in her workrooms. In return, Lydia had taught Louella the rudiments of the behaviour which was acceptable to the society to which her second husband, Hector Ramsay, belonged. This had also launched Lydia into a new career – one which amply covered the cost of sending her two boys to Wellington.

'She's been specializing ever since in knocking the rough edges off social climbers,' Louella explained. 'War profiteers' daughters of a marriageable age, for instance. They've got the cash and now they want the trimmings. And what with all the death duties the big estates had to pay as their owners died in Flanders or on the Somme, the landed gentry are desperate for new blood and the new money that goes with it, if only they can acquire it without social embarrassment!'

As she spoke, Louella felt a passing pang of sympathy for the Draycotts. If they'd had a daughter, they might well have been employing Lydia Matthews themselves. The sympathy gave way to determination. If she had anything to do with the matter, they would take her niece instead, and be glad of it.

'I shall contact Lydia tomorrow,' she said.

Daisy compromised over the issue of Rob's flight in a Tiger Moth.

'If he follows up the offer, then you can go. But you mustn't contact him about it.'

'Oh, *Mum!*' Rob was anguished. So far as he was concerned, this wasn't a compromise, this was a shattering of his hopes. 'He'll never remember. I'll never see him again. I'll never get to fly!'

But one weekend in November, collecting some gate hinges for his father from the ironmonger in Farnham, he bumped into Tom Searle at the bottom of Castle Street.

'Hullo, young Griffin. You never telephoned me about that flight.'

'No,' said Rob, feeling dizzy because his prayers had come true and the aviator had actually recognized him. 'Mum said I mustn't hound you.'

'But you still want to fly?'

'Oh, *yes*!' said Rob with fervour.

'Let's see. Tomorrow's Sunday and it looks like being fine. I could take you up tomorrow. Would that suit? I'd collect you in my car at about nine o'clock and drive you over to Croydon.'

'That'd be super,' Rob managed to say.

'Did your sister get my roses?'

'Ye-es.' The roses had stood in their milk bucket, largely ignored by the Griffins, until the water evaporated, at which point they had died. Rob didn't really understand what might drive a man to send flowers to his sister, but he didn't think that Tom would be much cheered by hearing of the reception given to his gift.

'Would she like to fly tomorrow too, do you think?'

'She can't. She's in London,' said Rob.

'Oh,' said Tom, sounding a little downcast by the news. 'When will she be back?'

'Dunno. When she's learned to be a lady, I suppose. Aunt Louella's going to show her how to dress grand and talk grand and impress people. I think it's daft,' said Rob disgustedly. 'All because she's soft on Gavin Draycott.'

'Oh,' said Tom again. He pursed his lips in a soundless whistle. 'Might have known there'd be *someone*,' he murmured, then shrugged. 'Never mind. See you tomorrow, then, young Griffin. Don't forget to wrap up well – it can get chilly at five thousand feet.'

Marion Brownlowe was slight of figure and deceptively fragile in appearance, but the management of her husband

Rupert gave her no problems at all. In part her strength came from her comparative youthfulness – in 1933, Rupert was nearing seventy and it wore him out to argue with Marion, twenty years his junior. She knew he needed her and the domestic comforts she organized for him; and she didn't love him, which left her immune to his anger. When he protested furiously about the hiring of the disabled Billy Marshall she heard him out calmly, then proceeded to make sure she got her own way.

'But Rupert, he was in some distress and I naturally assumed – as did Colonel Strover – that you would wish to help him. He's a former employee of yours, and wounded in the war at that. I know how you feel about making this country fit for heroes. I didn't think you would want it spread about the district that you had refused help to such a man.'

Rupert scowled, but was silent.

'And I thought it would help you, too, if he could get the stables into a better condition.'

'What can he do? Effectively, he's only got one arm.'

'He's lost a shoulder blade – it was shattered on the Somme in 1916. But he's had seventeen years to adapt to the condition, dear. I agree that he looks feeble at present, but that's because he's had a long period of semi-starvation, living in a damp, half-derelict house of which his landlord should have been ashamed. Once he's had some decent meals and slept under warm blankets for a few weeks, I think you'll be surprised at what he can do. And he'd work hard for very low wages,' Marion added, cunningly. She knew all Rupert's weaknesses.

'The stables aren't even being used,' Rupert pointed out, but his resistance was waning.

'I know, and I've always thought it a pity. I've often thought you must miss the horses – you've told me so many times about the days when your beautiful hunters won prizes, dear.'

'I'm past it now.'

'I don't believe that for a moment,' Marion said. 'Why

don't you start again? In a small way, of course, and see how you get on? It would give you an interest.'

Rupert snorted, dismissing the idea as impractical. Here he was, old, arthritic, plagued with debts . . . and on the strength of having engaged a one-armed weakling as an odd job man, his wife was proposing that he revive an enterprize that he had abandoned almost twenty years ago. Marion was simply out of touch with reality. All the same, her assumption that such a thing was possible gave him permission to dream. He did miss the horses, there was no denying it, and they had brought him success and respect that had eluded him elsewhere.

'I can't ride any more,' he said dismally.

'Surely you can get someone to do it for you, dear, if you direct them.'

Her phrase conjured up an appealing image. Rupert saw himself standing in one of his fields, leaning on his stick, while some suitably respectful employee cantered a well-broken animal to his instructions. His imagination crowded the gateway to the field with appreciative spectators and supplied their comments.

Brownlowe hasn't lost his touch . . . She's certainly a beautiful mover, no wonder she swept the board at the county show . . . wonder how much he wants for that mare . . . I'd pay pretty well any price . . .

The idea was lodged, and when he saw the notice of a farm sale in the local paper, he looked more closely at the details than he had done for years. Thirty heifers in calf, sheep, pigs and poultry, household furniture, assorted farm implements, a muck spreader, old but serviceable . . . and, 'Fine chestnut mare in foal to prizewinning hunter.' He circled the announcement in black ink. Of course he had no intention of buying the mare, but it would do no harm to look at her.

'I saw Rupert Brownlowe today at the sale,' Will Griffin said to Daisy as she dished up tea in the farmhouse kitchen. 'And I bought the muck spreader. It's rusty but it'll do.'

112

'Oh yes?' Daisy sliced into a cold pork pie and slid the wedges onto plates, automatically making the smallest wedge her own. 'What was old Brownlowe up to, then?'

'He was buying a horse.'

'Surely he isn't still riding?' said Daisy, surprised. 'I thought he gave all that up long ago. He sold all his horses to the army, didn't he, back in 1914? And that was why you went off and volunteered for the Horse Artillery?'

'Well, partly. Though I seem to recall that there was another reason,' said Will, with a mischievous sideways glance at his wife. 'Something to do with a housemaid I'd taken a shine to, who'd got herself engaged to someone else . . .'

'Get on with you,' said Daisy, blushing, because in the background Jem Wilkins was washing his hands at the kitchen sink. Not that he ever seemed to be listening to anything that went on and, anyway, Will had recently pronounced that he thought Jem was all right, which was Will's way of saying he liked him. But Daisy still felt uncomfortable about Jem, though she couldn't summon any evidence to back up her suspicions. She couldn't help wishing that Louella had never sent him here, just as she now wished that her husband hadn't bumped into Rupert Brownlowe. Neither event had produced any trouble as yet, but the potential was there.

In the year before the Great War, Will had been employed as a groom at Maple Grange. Will had disliked Rupert from the outset, but he'd loved the horses and taken a lot of satisfaction from their success in the show ring. And whenever Brownlowe's blustering arrogance tempted him to tell the man where to stick his job, he'd controlled the reaction because he was in love with Daisy, junior house-maid at the Grange. True, Daisy was supposed to be 'walking out' with someone else, but that fact hadn't altered the way he felt about her.

After war was declared the army had announced a nationwide requisition of horses for cavalry remounts. The rule was that half of every stables must be made available;

but fired with patriotic enthusiasm, Rupert had offered almost all his horses, a move which had coincidentally rendered Will redundant.

On the day the horses were sold, Daisy had announced her engagement. It had been an impulsive move, triggered by the news that Arthur Bright, a Volunteer Reservist with the Queen's Own Royal West Surrey Regiment, had been told to report to barracks. The first battalion of the Queen's was destined for France with the British Expeditionary Force. For Will, the loss of the horses and the apparent loss of hope where Daisy was concerned had been enough to send him into the recruiting office.

In the event he'd survived the war and Arthur Bright hadn't, and now he had Daisy and a farm and a family. He could afford to feel mellow towards his former employer, though once he'd hated the man.

'Poor old Brownlowe, he's certainly past riding. Walks with a stick. But I think he may be starting his stables up again,' Will told Daisy. 'I've heard his business is in trouble – he's had to borrow money just to keep it going. I suppose horse-breeding is one thing that's always worked for him in the past.'

'Well, good luck to him,' Daisy said, meaning the opposite. Daisy didn't often bear a grudge, but she made an exception for Rupert Brownlowe. Will failed to notice the sarcasm of her comment.

'He could certainly do with some luck. I heard he had a hayrick fire that wiped out all his last year's winter hay – replacing that must have cost him a pretty penny. Anyway, he hasn't lost his eye for horseflesh. This one was a brood mare, in foal to a good stallion,' said Will. 'She was a good-looking mare,' he added wistfully. 'Reminded me of Starbright.' He'd hankered after the mare himself, impractical though it was for a working farmer to indulge in such fancies. 'Should produce a first-class hunter.'

'But he's old,' said Daisy. 'He can't do his own schooling any more, surely?'

'I suppose he'll find someone,' said Will, suppressing a

pang of regret that it couldn't be him. The old man had been a pain in the neck, bumptious and bullying and mean towards his servants; but there was no denying that when it came to schooling horses, they'd made a good team, Will and Rupert Brownlowe.

He's starting up his stables again,' said Jem on the telephone to Louella. 'And he's had to borrow money to do it. He's got a brood mare and she's a good 'un. Do you want me to spoil it for him?'

'No,' said Louella. 'Not yet. Leave him to it for a while, let him get himself deeply involved. Build up his hopes. *Then* you can spoil it. How are you getting on with the Griffins?'

'Not too bad. *He* likes me – he'd like anyone who can do a day's work. *She's* not taken with me, but she likes Kitty. The lads are all right. The girl – Harriet – is a bit of a stunner, isn't she? I gather she's with you now and I'm not sorry to have her out of the way. Toffee-nosed bitch! She treated me like dirt.'

'Did she, now?' Louella was amused.

'Needs taking down a peg or two. I wonder how she'd feel if I told her I'm her uncle,' said Jem.

'Don't,' said Louella sharply. 'And you aren't, anyway. I'm only related to her by marriage.'

'Just joking.'

Louella wondered if that was true. She sincerely hoped so – Jem could do a lot of mischief among the Griffins if he wanted to. It was fortunate that he didn't know all there was to know. *A bit of a stunner*, he'd called Harriet, with an odd inflexion in his voice. Of course, she wasn't many years younger than Jem. Had there been an element of sexual attraction behind Harriet's disdain and Jem's wish to take her 'down a peg or two'? It was a disquieting thought.

But Jem knew which side his bread was buttered. Surely he'd got more sense than to throw away his advantageous connection with Louella for the satisfaction of scoring a point against a girl who treated him 'like dirt'? At any rate, it was fortunate that Harriet was here in London, out of his way.

'Jem, they think we're married.'

'So?' said Jem. He sat in the kitchen at Starling Cottages with a blanket round his bare shoulders while Kitty washed his only two shirts in the stone sink. 'We *are* married, as good as, aren't we? We're living as man and wife.'

'But we haven't been to church.'

'What does that matter?'

Kitty was silent, wringing out the shirts one by one and spreading them over the wooden airing horse to dry in front of the stove overnight. Jem watched her bare arms tensing as she twisted the cotton between her hands, idly anticipating the moment when he'd take her upstairs and teach her further how to please him, a lesson in which she seemed to take an unlimited delight. Then he realized that she hadn't answered him and that the subject of marriage, or the fact that they had undergone no such ceremony, was still in the air between them.

'So you want us to get married, is that it?'

'I'd feel better if we could, Jem. You did say, when I came with you . . .'

'So I did. All right,' said Jem. Kitty raised her head, relief plain on her features.

'Oh, Jem, can we really?'

'Course we can. I said I would, and I'm a man of my word. Now, where shall we have the banns read?' Jem said lightly. 'In the church at Bentley? Mind you, that'd mean letting the Griffins and everyone else round here know that we've been living in sin, wouldn't it? I wonder how they'd take the news. Or should we go back to Bethnal Green? Your Uncle George'll be delighted to see us, won't he? He might even be persuaded to give you away . . . once they let us out of prison for taking that money. Well?' Jem pursued the point. 'Which is it going to be? It's up to you.'

Kitty didn't answer. First, she had to deal with the disappointment. Then she had to convince herself that they wouldn't be at Welcome Farm for ever and that some day, in another place, Jem would make an honest woman of her. It wasn't much consolation for now.

Just for a moment something about her defeated, downcast look reminded Jem of his mother.

He hadn't thought about Agnes in the weeks they'd been at Welcome Farm. He'd left her some money but with her drinking habits it must be nearly spent. He supposed it was time to make a duty trip home – though he'd have to stay well away from the vicinity of the Crown and Cushion.

Jem stood outside his mother's house in Bethnal Green and an instinct told him that something was wrong. The house looked different – marginally cleaner, less neglected. When he opened the door and walked through to the kitchen, his instinct was confirmed. A young woman stood at the stove, stirring a pan of soup. The pan was unfamiliar to Jem, as was the chair in front of the stove and the curtains at the window, but he recognized the woman: Edie Perkins from the next street – he'd had a bit of a fling with her a couple of years ago, but she'd bored him very quickly and they'd parted on a sour note.

'Hullo, Edie,' he said. 'What're you doing here?'

'Jem!' The soup ladle clattered on to the brick floor.

'Where's Mam?'

'Trust you to sneak in and frighten a girl silly!' Edie scolded, scooping the ladle up from the floor. She straightened up, breathing quickly, and dropped it back, unwashed, into the soup pan. 'Where've you been? Police were round here a while ago looking for you. Reckoned you'd stolen some money from the Crown and Cushion – and run off with old George's niece into the bargain. Did you?'

Jem ignored the question. 'Where's my mam?'

'Your mam was buried weeks ago,' Edie said. Jem moved a spread hand, as if to fend off the news. He stood for a few long seconds, his expression frozen. Then, 'What happened?' he asked.

117

'She fell downstairs a week after you left and broke her neck. Doctor said she was blind drunk. Fairly pickled with gin – not that that was anything new for Agnes. Nobody knew where to find you and we couldn't just leave her to rot, so we got her buried on the parish. Anyway,' she told him, 'the landlord said we could have this place, Charlie and me. Did you know I got married to Charlie Coates, the coal heaver? We've got a nipper, too. Born in July, year before last. Nine months after you and me split up, funnily enough.' She put her hands on her hips, her eyes challenging him. 'Wondering if it might be yours, Jem? Charlie certainly did.'

Jem didn't answer. Disappointed by his lack of response, Edie turned back to the stove. 'Your mam's things are in the shed at the back,' she said, over her shoulder. 'Sooner you move them out the better. We live here now.' She wrapped a dishcloth around her hands before picking up the pot of soup by both handles.

'You hear what I said? Clear out. You're in my way,' she said.

Jem lashed out, tipping the scalding soup over her skirt. He left the house with her shrieks ringing in his ears. A mile down the road he wondered what had made him do that.

He would have said, if challenged on it, that he had no feelings for his mother. He had kept her fed and clothed, and supplied with the gin she craved, out of habit and not from any affection. She had taken her husband's taunts and blows year in, year out, till there was no trace of pride or spirit left in her. Jem had despised Agnes from the day he'd found the nerve to defy his father and take the beatings that went with that attitude; despised her for the compliant way she'd go to the cupboard under the stairs to fetch the stick his father kept to hit him with. And he despised her more for the fact that she'd known what Bert Wilkins, in his drunken moments, was doing to his children, and she'd let it happen.

There was something about her apathetic acceptance of the worst that life had to offer, even when Bert was dead and gone, which stirred up violent reactions in Jem and often he'd been tempted to beat her black and blue the way his father had done. But he never had and now he never would, because she was dead and underground, beyond punishment or understanding, forgiveness or love.

Instinctively he found an alleyway where he was alone, away from the curious gazes of passers-by. In the shadows, he covered his face with his hands, shoulders shaking, and found that someone was sobbing, in an ugly, spasmodic series of gasps and sighs that seemed to go on and on. Hard to believe it could be Jem Wilkins, who never cried.

Part 2

January–March 1934

8

Harriet came home to Welcome Farm just before Christmas. A letter announced her impending arrival and Daisy, reading the letter at breakfast in the farmhouse, found herself thinking that an 'announcement' was the right description for her daughter's brief note.

It was a shock to realize that more than six weeks had slipped away since Harriet's hurried and almost-tearful departure to London, but when Daisy had had time to think of her daughter it had always been the same Harriet – energetic, touchy, affectionate and a fraction late for everything – that she saw in her mind's eye, moving through Louella's elegent surroundings and not quite fitting in; hardly a bull in a china shop, but perhaps a slightly skittish young heifer.

This letter might have come from a stranger.

Dear Mother and Father, I shall be returning home for a while on Christmas Eve. There is so much to tell you. I have changed a great deal and I hope you will approve . . .

Daisy chewed unconsciously at her lower lip, frowning at the sheet of paper in her hand.

'What's up, love?' Will asked.

'Nothing. A letter from Harriet. She's coming home.'

'About time and all,' said Will, gulping his tea, already halfway up from the breakfast table. 'When?' he added.

'Tomorrow.'

'Which train? I'll meet it at Bentley, to save her walking with her suitcase.'

'She says Louella's sending her in a car.'

'Waste of money, just for one,' Will commented.

123

'I'd write and tell her,' Daisy said, 'but it might be too late.'

'Oh well, it's Louella's money . . . if she wants to spend it on hiring a car, that's her business!'

Will dismissed the subject with a shrug just as Jackie, reaching across the table for the jam, knocked the milk jug sideways and Daisy sprang up automatically to stem the flood. Later she would have liked to explain her nagging sense of unease about the contents of Harriet's letter to her husband, but Will had gone out to the sheds with Jem Wilkins at his heels and Daisy had her own mountain of tasks to carry out. All the same, the letter preyed on her mind for most of the morning.

Harriet shouldn't be encouraged to develop airs and graces by the provision of a chauffeur-driven car. She was a farmer's daughter, not a town socialite, young and healthy enough to catch a train and walk the two or three miles from the station, if need be. After all that time in London, she might have said something about looking forward to seeing her family again. And she had never called her parents 'Mother' and 'Father', always the warmer 'Mum' and 'Dad'. Even the handwriting, on Louella's thick, cream-coloured notepaper, seemed different – Harriet's bold, rounded characters tamed and diminished into a consciously graceful script.

I have changed a great deal and I hope you will approve. Stilted and formal, it didn't sound like Harriet at all. And what did she mean by, *I shall be returning home* for a while?

Harriet had left Welcome Farm with one modest suitcase. Now, the driver of the car hired by Louella carried so many boxes and bags into the house that Daisy wondered aloud, as he deposited them in the hall, how they would all fit into Harriet's small bedroom.

'Oh, they aren't all for me! Some are Christmas presents. Mother, how are you?'

Daisy looked up and there, framed in the doorway, was a Bright Young Thing.

At least, that was her first impression of her daughter. Harriet's hair had been cut short and marcel-waved. The colour on her lips and cheeks was too deep to be natural. She had lost weight, or perhaps it was the figure-skimming lines of the sapphire-blue, bias-cut dress that gave that impression. In response to her mother's concentrated gaze she gave a twirl, sending the flared hem of the dress flying out around her.

'Do you like it? It's one of Aunt Louella's designs, of course.'

'Very nice,' said Daisy, undecided whether to hug Harriet or stand back at a distance to admire this mannequin pirouetting in her hall, in strapped shoes with high heels that made her look taller.

'Lou's given me stacks more – I mean,' Harriet corrected herself, 'Aunt Louella has been very generous. She has provided a complete new wardrobe.'

'Very nice,' Daisy repeated.

'I'm to go back in the New Year. You won't mind, will you? Oh, and before I forget . . . she particularly asked me to find out what Rob and Jackie would like. I've brought Christmas presents, of course, but those are just for the time being. She said that I should let her know of their heart's desire.'

Yes, Louella had been generous to Harriet and it was kind of her to want to extend that generosity to the boys as well. So why should Daisy feel such a sharp pang of actual dislike towards her absent sister-in-law? Except that she wanted her daughter back.

'I'm riding Briony now.'

Rob stood in the black mare's stall with her saddle over his arm, his eyes daring his sister to argue. 'Dad said I was to take her over. After all, you went off to Auntie Lou. *Somebody* had to take care of her.'

'I suppose so.' Harriet, in her sapphire-blue dress, felt at a disadvantage. She had hurried out to renew her acquaintance with Briony, but had found Rob about to saddle the mare for what it became clear was a daily exercise session. She had known in the back of her mind that somebody would have to take her place in such duties; but she had let herself believe it would be Will, and that when she chose she could resume the schooling of Briony. Now she realized that her loss was final. She shrugged her shoulders, pretending not to care.

'You're welcome to her anyway. She's a proper little madam.'

'She's all right with me,' Rob said. 'She doesn't throw *me* off into puddles,' he added pointedly.

'That wasn't my fault, it was that aeroplane.'

'Oh, yes. The aeroplane! I've flown in it, since,' said Rob, distracted from sibling rivalry by a chance to enthuse about the most exciting event of his life. 'Tom Searle took me up. He's really decent, Harry. We looped the loop, and I wasn't sick. And he let me take the stick, just for a bit. He said I was a natural aviator. He said I should take lessons when I'm a bit older. Only they cost a lot,' Rob remembered sadly, 'so I don't suppose I'll be able to.'

'Aunt Louella said I should find out your heart's desire, so that she could help you to achieve it. Is flying your heart's desire, Rob?'

'Oh, *yes*.'

'Then maybe I'll tell her that what you really, really long for is a chemistry set,' teased Harriet, reverting for a moment to the Harriet that her mother knew and missed. Rob lunged at her but the new short haircut gave him nothing to hold onto; he chased her halfway across the farmyard before he caught her.

'Harry, you're a mean beast!' Fingers closing on her wrist, he swung her round and twisted her arm behind her back. Harriet was taller and in the past had always managed to outfight her brother, but in the new high-heeled shoes she was off balance, and she was further handicapped by the need to preserve the blue dress. She stood submissively still and Rob, who had been expecting the old tussles, slackened his hold.

'D'you think Auntie Lou might really pay for me to learn to fly?'

'If I tell her that's what you want.'

'Tell her, then, Harry. Promise?'

'We-ell . . . I don't know if you deserve it . . .'

'You pig!' He renewed his grip and applied an upward leverage.

'Ow! Let go of me, Rob, or I swear I'll never tell her. Let *go*. I really mean it, Rob.' She rubbed at the released wrist. 'All right, then. I'll do what I can. But only because I'm the best big sister that anyone ever had.'

As she was strolling away, Rob called after her.

'Tom Searle. He asked about you. He said I should let him know when you came home. Shall I do that?'

'Don't bother,' said Harriet, over her shoulder. 'I shan't be staying for long.' A thought occurred to her and she turned back to face him.

'Rob, did any letters come for me, while I was away? Or did anyone ask about me, apart from that pilot?'

'If by "anyone" you mean Gavin Draycott . . .' said Rob, 'No. He didn't. Sorry.'

A week ago, Harriet had written to Gavin from London. She and Louella had composed the letter together. Carefully casual, it contained no reference to the lovers' quarrel, or to the intimacy that had preceded it.

I hope you had a successful trip to Newcastle. Since we last met, I have been staying in London with my aunt, who has been introducing me to some aspects of her fashion business . . . ('That's to let him know that you have prospects,' said Louella.) *I am very much enjoying life in town, which is so different from that in rural Hampshire – but of course you know that much better than I do, as you lived in London for so long. I shall be coming home for a short while at Christmas. Perhaps we may see each other then?*

She had been constructing imaginary answers from Gavin

ever since, ranging from passionate declarations that he loved her, had missed her dreadfully and could not wait to see her, to cold reiterations that their different backgrounds made their engagement impossible.

What she had not anticipated was no reply at all.

'Happy Christmas, Lou.'

'What do you want, Jem?' Louella, on the telephone, was as curt to her half-brother as she had been during personal interviews.

'Nothing. Just checking if *you* want something from me. It's been a bit quiet lately. Isn't it time I gave this Brownlowe bloke another prod?'

'When I want you to do something, I'll tell you. All I want at present is information. Nothing to put him on his guard, and certainly nothing to get the police involved. Don't you like it at Welcome Farm? A break from a life of crime and violence should do you good.'

Jem had expected, when he came to Hampshire, that his commission from Louella would only last a few weeks. He'd planned to do a certain amount of damage to Rupert Brownlowe's property at Maple Grange to earn what Louella had paid him, then move on south with Kitty, perhaps to the coast.

The stealing of her Uncle George's cash bag from the pub had been a rash move, uncharacteristically careless. He'd only done it, as an afterthought to the abduction of Kitty, because he was reluctant to let the old man hang on to her small nest egg. He'd been shocked to learn that George Crowley had reported the theft to the police.

In Jem's own circle, people might rob one another blind, they might resort to violent revenge, but they sorted matters out among themselves – and in Bethnal Green, Jem's reputation as a 'sorter' was such that he'd confidently expected Crowley to cut his losses and keep his mouth shut. Now he knew better. The stupid old fool had called in the law.

He mentally chalked the action up on a score sheet, to be

settled in person one day. But for the time being there could be no open return to his old neighbourhood without risking an unpleasant interview with the local constabulary. So Jem had regretted the theft, not because he was particularly attached to the scenes of his childhood, but because it helped to have an area where you knew your way round and where you had built up a reputation as a dangerous man to cross. Then, too, there had been Agnes to consider. But now that his mother was dead, there wasn't so much point in going back to that part of the world. He and Kitty would have to start up somewhere else and, for now, Hampshire seemed as good a place as any.

Louella was paying him well to do not very much and she seemed in no hurry for him to move on. He liked the farm. He liked Will Griffin, who was spare with his words but made it clear that he appreciated Jem's willingness to work. He liked Starling Cottages, the best lodgings he'd ever had, and he liked living with Kitty. Agnes, drunk every night and sick every morning, hadn't been much of a housekeeper, whereas Kitty took good care of him. What with the regular meals, clean clothes, a warm bed at night and Kitty's yielding body and sweet mouth, endlessly available, life at Welcome Farm was beguilingly comfortable.

. . . Too comfortable. He was going soft.

Louella wanted him to observe Rupert Brownlowe but to leave the man alone for the time being. She'd decreed that there were to be no fires, no burglaries, no use even for the bundle of dynamite sticks he'd acquired during his navvying days on the railways and brought down to the farm hidden in his suitcase, just in case they might come in useful. Jem felt restless when reined in by such prohibitions. Too many days as an honest man might make it difficult to get back into the habit of wrongdoing.

He decided that, instructions from Louella notwithstanding, he would give Rupert Brownlowe a Christmas present – just a small one, to keep his hand in.

*   *   *

In London, Rupert's daughter Laura Allingham and her husband had planned a traditional family Christmas, incorporating a vast turkey, an enormous, decorated tree and days of unrelenting festivity.

'Oliver and Claire are coming,' Laura had told her father. 'With their boys. Edward and Caroline are so excited – they adore their cousins. And Tom is so good at keeping them all entertained.'

Rupert felt exhausted by the contemplation of such an occasion. He found it increasingly difficult, these days, to make himself comfortable in any but his own familiar surroundings, and Laura's town house near Kew Gardens would be bursting at the seams with the activities of his five boisterous grandchildren; their excitement driven to fever pitch by his stepson, Tom.

'Of course we are hoping that you will join us,' Laura said, doing her best to sound as if she meant it.

'I think perhaps not. I haven't been too well lately. The blood pressure, you know. We'll just have a quiet Christmas at home.' Rupert had noticed the effort behind Laura's words and the relief with which she heard his refusal, and for a moment he felt quite desolate. Long ago, he and Laura had been close – hadn't they? But the feeling between them had slipped away and he didn't know how to rescue it.

Christmas Eve and Christmas Day passed, for Marion Brownlowe, in a haze of boredom. She ached to be part of the lively household at Kew but Rupert's refusal had been for both of them. On Christmas night she excused herself early from the drawing room and another evening of petit point while Rupert dozed or fulminated about the state of the nation. Leaving him alone with his decanter of whisky, she retired thankfully to her own bedroom and the solace of a good book. At least these days he no longer knocked diffidently at her door in the small hours of the morning – months of feigning deep sleep had discouraged him from doing that.

Downstairs, Rupert poured himself a large whisky, and then another. The fire in the marble fireplace was burning low, but he couldn't summon up the energy to poke it into life again. The servants, in their own wing, were known to be celebrating their Christmas, but a green baize-covered door at the end of a long corridor kept the sound of their activities from disturbing the master of the house.

He had wanted Marion to stay down here with him, but he could not bring himself to admit it to her. She didn't say much as she stitched away at that fussy little embroidery frame of hers, turning out yet another cushion, too small to be useful, or another redundant footstool cover, but at least she was someone to talk to. He almost regretted that he wasn't in London with his children and grandchildren; but to be realistic he'd have felt tired and tetchy and out of place, and to be among people who are enjoying themselves when you are not is to be more lonely still.

A third generous glass of whisky followed the others down his throat. His head slipped sideways and he began to snore.

At a few minutes past midnight, Jem Wilkins inserted a knife blade up through the crack between the top and bottom sashes of one of the drawing-room windows and forced it sideways to spring the catch. Inch by cautious inch, he slid the lower half of the window upwards and parted the heavy velvet currtains.

The room was almost in darkness. Only one of the electric lights was switched on, and that was a table lamp standing on a small octagonal-topped table beside one of the arm-chairs that flanked the fireplace. Its light shone on the linen antimacassar laid over the back of the armchair, and on the thinning hair of the head which lolled sideways at its edge.

Jem hoisted a leg over the sill and slipped into the room. A regular, stertorous breathing came from the figure in the armchair. Jem padded noiselessly across the carpet and stood looking down at Rupert Browlowe.

His quarry. He'd never seen the man at close quarters. Asleep, Brownlowe didn't look particularly frightening, or even particularly detestable. Jem addressed him silently, his lips framing the words.

'You poor devil, Louella Ramsay hates you. She's working to ruin you. Do you know that? Do you even remember who she is?'

To business. He surveyed the room. The tantalus on the sofa table was open, showing cut-glass decanters with silver labels on chains around their necks identifying their contents as port, sherry, brandy. Those labels alone would fetch a respectable sum from the fences that Jem knew back in London.

A delicate brass carriage clock ticked away on the mantelpiece and the cupboards on either side of the fireplace were crammed with china ornaments which even he, no expert, could tell were valuable. It was tempting, very tempting, to tap the old man on the head with a poker to ensure his silence, take down a velvet curtain, roll up the contents of the cupboards in it and carry them away. But Louella had forbidden him to do anything that would involve the police or put her enemy on his guard.

On the Persian carpet beside the armchair, a few inches from the dangling hand of the sleeper, stood another decanter. Jem looked at it thoughtfully. Then he scooped up the decanter and carried it with him to the window. Outside in the frosty night, he cast a final look back into the room and its unconscious occupant before he eased the sash window down. He tried to slip the catch back into the locked position with his pocket knife, but it resisted his efforts and the blade was gouging the wood.

It didn't matter, he decided. With so little missing, an unlocked window, if noticed, would be put down to servant carelessness. As for the loss of one decanter of whisky – well, it wasn't much of a haul, but if his action sowed the seeds of a little domestic friction in Rupert Brownlowe's orderly household, his night's work would not have been wasted.

It was almost dawn when Jem returned to Starling Cottages. He had taken his time over the journey, stopping Rob Griffin's borrowed bicycle at intervals to take in a mouthful of Rupert Brownlowe's good whisky. Jem didn't know enough about whisky to recognize it as a ten-year-old malt, but he could tell it was smoother than any spirit he'd tasted before, and it seemed a shame to waste the stuff. He swallowed the last of the whisky a mile from the farm, registering hazily that the silver label was missing. He must have dropped it somewhere en route. A pity – it was old and ornately engraved, and would have been worth a bit. He dumped the decanter into one of the overgrown drainage ditches beside the road, then returned the bicycle to its usual place in an outbuilding at the farmhouse before making his unsteady way along the lane to the cottage.

He'd left Kitty asleep. It was a shock to find her sitting up in bed with a shawl around her shoulders.

'Where've you been?' she asked him, with an edge of reproach in her voice that he found irritating.

'Down the garden. Call of nature,' he said. The water closet was in a shed at the end of the garden path and it seemed to him to be a masterly reply, but Kitty was silent. Maybe she could tell he was drunk. Well, what of it? He sat down on the edge of the bed and unlaced his boots. When he looked up again she was still watching him with that sad, anxious expression.

'You've been gone hours, Jem, and on our first Christmas night together. What have you been up to?'

'None of your business. Don't ask no questions and you won't get told no lies.'

'It is my business,' Kitty persisted. 'I was so worried about you.'

'Then you're a fool,' said Jem with a gust of anger, his voice slurring because the whisky was getting to him. He knelt above her and took hold of her wrists, lifting her arms above her head. 'A stupid little fool.' She looked scared, and that stirred him further. He tangled one hand in the neck of her nightdress and jerked hard, sending the button which had fastened it rolling across the counterpane. Kitty, suddenly animated, shoved him sideways and taken by surprise, he toppled to the floor as she scrambled off the

133

bed. Spread-eagled on the wooden floorboards, he blinked up at her for a shocked moment.

'You bitch. Come back here.' Arms flailing, Jem reared himself on to his feet. Kitty backed away.

'Stop it, Jem! Not like this. You're in no fit state . . .' But his fingers closed on her wrist, jerking her towards him, flinging her back on to the bed. He rolled over on top of her, one hand still holding her wrist, the other hand groping inside the open nightdress.

'I don't know why I bother with you,' he said, breathing quickly. 'I don't know why I keep on doing this.'

Kitty uttered a smothered sound. He bent his head and caught her lower lip between his teeth, biting till he tasted blood. Then he kissed her hard with no affection, forcing her mouth open, his tongue pushing towards the back of her throat. His hand twisted savagely at her breast, his knee nudged her thighs apart. He reached down to unbutton his trousers, clumsy with haste and the effects of the whisky. Kitty tried once more to struggle free, but his weight pinned her to the bed.

'Whatever's happened to your face?' said Harriet on Boxing Day, as she and Kitty poured buckets of milk into the cooler. Above the swollen lip and bruised cheekbone, Kitty's pink-rimmed eyes avoided hers.

'Nothing.'

'But your mouth—'

'I stumbled and hit my face.'

On her stool beside the cooler, Kitty reached out for the handle of the bucket that Harriet passed up to her and the sleeve of her pullover slipped back an inch to reveal a wrist that was patched with black and yellow and purple.

'Oh, you've hurt your arm as well.'

'I banged it when I stumbled,' was all Kitty said. Harriet waited for further explanation but it didn't come and in the face of Kitty's determined silence, she didn't like to ask any more questions.

*   *   *

At Maple Grange, Rupert Brownlowe had woken in the early hours in front of a dead fire. Levering himself up from his armchair, stiff and chilly, he had taken himself upstairs to bed, resentful that because of the Christmas festivities in the servants' hall, none of the staff had done their usual late-night rounds of the house to check on his wellbeing. He'd overslept and risen for a late breakfast, followed by a visit to the newly refurbished stable yard to view his latest acquisition.

He'd been feeling headachy and liverish – too much whisky last night, he admitted, on top of the half-bottle of claret at supper and the port after it. And the wine bill still not paid . . . but his bad mood and his thick head cleared at the sight of the shining chestnut mare nosing peacefully at the contents of her feeding bucket. She really was a beauty. In just a few more weeks she'd drop her foal and then he'd know whether his venture had paid off.

Coming back into the house, he felt ready for another little snort of whisky before lunchtime. But the decanter wasn't on the sideboard, or on the floor by the armchair, where he remembered leaving it last night. Exasperated, he jerked at the bell-pull by the door.

'Sir?' said Doris, appearing in answer to the summons.

'Where's my whisky decanter?'

'Isn't it on the sideboard, sir, same as usual?'

'No, it isn't, or I wouldn't be asking you, would I?'

Doris annoyed him by looking over the range of decanters as if she didn't believe him.

'I told you, Doris, it isn't here. I assume that you, or one of the other servants, has moved it since last night.'

'Well, it wasn't me, sir. That I do know. I've been too busy to go shifting things around in here, sir.'

'Then kindly oblige me by asking the rest of the staff. I want you back here with it in ten minutes.'

Doris plodded silently away, but returned in less than the ten minutes he had stipulated, to say that nobody had any idea of the whereabouts of the decanter.

'It didn't just walk by itself, did it? Now look here, Doris, if you or one of the others has broken it and hidden the pieces, tell me now and I'll overlook it. Accidents will happen. It's trying to cover up for them and refusing to admit to them that I don't like.'

'I haven't had any accidents, sir,' Doris said, her lips quivering with suppressed emotion.

'Well, somebody's broken the bloody decanter, or stolen it,' Rupert exploded, running out of patience. 'And a pint of good malt whisky's gone missing into the bargain!'

Doris retreated woodenly, but by the time a slightly delayed lunch was served at Maple Grange the maid had given in her notice to Marion.

'I won't stay where my word's doubted, Mrs Brownlowe, ma'am. And I'm not used to being sworn at, not by a gentleman least of all.'

Marion tried to soothe Doris. Maids were hard to come by nowadays, particularly on the wages that Rupert was prepared to pay. And Christmas, however muted a Christmas, was no time to lose a member of staff. But Doris refused to be placated and retired to her room on the top floor of the house to pack her bags.

'I'll go to my sister in Croydon. She's been asking me to go for ages, only I didn't like to leave you in the lurch, ma'am. But there's plenty of jobs in the factories round her way – good jobs and good pay and all. And Mr Brownlowe's made it clear he doesn't trust me, so I don't see how I can stay.'

After Doris's departure, the rest of the staff were chilled and mutinous. An unpleasant atmosphere permeated the house. Rupert's headache returned and with it, his high blood pressure. Jem, who had planned to stir up domestic friction with the theft of the decanter, would have been delighted by the outcome of his night's activities.

In fact Jem, waking in the morning with a throbbing head and a tongue like sandpaper, hadn't been able to remember much about the previous night. He noticed the change in Kitty, though. In the past she'd welcomed his attentions, though after the first morning in London she'd never dared to make the first move. Now when he tried to kiss her, she turned her head away. It didn't matter, he told himself. He'd soon teach her not to do that. In the past two months he had learned the secrets of Kitty's body. She might put up a show of resisting him, but he could break down her resistance easily enough.

After he'd shown her who was master, she stopped turning away. But she still flinched when he reached out a hand for her, and he couldn't beat that tendency out of her. He wasn't sure what he was after, but he knew he wasn't getting it. The harder he handled her, the more apathetically she accepted the treatment. It wore out his patience.

She reminded him of his mother, that was the trouble. She bloody well reminded him of Agnes.

'Have you heard from Gavin?' said Louella, on the telephone.

'No,' said Harriet forlornly, from the telephone box at Bentley.

'He didn't answer your letter?'

'No.'

'Then he needs teaching some manners,' said Louella. 'I'll think about ways and means. Don't be downhearted.'

'What about you, Aunt Louella? How was your Christmas?'

'Oh . . . quiet.'

'You aren't lonely? I worried about coming away.'

'Bless you for thinking of it, Harriet. But no, I'm not lonely. If I want to be sociable I can contact friends. There have been plenty of invitations. Are you coming back in the New Year, as we arranged? What do Will and Daisy feel about it?'

'Oh, it'll be all right. I'm determined to come,' said Harriet.

Outside the telephone box, she turned up her coat collar because the wind was cold. Louella had told her not to lose heart, but if Gavin still had any interest in her, why hadn't he answered her letter? Unless he was still away? She tried to convince herself, as she walked home, that this must be the explanation.

As she reached the gate at the end of the farm drive, a car could be heard coming fast along the road from the direction of Bentley. Harriet, swinging back the five-barred gate, looked over her shoulder as it passed her – and wished she hadn't. The yellow Austin had its hood up but Gavin Draycott had been clearly visible behind the wheel.

Harriet gazed after the car as it sped along the road towards Hallows, her cheeks burning with humiliation.

He hadn't stopped. He hadn't acknowledged her in any way. Worse . . . there had been someone in the passenger seat beside him. All she had glimpsed had been fair hair and a blue scarf, but it was enough. She closed the gate behind her, fighting back the tears.

'Cheer up. A face like that's enough to curdle milk.'

Jem Wilkins stood in the shadow of the hedge, hands in pockets, watching her. It was plain that he'd seen the passing car and that he understood the reasons for her discomfort.

'Boyfriend let you down, has he? Never mind. Good looker like you'll find another one soon enough. Hell, I'd have you myself if I wasn't spoken for.'

Harriet found Jem Wilkins' appraising stare and flippant comments hard enough to take at the best of times. At this moment they were the final straw.

'I wouldn't have anything to do with you if you were the last man on earth,' she told him forcefully.

'Wouldn't you?' Under the peak of his battered cap, Jem's eyes glinted and his mouth curved up at the corners without showing his teeth.

'Running away, are you?' he said, as she hurried past him. 'Now if you stayed, you might learn a thing or two, Miss Griffin.'

'I don't imagine there's anything you could teach me,' Harriet snapped back, over her shoulder. His smile broadened.

'Don't you?' he said, softly. 'Oh . . . I do. About birds and bees, for instance. Maybe another time.'

It was only words, Harriet scolded herself. It was silly to let Jem upset her, it was only because of what had just happened with Gavin that she was being so sensitive. For all his bravado, Jem Wilkins wouldn't dare lay a hand on her. If he did, her father would have him thrown off the farm.

But she found that she was tingling all over, as if Jem had run his hands over her body, and not just his eyes.

9

'Louella, my dear, how nice to see you. And how brave of you to come.'

Louella had told Harriet on the telephone that she was not lonely, that if she wanted company she had only to accept one of the invitations that had arrived at Medlar House. Now, as she handed her black coat with the beaver lamb collar to a waiting housemaid, she was already wishing that she hadn't sent a last-minute acceptance to drinks with the Moffats. Stanley Moffat and Hector had been at school together but she had never warmed to Helen Moffat, who stood too close and presumed too much for guarded Louella's taste, and whose normal tendency to gush was exacerbated by the sight of her guest in widow's black.

'You have been in our thoughts, you poor thing. But we thought you would prefer to be alone at this sad time.' Helen was encased in shiny blue-green satin with black net trimmings, like a bluebottle. She seized and patted Louella's hand. 'How are you bearing up?'

Louella sensed that the invitation had been sent as a formality and that no-one had expected her to come. Withdrawing her hand as soon as she could, she repressed the urge to say something shocking and smiled wanly instead.

'Come and talk to some people, if you feel up to it,' breathed Helen.

'If I didn't feel up to it,' Louella heard herself saying, 'I wouldn't have come. I would simply *love* to talk to some people.'

Helen blinked. 'Oh, my dear. Of course you're lonely. Come along then, don't be shy.'

What was it about widowhood, Louella wondered, that was supposed to reduce you to the status of a quivering child? With Hector at her side, her hostess would not have dared to call her a 'dear', much less tell her not to be shy. She gritted her teeth and followed Helen into an over-decorated drawing room, crammed with strangers clutching cocktail glasses and talking at the top of their voices.

'Now, let's see. Do you know anyone here?'

Louella scanned the sea of faces. 'No,' she said. And then, 'Yes. I do. That man over there by the fireplace, talking to the blonde woman with the silver dress and the feathers.'

'You know Stuart Armitage?' Helen seemed taken aback.

'He's my solicitor,' Louella said, wondering why she should *not* know Stuart. 'Graham Madigan's junior partner.'

'Oh, *that's* the connection. Then he shall take care of you,' said Helen, with evident relief. She took hold of Louella's arm and led her guest towards the couple standing in front of the fire. Stuart was engrossed in conversation with the pretty blonde and looked round with a flicker of annoyance as Helen bore down on him ruthlessly.

'Stuart, here is poor dear Louella Ramsay. Do make her feel at home,' said Helen. 'And Bessie, you must circulate – there are stacks of people who are dying to meet you.'

Louella registered the blonde woman's chagrin as Helen dragged her away to be introduced to less attractive men. She looked wryly up at Stuart.

'I am so sorry – it's too bad of Helen to foist me on you like this,' she said. Stuart took her hand and bowed over it, gracefully.

'Not at all. To tell the truth, I was glad to be rescued – and I am delighted to see you, Mrs Ramsay,' he said.

'I think you might call me by my Christian name, as you are now my solicitor.'

'Louella, then. And how do you like being called *poor dear Louella Ramsay?*' he added, with a glint of amusement in his brown eyes.

'I dislike it intensely,' said Louella. 'I'm not sure how to behave, given that label. Should I wail and beat my breast, in the time-honoured manner of widows? Or should I be British and Brave?'

'Helen can be trying,' he said. 'You are looking very well.'

'You're the first person to say so in months. Everyone else insists on perceiving the symptoms of a decline in my pallid features.'

'Then they are blind,' Stuart said simply. 'Did you like my flowers?'

'Flowers?'

'I sent you some for Christmas.'

'Oh. I'm sorry. There were so many.' Stuart's could have been any of a dozen bouquets delivered to Medlar House in the days before Christmas – standard gifts from business or social acquaintances. Louella had told her maid to find vases and tossed the accompanying cards into a bowl on the hall console table to be acknowledged later. She bit at her lip, embarrassed. 'I really am sorry,' she repeated. 'If I'd realized they were from you . . .'

'It doesn't matter. I only wanted to remind you that I existed.'

'Oh, yes. We were supposed to talk about my will, weren't we? I did mean to contact you about that, but I've had my niece staying with me and what with one thing and another . . .'

'That wasn't what I meant,' Stuart said, quietly.

Louella dropped her gaze, aware of the sudden pounding of her heart. She had forgotten, or had failed to register before, how nice a voice Stuart Armitage possessed and it was sending distinct shivers down her spine. In that well-fitting dinner jacket, his good looks were dramatically enhanced. She touched her hand to her forehead to hide her confusion.

'Are you all right?' he asked, concerned.

'It's rather hot in here . . . and noisy.'

'Would you like to go?'

'I can't,' Louella said. 'I've only just arrived.'

'Does that matter? It's a dreadful party. Come on, I'll take you home.' His hand, cupping her elbow, steered her lightly but somehow irresistibly towards the door. As she watched him commandeer her coat, Louella was in the grip of a new sensation.

For most of her adult life she had been the most capable person she knew. Her business contacts treated her with deference. Her husband had allowed her to direct his life. Stuart Armitage, in contrast, had just taken control of the situation and seemed to have no doubts at all that she would do exactly as he told her. It made her feel absurdly young and fluttery and feminine. She discovered that she adored being bossed about by a decisive young man.

'We simply mustn't go yet,' she protested half-heartedly, as he held out her black coat to her. But she was already sliding her hands into the sleeves.

'I don't want to stay,' he said. 'Do you?'

'But what about making our farewells? And whatever will Helen say?'

'Oh, I expect she'll say, *Poor dear Louella Ramsay.*'

'Mr Armitage has been kind enough to see me home from the Moffats' party, Everett. I was slightly unwell.'

'Should I call the doctor, madam?'

'That won't be necessary. I am feeling better now. Mr Armitage and I will have a drink together, but we can manage by ourselves. You needn't wait up.'

In his room on the top floor of the house, Everett wondered whether he should stay awake until the visitor had gone. Then he shrugged. It wasn't his business when, or if, the fellow went home. His day would start at the usual early hour tomorrow no matter what Madam got up to in the interim. He supposed Madam knew what she was doing – and if she didn't, it was her look-out.

All the same, a part of him was shocked. He had, in his way, been fond of Hector Ramsay.

''Morning, Marshall.'

'Good morning, sir.' Raking the gravel of the drive, Billy

Marshall managed to lean the handle of the rake awkwardly against his shoulder and touch his one good hand to the peak of his cap as Rupert strolled by. Rupert smiled, appreciating the gesture. At least one of his staff knew the respect due to an employer.

He had resented being pressured by Marion to take the man on, and certainly another wage, even a wage as small as Billy's, was a strain on his purse. But Billy had turned out to be a bargain. As Marion had predicted, a few weeks of regular meals and weatherproof accommodation had made a big difference to his appearance and he was capable of achieving a surprising amount of work with that one functioning arm.

'Excuse me, sir. Can I have a word? I found this, down by the gate.' Billy had deposited the rake on the verge and followed Rupert past the morning-room window. Now he dug in the pocket of his jacket and held out a small object on the palm of his hand: a silver label shaped like a broad shield with scrolled edges, engraved with the word '*Whisky*' in flowing italic script. Rupert took it between his fingers and turned it over, frowning.

'By the gate, d'you say? Just this?'

'Yes, sir.'

It didn't make sense. The departed Doris might have been the thief responsible for spiriting away the whisky decanter, but surely she would have hidden her spoils away in the depths of her luggage, not so carelessly that the label could be dropped?

'Well, I'm glad to have it back, anyway. It's one of a set. Well spotted, Marshall. When you've finished that raking, can you cut back some of the winter jasmine around the drawing-room windows? It's beginning to shut out the light. And while you're at it, take a cloth and some vinegar-and-water to the glass, will you?'

An hour later, while he was in the drawing room reading a newspaper, Billy appeared outside the window with a bucket and cloth. Rupert sighed as he looked up from *The Times*. It was true that he'd ordered the window-cleaning, but he disliked the sensation of being observed from outside. He folded his paper and was about to move himself to his study when Billy tapped at the window and mouthed something through the glass.

Irritated, Rupert crossed to the window. He reached for the knob and lever which held it locked, and discovered to his surprise that the lever was, in fact, in the open position. He pushed the lower sash upwards.

'Yes, Marshall, what is it?'

'I'm sorry to disturb you, sir. It's just that I'd noticed that the catch wasn't closed.'

'Yes, you're right. I'll have to have a word with Mrs Barlow – someone's been careless.'

'That's not all, sir. Someone's been mucking about with the window, sir. Look here, where the paint's gone and the wood's been dented. As if someone's pushed a knife blade or a chisel or something in between the sashes and jiggled it about.'

Rupert felt a shiver of alarm. He peered closer at the place to which Marshall had pointed. There were indeed signs of tampering.

'And there's a footprint here in the flowerbed, and it's not from my boot. Nor from Stevenson's – he's got big feet, sir, you can always tell where he's been. And see this smear of mud on the window ledge? The way it looks to me is, someone's broken in, or at least tried to.'

'You're right. It does,' said Rupert slowly. 'But damnit, if they have, why would they just take a whisky decanter?'

'That I couldn't say, sir. Will you be calling the police?'

'No,' said Rupert. 'They're no use at all.' He had had enough of the local constabulary. They had been singularly unhelpful about his fires, asking endless silly questions and making copious notes but apprehending no culprits, and they would hardly be likely to produce a better result on the strength of a footprint, a scratch in the paintwork and a bit of mud, particularly when there was almost nothing missing. But if someone *had* gained entry to the house, and if the motive wasn't burglary . . . what was it?

There was always a possibility that one of the servants had a 'follower', who was being let in for the purposes of conducting an illicit passion. But when he mentally reviewed the staff it was difficult to imagine sedate Mrs Barlow or plain and comfortable Mary, or even Doris getting up to any such activity, and besides, it would be easy enough for any of them to admit a potential paramour by the back door rather than have such a person break in through a window.

It was all very disquieting.

'Marshall.' Rupert made a snap decision. 'I want you to switch your duties for the time being. I'll have to get some lad in from the village to help Stevenson and see to the mare. You can be night watchman – keep an eye out for intruders. Better safe than sorry.'

Louella was ashamed of herself. Weeks ago, she had decided to encourage Stuart Armitage in whatever advances he might be inclined to make, with the sole intention of begetting a child without the potential drawbacks of a marriage. She had cold-bloodedly assessed him as being attractive enough and healthy enough for such a purpose, but having made up her mind, she had postponed the plan in favour of transforming Harriet into a suitable bride for a Draycott. When and if she resumed the pursuit of Stuart, she intended to be fully in control of her emotions.

And now, too quickly for her to understand how it had come about, she was struggling to retain the shreds of that control.

He had brought her home in a taxi, had accepted her suggestion of a 'nightcap' of brandy and had identified the lilies in the drawing room as his bouquet.

'I should have guessed,' Louella told him. 'They are quite beautiful.'

'So are you,' said Stuart. 'I'm sorry. That sounds so trite. And you are probably about to rap me over the knuckles for being too forward . . . but I can't help it.'

'Actually, it's rather gratifying,' murmured Louella. Stuart had been standing a full three yards away. She wasn't sure how he crossed the space between them, but the next moment she was in his arms.

'Louella . . .'

And he is very good at kissing, she told her mirror, ruefully, as she repinned her chignon in the morning. Stuart had left in the early hours. To send him away had cost her an effort of will, but even as her bodily senses clamoured for his lovemaking, other instincts had told her to hold back. A man who conquers too easily may well lose interest in his quarry. Besides, it was unthinkable for him to be discovered in her bed when her maid came to light the fire. If they were to become lovers, it must be done with discretion.

And yet . . . she knew that if Stuart had tried to stay when she pushed him towards the door, her resistance would have crumbled. Facing herself in the mirror she stroked a finger across her mouth, swollen by kissing, and touched the area around it that had been rubbed rosy by the late-night shadow of a beard on his jaw.

Hector had been considerate, gentle . . . and old enough to be her father. Stuart was young, shapely, strong. Long ago, Robert Colindale had woken such physical responses in Louella, but when Robert died she had thought she would never feel passion again. She'd built a wall against emotional weakness in herself. Last night, Stuart had very nearly torn it down.

She selected a gold locket and chain from her jewellery box and was about to fasten the catch at the nape of her neck when she remembered the miniature photograph inside the locket. She turned the case over in the palm of her hand, undecided, before she pushed her thumbnail into the crevice which sprung the two halves of the locket apart.

Hector's face looked up at her from the oval frame.

The small, hand-tinted photograph had been taken when he was a young man, long before he met and married Louella; perhaps even before his first marriage and the birth of the son who had been lost in the Great War. He had had dark hair then, and an unlined face, but even as he faced the primitive camera of the time, his expression was already that of the man she had known: shy, kind, with a hint of a self-deprecating smile. He had been as handsome as Stuart, Louella told herself, but without Stuart's self-assurance.

Hector, I miss you so much. I don't know what I'm doing with this man. I know he can't compare with you . . .

It was a lie, she realized, with a jolt of shame that came like a blow to the ribs. She was lying to a photograph of her dead husband. She knew exactly what she was doing, and what she intended to do, with Stuart Armitage. She snapped the locket closed, because Hector's eyes seemed to reproach her.

A bell rang, somewhere in the house. A few moments later there was a knock at the bedroom door and her maid came into the room.

'Telephone call for you, madam. From a Mr Armitage.'

Louella made herself walk, rather than run, downstairs. In the drawing room, she snatched up the telephone and held the receiver to her ear.

'Louella Ramsay speaking. Stuart?'

'Hullo,' he said, and her stomach swooped. 'I wanted to hear your voice again.'

'It's only been five or six hours since you heard it last.' How delicious it was, Louella found, to flirt on the telephone.

'It feels like for ever,' he said. 'When can I see you again?'

'Jem, can you take this indoors for me? Give it to Daisy – or if she's not in the kitchen, stick it in the book with the red cover, inside the right hand drawer of the sideboard.'

Jem took the sheet of paper which Will held out to him. The figures scribbled on it in pencil were the morning's milk yields. In the kitchen, there was no sign of Daisy but a baking tin's worth of rock buns, thick with currants, were cooling on a wire rack on the table. He helped himself to one, cramming the warm, crumbly mass of it whole into his mouth before rummaging in the sideboard for the book that Will had described.

Automatically, while he was at it, he checked the other contents of the drawer: old ledgers, sheaves of household bills clipped together, and a wooden cigar box, still smelling faintly of Havana tobacco. Jem opened the box and found official documents, folded and faded: the title deeds of the farm . . . pedigree certificates for prize cattle . . . the marriage certificate of Will Griffin and Daisy Colindale, dated June 1917.

Jem eyed the certificate, calculating. That made the marriage less than seventeen years old. But surely the Griffins' oldest child, red-headed Harriet with the disdainful green eyes, was more than sixteen? He sifted through the papers and unearthed a trio of birth certificates: John Griffin, born 16 June 1922. Robert Griffin, born 26 September 1920. Harriet Colindale, born 25 April 1915.

Harriet Colindale . . . Well, who'd have thought it? So the imperious Harriet, pride of the Griffins, had been born on the wrong side of the blanket. Jem glanced down the entries on the certificate and his lips curved into a smile. It got better. The mother was listed as 'Daisy Colindale, housemaid.' The father: 'Arthur Bright. Occupation: Soldier.'

Jem whistled softly. Here indeed was an item of information that could prove useful.

The sound of footsteps and voices in the corridor made him tidy the papers hastily into their box and shove it back into the drawer as Daisy and Allie came into the kitchen carrying armfuls of bedlinen for the wash.

'What do you want, Jem?' Daisy's voice was sharp.

'Will sent me in with the milk yields. He said to put them in the book if you weren't here, missus,' Jem told her, flourishing the red book with its scrap of paper tucked into the cover.

'Oh. All right, I'll see to it.'

'I've a confession to make. I nicked a bun. Couldn't resist it, with that mouthwatering smell coming off 'em,' said Jem,

149

turning on the charm. 'You look a proper treat with that hairdo, Allie,' he added, from the doorway. 'You could be on at the pictures.'

Allie blushed. She might be pushing fifty but she wasn't past caring about her appearance and nobody else at the farm had thought to comment on her new permanent wave. 'Oh, get on with you,' she said, pleased. When he had gone, she told Daisy that she thought Jem was a very nice young man. 'I must say, I do wonder what made him take up with that mousy scrap of a wife he's got. He could have had his pick, I reckon.'

'That's as may be,' said Daisy tartly. She still found it hard to warm to Jem Wilkins.

Harriet returned to Medlar House in the New Year, looking for sympathy.

'I saw Gavin,' she confessed to Louella, with difficulty, 'but he was with someone else. I don't think he's interested in me any more.'

'Gavin?'

Louella echoed the name absent-mindedly. Something about her had changed in the fortnight that her niece had been away. Although still dressed in widow's black, she was bright-eyed and her hair, Harriet noticed, was pinned in a new, softer style.

Harriet had left behind her a family who didn't understand her need to transform herself and a one-time unofficial fiancé who seemed to have given up waiting for the transformation. Now she was confronted by an aunt who was supposed to be her one ally, and Louella wasn't even listening.

'How is everyone at home?' Louella said after a long pause, making an effort to pay attention to her niece.

'Very well, thank you,' Harriet said dully.

'Did you find out what Rob and Jackie would really like as a present?'

'Rob wants to learn to fly. Not just yet, of course, he's too young. But he'd rather save up any presents and put them towards the cost for when he is old enough to have lessons.'

'Well, that's a good ambition,' Louella approved. 'What do Will and Daisy think of it?'

'Dad wouldn't mind. He says kids will do what they want to do, and good luck to them – though of course he has to hope that in the end, Rob will want to stay on at home and be a farmer. Mum's rather hoping that Rob will grow out of it.'

'Do you think he will?'

'No,' said Harriet. 'Rob doesn't change his mind about things. He seems quiet and easy-going but when he gets stuck on something he just sort of puts his head down and plods on until he gets it. I suppose he takes after Dad like that. And now he's made friends with a pilot, so he scrounges flights whenever he can.'

'We'll see, anyway. What about Jackie? Does he want to fly as well?'

'No. What Jackie really wants at the moment is a radio – one of those kits that you put together yourself. He's cut out an advertisement from a newspaper – it's in my luggage somewhere. It said it costs four pounds for the kit and another seven shillings carriage paid home; but Mum says he shouldn't be asking you for expensive presents,' Harriet remembered. 'And neither should Rob. And she said I shouldn't have let you give me all those dresses, either.'

Louella shrugged. 'That's silly. She knows perfectly well that I can afford it and I like to buy things for you. After all, I've no children of my own. But Daisy has always had trouble accepting financial help from me – she hates having to be grateful. I've wondered sometimes if it's envy,' she added, 'because I married Hector and she married a penniless groom.'

'Mum's never regretted marrying Dad,' said Harriet sharply, 'even if he didn't have any money. And I'm sure she doesn't envy you. She just doesn't want us to aspire to what we can't afford. She says possessions suit you better when you've earned them – and maybe she's right.'

'And yet,' Louella said softly, 'she and Will aspired to Welcome Farm and my money helped them to buy it, however much Daisy hates to acknowledge that fact. And you aspire to Gavin Draycott.'

'I don't know if I do any more,' Harriet muttered, looking down at her clenched hands. 'After all the things he said to me, about loving me for ever and all that, he seems to have changed his mind very quickly. I never pretended in the first place, he knew exactly who I was when he said he loved me. Then all of a sudden he switched it off just because it wasn't easy for us. Well, now he's driving some other girl around in his car and I suppose it *is* easy for them, and I suppose the Draycotts think she's the right sort, and I don't care!'

'So you've given up,' said Louella.

'Yes. No. I don't know if I have any choice about it.'

'We must make enquiries,' Louella said briskly. 'I'll try to find out – discreetly, of course – if Gavin Draycott is seriously linked with anyone. If he is, of course, we'll have to accept that. Meanwhile, I think you should go on with your lessons here. After all, Gavin isn't the only young man in the world and unless you want to go home and fork hay about for the rest of your life, a good dress sense and a smattering of social polish will always be useful.'

'I suppose so.'

'Well, I can't deliver your handsome prince on a plate just yet, Harriet – though I'm doing my poor best to help you to achieve that ambition – but at least I can send your brother his radio.'

'I'm sorry if I sounded rude, Aunt Louella. Of course I'm grateful for everything you've done for us. And Mum and Dad are, too. I only meant . . .' Harriet's voice tailed away, because what she had meant, effectively, was: *We are a family and you're the outsider*, and there wasn't any way to say it nicely. Besides, it wasn't true any longer. The Griffins were a family, but Gavin Draycott and Louella, between them, had detached Harriet and now she didn't know who she was, or where she belonged. She had never felt so lonely.

*   *   *

Louella made a telephone call and wrote a cheque and, in due course, Jackie's present was delivered to Welcome Farm in a crate as big as a tea chest.

'What on earth's that?' said Daisy, eyeing the crate with disfavour. Parked in the middle of her kitchen floor, it was already getting in her way.

'It's a radio kit! From Aunt Louella.' Jackie's eyes shone. Since his toddling days he'd loved to tinker with machinery, spending long hours at his father's side while Will mended a tractor or repaired a malfunctioning car engine, absorbed in the magic that turned something silent and useless into something that came alive again. Louella's last big present, a Meccano set, had seemed to answer all his ambitions until the advertisement for the radio set had caught his eye. This was even better.

'Louella and her presents,' said Daisy with a sigh. 'Well, how long is it going to be there?'

'I dunno,' Jackie said, some of his happiness evaporating, because Mum sounded cross and he was confronted with his first problem – where to begin to assemble such a complex piece of equipment? You needed a table, for a start, and there wasn't enough space in the cluttered attic he shared with his brother.

Rob was already prising the lid off the crate, a task which Jackie wanted for himself.

'Leave it alone, it's mine!'

'I'm only helping.' Rob stood the lid on its side and delved among the woodshavings inside the crate. 'There's loads of it. Oh, here's a list of components. I'll lay them out, you check they're all there.'

The longed-for present was getting away from Jackie already. He had dreamed of assembling the radio in secret, of calling together his admiring family and having them applaud his unsuspected talents. But now that the kit was here, he wasn't sure if he could deal with it alone. The illustrated list that Rob flourished in front of his eyes was intimidatingly crowded. He hesitated, then fetched a pencil from the sideboard drawer while Rob lifted out a bewildering succession of outlandish-looking objects and laid them out on the kitchen table.

'Valves. Six. Tuning condenser . . .' Jackie frowned with concentration as he searched for and ticked them off against the list. 'What was that last one again?'

'Wave-change switch,' said Rob, consulting the list over his shoulder.

'Wave-change switch?' echoed Daisy. 'What on earth's that for?'

'Changing waves,' said Jackie, sounding more knowledgeable than he felt.

'Oh. Well, it all looks very complicated,' said Daisy dubiously. 'Anyway, you can't leave that lot all over my table.'

'Please, Mum. Just till I put it together. There's nowhere else. And it says it's easy,' Jackie wheedled. 'It says a child could do it.'

'Well, a child's going to have to,' his mother said. 'Your dad and I haven't got the time. And it's not as if we need a radio anyway.'

Louella's presents usually seemed to cause trouble, one way or another, and this one was no exception.

10

In the end, despite Daisy's declaration that she and Will had no time, the whole family became involved with the construction of the radio; partly because it was such a nuisance to produce and consume family meals amid the bits of it and partly because in itself the magic machine exerted such a fascination. Throughout every spare moment of the school holidays, Jackie was distracted by would-be helpers who wanted to interpret the wiring diagram and even Allie put in her two-pennorth of opinion as she mopped the kitchen floor around the legs of his chair.

'You'll never fit all of that lot into that little box. If you ask me, they've sent you the wrong cabinet to go with that machine.'

Eventually the radio was assembled and fitted, despite Allie's misgivings, inside its polished wooden cabinet. When the valves were in place and the batteries connected, a faint humming could be heard from the cabinet.

'Is that it?' said Allie, disappointed. 'What, no Harry Hall and his orchestra?'

'It needs an aerial to pick up broadcasts,' said Rob patiently. 'Up in that tree out in the yard. I'll do it.'

'No,' said Jackie, reasserting his rights of ownership. '*I* will.' With a rope looped across his shoulders he swarmed up the beech tree that Rob had nominated and hauled up the aerial, lashing it to the highest point he could reach in the face of his mother's anxious admonitions to be careful. By the time he reached ground level again, Rob was already synchronizing the tuning dials and sounds were emerging from the radio that were recognizable, though not always comprehensible.

'That's London! Paris . . . Hilversum . . . where's Hilversum?'

'Holland, I think,' said Will, coming in for his mid-morning tea. So, you've got it working. Well done! It isn't every lad your age could have done that.'

Jackie glowed. Rob went on twiddling the tuning knobs and picked up the sound of a military band, playing some unfamiliar piece of music. Then the music was replaced by a single voice, strident and emphatic. In a foreign language, the words meant nothing to the Griffins, but the effect was hypnotic and obscurely menacing. When the orator paused, wave after wave of cheering broke out from an unseen audience. Gradually it crystallized into two words, repeated over and over again.

'*Sieg Heil,*' Will said, listening. 'German.'

'That's right, Dad.' Rob peered at the dialling bar on the glass window. 'Hamburg.'

'What does it mean?' said Daisy. She carried a kettle from the kitchen range to pour hot water into the big brown teapot.

'It's to do with victory, I think,' Will told her. '*Hooray for victory*, or something like that.' He pulled out a chair from the table and sat down, frowning. 'I suppose it's that chap Hitler – the one they elected chancellor in Germany the year before last. Holding one of his rallies.'

'But they lost the war. Why should they be shouting about a victory?' said Rob.

'I don't think it's the last war they're shouting about.'

'Then what?' Daisy asked, joining her husband at the table.

'Maybe the next,' Will told her soberly.

'Oh, no,' Daisy protested. The Great War, though it had ended more than fifteen years ago, was still painfully clear in her memory. 'They can't start all that up again. Nobody could.'

'He doesn't sound very nice, does he?' said Jackie, in a small voice.

'No, he doesn't.' Will covered Daisy's hand in his own and tried to smile reassuringly at his son. 'We don't need to hear any more of that stuff, do we? Turn it off. Or better – let's see if we can find some nice dance music. Something to cheer us all up.'

'Mrs Moffat is here to see you, madam.'

'*Helen?* Oh, Lord.' Louella recalled that she had slipped away embarrassingly early from the Moffats' party. 'I'm not at home,' she told her maid.

'I'm sorry, madam, but I'm afraid if I tell her that now, she'll know it's not true.'

Louella mentally scheduled a short training session for Alice: how to keep her mistress's whereabouts a secret until the mistress had indicated that she was prepared to receive the visitor. She resigned herself to the inevitable.

'All right. Show her in. And you'd better fetch us some tea.'

Helen Moffat bustled into the drawing room on a cloud of scent, wearing a long-jacketed costume in striped twill with a fox fur collar which would have looked charming, Louella thought, on someone ten years younger and a stone lighter. She captured Louella's hands in her own gloved ones and kissed the air on both sides of her hostess's cheeks.

'My dear! I expect I'm intruding.'

'Not at all,' said Louella, bracing herself for half an hour of inconsequential chat. But Helen, removing her gloves, came to the point with uncharacteristic directness.

'I felt I had to come. I've been worried about you. You disappeared so suddenly the other night, without saying goodbye. So unlike you. Were you unwell?'

'A little,' Louella said. It had been easy at the time for Stuart Armitage to dispense with the conventions; he was not having to answer for it, days later, to an offended hostess. 'I . . . I felt faint. And breathless,' she improvised.

'I'm so sorry to hear that. But you should have told me,' Helen said reproachfully. 'I could have given you smelling salts, or somewhere to lie down. I am so distressed to hear that my party had that effect on you.'

'To tell the truth, I didn't want to spoil such a delightful event with my boring indisposition. With so many guests for you to look after, I thought it would be selfish of me to demand your attention. I made a mistake in going, I suppose. It was a little too much, so soon after Hector's funeral . . .'

'And Stuart Armitage took you home.' Helen cut short the excuse. Was it guilty conscience, Louella wondered, that made the words sound to her like an accusation of impropriety?

'Yes. So kind of him.'

Helen fiddled with her gloves.

'I feel I should warn you about Stuart,' she said.

'*Warn* me?'

'You won't thank me for it, I know – and why should you? We've never really got on, have we, Louella? You think I'm a silly old woman – no, don't bother to deny it. I'm not quite silly enough to believe you. And I don't really know why I should bother to say anything, except that we were so fond of Hector . . . and he thought the world of you . . . and for his sake if nothing else, it would be terrible to see you humiliated.'

There was a silence. In all the years that Louella had gone through the motions of a friendship with Helen she had never thought her capable of such perception, or been on the receiving end of such frankness.

'What is it that you feel I should know about Stuart?' she managed to say at last.

'In the first place, he's a married man. Were you aware of that?'

'*Married?*'

'A disabled wife, living with her family in Dorset. Confined by illness to a wheelchair. I believe he sees very little of her. I don't say that with blame, I daresay it's common enough for a man in such circumstances to detach himself, however hardhearted it may seem to onlookers.'

'So you thought I should know that Mr Armitage is married,' Louella said, suppressing her inner reactions to the news, to be dealt with later in privacy. 'Thank you for telling me, but I don't see that it affects his suitability as my solicitor.'

'I would have said the same, until recently,' said Helen. 'But when you left my party so abruptly, it caused comment. And it is that comment that I feel obliged to pass on to you, though I find it embarrassing, to say the least.'

Louella shrugged with feigned indifference. 'Gossips will always find a target. Let them talk about me for a day or two, if it makes them happy.'

'I wish I could believe that it was only gossip. But from what I've been told, there is some substance in it.'

'What exactly *have* you been told?' Louella said sharply.

'To put it bluntly, that Stuart specializes in rich widows,' said Helen Moffat. 'And you are regarded as his latest catch.'

At which moment, Alice brought in the tea.

When Helen had gone, Louella paced up and down in her drawing room, trying to make sense of what she had just learned.

Stuart was married, with a crippled wife in Dorset. The news conjured up an image in her mind: a shadowy figure in a wheelchair, sitting alone in an empty room with the curtains drawn. That was rubbish, she told herself irritably. So the unknown Mrs Armitage lived with a caring family while her husband earned a living for both of them in London? It was a perfectly sensible arrangement, and one that nobody was entitled to criticize. As far as Louella was concerned, it could be dismissed as irrelevant. She didn't want a husband, she wanted a lover, a temporary lover to father a child, that was all, and if Stuart's wife couldn't give him physical love, who could blame him for satisfying his needs elsewhere? But the image of the neglected wife persisted and, despite all common sense, the idea of Stuart as a married man tarnished what had happened between the two of them, even before she began to examine what else had been hinted at by Helen Moffat.

Stuart specializes in rich widows. That hurt. It was humiliating. Had he really been pretending to a passion that

159

he didn't feel? When she recalled his kisses, her head swam. *But why you?* her inner voice of common sense prodded at her. *You're older than he is. He hardly knows you. For heaven's sake, you're not so very irresistible, if it wasn't for your money . . . and he knows all about* that. *He has a schedule of your possessions in his filing cabinet . . .*

The telephone rang.

Her first thought was that it might be Stuart. She didn't know what to say to him. Her instinct was to let the bell go on ringing. Then Alice appeared at the door, pale and flustered because she knew that she had made a mistake in letting Helen Moffat in and that sooner or later, Louella would make her pay for it.

'Oh! I'm sorry, madam, I didn't realize you were still in here. Shall I get the telephone?'

'No, I will. It's all right, Alice.'

But the caller wasn't Stuart.

'I'm going mad with boredom here. I'll swear it rains more in the country.'

'Jem,' said Louella, and let out a long breath.

'Do you want me to do anything about this Brownlowe character or what? Isn't it time I gave him a few more pinpricks? I'll be getting out of practice.'

'I'm busy,' Louella said. 'I don't want to be bothered with all that now. You can do anything you like so long as it's only pinpricks.'

'That's all I need to know,' said Jem.

'And so long as you don't get caught.'

Around midnight on an evening late in January, Billy Marshall tipped another shovel of coal into the brazier in the harness room at Maple Grange. He sat down again on his stool, hunching one shoulder up against the cold. The other shoulder no longer obeyed such muscular instructions because Billy had lost the use of it in five hectic minutes on the Somme in July of 1916. The German surgeons who dealt with his wounds, when he was brought in through their trenches from No Man's Land, had taken out the shattered fragments of a shoulder blade and three more bullets besides, leaving him with a right arm that hung useless by his side and bouts of pain, exhausting and unpredictable, from the places where the other bullets had been. There was a fifth bullet, he had been told, too near the spine to be safely removed. It made itself felt on winter evenings.

Tonight there were no clouds to obscure the full moon, so there was a white skim of frost on the paving stones and the weeds in the courtyard. Billy shivered. His coat was too thin for this weather but if he built the fire in the brazier any higher, he'd pay for it another night when the coal ran out. Rupert Brownlowe, in assigning him to night watchman's duties, had taken no account of the fact that he would be up and about, instead of sleeping under a heap of blankets, throughout the coldest hours of the night. There was only so much fuel allocated to him for the winter and he'd calculated finely how many lumps he could use per night. This last shovelful was the ration for at least another two hours.

His dog Sally lay across his feet, more comforting than a hot brick wrapped in a blanket. She whimpered and twitched in her sleep. Sally was old now and half blind, and sometimes she staggered when she walked. She had maybe a month or two more to live before humanity would demand that he shoot her.

He hoped she'd last out the winter. He couldn't imagine life without Sally, who'd been given to him as a puppy early in 1919, soon after he came home maimed and despairing from a Prisoner of War camp in Germany. He remembered the day. He'd been slumped in a chair with his dead arm laid across his knees, and his mother dropped something warm and wriggling into his lap: a cross-bred pup with a silky black coat and tan-and-white patches.

'Here. She needs training.'

After the first jerk of surprise he'd relapsed into apathy, until Sally had scrambled up over the useless arm and licked his face. Then he'd laughed for the first time in what seemed like years.

But now she was fifteen, old for a dog, and he was thirty-four and felt very old for a man. His mother had died last March, not quite surviving another winter, and since then he'd been sleepwalking through half a life, with no purpose and no hope. Maybe someone ought to shoot him as well as Sally, out of kindness?

In her stall, Rupert Brownlowe's prize mare stamped and snorted. Billy spread his hands nearer to the glow from the brazier, feeling sorry for the mare, all alone and with her foal near to being born. Was she nervous, as a woman would be nervous at such a time? Automatically he fished his scarred tin harmonica out of his breast pocket. He'd learnt to play it in the war, at first for sing-songs at the rest camps in the days before he was wounded. Afterwards, in the German hospital, it had been one of the few things you could do efficiently with one hand.

It's a long way to Tipperary . . . He played the notes softly, not really thinking. In the stables the mare stood still, finding the sound soothing. But at his feet Sally stirred and raised her head, ears pricked though her cloudy eyes could see nothing but blurs.

'What is it, old thing?' Billy had broken off the tune. Sally unfolded herself on to her shaky legs and turned towards the open doorway, tremblingly alert. Her master laid a reassuring hand on top of her head but she bared her teeth and uttered a low growl of warning.

'Hush, now. I expect it's just a stray cat or a fox.' Billy pocketed the harmonica and followed his dog to the door. Sally padded out into the cold air. Stiff on her legs in the bright moonlight, she barked twice, sharply, across the yard. The brood mare neighed in response.

Billy never knew what hit him, but when he recovered consciousness he was lying face down in the yard outside the harness-room door. He struggled into a sitting position, limbs half paralysed with the cold. His head hurt and when he touched his hand to the source of the pain he found a sticky, swollen lump on his scalp. Then he became aware that beside him lay Sally, her cloudy eyes quite sightless now, her mouth still stretched back over her teeth in what had been her last warning snarl.

Blood had dried on the back of her head and on her smashed ribs. He scooped her up and cradled her for a while in his lap but there was no life in her. When he forced himself to his feet and stumbled towards the stalls that had housed Rupert's prize mare, the mare had gone.

Jem shed his clothes and slid silently into bed beside Kitty. She turned her face towards him, pale in the moonlight that filtered through a gap between the curtains.

'Where do you go at nights, Jem?'

'I've told you before, it's none of your business. Stay out of it.'

'Is there . . .' Kitty's voice trembled. 'Is there some woman you go and see?'

'Some woman? Now there's a thought.' Jem levered himself up on one elbow. 'Should I find myself another woman?' he murmured. 'One who doesn't ask questions when I've told her not to?' He took hold of her neck, his strong fingers pressed into the flesh around her windpipe, and held her like that till she felt limp under his hand.

'Next time I say *stay* out of it, maybe you'll do as you're told.'

He let her drop and turned his back. Within a few minutes his breathing was slow and even. Kitty lay awake till daylight, shuddering with fear.

At Maple Grange, its owner had been woken in the middle of the night with the news of an intruder in his stables. Hauling on his dressing gown and with a quilt clutched around his shoulders, he hurried to the stable yard where Billy Marshall, having raised the alarm at the house, had retreated to his stool by the brazier and now sat snivelling over the dying embers with a dead dog spread across his lap.

'*Where's my mare?*'

'I dunno, sir,' Billy told him hopelessly. 'Someone's made off with her.'

163

'Well, don't just sit there, man. Get on your feet and find her, damnit.'

'I dunno that I can, sir. I can't seem to walk properly. Dizzy. He hit me over the head, see. Knocked me out.'

'Who hit you?' Rupert demanded.

'Whoever it was that took the mare, I suppose. And he's killed my dog,' said Billy Marshall. 'Poor old Sal. Poor old thing.' He stroked a gentle hand over the stiffening corpse on his lap.

Rupert stared at his employee with mounting impatience. The man seemed to be crying.

'Never mind your damned dog! What about my *mare*?'

Marshall just went on crying.

'I gave him the sack,' Rupert told his wife at breakfast. 'What's the good of a night watchman if he can't see off intruders?'

'Oh, *Rupert*,' Marion said, dismayed. 'Poor Billy could hardly be expected to deal with some determined villain. It's not as if he's a hundred per cent fit.'

'Precisely,' said Rupert. 'I'm not a charity. I can't afford to keep on somebody who can't do the job. A good guard dog would have been cheaper than that cripple – *and* given the thief a run for his money. As it is,' said Rupert bitterly, 'I've lost Leonora, after all it's cost me to buy her and put the stables to rights *and* pay the wretched man's wages.'

'Where's Billy now?' Maybe, Marion calculated, if the police could be contacted and the mare recovered, her husband might be mollified and the whole mess sorted out in time.

'God knows. I borrowed from the bank,' Rupert remembered gloomily. 'I was going to pay them back when the foal was sold. Now what'll I do?'

Marion went down to the stables as soon after breakfast as she could, but there was no sign of Billy Marshall. His bed in the loft room had been stripped, the blankets neatly folded and the single small cupboard cleared of his belongings.

'Oh dear. Where could the poor man go?' she asked herself. Billy had first come to her attention through Colonel Strover of the 'Every Little Helps' organization, but from her experience of men like Billy, the poorer and more humble they seemed, the more stubborn was their pride in such situations. She doubted that Billy would contact the Colonel again, after being so unceremoniously dismissed by his employer. And until the missing Leonora was found, there was no chance that Rupert could be persuaded to rescind that sacking.

As she stood in the deserted room above the feed store she heard the clattering of hooves on the cobbles of the stable yard. When she hurried down the stone stairs, a man stood in the middle of the yard, hanging on to a restless horse at the end of a roughly constructed rope halter.

'Excuse me, missus.' His accent wasn't local. He sounded like a Londoner. 'Is this your 'orse?'

Marion stared incredulously at the swollen-bellied mare. Leonora showed signs of having come home unwillingly – her coat was damp with sweat and there were specks of foam about her muzzle and on her shoulders, but she was staring about her with recognition and for the moment she had ceased to dance on the end of her rope.

'Yes! Yes, she is ours. Oh, you can't imagine what a relief it is to see her – my husband will be quite delighted to have her back. But how on earth did you come by her?'

'She was wandering about in the woods under Crooksbury Hill, down near the river,' the man said. 'I heard her as I went by along the road and reckoned she shouldn't be out, not with her being so near to dropping her foal, so I put a rope on her and asked around and people reckoned she must've come from the Grange.'

'Well, they were quite right,' said Marion. 'Let's put her away in her stall and then you must come and talk to my husband. I'm sure he'll want to thank you properly.'

Rupert, on learning that Leonora had been returned, was so delighted that he underlined his thanks with what was for him the unwonted generosity of a five-pound note.

'Here you are, my man. It must be a few weeks' wages for you, I should think, so mind you do something sensible with it, now. Don't go spending it all on drink.'

The man touched his hand to his peaked cap as he accepted the proffered note and, having delivered a few words of thanks for the reward, he loped off down the drive.

'Have you called the police yet?' Marion asked her husband.

'Yes, but we may as well telephone again and tell them not to bother. There's not much point, now we've got Leonora back.' Rupert was already regretting the five-pound note – wouldn't a pound have done? After all, the honest return of stolen property was no more than any man's rightful due. 'I doubt if they'll put themselves out to catch a thief when the booty's been recovered,' he said.

'But there's still the fact that she was stolen in the first place. And after all, Billy Marshall was hit,' said Marion, though she was still unaware, because Rupert had not bothered to go into detail, that Billy had been clubbed unconscious and his dog battered to death.

'Well, *you* can report it, if you've the time,' Rupert said testily. But *I'll* tell Stevenson to get hold of a good, savage dog with a loud bark – that'll be more effective than a constable on a bicycle, asking silly questions.'

Later in the day, Rupert's predicted constable on a bicycle arrived at the front door of the Grange. Rupert, having provided the sketchiest of accounts of the night's excitement, left Marion to it.

'Where's this night watchman that you say was hit?' the policeman asked.

'Unfortunately, my husband dismissed him in the heat of the moment and now he's gone,' said Marion.

'Gone? Where to?'

'I'm afraid I don't know. I wish I did.'

'It *is* unfortunate,' the constable said. 'He might have been involved in the robbery, you see. There's often insider information in these country-house incidents – an employee with a grudge.'

'Not Billy Marshall – I'm positive of that,' Marion said decisively.

'Well, if you're sure . . .'

'Oh, Billy's honest. I'd vouch for him any day.'

'Well, any other ideas about who might have done it? Anyone who doesn't like your husband?'

It was not the first time that someone had asked that question in connection with a crime committed against Rupert Brownlowe, and Marion suppressed the usual reply, which was that a very long list of people disliked him. She could think of nothing useful to tell the policeman at the time, but after he had gone she found herself remembering something about the man who had brought Rupert's mare back.

It was such a small detail, nothing that she could justifiably have mentioned to the constable, but she had noticed that when the man smiled, his mouth curved higher on one side than the other and the lopsidedness of that smile had made her feel vaguely uneasy, as if she and her husband were being mocked. Rupert had spoken to him so patronizingly, as if to a simple-minded countryman, but there was more to him than that. It occurred to her now that his discovery of the mare, so soon after the theft, had been a remarkable coincidence and her speedy return to her rightful owner had been even more remarkable.

But it doesn't make any sense to go to all the trouble of stealing her, just to bring her back again, she reminded herself. Five pounds isn't much for a prize brood mare.

Jem Wilkins would have agreed with Mrs Brownlowe on that point. If Leonora hadn't given him so much trouble in the night, he would have led her further into the Hampshire countryside, hidden her somewhere safe and sold her on at the first opportunity. As it was, she'd played up to such an extent that he'd had to park her in the woods and make the journey back this morning to retrieve her. He'd also had to think up a good story to explain his absence from the farm and he'd had to walk all this way to do it – and all for a fiver and a condescending lecture from the old man.

167

Still, it was the pinprick he'd proposed to Louella, to shake up that old fool Brownlowe. The night watchman had been an unexpected complication but he'd dealt with him easily enough and had a bit of fun with his rickety old dog. He could always come back for the mare another time. But as he trudged the seven or eight miles back to Welcome Farm, Jem reckoned that Louella's vendetta aside, that mean bastard Rupert Brownlowe deserved all the trouble that was coming to him.

11

'Come and help me with pressing the cheeses,' Daisy said to Kitty, on a morning in January. 'Do you know about cheesemaking?'

'No, Mrs Griffin.'

'I'll show you how we do it, then.'

'I could do that, Mrs Griffin. I already know how,' Allie Briggs volunteered. She was in the middle of giving the stove its weekly rake-out, riddling to get rid of all the ash and taking out the clinker with a pair of tongs before re-laying and relighting the fire with new coal. It was a process which she detested and although she had done it for years, Allie didn't see why she should get lumbered with the dirty jobs while Kitty got the clean ones. But there was to be no reprieve.

'No, thank you, Allie. You carry on with what you're doing.' Daisy was worried about Kitty, who lately had looked even more thin and scared than she had done on her arrival at the farm three months ago. The dairy, being out of range of Allie's ever-twitching ears, seemed a suitable place for a heart-to-heart. She made sure that the door was shut firmly behind them before she broached the subject.

'Kitty, is everything all right? I mean, are you happy here?'

'Yes, Mrs Griffin.' It came out in a hoarse whisper.

'Is there something wrong with your throat?' Daisy asked. Kitty's hand flew to the scarf which was wrapped tightly round her neck.

'Oh no, ma'am,' she said, too quickly to be convincing. Her frightened eyes met Daisy's concerned ones, pleading for something which baffled the older woman. Did she want to be asked more, or to be left alone?

'If you're starting a cold,' Daisy ventured, 'I may be able to give you something to ease it. My family tease me sometimes about my herbs and potions, they say in another age I'd have been swum for a witch. But my mother showed me some of the old country cures and Mrs Driver at the Grange taught me some more, and I reckon they really *do* work, even if they don't come out of a smart book or from the doctor.

'I haven't got a cold,' Kitty said.

'But you aren't well. Or at any rate, you aren't happy. I wish I could help,' said Daisy. There was a pause while very slowly, two great tears welled up in Kitty's eyes and slid down her pale cheeks.

'Oh, my dear,' said Daisy gently. She reached out and touched the girl's fist which was clenched so tightly that the knuckles were white. It was the final push for Kitty, who hid her face behind her hands and subsided into helpless sobs. Daisy gathered the fair head against her shoulder and patted her on the back in a motherly way.

'There now, cry it out,' she said. 'And then you can tell me all about it.'

'Lovely strawberry jam you make, Mrs Griffin. Strawberry's difficult – mine always comes out runny unless I mix it with apple, but you got yours to set beautifully last summer, and the fruit's so nice and chunky.'

Allie Briggs, having relit the stove, had moved on to the tidying of the larder. For Allie, this meant rearranging the plates of half-consumed pies and cold meat, eating up odds and ends to get them out of the way and casting covetous eyes at the pots of preserves stored in the cool, dark recesses underneath the stone shelves.

'You can take a pot home with you if you like, Allie,' Daisy said, accustomed to the drift of Allie's compliments. She fished out the promised pot of jam from the dozens of jars stored at the bottom of the larder.

'Well, I won't say no, Mrs Griffin. My Stanley does love a bit of strawberry jam on his toast. Where's that Kitty gone, then?'

'She wasn't very well so I sent her home for a lie-down. Time you were on your way as well, Allie.'

Kitty, washed-out with weeping, had been dosed with a tisane made from dried comfrey leaves for her bruised throat and packed off to Starling Cottages to recover. While Allie donned her coat and hat, Daisy remembered the neglected ritual of tightening the screws down on the row of cheese presses waiting in the dairy. And it was only as Will came in for his midday meal that she realized that the cottage pie she'd prepared after breakfast was still sitting on the kitchen table instead of browning in the oven. There was no help for it but to give him cold meat instead, an action which by Daisy's normal standards amounted almost to criminal negligence.

'Sorry about this,' she apologized as she laid a plate of leftover chicken and hastily boiled vegetables in front of her husband. 'I was busy in the dairy and Allie didn't think to put the cottage pie in the oven. Jem not coming in for his dinner?'

'No, he needed his boots repaired and we weren't too busy this morning, so he took them over to Wrecclesham to Mr Wilkinson for a stitch.'

'It shouldn't take him half the day to get to Wrecclesham and back,' Daisy observed.

'Well, maybe he's got chatting, or remembered some other chores while he's over there. I told him there was no hurry.' Will ate a mouthful of his food before adding, 'I know you don't like Jem, love, but I'll say this for him, he's a good worker. He's more than earned a morning off.'

'You're right that I don't like him,' Daisy said. 'But it's nothing to do with the way he works. It's how he treats Kitty that I mind. He hits her, Will. We had a bit of a talk this morning. She didn't say a lot, poor soul, but that much I did manage to gather.'

'That's bad,' said Will, cautiously.

'Bad? It's terrible. She's such a wisp of a thing, how can she stand up for herself against a bully? We have to stop him. *You* have to stop him,' Daisy elaborated. 'He'll listen to you.'

'I dunno. Might be difficult,' Will commented, brow furrowed. 'I mean, as far as I'm concerned he's done nothing to complain about.'

'*Nothing?*' Daisy's voice climbed. 'You should have seen her throat this morning.'

'We haven't heard both sides of the story, have we?'

Daisy was taken aback. Usually, she and Will were so much of a mind that they hardly needed to put things into words before reaching an agreement, but on this subject, he was being surprisingly unhelpful.

'You have to mind what you're doing,' he said, 'when you interfere between husband and wife. *Those whom God hath joined together, let no man put asunder*. Isn't that part of the wedding service?'

'I don't want to put them asunder,' Daisy pointed out tightly. 'I just want to make him see that he has to be a bit kinder to her. Promising to love and cherish is in the service as well, as far as I remember. And anyway,' she remembered, 'they aren't married.'

It was Will's turn to look startled. 'But I thought Louella's letter said—'

'No. She wrote that she'd sent us Jem Wilkins and Kitty. We just took it for granted, and Kitty didn't dare contradict because she felt ashamed about it. Jem promised to marry her but now he's dragging his heels over it.'

There was a splintering crash and a muffled cry of dismay from outside the door that led into the hall. Daisy leapt up and wrenched open the door. Allie Briggs faced her guiltily over shattered glass fragments in a puddle of lumpy crimson jelly.

'I forgot my pot of jam, Mrs Griffin, left it on the stairs while I put on my coat, so I came back for it. And now I've gone and dropped the blessed thing.'

*   *   *

'D'you think she heard?' Daisy asked Will, when the sticky mess had been hastily cleared up and Allie seen off safely down the lane on her bicycle – denied a replacement pot of jam, because Daisy took her for a snooper.

'Bound to have,' said Will.

'Oh dear. She's the biggest gossip in Bentley . . . Oh well, we'll just have to deal with it when we know the damage. But to get back to what I was saying before, Will, Jem promised to marry Kitty and he hasn't.'

It was a familiar enough story, Will thought, faintly exasperated. He wanted to tell his wife that these things wouldn't happen if women would only hang on to the goods till the banns had been called and the knot well and truly tied; but he reckoned that Daisy wasn't in a mood to hear such observations – and besides, she might take them personally, given the circumstances of her life before her marriage to Will.

'I suppose that's their business,' he said. 'People make their own decisions about the way they live, and so they should, just so long as they don't go hurting anyone else by it.'

'Oh, *Will*. I'm disappointed in you. I expected you to be more sympathetic.'

Will sighed. Daisy had made up her mind about the situation and now he was being harried over his dinner, the precious half-hour's break in a hard day, just because he didn't automatically take the same side. His loyalty to Daisy was a high priority, but why should he get involved in an argument against a man he rather liked, on behalf of a girl he barely knew? Daisy saw a lot of Kitty and very little of Jem, but with him it was the other way round, and there was plenty of room for misunderstandings. He stuck to his guns.

'If you're disappointed I'm sorry, love. I'm only saying it the way I see it. Anyway, it makes things simpler for Kitty if they aren't married, doesn't it? If she doesn't like the way Jem treats her, there's no bit of paper that says she has to put up with it. She can always leave him.'

'Trouble is,' said Daisy, 'I think she loves him, even if he does treat her rough. And besides, she's got nowhere else to go.'

Your father's mare has foaled, wrote Marion Brownlowe to her stepdaughter, *and Rupert is so pleased and proud. He spends all his time at the stables, gloating over the new arrival, which is a colt, a lovely chestnut like his dam, and with a white star on his forehead. I gather he's the image of a mare that Rupert used to own before the war – he says you would remember her. So the foal is called Starbright, in her memory.*

Edward must be back at school now, of course, and I daresay James will be too busy as usual, but do come and visit for a few days yourself if you can, and bring little Caroline. Your father said only yesterday how sad he felt that his grandchildren are growing up so quickly and he sees them so seldom. He would be delighted if you came, and he would love to show Starbright off to you.

Laura Allingham sighed. Marion was a darling, but she was also an adept emotional blackmailer. She would know perfectly well, in writing her letter, the degree of guilt it would induce in its recipient, but the last thing that Laura wanted, now or at any time, was a visit to Maple Grange. The house held too many memories . . . and encounters with her father invariably stirred them up. She postponed replying until Marion telephoned her to press the invitation.

'Oh, it's so kind of you and I would love to see the foal,' Laura said. 'But I don't see how I can manage it at present. You know all about my activities with the Fabians and the Anglo-German Friendship League and the Peace movement; and now James is thinking of standing as a parliamentary candidate for the Labour Party – you can imagine how Pa would react to that news! And his involvement has generated an enormous amount of correspondence, which I am trying to deal with for him on top of my own work. Of course I'd love to see you here at any time that you can get up to London,' she added.

'Your father will be so disappointed,' said Marion, reproachfully.

'I'm sorry, but I honestly can't find the time at present,' Laura defended herself.

'How soon *would* you be able to?' Marion said. Rupert kept badgering her to repeat the invitation and exasperating though Rupert frequently was, there was something about his bruised hopefulness where Laura was concerned that touched his wife's heart and prompted her to transfer some of that exasperation to his daughter.

Caught on the prongs of Marion's persistence, Laura squirmed. 'Perhaps next month,' she hedged.

'Good. That's settled then. I'll tell Rupert you'll be coming in February,' said Marion, neatly converting an evasion into a promise.

Louella had refused to take telephone calls from Stuart Armitage ever since the visit from Helen Moffat, and now Stuart had called upon her to find out why.

'I'm not sure if Madam is at home. I'll enquire.' Alice was newly trained to prevaricate, but she didn't know how to resist the determined invasion of a young man who had known a warmer reception from Mrs Ramsay and wanted to know what lay behind her current coldness.

'I'm sorry, madam, he pushed past me.'

'All right, Alice, I'll deal with it. You can go.'

'What's happened, Louella? Why won't you talk to me?' Stuart demanded as soon as the maid had left the drawing room.

'Why didn't you tell me you were married?' countered Louella. She stood in front of the fireplace, only a few feet away, but from her expression and the tone of her voice, she was no more touchable than if she had been surrounded by a brick wall.

Stuart's healthy complexion changed colour. 'Who told you that?' he said.

'Never mind that. I should have heard it from you.'

'I suppose it was one of those jealous old women, the

175

ones who can't bear to think that anyone else might get what they can't have.'

'Why didn't you tell me?' Louella repeated.

Stuart came closer. 'Louella,' he said softly. He saw the shiver of reaction in her and thought he recognized some involuntary fission in her resistance. 'For God's sake, look at me. Please.'

Louella had been stung and shamed by Helen Moffat's words and by the memory of her own responses to a man who, if Helen was to be believed, was a cynical exploiter of women in her position. Her expression as she looked at him was not inviting but Stuart ploughed on.

'The fact is, I love you. I fell in love with you from the first time I saw you, all in widow's black, so alone and so proud, untouchable and yet waiting to be touched. It was like a light bursting inside me – oh, I know that sounds clichéd, but I don't know how else to describe it. And I desperately wanted to make you love me in return.'

'You very nearly succeeded.' It was said so matter-of-factly that Stuart took a moment to interpret it as an encouragement. When he did, he tried to kiss her but she turned her face away.

'Don't. I spoke in the past tense. Why weren't you honest with me?'

'About my matrimonial state? Because I was afraid that it would lose me whatever chance I had, if I told you too soon. Yes, I am married,' he said bleakly. 'I was married when I was barely twenty-one, to a girl who was even younger. We never learned to understand one another's needs. We started almost as strangers; maybe that's usual, but most couples grow together as the marriage progresses. We just grew further apart. Oh, I tried to talk about what was happening, but she would never discuss anything, she was so icily determined not to quarrel that she'd never admit there was anything to quarrel *about*. And even though we had no emotional contact, she demanded attention. She ate up every moment of my time, she wanted it for little things, not for what really mattered. It was like being throttled by ivy. As for sex—' He broke off. 'Do you want to hear this?' he said. 'It didn't work, is that enough?'

'And the wheelchair?' said Louella, in the same barely interested tone she had used throughout the interview.

'That came later. She fell from a horse out hunting and damaged her back. Her horse, her choice to go hunting; but I think she blamed me for it in some obscure way; she blames me for everything bad that happens to her. The doctors said she might recover the use of her legs if she tried, but she didn't try. She took to that damned wheelchair as if it was the height of her ambition to be an invalid. Then she said she wanted to go back to her parents, and it seemed the best thing for both of us. I still support her financially. But I'm a man, Louella, I'm human, I've wanted . . . all the usual things that a man tends to want,' he said wryly. 'I can't court young girls, that wouldn't be fair. And I'm too proud or finicky to go to prostitutes, and too much of an idealist, in my own way, to settle for an intrigue with a married woman.'

'So you fall back on rich widows,' said Louella.

'*Rich widows?* Is that what you've heard? Someone has a wicked tongue,' complained Stuart. 'And like any really efficient libel, it contains a small grain of truth which makes it hard to swallow. I've found that older women can be sympathetic, and wise, and generous with their sympathy and their wisdom.'

'And their bodies.'

'And their bodies,' Stuart admitted. 'Oh, how can I explain? Do you know those lines from John Donne? "*If ever any beauty I did see, Which I desired, and got, 'twas but a dream of thee.*" Well, until you, I never wanted anyone so much or so badly.

'And that,' said Stuart, 'is the honest truth. The question, now, is what are you going to do about it?'

Harriet had spent the afternoon with Lydia Matthews, learning to understand and order from a menu in French.

Aunt Louella had suggested that this was one of the many experiences which a girl should undergo if she wanted to marry someone like Gavin Draycott; but after two hours of reciting *filet de boeuf rôti* and *potage crème Dubarry* until her accent passed muster, Harriet was feeling tired, headachy and distinctly rebellious.

Walking back to Medlar House across the green, she wondered why she had ever embarked on this arduous process of becoming a lady. Before Christmas, she would have gone to any lengths to regain Gavin's interest and since her return to her aunt's in the New Year, Louella had continued to assure her that if she could only acquire the right degree of polish, Gavin would come to his senses and realize what a catch he'd thrown back. But then, Louella had not seen the Swallow swirl along the lane outside Welcome Farm with a pretty girl in the passenger seat and Gavin at the wheel.

Harriet still smarted at the memory of that humiliation. As for Lydia's lesson today, which was supposed to improve her chances, what kind of a love was it that depended on its recipient knowing the difference between *steak entrecôte* and *steak tournedos*? Harriet Griffin, farmer's daughter, considered that she knew what really mattered where food was concerned – and that was knowing how to rear a bullock, kill and cook it, not how to describe the results in another language. For two pins she would abandon the whole silly enterprise and go home.

And yet it would be such an anticlimax to admit defeat and go tamely back to Welcome Farm. Her family seemed to have grown thoroughly accustomed to the idea that she was living away from home. Jem was more than compensating for her absence with his work on the farm, her mother wrote to Louella that Kitty was a dear and very good company, and even the flighty mare Briony was reportedly behaving far better under Rob's schooling that she ever had for Harriet. At Christmas she had felt awkward and out of place and she had a miserable feeling that her boats had been burned. As for the brief 'engagement' to Gavin, it had been a mistake. There was no hope of reviving it. What was her future to be?

'Where is my aunt?' she asked Everett, when he opened the front door.

'Mrs Ramsay is in the drawing room, Miss Harriet.'

'Thank you, Everett.'

'Mr Armitage is with her. I think you had better not disturb her,' added the manservant, a fraction too late. Harriet was already pushing open the drawing-room door.

Louella was in the arms of a man. Her dress had been unfastened to the waist and the bodice was spread open so that it slipped down over her shoulders. Her black hair was unpinned and one of the man's hands was entangled in it as he kissed her. The other hand was caressing the bared skin of her back.

For Harriet, the sight was an unbearable echo of her own last kiss with Gavin, so disastrously interrupted by Jem Wilkins.

The sound of the door opening, and Harriet's sharp intake of breath, had sprung the interlocked figures apart. Two startled faces turned towards the intruder. For a moment Louella was as shocked as her niece; then she regained her composure. She stepped away from the man, tucked strands of hair behind her ears, hitched her bodice into place and spoke calmly.

'Ah. Harriet. I don't believe you have met Stuart Armitage, my solicitor.'

Harriet stammered an incoherent apology and fled.

In her blue-and-white bedroom at the top of the house she sat on the bed, confused and miserable, remembering the funeral of Hector Ramsay which seemed in some ways to have taken place only yesterday and in other ways to belong to a very distant past. She hadn't cried for Uncle Hector at the funeral, but she cried for him now because Aunt Louella, who was supposed to have loved him, had forgotten him and it was too soon, too soon entirely, to forget the quiet, grey-haired man with the kind eyes.

Much later, as she sat on the bed drying her reddened

eyes, there was a knock at the door and Louella came in, her normal well-groomed appearance restored.

'Harriet,' she said. 'We should talk.'

'I'm sorry, Aunt Louella. I didn't expect – I never dreamed—'

'It is I who should be sorry,' said Louella. 'You saw something that you should not have seen. I am so accustomed to being private in my own house, and the staff know better than to walk into a room without knocking. To be honest, I had forgotten about you.'

'Who is he?' said Harriet.

'I told you. My lawyer. His senior partner in the firm was Hector's solicitor.'

'Are you going to marry him?' Harriet asked, almost inaudibly this time.

Louella laughed. 'Marry him? Certainly not.'

'But you were . . .'

'We were kissing. In London society, this does not automatically lead to marriage, Harriet. If Lydia has not yet explained such things to you, I had better make a note of it.'

Louella was smiling, but her tone had been sharp and there was something very cold about her eyes. Once, a few months ago, Harriet had overheard her parents discussing her aunt. Will had said, *Louella's as hard as nails and twice as dangerous.* And Daisy had said, in defence of the absent Louella, *But she wasn't always. Something shut down in her after Robert died, and then her poor little baby . . . After that it seemed like you couldn't get to the heart of her any more.*

'You never loved Uncle Hector, did you?' Harriet said. She wasn't sure, afterwards, what had made her say it, but it dissolved Louella's smile. She slapped Harriet, hard, across the face.

'How dare you say that? How dare you? What do you know about love, you silly girl? You and your mawkish infatuation with that *boy*.' She ground out the last word with utter contempt, eyes blazing.

There was a long silence.

Then Harriet said dully, with the stinging imprint of Louella's hand on her cheek, 'I think I should go home.'

'As you wish,' said Louella.

'Harriet's back. I don't know what happened,' Daisy told Will next day. Her daughter had arrived without warning, carrying a single suitcase, having walked from the station at Bentley. 'She's upset, but she won't talk to me about it. I *knew* we shouldn't have let her go to Louella and have her head turned.'

'Where is she now?' Will said.

'Out in the orchard, I think, probably catching her death of cold. Take a coat out to her if you're going, Will. It looks like snow.'

In the gathering gloom of snow-laden clouds, Will walked down to the orchard with Daisy's old winter coat over his arm. Harriet was standing among the bare trees, looking forlorn. He went quietly up to her and spread the coat across her shoulders.

'Here. Mum's instructions. You know how she worries.'

'Oh, Dad . . .' Harriet rubbed the back of her hand across her nose and sniffed. Will put his arm around her shoulders and she leaned against him, finding his silent presence comforting. With Will there were no questions. He would give you all the time in the world to tell him what you needed him to know.

'Good to have you back,' was all he said.

'Mrs Griffin, could I have a word?'

Usually Allie arrived a few minutes late for work with a breathless story about how the postman had waylaid her on her doorstep and insisted on a chat, or her bike had a puncture, or the wind had been against her on the road from Bentley. Today she was on time. She stood in the middle of the kitchen, making no move to take off her coat.

'All right, Allie, what is it?' Daisy paused in the middle of stacking breakfast dishes beside the sink.

'It's about that Kitty Wilkins – or whatever her name is,'

said Allie. 'I couldn't help but overhear what you were saying to Mr Griffin yesterday, about her and Jem Wilkins – how they aren't properly married, for all that they're living together as man and wife, bold as brass. And when I was talking to my Stanley last night, it just slipped out—'

'As it would,' said Daisy.

'Pardon?' Allie wasn't sure what to make of the comment. It seemed harmless enough, but there had been a hint of steel in her employer's voice.

'You were saying?' Daisy prompted.

'Well, my Stanley doesn't like it. He says he doesn't like to think of me working alongside an immoral woman.'

'That's a pity.' Face averted, Daisy rinsed her hands under the tap. 'In that case I shall be sorry to lose you, Allie, but if you can't work with Kitty, I suppose it can't be helped.'

It was not the answer that Allie had expected. Last night, talking to Stanley about what she had learned in a scrap of overheard conversation, she had assumed that it was Kitty, the newcomer, who would be given her marching orders now that her shameful secret was uncovered.

'I didn't exactly mean that, Mrs Griffin,' she said hastily. 'I like working here. I wouldn't want to leave. I just thought I'd better tell you about what Stanley said, in case it causes any trouble.'

'We'll have to hope it won't then, shan't we?' said Daisy. She dried her hands, a finger at a time, on the towel hung on its wooden roller beside the sink before turning to face Allie.

'I'd be at least as upset as Stanley is now, if I found he'd been spreading gossip about Jem and Kitty down at the Red Lion. You'd better pass that on, Allie. Because he wouldn't have known anything to get unhappy about, would he, if you hadn't eavesdropped on a private conversation?'

Allie gaped.

'You can wash this lot up, if you're staying,' said Daisy. She unhooked an apron from the peg behind the back door and held it out to the chastened Allie, who took it like a lamb.

12

Being a realist, Will Griffin had recognized that the future for farming lay with the combustion engine, but his heart was with the heavy horses that the tractor was replacing on farms across England. 'A horse'll keep you company,' he said. 'It'll learn the job as well as its owner. It'll start easier on a cold morning than a tractor, and it'll give you barrowfuls of muck as a bonus.'

Harriet, mucking out the adjoining stalls of Captain and Charlotte, the two bay Shires that made up Will's match-winning ploughing team, might have disputed the concept of stable manure as a bonus. In Captain's stall she tossed a forkful of stained straw on to the reeking pile in the wheelbarrow at her side, leaned on her pitchfork and straightened her aching back, ruefully inspecting the blisters forming on her palms.

'The trouble with you is you've had too many weeks of soft living at Aunt Louella's,' she scolded herself. 'Well, this is your life, like it or lump it, so you'd better get back into the habit, hadn't you?'

'So you're back. And planning to stay by the sound of it.' Jem Wilkins stood watching her, his arms resting along the chest-high wooden partition that divided the stall from the main passageway.

'What if I am?' said Harriet, self-conscious about being overheard and uneasy as always in the presence of Jem, whose eyes seemed to laugh at her whatever his mouth was doing.

'No need to be surly. I was just passing the time of day.'

'Maybe you've got the time. I haven't.' Harriet took a fresh grip on the pitchfork and prepared to ignore him; but

183

Jem, stepping inside the stall, took hold of the wooden handle six inches above her hand and without any apparent exertion, held it immovable.

'I was going to say you brighten the place up a bit. No harm in paying you a compliment, is there?'

'No point in it either. What do you want, Jem?'

Jem grinned. 'Depends what you're prepared to give me, doesn't it?'

The implication was deliberate and obvious. Harriet turned scarlet, not merely from annoyance but because Jem's behaviour was having a very disturbing effect. It had started with that long, considering look he had given her at Christmas. She told herself that he repelled her, but she could not entirely shake off a physical awareness that was as alarming as it was powerful.

'Whatever would Kitty think if she heard you talking like that?'

'Kitty? What does it matter what she thinks? She wouldn't have the nerve to complain anyway, she's too much of a mouse. You're twice the girl she is . . . but you don't know how to use it, yet, do you?'

'I don't like it when you talk like that,' said Harriet, with an effort. 'And if you don't stop it at once, I'll tell my father.'

'Will you?' For the moment, Jem had lost whatever battle was being waged. He abandoned seduction for blackmail. 'That wouldn't be wise. I might know a thing about that father of yours that you don't, and you might regret it if I told people what I know.'

Jem unclosed his fingers from the pitchfork handle and strolled out of the stall. Harriet stared after his departing back, trembling with reaction. She wanted to run in search of her father and have him throw Jem off the premises. That way she would be safe; but from what?

'Hurry up, Rob. You'll be late for school and so will Jackie if you keep him waiting.'

'Don't panic, Mum,' said Rob, looking up from the letter in his hand. He snatched up a last piece of toast-and-marmalade from his plate, then paused on the verge of cramming it into his mouth. 'Jackie, will you do my chores on Saturday morning?'

'What'll you give me if I do?' said Jackie, hovering in the kitchen doorway.

'My book about how car engines work?' Rob offered.

'What else?'

Rob groaned, but he had been expecting a hard bargain. 'Sixpence on top? And I'll do double chores on Sunday.'

'All right,' said Jackie. 'But not if you get me kept in for being late this morning.'

'What's happening on Saturday?' Daisy remembered to ask, as the boys wheeled their bicycles across the yard from the barn. Rob glanced back over his shoulder, beaming, and patted the pocket where he had stowed his letter.

'Tom Searle asked if I'd like another flight,' he called, and was off before his mother had time to protest.

Daisy sighed as she went back into the house. Another flight for Rob, another time of tension for her as she waited for him to come home in one piece. She knew it wasn't logical to be so fearful of him flying, or at least Will assured her that it wasn't logical . . . but the idea still gave her cramps in the stomach.

She sent Kitty out to feed the hens and hunt out eggs, just as Allie arrived for work, out of breath as usual. At least Allie seemed to have settled down after the flurry of trouble over Kitty, and even seemed to have taken a liking to the girl; but the problems with Kitty herself were no nearer to being solved. Will stubbornly refused to intercede with Jem, and Daisy supposed that her only option was to be sympathetic as and when required, and to try to infuse some spirit into the downtrodden girl.

'I'll do the washing up. You lay a fire in the parlour, would you?' Daisy instructed Allie, remembering a letter of her own that the postman had delivered before breakfast. 'I'm expecting a visitor this afternoon. And can you run a duster over the furniture in there and make sure the best tea service is clean?'

Allie raised her eyebrows. For reasons of economy the parlour at Welcome Farm was generally left unused and unheated through the winter, while the Griffins shared the warmth of the kitchen range.

'Somebody important, I take it, Mrs G?'

'Important enough for a fire anyway,' said Daisy unhelpfully. She didn't believe in supplying any free fuel for Allie's gossiping tendencies, even if the district had so far remained unenlightened about the Wilkins' unblessed state.

'Lucky I brought you in some of our newspapers, then,' Allie said. 'I noticed you were running low on papers for getting a fire going. Mr G does like to hang on to his old *Farmers Weekly*, doesn't he?'

'He keeps them for a spare moment,' said Daisy, 'and spare moments don't come very often. Thank you for bringing us some of yours, Allie. The fire, please. Time's getting on.'

Allie carried a stack of newspapers into the parlour. After half an hour's silence, Daisy investigated and discovered her on hands and knees on the hearth, reading old copies of the *Daily Mirror*.

'Sorry, Mrs G,' said Allie, caught red-handed. 'You know how interesting they always are when you're about to throw 'em away,' she excused herself. 'This one, for instance. It's all about them Nasties walking out of the League of Nations Disarmament Conference last October. The chap who wrote this is getting in a rare old twist about it. Listen: "*The German people are today a desperate people who have lost all. And no man is so dangerous as the man who has nothing to lose.*" Sounds awful, doesn't it?'

'The fire,' Daisy reminded her.

'Any minute, Mrs G. It's nearly done,' Allie lied unblushingly, 'but there's something else I wanted to show you. You don't get the *Mirror*, do you? I meant to bring it in with me right at the beginning of last November, only I forgot. This'll interest you.'

'What is it?' Daisy said, resignedly.

' "*If there was another war, would I go again?*" ' Allie

quoted. 'Fifty words on a postcard from anyone who saw active service in any capacity in the Great War, it says here, and a guinea for every answer published. I thought Mr Griffin might like to write in, seeing as he was with the gunners. Only it's too late now,' she added. 'There must be the paper with the winners they picked, somewhere in this heap.'

'Thank you for telling me about it,' said Daisy hastily, backing out of the door, 'but I must get back to my bread.'

She returned to the kitchen, where a row of loaf tins held bread dough, newly risen and ready for baking. As she checked on the temperature of the oven, half her attention was on the job in hand, the other half on what Allie had just said.

If there was another war, would I go again?

During the war, Daisy had filled artillery shells at the Woolwich Arsenal. Over in France and Belgium, Will had been with the Horse Artillery, perhaps firing the very shells that she had helped to make. The enemy had fired back, with shells made by women in their own country, women who were probably just like her. Each nation in the war had believed they had God on their side against a wicked enemy, but it didn't make sense that God would side with everyone; and she had wondered, since the Armistice, if all the enemy had really been quite so wicked as they were painted.

Sometimes when a shell landed, Will had told her, you could see bits of bodies flying up into the air. 'Enough to turn your stomach over,' he had said. And when you thought about it, they had been the bodies of men who were mothers' sons just as much as the Englishmen who were trying to blow them to smithereens. If there was another war now, would Will be expected to go again? Would he want to go? And what about the boys? They were young now, but the Great War had lasted for four terrible years, and had sucked in lads as young as fifteen or sixteen.

She remembered the shouting and the cheering that they had heard on Jackie's radio, and how threatening it had seemed, and despite the heat of the oven blasting in her face

187

she found she was shivering. Why, after all that suffering and slaughter, couldn't 'the War to end all wars' have achieved its purpose?

'I found them answers!' said Allie, bustling into the kitchen with a crumpled newspaper and an air of triumph, as if she had been carrying out a commission instead of taking time off from her proper duties. 'They reckon two out of every three of the ones who wrote in would fight again if they have to. That's us British, we don't shirk a fight, do we? But there's one here from a woman who made shells like you, Mrs G.'

'What did she say?' Daisy asked.

'She said she'd seen what shells do to people. She said, "*Never again.*" '

Harriet had been worrying about Jem's comment all morning – did he really know some dark secret about her father? She made up her mind to confront him about it. Asked about Jem's whereabouts, Will said that he was back at Starling Cottages, making a start on the neglected roof of the empty cottage next door to his own.

'Where's Kitty?'

'Your mum'd know that. I think she's feeding the chickens.'

Harriet walked out to Starling Cottages. Jem was at the top of a wooden ladder propped against the eaves, with a canvas satchel of replacement tiles over his shoulder, but when he saw her he unslung the bag, hooked it over the top of the ladder and started down again. Harriet pulled her coat closer round her, shivering.

'You wanted me?' Jem said, dropping from the third rung to the ground with the easy athleticism of a cat.

'I wanted to ask you something.'

'I'm at your service, Miss Griffin. Any time.' He touched a hand to the brim of his hat and smiled that secretive smile that she found so disconcerting.

'You said you knew something about my father. What is it?'

188

'Come inside a minute and I'll tell you,' said Jem, heading for the cottage door. Harriet hung back.

'I'd rather you told me out here.'

'It's too cold for an out-of-doors conversation,' Jem said. 'And I don't know about you, but I fancy a cup of tea.'

'I won't come inside.'

'Pity. Then you'll never know what it's about, will you?'

He disappeared inside the house, leaving the door open. After thirty seconds of indecision, Harriet followed him. The small front room was empty and she walked through to the kitchen. Jem had tossed his hat on to the table and was filling a kettle at the sink. There was nothing particularly alarming about that, she told herself, fighting down her nervousness. There was an artist's pad of drawing paper on the kitchen table, with a tobacco tin of coloured crayons lying open beside it. Harriet lifted the cover and found a sketch of the cottages seen from the road. The colouring was crude but the building had been skilfully drawn.

'Did Kitty draw this?'

'No. I did,' said Jem. 'It's a hobby of mine.' He lifted the lid of the range and stood the kettle on the hotplate.

'I didn't think you'd have the time to be an artist.'

'It's difficult when the days are short. I don't cheat Will Griffin out of the hours I'm paid for, if that's what you think. But I cut back here for my dinner sometimes and do a bit.'

'They're good,' said Harriet. She turned more pages, and found a sketch of a robin which had captured not only the accurate shape of the bird but also its jaunty personality. On the page beneath it, there was a drawing of her.

'It don't do you justice,' said Jem. 'Only I didn't reckon you'd pose for me, so I did it from memory.' He had come nearer while she was inspecting his work and now his warm breath was so close to her cheek that it made her gasp.

'Scared are you?' he said, amused. His dishevelled hair was very black and his eyes looked directly into hers. She wanted to look away and couldn't.

'I'm not scared of *you*,' she said, with assumed bravado.

'Course you're not. That's what I like about you – you've

189

got guts. *One* of the things I like about you,' he amended. 'Mind you, your manners could do with a bit of improving.'

'My manners are better than yours.'

'Not the way *I* meant. I heard you've been learning how to act the grand lady, up in London,' said Jem. 'Lot of good that'll do you when it comes to catching a man. What you need is a lesson in what *really* pleases – the sort of thing that'd hook your fancy man and keep him groaning for more.'

For Harriet, the comment pressed on a secret bruise – the ease with which Gavin had shrugged off their relationship. She had told herself defensively that he was merely shallow, but the nagging insecurity remained. Had her inexperienced kisses been too clumsy?

'Get to the point,' she said, trying not to let Jem see that his words had hit home. 'What is it you brought me in here to tell me about my father?'

'What's it worth?'

'I don't have any money.'

'You know that's not what I'm talking about,' he said. 'A kiss, now, that might do the trick.'

'Don't touch me!' Harriet snapped.

'Easy, now.' Jem might have been soothing a frightened horse. 'What's a friendly kiss between relations?'

'What do you mean? You've said that before.'

'Give me the kiss and I'll tell you.'

Harriet backed away, but Jem had hold of her wrists now. She struggled vainly against his grip, fighting down panic. It was no use screaming; nobody would hear. He was too strong for her to break free . . . she wasn't even sure if she wanted to break free.

Jem was unprincipled and dangerous, the kind of man that any girl of sense would avoid. And there was Kitty to be taken into account. But the shaming truth was that on some level that had nothing to do with sense, Harriet wanted to learn whatever Jem Wilkins could teach her.

'All right. A kiss, then, for a secret.'

'That's more like it.'

Still holding her with that deceptively light, steely grip, Jem put her wrists behind her back in a movement that brought her body against his. 'Act like you mean it, now, or it won't count,' he said softly. His breath travelled across her cheek. When he kissed her, it was with surprising gentleness.

'There, now . . . that wasn't so bad, was it?' He kissed her again. This time his tongue explored. Jem, she recognized over the pounding of her heart, was better at kissing than Gavin.

'No! Don't!' she said with renewed struggling, because what she had felt a moment ago was too strong and too frightening to acknowledge.

'You don't mean that,' he said, his eyes glinting. 'You were enjoying it, same as I was.'

'Tell me what you meant about my father. And then let me out of here.'

'Bitch,' said Jem. 'Cock teaser.' He released her so suddenly that she staggered. 'All right, then, have it your own way. Be a bloody nun. Save yourself for your fancy gentleman friend – the one who doesn't want you any more.'

'Tell me. We made a bargain. A secret for a kiss. You've had the kiss, so tell me about my father.'

Jem pulled out a kitchen chair and dropped on to it. He leaned back, legs sprawling, and grinned mockingly up at her.

'Ever seen your birth certificate? Ask your mum. Will Griffin married her in 1917, when you were two years old.'

'The war . . .' said Harriet desperately.

'The war killed your real dad. Soldier by the name of Arthur Bright. You were a little bastard, Harriet, till Will took you on.'

Harriet stumbled towards the door. His voice followed her.

'And if you let on that it was me that told you, or tell him anything about what happened just now, I'll make sure the whole district knows about the Griffins and their family secret.'

Harriet turned in the doorway. 'Why are you doing this?' she said shakily. 'I've never done you any harm.'

'Haven't you? Oh, come on,' said Jem. 'You can't be *that* naive. There's a part of me that aches because of you, a sight too often for comfort. And I reckon there's a part of you that'd ache for me, only you won't let it happen. I've seen you twitch when I come near you. And it's not because I disgust you, either. It's because your body wants to know mine, even if your mind tells you otherways. And you won't stop it by running away,' he called as a parting shot, but she was already at the front door and he wasn't sure that she'd heard him.

Jem shrugged dourly and as the kettle boiled, he made himself the promised cup of tea. When he had drunk it he tore up the sketch of Harriet, and dropped the pieces into the stove. Turning to the back of the pad, he made another drawing, swift and explicit, of what he thought she would look like naked. He burned that as well.

'I want to see my birth certificate,' Harriet told Daisy, erupting into the farmhouse kitchen where her mother was laying out plates and cutlery for dinner.

'Why?' said Daisy, startled by the sight of Harriet's clenched fists and cheeks patched scarlet with emotion.

'I just do. Where is it?'

Daisy recognized that this was not a moment for prevarication.

'In the sideboard, along with all the other papers. Harry, what's happened?' But Harriet was already at the drawer, sorting rapidly through the certificates until she found the one she wanted. She unfolded it and scanned the information it contained while Daisy watched, bewildered and anxious.

When Harriet looked up, angry tears brimmed on her lashes. '*Arthur Bright. Soldier.* Why didn't you tell me?'

'It never seemed to be the right moment,' Daisy said, helplessly.

'All these years you've let me think someone else was my father.'

'Will came back from the war . . . we were a family. I meant to tell you one day, but . . . we were happy, there didn't seem any point in spoiling it.'

'But it was all a lie!' cried Harriet, on a long note of grief and rage. So many things seemed comprehensible to her now: small and stupid things like the way Rob's instinctive skill with horses and Jackie's ready understanding of machinery had passed her by; that and Will's calm and sensible approach to life, so different from her own erratic emotions. And perhaps, her wounded heart told her, it also explained something else: the reason why Will and Daisy had let her go so unprotestingly to Louella in London. Was she, the 'little bastard' of Jem's scathing phrase, not wanted at Welcome Farm?

'She's taken it badly,' Daisy told Will, so troubled that her dinner lay untouched on its plate in front of her. 'She's locked herself in her room and she won't answer me when I knock. I don't know what to do.'

Will pushed his plate away, resolutely ignoring the clamour of his growling stomach and the appeal of boiled beef and carrots, and climbed the attic stairs to reason with Harriet through the locked door.

'Harry? What's up, love?' But there was no sound from inside the room.

'Not a word. She'll calm down eventually,' he said, coming downstairs. 'Best leave her alone for a bit, till she's ready to talk it over. How did she find out?' he asked, as an afterthought.

'She wouldn't tell me,' said Daisy. She propped her aching head in her hands. 'Oh dear. My poor little Harriet.'

In the middle of February, Marion had reminded her stepdaughter of her promise and Laura Allingham came to stay at Maple Grange. She brought with her four-year-old Caroline, Caroline's nanny and a fat file of letters to be dealt with on behalf of her husband James.

'Is Tom here?' she asked Marion, while her luggage was

being unloaded from the car. 'James asked me to pass on various messages.'

'No, he's away,' Marion told her. 'He gave up the job with the aerial photography firm – or they gave him up, I'm not sure which way round it was. He's gone off to chase another job, also flying, but he wouldn't tell me anything about it in case they wouldn't have him.'

Laura pulled a face. 'Pity. I was rather counting on him to draw some of Pa's fire.'

'Oh, Laura, promise me you aren't going to quarrel with your father this time.'

'I'll do my best not to,' Laura said, smiling affectionately at the tall woman with the threads of grey in her brown hair, whom Pa had married without ever seeming to appreciate his luck. 'But you of all people must know how aggravating he can be.'

Marion returned the smile knowingly. 'Well, come and say hullo.'

Laura took her small daughter into the drawing room and Rupert rose stiffly from his chair, reaching for the stick that leaned against the arm of it.

'Hullo, Laura. Hullo, Caroline. Goodness gracious, you are growing into a very pretty little girl. Come and give your grandpa a kiss.'

Caroline recoiled, turning her face into the hem of her mother's skirt.

'Don't you recognize your old grandpa, then?'

'Caro, you remember Grandpa Brownlowe,' said Laura. 'Say hullo.'

Caroline peered warily at the loud-voiced stranger. Rupert, clumsy because he wanted too badly to succeed with his granddaughter, rushed things by trying to tickle her under the chin. Caroline burst into tears and the visit began on a sour note.

The admiring of Leonora and her foal Starbright helped to restore the peace and when Caroline had been despatched to the old nursery with her nanny, the adults turned to discussing family news.

'How is Edward getting on at school?' Rupert asked.

'All right now, I think. He was very homesick for the first term. Seven seems so young for them to be sent away.'

'Rubbish. Toughens them up,' Rupert said. 'Never did me any harm. I'm glad you took my advice and sent young Edward to the same prep that we chose for your brother.'

So far, so good. But over supper the talk moved to questions about Laura's husband, the absent James, and as she had gloomily foreseen, Rupert reacted sarcastically to the news that his son-in-law proposed to stand as a Labour Party candidate.

'Silly ass. Still, with his background, I suppose he can't help it. Parents are of the same persuasion, aren't they? Damn fools the lot of them. D'you hear me, Laura?'

'Yes, I hear you, Pa.'

Laura could remember so many similar scenes from her childhood days. Always Rupert used these obligatory family gatherings to hand down his convictions and sneer at those of other people. She had thought that as an adult, a married woman with children of her own, she could control her reactions; but something about her father's insistent voice and the arrogant jutting of his jaw stirred old resentments.

'I'd have hoped a daughter of mine could make him see sense. Good God, any half-wit can see that the Communists'll be the ruin of this country.'

'I am entirely in agreement with James about politics, Pa, so I don't see how I can be expected to convert him to your idea of "sense". And your comment about Communists is a non sequitur, because neither of us *is* a Communist.'

'What's the use of giving women an education,' said Rupert, 'if all the use they can find for it is to spout silly bits of Latin at you? Nonsense anyway. Labour, Communists, they're all the same.'

'I daresay the difference *is* beyond your powers of perception.'

On the far side of the table, Marion made urgent hand signals at Laura but her stepdaughter ignored them.

'Pity you ever married Allingham,' said Rupert. 'If Charles McKay had been alive now he'd have kept you in order. *He* had a sound head on his shoulders.'

'Did he?' said Laura. '*I* heard they shot bits of it off in France in 1916. But then, I never did get the opportunity to check on the accuracy of that report, did I?'

Abruptly, she pushed back her chair and left the room. After a moment, Marion put down her napkin and followed her stepdaughter out into the hall and along the passage to the point where it widened at the foot of the stairs. Laura was running upstairs, but when Marion called her name she came unwillingly to a halt on the half-landing, under the stiffly formal portraits of ancestral Brownlowes and Cathcarts which hung above the second flight.

'He doesn't mean to hurt you,' Marion said, joining her on the landing.

'And yet he always does,' said Laura.

'He was so looking forward to you coming,' Marion said sadly. 'And as soon as you're here, there's tension and bickering. He can't seem to help saying the worst things. What is wrong between you, Laura? He doesn't understand it, and I have never asked you.'

'No, you're far too tactful.'

'But I'm asking now.'

'I suppose . . . oh, so many things. When I was small, Pa seemed so tall and splendid, almost godlike. Then, after Ma died, I could see that he was sad and I felt close to him then. But as I got older, I began to be more and more uncomfortable about the things he said and did. He was generous, in his way, to *me*. I suppose he still saw me as his little girl, to be rewarded for good behaviour with praise and presents – but at the same time, he was being so hard on Oliver. When you're a twin that hurts as much as if it's being done to you. And where the rest of the world was concerned, he seemed to be lacking in charity and kindness. I suppose it was what happened in the war that finished it. Did he ever mention to you,' Laura asked, her voice hardening, 'that he killed my husband?'

Marion drew her breath in sharply. 'No. You'll have to explain.'

'My first husband, Charles McKay, was a serving officer in the Blues – the Household Cavalry. They went out to the Western Front and he was badly wounded by a shell explosion. Facial wounds. Pa opened a telegram addressed to me,' Laura said, 'and decided to keep the contents from me. Instead he went to France in my place, to the field hospital where Charles was being nursed, and . . . after the visit from Pa, Charles died. By the time I was told of his wounds, it was too late.'

'I'm sorry,' Marion said, inadequately.

'There's more. Something he said when he came back led me to believe that Charles . . . may have brought about his own death because of what my father said to him. I heard Pa tell my aunt Jessie that Charles had been encouraged to do the decent thing, to spare me a life shackled to a monstrously deformed man.'

Knowing Rupert as she did, such behaviour sounded chillingly probable to his wife. Marion groped for a response. 'I suppose he was trying to protect you, as he understood it,' she ventured.

'Oh, yes! Pa always thought he knew what was best for everyone else. He decided I wasn't up to caring for Charles, so he put it out of my power to do so.' Laura stared down over the bannister into the hall below, seeming not to be aware of Marion's hand covering her own in an awkward attempt at consolation.

'He had no right,' she said bitterly. 'No right at all.'

13

Somehow Marion, exerting all her skills of diplomacy, smoothed down the quarrel. At breakfast the conversation was civil, if stilted, and to her step-grandmother's relief, Caroline was persuaded to accompany Rupert unprotestingly down to the stables for a further session of foal admiring.

'I'm glad she's settling in,' Marion said, watching the old man and the small girl walking past the drawing-room window. Rupert leaned heavily on his stick but his expression had an unaccustomed softness as Caroline skipped eagerly alongside, yesterday's shyness forgotten because the chestnut foal might take a sugar lump from her open palm as he had done yesterday.

'Oh, Caro's good at adapting quickly to unfamiliar faces. Lord knows, she's had to be, considering the unreliability of nannies. This one's the fourth – and *she* told me just before we left London that she was getting married at the end of the month, which doesn't leave long to find a replacement. Ah well, I'll tackle that problem when I get home,' said Laura with a sigh.

'What would you like to do today, Laura?'

'I thought I might go into Farnham, just to walk round for a bit. I haven't seen the town for a long time.'

'I'll come with you. I have a few things to do.'

'Oh – and I want to look up a woman who used to work here years ago,' Laura said, 'when my aunt Jessie kept house for Pa. She married one of the grooms from the Grange after the war and now they have a farm in Bentley.'

'I'm glad you still keep in touch with your old servants,' said Marion, knowing that Rupert didn't bother with such niceties.

'To be honest, I haven't had any contact with anyone from the Grange for a long time. But Daisy was a dear.' Laura smiled reminiscently. 'She wrote to congratulate me when I married James – I suppose she saw the announcement in the papers – and we've kept in touch vaguely ever since. I've always meant to pay a visit, but never got round to it until now. I sent her a letter from London yesterday, to say I planned to call this afternoon.'

In Farnham, Marion had to buy skeins of embroidery silks. She chose the colours carefully while Laura hovered restlessly, already bored.

'What are all those for?'

'I'm doing new covers in Florentine work for all the dining chairs.'

'However do you find the time?'

'There isn't much else to do here in the evenings,' Marion said.

Laura gave her a sharp look. 'I've often wondered how you stand it. Marion, this is probably frightfully disloyal of me, but why ever did you marry Pa? You're much too nice for him.'

'Needs must when the devil drives,' said Marion frankly. 'At first it was an entirely practical step – a roof over our heads for Tom and me. After the war there were a lot of women in my position: widowed, but unqualified for anything except the duties of a wife. And Tom's father had been a charmer, but a bit of a spendthrift. There wasn't much left when he died and by the time I met your father things were getting desperate.'

'So you sold yourself into slavery for Tom's sake,' said Laura soberly. 'How awful.'

Marion laughed. 'Good gracious, that's far too dramatic! "Slavery" is hardly the way to describe the far-from-onerous task of running Maple Grange. And . . . Rupert and I were never a love match, but there *is* a good side to him, Laura. He's a product of his upbringing. Sometimes he sounds hard and unfeeling because that's the kind of treatment he had as a boy, but inside the shell there's a lonely man. Actually, I've become rather fond of him.'

'Then you're a saint,' Laura said as they emerged from the haberdashery into West Street.

'Listen. Somebody's singing.' Marion's ears had caught a distant sound.

'You're right. A whole bunch of them,' said Laura, head turned in the direction of the voices. 'I wonder what's going on. Let's go and see.'

They walked towards the corner where the broad Georgian thoroughfare of Castle Street sloped down from the ruins of Farnham castle to meet The Borough. Down the centre of the road marched a group of young men in workmen's clothes, led by an older man with an accordian. The wavering strains of the tune changed and the voices gathered strength.

'It's the *Internationale*,' said Laura. ' "Arise you starvelings from your slumber, Arise you prisoners of want". I didn't know you had hunger marches in rural Surrey.'

'We don't, usually. Oh, there's Colonel Strover, he'll know what's happening.' Marion crossed the road behind the marchers to speak briefly to a tall man in a tweed jacket, standing among a group of spectators.

'They aren't local,' she reported back to Laura. 'They're on their way from Portsmouth to London. But we do have our hungry mouths in this area, though not on the same scale as in the industrial towns, of course. Our time of hardship was ten or eleven years ago when the cheap food imports from abroad and the fall in grain prices hit farming profits. There was a lot of very real misery then. Things have settled down since, thank goodness. But I believe our local unemployed still feel the pinch of hunger and the shame of having to beg for hand-outs as badly as a Welsh coalminer or a Tyneside shipbuilder. It may even be worse for them in one way, because they are fewer in number and more isolated in their trouble.'

'Do you think so? James was in Wales before Christmas,' Laura said, 'on a fact-finding visit for the Party. He said it

200

was terribly depressing to be among whole communities left without hope for the future. But what can we do?'

'Not much,' said Marion with regret. 'Little things. For today we Farnham residents can make sure that this particular group of hunger marchers don't have to go on their way without a good dinner. Colonel Strover said a meal has been arranged for them at the Co-op premises.'

They watched the band of marchers striding along The Borough towards the top of Downing Street.

'It's tragic, isn't it?' Marion commented. 'Young men like that, most of them can't be more than twenty-five, and there's no work. It must seem to them that their lives don't—' She broke off, staring at a man who was standing under the arched colonnade which ran along the north side of The Borough.

'Why, it's Billy. Billy Marshall!' and she hurried along the pavement, waving and calling. After a moment's bewilderment, Laura followed her.

Billy seemed embarrassed rather than pleased to be accosted. He was even more ragged and unhealthy-looking now than he had been when Marion had first set eyes on him, several months before, at Colonel Strover's house.

'I am *so* glad to see you,' said Marion. 'I've been trying to trace you ever since that awful night.'

'What awful night?' Laura asked.

'I'll explain later. Billy, how have you been getting on? Have you found any work?'

'Odd jobs here and there.'

'Do you remember me, Billy?' Laura said.

'Miss Laura,' he said, out of old habit.

'I'm Mrs Allingham now. Were you watching the hunger march?'

'Yes,' said Billy drearily. 'Fine for them as have got the energy to march, I suppose. And they'll get fed in the towns along the way.'

'What happened to your arm?' Laura asked.

'War wound, Miss Laura.'

'Oh, bad luck. And you're finding it difficult to get work?'

'Difficult enough.'

'Where are you living now?' Marion asked.

'Here and there.'

'We must be able to help.' Laura turned to Marion. 'What do you think, Marion? Perhaps Pa—?'

'No,' said Marion. She laid a restraining hand on Laura's arm. 'I'll explain later,' she repeated. 'Billy, I have been so worried about you, but now that you're here, I'm sure we can do something. But first things first. Here, take this money,' she fumbled in her purse, 'and go and buy yourself a really good dinner, while Mrs Allingham and I finish our shopping. Meet us back here in half an hour and we'll have thought of something.'

Billy's thin face went scarlet. He looked down at the money that Marion held out to him but made no move to take it.

'It's very good of you,' he said, with difficulty. 'But I don't see how I can take this. I've not earned it.'

'You have. You worked very hard for Mr Brownlowe,' said Marion. 'And what happened wasn't your fault. Please, Billy, don't make me feel worse about it than I do already.'

Dubiously, Billy took the money.

'Promise me you'll come back here in half an hour?' Marion insisted.

'All right.' He walked away stiffly in his threadbare, shapeless coat, useless arm dangling.

'I'm sure he's been sleeping rough,' said Marion worriedly. 'And in this awful, cold weather. Laura, whatever can I do about him?'

'For a start, you can tell me what's been going on.'

'Oh, it's lovely to see you again, Miss Laura!' Daisy exclaimed, then corrected herself, blushing. 'I'm sorry. I meant Mrs Allingham.'

'I rather like *Miss Laura* – it reminds me of the old days,' said Laura, smiling. 'I still don't feel like a "Mrs", even after all these years – it sounds so sober and matronly.

Daisy ushered her visitor into the parlour. The room smelt

damp from disuse and Allie's morning dusting had been a hit-and-miss affair, but at least the specially lit fire was still burning.

'Please make yourself at home. I'll get the tea.' She wheeled in the tea trolley, so carefully prepared earlier in the day, feeling self-conscious and unsure how to behave towards this self-possessed adult that Miss Laura had become. The Griffins had come up in the world since their days as Rupert Brownlowe's under-housemaid and second groom, and Miss Laura had never been one to stand on ceremony, but all the same she couldn't be treated as an equal. As Daisy poured tea and offered bread-and-butter – carefully de-crusted and cut extra thin as befitted a lady – she was torn between questions of etiquette, her pleasure at the fact that her old mistress had come to see her, and worry over Harriet, who was still in her room with the door barred and would have to be placated, somehow, when the visitor had gone.

'Actually, Daisy, I've got a favour to ask you.'

Laura, having skimmed over the events of her married life and recounted the gender, ages and temperaments of her two children, paused with her teacup halfway to her lips and looked expectantly at her hostess.

'What kind of a favour?' said Daisy cautiously.

'Do you remember Billy Marshall? Gardener's boy at the Grange? He volunteered for the Queen's in the Great War.'

'I think so.' Daisy's memory conjured a picture of a shy, skinny lad with a pale face, delivering cut flowers for Miss Laura's vases to the kitchen door at the Grange. He'd gone to Stoughton Barracks on the first day of the war to enlist with the Queen's Own Royal West Surrey Regiment, and had come back crestfallen at being rejected. 'Only they wouldn't have him because he wasn't tall enough to lie about his age?'

'That's right. They did take him eventually, though,' said Laura. 'He was sent out to the Somme in time for the big offensive in 1916. He got shot to pieces almost immediately and ended up in a German hospital for the duration of the war.'

'Oh, the poor lad.' Daisy's too-ready imagination gave her the pale boy swathed in bandages on a hard cot in an alien land, all his patriotic fervour dissolved. It had happened to so many people. Fifteen years later, the nation had stopped being grateful to its heroes but the casualties still bore their mutilations, living out their limited lives. You saw them on street corners sometimes, even here in the prosperous countryside of the Home Counties, with their crutches and their wheelchairs, cynicism etched deeply on prematurely aged features.

'What is Billy doing now?' she asked.

'That's the point,' Laura told her. 'Nothing. He lost a shoulder blade and the use of one arm entirely and lately it's been more and more difficult for someone who's not able-bodied to get work. And he didn't even get a disability pension. Apparently he was told that it was his own fault he got hurt, because he'd lied about his age and shouldn't have been in the army at all. *Contributory negligence*, they called it – any excuse for the government to wriggle out of its debts. And this is supposed to be a country fit for heroes to live in!' said Laura with disgust.

'I don't know who still believes that claim,' Daisy said sadly.

'Anyway, what he needs is work. Any work with tied accommodation – and living on a farm would suit him perfectly.'

'I don't think we could afford to take on anyone else.'

'Oh, he'd work for a song,' Laura said airily. 'Actually, I was so sure that you would want to help that I brought him along with me. He's in the car now, waiting.'

'Well . . . I suppose I could talk to Will about it . . .'

'Oh, bless you, Daisy. Billy will be *so* grateful. I'll fetch him in and you can tell him now.'

'But I haven't said—'

It was too late. Laura had gone.

* * *

'It's a good thing I had Jem patch that roof on Number Two,' Will said resignedly. 'It's a bit rough in there, rotten floorboards upstairs and plaster that needs replacing where the rain got in, but the downstairs rooms are habitable – and from what you say, Billy won't be expecting luxury.'

'I thought you might mind,' Daisy said, relieved that her husband was taking the news of another unplanned addition to the work force so calmly.

'Oh, I remember Billy. Poor devil. We ought to do what we can. How was Miss Laura?' asked Will. 'Still expecting the world to fit in with her plans, the way she used to?'

'No, she's changed a lot – although I suppose she *does* still tend to organize people,' Daisy admitted, thinking of the deft way that Billy had been imposed on the Griffins. 'And I'm sure she thinks it's for their own good, and that she knows what's best for them. She gets that from her father, although I daresay she'd hate to admit it! She said she's very busy with the Peace Movement, and her husband's going to be a Labour Member of Parliament if he gets elected. She married that nice James Allingham, you know, her brother's friend who was in the Flying Corps in the war. Oh, and she had a bit of a moan about the problems of getting reliable staff,' Daisy recalled wryly. 'Her nanny that looks after the little girl has given in her notice, and she's got to find another one as quick as she can . . .' She trailed off, because Will had stopped listening. Harriet was standing in the kitchen doorway.

'Hullo, love,' Will said awkwardly. 'Feeling better?'

'Milking time. Rob's fetching them in,' was all that Harriet said, stony-faced, before she walked away.

In the morning room at Maple Grange, after breakfast on the following day, Laura was rereading a Fabian Society pamphlet entitled 'Labour's Foreign Policy.' She wondered why she was bothering; foreign policy was having to change faster than it could be written, as Germany's Chancellor, Adolf Hitler, systematically challenged all the arrangements for peace that had been set in place after the Armistice.

Laura's husband James said that for the last decade the losers of the war had been made to shoulder too heavy a burden in reparations by the winners, and that it wasn't surprising there had been a backlash. But when it came to making ethical judgements about the conduct of nations and individuals, there was always a conflict between what was fair and what was practical. One might sympathize with German humiliation and frustration, Laura thought despairingly, but one still had to deplore Hitler's behaviour in the League of Nations. There were moments when she envied her father his blinkered certainty that in all matters international, England was in the right and everyone else was in the wrong.

A housemaid came into the room.

'Excuse me, Mrs Allingham, there's a young woman at the back door asking to speak to you.'

'To see *me*? Did she give her name?'

'Harriet Griffin.'

'Oh, *Harriet*.' Laura rose eagerly from the armchair. She hurried to the tradesmen's entrance, where a red-headed girl waited. Laura, who had last encountered Harriet as an engaging baby in a pram, was expecting someone like Daisy, small and shy and friendly. This girl was tall and unsmiling, nervous but determined.

'Excuse me for coming here without writing first, Mrs Allingham, but I heard you had a vacancy for a nanny and I wondered if you'd consider me.' Harriet's need to escape from the truth at Welcome Farm was such that she had thrown caution to the winds. She knew that Laura Allingham was step-sister to her own unwanted airman admirer, and therefore that Tom Searle was uncle to Laura's children, but she wanted a job and the connection did not deter her.

'Oh.' Laura was taken by surprise. 'Well, I do need someone . . .'

'So my mother said.'

'Do you have any experience?'

'I've got little brothers. And common sense,' Harriet said. 'Would you give me a try?'

'Well, it *would* solve a problem. But I'd better talk to your mother about it before I decide,' said Laura, feeling that the conversation was moving too fast for her. 'I wouldn't have thought your parents would want to part with you from the farm.'

'Oh, they won't miss me,' said Harriet bleakly. 'Especially now they've got that new man you brought yesterday,' she added, making it doubly difficult for Laura to refuse her.

'Do you mean that you *never* told her about her real father?' Laura was paying a second visit to Welcome Farm.

'No,' admitted Daisy. 'We meant to, but we never seemed to find a way.' She wanted to tell Miss Laura that this was a farm. There was always something to be done, a daily round of tasks that got in the way of family discussions like the one that would have been needed to break such delicate news to her daughter. And besides, for years now it had been difficult even to remember Harriet's natural father, the late Arthur Bright, who had been killed at First Ypres in October of 1914 less than three months after the single hasty tumbling in a hay barn, on the day that the Reserve were called up, which had resulted in Harriet.

Daisy vaguely recalled that the news of Arthur's death had hurt at the time, but there had been so many seasons and so many harvests in between. And there had been Will, an effective banisher of ghosts. Harriet had been happy as Will's daughter, and if it hadn't been for this sudden, unexplained discovery of her origins, she would have been happy still.

'But she's feeling bruised, of course. And it's come on top of a disappointment about a young man,' Daisy told Laura. 'So if you *could* give her some employment for a while, it might be the best thing.'

'Well, if you really don't mind? Perhaps she'd better come back to the Grange with me straightaway, so that she can get to know Caroline while the current nanny's still with us to make the transition smoother.'

'That would be all right,' said Daisy. Ever since

yesterday's confrontation, Harriet had been carrying out her duties with icy control, rebuffing all peacemaking overtures. The tense atmosphere was hurting Daisy and although Will hadn't said so, she knew it was hurting him too. If Harriet wouldn't talk about the situation, it seemed best for her to take her smouldering resentment somewhere else for now.

'I hope I haven't made a mistake in taking her on,' Laura told Marion on her return to Maple Grange. 'I didn't see how I could refuse the girl, when her parents had found a place for Billy just to oblige me. But I do wonder if she isn't rather young to be trusted with Caroline? She's certainly inclined to be headstrong, and Daisy did hint that there'd been some young man in the picture, on top of all this bother about her father.'

'I only saw her for a minute or two,' Marion said, 'but it seems to me that it would be quite surprising if there *hadn't* been a young man in the picture! She's a very striking-looking girl, isn't she, with that red hair and those eyes?'

'Precisely,' said Laura grimly. 'Which means I'll have to keep a close eye on her – I don't know how I'd face Daisy if her daughter got herself into trouble while in my employment.' She sighed. 'As if I didn't have enough to worry about already! Oh well, what's done is done. At least we're going home tomorrow.'

'Won't you stay a little longer?' Marion said. The visit from Laura had highlighted the normal dearth of feminine company and she was going to find it hard to settle again to the long evenings with Rupert and her petit point. 'Just a day or two? I heard from Tom this morning,' she wheedled. 'He'll be home before the weekend.'

'No. It's a shame to miss Tom, but we must go,' Laura said firmly.

'When shall we see you again?'

'Perhaps in the Easter holidays, when Edward's home from school.'

*   *   *

Harriet's sudden departure took Jem by surprise. He wasn't used to being rejected by women and this particular girl had got him bothered to a degree that he couldn't remember before. He was aware that he had taken a big risk in making a play for her. He'd stood to lose his position at Welcome Farm and his retainer from Louella, not to mention the probable impact on Kitty if she knew what he was up to. And yet he'd stuck his neck out and kissed the girl, and told her more about how she affected him than was sane, let alone sensible . . . and she'd gone just far enough to get him into a lather and then pulled away from him and taken herself off to London. Hurt and frustrated and inwardly raging, he wanted to break something and didn't know what to break that would vent the feeling.

When his work for the day was finished, instead of going home to Starling Cottages he walked down to the Red Lion at Bentley, where he was beginning to be recognized as a regular customer, and demanded a whisky. When he'd drained the glass, he called for another.

Kitty, waiting and worrying beside the front-room window as darkness fell, saw Billy Marshall arrive at the neighbouring cottage. He carried a lantern in his left hand and under the same arm was tucked a brown paper parcel, tied up with string.

Kitty had been introduced by Daisy to the shabby, diffident stranger earlier in the day. Now she thought that as a neighbour he should be given a proper welcome, so she took up the oil lamp from the kitchen and went next door.

The front door stood open. In the little sitting room, Billy had hung up the lantern from a hook in the ceiling and laid his jacket over the back of the only chair. The iron frame of a bed and a mattress leaned against the wall, not yet assembled, and bedding was heaped beside it. Billy's brown paper parcel lay open on the floor beside the fireplace, revealing its contents: a few rolled-up items of clothing, a watch, a harmonica and a couple of large, sepia-tinted photographs mounted on stiff card, dog-eared at the corners.

Billy, unconscious of being watched, picked up and

studied one of the photographs. When Kitty knocked at the open door, he looked up, startled.

'Hullo. I'm Kitty, remember? We met earlier. You know we live next door, don't you – me and Jem? You'll have met Jem?'

'Yes, I've met him,' said Billy.

'Is he still at work, do you know?' Kitty asked. She wondered what it was about Billy's brief reply that hinted that he and Jem had not liked one another.

'He finished the same time as me. I saw him walking off down the road towards Bentley,' Billy told her.

'Oh.' For a moment Kitty's shoulders drooped as she faced the prospect of Jem coming home late and drunk from the Red Lion. She made an effort. 'Have you got everything you need here?'

'Mrs Griffin's boys brought some food and kindling down this afternoon. And bedding and things.'

'If you need any washing done, I could easily put yours in the bowl with Jem's, while I'm at it,' Kitty offered shyly.

'I can manage, thanks,' said Billy. He propped the photograph he had been holding on the mantelpiece and bent to pick up the other.

'Oh. Well, I'm glad you're all right.' But Kitty lingered, putting off the moment when she would have to return to her silent cottage and wait alone for Jem.

'Is that your mum and dad?'

'That's right. More than forty years ago, mind you,' Billy said. It was his first response that had not been strictly informative, and thus encouraged, Kitty ventured into the room.

The photograph he held was a full-length portrait of a man and woman, standing stiff-backed in the dark, old-fashioned clothes that belonged to the reign of Queen Victoria. 'It's the only one I've got of them,' he said. 'There were more, but they must have got lost or thrown away after Mam died, while I was—' He broke off, then finished the sentence. 'While I was away.'

'She was very pretty. And kind-looking,' Kitty said. She

turned to the other photograph, which Billy had already stood on the mantelpiece: a young man in soldier's uniform, smiling out with shy pride at the camera. It was the sort of studio portrait routinely taken for proud parents, and wives and sweethearts, as their men had flooded to join the fighting forces in the Great War.

This one was *very* young to be a soldier, Kitty thought – hardly more than a bright-eyed lad. His hair had been cut brutally short at the sides, but still a rebellious lick of it flopped over his forehead. It dawned on her that the photograph was of Billy Marshall, though at first she hadn't spotted the resemblance; Billy as a boy, before the years – and the war – had stamped lines on his face and drained the pride out of him.

'Mam *would* keep it,' Billy said, beside her.

'I bet she was proud of you,' said Kitty.

'Yes, she was,' Billy said, his voice softening. 'Any rate, she *said* she was. Even when I came home a cripple 'stead of dying a hero. She was a good woman, my mam,' he added, remembering the day of his homecoming and the way his mother's face had seemed to flood with light when she first caught sight of him.

'Kitty.' The voice from the doorway was Jem's. 'Where's my supper?' he demanded belligerently.

'I'm coming,' Kitty said hastily, and hurried towards the door. Jem nodded towards Billy with the minimum of civility and taking her wrist, almost pulled her over the doorstep.

Billy stowed the remainder of his possessions away in the cupboard built in beside the chimney breast, and assembled the bed which Rob and Jackie Griffin had brought over to the cottage earlier. He was used to his disability, but it took some ingenuity to slot the side irons into the two end pieces with only one hand to hold everything steady, and his forehead was damp with sweat by the time the bed was up and made.

He was brewing himself a cup of cocoa in the kitchen when he heard something that sounded like a glass shattering on a brick floor in the house next door. Through the thin wall, Kitty's voice said something he couldn't distinguish. Jem answered sharply and there was another splintering crash which might have been a chair tipping over. When Kitty spoke again Billy thought she sounded frightened, and then her voice cut off suddenly.

Feeling uneasy, he went to the door and stood there listening for a few minutes, but there were no more recognizable sounds from the neighbouring house. Later, as he drifted off to sleep, he thought he heard something that might have been sobbing, but in the morning he couldn't be sure whether it had been real or only a dream.

Kitty was crossing the farmyard with a bowl of vegetable trimmings and potato peel for the pigs when she encountered Billy, precariously trundling a straw-laden wheelbarrow across the yard with his one good hand.

'Morning.'

'Morning. Are you all right?' he asked her.

'Yes, thanks.' But Kitty looked away as she said it.

'. . . Only I heard noises, last night,' said Billy.

'Oh, that would just have been Jem and me larking about.' Kitty's fingers pinched at the skirt of her dress and colour stained her thin cheeks as she tried to work out which of last night's events might have been overheard through the party wall.

'It didn't sound much like larking,' Billy said. 'It sounded like you were in trouble.'

'Well, I wasn't,' said Kitty, with unexpected sharpness. Her chin went up. 'We'll try and keep the noise down. Sorry if it bothered you.'

'And *that'll* teach you to mind your own business, Mister Marshall,' Billy told himself wryly, as she walked away.

'Didn't your sister want to come, then?' Tom Searle greeted Rob in the lane in front of the farm, at seven o'clock on a Saturday morning at the end of February. 'If she's got jobs to finish, we could wait a bit longer.'

'Oh, Harry's gone away again.'

'Gone? Where to?' said Tom.

'Up to London again.'

'To the educating aunt?'

'No, not this time. I think she's quarrelled with Auntie Lou, but she wouldn't tell me about it. And then something happened at home, but she wouldn't tell me about that either. Nobody ever tells me *anything*,' Rob commented with disgust. 'Anyway, she's gone to be a nursemaid to somebody's children.' Rob did not know that the children in question were Tom's own step-niece and step-nephew.

'When did this happen?'

'A few days ago. It was all arranged very quickly.'

Tom made an effort to hide his chagrin at the news. When he had written to Rob with the invitation for today, he had added a casual enquiry about how the red-headed angel was getting on, and Rob had replied equally casually that if he meant Harriet, she was back from London and fed up, perhaps because her Gavin seemed to have lost interest in her. The news had rekindled Tom's own interest; but to no avail because now she was off again. Tom concluded wryly that when it came to red-headed angels, the fates were against him.

'But I don't think she was all that keen on flying anyway,' Rob said, dimly aware of his companion's disappointment. 'Not like me.'

'*Nobody's* as keen as you, young Griffin. Well, we'd better get cracking,' Tom said. 'I've got an Avro 504 booked for the day at Brooklands. By the way, this flight is in the nature of a goodbye present for the time being,' he added.

'Goodbye?' Rob echoed disconsolately.

'Like your beautiful but elusive sister, I've got a new job which will take me away for a while.'

'Is it to do with flying?'

'Of course it's to do with flying,' Tom said. 'And when I tell you what kind of flying, you'll be green with envy.'

Part 3

April–December 1934

14

When Laura and James Allingham returned to Maple Grange after the second week in April, they were accompanied by eight-year-old Edward, on holiday from his boarding school, as well as by Caroline and the new nanny.

'Your Harriet seems to be a success with the children, anyway,' Marion commented, watching through the drawing-room window as a helplessly giggling Caroline snatched vainly at the ball which Harriet and Edward were tossing to-and-fro just above her hands.

'Oh, yes, Caro adores her.'

In the two months that Harriet had been part of the Kew household, Laura's fears that she might be a magnet for unsuitable young men had proved groundless. Harriet's devotion to the care of her small charge had been beyond reproach.

'But frankly, there are times when I wish they didn't hit it off quite so well!' Laura said. 'They play such boisterous games and Harriet doesn't check Caro at all. In fact, she encourages her to run about and make a lot of noise, and when I commented on it the other day, she just laughed and said, "She's only letting off steam, like any normal child." Well, that might be normal for children from *her* background, but I'd rather Caroline behaved with a little more decorum. And now Edward's home for the holidays, the three of them are quite exhausting.' Laura chewed her lower lip. 'I'm sure I'm a very liberal-minded employer, but I must maintain *some* standards. But if I sent her home now, Caro would be devastated. What *is* one to do?'

Privately, Marion agreed with the new nanny that children must be allowed to let off steam. It was an approach that she had adopted with her son Tom, to the distress of his stepfather. Laura, of course, was Rupert's daughter, a product of the *'Children should be seen and not heard'* school, and it must be difficult for her as a mother to reconcile her innate humanity with her strict upbringing.

'Will Harriet be wanting to visit her family while she's here?' Marion asked, thinking that such a visit would be an excuse to check on the welfare of Billy Marshall.

'I wondered that too, but she says she doesn't need to see them.'

'How odd.'

'It's up to her,' said Laura, with a shrug. 'And it's certainly easier for me if she doesn't ask for any time off at present. James has some visits to make on Party business while he's here, and I should very much like to go with him.'

'That reminds me . . .' Marion said. 'There's something I hope to interest you both in while you're here. The Surrey Fund, with which I'm involved, has launched a scheme to help the people of a northern town where the shipbuilding industry has closed down. What do you know about Jarrow?'

'Harriet, please, *please* can we go to the air show?' Young Edward Allingham stood in front of Harriet with an air of agonized expectation.

'What air show is that?'

'The one at Guildford. It's in the local paper,' said Edward eagerly, brandishing a crumpled copy of the *Surrey Advertiser*.

Harriet scanned the advertisement he showed her. '*Sir Alan Cobham's National Aviation Day Tour.*' The name rang a bell. Hadn't Rob mentioned the Cobham displays? She seemed to remember a breakfast-table conversation in which he'd told his family about the countrywide tours, launched two years ago in an attempt by Cobham to revive the public's interest in flying. 'A whole fleet of aeroplanes, doing all sorts of stunts! They've been to Guildford two years running and I've never even *noticed*!' he'd lamented.

'So can we go?' Edward awaited her verdict, jiggling with

excitement. 'There's going to be a full aerobatic display and flying races and a lady glider pilot and a wing walker and a free fall parachuter . . .'

'Well, I don't know . . . what would your parents say?'

'I didn't see the notice in time to ask. They've all gone to lunch in Godalming with some friends of Granny and Grandpa, and it starts at one o'clock, and they won't be back till tea time, and then it'll be too late. Oh *please*, Harry, say we can go,' Edward pleaded, his eyes eloquent with longing.

'But how are we to get there? Your parents have taken their car.'

'Stevenson drives Grandpa's motor sometimes, and he'll go if you will. I've already asked him.'

'Oh . . . all right, then. I don't see why not.'

Edward threw the newspaper up into the air and executed a Red Indian war dance with whoops of delight. He might have been Rob at the same age, Harriet thought. These boys and their passion for flying . . .

Stevenson, Rupert Brownlowe's gardener, confirmed that he was prepared to ferry the Maple Grange contingent to Newlands Corner, but only when he'd finished rooting out some seedlings from the greenhouse. Waiting was torture for Edward.

'We'll miss the fly-in. I know we will!'

'That's all very well, young sir.' Stevenson dug his trowel into another patch of earth and his fingers eased a seedling from the wooden tray. 'But if I don't get these here seedlings out into this here herbaceous border, your grandpa'll be missing his flower display come summer, and I'll be missing my job.'

At last they set out for Newlands Corner, on the far side of Guildford. Edward's fear was confirmed: by the time they arrived, the aeroplanes of the Cobham Circus had already flown in, dropping out of the mist to land in an impressively small area. Many spectators were already inside the display enclosure, but a sizeable queue still straggled alongside a tall yellow canvas screen, painted with advertisements in bold black lettering, which had been erected between the masses of parked cars and the arena.

'They don't plan to let us see anything we ain't paid for,' grumbled the man ahead of them in the queue.

'How much is the entrance fee?' It occurred to Harriet that she hadn't much money with her.

'One-and-six to get in, extra for the flights.'

'I ain't paying one-and-six,' said Stevenson dourly, and went off to have a nap in the car. Harriet checked her purse. There was enough to get Edward and Caroline into the enclosure and perhaps buy them something to eat. She hoped.

The queue shuffled forward. From the other side of the screen could be heard a happy din of revving aero engines and expectant voices, mingled with the raucous strains of dance music, broadcast from the great trumpet-shaped loud-speakers mounted on top of vans parked around the field.

'My dad was in the Royal Flying Corps in the Great War,' Edward told Harriet, as they neared the gap in the screen which marked the entrance. 'He was an Ace. He shot down ever so many enemy aeroplanes.'

'Was he? I didn't know that,' Harriet said. She tried to reconcile this information with her impression of Edward's father. Since she had joined the staff at Kew she had seen little of James Allingham, who seemed much occupied by his working life as a London solicitor and his political ambitions as a prospective Labour Party candidate. She had wondered in passing if the quiet man with the harassed air was entirely happy in his marriage to the extrovert Laura, and had told herself that it was none of her business.

'Oh, yes,' said Edward, with pride. 'He's got loads of medals. He even got a Legion of Honour from the French, though he doesn't brag about it. But the chaps at school think he's ever such a hero.'

'I'll have to tell my brother Rob,' said Harriet, and then remembered with a pang that it was two months since she had spoken to Rob. Suddenly she was homesick, for the hazel catkins and the daffodils that had sprouted without her this year in the lane beside the farmhouse. And her mother's bees would have worked the apple and plum blossom in the orchard, and now they would be feeding on the dandelions in the meadows . . . She pushed the thought away. 'Rob is mad about flying,' she told Edward. 'He's been for a few flights and wants to have flying lessons when he's older.'

'Oh, so do I!'

At the gap in the screen, Harriet argued briefly and successfully that Caroline was too young to be charged the full entrance fee. Then they were through and had their first sight of the aeroplanes, drawn up in a line at the edge of the field.

'I want an ice cream.' Caroline, having spotted the row of catering vans and the refreshment tent, set up an insistent plea.

'Oh, Caro, it's too cold for ice cream,' Harriet protested vainly.

Edward insisted that he only wanted to look at the planes.

'But if we split up, you'll get lost,' said Harriet. 'Well, all right . . . but you must meet me again in ten minutes, by the booking tent. And don't you dare be late.'

Ten minutes later the flying displays had begun and there was, predictably, no sign of Edward. Grimly, Harriet hauled Caroline around the field in search of him. Her head ached with the noise. She wondered what Laura and James Allingham would have to say about the loss of their son and heir. Finally she found the source of the Tannoy broadcasts, where the music from a portable gramophone had now given way to a man announcing the thrills to come.

'Book here for your experience flights. See Guildford as you've never seen it before, from a Handley Page Clive, twenty-two seats, unobstructed views, cruising at a hundred miles per hour. Or try the Airspeed Ferry, designed and built especially for our display. Ten seats and a quiet flight! Be a part of the great air race in one of our three Cadets . . . or try a hop in an Avro 504 for a mere five shillings . . . and for the truly intrepid, we offer the full aerobatic flight with Captain Phillips, in which you can taste at first hand the thrill of looping the loop in a Tiger Moth. One pound for an unforgettable experience . . . only a pound.'

Harriet stopped dead, so suddenly that Caroline bumped into her, leaving a smear of ice cream on the skirt of her coat. 'Why it's Tom Searle,' she said. 'Your uncle Tom! That's him, on the Tannoy.'

'Will Edward Allingham report *immediately* to the Public Address system!' The announcement, booming across the ground, brought a guilty Edward running to the Tannoy, where Tom remembered to switch off the loudspeaker before reading his nephew a brief, telling lecture about the folly of testing his luck with kind-hearted adults. He succeeded in shaking Edward thoroughly while at the same time, he hoped, managing to conceal from Harriet Griffin how delighted he was to see her. He had learnt of her new rôle from his mother Marion, but this was the first time he had seen her carrying it out.

'My official job is to handle the announcements,' he said, having temporarily delegated his duties on the loudspeaker to someone else, in order to take Harriet and the children to the refreshment tent. 'But I'm probably going to get in some flying as well. That's the idea, anyway.'

'Are you going to loop the loop in a Tiger Moth?' Edward asked, with awe.

'No, that's Captain Phillips' speciality,' Tom admitted. 'The fancy display stuff goes to the ex-Flying Corps types. I'm only a general dogsbody, but if there are enough takers for the air experience flights, I'll be obliging some of them later in one of the Avro 504s. Do you fancy going up?' he asked Harriet. 'I still owe you the flight I promised from that day on your farm.'

'*I* want a flight,' Edward interrupted. 'Please let me have a flight, Harriet. I want to loop the loop,' he added.

'Oh, I think something a little less dramatic . . .' Harriet said doubtfully. 'Anyway,' she remembered with relief, 'I haven't got a pound left.'

'Let me take you up in a 504,' said Tom to his

222

disappointed nephew. 'Save the aerobatics for another time, when you're a bit more used to the feeling. Most people'd be sick if they tried that their first time. Though your brother wasn't,' he added in an aside to Harriet. 'Have you seen Rob, by the way?'

'No. Is he here?'

'Oh, yes. I got him a job for the day. He's over there on the far side of the field, helping to organize the short-hop flights. We have to get 'em in and out of the plane as quickly as possible, to keep the costs down,' Tom explained. 'Twelve flights an hour is the aim for the five shilling hops. So Rob's shoving another passenger in up the ladder as fast as his partner's hauling the last one out. But don't you worry,' he added to Edward. 'If you wait till the end of the afternoon, I'll see you get a bit longer when it's your turn. Tell you what, we'll go and buzz Grandpa Brownlowe's house.'

Harriet had almost given up hope of being able to talk to Rob. Whenever she approached him he was too preoccupied with the task of getting the air-experience passengers into their plane even to notice her presence. But finally the queue for the five-minute flights dwindled to a handful and Tom was able to negotiate with the pilot to take the Avro for a slightly longer spin with his nephew in the passenger seat.

'And you can go off and get yourself some tea,' he told Rob. 'I don't suppose anyone's remembered to give you a break all afternoon, have they?'

'No,' Rob admitted. 'I don't mind, though.'

'Well, your sister's here and I expect she'd like some tea as well,' said Tom.

'Harry's here? Really?' Rob looked round eagerly and saw Harriet standing at a little distance. If Harriet had been unsure how to greet her brother after a couple of months and the discovery that he was in fact her half-brother, Rob had no such reservations. He ran over to her and gave her an uninhibited hug.

'How are things at home?' she asked him, walking towards the refreshment tent.

'All right. We've got a new vacuum milking machine,' Rob told her. 'At least, it's an old one, Dad picked it up from a farm sale, but it works – most of the time. You have to stick these suction cups on the udders, which is quite a performance, and sometimes the cow kicks over the container and the cups fall off in the dirt. And then you have to clean them off with disinfectant, which is an even bigger performance, only Dad says we'll get better with practice. There's another new farmhand, a man called Billy. He's only got one arm – I mean, the other arm's there but it's not properly connected, if you see what I mean. You'd have thought he wouldn't be much use like that, but he can do an awful lot with one arm.'

'I know about Billy – he came the day before I left. What about Jem Wilkins?' said Harriet. 'In a minute, Caro,' she added, because Caroline, bored, was tugging at her skirt and claiming to be thirsty.

'Oh, Jem's still around. Dad thinks he's very good – he's been teaching him to drive the tractor. What else? Allie's the same as always – late for work unless the wind's behind her. That Kitty's getting quite good at making cakes, but she still looks like a wet weekend. Jackie came top of his class at sums in a test, so he's being a right show-off, but his wireless is still working a treat. Dad says the Farming News is really useful. Mum has it on sometimes in the daytime to listen to the dance music while she's working, though she tries to pretend she doesn't because of using up the battery. Oh, and Aunt Louella's written to say that she's coming to see us tomorrow. Will you be able to come home to meet her?'

'No,' said Harriet flatly.

'Mum seemed to think her visit has something to do with you.'

'I can't think why it should have,' said Harriet, with bitterness, trying to ignore the increasingly insistent demands of Caroline for orange juice. 'When I was staying with her before, she seemed quite keen to get rid of me.'

'Hey, kid!' A man called to Rob from further down the field. 'Come and help me haul this kite round ready for take-off.'

'I must go,' Rob told Harriet, forgetting about tea breaks.

'Rob . . . In a *minute*, Caro! Rob, do Mum and Dad ever talk about me?'

'What do you mean, talk about you?' Rob called back as he hurried towards the waiting aeroplane and an impatient pilot. Harriet spread her raised hands in a cancelling gesture.

'Nothing. It doesn't matter,' she said.

It was late afternoon before Harriet brought her charges back to the car, where Stevenson had spent the time asleep. Caroline was fractious as a result of missing her afternoon nap, but Edward was still silenced by the remembered glory of the day's experiences, crowned by a flight with his uncle Tom.

'Where's your school cap?' Harriet asked him as they climbed out of the car in the stable yard behind the house.

Edward looked dismayed. 'I had it before I went in the aeroplane. It must have blown away when we were up.'

'Oh dear,' said Harriet. 'Your mother isn't going to be very pleased about *that*.'

'How dare you?' panted Laura. Her eyes blazed in a pale face. Even her lips were white. 'How dare you take such a risk with my son's life?'

'Steady on, Laura. There's no harm done,' said James, laying a restraining hand on her arm. She shook him off.

'No *harm*? He might have been killed!' cried Laura, her voice climbing. 'He might have been smashed to . . . oh, God.' She rounded on Harriet, who was clasping a confused and apprehensive Caroline in her arms. 'Give my daughter to me this instant!'

'Laura, for heaven's sake!' James raised his voice but his wife seemed not to hear him.

She hauled at the little girl's resisting body as Caroline

225

clung, terrified, to the one adult who wasn't shouting. 'You're not fit to be in charge of my children,' Laura was screaming. 'You're dismissed. Get out of my sight.'

'Laura!' James's hands shoved Harriet and Caroline firmly to one side. He took hold of Laura's wrists and shook her. 'Laura,' he repeated, his voice battling against her hysteria. 'Stop it. *Stop it*. You're frightening Caroline.'

Laura's breath was coming in quick gasps. She stared, wild-eyed, at her husband. James glanced over her head at Harriet and said something which Harriet, trying to soothe the wailing child, was too shaken to hear; but she guessed it was an instruction to make herself scarce, and she did, taking Caroline out of the room with her.

'My wife was a bit overwrought,' James told Harriet, later. He looked tired. 'Of course she didn't mean what she said about terminating your employment. It was just the shock of hearing that Edward had been flying.'

'It was only an air experience flight,' Harriet excused herself. 'I didn't think there was any harm in it. He was so keen, and it *was* with his uncle. Tom said he'd take care of him, and they couldn't have been up for more than fifteen minutes.'

'You must forgive Laura,' said James, 'for what may have seemed like an extreme reaction. During the war she saw someone killed in a flying accident – someone to whom she was very attached. This afternoon, when the Avro came so low over the house, that stirred up bad memories . . . and then when we found that Edward had been in the plane, it did frighten her very badly.'

At Caroline's bedtime Laura reappeared, pale but composed, to bestow the usual goodnight kiss on her daughter's cheek.

'Good night, Caro. Sleep tight.'

'Good night, Mummy.' But Caroline was still upset by the scene she had witnessed earlier and she hung back from the embrace, lower lip quivering.

'What's the matter, darling?' Laura asked.

'I don't want Harry to go away,' whispered Caroline.

'No. No, it's all right. Harriet won't be going. It was a misunderstanding. We're friends again now.'

A little reassured, Caroline climbed into the high brass bed and allowed herself to be tucked in. Outside the bedroom door, Laura turned to Harriet.

'My husband has explained the situation to me and on this occasion I'm prepared to overlook what happened. But in future I want you to consult me before you allow my children to take part in any unusual activities. And if that means they miss out on something, it can't be helped.'

If this was meant to be an apology for a too-hasty dismissal, it was distinctly lukewarm, thought Harriet. 'I'm sorry you were upset, Mrs Allingham,' she said stiffly. 'But I thought it would be all right, what with the pilot being Edward's uncle . . .'

'Oh, I accept that you didn't know any better,' said Laura. 'But as for Tom . . . well, *he* knows perfectly well how I feel about Edward flying, and he chose to ignore it.' Her mouth tightened. 'And for that,' she said grimly, 'I won't forgive him.'

When Harriet had stumbled on her private moment with Stuart Armitage, Louella had found the incident embarrassing and distasteful. Instinct had told her that the easiest way out of the mess was to send Harriet home; but she had always intended, when her own emotions were more stable, to fetch the girl back to Medlar House.

The affair with Stuart proved more unsettling than she had anticipated. For a period, Louella openly admitted to herself, she had behaved like a besotted schoolgirl. But in time, the early excitement and the sense of danger had given way to a routine of clandestine but well-organized trysts in a rented house in Kensington.

It was Louella who had found the house, paid the rent and hired the discreet maidservant who kept the place clean. She even paid for the flowers that the girl arranged in cheap glass vases around the rooms, to counteract the depressingly insipid standard of the decorations. Stuart, though he was still gratifyingly amorous, had given up sending bouquets. Nowadays he seemed to take it for granted that she would bear the costs of their liaison – an assumption that Louella was beginning to resent.

The waning of passion freed Louella's attention for another matter. Over the years of her marriage, she had built up a wife's pin-money hobby into a small but thriving fashion empire. Hector had hardly been aware of its importance, but the employees who carried out her instructions and the department-store buyers who placed their orders, season after season, were well aware of what the company's balance sheets confirmed: Louella was a success.

But she couldn't last for ever. If the name 'Louella Ramsay' was to go on adorning the woven labels that the seamstresses stitched into those stylish blouses and well-finished suits that came out of her workshops, she should pay some attention to the matter of who was to inherit her labours and their fruits . . . and so far, despite all her hopes and Stuart's athletic attentions, there was no sign of a pregnancy.

An heir in the hand, Louella reminded herself, was worth several babies in the bush. Harriet had shown promise as the future caretaker of the Ramsay reputation, if only she could acquire the necessary polish and outgrow a tiresome tendency to get herself involved with unsuitable young men such as Gavin Draycott. And, hard-headed considerations aside, there were memories of the wartime days when baby Harriet had been in her aunt's care while her mother worked at the Arsenal. Old attachments, long buried, were apt to surface without warning, leaving Louella vulnerable to a nostalgic longing for her niece's company. So in mid-April, when she came down to Welcome Farm, it was with every intention of carrying Harriet back to London.

'But Harry's not here,' said Daisy. 'She's gone off to Kew, to work as nursemaid. You remember Miss Laura – Laura Brownlowe that was, of Maple Grange? Well, she happened to come here one day on a visit, and she was in need of a nanny for her little girl, and Harriet thought she would go.'

'But why? Why be a nanny? She's worth far more than that,' protested Louella, exasperated by the frustration of her plans.

'It's what she wanted.'

'There must have been a reason. What happened, Daisy?'

'Well . . .' Daisy said, reluctantly. 'As a matter of fact, there *was* a bit of trouble here. She found out, Lord knows how, that Will isn't her real father. And it upset her, and what with Miss Laura's visit coming just at that moment . . .'

'Oh, *Daisy*. I always said you should have told her,' Louella scolded.

'So I would have, sooner or later. But it's not something you can blurt out just like that, is it?'

'How exactly *did* she find out?'

'I don't know.' Daisy sighed. 'I'd have said that of the people she's had any contact with, there was only Will and me – and you, of course – that knew about Arthur. And you'd always promised me you wouldn't say anything.' Belatedly, Daisy remembered her daughter's unexpected return from London in January, and her tone sharpened. 'Louella, I suppose you didn't . . . ?'

'No!' Louella flatly denied the implication. 'I wouldn't dream of breaking such a confidence, however much I thought privately that she ought to know. I left it entirely up to you.'

'Then heaven knows how she got wind of it. But she did, and off she went, and that's that for the time being. Will misses her terribly. He couldn't be more upset if she really was his daughter. I reckon he stopped remembering she wasn't, long ago,' Daisy said sorrowfully. 'She's family, his and mine, that's all. The best we can hope for is that she'll come home again once she's got over it.'

Louella went in search of Jem Wilkins and found him grinding cattle cake in one of the sheds. Fingers tapping on her folded arms, she waited until he turned off the clanking machine.

'I gather that someone's told my niece a family secret that she wasn't supposed to know.'

'Oh yes? Whatever might that be?' Jem enquired innocently. 'And I'm very well, Lou, thanks for asking, and how are you?' he added, with deliberate sarcasm.

'Never mind that. As I recall, you've got quite a talent for poking family skeletons out of cupboards, haven't you, Jem?'

Jem pushed back the brim of his hat with a work-scarred forefinger and considered the question.

'Now when it comes to skeletons,' he observed thoughtfully, 'some families do seem to have more than their fair share. Interesting, that. Not that anyone ever lets *me* in on any of them. I suppose you wouldn't care to give me the details of this particular bag of bones, seeing as you've roused my curiosity?'

He favoured her with an impudent smile which left her with two distinct impressions: one, that he knew very well what had sent Harriet away from Welcome Farm; and two, that he'd very probably had a hand in it, but wasn't about to admit it. Defeated, she turned to go back to the house.

'By the way, Lou,' he said. 'Seeing as you've shown up . . . It's been six months, near enough, since I came here. You said it was to pursue that little matter of that man Brownlowe at Seale . . . but time's gone by and the instructions you've given me have been precious few.'

'I told you to use your initiative.'

'True, but then you tied my hands. *Don't do this, don't do that, no* fires, *no* explosions. Pinpricks, that's all I've been allowed.'

'I suppose I can't expect you to understand the concept of finesse,' Louella commented scathingly. 'It's a slow process I wanted, and a slow process I paid for.'

'Only thing is, Lou, I don't fancy dragging out the rest of my life on this farm or any other farm, waiting on your idea of . . . *finesse*, was it? You see, Mam's dead. The pressure to earn money's got less now there's one less to feed. I wouldn't have put her in a pauper's grave, but it's done now. And you never answered that letter I wrote when I found out about her,' said Jem.

Louella shrugged. 'What was there to say?'

'You might have said you were sorry to hear it. You might even have wondered,' Jem suggested gently, 'if she'd still have died if I'd been there to keep an eye on her, 'stead of sweating it out on *your* business, down here in Hampshire.'

'What's the use of speculating,' Louella said. Her patience snapped. 'Frankly, Jem, it suits me to know where you are and what you're up to. You've been paid to await my instructions, and you'll do as you're told.'

Jem's expression was an unreadable as his voice. 'Will I? Maybe. But if I was you, Lou, I wouldn't count on it.'

15

Hector Ramsay's musical tastes had extended to opera and he'd been a regular subscriber to a ten-guinea box at the Royal Opera House at Covent Garden. At first Louella had found his enthusiasm hard to understand, but she had tolerated the long hours in the box in the Grand Tier for his sake. When the details of the 1934 programme arrived at Medlar House, she realized to her own surprise that she had grown used to the music. Almost, it seemed, April would not be April unless it closed with an attendance at the first night of the Grand Season.

Fidelio was the work with which the Opera House would open its short season on the last day of April. Beethoven's only completed opera would star the German tenor Franz Voelker as the political prisoner Florestan, and the mezzosoprano Lotte Lehmann as his devoted wife, Leonora. Sir Thomas Beecham would conduct.

How Hector would have loved such an occasion . . . Louella fingered the programme, remembering how distinguished he'd always looked in a dinner jacket. The tide of misery that washed over her at the recollection was so powerful that it frightened her.

What to do? Her mind scrabbled for distractions. Stuart Armitage had been out of town for a fortnight, on what he described as a 'tedious formality' – a duty visit to his estranged wife and her family in Dorset. He'd been vague about the date of his return, saying that it depended on his wife's state of health – and she, no doubt, would play the invalid to the hilt. The unknown Mrs Armitage was no wife at all – these days it was the Widow Ramsay who satisfied Stuart's physical needs, and a good proportion of his material needs too, Louella reminded herself, bitterly. Yet a peevish cripple in Dorset had rights which, whenever she chose to exert them, could topple Louella Ramsay into the abyss of boredom and loneliness that was London without Stuart.

Well, let him get what amusement he could in the country! And while he was playing the dutiful husband, his redundant mistress would come out of mourning. She would go to the opera.

As usual, having something to plan brought relief. Louella had reserved a box and decided on her dress and her jewels before she recognized the problem of the choice of companions. It was as unthinkable to appear alone in a box at Covent Garden as it was difficult to find an escort to fit the occasion. Eventually she sent a carefully worded note to Hector's old solicitor, Graham Madigan, inviting him to join her if *Fidelio* appealed. At least Graham was old enough and sensible enough to see such an approach as a chance to hear good opera at someone else's expense, nothing more.

Graham accepted immediately and with a box for four to fill, Louella gritted her teeth and sent another invitation to Helen and Stanley Moffat.

Helen's acceptance contained a barb or two.

How lovely to hear from you and to know that we aren't forgotten. Of course Stanley and I would be delighted to hear Fidelio *again. It has always been a favourite of ours – such a lovely story of a brave woman keeping faith with her husband and her moral standards against all the odds.*

I hear that Stuart Armitage is still keeping you company. What a pity he's had to go to Dorset.

'Oh, you *bitch*,' said Louella, and crumpled Helen's note into a ball in her hand before hurling it into the fire.

Schon sinkt die Nacht hernieder
Aus der so bald kein Morgen bricht!

Louella had read the libretto and thought the closing lines of the first act had something to do with descending nights and unco-operative mornings. For a while the music had absorbed her but now that the curtain had descended and the soaring voices blending with the strains of the orchestra had been replaced by the relentless chatter of the interval, she was aware again of how small and hard the wooden-backed chairs were. Everyone else seemed to be in couples and the impression emphasized her loneliness.

'It's uneven, of course,' Stanley Moffat was saying. 'Beethoven didn't really understand theatre. It was a flop at its first performance, and heaven knows how much revising it took to get it to its current acceptable level. But can anyone resist that overture?'

'Don't lecture, Stanley,' said Helen. 'I'm dying for coffee. Come on, or there'll be too much of a crush to get served.'

Graham Madigan declined the prospect of the crush, as did Louella. It was a relief to see the Moffats go; except that it imposed a duty to make conversation with Graham, and Louella couldn't think of anything to say.

Nor, apparently, could Graham. He stared at the empty stage and the curtain for several silent minutes before he said, suddenly, 'I was surprised to get your invitation, Mrs Ramsay. I had rather understood from my junior partner that you regarded me as an old fool who couldn't add up his sums any more.'

'Excuse me?' said Louella blankly. 'I don't understand.'

'Hector trusted me to handle his affairs for upwards of twenty years. You don't. To be frank, Mrs Ramsay, that hurt.'

'But Stuart suggested . . . that is, he said *you* had suggested . . . that he might take over my portfolio,' Louella explained. 'He said you both felt it was time you took things more easily.'

'*Did* he? Stuart,' said Graham Madigan grimly, 'is a young man of ambition unfettered by moral scruples. As I have learned to my cost.'

The first warning bell rang to mark the end of the interval and Stanley and Helen returned to the box. 'It's so crowded out there,' said Helen, fanning herself energetically. She turned to Louella. 'But who do you think we spotted just now in the stalls? Stuart Armitage and his wife. Isn't it *lovely* to see her walking again? And looking so *pretty*.'

'It meant nothing,' Stuart protested the next day, in the Kensington house to which a terse note from Louella had summoned him. 'For heaven's sake, Louella, I *am* still married to Anne. She'd got out of her wheelchair. She said she was bored with country life and she wanted a taste of town. What else could I do?'

'You could have warned me.' Louella, looking at his flushed, guilty face, thought he was like a little boy who had been caught stealing apples. She clenched her fists at her sides because the idea didn't reduce his physical appeal and after almost three weeks of separation her body was hungry for him. But her mind was engaged in hating him. 'How do you think I felt, knowing you were together at such an event?' she demanded. 'And with that gossipmonger Helen Moffat watching every twitch I made?'

'There wasn't time to contact you. It was a sudden decision and her parents produced the tickets. In any case, how was I supposed to know you'd be there? Oh, *Christ*, Louella!' Without warning, Stuart exploded into anger. 'Can't you begin to understand what it's like for me? I'm treading a tightrope between the woman I stupidly married and the woman I really want, and it's driving me crazy.'

His arms closed round her, and when he kissed her, it was with the same desperation that his voice had just conveyed. Louella closed her eyes and gave way to his urgency. After all, it was what she had wanted.

So why, she asked herself after he had gone, was she left with this hollow, degraded feeling?

As part of its 1934 tour, Cobham's Circus had come to Guildford on the fifteenth of April. The Allingham family returned to Kew on the sixteenth. If Laura remembered her explosion over her son's air experience flight, she made no further reference to it. Edward went back to his prep school in Sussex at the end of the Easter holidays, his head still filled with the glory of having flown, though he recognized that it was not a subject to be mentioned in the presence of his mother.

The Kew household settled back into its routines. On daily walks in Kew Gardens with Caroline, Harriet began to recognize and greet a cheerful, big-boned girl who, like Harriet, was in charge of a small child. While Caroline struck up a cautious acquaintance with four-year-old Jennifer, the two nannies built their own friendship.

'I'm glad we met, I don't mind telling you,' said Vera, strolling with Harriet beside the Palm House pond. 'When I first started here after Christmas, the weather was so cold and nasty and I was that lonely, I thought I'd die. I come from a big family at home, you see. It has its drawbacks but I'll say one thing for it: there's always someone there if you fancy a chat. The people I work for now are all right, but they don't talk to you. You're there for the job and that's it. And little Jenny . . . well, she may look as if butter wouldn't melt in her mouth, but she can be a real spoilt brat sometimes,' she added feelingly. 'If my mum had her back at our house, she'd soon show her what's what . . . How about your family? Where do you come from? Not London anyway, from the way you talk.'

Harriet was silent. Mostly she tried not to think about her lost life at Welcome Farm, because if she did it was apt to trigger a hollow sensation under her ribs and a wave of misery that made her want to howl. Half of her desperately wanted to go home and pretend that Jem Wilkins' revelation had never happened, but the other half recoiled at the idea. It wasn't 'home' any more, it was all tainted. The two people she had trusted utterly hadn't been honest with her. If Will as her father had been a lie, what else in her seemingly secure life was built on quicksand?

Sometimes she had nightmares in which she went back to the farm and instead of the familiar buildings there was nothing but empty fields and rampant weeds, and Jem's smile and his mocking voice: *You were a little bastard,*

Harriet, till Will took you on. Then his face would fade and change into Gavin Draycott's face, saying, *You and I come from different worlds.* Gavin had rejected Harriet Griffin, daughter of a successful farmer. What would he have said to Harriet Nobody, illegitimate offspring of a dead soldier?

'I don't have any family,' she said eventually.

Vera was impressed. 'Blimey, are you an orphan?'

'Yes.' It was simpler than explaining.

'What do you do with your days off, then?'

'I don't bother with them.'

'Well, you should. You mustn't let your employers get used to that, or they'll take you for granted. Tell you what, why don't you take them on the same day as me, then you could come home with me next time? It's a madhouse, but you'd be very welcome. As my mum always says, *the more the merrier.*'

The weekly visits to Vera Birkett's exuberantly rowdy family gave Harriet something to look forward to. She had coped grimly with the loneliness and told herself that it didn't matter, but Vera's companionship made a surprising degree of difference to her life in Kew.

At the end of April she had her nineteenth birthday and two parcels arrived by carrier at the Allingham house: a brown-paper package from Daisy and a box from Louella, which had been sent to Welcome Farm and forwarded.

Inside Daisy's parcel was one of the rich, moist and crumbly fruitcakes that the cook at Maple Grange had taught her how to bake to perfection in her housemaid days, together with a note wishing Harriet a happy birthday from all her family. The awkward phrasing of the note was doubly pathetic because of what it didn't say and because a few months ago, Daisy would undoubtedly have signed it: *With all our love, from Mum and Dad.*

Harriet took the parcel to Vera's house, telling the Birketts it was from her employer, and the younger children fell avidly on the fruitcake. The sight of them devouring the last crumbs brought home to her what she had not noticed before:

that food in the Birkett household was not plentiful, and that the jam she scooped so carelessly out of the pot at tea time was spread far more thinly on the family's slices of bread. Mrs Birkett often didn't eat anything herself, saying that she wasn't hungry. Now it occurred to Harriet, with a pang of conscience, that it was self-sacrifice rather than lack of appetite that prompted such behaviour. On future visits, she resolved, she would always bring some contribution to the meal.

Louella's box contained a tea dress in black lace over a satin slip. Tucked into the tissue-paper lining of the box was a scrap of paper on which she had scribbled: *I don't know if you have the chance to wear such things in your new situation. If not, and you would like to, contact me and we can arrange something.*

It was, Harriet supposed, a peace-offering. She resisted the allure of the dress for a week before she tried it on in the privacy of her room. It made her look slim, graceful and dramatic. She would have liked to test its effect on Gavin Draycott . . . but it had come far too late for that.

She considered telephoning or writing to her aunt, if only to find out whether Louella, too, had known and kept the secret that Will Griffin was not her father. But Caroline came down with tonsillitis and the doctor decided that it was necessary to remove the offending tonsils and adenoids. After three days in hospital she came home to Kew and between them, Harriet and Laura nursed the hot and fretful little girl on fruit juice and glucose, bread and milk. When she cried they gave her an inhalation of ammonia, camphor and sal volatile to soothe the pain in her throat.

Harriet had been rather in awe of Laura, especially after the explosion of anger at Maple Grange, but her employer seemed much more human and likeable after she had been found asleep in a chair beside her daughter's bed at three in the morning, still holding Caroline's hand.

Caroline got better. It rained steadily throughout June and Harriet, thinking of the effect on the first hay crop at home, reminded herself dourly that *this* was her home now and that hay crops were no longer her concern. If she had felt tempted to respond with anything more than the barest thanks to her mother's wistful note or to Aunt Louella's guarded invitation, the moment had passed.

'Christ!' said James Allingham, reading his morning newspaper at the breakfast table at the end of June.

Laura looked up sharply. James wasn't in the habit of blaspheming.

'Sorry,' he apologized belatedly. 'But something rather dramatic has been going on in Germany.'

'What's that?' Laura asked.

'Hang on, I haven't read it yet.' He finished scanning the report then looked up again. 'Hitler's uncovered a plot for an uprising – apparently a lot of the top-ranking army officers were involved, including Röhm, the head of the SA.'

'Röhm?' Laura echoed. 'But isn't he supposed to be one of Hitler's staunchest supporters?'

'He was certainly instrumental in getting the *Herr Chancellor* elected to his current lofty position – he and his Brown Shirt bully boys of the *Sturmabteilung*. But he must have gone sour on the idea because according to this, he was plotting like mad to stage a *putsch*. Hitler mopped up the whole operation, apparently, in one co-ordinated swoop.'

'Well, I don't think I'll waste any tears on Röhm,' Laura said. 'He's a nasty piece of work, by all accounts. He probably deserves what's coming to him.'

'True. Except that he's already got it – widespread, summary executions. I won't say it wasn't justified, but that kind of thing does leave you fairly breathless. One tends to think, living in a democracy, that all men have the right to a fair trial, whatever their crime; but then, Nazi Germany's hardly a democracy. I read that in last November's elections – in which there were only Nazis standing anyway – any "anti" votes were promptly declared invalid, but the electors were still forced at the polls to buy a metal token to prove they'd voted. Then the thugs went round from door to door checking on who had their tokens – and who didn't.

That's one way of ensuring a hundred-per-cent vote in your favour! At any rate, I'll be able to pick up more details of this latest incident when I'm over there next week.' James folded his copy of *The Times* and resumed his interrupted breakfast. 'What a stroke of luck,' he said, stirring his coffee, 'that I agreed to produce that report on the reorganization of the German railway system for the Party – the timing couldn't be better!'

James would be away for several weeks, travelling through Germany on his observation trip, then on into Austria to pay a visit to an old acquaintance. Jurgen Reinhardt had become a friend by an accident of war: in 1915 he had shared a shell-hole on the Western Front for a few hours with Laura's twin brother Oliver, before becoming Oliver's prisoner. Jurgen's excellent command of the English language, his obvious decency and not least, the discovery that he had an aunt married to an Englishman and living in Weston-super-Mare, had sown the seeds of a friendship between the two young officers of opposing armies, which they took up again after the war. Nowadays, visits to Jurgen's home in Vienna were a regular feature of continental holidays for Oliver's family, and the link had extended to James and Laura too.

When James had actually gone to catch the boat train, Laura wandered into the nursery. 'Well, Caro, your daddy's off on his travels.'

'Won't you miss him?' asked Harriet, and then wondered if the question had been too forward. It was always difficult to know how to behave towards Laura. There was the old connection through Daisy which had won her the position, but set against it was the black mark of her mistake with Edward and the Cobham's Circus flight. Then, nursing Caroline through her illness had lowered some barriers between nanny and employer, but there were still times when Laura was very much the lady of the house. At other times, as now, she seemed quite simply rather lonely and ready to chat.

'Oh, I'm used to it. We made an agreement when we married that we would never stand in one another's way. I thought at the time that he was promising not to tie *me* down,' remembered Laura ruefully. 'And now he's a man of ambition and I'm the stay-at-home wife. And he'll be away for his birthday . . . but that doesn't matter, I suppose. James doesn't care about birthdays – or not about his own, anyway.'

'My dad's like that,' said Harriet. 'He pretends he doesn't want any fuss, but it's only because nobody ever did make a fuss of him when he was little – like saying *No flowers by request* at a funeral because you're afraid nobody will send any. Mum always bakes a cake anyway, and we wrap up presents and sing songs and he loves it really. I mean my stepfather,' she amended, colouring, and then fell silent because the memory hurt and she didn't want it to.

'I do believe you're right,' said Laura. 'Oh, poor James! All these years and no happy birthdays.'

The Allingham house at Kew was built of grey stone, with a sober Georgian façade and tall, many-paned windows. It stood in a quiet street close to the Royal Botanical Gardens in which Caroline, Jennifer and their nannies took their daily walk.

'I want to go in the Palm House and run on the noisy staircase,' said Caroline, on a day in early July, soon after James Allingham had left for Germany.

'Oh, *no*, Caro, it's much too hot for running.' But Caroline had set off with Jennifer in tow and reluctantly, Harriet and Vera followed the children around the edge of the Palm House pond towards the huge Victorian conservatory. Inside, the air was warm and heavy, with a scent of damp earth and greenery. The tall palms with vast, serrated leaves rioted towards the vaulted glass roof.

In a rash moment, one wet and miserable afternoon in spring, Vera had introduced the children to the joys of being chased up one white-painted spiral staircase, then of scampering along the aerial balcony which circled under the roof, and down the other staircase to play hide-and-seek among the palm fronds. Now it was being demanded as a regular feature of their walks.

'You're a tiger,' prompted Jennifer.

'We really shouldn't do this, Vera,' Harriet said. 'If one of the curators catches us, there'll be hell to pay.'

'Oh, if we get told off, then we'll stop. All right, Jenny, I'm a tiger.' Vera snarled convincingly and made snatches with her hands. 'And if I catch you I'm going to eat you up.'

Shrieking with laughter and mock terror, the two little girls pounded up the staircase, shoes clanging on the iron treads, with Vera in hot pursuit. Harriet, refusing to co-operate, waited at the bottom of the stairs, with a palm leaf tickling the back of her neck.

. . . Or she thought it was a palm leaf, until a voice beside her ear said, 'I'm glad to see, Miss Griffin, that you are too sensible to subscribe to such madcap activities.'

Harriet spun round, gasping, and found herself face to face with Tom Searle.

It took her a moment to steady her pounding heart after the fright, and another to realize that Tom's left hand, swathed in white bandaging, was held against his chest in a sling made out of a strip of the same *crêpe* material.

'What's happened to you?' she asked.

'Oh, I was helping to start a plane by cranking the propeller, and the idiot of a pilot had left a switch on. So the damned thing caught unexpectedly and nearly took my hand off,' Tom said. 'As it is, my fingers were fairly mangled, so I'm grounded for the time being. I thought I'd come and see how Laura's getting on, so I asked at the house and they said she's out for the rest of the afternoon, but that Miss Griffin was in the park with Miss Allingham.'

'Uncle Tom!' Caroline, tearing helter-skelter along the balcony, had spotted her favourite uncle. She stopped dead, with a joyful shrieking of his name, at the precise second that Jennifer cannoned into her full tilt from behind. There was a heart-stopping crunch at the moment of collision and

242

then another horrible crack as Jenny's small chin hit the cast-iron floor of the balcony.

'Oh, God!' Tom ran up the stairs with Harriet behind him. When they reached the scene of the accident, Caroline was crying with fright rather than hurt, and Vera was nursing Jenny in her arms. White-faced, Jenny was too shocked to cry. One of her front teeth showed a jagged edge above a cut lip, from which blood was trickling down her rapidly swelling chin.

'Oh, 'eck,' said Vera grimly. 'Now there really will be hell to pay.'

When Vera didn't come to collect her for their afternoon off the next day, Harriet caught the bus round to her family's house in Hammersmith. Vera opened the door, pink-eyed, and said with assumed bravado that she'd got the sack but she had never much liked the job anyway.

'Oh, Vera. I'm so awfully sorry.'

'Oh, it was my own fault for playing that silly game, I suppose.' Vera tried to smile. 'Still, it could have been worse. As Jenny's mum pointed out, we were lucky she didn't fall off the balcony and get killed.'

'Was she *very* angry?'

'Put it this way,' Vera said. 'I thought it was the worst half hour of my life – till I had to tell my dad what had happened. And if I can get through the rest of my days without another evening like *that*, I'll be blooming thankful.' She joined Harriet in the street. 'Let's go for a stroll. I'd ask you in, only Mum and Dad aren't really talking to me at the moment and I wouldn't want them being rude to you. Oh, and I'd better warn you: Jenny's mum wanted to know who you were, so she could complain to your Caroline's family about you as well. I wouldn't tell her your name, but I wouldn't put it past her to find out.'

'Oh,' said Harriet blankly. 'I hope she doesn't . . . But what about you, Vera, what are you going to do now?'

'Well, my family needs the money, that's for sure, so I'd better get cracking and find myself another job. Trouble is,'

Vera said with a sigh, 'I don't suppose I'll get another nursemaid's job in a hurry, because I haven't got a reference. So it looks like the factories for me. Oh, let's talk about something a bit more cheerful!' she added determinedly. 'Who was that young man that was talking to you? Didn't Caroline call him her uncle?'

'That's right,' Harriet said. 'He's my employer's step-brother.'

'Well, he likes *you*,' Vera commented. 'Anyone could see that from the way he looked at you. And he's awfully good-looking, isn't he?'

'I hadn't really noticed,' said Harriet.

'Well, just in case you had . . .' Vera warned, 'Remember he's gentry and you're the servant class and the two don't mix, do they? I nearly got into that kind of trouble once, with the son of some people I worked for, and now I'm only glad I didn't make a fool of myself. Those young gentlemen, they'll say one thing and mean another.'

'I know,' Harriet said grimly.

'Well, I'd better be getting back,' Vera remembered. 'I have to get some clothes packed. I'm off to stay with my aunt in Sutton in the morning – there's more chance of a factory job round her way. So it looks like we won't be seeing each other for a while.'

They hugged one another goodbye in the street.

'I'll send you my address when I'm sorted,' said Vera. 'You will keep in touch, won't you?'

'Oh, *yes*,' said Harriet, and walked away forlornly down the road.

Tom Searle encountered Harriet in the hall as she came in from her afternoon off, and made the mistake of asking her if she'd had a good break. Harriet had spent a miserable four hours wandering around unfamiliar streets and had ended up sitting on a bench in Kew Gardens to kill time, precisely because she didn't want to face any questions about her early return. Tom's cheerful greeting was the last straw and she informed him of Vera's dismissal in a few terse sentences that left him in no doubt about whom she considered responsible for the situation.

'I'm sorry to hear about your friend,' Tom said, his smile fading, 'but I don't see why you're blaming me.'

'Don't you? Every time I see you,' Harriet said, with controlled fury, 'something awful happens. First my horse throws me and I miss seeing . . . someone very important because of it. Then you give Edward a flight – when you knew perfectly well that you shouldn't – and nearly lose me my job. And then you turn up in the Palm House and take us all by surprise and Jenny cracks her chin and Vera gets sacked and now I've lost the only friend I had in London.'

'Be fair, Harriet,' Tom protested. 'It really wasn't my fault, what happened.'

'I don't care whose fault it was. You're like an albatross,' Harriet told him bitterly. 'Like the one in the poem that the sailor had tied round his neck. You're bad luck. Why can't you just go away?'

'As you wish,' said Tom. He touched a hand to his forehead and turned away. He'd taken her dismissal with apparent good humour, but watching him run up the stairs towards his own room, Harriet recognized that the mock salute had been preceded by a flicker of hurt. She pushed the thought away. All right, she *had* been unfair . . . and her outburst was rash as well, given that Tom was her employer's stepbrother. But she wasn't about to call him back and apologize – she had enough problems of her own to deal with, without worrying about the feelings of Tom Searle.

245

16

Although Laura had vowed that she wouldn't forgive Tom for taking her son for a flight in a biplane, she was prepared to suspend hostilities because his arrival fitted so well into her newly formulated plans.

'Since you're at a loose end, you can help me out. I want to go to Austria, to meet up with James at the end of his German tour. I didn't see how I could manage it without a male escort, but now that you're here, the whole thing becomes much simpler.'

'Austria?' Tom said doubtfully. 'I wasn't planning any foreign travel. To tell you the truth, my hand is pretty sore—' The injured hand was out of a sling by now, but was still swathed in bandages, and only he knew how it throbbed in the night, keeping him tossing and turning till dawn as he tried to escape from the pain of it.

'Edward will be home for the holidays in a few days,' Laura interrupted him briskly. 'We can go then. We'll be able to see Jurgen's family – have you ever met Jurgen? He's a delightful person, so civilized. A solicitor, like James. And Kirsten has a new baby, only two or three months old, whom I'm longing to see. We'll be there in time for James's birthday, and we should be back at the end of July, by which time your hand will be better and you can go back to your Flying Circus. It all works out perfectly!'

'Oh, you're taking the children? What about Caroline's nanny?'

'Harriet? She'll come too, of course. I'll drop her mother a line to OK it.'

'In that case, she would probably rather I wasn't part of the expedition,' Tom said, with memories of his last encounter with Harriet fresh in his mind. 'She informs me that I'm bad luck, like the Ancient Mariner's albatross, and she wishes I'd go away. And actually, I feel rather inclined to do just that.'

'Oh, rubbish,' Laura said, bridling at the suggestion. 'It's certainly not up to *Harriet* who comes with us! If it's a choice between her and you, I'm perfectly happy to leave her behind. Oh, Tom,' she added on a note of misgiving, as the gist of his words penetrated, 'Don't tell me you're about to get yourself into a silly situation with Harriet Griffin? If there's the least risk of it, I shall simply have to pack her off home to her mother.'

'If you mean a *romantic* situation, it couldn't be more unlikely,' Tom assured her.

Laura heard the conviction in his words and missed the regret. 'Well, thank goodness for that!' she said with relief, and turned to more pressing matters. 'Hand me that copy of Bradshaw from the bookshelf behind you, Tom. I want to check on the train connections.'

In the end, the party for Vienna consisted of Laura, Tom, Harriet and Caroline. On his return from boarding school, eight-year-old Edward had told his mother that if she didn't mind, he'd rather stay in Dorset with Colborne Minor, actually, because Colborne's pater had offered to teach him all about fly-fishing.

'But don't you want to see Daddy?'

Edward shrugged. 'I can see him when he comes home.'

Laura looked at her son and for a chilling moment she heard echoes of his grandfather Brownlowe in his voice. Rupert had always had that same detachment from family ties and affections – had it been learned in the same way? At times Laura had thought there was still an emotional human being behind the gruff, cold mask that her father presented, and sometimes she thought she was within reach of that human being, but he always slipped out of her grasp and in the end she had given up trying.

A year ago, when Edward had set off for his first term at

boarding school, he'd been heartbreakingly young and vulnerable. Laura had seen the panic in his eyes at the moment of parting, and the valiant attempt to disguise it, and her instinctive response had been to call him back and keep him by her. But that wasn't how sons of Edward's background were brought up, so she'd let him go, to the prep school that had been Rupert's in his childhood. And already Edward had withdrawn into the private world of boys and was lost to her.

She wanted to hug him and ask what was wrong, what she could do to make it right and win him back again. Instead she heard herself agreeing to telephone Mrs Colborne and make the arrangements for Dorset.

But if Edward had been unmoved by the prospect of a trip to Vienna, Harriet had no such blasé reaction. She had never been out of the country before and Vienna seemed inexpressibly glamorous. As she packed Louella's birthday tea-gown, swathed in tissue paper, among her clothes, she couldn't suppress a rising conviction that her life was about to change for the better.

The only drawback was that Tom Searle was going to be part of the proceedings. Increasingly, Tom represented a threat to her peace of mind, and not just because of his propensity for bringing bad luck. His interest in her was obvious, and there were moments when she felt tempted to respond to it. If she hadn't been haunted by the memory of Gavin Draycott, she would probably have done so – there was something very appealing about his frank and friendly manner. But Harriet's brief romance with Gavin had come to a bruising conclusion and she had no intention of making the same mistake again.

The Allingham contingent took the boat train from Victoria on Friday the twentieth of July, spent the night in a Paris hotel and boarded the Orient Express the next day. Travelling via Ostend, they were due to arrive in Vienna on Sunday afternoon.

The *wagons-lits* of the Orient Express were as comfortable

and luxurious as attention to decorative detail could make them, with marquetry panelling, stylish glass-shaded lamps and deep, comfortable upholstery; but they were, of necessity, limited in space. Harriet shared a compartment with Caroline. Laura's compartment was on the other side of an interconnecting door between the two washbasin cubicles.

Unpacking Caroline's washing kit from a suitcase, Harriet heard Laura's voice from the neighbouring compartment.

'I suppose they'd better share our table. I've asked for an early sitting so that Caroline won't be kept up too late. I do hope Harriet will manage without feeling too awkward – I imagine she's not used to eating in such sophisticated surroundings. The menu will be in French, of course.'

'Oh, I daresay she'll cope. Harriet has a lot of poise, for a country bumpkin.' The voice was Tom's and he sounded amused, Harriet thought, the colour flaring in her cheeks at the realization. 'We can always give her a bit of guidance if need be.'

When Harriet brought Caroline down the swaying train later that evening, she found that Laura had been right in describing the ambience of an Orient Express dining car as sophisticated. Confronted by snowy table-linen, fresh flowers in silver centrepieces, delicate porcelain and sparkling crystal, Harriet was heartily grateful for the tuition she had rebelled at in London from Aunt Louella's friend, Lydia Matthews, and even more grateful for the gift of the black lace dress from Louella. As she passed along the dining car, she collected admiring male glances, and when she joined Tom and Laura at their table, Tom's expression confirmed that the dress suited her. She studied the menu card, aware that he was having difficulty in keeping his eyes off the 'country bumpkin'.

'*Madame?*' The white-jacketed waiter hovered with pad and silver-cased pencil. Laura ordered briskly for herself and Caroline.

'*Et pour Mademoiselle?*' It was Harriet's turn.

'Would you like a hand with interpreting the menu?' Tom offered.

'No thank you, I've chosen already.' And Harriet ordered *gigot d'agneau à romarin* in a passable French accent. Out of the corner of her eye she caught Laura's raised eyebrows and Tom's quick glance of startled appreciation, and felt that she had scored a very satisfying point.

When they returned to their compartments at the end of the meal, the sleeping-car attendant had achieved a transformation, lowering and making up the bunk beds that had been folded into the walls. Caroline was enchanted. Given the lower bunk for safety's sake, she spent half the night climbing up the shining mahogany ladder into Harriet's bunk overhead, on the flimsiest of pretexts, to share in the thrill of going to bed on a shelf.

Laura had booked her train tickets without contacting Jurgen Reinhardt. She had taken her welcome from an old friend for granted and had only remembered to despatch a telegram at the last minute to announce their impending arrival. Jurgen, it transpired, had sent a return telegram, too late, urging her to put off the visit. He arrived at the station to meet them, looking harassed.

'This is not a good time for you to come – the country has been almost in a state of civil war. Didn't you hear of such things in London?'

'No. I'm sorry,' Laura said. 'It's James who usually keeps me informed about overseas developments, and he's been away for nearly three weeks. And Caroline's been getting over tonsillitis, so I haven't been reading the papers. I heard there were some terrorist outrages, but that was months ago and I thought your government had dealt with the situation.'

'I wish that was true. But there have been more incidents,' Jurgen told her. 'There were even bombs on the trains in the middle of last month – so many that a special force has been formed to try to keep the federal railways safe. And I believe that another bomb was set off early this morning on the Danube shore railway track, though from the reports I've heard, not much damage was done. But it is not safe for you to be here on a pleasure trip, especially with a child.'

'Oh. Well, anyway, we're here now,' said Laura briskly. After travelling for nearly two full days to reach Vienna, she refused to be dashed by the news. Besides, she had an innate belief that *foreigners* might behave badly towards one another but that an Englishwoman would be somehow sacrosanct. 'If it's a nuisance for you that we came, Jurgen, don't worry about us, we can look after ourselves.'

'No, no. Forgive me. Of course it is good to see you. *Wilkommen in Wien.*' Jurgen's hospitable instincts surfaced belatedly. He shook hands with Tom, clicked his heels at Harriet and reduced Caroline to giggles by kissing her hand. 'Do you have hotel reservations?'

'I haven't made any advance bookings. I hoped you might be able to suggest somewhere,' said Laura.

'There is a hotel near the Graben that should have rooms and it is not far to walk to our apartment in Rosengasse. I wish that we could put you up ourselves, but the apartment is very cramped,' he apologized. 'And we already have an English visitor, my cousin Peter, who is working for a while in Vienna. He has gone to Salzburg for a few days, but he has use of our only spare room at present. Of course you will take your meals with us, at least.'

Within half an hour they had been booked into the hotel that Jurgen suggested in Dorotheegasse, just off the large shopping square of the Graben. The street was narrow and the hotel reception area gloomy, with an iron-balustered stone staircase rising from the reception hall and a clanking lift which carried the new arrivals up to their rooms. The rooms themselves were dark too, with windows that opened on to a small central courtyard which was little more than a well.

'I am sorry, the rooms are not the best. But without a reservation . . .' Jurgen apologized again.

The hotel made Harriet nervous, partly because she had never been in a hotel before, let alone a foreign hotel, and partly because the clerk on the reception desk had seemed brusque and impatient. So far, Austria was a daunting place. But she liked Jurgen Reinhardt. He was about forty years old, tall and fair-haired, serious-looking, very correct in his manners – the heel-clicking had impressed her enormously – and very competent in organizing the co-operation of railway porters, cab drivers and hotel desk clerks.

'Now I hope you will come to the apartment for some coffee,' said Jurgen. 'Or perhaps it should be tea,' he added, his pleasant face breaking into a smile. 'Tea is your national drink, isn't it?'

The Reinhardts' apartment was in a tall, stone-faced house in one of the smaller streets off Herrengasse, only a few minutes' walk from the hotel. When they arrived, a flustered maid opened the door and launched a flood of German at Jurgen. He stemmed the flow with a few terse questions then turned to his guests.

'I must ask you to excuse me for a few minutes – something has happened to my wife. If you will go into the drawing room, Anna will bring you tea.'

'What is it? Nothing serious I hope?' Laura said quickly.

'I hope not, too. Please. Go in.'

They sat uneasily in the drawing room, conscious of the red eyes and distracted air of the maid when she brought in tea on a silver tray. Nobody wanted it except Caroline, who took advantage of the adults' preoccupation to eat more biscuits than would normally have been considered good manners.

When their host rejoined them fifteen minutes later, the worry line between his eyes was even deeper than before.

'Someone threw a stone at Kirsten while she was out walking with the baby.'

'Oh, how awful!' Laura exclaimed. 'Is she hurt?'

'Fortunately it only grazed her forehead a little.'

'How awful!' Laura repeated. 'But why on earth would anyone do such a thing?'

Jurgen shrugged. 'I suppose she is on a list, somewhere, as a target . . . That kind of thing has been happening lately, in Vienna. The Nazis are becoming increasingly out of control.'

'Nazis?' Laura echoed. 'Oh . . . We heard in England that they are behaving badly, but I understood that they were only a problem to the Jewish population.'

'But didn't you know?' Jurgen said. 'Kirsten is Jewish.'

The words dropped among his visitors like a stone. Even Harriet had heard scattered reports of the increasing harassment of Jews in Germany and Austria, and had felt a passing sympathy for their plight.

There was a moment of shocked silence before Laura said, 'I didn't realize. She doesn't look—'

'How is a Jew supposed to look?' said Jurgen quickly. 'It is not just a breed, it is an ancient code of beliefs and rituals that has spread among the people of many nations.'

'I meant . . . how silly of me, but I had thought that they didn't marry outside their own kind . . .' Laura's voice trailed away as she became aware of further pitfalls.

Jurgen rescued her. 'It's true that to marry a Gentile isn't encouraged,' he said, more gently. 'Kirsten's family disapproved of our marriage – you might say that they disowned her for it. She is not a practising Jew, and our child will not be brought up in the faith, but I am sure that where such things are noted, she will be recorded as being of Jewish descent. As matters stand, it's not a very safe heritage,' he added wryly, 'but that can't be helped.' He changed the subject to something less fraught. 'And that reminds me, it is high time that you were introduced to the baby.'

He left the room and returned a few minutes later followed by a plump girl with a good-humoured face, who carried a bundle swathed in a shawl. The shawl was folded back to reveal a miniature human being with a neat cap of dark hair and a challenging stare.

'Allow me to present to you Gilda Magdalena Reinhardt,' Jurgen said with mock formality and undisguisable pride as the visitors clustered round the nursemaid.

'What a darling,' said Laura, holding out a finger to the

baby, who clutched at it, blinking up at her impassively. Laura had a sudden clear memory of making exactly the same gesture to Harriet Griffin nineteen years ago, and was reminded that babies grow up very quickly. Then she noticed that her own daughter was hanging back shyly, and Caroline had to be sat down and given Gilda to hold on her lap, so that she wouldn't feel left out of things.

Kirsten Reinhardt appeared for the evening meal. She was a pale, slender woman, a few years younger than Jurgen, with sleek almost-black hair parted in the middle and coiled on either side of her face. The graze on her forehead was clearly visible but nobody mentioned the incident that had caused it. While her husband and the guests made conversation around her she sat in silence, pushing the food about on her plate rather than eating it. When Harriet glanced across the table at intervals she noticed that Kirsten's hands were trembling; and that, unobtrusively, she was drinking too much wine.

As the maid was serving coffee the telephone rang and Jurgen excused himself from the table to answer it.

'A contact in the police rang,' he said on his return, 'to inform me that two men have been arrested for the bomb explosion this morning.'

'Oh, that's good, isn't it?' Laura said. 'I mean, that they've been caught and will be punished.'

'Were they Nazis?' Kirsten asked.

'No,' said Jurgen. 'This misguided pair were Social Democrats – full of fervour and lacking in efficiency! The only damage done by their wretched bomb was to the cement base of a railway signal, but unfortunately, one of them shot and wounded a policeman while resisting arrest. So the whole incident becomes much more serious and the terrorist responsible – he's hardly more than a lad – will be tried by court martial, under the new law which was passed nine days ago to deal with political acts of violence.'

'You sound almost as if you sympathize with him,' Laura said.

'I feel sorry for him, if that's what you mean.' Jurgen poured himself a glass of wine. 'Poor devil. If he is convicted, which he will be, he is liable to hang.'

Kirsten said something to her husband in German and he forced a smile. 'But this is not fit conversation for the dinner table. Excuse me. We shall talk of more cheerful subjects. What are your plans for tomorrow?'

Laura's party had arrived in Vienna on the twenty-second of July, but James was not expected until Tuesday the twenty-fourth, which was also his birthday.

'So we have a few days to be tourists,' Laura said happily, and drew up a list of unmissable sights for the benefit of Caroline, who should not miss this early opportunity to be introduced to culture, and for Tom, who had not been to Vienna before. Harriet she included automatically.

Vienna was not a big city, but as the centrepiece of the Austro-Hungarian empire it had been crammed by the Hapsburg dynasty with imposing buildings, grandiose statues representing mythological scenes, and museums bursting with important works of art. By Tuesday afternoon Caroline had reached saturation point and so, privately, had Harriet. The noise of traffic and the clamour of voices in the streets bombarded her senses and she thought that if she was called upon to admire one more gilt-framed portrait of a Hapsburg on a horse, or one more domed-and-cupola'd stone façade, she would probably scream.

'And now for the *Kunshistoriches* Museum,' announced Laura, showing off her German. 'There are some wonderful Breughels.'

'I think Caroline would prefer an ice cream,' said Tom. They had reached Maria-Theresien-Platz, the lawned square between the twin buildings of the Fine Art Museum and the Natural History Museum, and now he seated himself firmly on a park bench. 'And so, frankly, would I. You go and look at the paintings if you like, Laura. We'll meet you here in a couple of hours.'

Harriet was torn between admiration for his mastery of

the situation and a reluctance to fall in with his plans, whatever they might be. But her aching feet and Caroline's evident exhaustion dictated her co-operation. For two hours she let him take control and while Laura toured the *Kunshistoriches* alone, the rebels took a taxi to a coffee-house and Caroline ate ice creams to her heart's content.

For days now, ever since she had called him an albatross, Tom had hardly spoken to Harriet. But in the Café Central, with its bentwood chairs and marble pillars, under a vaulted ceiling picked out with painted flowers, he turned on the full force of his easy charm and she discovered how much she had missed it.

'You were wonderful with the *gigot d'agneau* on the train,' he told her. 'Laura was flabbergasted. I would have been too, except that I already know how astounding you can be.'

Harriet added water from a carafe to her strong black coffee and sipped it without replying. Tom spoke to her like an equal. He shared jokes and squabbled with her good-naturedly and he might have been a favourite older brother except for a look in his eyes, sometimes, that was not brotherly at all. She reminded herself grimly of Vera Birkett's comment, that these young gentlemen said one thing and meant another.

James Allingham had sent a telegram postponing his arrival for twenty-four hours. Jurgen Reinhardt was preoccupied with work and with keeping track of the repercussions of the bombing incident which had occurred on their first day, but with Kirsten's help, Laura had organized the trimmings of a surprise birthday supper for James. Now the scheme had fallen through.

'Never mind. It can be lunch tomorrow instead,' said Kirsten as the Reinhardts and their guests sat down at the elaborately set table which was no longer appropriate.

'A day late. It won't be the same,' uttered Laura dismally. 'It's just that I was looking forward to seeing his face, when he realized we were here.'

'You have been missing him. I understand. Jurgen and I have never been parted for more than a day,' Kirsten said softly. 'Not since we were married. Though of course, when we were engaged and he was away at the war . . .'

Laura felt a stab of envy. Had she and James ever been that close? She could remember, the year after the Great War ended, coming home from nursing on the Western Front to the relief of discovering that she was loved by James Allingham. But by then she had lost a husband and one other man, for whom her feelings had been so much more intense. In the aftermath, James, a rock of steadiness, had always seemed to accept that for all the affection between the two of them, he was only a substitute for the dead soldier and the dead airman who had been the real loves of her life.

Now Laura had to recognize the degree to which she had come to depend on James. All the time that he had been away on this German trip, she had been pacing herself to cope with his absence. Three weeks more, two weeks more, the plan to travel to Vienna to meet him, then a countdown of days . . . and now the disappointment of his non-arrival was sour and sharp, and it wasn't just because of the wasted birthday cake and the unopened bottle of champagne.

Frustrated expectations kept her awake for most of the night in the hotel room in Dorotheegasse. The next morning, edgy and hollow-eyed, she nagged Tom, Harriet and Caroline into setting off too early for the Reinhardts' apartment and on their arrival she offended the maid with too many questions about the substitute lunch.

The Reinhardts were no help. Kirsten was worried about the baby, who had spent a restless night which might or might not only be due to teething. Jurgen's cousin had come back from Salzburg and he and Jurgen seemed to be interested in only one subject. On the previous day, the bomber Josef Gerl had been condemned to death under the new, steeply punitive anti-terrorist law, and despite appeals to Chancellor Dollfuss for a stay of execution, he had been hanged on the same evening.

'I don't see why that's so bad,' Laura said. 'Surely, it's

important for an example to be made? Of if he needed to be let off with a lighter sentence, the Chancellor would have seen that and acted accordingly?'

'He didn't act at all,' said Jurgen abruptly. He folded his copy of the *Neue Freie Presse* carefully, with the deliberate air of a man who is trying to keep his temper in check. 'He promised to be in his office to discuss the situation with a political opponent who was appealing for clemency, and then he simply disappeared. The sentence was carried out without his making any positive commitment for or against it – like Pontius Pilate washing his hands. That won't save him from the resentment of the Reds. They'll know he let Josef Gerl hang because he was a Red and not a Nazi. Our little Chancellor may think that having used military and police might to crush the Social Democrats' resistance and to dissolve their party in February's civil war, he's removed their power to damage him . . . but when the Nazis turn on him, he may well wish the Social Democrats were still strong enough to keep them in check.'

Laura gave up trying to understand the complications of the Austrian political situation. Yesterday, to stave off her disappointment at James's non-arrival, she had bought him an extra birthday present from an antique shop in Dorotheegasse, and now she carried it into the drawing room to balance on top of the stack of parcels already waiting on an occasional table under one of the long windows.

'What's in there, Mummy?' Caroline had followed her mother into the room and reached out to prod curiously at the new parcel in its gold-and-blue wrapping paper. It teetered and toppled and Laura just failed to catch it in time as it thudded onto the polished floor.

'Oh, *Caro*! Must you meddle with everything!' Laura, in trying to make up for too many neglected birthdays, had overspent wildly and the parcel contained a ridiculously expensive Lalique glass vase. With shaking hands she tore off the wrapping, but protected by its box and swathed in tissue paper, the vase seemed undamaged.

She lifted it out. Somehow it looked less attractive than

it had done amid a cluster of others on a carefully lit shelf in the shop. She became aware that she had paid far too much, and James probably wouldn't even like it anyway; and also that Caroline was biting her lip and blinking back tears.

'I'm sorry, Caro,' Laura said contritely. 'I didn't mean to shout at you. You couldn't help it, and there's no harm done. I'm just a bit nervy, waiting for Daddy to arrive. I'm so looking forward to seeing him, and so are you, aren't you, darling?' She reached for her daughter's hand, but Caroline had retreated into the consoling arms of Harriet, who had followed her into the room and was now gazing reproachfully at Laura over her head. In the doorway behind her, Jurgen and Tom exchanged glances which were equally expressive.

'Oh, *damn*! Damn everything!' Abruptly, Laura subsided onto the carpet beside the ripped gift-wrappings and buried her flushed face in her hands. Jurgen beckoned Harriet and Caroline out of the room and closed the door tactfully on Laura.

'She is a little tense. It will be better if you and Harriet and the little girl are somewhere else for the rest of the morning,' he told Tom in an undertone.

'I agree. But what do you suggest we do?' said Tom.

'Have you visited the Spanish Riding School at the Hofburg in Josefsplatz? My cousin Peter knows someone there who is a *bereiter anworter* – an assistant rider at the school. If you go along with him this morning, I am sure you will be welcomed.'

Tom seized on the suggestion with alacrity – he hated being around distressed women, who made him feel helpless and correspondingly irritated – but Harriet hesitated.

'Perhaps I should go in to Laura?'

'She is best left alone, I think,' Jurgen said. 'She will be all right once her husband arrives. You go along.'

Peter Morris was about the same age as Tom, tall and thin, with dark hair and a pleasant, rather shy manner. On the way to the riding school he explained his connection with Jurgen Reinhardt.

'I don't know what the exact relationship would be. We're sort of distant cousins, I suppose. My grandmother, Frieda, is Jurgen's aunt. She met my grandfather in Bayreuth fifty years ago – they had a passion for Wagner's operas in common – and married him and moved to England, to Weston-super-Mare. When I wanted to come to Austria, my grandmother wrote to ask Jurgen to help me, and he and Kirsten have always made me very welcome in Vienna.'

'So you've been here before?' Tom asked.

'Half a dozen times, since I was a schoolboy. At first I wanted to improve my German and later I needed to learn more about the European situation for my job – I started out as a junior reporter on an English provincial newspaper but of course I had absurd aspirations! I hope eventually to be a foreign correspondent on a national paper, either in England or in Austria,' Peter said. 'I haven't decided which, yet. I have divided loyalties, you see – I'm English, but I've always felt a great liking for Vienna.'

At the Spanish Riding School, Peter demonstrated his fluency in German when he explained the presence of his companions to his friend Andreas. Like Jurgen, Andreas clicked his heels on greeting the visitors, but with Andreas the movement was doubly effective because of the highly polished leather riding boots he wore.

'They are in the middle of the day's schooling of the horses, and in fact they are about to begin a full rehearsal for the display. He says if it would amuse us to watch, we can go up to the gallery,' Peter translated. A porter escorted them up a flight of stone stairs to the viewing gallery which ran all round the arena of the Winter Riding School.

'Now I see why it's called the most beautiful riding hall in the world,' said Tom in an undertone to Harriet. The architecture of the hall was Baroque, with the second tier of gallery supported on marble columns rising from the first, and stone-carved swags of fruit ornamenting the walls. Under the vaulted roof, huge cut-glass chandeliers hung on long chains from the moulded ceiling above a pristine rectangle of raked earth.

Harriet knew nothing about the Spanish Riding School with its Lippizaners, once the carriage-horses of the Hapsburgs and now bred and schooled for dressage in the élite academy in Vienna. But her upbringing had given her an eye for horses and the first entry of eleven white stallions into the arena below brought a shock of pure pleasure.

They were beautiful: proud and strong and showy, with the dished noses, delicate muzzles and flowing tails of their Arab antecedents. Harriet picked out Peter's friend Andreas from the riders in their uniform of dark brown frock coats and cream breeches. Under the two-cornered hat trimmed with gold braid, his expression was very serious and his concentration absolute. The stallions circled the ring in a deceptively easy, controlled canter, with the riders sitting motionless in the saddle, as if horse and rider were welded together. There was classical music that she recognized from the lessons in Lydia Matthews' drawing room, played on a hidden gramophone.

'They're dancing!' said Caroline, eyes shining as she watched the intricate movements flow together in the arena below. The display had reached a *pas de deux* and as two stallions passaged delicately away from one another, Harriet was reminded of Captain and Charlotte, Will Griffin's plough horses, as they turned at the end of a furrow. There was a world of difference between the elegant Lippizaners and the big, patient Shires, but they had the same precision of movement and the same calm, intelligent eyes as their hooves crossed, sending them sideways across the arena. Standing in the high gallery, amid the splendour of the Spanish Riding School, Harriet suddenly wanted quite desperately to be at home.

'You're looking sad,' noticed Peter Morris in an undertone. 'What's the matter?'

'Nothing,' said Harriet, and turned her face away so that he wouldn't see the tears glittering on her lashes.

17

Caroline was enchanted by the riding display and the tour of the stables which followed it. When she came out of the building two hours later, she skipped rather than walked along the stone passageway that led from the stables, brimming over with questions which Peter did his best to answer.

Harriet proceeded with more decorum, but her inner mood echoed Caroline's. Her moment of homesickness in the gallery had given way to an equally unexpected sensation of buoyancy. It was partly to do with the familiar trappings that went with horses – the stalls, though splendid, still had straw underfoot, and the decorative harness still smelt comfortingly of saddle soap – but if she was honest with herself, her recovery was not entirely unconnected with the presence of Peter Morris, walking beside her with the sun glinting on his dark hair, and an echoing glint in his eyes that told her he found her attractive.

Peter was explaining the history of the Lippizaner horses and of the *haute école* movements which had their origins in ancient Greece. 'That's two thousand, five hundred years ago,' he told a wide-eyed Caroline. 'The schooling then was designed to train the horses for war, as well as being beautiful to watch. Of course, we hardly use horses to fight wars any more since tanks were invented,' he added.

'My mummy was married to a cavalryman, but he was killed in the Great War,' Caroline announced. 'And so was everyone else that she liked. So she married my daddy instead.'

'Poor old James,' Tom muttered sourly. Caroline didn't hear the comment but Harriet did, and she shot him a sideways frown. Until now, Tom had been silent and vaguely sulky and it occurred to Harriet, with a *frisson* of pure delight, that he was resenting the attention paid to her by Peter Morris.

They crossed Michaelerplatz, in front of the splendidly ornate semicircle of buildings which was part of the imperial palace, pausing to look up at the four statues which flanked the tall archway leading through to the central courtyard. On top of their stone plinths, four aggressively muscular, bearded figures brandished clubs over fallen victims.

'What are those men doing?' asked Caroline.

'I suppose they are gods conquering their enemies,' Peter told her. Then he realised that Caroline wasn't looking at the statues but at the shadowy area under the archway, where half a dozen young men in brown uniforms were clustered around something in their midst.

'*Nazis*,' said Peter, with an edge in his voice, and now his companions could see the swastika armbands. The lads were laughing, but in the jostling figures, with their spread hands and shifting feet, there was an unpleasant echo of the stone statues nearby – the attitude of the dominant mocking the weak, Harriet thought, with a shudder of distaste. Then one of the lads swayed sideways and the object of their attentions became visible.

An old man was trying to make his way through the cordon of jeering youths. Confused and frightened, he turned from side to side as a gap opened invitingly, then closed again. The laughter from the brown-shirted boys and the hissed comments that accompanied it grew uglier. Without warning, one of the youths chopped a hand at the side of the old man's neck and he crumpled to the ground.

Peter said something under his breath and started forward.

Tom grabbed at his arm. 'Leave it. It's not your business. And there are too many of them.'

Peter shook his head. 'There are some things you can't walk away from,' he said quietly.

Tom hesitated, still retaining his hold on Peter's sleeve. The old man was on his knees on the pavement, staring hopelessly up at his tormentors. Even at that distance Harriet could hear his sobbing snatches of breath.

'We must stop them,' she said, feeling sick. Beside her, Caroline's hand stole into hers for reassurance.

Tom took in a long breath and visibly straightened his back. 'All right. Harriet, you wait here with Caroline. Come on, then, Peter.'

'No, not you – not with an injured hand. We must be practical. I'll deal with this,' said Peter. 'And you must escort Harriet and Caroline safely home.'

'Don't be silly. You can't take that lot on alone.'

'I can. One of us might be able to interrupt without provoking a confrontation. Two would seem like an invitation to a scrap. In any case, there isn't time to argue.'

The old man had been hauled to his feet by now, and was being buffeted and spun between the youths like a rag doll. Peter pulled free of Tom's restraining grip and walked steadily towards the archway, telling the others, 'I'll catch up with you as soon as I can.'

'He's right,' Tom told Harriet. 'I hate to admit it, but two won't be much better than one against those thugs, and with this hand I'm useless anyway. We must go back to the Reinhardts and fetch some able-bodied help. Come on.'

Harriet hesitated. 'What'll happen to Peter?'

'I expect they'll beat him up,' Tom answered her grimly. 'And there's not a thing we can do about it. Come *on*.' He caught hold of Caroline's free hand and set off, running, in the direction of Rosengasse. Harriet was pulled with them, still protesting but not daring to look back at what might be happening in the Michaelertrakt arch.

At the Reinhardts' apartment, James Allingham sipped coffee and tried to conceal his dismay at being greeted not only by his friend Jurgen, but also by his wife Laura, who was supposed to be safely at home in Kew.

'I wanted to surprise you,' Laura said.

'You've certainly managed that.'

'I meant it to be for your birthday, but you came too late.'

To Laura's chagrin, James ignored her reproachful comment and instead, spoke over her head to the tall Austrian who hovered behind her chair. 'There were some disturbing rumours flying about across the border Jurgen – I must talk to you about them.'

'Kirsten and I had planned you a birthday supper but that was no good, so now we've made an after-birthday lunch,' Laura persisted. 'Where can Harriet and Caroline have got to? They knew they had to be back here before one o'clock.'

'You've brought *Caroline* to Vienna?' James exclaimed. 'Laura, how could you?'

'Of course I brought her. I wasn't going to leave her behind. What sort of mother do you think I am? It was supposed to be a birthday treat for you,' said Laura, miserably aware that her idea had gone wrong and that James, apparently, wasn't the least bit glad to see her.

'But for heaven's sake, Laura, to bring *Caro* to Vienna when the situation here is so unsettled . . .'

'How on earth was I supposed to know that—' But Laura's defence was cut short by an insistent hammering at the front door and a few moments later, Caroline hurtled into the room.

'Daddy! Oh, *Daddy!*'

It took time for James to extricate himself from his daughter's passionate embrace and to comprehend that, behind her, Tom and Harriet were breathlessly explaining to Jurgen the need to mount an urgent rescue operation for Peter. It took even more time to persuade Caroline to stay with her mother, and to convince Laura that he must go with their host.

'In that case, I'm coming too,' said Laura. 'Harriet can stay here with Caroline. Harriet?' she said, but in vain.

Harriet had already disappeared with Jurgen and Tom. They had almost reached the Michaelerplatz, running, before James caught up with them.

Under the Michaelertrakt arch there was no sign of the gang of Nazi youths or of their elderly victim. But Peter was still there, slumped against a wall with his legs splayed out on the paving in front of him, while blood coursed steadily from his nose and dripped from his chin on to his stained shirt. He peered up at the rescue party through the rapidly swelling flesh around a black eye and managed a travesty of a smile.

'I tried the reasonable approach,' he said ruefully, 'but they didn't buy it.'

'I should have stayed,' lamented Tom, squatting on his heels beside him.

'No point in two of us being involved when one would do,' croaked Peter. He manipulated his jaw experimentally and prodded with a forefinger at a loosened tooth, then caught sight of Harriet's appalled face behind Tom's shoulder. 'It's not as bad as it looks,' he said. 'At least, I don't know how it looks, but it can't be as bad as all that!'

'We must get you home. Can you walk?' Jurgen asked.

'I don't know. Let's see.' Peter struggled to his feet, then winced and doubled forward, arms folded against his chest. 'I think they may have cracked a rib or two,' he said, drawing shallow breaths. 'They did rather kick me about once they had me down.'

Jurgen swore briefly and explicitly under his breath, his face stiff with anger as he hooked an arm under Peter to support him.

'What happened to the old man?' Tom asked.

'He managed to get away when they turned their attentions on me. So at least something was achieved.'

With Tom on one side of Peter, and Jurgen on the other, they made their way slowly past the stone gods on their plinths towards Herrengasse. As they crossed the eastern corner of Ballhausplatz, a lorry shot across the cobbles on the far side and halted in front of the Chancellory building, disgorging a stream of men in uniform.

'Police. We could have done with them earlier,' Tom observed wryly. 'Police *and* army,' he added, as the troops swarmed into the building through the double doors which stood wide open. 'I wonder what the hell's going on?'

'Changing of the guard, I suppose,' said Jurgen, barely

interested because it was obvious that Peter was in pain and couldn't be expected to walk much further.

'It's a heavy guard if that's the case,' Tom said, as further lorries arrived and their human cargo spilled out and ran into the Chancellory. 'There must be well over a hundred of them.'

'Oh. I was on the point of telling you, Jurgen,' said James. 'Something I picked up from one of my contacts across the border before I left Berlin . . . there was talk of the possibility of a Nazi-led coup against Dollfuss. Extra troops must have been drafted in to protect the Chancellor.'

Outside the building in Rosengasse that housed the Reinhardts' apartment, Kirsten stood anxiously scanning the street. As they turned the corner, she hurried forward.

'Oh, Jurgen . . . I just heard it on the radio – they say that the Chancellor has resigned!' Then she took in Peter's battered face and bloodstained shirt and the problems of the government were shelved for more immediate concerns.

A taciturn grey-haired doctor who was one of Jurgen's Rosengasse neighbours strapped up Peter's ribs and dealt briskly with his cuts and bruises, asking a few questions about the way in which they had been acquired before he pronounced the injuries to be less severe than his patient's appearance had at first suggested.

'Bed rest, no excitement,' he prescribed prosaically as he replaced rolls of bandage and bottles of liniment methodically in his bag. He snapped the catch shut, saying, 'There will be no charge for my attendance. There are not many who will stand up to those ruffians nowadays. I am honoured to have been of assistance to you.'

Later, as the Reinhardts and their guests sat down to the ruined remains of James Allingham's delayed birthday meal, they heard a staccato stutter of noise from another part of the city.

'That sounded like gunfire,' said Tom, startled. Jurgen left the table abruptly and headed for the telephone, returning frustrated because the lines were jammed with callers as anxious as he was to discover what was happening. But by evening he had managed to contact a few friends and the rumours were crystallizing into facts.

'Those whispers you heard in Berlin were true,' he reported to James. 'The Nazis did attempt a *putsch* – and we actually witnessed part of it, though we didn't realize it at the time. The troops we saw going into the Chancellory this afternoon were an SS regiment, disguised in police and federal army uniforms. Another group took over the radio station in Johannesgasse and broadcast the announcement that Kirsten heard. But it would seem that the situation is under control now. The real police soon recaptured the *Ravag* and once the military had the Ballhausplatz surrounded, the conspirators were induced to give themselves up. Their nominated replacement for Dollfuss, Dr Rintelen, had already disassociated himself from the attempt anyway.'

'So the *putsch* has failed.' James let out a long whistle of relief.

'. . . And everything's all right,' said Laura, hoping that at last her husband might be persuaded to pay attention to his neglected birthday parcels.

'Not quite,' Jurgen told her. 'During the attempt our Chancellor, Engelbert Dollfuss, was shot in the throat. He died at about three forty-five this afternoon.'

The next day, in a city shocked by the murder of its head of government, the Allinghams made arrangements to return to England.

'Thank goodness you came across the border from Germany yesterday. It's closed today, and heaven knows how long it will stay that way. I'll be glad to get away from here,' Laura told James. 'I used to think Vienna was such a lovely city, but it's different now. Dangerous.' She shuddered. 'Just in the short time since we arrived, there's been an attack on Kirsten, and then Jurgen's cousin gets into a fight with a gang of thugs and now there's this business of the Chancellor's assassination . . . The Nazi coup failed, thank goodness, but what if it hadn't?'

'Then Adolf Hitler would have controlled Austria as he controls Germany now,' said James. 'And from what I've witnessed over the past few weeks that's a frightening thought, especially for the Jewish population.'

'Did you know that Kirsten is Jewish?' Laura asked.

'Yes, I did.' Unconsciously, James gnawed at a thumbnail, his brow creased with worry. 'God knows what the end of it will be. I hate to think. We can go home and leave it all behind, darling, but for the Reinhardts – well, this *is* their home. And this *putsch* may have failed, but I don't doubt that the Nazis will try again.'

It was with some relief that the Reinhardts greeted the news that their English guests were about to leave Vienna.

'Next time you come,' said Kirsten, 'we will make you so welcome. Everything will have settled down again and then you will see the *real* Austria,' she added, with more hope than conviction.

'May I say goodbye to Peter Morris before we go?' Harriet asked. She looked hopefully at Laura. 'Of course, I *could* take Caroline in with me . . .'

'No, better not to.' Yesterday, by the time Peter was half-carried into the apartment, Caroline had already been removed to the nursery by her mother – ostensibly to help distract baby Gilda from her teething problems, but in reality to ensure that she wasn't exposed to the sight of blood.

'Caro can stay with me while you go in to Peter,' Laura said, now. 'But don't take too long about it,' she stressed, uncomfortably aware that a regular nanny wouldn't expect to take private leave of a relation of her employers' hosts. A *regular* nanny would know her place and would have remained too discreetly anonymous for such a farewell to be necessary. Laura sighed and regretted, not for the first time, that she had ever taken on Daisy Griffin's untried and unsuitably pretty daughter for such a sensitive occupation.

'I'll come with you,' Tom said, as Harriet rose from her

chair. 'It'll be another chance to admire the wounded hero,' he added, with a flash of sarcasm.

Peter was sitting up in bed, propped against several pillows and reading the day's copy of the *Wiener Zeitung*, when they came into his room. He put down the newspaper, with its black-framed headline announcing the death of Chancellor Dollfuss, and smiled a welcome.

'How are you?' said Harriet.

'I'm almost recovered, as you see.' It wasn't true; above the open neck of his striped pyjamas, the swollen, multi-coloured bruises were still shockingly obvious and when Peter gestured his visitors towards the chairs beside the bed, he did so with a caution that suggested it hurt him to move too abruptly. 'Kirsten is making a fuss about it, but I hope I'll be able to join you for supper this evening.'

'We won't be here. We've come to say goodbye – we're starting for England today,' Harriet told him.

Peter's smile faded. 'I am sorry to hear that,' he said, with unmistakeable sincerity. 'What I mean is, I expect you're looking forward to going home, but I'm sorry I shan't have a chance to get to know you better.'

Harriet wanted to tell him that she felt the same, and to say how much she admired him for going to the defence of the old man in Michaelerplatz but she found it difficult to do so with Tom glowering silently in the background, so she stammered and made a mess of it; and told herself afterwards that it didn't matter if Jurgen's cousin thought she was a tongue-tied fool of a girl, because she wasn't ever likely to see him again anyway.

The Orient Express, emblazoned with the sign of the *Compagnie Internationale de Wagons-Lits*, powered its way across Europe. In one of the sleeping compartments, Harriet entertained Caroline with interminable stories and card games and sessions of 'I Spy'. In another, the Allinghams were closeted; emerging only for meals, when they remained absorbed in each other's company. For Laura, it seemed the old adage that 'Absence makes the heart grow fonder' had proved true, and now she was intent on recapturing the lost emotions of her marriage.

Harriet was glad for James, who seemed delighted if bewildered by his wife's newly demonstrative behaviour, but she was less happy about the conduct of Tom Searle. On the outward journey he had been instrumental in keeping Caroline cheerful and occupied, and Harriet had been counting on his company going home. Instead Tom, like the Allinghams, stayed in his compartment and at supper in the dining car, she was miserably aware of his silence. When their eyes met, he looked quickly away.

After supper, when Caroline had finally drifted off to sleep in her converted bed, Harriet came out into the corridor illuminated by bulbs behind glass shades, their glow reflected in the polished panes of the windows. She stood for a while, leaning against the closed door of her compartment, her legs automatically braced to accommodate the swaying motion of the train. Outside in the blackness of the night, unknown countryside flashed by.

What was happening with Tom? Until the trip to Vienna, whenever they met he had shown an obvious interest in her. She hadn't taken it seriously at first, reminding herself that in Vera's words, 'Those young gentlemen, they'll say one thing and mean another.' Besides, with the memory of Gavin Draycott still fresh in her mind, Tom's attentions had seemed more of a nuisance than a compliment. But in Vienna, she had begun to know him, and almost against her will, to like him. There had been *something* between them . . . some feeling, hard to pin down but persistently present, which she had acknowledged, without knowing how to deal with it. Now it had gone. And she minded.

Further down the coach a door opened and Tom stepped out into the corridor. He had already turned to close the door behind him by the time he noticed Harriet and his first instinctive move to reopen it was a wounding confirmation that he wanted to avoid her.

'Tom. Don't go,' she called quickly. 'I want to ask you something.'

Tom stood with his hand on the jamb of the half-open door, face turned towards her, his expression distinctly unfriendly.

Harriet walked down the corridor towards him, feeling even as she did so that his refusal to approach was deliberate, an exercise in power to see if she could be made to go to him. Resentment of the gambit brought a sharp note into her voice.

'What's the matter with you, Tom? You've been in such a bad mood, ever since the Spanish Riding School.'

'Have I?'

'Do you mind that it was Peter Morris who intervened with those Nazis, and not you?'

'Of course I mind!' Tom's explosive reaction took her by surprise. 'Wouldn't any man with a scrap of pride mind being packed off to safety with the women and children while someone else takes on a mob of bully boys single-handed?'

'But you wouldn't have been much help anyway,' said Harriet, and realized too late that it was the wrong thing to say.

'Morris was of the same opinion, as I recall. Well, when you're set on making a martyr of yourself, a one-handed deputy *would* be a bit of a liability. It would dilute the glory, wouldn't it?'

'Peter didn't do what he did for glory, he did it because as he said, there are some things you can't walk away from.'

'Only I did,' said Tom.

'You couldn't help being injured at the time.'

'Don't be so bloody patronizing. Having both his hands didn't save Morris from getting smashed up, did it? I could have taken half of it, if I'd had the nerve to stand beside him. I should have stayed,' Tom declared passionately. 'I should have damn well stayed, and you know it. And I know it. And *everyone* knows it. But I ran away . . . and it's too bloody late now, isn't it?'

'Tom, nobody thinks the worse of you for it.'

'Don't they? Don't *you*? I saw the way you looked at him

back in Vienna – and gushed at him for being so *frightfully* brave.' Tom flung the words at her. 'And I saw the way he looked at you, too,' he added sourly.

'You're jealous!' Harriet realized.

'Oh, well *spotted*,' said Tom, on a gust of rage. Without warning he hooked his undamaged hand behind her head and kissed her, his hand tangling in her hair. There was nothing gentle about the kiss.

'One thing – if those krauts had knocked *my* mouth about, I couldn't have done that,' he said, releasing her suddenly. In the dim lamplight, his eyes seemed almost black with an anger which might have been directed either at Harriet or against himself. 'So there are some consolation prizes for cowards after all!'

He hauled open the door to his compartment and retreated inside it, leaving Harriet standing in the corridor, her mouth and her emotions bruised by his assault.

She stood there for a minute, wondering what to do. His door remained closed and although she knew that sooner or later this situation with Tom would have to be dealt with, Harriet lacked the nerve to confront it now. She walked slowly back towards her own compartment and as she did so, she thought she saw the handle of the Allinghams' door move very slightly, as if it was being surreptitiously closed. But when she looked again the movement had ceased and she couldn't be sure if she had imagined it.

'I don't know what to do about Harriet,' Laura told James, in the maple-veneered splendour of their carriage. 'Tom swore there was nothing between them or I would never have brought them both on this journey. But there is – I should have trusted my instincts. Just now he was kissing her out there in the corridor.'

'People do funny things on trains,' said James. 'It's being away from home, I suppose. It frees the inhibitions.' Having profited lately from the freeing of Laura's inhibitions, he felt a certain generosity towards Tom and Harriet. 'I

273

expect they'll settle down once they get home,' he added soothingly.

But Laura refused to be soothed. 'It's so irresponsible of Tom. He doesn't pay any attention to social distinctions, he's picked up all these impractical ideas from the people he mixes with, and he hasn't really thought about the consequences. You know he was involved with one of those society girls who goes around with the racing crowd? It was never intended to end in marriage, according to Marion. They parted last year and I suppose he's ready for a replacement now. I daresay he wouldn't think twice about having an affair with someone who's his social inferior – which is all very well for him and his friends,' Laura said with asperity, 'but a girl in Harriet's situation can't afford to be that modern. And I don't want to be responsible for her reputation. And besides, I'm not sure she's the proper person to look after Caro.'

'Why not?'

'She lets her run wild.'

'Caro seems very happy with her, though,' said James. 'Anyway, there's nothing you can do about it on a train in the middle of Europe, so let's deal with it when we get home, shall we?' He reached out and pulled his wife closer and Laura allowed him to distract her because she didn't know how to voice her secret fear, which was that Caroline might be falling too much under the influence of her lively and sympathetic young nanny at the expense of the attachment to her own mother.

Amid the pile of correspondence awaiting Laura's attention on her return to Kew, there was one particularly disquieting letter.

Please forgive a total stranger for writing to you, but I thought you should know that the young woman you have hired to look after your daughter is not a fit person to have such a responsibility. She and my daughter's nanny encouraged their charges in some very silly,

*uncontrolled games in Kew Gardens and as a result
my daughter was badly injured in an accident and may
have been permanently disfigured. Indeed, it is lucky
that she wasn't killed. Naturally I have dismissed the
young woman responsible for the incident from my
employment and I would strongly advise you to do the
same with your nanny, if you care at all about the safety
of your child.*

Coming on top of Laura's existing reservations about
Harriet, this warning from Vera Birkett's former employer
was the last straw. She steeled herself for an unpleasant
interview.

'I'm sorry, Harriet, but I'm going to have to let you
go.'

On the Orient Express, in the aftermath of the kiss which
had taken both of them by surprise, Tom had made a
resolution to avoid Harriet Griffin like the plague for the
foreseeable future. He had been strongly attracted to her
from first acquaintance, but when he thought about the
situation seriously, it wouldn't do.

She was a farmer's daughter. Despite the veneer of
sophistication that a few months of living with her London
aunt had given her, she was still basically a country girl,
too soaked in the moral standards of her upbringing to be a
sensible marriage prospect for someone from his background
– not that he had the slightest intention of getting married,
however suitable the candidate. Among the young people
of his set, you didn't get married these days. That was
bourgeois. You had a love affair, you had fun together and
when it was over, you went your separate ways.

He suspected that such an arrangement wouldn't appeal
to the Griffin girl from Welcome Farm . . . but there was
something about Harriet, something to do with her spirit as
well as her undeniable physical attractions, that kept him
awake at night, and if he wasn't very careful he'd get himself
into something deeper than he intended. Better to stay away

from her and stick to the barest civilities when her company was unavoidable.

For the remainder of the journey home he had kept to his decision; but today, when he met her as she climbed the stairs, she had looked so thoroughly miserable that he had found himself asking her what was the matter.

'I've got the sack,' Harriet told him bleakly. So now here she was, sitting on the bed in his room, sniffing hard and dashing tears of humiliation from her cheeks with the heel of one hand, while he rooted through his chest of drawers in search of a clean handkerchief.

'I'll talk to Laura,' Tom said. 'I'll explain that accident in Kew Gardens wasn't your fault.'

'I don't think it would do any good. Laura was already thinking I'd have to leave because she saw you kissing me on the train. She said she'd had your assurance before we left England that nothing like that would occur, but now that it has, she doesn't want to be responsible for anything else that might happen. I told her it was just the one kiss, it was just a passing impulse that you had and there really wasn't anything going on between us, but she didn't believe me. And if you try to persuade her to let me stay, it'll only make her more convinced that she was right.'

Tom ruffled a hand through his hair, trying to think straight. In the first place, it seemed he was at least partly responsible for Harriet's dismissal. In the second place, although he had intended to go back to the Cobham team and immerse himself in work and flying to forget her, he had meant to do it at the moment of his own choosing. The news that she was going so soon and so suddenly had caught him off balance and it hurt.

'So what will you do?' he asked, after a pause.

'Go back to Welcome Farm, I suppose.'

'Do you want to?'

'It's the last thing I want, but what else can I do?'

'Hang on, let me think . . .' Tom searched his brain for solutions. 'I suppose you could come back with me to Maple

Grange. My mother might be prepared to let you stay for a bit.'

'That's hardly likely, is it, after Laura's sent me packing? What would she think, anyway, if you asked her to take me in? She'd come to exactly the same conclusion as Laura, that you and I were involved in some way. And we're not, are we?' Harriet said.

It was a direct question. Tom hesitated. He wanted to kiss her again. He knew he shouldn't, because it would complicate matters even more than they were already complicated, but he could imagine the warmth of Harriet in his arms so clearly and the way that the tears drying on her cheeks would taste of salt.

'No,' he said, with an effort. 'You're right, that kiss was just a passing impulse.'

'I'd better get on with packing my things, then.'

'Hang on a minute . . . I'm supposed to be going back to the Cobham tour in a couple of weeks – they'll be at Winchester on the sixteenth of August and I've written to say I'll join them there. But while I'm in Seale I'll ask my mother if she knows of anyone who wants a nanny. With any luck she needn't know about what's happened here and I can persuade her to give you a personal recommendation. If I come up with anything, I'll get a message to you at the farm.'

'Thank you,' said Harriet stiffly. 'And now, I really must go and pack.'

'Cheer up,' Tom said as she was leaving. To make her smile, he tried a joke. 'If all else fails, you could always run away with me and join the Flying Circus!'

An hour later, when Tom knocked at the door of her room on the top floor, there was no answer. He ran down to the kitchen to quiz the housekeeper.

'Harriet? Packed her bags and gone, she has, all in a rush. Needed at home, Mrs Allingham says, and she won't be back. Young Caroline's taking on something awful.'

Tom swore softly under his breath, then shrugged. Harriet's headlong departure without saying goodbye was

277

frustrating, but it was another example of the spirit he admired in her. And to apply common sense, it was no bad thing that she'd gone. For a minute back there, he'd been perilously close to losing his head and saying something he might regret.

18

At Welcome Farm, Daisy tipped the telegram delivery boy sixpence and tore open the envelope. Telegrams were rare, and to receive one still gave her a momentary sick feeling which was a legacy of the days of the Great War, when they had so often carried the worst possible news. She scanned the form rapidly before carrying it back to the kitchen table, where Will was finishing his breakfast.

'What do you make of this?'

Will glanced at the telegram. *Have left Allinghams. Arriving Bentley 3.15 p.m. today. Harriet.*

'She's coming home,' he said. 'That's good news, isn't it?'

'But it's so brief,' Daisy worried. 'And for her to be coming back so suddenly, without any warning . . . You'd think she'd have put in a bit about why she's left, wouldn't you?'

'I expect she was economizing on the telegram,' Will commented practically. 'Anyway, we'll find out the details when she gets here. The important thing is, she's coming. I can't go to the station, worst luck,' he added. 'The fellow from the Milk Marketing Board's coming this afternoon to check us over before he renews our "tuberculin tested" certificate. But I'll send Jem down to the station with Joseph and the trap to meet her.'

'Do you think you should, Will?' Daisy looked dubious. 'Jem's not had that many lessons at driving the trap.'

'Oh, he'll manage. Like he said when he came, he picks things up quick enough for a townie. Anyway, Joseph's as safe as houses. I reckon if you sent him down by himself, he'd come back with Harriet, right enough.'

Joseph was the good-tempered grey gelding on whose back the Griffin children had first learned to ride. Nowadays he spent most of his time grazing peacefully in the paddock near the house, but Will used him occasionally for tasks which were mechanized on wealthier farms. It was Joseph who had plodded round in patient circles last autumn, harnessed to the geared bar which drove the hay elevator, or pulled the swath turner through the mown hay to turn and aerate it after it was cut.

Will had bought the trap at an auction in the spring and he and Rob and Jackie had spent a few hours cleaning it up and replacing the woodworm-infested bench seat. Daisy had made a new cushion for the seat and sometimes she and Will took the trap down to Bentley Church on a Sunday, where Joseph could be trusted to stand outside, reins knotted on his neck, for the duration of the service.

There was nothing that even a novice driver like Jem could do that would make Joseph unsafe, Will reasoned . . . and Harriet would enjoy a ride home in the trap. She would be able to smell the wild honeysuckle in the hedgerows that fringed the lane. Will hoped that by now she'd have got over her distress at discovering that he wasn't her real father and be ready to settle down again at Welcome Farm. Real father or not, he'd missed her.

Daisy was washing up dishes at the stone sink when Kitty arrived from Starling Cottages.

'I'm sorry I'm late, Mrs Griffin. I didn't feel too well, first thing.'

Daisy had meant to ask Kitty to make up the bed in the top floor room for Harriet, but the girl's face was waxy pale and having put down the basket she carried, she was holding on to the edge of the table to steady herself. Daisy shelved thoughts of her daughter's return in order to deal with more immediate concerns and guided Kitty to a chair.

'You don't look too good now, either. What is it, Kitty?'

'I don't know. But oh, I do feel peculiar.'

In the past, Kitty feeling 'peculiar' had coincided with

the appearance of bruises which she didn't explain and which Daisy had stopped asking about; but today there was no such evidence of what Daisy strongly suspected to be Jem Wilkins' brutal treatment. Kitty leaned forward across the kitchen table, eyes closed, one hand pressed to her mouth. Her face was dewed with perspiration. An explanation born of personal experience occurred to Daisy.

'Kitty . . . you don't think you might be pregnant?'

'Oh, *no*, Mrs Griffin . . .'

But Kitty's moan of distress was answer enough.

Jem hummed softly to himself as he tacked up Joseph and backed him between the shafts of the trap. He knew the grey gelding went well for him and he looked forward to showing off his new skill to Harriet Griffin – not that she'd give him much credit for it, the uppity bitch.

He could still remember the way she'd looked at him at the end of their last encounter – as if he was something that had just crawled out from under a stone. All the same, he reckoned the blood in her veins didn't run as icy as she tried to make out – not judging by the way she'd switched on at first, when he'd kissed her. And he'd had his own back on her with that bit of news about her origins. That had shaken her up good and proper. It had also sent her away from the farm, which had felt like a kick in the guts at the time . . . but now she was coming back.

It wasn't until he led Joseph out of the stable yard and into the lane that he noticed the horse was lame in his off hind leg, putting it gingerly to the ground with every step. When he bent to examine the offending hock, Jem found it was hot and puffy to his touch. Joseph currently shared a paddock near the farmhouse with the black mare Briony, who had a temper that matched Harriet Griffin's, and it wasn't hard to guess how the gelding had come by a swollen hock.

Will and Daisy were in the dairy with the man from the Milk Marketing Board and wouldn't welcome an interruption. Harriet was due to arrive at Bentley at a quarter

281

past three. Jem reviewed his options. He could take the car, but his lessons in driving a car were at a far more rudimentary stage than his lessons in driving a horse. He could leave Harriet to walk home by herself – or he could take Briony instead of Joseph.

The black mare's owner had lately requested that she should be broken to harness – perhaps as a way of postponing her return to his stables and the moment of truth for her less-than-confident rider. Will and Rob had reported that, so far, Briony was resisting the experience with some determination, but was gradually settling down to it. And if a mere lad like Rob Griffin could manage her, Jem told himself, then so could Jem Wilkins.

He led Joseph back to the paddock. Briony proved surprisingly easy to catch – curiosity brought her to his call and she let him slip a halter on her without much fuss. In the stable yard she played up a bit when he laid the padded collar on her, but he managed to get her harnessed up to the trap and drove out of the farmyard.

She fought him hard all the way to Bentley, so he had to hold her to a skittering semblance of a walk rather than risk letting her break into anything faster, and by the time he arrived within sight of the station the London train had come and gone. Harriet was stalking along the lane, lugging a suitcase and looking put out because no-one had come to meet her.

'Hullo,' he said, dragging Briony to a halt. 'I'm your transport.'

'Oh.' Harriet scowled ungraciously up at him. 'I was expecting my father.'

'Oh, you mean Will?' Jem clarified the point deliberately. 'He couldn't come, he's too busy, so he sent me instead. Hop in.'

After a moment of hesitation, Harriet heaved her suitcase over the tailboard of the trap and climbed up beside him. At the change of weight behind her, Briony threw up her head and capered on the spot, her eyes rolling backwards.

'Are you sure you're safe with this animal?' Harriet asked, eyebrows lifting.

'Safe enough.' But Jem's shirt was damp with sweat and it wasn't just from the physical effort of holding in the black mare. In truth, she was more of a handful than he'd anticipated, and he would be glad to get back in one piece. 'Why, are you nervous?' he jibed.

'Not of Briony,' said Harriet, arranging her skirts. They progressed along the lane in a series of fits and starts.

'Enjoy yourself in London?' Jem enquired.

'Not particularly.'

'Missed us, did you?'

'No.'

'I'll say this, it hasn't been the same here without you.' Jem glanced sideways and noted with satisfaction that Harriet was looking flushed and self-conscious. At least he still had the power to shake her up. He was wondering how best to exploit it when he heard the sound of a revved car engine. A few seconds later a yellow motor with bright red mudguards shot into sight round a bend in the road.

Harriet registered two things in rapid succession: firstly that the driver of the yellow car was Gavin Draycott and secondly that on the narrow Hampshire lane there wasn't room for the car to pass the trap comfortably. There was a squeal of brakes and Gavin pumped furiously at his horn. Briony jerked her head up and plunged sideways onto the grass verge, dragging an extra foot of rein through Jem's fingers. As the car shaved past, she took off down the lane at a gallop, hauling the bouncing trap behind her.

Jem, sawing ineffectively at the reins, made the discovery that when Briony had the bit between her teeth, his own wiry strength counted for nothing. Beside him, after her first stifled exclamation, Harriet hung on grimly with both hands to the bench seat. At the open gateway to the farmyard the mare turned without slackening her speed and the trap, crossing at an angle behind her, hit the gatepost.

The collision brought horse and trap down, catapulting its passengers into the dust of the yard.

Briony rolled and snorted and managed to get upright. She stood trembling, head hanging, thoroughly frightened by her own performance. Harriet lay still for a few seconds, shocked and winded. Then Jem knelt above her, the sun overhead creating a halo of light behind his head and shoulders.

'You all right?' he said.

'If I am, it's no thanks to you.' Harriet struggled into a sitting position and tested her limbs for possible fractures.

'It wasn't my fault,' Jem said. 'It was your fancy man from Hallows in that yellow car that started Briony off.'

His eyes travelled downwards. The skirt of Harriet's cotton dress was skewed upwards and twin grazes oozed blood amid the dirt on her knees. Flushing, she moved to tug down the skirt but Jem beat her to it, stroking a fingertip, light as thistledown, along one bare thigh.

'Nice legs you've got. Even if they are a bit the worse for wear,' he said, and grinned his lopsided grin as he heard her gasp and saw her shiver at his touch. He uncoiled himself and strolled towards the overturned trap to unharness Briony from the broken shafts.

'Anyway,' he added over his shoulder, 'I thought you might like a bit of excitement, to welcome you home.'

The inspector from the Milk Marketing Board paused in the middle of a one-sided conversation with Will about the comparative milk yields of Friesians, Jerseys and Short-horns, to announce to Daisy that he didn't half fancy a cup of tea.

'I'll go and put the kettle on,' said Daisy, but behind his back she pulled an expressive face at Will. The inspector had the gift of the gab and Will was doing nothing to discourage him, and it was four o'clock. Harriet must have arrived by now and Daisy was longing to go in search of her daughter and give her a welcome-home hug and a kiss, to get things started off on the right footing this time. But when Daisy came into the kitchen, Harriet was sitting on a chair by the kitchen table, swabbing blood and dirt from her knees with cotton wool dipped in a bowl of disinfectant.

'Oh, Harry, whatever's happened to you?' Daisy's heart sank, as much at Harriet's thunderous expression as at the evidence of a mishap.

'That idiot Jem Wilkins managed to overturn the trap,' Harriet said. She dunked her blood-soaked cotton wool into the enamel bowl and the cloudy water became tinged with pink. 'I got a few grazes, that's all. For heaven's sake, don't fuss about it.'

'Oh dear, I knew Will shouldn't have sent Jem to fetch you,' Daisy said, 'but he said even a novice driver like Jem would be safe with Joseph.'

'It wasn't Joseph, it was Briony.'

'*Briony?* Jem drove *Briony*?'

'Why not?' said Harriet with unmistakeable bitterness. 'I gather Will was far too busy to come himself.'

'He would have done, love, he really wanted to. But the man from the Milk Marketing Board was here and your dad – and Will *had* to see him,' Daisy corrected herself. 'And I'm supposed to be making him a cup of tea,' she remembered, distractedly.

'You'd better get on with the *important* things, then. I'll get out of your way.' Harriet picked up the bowl and limped towards the door which led into the hall. Daisy wanted to follow her but she could hear the voices of Will and the inspector coming in from the dairy, and after a moment of helpless indecision, she supposed she had better make the wretched man his cup of tea and be done with it.

'Where's Harry?' Will asked, when the official had gone at last.

'Upstairs,' Daisy told him.

'How'd she seem?'

Daisy's distress over the encounter with Harriet resurfaced. 'Oh, Will,' she said, 'things are just as bad as before. She hasn't got over it at all.'

In her attic bedroom, Harriet sat on her bed and stared at the wall. The bed had been stripped of sheets and blankets when she went away and apparently nobody had been bothered enough about her return to make it up in anticipation. There was dust on the chest of drawers. The pot pourri in the bowl on the windowsill was bleached colourless by sunlight and had long since lost its scent. The room with its sloping eaves seemed smaller than she remembered, and in the heat of late July it was stifling.

Perversely, she elected not to open the window. In her current mood she wanted everything to be as bad as possible, because it couldn't ever go back to being the way it was, before Jem Wilkins had told her that Will Griffin wasn't her father.

Last winter, as part of her timid early efforts to make a home for Jem, Kitty had cleared a patch of earth behind Starling Cottages for a vegetable garden. In the spring she had planted the seed for runner beans and peas and rows of lettuce because it seemed a shame to waste the raked soil, but by then she had already discovered that Jem didn't care about having a home made for him and, indeed, didn't care about Kitty either. Although he continued to climb on top of her in the creaking iron-framed bedstead whenever he felt that way inclined, he had given up kissing her on the mouth or calling her 'Kitten', or any of the other small signs of tenderness that had at first been some compensation for his harsher moments.

He didn't say anything and Kitty had never dared to ask, but her intuition told her that his loss of interest was partly to do with Harriet Griffin. There had been a tension between the two of them that was clearly visible to Kitty, and it had been a relief when Harriet went away. It didn't make Jem any kinder, but it did release Kitty from the pain of having to watch him watching Harriet.

Ironically the vegetable garden had flourished, though its produce was not really needed. Daisy Griffin was prepared to cook for the farm workers as well as for her family, so most of Kitty's vegetables went to join the already ample store in the farmhouse larder, but she kept on tending the vegetable patch because she couldn't bring herself to let the plants die.

Today, after her bout of sickness in the morning, Kitty had unexpectedly been given the day off. At first she had felt so poorly that she had wondered whether she would even manage to reach Starling Cottages, but by late afternoon she was feeling better. She considered returning to work, but after all, Mrs Griffin had sent her home to rest without attaching any conditions; so instead she washed the windows, blacked the stove and scrubbed down the pine table in the little kitchen, then ironed one of Jem's two shirts, wishing that he was the sort of man who appreciated such things. By early evening the house was thoroughly clean and Kitty went out to hoe the vegetable garden.

'You've got green fingers. Those runners are coming on a treat.'

Billy Marshall had appeared at the back door of his cottage and stood watching her. Kitty straightened up and pushed a strand of hair back from her face.

'Oh, you've finished work. I didn't realize it was so late.'

'It isn't,' Billy said. 'I'm early. Mr Griffin said I could knock off because he and Mrs Griffin wanted the family to have supper tonight by themselves, on account of Harriet coming home.'

'Harriet?' Kitty echoed. 'Oh.' A spasm of apprehension crossed her face, and was erased. 'Is Jem on his way, do you know?'

'I couldn't say,' said Billy. He hesitated, then added, 'He finished the same time as me, but I think he might have gone down to the Red Lion in Bentley.'

Silently, Kitty propped her hoe against the wall of the cottage and scooped an old tin watering can into the butt of rainwater beside the back door. She started to lug the brimming can towards the neat row of plants which were trained on wire stretched between two upright canes, with their scarlet flowers that would soon be runner beans.

'Here. Let me.' Billy's left hand closed on the handle of the can beside hers, taking on the weight of it. Kitty was

287

too surprised to argue. He'd changed a lot since he'd come to Welcome Farm, she thought, watching him as he watered the beans. When he'd first appeared he'd looked half-starved and thoroughly down on his luck, but a few months of Mrs Griffin's good dinners had restored his health and his optimism. Now, although nothing could give him back the use of his dead arm, he was at least recognizable as the Billy of the photograph on his mantelpiece.

'What'll you do about supper, if you aren't having it up at the farmhouse?' she asked, when he came back to her side with the empty watering can.

'Oh, Mrs Griffin gave me a parcel of cold chicken and some tomatoes to bring home with me. There'd be plenty for you, too, I should think,' Billy said. 'Hang on a moment and I'll bring some out, if you like.'

'I've got a better idea,' Kitty found herself saying. 'Why don't you come and have supper with me? I could easily do a salad – those lettuces are going to waste with no-one to eat them.'

Harriet's unexpected return to Welcome Farm was a problem in more ways than one.

'What work do you want me to do?' she asked Daisy over supper.

'I don't know . . .' Daisy and Will exchanged glances. Once, Harriet had been almost indispensable, but after nearly half a year of doing without her, things were different. Last week another worker would have been more than useful, but now haymaking was over and for the time being Will and Jem were coping with the farm work. Billy Marshall, who had looked like being such a liability when he arrived, could turn his one good hand to a surprising variety of jobs. Rob saw to Briony and helped with the milking; Jackie had his rota of tasks and as far as housework was concerned, with Allie and Kitty to help her, Daisy had never been so spoiled. Offhand, there wasn't anything for Harriet to do at this precise stage that wouldn't involve taking the work away from someone else who was already geared to doing it.

'Why don't you have a little holiday,' Will suggested, 'till I start cutting the wheat -- that'll probably be next week some time. Give yourself a chance to get settled in again.'

He had meant it kindly but Harriet, watching his face, understood that she wasn't needed. 'I'll go to bed now, if that's all right with you,' she said abruptly, pushing her plate of cottage pie away almost untouched.

'Your bed's not made yet,' Daisy remembered, half-rising from the table. 'I'll get you some sheets and things.'

'I can manage. I did live here once, remember?' said Harriet.

When it was closing time at the Red Lion, Jem made his way back along the lane from Bentley. Usually he could hold his drink better than most, but tonight his walk was unsteady. He'd had an uncomfortable interview with Will Griffin at the end of the afternoon, in which he'd been informed bluntly of Will's displeasure over the incident with Briony and the trap, and he'd awarded himself an extra few pints of beer to wipe out the memory.

At Number One, Starling Cottages, the curtains were still undrawn in the little living room, but there was a light showing through from the open doorway of the kitchen beyond. The neighbouring cottage was in darkness. He soon discovered why.

Billy Marshall and Kitty sat facing one another across the remains of a meal on the kitchen table, with the lamp between them. They were laughing at some shared joke and the sight of Kitty being happy with another man was offensive to Jem. He stood on the threshold, waiting till the two of them had had time to take in his hostile expression. The laughter died abruptly.

'Time you were in your own place I reckon, Marshall.' Jem jerked a thumb in the direction of the party wall. Billy stood up obediently, then hesitated, looking at Kitty.

'Will you be all right?' he asked. She nodded mutely.

'I'll be getting along, then.'

As soon as Billy had gone, Jem stumbled up the narrow stairs to bed. When Kitty followed a few minutes later, after tidying away the debris of her supper, he was asleep, sprawled fully clothed on the bed.

Carefully, she removed his boots and unbuckled his belt, but she was afraid to undress him further in case he woke up. All day long, ever since Daisy's guess had reinforced her own fears, Kitty had been wondering how to tell Jem that he was going to be a father. The unexpected pleasure of the evening spent in Billy's company had put it out of her mind. Now, as she looked at Jem's flushed face and listened to his drink-drugged breathing, she thanked her merciful stars that she had been able to postpone the announcement for the time being.

'I heard you were back,' Allie Briggs told Harriet the next morning, bustling into the kitchen at Welcome Farm. 'I met that Gavin Draycott down the lane just now. He asked me about you, were you all right and so on. Mind you, he's quite often stopped me to ask questions about you, since you went away.'

'And of course you told him you couldn't possibly answer them,' Harriet said sarcastically. Undeterred, Allie glanced around to check that they were alone, then lowered her voice conspiratorially.

'He said I was to tell you he wants to have a word with you. He's out there down the lane now, waiting.'

'If he has anything to say to me,' said Harriet, 'he can come here, to the farm.'

'He said you'd understand why he can't. Go on, Harriet, at least see what he wants. He seemed quite anxious. If you ask me, he's still a bit sweet on you.'

'I don't ask you,' Harriet snapped, flushing to the roots of her red hair. If Allie was a party to the knowledge that Gavin Draycott had once been 'sweet' on her, what else did she know?

'So you won't talk to him?' Allie asked, disappointed.

'Don't you have anything better to do than minding other

people's business, Allie? I thought this was your day for polishing in the parlour.'

But when the home help had been safely distracted, Harriet ran upstairs to brush her hair and check in the mirror that her flower-patterned green dress concealed her scarred knees, before walking out to the lane.

Gavin Draycott was leaning against the side of his Austin Swallow in a pose that reminded her powerfully of last autumn's surreptitious meetings by the crossroads. His face lit up at the sight of her and she realized that there had been some truth in Allie's comment. He *was* still sweet on her . . . or at least, for the moment he was feeling inclined to revive an old flame.

'Harriet! It's good to see you.' Gavin unpropped himself from the Swallow and advanced towards her with his arms extended, smiling a welcome.

'*Don't*, Gavin.'

He had been about to hug her, but her tone made him check the gesture. His hands fell to his sides.

'I wanted to make sure you were all right,' he said, with a new uncertainty. 'By the time I realized it was you in that trap yesterday, you'd gone.'

'I didn't have much choice about it,' Harriet pointed out, 'since Briony was bolting at the time.'

'Oh, yes. Briony. I seem to remember that mare from the blacksmith's forge last autumn. She's a bit on the wild side, isn't she?'

'She's not used to road-hog drivers.'

Gavin opened his mouth to refute the charge and thought better of it. He cleared his throat and produced a smile. 'Well, I can't tell you how glad I am to find that you're still in one piece. As a matter of fact, you look terrific.'

The smile, and the tone, were too practised to be convincing. *He used to remind me of a Greek hero*, Harriet thought. Now the only myth that came to mind was that of Narcissus, besotted by his own beauty. It was a liberating discovery.

'I've missed you, Harriet,' he was saying. 'I know we didn't part on the best of terms . . .'

'No, we didn't,' Harriet agreed pleasantly. 'But that was ages ago, wasn't it? It hardly seems worth talking about now.'

'. . . But I haven't been able to forget the way things were between us, have you?' Gavin persisted, his voice husky.

'Yes, actually. I have.' Harriet saw the smile freeze on his handsome face and felt an unworthy exultation. 'I was very young and very silly and I know better now. Was there anything particular you wanted to talk about, Gavin? No? Well then, I must be going. Things to do, you know.' She held out her hand and Gavin took it dazedly. *Poor Narcissus*, she thought. *He isn't used to rejection.* 'It's been *so* nice seeing you, Gavin,' she continued briskly, in her best London-with-Aunt-Louella voice. 'Perhaps we'll run into each other again.'

Whatever else in her life might be less than perfect at the moment, Harriet told herself as she watched him driving away down the lane towards Hallows, at least she was well and truly cured of her infatuation for Gavin Draycott . . . and she had just had the very considerable satisfaction of letting him know it.

'Nicely done. You certainly told *him* where to get off.'

Standing just inside the farmyard gate, half-hidden by the drooping branches of the apple tree, Jem Wilkins clapped his hands in an ironic gesture of applause. Harriet flushed crimson, and her moment of triumph lost its savour.

'Oh, leave me alone!' she snapped. Jem didn't move.

'Is that what you really want?' he said, softly. 'Or is it something else altogether? Think about it, my lady Harriet.'

What is it about me? Harriet asked herself as she stalked moodily towards the kitchen door. The *femme fatale* who could make Gavin Draycott rue the day that he had dropped her was just an illusion. The reality was that Gavin had cancelled her after a few weeks of furtive fumblings in his hideously uncomfortable little yellow car, and today's encounter couldn't wipe out the memory of his parting words last year. Then there was Tom Searle, who had flattered her and flirted with her, but had followed up his kiss by admitting that it had only been a passing impulse. *Other* girls were courted properly by young men who loved them. In due course they got engaged, with proud announcements from their parents in the newspapers, and then married in church with pomp and ceremony. But not Harriet. Was her bastard status so very obvious? Did it somehow label her as a mere plaything, to be dropped as soon as you were tired of the game? It was a humiliating thought.

As for Jem Wilkins, his interest was crude and confined to her body. He was her father's employee, he belonged to Kitty, and even if he was the most desirable man in the world – which he wasn't, Harriet told herself furiously – he had no right whatsoever to behave as he had done. But at least his conduct had a sort of honesty to it. He didn't tell her any lies about 'love'.

19

By the second week in August there was still no word from Tom Searle about alternative nannying jobs and Harriet was getting increasingly desperate.

She felt like an intruder at Welcome Farm. She missed the Allingham household, the companionship of the staff sitting room and the daily walks in Kew Gardens with Caroline. She tried to avoid Will as much as possible because she didn't know what to call him: 'Dad' was unthinkable, but nothing else seemed right either. The conviction of having been betrayed by Daisy's silence over the unknown man who had been her natural father was no less strong than it had been all those months ago, when she had fled to Kew with Laura Allingham.

To add to her emotional turmoil, Jem Wilkins seemed to be forever lurking in the background, his watchful eyes missing nothing. Harriet didn't know what to do about Jem. She kept telling herself that he disgusted her but she was haunted by the sense of his presence. He seemed to represent something that was as alluring as it was abhorrent. Behind his crooked smile lay all the secrets of sex that she had barely begun to explore with Gavin Draycott, and at which she had apparently failed so miserably that Gavin had abandoned her. Nor, she recalled with shame, had Tom Searle seemed particularly impressed by their one embrace. He certainly hadn't attempted to repeat it.

At night, lying in her attic room with the window open to let in the cool air, she found herself fantasizing about Jem, conjuring up scenes in which he found her alone and forced his kisses on her. Increasingly she let these imaginary scenes progress further and further along the paths of intimacy. Once or twice she dreamed about him.

Lonely and restless, she would have liked to befriend Kitty, one of the few females of about her own age whom she had come across since leaving school. But the pale girl was guarded and distant and Harriet had the uncomfortable feeling that she knew about Jem's kiss at Starling Cottages back in February, and even about the unsettling effect he was having on Harriet now. No, there could be no friendship with Kitty.

At least once the wheat harvest started, there was work for even Harriet to do, stooking the sheaves after Will had gone round the twenty-acre wheatfield with the tractor binder. Through the blazing days she rediscovered old skills, driving the butt of each foundation sheaf hard into the ground so that the finished stook would stand up against the wind. Her back ached and her town-softened hands were blistered but it could not be denied that she was earning her keep, working like a man alongside Will and Rob . . . and Jem.

'Time for afternoon milking. Rob, can you get the cows in? I'll be along as soon as I can.'

With the cutting of the wheat finished, Will had left his tractor by the gate and joined the trio of Jem, Rob and Harriet to help with the stooking. 'You and Harriet carry on here,' he said to Jem. 'I'd like you to get this field finished by tonight if you can manage it. Rob and I can see to the milking by ourselves for today.'

'All right, guv'nor,' Jem said, looking across at Harriet, who looked away. She didn't want to be left with Jem, even in a wheatfield with work to do. But Will was already climbing onto the tractor and she couldn't think of any way to state her refusal without sounding like a hysterical female. It *was* silly, she told herself, to suppose that she had only to be alone with Jem for him to try to make love to her.

It wasn't. Once the tractor had gone, Jem abandoned his task and stood watching her instead. His eyes dwelt appreciatively on her movements as she stooped to pick up and swing the sheaves into place, her cotton shirt and man's trousers clinging to her body in the heat and her hair darkened at the roots with the sweat that trickled down in rivulets.

'Will you stop staring at me?' she said at last.

'Why? You're worth staring at. I'm enjoying it. Course, there's other things I'd enjoy even more.'

'That's it, Jem, I've had enough!' Harriet dropped a sheaf and confronted him, hands clenched. 'What makes you think you have the right to say things like that to me?'

Jem considered the question. 'It's more a case of *Can I help it?* than *Do I have the right?* A man can't help looking at you. And he can't look at you, Harriet, without wanting to have you. Mind you, some men might not admit it.' He took a step towards her and Harriet backed away.

'Don't come too close, Jem.'

'How close is *too close*?' Jem teased her. 'Is it here?' He moved nearer. 'Or here? Or here?'

The last step brought him within reach. Harriet turned to run but he caught her by the wrist and swung her back towards him. She fell against his chest and his other arm closed round her. His mouth, inches from hers, wore that twisted smile that so alarmed and haunted her.

'You liked this the last time, though you tried to kid me you didn't. Remember?' His free hand caught a handful of her hair and tugged her head back. His mouth descended. Harriet struggled against his grasp but there was no escaping, and by the time he released her wrist to use his hands elsewhere, she was past noticing. One hungry kiss blended into another in a relentless progression. The sky swung dizzily behind his head, the sunlight dazzling her, then she was on her back amid the wheat stubble and Jem was kneeling above her, his hands ripping her shirt open.

This must be what happened to my mother!

The idea came from nowhere, but with it, sense came flooding back. There was something in Jem's expression that gloated over her submission. Daisy's moment of weakness nearly twenty years ago had resulted in a bastard child.

Like mother, like daughter? No, Harriet could not, *would* not go the same way. Once her power to think clearly was restored, she knew what she had to do. She lay still and apparently compliant while Jem spread the edges of her shirt aside and surveyed her half-naked body, then suddenly, viciously, she jerked up a knee.

Jem let out an agonized grunt and toppled sideways, his hands clutching at his groin. Harriet rolled clear and scrambled upright, sprinting for the gate. A pitchfork was leaning against it and by the time Jem was on his feet again, she had hold of it. Jem, lunging for her, his face distorted, was brought up short by two iron prongs prodding at his chest.

'I'll use it if I have to,' panted Harriet.

'Christ! You little spitfire,' said Jem, and a note of reluctant admiration crept into his voice. 'I thought I had you, just then.'

'You didn't,' hissed Harriet. 'And you never will!'

'Won't I? Remember there's things I know about you. How'd you fancy having the whole district talking about you and your respectable family, Harriet Griffin-or-should-I-say-Colindale? Want me to spread the word?'

'That threat's worn out,' said Harriet. 'I'll never let you near me again, whatever you say.' She backed away, still holding the pitchfork aggressively in front of her with one hand while with the other she fumbled behind her for the gate latch. Once safely through and with the gate slammed shut behind her, she jettisoned the pitchfork and took to her heels.

Jem didn't attempt to follow her. Now that his first impulse of rage had ebbed, he was having difficulty in staying on his feet – Harriet's knee-jerk blow hurt more than he had wanted her to know. Grudgingly, he had to acknowledge defeat. He'd counted on being able to overcome her resistance but it hadn't worked . . . and however powerfully he wanted her, he couldn't afford to take on the consequences of an out-and-out rape, not now. He watched her flight with narrowed eyes. She could certainly run.

When Billy Marshall came back to his half of Starling Cottages late in the evening, the kitchen range had been raked out and topped up with coal from the hod on the hearth, and the kettle was filled ready to brew up a cup of tea. So Kitty must have come in earlier. Billy scolded himself for the rush of warmth that the thought provoked. Kitty was a kind girl, the kindest he'd ever met, sweet and slim and pale like a saint from a stained glass window . . . and married to Jem Wilkins, who didn't treat her right. And it was none of his business.

It was growing dark in the kitchen. He lit the oil lamp, holding the box of Vestas steady between his knees while he struck the match. Soon he would have to close the kitchen door or the lamplight would attract moths and midges, but for the time being he was reluctant to lose the scent from the honeysuckle climbing up the wall beside the door. He stretched his one good arm above his head to relax his tired body, considering what was to be done with the precious remaining hour or two of the day. He decided to darn a hole in one of his socks.

He'd been putting it off for a week because it was such a frustratingly slow, fiddly process, but now he took out the little wooden box which held his sewing equipment from the cupboard on one side of the chimney breast. He chose a darning needle from an assortment of needles and pins stuck into a cloth stretched over the top of a tin that contained talcum powder to stop the needles from rusting.

Next, he shook out a length of grey wool from a ball that had been unravelled from an old jumper. He held one end of the wool between his teeth and clamped the ball between his knees while he cut through the wool with a kitchen knife. He dug the sharp end of the needle into a crack in the kitchen table so that it stood upright, moistened the wool between his lips and threaded it, after several bodged attempts, through the eye of the needle. Lastly he inserted his mother's old wooden darning mushroom into the sock, shaking it down into place behind the hole. Gripping the sock tightly between his knees he began to thread the needle in and out round the edge of the hole.

'I could do that for you.'

Kitty stood watching him. Framed in the doorway as she was, her slim fragility reminded him again of a saint from a stained glass window.

'I can manage,' Billy said, embarrassed at having been watched being clumsy in a task which Kitty and anyone with two useful hands could have accomplished with ease.

'I know you can. I know you don't *need* things done for you. I was just being friendly, that's all.' She sounded hurt and Billy mentally cursed himself for being so surly. He wanted to tell her that she already did too much for him, but then that would sound wrong too.

'Jem not home yet?' he asked, because it was the first thing that came to mind.

'No. I expect he's down at the Red Lion again,' Kitty said dispiritedly, then flinched as a large moth swooped through the open doorway, skimming over her head and stirring her hair with its wings. It collided with the heated glass of the lamp and flopped onto the surface of the table, stunned.

Billy stood up quickly and reached for a mug on the draining board behind him.

Kitty clapped a hand to her mouth. 'Don't—' she began to say, but instead of crushing the moth, Billy had inverted the mug over it. One-handed, he was left with the problem of how to scoop up the trapped insect.

'Slide it across the table and I'll put my hand under it,' Kitty said, understanding what was needed without any need for explanation. They moved in unison to the doorway. Inside the mug, the recovered moth fluttered frantically against the palm of Kitty's hand but a moment later Billy had shaken it out into the night.

'Better shut the door,' he said, doing so. 'Or we'll have more of them in.'

'I'm glad you didn't kill it,' Kitty said quietly. They were still standing shoulder to shoulder. The lamplight shone on her straight, silky fall of hair and her blue eyes seemed very dark, the pupils enormous.

'Oh, I don't reckon we've a right to kill things just because they're a different species.' Aware of her nearness, Billy was finding it difficult to keep his voice steady. 'Moths don't do us any harm. Leastways, not until they get at your jumpers.' *Shut up, Marshall*, he berated himself, *unless you can think of something a bit cleverer than that to say to her!*

'Jem stamps on them. He doesn't like moths.'

To Billy's mingled relief and regret, Kitty had moved away as she spoke. At least the increased distance between them restored his capacity to breathe. Her words reminded him of what he had been trying to say before the insect's invasion. 'I don't think Jem'd like it if you help me out too much, either,' he said.

'I suppose you're right.' Kitty sighed. 'Not that *he* wants anything from me,' she added, with an unexpected flash of bitterness. 'He just doesn't want anyone else to have it, either.' She lifted her head and her voice became stronger. 'Well, Jem doesn't own me. If you want your socks darned, or anything else done around the house, I'd be glad to come in and help. He needn't know, if that worries you. But if you want to be left alone, just say so.' She faced him directly. '*Do* you want to be left alone?'

'No,' said Billy. 'It's very kind of you to offer. Thank you.' He realized as he spoke that in agreeing to the surreptitious filling of kettles and darning of socks, he was agreeing to much more – a conspiracy between the two of them against her husband. And it would be playing with fire: not just with Jem's capacity to be jealous but with the tinderbox of Billy's own emotions. He'd never felt for any girl what he was beginning to feel for Kitty and he'd be insane to let it grow, but it was too late for sanity. He was powerless to stop it.

Once Jem had got his wind back he'd ignored the pain between his legs and finished the stooking alone. Somehow he didn't think Harriet would go bleating to Will Griffin about what had happened, but he wasn't in the mood to test the theory. By the time the last of the wheatsheaves was in place, the sun was setting. He could go back to the farmhouse for a meal, as usual, or he could go on down to the Red Lion in Bentley, get drunk and forget about being bested by bloody Harriet Griffin. It was an easy decision.

In the public bar at the Red Lion, sitting in a corner on one of the wooden bench seats, he had just downed most of his fifth pint of beer, without any noticeable mellowing of his mood, when a shadow fell across the table in front of him and someone slid into the opposite seat.

Jem looked up, resenting the intrusion.

'You're Jem Wilkins, aren't you?' said the newcomer, planting his own beer mug on the table between them. 'I'm Stanley Briggs. My wife Allie's told me about you.'

Jem grunted discouragingly and drained his mug.

'Same again?' Stanley gestured at the barman to bring a couple more pints over. He was curious about Jem. Allie had started off by being charmed by the Londoner – it had been *Jem this* and *Jem that* until he was sick of the sound of the man's name. But lately she'd stopped praising Jem to the skies and had even been known to utter a word of criticism. Stanley gathered that this had something to do with Allie's growing liking for Kitty, the girl Wilkins had brought with him to Welcome Farm.

Allie had been shocked, and he had too, to learn that Jem and Kitty weren't married, and at first Allie had been inclined to blame Kitty and her lack of moral standards for this regrettable state of affairs. But nowadays it was reckoned to be more a case of Jem exploiting the poor girl and denying her the security of wedlock. Stanley had had a lively debate or two with his wife over the rights and wrongs of the situation and he was interested in hearing Jem's side of things.

Jem accepted the pint that had been offered, but it didn't make him sociable. He gulped it down steadily and wiped the back of his hand across his mouth when he had finished, without saying anything to his drinking companion. Stanley decided to try direct questions.

'How d'you like working for the Griffins, then?'

'S'all right,' said Jem, staring moodily into his empty glass.

'Tolerant pair, Will and Daisy.'

'Mmm.'

'It isn't every employer would have let you stay on in a tied cottage,' Stanley said, greatly daring, 'not once they knew about the situation between you and that young woman of yours.'

Jem's head lifted and Stanley found himself the object of a very penetrating gaze. 'What exactly do you mean?' said Jem.

'Well . . .' Stanley floundered, suddenly aware of a menace that hadn't been detectable a moment ago from the taciturn young man opposite. 'My wife says you two aren't married.'

'Your wife is a nosy cow,' Jem said with precision, 'and it she knew what was good for her, she'd watch her tongue.'

Stanley cleared his throat. 'No offence meant,' he said. 'And none taken, I hope? Allie *is* a bit free with her opinions. Care for another beer?'

Jem grunted, Stanley beckoned the barman and by the time the bell rang for closing time, the two men had assembled an impressive cluster of drinking mugs on the scarred surface of the table between them. They left together. In the starry night outside, Jem turned to Stanley with a ponderous dignity and remarked that the Griffins were not so much tolerant of the sinning as fellow sinners.

'How d'you reckon that?' asked Stanley.

'You know Harriet?'

'Will and Daisy's daughter?'

'She may be Daisy's,' Jem informed him, his speech slurred, 'but she isn't Will's. Oh, no. Harriet's dad was a soldier name of Bright, back in 1914.'

'You don't say?' Stanley gasped. 'D'you mean that Daisy—?'

'Before she was married to Will, Daisy Griffin was unchaste, impure, loose, a wanton, a fallen woman . . . she tasted of carnal pleasures outside the holy condition of matrimony . . .' Weaving down the road beside Stanley, Jem explored the vocabulary attached to Daisy's former behaviour.

'Blimey,' said Stanley simply. 'So Harriet—?'

'. . . is a by-blow. A bastard. Born on the wrong side of the blanket. To sum it up,' Jem finished, 'for all her airs and graces, the lovely Harriet is illegitimate.'

Over the stewed remains of the supper that Allie had kept hot for him, Stanley gave his wife the gist of Jem's revelation.

'Small wonder that Mrs Griffin was so understanding about Kitty Wilkins-as-isn't!' he announced, chasing the last of the gravy round his plate with a wedge of bread. 'Couldn't point the finger, could she, not with her own little secret? That'd have been a case of the pot calling the kettle black and no mistake!'

Allie looked at him with distaste. There was a smear of gravy on his chin and another on the front of his shirt. As she bent over him to clear away the plate, he smelled of sweat, ale, machine oil and bad teeth.

'Anyway, that settles it. I won't have you working up there no more,' he said.

'I'll work where I want to,' said Allie tartly. She dumped the dirty dish in the sink, making a lot of noise about it to cover her confusion over what she'd heard. She was torn between shock at the news about Harriet's status and chagrin that she wasn't the one to have discovered it first.

'But the Griffin woman's had a bastard baby and there she is in church on Sundays, saintly as they come, butter-wouldn't-melt,' Stanley said. 'Hypocritical bitch.'

'Mrs Griffin's been good to me,' Allie told him. She discovered to her own surprise that she meant it. 'So you can stop saying bad things about her, Stanley Briggs – and don't you go spreading any gossip about the Griffins, neither. If Jem Wilkins wants to go telling people what he knows, that's his affair, but we don't have to get mixed up in his nasty little game, do we?'

Coming from Allie, who was usually a front runner when it came to spreading gossip, this was hardly fair. Stanley opened his mouth to argue, then changed his mind. The way Allie was clashing pots and pans about, if he wasn't careful he'd have one of them flying his way . . . and he already had a considerable headache from trying to match Jem Wilkins beer for beer at the Red Lion. If his wife wanted to go on working at the farm he supposed it was her lookout. Anyway, her wages came in useful and who could tell when she'd find another job if she quit working for the Griffins? He abandoned high principles and went to sleep in his chair by the hearth instead.

Allie regarded his dozing form with relief. This being Friday night she'd anticipated without enthusiasm that he'd probably try to force his attentions on her once he'd got her to bed. Nowadays it wasn't all that difficult to repel the fumbling remnants of his manly ambitions, but tonight she was tired and she welcomed the prospect of a peaceful hour or two before he woke again and climbed the stairs. He lay slumped sideways in the chair, his mouth hanging slackly open, his breathing noisy, and she wondered for the umpteenth time why she'd been fool enough to marry him. She supposed he'd seemed something like a man at the time.

If only she'd had the sense to try him out first, like Daisy Griffin had apparently done with Harriet's unknown father, she might not have been stuck with him for all these years.

Jem was in a black mood. Kitty could tell as soon as he came through the bedroom doorway. Something in the day had made him angry and, with Jem, anger wasn't contained inside him; it seemed to emanate outwards like a black aura held in suspension a few inches from his hard body. She shrank down in the bed and gathered her courage.

'Well?' he said, in the edgy, sarcastic voice of such moods. 'Nothing to say? *Good evening, Jem*, would be nice.

Did you have a good day, my dear? would be friendly. But that's too much to expect from you, isn't it?'

Another day, another bad mood and *Good evening, Jem*, would have provoked his rage just as much as her silence had this evening. Kitty had learned that nothing was right at such times except to leave him alone to work his way through the mood. If she'd known this was coming, she could have gone to hide somewhere for a few hours and hoped the storm had evaporated by the time she came back. But she'd let exhaustion take her to bed before he came home and now it was too late. She saw the shape of the night and its inevitable conclusion. She was in for a beating.

Standing by the bed, Jem dragged the covers back and stared down at her. Deliberately he gripped her by the shoulders and hauled her up like a doll. Then he hurled her sideways with all his strength. Kitty landed on her back on the boarded floor with a crash that knocked all the breath out of her and, as she lay there, Jem kicked her in the stomach.

Since Billy had come to live in the neighbouring cottage, Kitty had learned to take whatever Jem handed out in silence, and to feign unconsciousness as soon as she could convincingly do so. Jem, too, was aware of Billy next door and of Daisy Griffin's sharp eyes in the mornings, and he had taken to hitting Kitty where it didn't show. But this kick was worse, far worse, than any blow he had inflicted on her before. Kitty cried out, helpless against the pain that seared through her body.

Jem stood over her, breathing heavily and she knew he was going to kick her again. Instinctively she drew up her knees and huddled herself for protection, eyes closed tightly to shut out the image of his distorted face.

The blow never came. She was dimly aware of the sound of footsteps running up the stairs. The door to the bedroom crashed back on its hinges.

'You bastard! Leave her alone!' panted Billy Marshall.

'Who's going to make me?' Jem glared at him, eyes

narrowed. 'This is a private quarrel, Marshall. And if you know what's good for you, you'll get out of here.'

'And leave her with you? You'd have to kill me first.'

There was a pause. In the background, Kitty struggled into a sitting position. The two men ignored her, circling one another warily.

'For Christ's sake,' said Jem with disgust. 'I'm not going to hit a cripple.'

'Why not? You'll hit a woman,' said Billy.

Jem advanced on Billy, fist clenched, but at the last moment he swung his arm out sideways instead and swept a flower-sprigged wash basin off the chest of drawers. Shards of smashed pottery flew in all directions. He swore once under his breath, then thrust Billy aside and blundered past him down the stairs.

'Are you all right?' Billy asked, helping Kitty to her feet. He wanted to put his good arm round her, to still the shaking of her body, but he didn't dare. She stared at him dazedly, one hand pressed against her stomach, then she put her other hand down between her legs. A crimson stain seeped through the thin cotton of her white nightdress.

'I'm bleeding,' she told him. She looked down at her fingers, smeared red. 'I'm bleeding,' she repeated stupidly.

Billy drew in his breath. 'Did he cut you?'

'No,' said Kitty in the same toneless voice. 'But I think I'm having a miscarriage.'

Billy ran to the farm and hammered on the back door until Will appeared in his pyjamas with Daisy at his shoulder. 'You'd better telephone for the doctor,' she said, when she had heard Billy's breathless account. She hurried down to the cottage in her dressing gown and the doctor, summoned by Billy from the telephone box at the cross-roads, arrived shortly afterwards; but there was nothing much he could do except give Kitty something to calm her down, and Daisy held her hand while the blood that would have been a baby drained away.

Later, Will came to find out what was happening and to

report that there was no sign of Jem Wilkins anywhere around the farm outbuildings.

'Do you think we should call the police?' Daisy asked, still with her hand in Kitty's, though by now Kitty seemed to be sleeping.

'On what charge?' Will said doubtfully. 'Drunk and disorderly?' He could remember an experience of his own in the Great War when he had come home on leave. He'd searched for Daisy and having failed to find her, had drunk more whisky than was good for him and ended up in a bar-room brawl. He'd spent a couple of days in the cells then, and it had left him with an instinctive wish to avoid police involvement.

'Grievous bodily harm. He was drunk and he kicked Kitty, Will. Kicked her in the stomach. It's his fault she's lost the baby.'

'Oh,' said Will blankly. 'Well, if that's the case then I suppose we *had* better report it to the police.'

'No,' said a voice from Daisy's elbow. Kitty's eyes had opened. 'No. Please. I don't want you to.'

She sounded faint but determined, and Daisy shelved the idea for the time being. Next day there was still no sign of Jem, but something else had happened which took precedence in Daisy's mind.

'We're short-handed for milking without Jem,' Will said in the early morning, bleary-eyed from the disturbances of the night. 'Ask Harriet if she'll help out, will you?' But when Daisy knocked at Harriet's door there was no reply, and when she went into the room it was empty. The bed had been made and resting on the pillow was a folded piece of paper.

Dear mother, for a number of reasons I feel it is best if I don't stay here. Don't worry about me, I am going to be with a friend.

'What do you think?' Will said, when Daisy showed him the note. 'Do you reckon she's run off with Jem?'

'Oh, Will! She can't have.' Daisy was shocked. 'Not Harriet.'

'Looks awfully like it to me,' said Will grimly.

                              *   *   *

'What if she's dead?' said Allie Briggs. 'She might turn up in a suitcase somewhere.'

'Oh, don't be so melodramatic, Allie!' But Daisy was worried sick about her daughter and Allie's suggestion came uncomfortably close to her own worst fears.

'It happens,' Allie told her starkly. 'Think of those poor women in the Trunk Murders.'

Daisy didn't want to think about them, but like anyone else who read a newspaper, she hadn't been able to ignore the Trunk Murders. The gory details had been fascinating the nation since the day in June when a lost-luggage attendant at Brighton Station had investigated an unpleasant smell and signs of sinister leakage coming from a large brown suitcase deposited at his office nearly a fortnight earlier, and had found the torso of a woman, wrapped in brown paper and tied up with Venetian blind cord. On the same evening, another left-luggage attendant opened another suitcase at King's Cross Station and discovered two legs.

'But they still haven't found the head or arms,' Allie reminded Daisy, with grisly relish. 'Course, she was pregnant – they reckon that must be why her gentleman friend did her in, didn't they? And cut her up and spread her about to make it harder to work out who she was. Then while the police were looking for the missing bits, they found that other body in *another* trunk – though at least she was still in one piece. They've got the man that did it – at least, he hasn't been tried yet, but everyone says he must be guilty. So there's one comfort: at least he can't have done for Harriet. But that Jem Wilkins could have,' Allie added. 'You never know.'

In the absence of both Jem and Harriet, and with Kitty bedridden, the Griffins were suddenly faced with a crisis of manpower; but in spite of it, Daisy went up to London on the train to talk to Louella.

'Is Harriet here with you?'

                              308

'No,' Louella said. 'I haven't seen her since she left in the New Year. I sent her a birthday present in April and she wrote back, but very briefly, to thank me for it. There's been no word since. Why, what's happened?'

'She's gone,' Daisy told her. 'And Jem's gone, too. Louella, you sent him to us. What do you know about him? You have to tell me.'

'All right,' Louella said after a pause. 'Do you remember when you and I first came to London years ago, when Harriet was a baby, and we went to see my mother and my stepfather in Bethnal Green?'

'Yes, I think so,' Daisy said doubtfully.

'You met Jem then, just for a moment or two. A little boy playing in the street with an old bicycle wheel. He's my half-brother,' said Louella.

'Oh!' Daisy tried to absorb the information, but was momentarily rendered speechless. When she found her tongue again, she struggled to hit the right note. 'Well, I'm sorry, Lou, but I still don't trust him,' she said.

'You're quite right not to. I don't trust him either. He's an evil little brute. Capable of anything. I suppose it's hardly surprising when you consider that his father beat him up regularly – and buggered him too, when he was drunk enough not to be fussy. Jem was his victim – but I'd say he's got a streak of Bert's cruelty in him as well.'

'Oh, Lou!' Now Daisy didn't know where to begin to be appalled – at Louella's language or at the gist of what she was saying. 'But why . . . if he's like that, why do you . . . ?'

'I just find him useful sometimes.'

'You wrote that he had work to do for you, when he came to the farm. What kind of work?'

'You don't want to know.'

'I do, if it involves Harriet,' Daisy persisted, angry that Louella had sent someone whom she knew to be 'an evil little brute' to Welcome Farm. 'Suppose something's happened to her? What if Jem—' She couldn't go on.

'Listen to me,' Louella told her. 'I wouldn't put it past

309

Jem to have made a play for Harriet, but I'm quite sure that Harriet won't have run off with him. I don't know where Jem is now but I'm sure he'll contact me once he's had time to sober up and calm down – he does too well out of me financially *not* to get in touch. In any case I'll have some enquiries made in his old neighbourhood and leave some messages with his old cronies. And of course, if Harriet comes here or gets in touch with me, you'll be the first to know.'

Defeated and cross, Daisy boarded the train for Bentley. Will met her at the station with the car.

'Any luck with Louella?'

'No. I don't know if I'll ever forgive her for sending Jem Wilkins to us, Will, when she knew what he was like.'

'What exactly *is* he like?'

'I'll tell you later. Can you stop by the crossroads? I want to telephone Laura Allingham.'

But Laura couldn't give Daisy any idea of Harriet's whereabouts either.

20

'Mr Wilkins is here to see you, madam.'

'Thank you, Everett. Show him in.'

Jem sauntered past the butler into the study even as Louella spoke. His manners hadn't improved, she thought . . . but his appearance had. When she last saw him he had been lean almost to the point of emaciation, with a sallow, unhealthy complexion, but in the intervening months his frame had filled out and above the red scarf knotted round his neck, his face was tanned by hours of working in the sun.

'You look well. Country life obviously suits you,' Louella commented dryly.

'Like hell it does,' said Jem. 'Word is out that you wanted to see me.'

'Yes. I'm surprised my messages reached you so quickly.'

'Oh, the jungle drums are quite effective. What do you want, Lou?'

'I gather you left Welcome Farm somewhat abruptly.'

'I got fed up with it,' Jem said. 'I reckoned I'd earned that money you gave me last year and I fancied a change of scene. Any complaints?'

'I'd have preferred you to discuss it with me first.'

'Asked your permission, d'you mean? I didn't get around to it.' Jem stared her out and Louella decided that now was not the time for a confrontation.

'Did my niece Harriet leave the farm with you, by any chance?'

'Harriet?' Jem looked startled, then he laughed. 'No, she didn't – not that I'd have complained if she did, she's a good-looking bit of stuff, when she isn't spitting in your eye. But no, she didn't come with me. Why do you ask?'

'She went missing at about the same time as you and her parents are worried about her. I didn't think she'd be with you – she'd got more sense,' Louella said pointedly. 'Can you suggest any reasons *why* she might have left?'

'She didn't confide in me. We weren't exactly close,' Jem said, but to Louella's sharp ears he sounded evasive.

'If you know something, Jem, tell me.'

'There's nothing to tell. We had a bit of a barney the evening I came away, but that's all. I don't know where she went or what she's up to now, Lou, and that's the honest truth. This is the first I've heard that she's left the farm. Anyway, about that Brownlowe fellow I was supposed to harass for you,' Jem said, changing the subject with determination, 'I've got one more pinprick to report: as I was leaving the district, I sent some of his cows in to mess up his garden. That'll have to do you for now.'

'All right. I've got something else planned for him actually. What are you going to do next?'

'Thought I'd try a spot of road-building. They're paying good wages for navvies on the new road from Guildford to London.'

'Can you leave me an address in case I need to contact you?'

'I'll write when I have one.'

'What are you going to do about that girl you took down to the farm?'

'Kitty? Leave her to it. She got on my nerves. We weren't married or anything. The Griffins'll look after her – they're soft like that. Anyway, I think she's got herself another man. You're being dead calm about all this, Lou. I'd expected a roasting. Are you in love or something?'

'That,' said Louella, 'is none of your business.'

'I'll be going, then, if there's nothing else.'

With her hand on the bell-pull to summon Everett, Louella remembered something. 'By the way, Jem, I've always meant to ask you: whatever happened to Bert Wilkins?'

'Dad? Oh, I disappeared him years ago,' Jem told her easily.

'*Disappeared* him? What exactly does that mean?'

'Work it out.'

'I'd rather you told me. I admire the way you operate, Jem. I'd like to know the details.'

Jem stuck his hands in his trouser pockets and tilted his head back. 'All right. If you insist. After all, you're hardly likely to shop me, are you, with what I know about *you*? Well, there came a day when I was about fourteen that I realized I was stronger than him and smarter than him, and quicker on my feet. And he'd hit Mam once too often . . . So I lured him down to the river one dark night – told him I'd fixed up a deal to work over some geezer that was giving a mate of mine some trouble, only it needed two of us to do it properly. Told him there was good money in it. He came along like a lamb. Down by the wharf I stuck a knife under his ribs and he went into the water in a good strong sack, along with a chunk of masonry I'd nicked off a demolition site downriver to anchor him down. I heard he floated to the surface eventually, though,' Jem added un-emotionally. 'I suppose the sack must've rotted. But by then, of course, he'd rotted too, and he was just another unidentifiable corpse that nobody was laying claim to.'

His eyes were on Louella, searching for a squeamish reaction.

'Well,' she said, after a short pause, 'Good riddance to bad rubbish, I suppose.'

Jem laughed. 'You never did have much time for Bert, did you? Kept him at arm's length, as I recall. He was hot for you, though – that's what made him come after me on a Friday night when I was a nipper, when he was too blind drunk to know the difference. God, I hated the man. Funny thing is,' Jem added reflectively, 'Mam cried when he went. Course, she didn't know he was dead, she just thought he'd scarpered. But you'd have thought she'd be glad to get shot of him 'stead of bawling her eyes out like that. It's not as if he ever gave her anything except bruises. Daft old

313

woman.' There was a catch in his voice. He steadied it. 'It was after that she went on the gin.'

In the hall, on his way out, Jem passed Stuart Armitage coming in.

'Who on earth was that disreputable-looking man?' Stuart asked as Louella emerged from the study.

'Nobody you'd care to know, Stuart.' At that moment, Louella was wishing that she didn't know Jem either. She was beginning to think that he might be a little too dangerous for her to have further dealings with, half-brother or not. She'd hated Bert Wilkins herself, but even so, the news that Jem had murdered his own father shocked her. The question was, how to distance herself. At least he'd said he wasn't responsible for Harriet's disappearance . . . was he telling the truth? She'd think about it later.

She led Stuart back into the study. As soon as the door was closed behind them he put his arms around her, but she averted her face and his kiss landed on her jaw.

'Not now, Stuart, I'm not in the mood. Have you made any progress yet with that loan to Rupert Brownlowe?'

'Yes, I have. We got it all tied up this morning,' said Stuart, sulky because Louella had pushed him away. 'He was supposed to see me several days ago, but he didn't turn up for our appointment. Apparently someone drove a herd of his own livestock on to his garden the night before and he had to spend the day rounding them up. He was still fairly frothing at the mouth when I saw him.'

'But he's signed now, anyway?'

'Oh yes, he's signed. Here are the papers. I wouldn't say you own the man lock, stock and barrel but he certainly owes you a considerable sum. And it's secured against his house, so let's hope for Brownlowe's sake that his business takes an upward turn.'

Louella carried the file of documents that Stuart had given her to her desk and locked it safely away. Stuart followed her.

'You're looking particularly seductive today. It's been days since we were alone together. Can't you take time off from being the brisk businesswoman for an hour or two, and come with me to the other house?' he wheedled.

'I shouldn't. I have things to see to.' Louella was torn between irritation and temptation. These days she was becoming more and more resentful of the things that Stuart took for granted, not least her willingness to go on maintaining the 'other house' for their occasional assignations. He wound his arms around her from behind, turned her round and planted a kiss in the hollow at the base of her throat and another at the side of her neck where the pulse was beating.

'Well . . . perhaps for an hour,' she conceded, ashamed of the weakness that betrayed her time and again where Stuart was concerned.

'I'll call us a taxi,' he said.

And I'll pay for it, as usual, thought Louella.

. . . But he was still a very good lover. It was a pity that he couldn't get her pregnant – that, after all, had been the main object of her liaison with him, she reminded herself later, as Stuart lay beside her, arm crooked across his face, half asleep in the aftermath of their lovemaking. And to further this object, she had deliberately told him that she was barren – so that he had never suggested any form of contraception. She pushed away the thought that there had been more to it than that, not wanting to own, even to herself that for a while she had lost her head, and her heart, to the practised wiles of a handsome young man.

Anyway, if she had, she was getting them back again. Sooner or later, probably sooner, it would be time to part with Stuart; but that would require as careful an approach as the other matter of dispensing with Jem. If only she could 'disappear' her troublesome and sinister half-brother as finally as he had dealt with Bert Wilkins, she thought wryly. But it was far more complicated than that.

And as for complications, what was she to do about Harriet? Jem had told her that he didn't know Harriet's whereabouts and Louella assumed that was true. From what she knew about Jem, if he had actually succeeded in persuading her niece to run away with him, he would have said so. He wasn't likely to pass up an opportunity to crow about it to Louella.

But if Harriet wasn't with Jem, where on earth was she?

In fact, Harriet had spent the night after her struggle with Jem at the Bush Hotel in Farnham, though she'd flinched at the hole it made in her savings from nannying for Laura Allingham. In the morning she squandered further precious cash by taking a taxi to Maple Grange, where she asked the maid who opened the front door if she could speak to Tom Searle.

Summoned by the maid, Tom seemed distinctly uncharmed by her arrival. Ignoring her tentative greeting, he took hold of her elbow and hustled her out into the porch, pulling the front door shut behind him. 'What are you doing here? I thought we'd agreed it was best for you not to turn up here? I said I'd contact you at Welcome Farm.'

'But you didn't,' said Harriet, taken aback by this reception.

'Mother's put the word around among her friends that you were looking for work, but there's been no result yet. And now's not a good time to pester her about it. My stepfather's throwing fits because last night some joker rounded up the cows from the home farm and herded them down the road and into his beautiful paeony garden. You'd better go back home and wait to hear from Mother when she's had more time to work on your problem.'

'I can't,' said Harriet. 'Something's happened and I had to leave.'

Belatedly, Tom registered the existence of the suitcase at her feet. His face paled with dismay.

'Harriet, what have you done?'

'I've left home, that's all.'

'Well, I don't see what I can do about it. I don't want to seem unfeeling, Harriet, and I'd help you if I could. But I'm planning to rejoin the Cobham outfit when they reach Winchester tomorrow, and I don't intend to postpone that.'

'Take me with you,' said Harriet. 'You said you would if all else failed,' she reminded him.

'For heaven's sake, Harriet, I was joking! It's hardly the life for you, is it? Living out of a suitcase, never in one place for more than a day or two.'

'I wouldn't mind,' Harriet declared. 'I'd work. I'd do whatever was needed.'

'But what *can* you do that'd be of any use to Cobham's crew? You can't fly an aeroplane, or wing walk, or anything like that.'

Somehow in the interval between their last meeting in Kew and today, Harriet realized, Tom had erased her from his life. Whatever had been in the air between them before, she was nothing but a nuisance to him now. It was galling to have to plead for help in such circumstances, but what alternative did she have?

'I could be useful. I'm quite strong and I'm not stupid. Rob helped to load the passengers for the joy rides at Guildford. I could do that.'

'It's the sort of thing they might take a lad like Rob on for, on a daily basis. But they wouldn't want a permanent loader. I suppose there's the refreshments team,' Tom said doubtfully, 'but I doubt if they'd be looking for another helper at this stage of the season.'

'At least let me come with you and ask.' Anything, Harriet reasoned desperately, would be better than going back to Welcome Farm and having to face Jem Wilkins and the consequences of whatever information about her he might have chosen to broadcast to the inhabitants of Bentley.

Tom glanced apprehensively over his shoulder at the closed front door. At any moment Rupert or Marion might appear and ask awkward questions about the young lady with the suitcase on their doorstep.

'All right,' he said reluctantly. 'But not now. Tomorrow. And you can't stay here in the meantime.'

'I stayed at the Bush last night. I'll go back there and wait until nine o'clock,' Harriet said, 'but only if you give

317

me your solemn word that you won't go without me tomorrow.'

The next morning Tom turned up at the Bush Hotel driving a smart little two-seater MG painted a glossy emerald green. He was an hour late, for which he didn't apologize, but Harriet didn't complain because she was relieved to see him at all. The day promised to be hot so the hood of the MG was down and as the sun climbed, Harriet, who had spent a second thoroughly restless night in her hotel bed, slipped down in her seat and let her eyes close. Soon she was fast asleep.

From time to time as Tom drove he glanced sideways at Harriet's unconscious head tilted back against the soft squab of the black leather seat. The wind stirred her red hair, her lips were slightly parted and her surprisingly dark eyelashes fanned out over cheeks on which the sun had brought out the lightest powdering of freckles. Under the white linen blouse, her chest rose and fell with her light breathing. There was no denying it, he conceded realistically – she was devilishly attractive . . . but what on earth was he to do with her?

'Wake up, Harriet. We've arrived!'

Harriet opened her eyes on a scene like the one she had witnessed at Newlands Corner in the spring, on the day that Cobham's Air Circus had come to Guildford: a grass field ringed by bright yellow canvas barriers, with a dozen or more biplanes drawn up on the far side; ranks of parked cars; a row of loudspeaker vans; vending stalls with canvas awnings; display advertisements on hoardings and everywhere a seething, chattering mass of spectators. There was the same smell of aviation fuel that she remembered and the sound of droning engines above the excited buzz of the crowd. She climbed stiffly out of the MG, pushing back her disordered hair with both hands.

'Wait here,' Tom said, 'while I have a word with Johnnie Johnson – he's that fellow in the flying suit, over there. It'll be up to him whether you can stay.'

'I thought the show was run by Alan Cobham?' said Harriet.

'Oh, he's always dashing about the world; he leaves the hiring and firing to Johnnie.'

Harriet leaned against the side of the car and watched Tom walking diffidently up to the man he had pointed out. It made a change to see Tom, who was normally so confident, looking so shy. She guessed that Johnson was something of a hero for him. The two men exchanged a few words then turned to look in her direction and she smiled nervously, aware that her immediate future hung on being judged acceptable by Johnnie Johnson. Tom seemed to be saying something about her but the other man cut him short. Picking up a small suitcase that had been standing at his feet, he thrust it into Tom's hands. Tom returned to Harriet and placed the suitcase on the bonnet of the car.

'Initiation test. You'll enjoy this,' he told her.

'What are we going to—?'

'You'll see. Stick this on your head.'

He took a gauzy white square of fabric out of the suitcase, dropped it down over Harriet's hair and topped it with a chaplet of white silk flowers, then scooped her up bodily and dumped her over the side of the car into the passenger seat. While she was still spluttering with indignation at this rough handling, he tossed the suitcase into the storage space behind the car's seats, raced round the rear, vaulted into the driver's seat and switched on the ignition.

Harriet hauled herself upright, chaplet askew, as the MG raced across the field. She had never been driven so fast in her life – not even by Gavin showing off in the Swallow last autumn. The loudspeakers blared out a commentary that she couldn't catch and the crowd set up a hum of expectation, which was almost drowned out by the roar of an aero engine as a Tiger Moth swooped low overhead. Something round and heavy tumbled over the side of the plane and Harriet let out a stifled scream, clapping her hands to the sides of her head and screwing her eyes shut as she waited for the impact.

There was a soft crump of sound and a feathery sensation across her cheeks. When she opened her eyes again Tom, at the wheel, was ghostly white, his hair, face and body comprehensively dusted with a fine powder. Looking down, Harriet discovered that she, too, was covered in the powder.

'Don't worry, it's only flour in paper bags,' said Tom, grinning through the mask. The Moth executed a steep climbing turn then dived again, and again Harriet closed her eyes, shrinking down in her seat in anticipation of what seemed like an inevitable collision. But the plane pulled out seemingly only feet above their heads and shot upwards, engine screaming, as Tom wrenched the steering wheel over and the MG slewed sideways. There was a concerted bellow from the crowd as a second missile that had toppled from the plane missed the car by inches and exploded its contents over the grass.

'What in heaven's name is going on?' shrieked Harriet, clutching at Tom's arm as the nearest solid object. The wind had already snatched away her veil and chaplet of flowers and blown them across the field.

'Gretna Green Race,' he shouted back. 'It's part of the show. I'm a cad, you're an heiress, we're eloping and that's your father in the plane, trying to stop us and save your honour. Hang on.'

Teeth gritted, hair whipped across her face by the wind, deafened by the noise of the Moth's engine and the baying of the spectators, and growing whiter by the minute as more and more flour bags found their target, Harriet hung on. At last the car came to a shuddering halt and seconds later the Tiger Moth touched down and taxied bumpily over the grass to draw up alongside them.

Even before the propeller had stopped spinning, a figure clad in a brown flying suit and leather helmet jumped down from the lower wing of the biplane, sprinted to the side of the car, dragged open the passenger's door and hauled Harriet out. He ripped off his goggles, leaving two pale circles like an owl's eyes in the darkness of his oil-spattered face, and she found herself briefly clasped to his chest before

320

he thrust her aside. Meanwhile, Tom had climbed out of the car and with the exaggerated movements of a silent movie star, tried to make his escape, only to be pursued and caught by the pilot, who punched him once, twice, three times on the jaw, with musical punctuation supplied by the loudspeakers. At the third blow he toppled backwards and landed spread-eagled, his legs rising into the air theatrically before he lay still. The pilot ran back to Harriet, caught her hand and raised it skywards.

'Curtsey,' he hissed at her. Dazedly, she obeyed and beside her, he sketched an elaborate bow. The crowd applauded and catcalled. Tom scrambled up, dusted himself down and came to take her other hand. The three of them bowed in unison, to one last cheer from the crowd. Then another Tiger Moth, startlingly inverted, shot overhead and the eyes of the spectators were dragged away from the breathless participants in the Gretna Green Race.

'Sorry you didn't get much notice of that. The team that normally do it had broken down in their car on the way here but nobody realized till the plane was airborne. Well?' said Tom. 'How did you like it?'

'It was fun,' Harriet discovered.

'You're a good sport.' Tom lifted a wayward lock of hair from Harriet's face and tucked it behind her ear, then unexpectedly followed it up with a kiss on the cheek. 'Mmm. You're all floury.' He extracted one end of his scarf from inside his jacket and wiped some of the flour from her face, then gave her an affectionate grin.

'Welcome to Cobham's Flying Circus.'

Johnnie Johnson said that he was prepared to recruit Tom's charming young lady friend to the refreshment team but that it was Tom's responsibility to arrange accommodation for her.

'She can start right away in the tea tent if Ma West's agreeable. But if she gives us any problems, you'll both have to go. I've got enough to worry about already. Understood, Tom?'

'Understood,' said Tom, relieved. It was only at the end of the day, when the crowd had dispersed and the screens and the impedimenta of the show were being dismantled, that he recognized a further problem. He went in search of Harriet. She was stacking cups in a tea chest, ready to be transported to the next day's venue at Bognor Regis.

'I'm afraid there's no alternative. You'll have to share my hotel room tonight.'

'I beg your pardon?' said Harriet, startled.

'The chap who did the booking for us this morning says the hotel's got no more rooms available – and even if there was one it would be fifteen shillings for the night. I was supposed to be sharing the room with another chap but he reckons he can double up with one of the others. Don't worry,' Tom added. 'There are two beds and I guarantee your honour's safe with me.'

But it wasn't going to be easy to keep that guarantee, he reflected ruefully later. He'd rigged up a rope down the centre of the room between the two single beds and hung a sheet over it, but with the light on in Harriet's half her shadow was projected on to the makeshift screen like a magic lantern show, making him an enforced spectator of most of the details of her undressing for the night. And what he couldn't see, his imagination readily provided. He was only human, after all.

'We've had a setback with the Surrey Fund to help the people of Jarrow,' Marion Brownlowe said to her husband at the supper table. 'The administrators decided that one way to benefit the townspeople who've lost their livelihood would be for them to redecorate their houses, with the Fund paying.

'It seemed like a good idea, one that would keep them gainfully occupied and brighten up their surroundings. But the response was quite hostile – according to their representative, the housing is rented anyway, and their landlords are responsible for refurbishment, so for our Fund to pick

322

up the bill would only let the landlords off the hook and enhance the value of their assets, not help their tenants. And they said very bluntly that they don't want charity, they want work.

'I suppose you can see their point of view, but it's rather a slap in the face. After all, the people who subscribed to the Fund meant well. It's not our fault that their shipyards closed . . .'

On the far side of the table, Rupert went on staring into his glass of wine, thankful that Marion had too much on her mind, agitating about yet another of her wretched charitable activities, to notice his low spirits. In his current mood he was damned if he could spare much sympathy for the townsfolk of Jarrow.

In a sense he should be jubilant, not depressed, because for the time being his money worries were over. Some unknown woman had come forward with a loan which would pay for the long-overdue modernization of equipment and repairs to the building that his factory manager, Pritchard, had been nagging about for ages. Rupert hadn't been able to find out much about the woman from the smooth and slightly supercilious young solicitor who represented her at the negotiations, except that she was rich and newly widowed and already owned a factory that made ladies' clothing. The lawyer had delicately hinted that she had more money than sense and wanted to play at being a businesswoman, and Rupert was too relieved at getting the loan to question this assessment of his benefactress, although it reflected poorly on his particular business as an investment.

But he wished he hadn't had to put Maple Grange up as a guarantee for the loan. He had taken a gamble and signed a paper which could, if the gamble didn't pay off, ultimately lose him the roof over his head – but what alternative was there? He had no other collateral, and nobody else had even been prepared to let him mortgage the Grange.

The trickiest part of it was working out how to tell Marion what he'd done. After all, it was the roof over her head, too.

He knew that she'd only married him for the sake of security for herself and her son, and he inwardly quailed at the prospect of having to admit the extent to which he was currently risking that security.

Perhaps it would be better if he didn't tell her. With any luck, she'd never have to know.

Another sunny August evening rounded off another glorious day; but Kitty was shivering as she stood in the lane outside Starling Cottages. She hugged her thin arms against her body, over the still-livid bruises that Jem's boot had imprinted on it. Outwardly she'd made a good recovery, but the deeper, unseen damage remained.

In the first days after Jem went she'd been afraid that he would come back. Now she was more afraid that he wouldn't. How long would the Griffins let her stay on at Welcome Farm without him? After all, he'd been the one they'd taken on – she was only the bit of extra baggage he'd brought with him. Daisy Griffin had been kind, but surely soon Kitty would be told to leave Number One, Starling Cottages, and she had nowhere else to go. She saw the future as a black void: no Jem, no money, no home, no baby to love . . . A sob escaped her, then another. She rammed her fist against her mouth to suppress the sounds, but they would come in spite of it. She cowered there until the storm of weeping had subsided, then her body stiffened with a new determination and she set off along the lane.

The months with Jem had brought her low and the loss of the unborn baby had finished the job. Now she had made up her mind what to do.

As Billy Marshall drove Joseph in the trap towards Welcome Farm, he was half-asleep in the evening sunshine. Jeffrey, the blacksmith at Bentley, ran a battery-recharging service as a sideline and after evening milking was finished, Will had sent Billy down to the forge with a battery from Jackie's radio. Jeffrey had been in a sociable mood, insisting that his customer should join him in a glass of last year's elderflower wine and Billy, who wasn't used to alcohol, found that it had gone to his head a little.

The air was heavy with the stored warmth of the day, and loud with evening birdsong, making him feel pleasantly lazy, and he was in no hurry to get back to the farm. Perched up high on the bench seat of the trap as the grey horse ambled along the lane, Billy saw a formation of wild geese flying over the fields towards their night-time nesting-ground of Frensham pond. He raised his good hand to shade his eyes, letting the loose rein slip along his arm to the elbow, while he charted their progress. As the geese and the sound of their honking receded into the distance, his attention was caught instead by a pale shape moving across a neighbouring field.

Screwing up his eyes, he identified the shape as a woman and then as Kitty, and wondered idly where she was going. There was nothing in the north-easterly direction she was following except the open fields and the road to Alton, and on the far side of it, the river.

Puzzled, Billy tugged at the reins to bring Joseph to a halt and walked back on foot to the field gate. Kitty had already disappeared over the rise. He scrambled over the gate and hurried after her. As he topped the crest of the rise, Kitty had reached the gate on the other side of the field which gave access to the road. He called, but she gave no sign of hearing him. There was something odd about the way she moved . . . like a sleepwalker, he realized. With a growing presentiment that something was wrong, Billy began to run.

Across the road and alongside it, the river wound in a series of curves between grassy banks, fringed by willows. In some places the water was shallow, with the small fish that flicked to and fro over the stony bottom clearly visible. Elsewhere it deepened, becoming dense and murky. Still with the same trance-like movements, Kitty advanced to the bank. There she hesitated for a moment, shook her head as if trying to clear it, then stepped down into the water.

It was shallow at that point. She stood knee-high, looking up and down the liquid stretch before she leaned down and began to scoop up stones from the riverbed, loading them into the patch pockets of her cotton dress with jerky movements. Billy waved and shouted, in vain. Her pockets filled, Kitty waded upriver.

For the first few yards the going stayed shallow. After that the river turned a bend and in the crook of the bend the current had scooped out the soil over the years, creating a pouch of deeper water. One step too many and the brown water closed suddenly over her head.

Billy stumbled down the bank, slipping and sliding, his good arm flailing wildly for balance. Kitty's hair floated on the surface like tendrils of water weed. Billy plunged into the river and the coldness of it made him gasp. Then one of Kitty's hands broke the surface and snatched at the air. He made a desperate grab but overbalanced and toppled forward into the deeper water.

In the several panicky seconds it took to get his head up to the air again, choking and spluttering, Kitty had gone under once more. Heart thudding furiously, he kicked out and to his unspeakable relief managed to locate solid ground underfoot. When he stood upright the water came as high as his chest. A widening circle of ripples showed him where Kitty was and he launched himself towards it, his lifeless arm dragging through the water, the other stretched out to help his balance as he kicked about to locate her body.

His knee bumped against something bulky and he ducked under again, groping to find Kitty's body and lift it till her head was clear of the water. Somehow, sobbing for breath, he struggled towards the bank, towing the inert weight of her behind him.

On the grassy slope he laid her down. She lay so still that he was afraid she was dead. He racked his memory for details learned long ago as a boy scout: how to resuscitate someone after a drowning accident. It needed two hands. *Dear God, let this work somehow.*

Levering Kitty over so that she lay face down, he knelt above her and spread his good hand against her lower ribs on one side, swinging his weight forward, stiff-armed, then transferred his hand to the other side and repeated the process. He lost track of how long he kept at it, until he was finally rewarded by a stir of movement under the soaked bodice as her lungs responded. A moment later, she raised herself on her hands and coughed up water.

'You gave me a fright there,' Billy said jerkily, sitting back on his heels. He felt like crying with relief. 'I thought you'd gone.'

'Why did you stop me?' Kitty whispered, rolling over and levering herself up into a sitting position. 'I wanted to die.' She rested her forehead on her drawn-up knees. Tears trickled from her closed eyes and her body shook with silent sobs.

'Please don't,' Billy said, touching her shoulder. 'Please . . . I've felt like that. I've thought I couldn't take any more. After Mam died . . . but things get better. People are kind. Life gets bearable again.'

'But what'll become of me now that Jem's gone?' cried Kitty despairingly.

'Jem? Why d'you care about him? He wasn't good enough for you,' Billy protested with sudden force.

Kitty raised her head. 'He was all I'd got,' she said simply. 'I'm no good alone. I'm too much of a coward to manage by myself, I suppose.'

'You won't have to be alone. I'll look after you,' offered Billy. 'I'd give my right arm for the chance . . .' He broke off suddenly as he remembered what a poor, maimed thing it was that he had to offer. 'I'll do the best I can, anyway,' he said wryly, with a downward glance at the lifeless arm.

Sodden and shivering, wet hair dripping into her eyes, Kitty saw Billy's surge of protectiveness, then his shamed recollection of his disability, and her own misery gave way to a sharp ache of sympathy for him. It was followed by a rush of gratitude and tenderness. He'd done more than save her life, he'd given her something even more precious: a reason to go on living. Someone to care for. She took hold of the cold, bent fingers of the disabled hand and carried them to her cheek.

21

The front doorbell rang and in the kitchen Daisy looked up, startled. Nobody ever came up the garden path to the front entrance at Welcome Farm, always round the side of the house to the kitchen door. She hurried through the dining room and along the passageway, and stood nonplussed by the need to unbolt the stiff top and bottom bolts and turn the key before she could open the door.

The bell pealed again. Daisy bent down and lifted the flap on the letter box. All she could see was a female midriff clothed in some kind of tailored pearl-grey outfit with tiny cut-glass buttons on the jacket.

'Who is it?' she called.

'Laura Allingham.'

'Oh! Oh, I'm awfully sorry, Miss Laura. I mean, *Mrs* Laura. Please can you just wait a moment.' Flustered, Daisy wrestled with the bolts. Two minutes later, scarlet with embarrassment, she was at last able to admit her visitor into the hall.

'I am sorry to have kept you waiting on the doorstep like that. Whatever must you think? Do come in. Allie, put the kettle on, will you?' Daisy called in the direction of the kitchen.

'Don't do that for me, I can't stay long,' said Laura hastily. 'I've just popped over, because I didn't know if you'd heard from Harriet and thought you might still be worrying about her.'

'Well, no, we haven't heard,' Daisy admitted, biting her lip. 'I know it's silly, but you can't help imagining all sorts of things, can you, when you don't know where—'

'Then this might help,' Laura interrupted. 'Or perhaps not.

329

It's good news and bad news at once. I'd better explain. Caroline and I came down to Maple Grange last night for a visit and this morning I happened to overhear a couple of the servants gossiping about a girl who turned up there a few days ago. She told the maid who answered the door that her name was Harriet Griffin, and she asked to see my stepbrother, Tom Searle.

'The maid eavesdropped on them afterwards, which was very improper of her – I gather she has a bit of a crush on Tom – and heard the girl asking to be taken with him to join the Cobham Aviation Day tour. So it would seem that's where she is, for the time being anyway.'

'Oh,' said Daisy blankly.

'So the good news is that she's safe. The bad news . . . well, I don't know if Harriet told you this,' Laura continued, 'but it was partly because I was concerned that something might be developing between her and Tom that I asked her to leave. I'm very fond of Tom, but I have to say that he's not the most reliable of young men. He has a lot of modern ideas and when it comes to his dealings with girls some of those ideas are rather *too* modern for my taste, if you understand me. I'd hoped that by sending Harriet back to you I might have nipped the situation in the bud, but apparently not.' She looked with concern at her former housemaid, who was now standing with her hands pressed to her mouth, eyes wide with alarm. 'Daisy, I am so sorry.'

When Laura had gone, Daisy went back to the kitchen. Will had come in to record the morning's milk yields and stayed to glance at the newspaper. He looked up as she came in, his face serious.

'That was Miss Laura,' said Daisy heavily. 'She says she's found out that Harry's gone off with that airman, Rupert Brownlowe's stepson.'

'She's all right, then,' Will said. 'Thank God for that.'

'But from what Miss Laura said, he's a bit of a rake, Will. She said there was something going on between them. What if he doesn't marry her? And what if he makes her fly?' Of the two prospects, Daisy couldn't decide which was more disquieting.

'We can't do much about it, can we, love? She'll just have to go her own way.' Will handed his wife the folded newspaper. 'Have you seen this? The Germans are calling Adolf Hitler their *"Führer"* now.'

'Führer? What does that mean?'

'According to this report it means "leader". I wonder what he's supposed to be leading them *into*? Not another bloody war, I hope,' said Will, giving Daisy something else to worry about.

Sorting through the contents of her suitcase for a clean petticoat, Harriet found a crumpled envelope, addressed to her, which she remembered collecting from the salver on the hall table of the Allingham house as she left and tucking unopened into her luggage. It proved to be a letter from Vera Birkett.

Dear Harriet, I thought I would just drop you a line to let you know that I am very well and having a good time in Croydon. I wasn't too keen to come here, I thought I was going to have to work in a factory and I didn't fancy it, but I found a job in a flower shop and I like it very much.

The customers are very cheery and what is more, I have a boyfriend! His name is Fred and he is ever so nice. He came to the shop to buy some flowers for his mum's birthday and I helped him to choose a specially nice bunch. I knew he liked me – you can tell, can't you? Anyway, he came back the next day and all the rest of the week and kept on buying bunches of flowers. So I said, 'She must be a smashing mum, but I don't know how you can afford to give her all these flowers.' And he said, 'I can't. I'm going to be stony broke at this rate. But I don't know how else I can go on meeting you.' So I said, 'Why don't you just ask me out then, you daft ha'porth?' So then he did.

331

We are saving up to get engaged, and once we have done that, we can start saving to get married, though I expect it will take a few years yet because neither of us earns very much. Fred isn't half romantic – he's a lovely kisser! It's very tempting to misbehave, but I am determined to be a good girl and start out married life on a proper footing. Please write back and tell me all your news. With love from Vera.

Harriet envied Vera the happy certainty of her relationship with the unknown Fred of the flowers. She herself had gone on sharing hotel rooms with Tom Searle because she couldn't afford to pay fifteen shillings a night for a room of her own, but after five days of enforced togetherness, she was no nearer to understanding his attitude towards her than she had been in Vienna or London.

The kiss on the Orient Express had been passionate, but it could have been prompted by wounded pride after the incident of the Nazis in Vienna as much as by interest in Harriet. The kiss on arrival at Winchester had seemed distinctly brotherly, and he had made no move to repeat it. He'd been reluctant to let her come with him and she supposed it was perfectly possible that he didn't care about her at all. Her own feelings towards him were equally confused.

One thing she could predict with certainty: Tom wasn't about to shower her with bouquets of flowers.

'Harriet, come with me.'

As the queue of joy-riding customers dwindled at the end of a long, hot day's flying, Tom summoned Harriet from the tea tent and marched her towards a Tiger Moth standing at the edge of the field which had been the scene of the day's activities.

'As you are now a member of Cobham's Air Circus, I think it's high time that you went aloft. What's the matter?' Tom added, watching her face. 'Don't you want to?'

'Of course I want to. You just took me by surprise.' But

Harriet was nervous. Flying was so important to Tom . . . she felt that she was about to undergo some kind of test.

'Put your foot on that patch on the lower wing that's coloured differently,' he instructed her. 'That's the re-inforced bit. Step anywhere else and you're liable to go through the fabric. Take hold of the padded rim of the cockpit – that's right. Now haul yourself up. There's a flap on the side of the cockpit which you lower to get in. Yours is the front cockpit, not the rear – that's where I'll be. This plane's got dual controls because it's designed as a "tutor" – used for flying lessons. Don't touch the joystick, that's what we call the control column in front of you, and keep your feet clear of those pedals when we're in the air or the plane might do something very odd!'

In the cramped cockpit, Harriet's stomach fluttered as she arranged her legs gingerly in whatever small space wasn't occupied by touch-sensitive controls. Tom leaned over and helped her to assemble the safety harness with its various buckles held together by a locking pin, and handed her a leather flying helmet and goggles before he lowered himself into the second cockpit behind her.

'Throttle set . . . fuel on . . . switches off . . .' Tom ran through the engine checks with another man who stood beside the plane. 'OK, swing the prop.'

The mechanic grasped the metal strip which edged a blade of the propeller and swung it downwards until the engine coughed and caught, and the propeller began to spin of its own accord.

'Contact.'

The Moth taxied across the grass, slowly at first, then gathering speed. Harriet sat rigid in her seat, unsure what to expect; but the moment of take-off, when it came, was so smooth that it took her by surprise. The field dropped rapidly away beneath the biplane's wings as they climbed. She could see nothing over the nose of the plane except the tip of the propeller spinning steadily, but when she looked over the side, with the wind beating against her face, the ground was already a patchwork quilt of fields and tiny houses and trees, with the miniature aeroplanes of Cobham's Flying Circus assembled in one field and the dots that were cattle in another.

Almost deafened by the noise of the engine, buffeted by the wind but enchanted by the sense of openness and space, Harriet gazed at the golden landscape dappled with cloud-shadows that unrolled beneath her. Almost she could understand Rob's ecstatic reaction to the experience. Tom tapped her on the shoulder and when she turned he was mouthing something at her. She tried to lip-read and failed, but thought he had asked whether she was enjoying herself. She nodded vigorously and he smiled and raised his thumb.

With a lurching suddenness, the wings tilted and the plane seemed to slip sideways in the air. The sky and the horizon swung crazily and merged into a spinning pattern like the colours in a toy kaleidoscope. Harriet gripped the sides of the cockpit and closed her eyes, but the spinning sensation was only worse like that. Waves of heat flooded through her and she swallowed desperately to keep down the rising tide of nausea. The landscape hurtled up to meet them and it dawned on her that the plane was about to crash, but she was too sick and dizzy to deal with the realization.

Then the Moth levelled out, and what rushed past on either side was no longer empty air but a field of aeroplanes. Tom touched the plane down and taxied it to a halt. He switched off the engine and as the propeller slowed and stopped he had already released his harness and was climbing out on to the wing.

'How did you like it?' he asked her.

Harriet smiled weakly, not trusting herself to answer. A moment later she was bolting for the nearby hedge, where she deposited the remains of her last meal. Tom watched her without comment. If she had undergone a test of her ability to adapt to flying, Harriet recognized sadly, she had just failed it.

'I thought we were going to crash,' she admitted when the churning sensations in her stomach were showing signs of settling down.

'What on earth gave you that idea?'

'When the plane went down like that . . .'

'That was only the spin,' Tom said. 'Basic aerobatics. I asked you if you fancied trying a spin and you said yes.'

Harriet closed her eyes. And that, she thought, would teach her not to nod in answer to unheard questions in aeroplanes.

'Well, that's that lot sorted out.' Beside Harriet, the woman who had been drying up teacups and packing them away in a cardboard box ready to transport to the next site tossed her soggy tea towel to one side and started to unfasten her apron. 'I hear there's going to be a sing-song down at the pub in half an hour, girls, if anyone's got the energy to go.'

The other women murmured their assent, but Harriet was silent. She had been with the National Aviation Day team for a week and in some ways it might have been for ever, but in other ways she had hardly broken the ice with her fellow workers.

All day, in Ma West's refreshment marquee she helped serve food to the spectators of the air show, a blur of anonymous faces passing on the far side of a long table, behind which she slapped thousands of sausages and scoops of chips or mash onto the thick pottery plates, or slopped dark, stewed tea into long rows of teacups from a vast, heavy teapot. In the evenings the others went to their caravans and tents and sing-songs at the nearest pub. Harriet went to a hotel with the pilots.

She had given up speculating whether Tom still felt romantically inclined towards her – he so obviously didn't. Some days he hardly talked to her at all, sitting silently over the late-night suppers or early breakfasts in the shabby hotel dining rooms which were all that the Cobham fliers could afford. Nor did he talk much to his fellow pilots.

At first Harriet had wondered uneasily if Tom's isolation was because of her arrival. Finally she concluded that it wasn't. The official display team were older, with Royal Air Force experience and a cameraderie in which Tom, the new boy, was not included. Officially he was supposed to make the loudspeaker announcements and help out generally. On good days, when another pilot was away, this meant that he took eager schoolboys and curious townspeople aloft on joy rides in an Avro 504K for as long as the daylight or the queues lasted. On such days he would drag himself up to their hotel room afterwards and collapse, exhausted but reasonably happy. But after a day when there had been no flying, he was edgy and remote and Harriet guessed that he minded his subservient rôle in the Cobham team.

She had her own problems. The refreshment marquee workers saw her as being attached to a pilot. The few fliers' wives who travelled with the tour ignored her. If her apparent relationship with Tom had attracted their contempt nobody said anything, so there was nothing for Harriet to refute.

Once or twice she had tried to compose a letter to Vera Birkett, but although she longed to confide in someone, she abandoned the attempt because too much had happened. It was difficult to conduct a correspondence when her address changed every day or two and, besides, how could she begin to explain that after a dramatic visit to Vienna and a brief return to her family, whose very existence she remembered denying before, she had run away to the Flying Circus with the 'young gentleman' that Vera had warned her against?

Vera, saving up to get engaged and married like a 'good' girl should, wouldn't approve at all.

By the beginning of September, Harriet was still an outsider in the Cobham team, and she was afraid that Tom was regretting that he had allowed her to come with him. He had been particularly morose over supper and to escape from his oppressive moodiness she went up to their shared room early.

At least she was used to the routine of sharing hotel rooms. She shifted a chair to the door and climbed on it to loop one end of a length of rope round the hook on the back of the door, then moved the chair and tied the other end of the rope to the curtain pole above the window opposite. She

336

had just draped a sheet over it and was about to duck under a corner of the suspended sheet and retire to her half of the divided room, when Tom came in.

'Harriet, we need to talk,' he said.

'What about?' Harriet asked apprehensively.

'About us. About you being here. It's time we sorted this situation out.'

Harriet braced herself for a dismissal.

Instead, he said, 'You must have realized that I find you awfully attractive, Harriet, and to be honest, it's damned difficult sharing a room with you and knowing that you're there every night, just a few feet away from me. I can hear your breathing when you're asleep, and when you're getting ready to go to bed . . . All in all, I don't know if I can take much more of it.'

Harriet gazed at him, heart thumping. 'What do you want to do about it?' she asked at last.

'I want to take down that damned sheet,' Tom said frankly, 'and do what we should have done days ago. I want to make love to you. Properly.'

'Tom . . .'

'But before we go any further, I'd better make this quite clear,' Tom hurried on. 'I'm not the marrying kind. The way I see it, you don't have to go through all that wedding business to be with someone you like. You just are.'

'You mean, living in sin?'

'That's not the phrase I'd use. Call it living in *freedom*. No ties, no regrets, no expectations. That way, when it's over, nobody gets hurt. And if you're worried about getting pregnant, you needn't be. I know what precautions to take. I'd like you to stay with me – but if you do, it'll have to be on those terms,' he concluded resolutely. 'Otherwise you'd better go back to your family. I've had enough of things the way they are.'

Harriet let out a long breath, her face pale. Whatever she had expected from Tom, it wasn't this businesslike stating of conditions. She wasn't sure whether to be offended or whether, if she thought about it, what he was suggesting might not be a good idea. She wasn't entirely in love with him – was she? But she too had lain awake at night listening to *his* breathing.

The other thing to be taken into consideration was that if she didn't do what he suggested, the alternative would be to leave the Cobham tour, and the prospect was daunting. She probably had enough money left to survive for a week or two in a boarding house somewhere, but after that, if she hadn't found work she would have no alternative but to go back to Welcome Farm.

'Well, thank you for your proposition. I'll think about it,' she said, in a small, cold voice. She ducked under the makeshift curtain and switched on her bedside light.

Tom climbed into his own bed and lay still, staring up at the fine network of cracks running across the ceiling to avoid watching her shadow on the sheet. After a few minutes Harriet's light was switched off. There was silence. Then he heard her low voice.

'Tom? Are you still awake?'

'Of course I'm awake,' said Tom bitterly. 'Like I told you, it's difficult to get to sleep in these circumstances.'

Harriet's light came on again with a click. There was a sound of movement from the other side of the sheet as she climbed out of bed. She lifted a corner of the curtain. The light behind her showed up the silhouette of her figure through the thin cotton of her nightdress and Tom drew in his breath sharply at the sight.

'I've thought about it,' she said.

But it hadn't been right, Harriet told herself afterwards, lying wedged between Tom and the wall in his bed. The bed was so narrow that half their attention had been concentrated on not falling out of it. Now she lay with her arms above her head, because with Tom asleep on his back, there was no room to bring them down to her sides. She was acutely uncomfortable. To add to her uneasiness, Tom had been so ... detached – and it wasn't just because he was experienced and she wasn't. She'd had the impression that he was holding himself back deliberately, putting what was happening between them at a distance, that he was *watching* her, somehow. She had wanted to be overcome by passion, to drown out her qualms about what she was doing; instead of which she was now left with the feeling of having parted with something precious, to someone who didn't value it enough.

On a Sunday morning in the middle of September, Allie Briggs got up earlier than usual and rummaged among the jumble in the attic for the box containing her best straw hat. When she found it, she lifted out the hat and surveyed it ruefully. It didn't look as smart as she'd remembered. She'd have to replace the faded ribbon and throw away those rather battered wax cherries and buy some artificial flowers to trim it with if it was to pass muster at Bentley Church.

She sat at the kitchen table, picking the stitches out of the ribbon with the end of a pair of scissors. She could remember the first time she'd worn this hat, for her daughter Phyllis's wedding to Jim Jarvis the plumber, and that must have been – how long ago was it? Six years? Time seemed to fly by these days, and every year since then she'd had to put on the hat for the christening of one of Phyllis's babies. No wonder it was looking so shabby now! Phyllis had four little ones at home, and another on the way, and it hardly seemed worthwhile any more to dig out her best hat for the christenings.

Stanley shambled downstairs, still in his vest, yawning and scratching at his stomach. 'You're up early. What're you doing?' he asked her.

'Changing the ribbon on my hat.'

'What for? Phyllis isn't due for another four months yet.'

'It isn't for Phyllis. It's for Kitty.'

'Kitty?' Stanley echoed uncomprehendingly. 'D'you mean the girl at Welcome Farm – the one that was living with Jem Wilkins?'

'That's her.'

'Died, has she?'

'No,' Allie told him. 'She's getting married.'

'Blimey,' said Stanley. 'Has Wilkins come back to make an honest woman of her, then?'

'No. He's gone for good, that's what Kitty reckons. She's going to marry Billy Marshall.'

'The cripple?'

'He's not all that crippled,' Allie said tartly. 'And he and Kitty are in love.' Her voice softened. 'It warms your heart to see the way they look at each other – like something out of a Hollywood film, it is. And they're getting married in Bentley Church, and I'm going to be matron of honour,' she added, with pride.

It was Daisy who had suggested this solution to Kitty's problem of finding a bridesmaid. Since Kitty had no-one to be her 'family', Will had been volunteered as best man and Daisy would have been happy to stand as matron of honour, but she had reckoned that asking Allie would dispel the last faint traces of the hostility that had been the older woman's first reaction to Kitty's arrival at Welcome Farm. And so it had proved. Allie had been over the moon.

Stanley's response was less generous.

'I don't like the thought of you standing up behind that slut in God's house,' he said. 'If you ask me, she's not entitled to the blessing of the church, hardened sinner that she's been, and you wouldn't catch me going to the wedding.'

Allie put down her scissors and the hat and eyed him coldly. ' "Let him that is without sin amongst you cast the first stone," ' she quoted.

'What's that supposed to mean? I've never strayed in all the years we've been together,' said Stanley.

'Haven't you? Maybe that's because nobody'd have you if you tried. But there's more ways of sinning than one, you'd know that if you knew your bible better – only you fall asleep in the vicar's sermons, don't you? Well, there's sloth and envy and gluttony for a start; *and* taking the name of the Lord in vain, which I've heard you doing many a time, Stanley Briggs, and don't you deny it. Anyway,' Allie continued briskly, '*I'm* going to the wedding. You can stay away if you want to. I reckon it'll be nicer for Kitty and Billy if it's just their friends that turn up, the ones that really wish them well. Now get out of my way if you can't think of anything useful to do.'

Scowling, Stanley went back to bed for another hour. In church later that morning, he was still not speaking to his wife and when the banns were called for Kitty Crowley, 'spinster of this parish', he snorted audibly. But when they came home from church, Allie silently put a cup of tea by his elbow and Stanley grunted his thanks and drank it, because after all, their years of living together were too long to be dismantled for the sake of a few cross words and a difference of opinion.

Harriet had been aware for some time that the Cobham team would finish their tour for 1934 on the last day of September, but she had pushed the prospect to the back of her mind because her affair with Tom was too new and too fragile for her to be able to assume that they would stay together once their current itinerant existence came to an end. But as the last day of the month drew inexorably closer and Tom still made no reference to future plans, she was forced to ask him about his intentions.

'Well, it's a problem. I can't go back to Maple Grange,' he said. 'Not with you in tow.'

Harriet had mixed feelings. Tom spoke of her as an impediment, which was wounding, but at least he seemed to be taking it for granted that they would stay together. 'And you won't go back to your family, will you?' he asked.

'Not if I can help it,' Harriet said grimly.

'I never did understand what all that was about. I mean, I know you found your father wasn't your father after all, but is that such a big problem? I don't have a father, only the odious Rupert, but I don't make a song and dance about it.'

Not for the first time, Harriet was stung by Tom's lack of sympathy for her situation. Was she making 'a song and dance'? 'It's not only that,' she defended herself. 'There's someone working at the farm who I don't get on with.' She flushed, remembering Jem Wilkins and a hectic few minutes in a wheatfield.

'Well, anyway,' Tom said with a trace of irritation, 'if you won't go home, you won't. We'd better go to London. The problem is shortage of funds. I haven't earned much this season because I missed a lot of the tour through that damned hand injury and anyway they pay me a pittance. And I spent most of this half-year's allowance buying the MG. Any ideas? Oh, sorry, I keep forgetting that you don't have any money, or any access to money. My last girlfriend, Diana, has a flat in town and I used to stay there whenever I was stumped for cash. Now, why didn't I think of that earlier?' he added. 'We can go to Diana!'

Harriet regarded him, stony-faced. 'I don't think your former girlfriend would be all that pleased if you brought me to stay, any more than Rupert Brownlowe would,' she said carefully.

'Oh, Diana won't mind,' Tom said. 'She's a good sort. We're friends now that it's over between us. And she's got a new boyfriend, anyway.'

He seemed to regard the problem as solved. For Harriet, it was not so simple.

The wedding of Kitty Crowley and Billy Marshall was a very quiet affair.

'I reckon my poor old hat was the grandest thing about it,' Allie said afterwards, a little disappointed because she had gone to a lot of trouble to look smart and, having overcome his resistance to attending, she had even taken Stanley's good suit out of the wardrobe several days beforehand to air it so that he wouldn't smell of mothballs.

Kitty and Billy were as poor as the proverbial church mice and didn't know anybody in the parish, so the only guests apart from Allie and Stanley had been the Griffins. It had made the singing a bit thin in the hymns, but that couldn't be helped, and Allie cheered up at the memory of their faces when the vicar had pronounced them 'man and wife'. Who'd have thought that Kitty, once so pale and scrawny, could be transformed into such a radiant bride? And, if you ignored his arm, Billy when happy was downright handsome.

'It's a real happy ending, isn't it, Mrs Griffin?' Allie said to Daisy when the wedding party were back at Welcome Farm, eating a lavish tea before they got on with afternoon milking. 'Pity your Harriet isn't here to see it, though.'

'Yes, isn't it,' agreed Daisy quietly. Allie, with her usual tactlessness, had just ruined the day for her. She tried not to let it show.

22

'Mrs Moffat has called to see you, madam. She's brought a young friend with her.'

Louella looked up irritably from a sheaf of papers on her desk and said something indistinct but probably profane. Everett waited, his face impassive, while his employer considered whether she could afford the luxury of telling Helen Moffat to go to hell. She decided that in view of Helen's connections she couldn't – not quite.

'All right, Everett.' Louella opened the top drawer of her desk and swept the papers into it. 'You can show them in. Who is this friend, by the way?'

'She wouldn't say, madam. She said she wanted to surprise you. Should I take them into the drawing room, madam?'

'No, I'll see them in here.'

'Shall I serve sherry, madam?' the butler suggested smoothly.

Louella darted him a sharp look. 'Not unless they stay for more than ten minutes. I hope they won't.'

Helen flowed into the room in a brown worsted suit, with a chocolate-brown felt hat tilted at an angle on her forehead and a dead fox arranged around her shoulders. Strictly speaking, it was too early in the year for fur; but Helen was a cold-blooded mortal, Louella reminded herself, and the fox was probably a status symbol. At any rate, its presence was a disguise for Helen's narrow shoulders.

'*Dearest* Louella, I hope we're not intruding. I know how terribly busy you always are – you keep telling me so whenever I invite you to one of my little soirées.'

'I *am* rather busy. What can I do for you?' Behind Helen,

her companion waited. She was a good-looking young woman of about thirty, in a quiet beige outfit which complemented her soft brown hair and shy manner. She was discernibly pregnant. Suppressing the usual pang of envy, Louella gestured her visitors towards the two Hepplewhite shieldback armchairs set against the wall opposite her desk. They were valuable, antique and uncomfortable, specifically chosen for the study to encourage unwelcome visitors to state their business and go.

'We won't stay. We were just passing and we hoped we might persuade you to donate a little something to a fund for which we're collecting,' Helen said. 'You are always *so* generous.'

'And your good causes are always so deserving.' The conversation was like a fencing match, Louella thought: *thrust* and *parry*. Since the night of the opera, she and Helen had abandoned the pretence of being friendly. Nowadays they just crossed swords, and Helen's visits normally meant that she had some barbed piece of information to impart, so it was a welcome relief that she was only after money. Resignedly, Louella reached for her chequebook. 'What's this particular fund for, Helen?'

'Doctor Barnardo's Homes.'

Louella scribbled an amount, tore the cheque out and passed it over.

Helen raised her eyebrows. 'Goodness, that *is* generous.' She turned to her companion. 'Look, dear, isn't this a marvellous boost to our fund?'

'Oh, it's so kind of you, Mrs Ramsay,' said the other woman, with real gratitude.

Louella shrugged. 'It's in a good cause.'

'Yes, isn't it,' the woman said eagerly. 'It's so awful that we still need to support these institutions – one would have hoped that children wouldn't be in such need of help, nowadays. But I don't know if you've ever been in the slums of the East End?'

'I was brought up in Bethnal Green,' said Louella dryly.

Helen Moffat's eyes stretched momentarily and Louella

chided herself for letting something slip that could be investigated and used against her. But she found herself warming to the other woman and wondered what she really thought of the artificial and affected Helen.

'Oh, Louella hasn't time to listen to your campaigning,' Helen said airily. 'Louella, I don't believe I've introduced you. How remiss of me. This is Anne Armitage, your accountant's wife.'

She paused to enjoy the impact of her words. There was only a momentary dropping of Louella Ramsay's guard, but it was telling, all the same. So Louella *hadn't* known about the pregnancy . . . it was moments like this that made Helen's spy network so worthwhile.

Liar. Cheat. Fraud.

Louella wanted to cry and she couldn't. She wanted to break things . . . starting with the neck of Stuart Armitage.

A young man of ambition, unfettered by moral scruples – wasn't that what Graham Madigan had called him?

And somewhere in the middle of his liaison with herself, Stuart had managed to conceive a child with his wife – the peevish cripple who had turned out to be a gentle, warm-hearted woman whom Louella could have liked. And their child would be the child that Louella didn't have, and would probably never have, and the knowledge cut into her worse than any knife. Above all, it strengthened her long-cherished resolve to see Rupert Brownlowe go under. She needed no reminding that but for his spectacular lack of charity when she'd been pregnant with her poor doomed son, that son might be alive today.

'I've been looking at my accounts, Stuart, in some detail. I notice that since I let you handle my shares for me, you've been buying and selling on my behalf with a most admirable zeal.'

Stuart fidgeted, recognizing that Louella was in a difficult mood. 'That's what I'm supposed to do, isn't it? Maximize the yield of your holdings?'

346

'This zeal is not unconnected, I deduce, with the fact that you take a commission for each transaction.'

'It's the norm in such situations. I thought you knew,' he defended himself. 'It would look odd if I didn't claim my commission. I don't want to compromise you.'

'Of course you don't,' Louella murmured ironically. 'How fortunate for both of us that the best way to safeguard my reputation should also be of such financial benefit to you.'

'Louella . . . What's the matter? Are you all right?'

'Thank you, Stuart, I am very well. And how are you? And Mrs Armitage? How is her pregnancy progressing?'

'So that's it. You know,' said Stuart.

'I know,' Louella confirmed. 'I was bound to, eventually, wasn't I? I'd rather have learned about it from you.'

'I didn't know how to tell you.'

'I'm not surprised. In view of what you've led me to believe about the situation between you and your wife, her condition is a miracle second only to the one on which nearly two thousand years of Christianity were founded.'

'You know I care about you,' Stuart said lamely. 'Does this stupid business with Anne have to be so important?'

'Get out.' Under her desk, Louella's hands were gripped so tightly together that afterwards she would see the marks of her nails in her flesh. 'Graham Madigan can resume the management of my business from now on. We need have no further contact.'

'I never knew you could be so hardhearted,' said Stuart.

'You underestimated me,' said Louella.

But it was she who had underestimated what the salvaging of her pride would cost her. She had cut the connection. Now she had to deal with the pain.

'Mr Pritchard, when I was last here, you very kindly said that I was welcome to come again at any time. I thought I would take you up on that offer.'

Louella's decision to revisit Rupert Brownlowe's lawn-mower factory, in which she was now the major investor, had been taken on an impulse. But to say that Rupert

Brownlowe's manager looked taken aback by her un-heralded arrival was to put it mildly. His face was ashen. *Intriguing*, Louella thought. *I wonder what he's hiding?*

'I don't want to disturb you or disrupt production, of course. Just get on with your usual routine and I'll walk round, if I may?'

'Of course I'll accompany you, Mrs Ramsay,' said Pritchard.

'There's no need.'

'I insist.'

He wasn't a very good dissembler – too honest, Louella thought wryly. She detected within a very short time that he was sensitive about a small storeroom at the back of the main factory building. She played with him for a bit, letting him steer her away, then turning purposefully back, watching the spasms of tension that crossed his features each time.

Finally she said, 'What is in the storeroom, Mr Pritchard?'

'Nothing. Boxes. Spare parts.'

'I'd like to get an idea of storage facilities. May I?'

She crossed the remaining floor in a few strides and opened the heavy door. Inside the room a factory worker in a brown overall stooped with his finger to his lips in a shushing gesture. Watching him with wide eyes, amid a debris of wooden building blocks and soft toys, were two small children.

'Mr Pritchard?' Louella was charmed and amused. She tried to disguise it by making her voice stern. 'I'm sure there's an explanation for this. Are you running a nursery here as a sideline?'

'They are my sister's children,' Pritchard said, shame-faced. 'She's in hospital having her third, and there have been complications with the pregnancy. She's been hospital-ized for the last week, with maybe another three or four weeks to go. My brother-in-law was at the end of his tether – he's afraid of losing his job if he takes the time off, and there's nobody else to help except me. I thought they wouldn't be too much trouble here. I haven't let them distract the workforce – but if you tell Mr Brownlowe, he probably won't believe that,' he finished, on a note of pleading.

'I have no intention of telling Mr Brownlowe,' Louella reassured him. She smiled at the children and was rewarded by answering smiles. She squatted on her heels and addressed them directly. 'Hullo. I'm Louella. What are your names?'

Within two minutes, she was on the floor with the building blocks.

'Do you have children of your own, Mrs Ramsay?' Michael Pritchard asked Louella, later.

'No. I haven't been that blessed,' Louella said. 'I had a baby once, but he died.' She did not add that she held Rupert Brownlowe responsible.

'You should have seen her face when she told me,' Pritchard told his sister that evening, sitting by her hospital bed. 'There was such sadness in her eyes . . . it really brought a lump to my throat. It seems almost presumptuous to pity a woman in her position, wealthy and successful as she is, but I did feel sorry for her.'

'I remember you saying that you liked her when she first came round the factory.'

'Yes, I did. But she seemed harder and sharper, then. Anyway, the thing is, she's offered to have the children to stay, for a month or whatever you need. She has a big house in Blackheath – with a nursery on the top floor, she says, and a staff to help her. She was so good with them, Jean – you should have seen her. And they really took to her, as well.'

Tom's friend Diana Somerville, the 'good sort', lived in Clapham. Her flat, Tom explained in advance to Harriet, was furnished in the Modernist style. 'Her people are rather well off, you see.'

In spite of having been forewarned, Harriet was rendered speechless by her first sight of the flat. The sitting room was

349

like nothing she had ever seen before, with its thick pile carpet patterned in uncompromising squares of black, grey and white overlaid with contrasting circles of the same colours, and the austere lines and pale wood of its furniture. It looked artistic and rather self-conscious. It was certainly expensive, as were the white hothouse lilies in an unadorned white porcelain vase, standing in the fireplace.

Diana herself was the reverse of austere; a slender blonde in floating moss *crêpe*, with a retroussé nose, china-blue eyes in a childlike face and a marcel-waved hairstyle very like the one which Harriet had acquired last year with Aunt Louella's guidance and had not been able to afford to keep.

'Darling! How divine to see you!' She embraced Tom with enthusiasm, then turned her attention to Harriet – or rather, she surveyed Harriet briefly and returned her attention to Tom.

'And who is this you've brought with you? Do tell!'

Harriet felt that she had seen Diana somewhere before. She mentioned this in an undertone to Tom while their hostess was dispensing cocktails from an angular cabinet in a corner of the room.

'I expect you have,' Tom whispered back. 'She's from our area, originally – her parents still live in Farnham, which is how I first met her.'

Harriet, perched on the edge of one of the very deep, square sofas, was feeling distinctly ill at ease. She had thought that Aunt Louella's house had given her enough experience of a grander lifestyle to get by with Tom's friends, but the opulence of her surroundings and the cold, assessing look that Diana had swept over her were rapidly dispelling that illusion.

'Tom, did you hear I'm engaged?' Diana asked, returning with black-stemmed glasses in which a pale lemon liquid sparkled.

'Yes. What kind of ring did he give you, Diana?'

'Diamond and sapphire half-hoop.' The blonde girl flourished her left hand with its crimson-painted nails in front of Tom's nose. 'Not nearly so nice as yours, darling, but he's awfully good-looking to make up for it.'

So Tom had once been engaged to Diana. Harriet felt a spasm of pure jealousy.

'He'll be here at any minute,' Diana continued. 'When I telephoned and told him that my ex-fiancé and his lady friend were coming to stay, he was absolutely eaten up with curiosity . . . Tom, can you be a dear and run down to the wine shop on the corner for a bottle of champagne for us to have with supper?'

When Tom had gone, she folded herself into the armchair opposite Harriet and took a cigarette from a silver box on the low table between them. Having inserted it into a long tortoiseshell-coloured holder, she applied a flame from a silver lighter to the tip and blew a long, considering stream of smoke into the sir.

'So, you're Tom's latest girlfriend?'

'Yes,' Harriet admitted.

'How fascinating. I'm his last – did he tell you?'

'Yes.'

'We're the best of friends now. Of course, we've known each other for a long time.' The doorbell chimed. 'That must be my fiancé,' she explained, rising to her feet.

In the hall outside the room in which Harriet waited, she heard the visitor being admitted.

'Darling!'

'Darling! Have they arrived?'

'Yes. Tom and his little provincial. Wait until you see her, darling! I suppose he must have felt like slumming it for a bit, after me.'

Harriet had disliked Diana on sight. Now she hated her. While she was grappling with this emotion, the new arrival was led into the room.

'Darling, this is Harriet – I'm sorry, I didn't catch your name.'

'We've already met,' said Gavin Draycott.

Too late, Harriet equated Diana Somerville with the girl she had seen in Gavin's car last Christmas.

*　　*　　*

'I can't stay here.'

'Why not?'

'I just can't.'

'Harriet, I don't think you understand the situation. Until my trust matures when I'm twenty-five, I'm limited to the income from the shares. I've spent this half-year's income. I'm stony broke until Christmas. Diana's willing to let us stay in her guest room for a week or two at least. Unless you can think of somewhere else for us to go, this is where we live until one or other of us can bring in some kind of wage.'

'Miss Harriet,' said Everett. 'We haven't seen you here for a long time. Is Mrs Ramsay expecting you?'

'No,' Harriet said. 'I should have telephoned before I came, I suppose, but I hoped . . .'

'I'll tell her you're here, miss.'

Harriet waited in the hall, wondering what kind of welcome she was about to receive from her aunt. She had not seen Louella since surprising her in the arms of a man, and they had quarrelled. Louella had hit her, the first blow that she had received in her life, and the shock had sent her storming back to Welcome Farm, only to have the illusions on which her life had been built shattered by Jem Wilkins' revelation.

Several months later her aunt had sent her the birthday present of a black tea gown and a note which, if you knew Louella, could be interpreted as a peace overture. She had snubbed it at the time. She was wishing she hadn't.

'Harriet, how lovely to see you!' The greeting was whole-heartedly welcoming, and Harriet heaved an inner sigh of relief. 'You are heaven-sent,' Louella continued, taking her hand. 'You know about children, don't you?'

Louella's spell as a substitute mother for baby Harriet while Daisy worked at the Woolwich Arsenal, nearly two decades ago, in the Great War, had given her a misplaced confidence. She was older now, and more easily tired; and in taking Michael Pritchard's niece and nephew into her well-ordered household, she had blithely bitten off more than she could immediately chew.

'And who is this young man of yours, Harriet?'

'He's Tom Searle, Rupert Brownlowe's stepson from Maple Grange.'

'Really?' Louella said, after the briefest of pauses. 'Is he close to his stepfather?'

'Not at all. He detests him.'

'Then I'm sure I shall like him,' said Louella.

'So it's really all right for us to stay? You don't mind that we're not married?'

'Dear Harriet, I am simply happy to see you.'

'I have one more favour to ask, Aunt Louella.'

'In return for your services as a nanny there is not much that I wouldn't grant you. What is it that you want?'

'I'd rather you didn't tell my mother that I'm here,' said Harriet.

'Your Tom is charming,' Louella told Harriet, after the first evening. 'But I have the impression that he may be a little difficult to pin down,' she added acutely.

'I expect you're right,' said Harriet, and for a moment a hunted look crossed her face.

'Has he said anything about marriage?' Louella asked.

'Only that he doesn't believe in it.'

'Ah,' said Louella, and pressed her lips together. 'Do you love him?' she asked, after a pause.

'Yes,' Harriet admitted unhappily. 'When we first started, I wasn't sure if I did. I know it was bad of me, but I was in a situation that I needed to get away from and I suppose I thought I could use him. Only when you've been living with someone for weeks on end, it's hard not to get involved.' She recognized even as she said it that her involvement was one-sided. Tom seemed as detached now as he had been at the beginning.

*   *   *

All through October, Harriet stayed in Blackheath, helping Louella to look after her small visitors, while Tom pestered old friends and acquaintances in his search for work. At the beginning of November, the two children went back to their parents and a new baby brother.

'I'm going to miss them awfully,' Louella told Harriet. She escorted the children down to Guildford by train and later telephoned to warn Harriet not to expect her back that night.

'Michael Pritchard insists on taking me to supper at the Angel, to thank me for my help, and it seems easier to stay on there overnight and come back tomorrow,' she said. She sounded oddly breathless and girlish, Harriet thought, and then forgot about it because Tom had come back in triumph to report that at last he had found a job.

'It's flying a mail plane from Croydon airport to Paris. It'll mean finding somewhere to live in Croydon, though. It's too far to travel from here.'

'I know somebody who lives in Croydon,' Harriet remembered. 'Vera Birkett – you met her in Kew Gardens when the little girl she was looking after had her accident. I could contact her and ask her to help us find somewhere to rent, if you like.'

'Don't you want to stay on here for the winter?' Tom asked. 'Your aunt's house is far more comfortable than any lodgings we might be able to afford in Croydon.'

'I'd rather be with you,' said Harriet. 'I'll write to Vera now.' It was only later that she worried about how easily Tom had seemed prepared to leave her behind.

'Christmas seems to come round quicker every year,' said Allie Briggs, watching as Daisy fastened a wreath of holly trimmed with red ribbon to the back door of the farmhouse. 'There's mistletoe on that dead apple tree down in the orchard,' she added. 'I saw it as I came past the wall this morning on my way here.'

'I don't know that we'll need mistletoe,' Daisy said practically. 'We've no young lovers here needing an excuse for a kiss.'

'I suppose not, now Billy and Kitty are a married couple – though your boys'll be at it before you can catch your breath, Mrs G. Still no news from Harriet?'

'No,' Daisy answered, and winced because she had pricked her hand on the holly.

'She's a naughty girl, letting you worry like this . . . If my Phyllis did the same, I'd give her what for.'

'You'd have to find her first,' said Daisy.

Part 4

1935–1936

23

'If you ask me, Madam's in love.'

Rose was the first of the staff at Medlar House to recognize the symptoms, but Everett soon conceded that she was right. After months of tight-lipped misery, their mistress was as bright-eyed and luminous as any schoolgirl in the grip of first passion.

'Well, I hope this one's better for her than the last,' said the butler. 'Anyone could see that he was just after her money. Anyway, it's put her in a good mood, so who's complaining?'

At first Louella's trips to Guildford had been weekend visits to the Hartley children and the new baby. Michael Pritchard was invariably there, at first by coincidence, or so he claimed. Then he stopped pretending and said openly that he hoped to see her again soon. Finally, in the early spring, after much hesitation and clearly bracing himself for a rejection, he asked her to accompany him for a walk in the country the following Sunday.

'We could go to Saint Martha's hill and down into Shere. The scenery is very pretty round there, and the daffodils will be out,' he said.

'I would love to,' said Louella, and then worried uncharacteristically about acquiring the right slacks and shoes for such an untried experience.

The rest of the nation had taken up country walking on a grand scale, the trains out of London being packed every weekend with hikers in shorts with haversacks. There had even been a hit song, 'I'm Happy When I'm Hiking.' But sophisticated, busy Louella had not walked anywhere for the mere pleasure of it for years. Rather to her surprise she found that she enjoyed herself immensely. More walks followed, with afternoon teas in tudor-beamed teashops. In the time she spent with Michael, he reminded her more and more of Hector for his decency, but also of her first husband Robert for the blessed simplicity of the things in which they both took pleasure.

After so many years of pretending to be a lady, with the appropriate tastes in music, art and literature, Louella found it an indescribable relief to relax and admit to a liking for popular ballads like 'Sunny Side of the Street' or 'Happy Days Are Here Again.' With Michael she could even sing them, shyly at first, then at the top of their voices, laughing.

The daytime walks were extended to evenings at the 'pictures' in Guildford, where they saw Greta Garbo and Anna Neagle, the Marx Brothers or Charles Laughton. Coming away afterwards and walking to the Angel Inn in the High Street, where Louella would stay the night, she longed for Michael to hold her hand. His slightly crumpled ordinariness had become very attractive to her now that she knew the man behind it.

At home in her elegantly furnished bedroom at Medlar House, after returning from one of the Michael days, she found herself talking to Hector's photograph in its silver frame.

'Please forgive me that I care about him, dear. It isn't betraying you, is it? He's so much like you in some ways.'

In others, he was not. The physical yearning for Michael was growing beyond anything she had felt for Hector, or even for Stuart Armitage, untainted as it was by the guilt and self-scorn that had been part of her adultery with Stuart. Michael liked her. Louella liked him; though 'like' was an inadequate word, she admitted to herself eventually. However much she shied away from 'love', it was the truth behind her feelings . . . but still he made no move to cross the gap between friendship and physical intimacy.

There was a gulf between their social and economic standing and perhaps that was what inhibited him, Louella told herself, struggling against the urge to confront him with her own seething emotions. Long used to taking control of her life, she knew instinctively that any attempt to control this particular situation would be to risk damaging it beyond repair. However much her inner self screamed at the delay, she must wait until he was ready to declare his feelings. What made the restraint bearable, though only just, was the sense that however long it took, the declaration would come. There was a vibration in the air between them that was impossible to misconstrue.

In Croydon, while Tom flew mail planes across the Channel, Harriet had enrolled on a course to teach her how to be a stenographer. At the end of it she found herself a job as a junior typist in a solicitor's office and began to learn the jargon of contracts and leases, wills and codicils. At first this meant frequent referrals to a dictionary and pages coming back with red ink corrections which had to be typed all over again, a careful key at a time, with much frustration and occasional tears.

'But you're learning fast,' said her employer approvingly, and spoke vaguely of a rise in salary in a month or two. When Harriet told Tom, with pride, he barely let her finish.

'You'd better give in your notice,' he said.

She stared at him uncomprehendingly. 'Why?'

'We have to be at Fareham by April the twelfth. We're going back to the Flying Circus.'

Louella was tired. On a warm day in May, seven miles of rambling with Michael had brought them to a stile near Compton on the Pilgrim's Way, where once Chaucer's Canterbury pilgrims might have entertained one another with stories that were sad or funny or bawdy.

Louella wished that, like the pilgrims, she had a horse or a donkey to ride. Although Michael had climbed the stile with ease, she didn't know if her legs would get her over it. She made an effort, hauled herself up, negotiated the top bar and stepped down on to the footpath; at which point her weary thighs betrayed her and she lurched forward, into Michael's arms.

His face was inches from hers. She heard her voice spilling out incoherent excuses for her fall, and his voice saying, 'Shhh . . .' and then his mouth came down on hers.

Louella closed her eyes. After months of hoping, with a patience she had not known she possessed, for Michael to make this move, her waiting was finally over. She let herself give way to the exquisite relief, the dazzling happiness of the moment. Time and place ceased to matter, there was only Michael.

Then it stopped. Abruptly, he lifted his head and pushed her away. 'No. I'm sorry. I shouldn't have done that.'

Shocked, Louella gazed at him. Already her long familiarity with situations that went wrong had supplied the sick feeling that accompanied loss.

'What is it, Michael? What's the matter? I'm not angry with you,' she blurted. 'I'm glad. It's what I've wanted for a long time . . . surely you have too?'

Michael put his hand to his forehead and closed his eyes momentarily. He looked deathly tired. He sat down on the step of the stile and reached for her hand, drawing her towards him so that she was standing beside him, their knees touching.

'Yes, I've wanted it,' he admitted. 'You can't know how I've wanted it. But it's no good, Louella. It isn't possible.'

'Why not? I don't understand. If it's the money, it doesn't matter, really it doesn't.'

'It's not the money. Louella, I should never have let this grow. It wasn't fair of me. But I enjoyed your company so much, I've come to like you so . . .'

'Michael, what are you trying to say? Are you married?'

'No, I'm not married.' Michael laughed, but without any gladness. 'That's the whole point. I'm not married and I never have been because I'm not . . . *equipped* for marriage.' His mouth twisted, cynically. 'I suppose that's one way of explaining it.'

He looked up at her and his brown eyes were bleak.

'I fought in the Great War, Louella, like just about every other man of my age. I was twenty-two and engaged to be married when I climbed out of a trench on the Somme in 1916. That was the end of my fighting days. I suppose I was very lucky; I survived. But my particular wound . . . oh God, I hate telling you this . . . it emasculated me.' He spoke with brutal clarity. 'It doesn't show, it doesn't incapacitate me in any other way. I feel all the emotions, I feel all the longings, but I can't . . . I can't make you, or any other woman happy.'

'Oh, Michael . . .' Louella said inadequately. With a sudden movement, he turned and pressed his face against her ribs. His shoulders shook. She stood there, heartsick, her dreams dissolving into air, not knowing how to comfort him, or how to comfort herself.

'My fiancée offered to go on with the engagement,' Michael said when he'd recovered himself. 'But I wouldn't let her sacrifice herself like that. She was young, pretty, she deserved to lead a normal life and have babies. I think she did get married eventually, but we've lost touch.'

'I'm not young,' Louella said. 'And having babies is a likelihood that becomes less so with every day that passes.' At this moment she was telling herself desperately that just to be held and kissed and caressed by him would be enough, to be with someone she cared about, who cared about her in return. A rescue from the arid loneliness of her widow's existence. She had done without the hope of children, and largely without sex, during her sixteen years of marriage to Hector. Her liaison with Stuart had made her aware of the depths of her frustration, but surely that could be conquered again?

'It wouldn't matter, with us,' she said, closing her mind to the conflict of emotions inside her.

'It would,' Michael said bluntly. 'You say that now, but I'm no Darby and you're no Joan. You're a beautiful, powerful woman in the prime of life, you could have the real thing. And I know my limitations as well. I have to live with the wanting – I've learned to – but I don't think I could stand it if I shared a house with you. In the weeks and months and years ahead, we'd find that it mattered more and more. I made up my mind nearly twenty years ago that there was no prospect of marriage for me, and I still hold to that. I've been weak in not telling you before, and it was unpardonable of me to kiss you just now; it's made things worse for both of us. But friends is all we can ever be,' he concluded. 'And I hope we can still be that,' he added, his eyes pleading.

Why does it always have to happen to me? Louella cried silently that night in her bedroom at Medlar House. *Why can't I ever be happy?* And she pressed her face into the pillow while her mouth twisted with the effort of stifling her sobs and the tears soaked into the cotton pillowcase. But nothing she could say would shake Michael's decision; and so she would have to make the painful journey back from love to friendship.

'Everett, I understand that it's one of the tacitly accepted perquisites of a butler's life to help himself to the sherry on occasion – but not, if you please, to the vintage port. I've checked the cellar list and there is a marked discrepancy between what my late husband laid down and what remains to be brought up. If I detect any such shortfall again, you may look for alternative employment. And Cook has become very careless lately – the food is unimaginative and the butcher's bill has escalated to a quite unjustifiable level. I shall expect to see a marked improvement. And kindly inform Rose that I won't have her canoodling with her young man on my premises. She can avail herself of the back row at the cinema, like everyone else.'

'I think we can assume,' Everett told the rest of the staff gloomily, in the servants' hall that evening, 'that Madam's little fling is over.'

In May of 1935, King George the Fifth celebrated his Silver Jubilee. The nation, tired of twitching about the goings-on in Europe, where Germany had recently overturned the military provisions of the Versailles Treaty, celebrated with him. In London there was an orchestrated programme of state occasions in which the king, old and ill, took part. Elsewhere in his kingdom there were street parties throughout the land, for which children were laboriously and expensively kitted out by their parents in red, white and blue.

Harriet Griffin, touring with Cobham's National Aviation Day team, barely noticed the furore.

On 30th May, 1935, Cobham's fliers reached Woodford in Cheshire. Harriet, who was back in the refreshment marquee and hating it, took a few minutes' break from the ceaseless supplying of cups of tea and emerged to watch the parachute fall.

The two parachutists, Ivor Price and Miss Naomi Heron Maxwell, would make their dual jump simultaneously from two Avro Cadets, the loudspeaker announced. Harriet knew the careful timing that such co-ordination would entail. With an insider's interest in such professional details, she watched while the Cadets climbed to two thousand feet.

The aeroplanes droned above the upturned faces of the crowd and two figures bundled out. One parachute opened almost immediately, the other didn't. Watching as Ivor Price toppled through the air, Harriet reminded herself that he made a habit of delaying the opening of his parachute until he had fallen the first thousand feet. It thrilled the crowd, he said.

As Ivor went on falling, she heard the first gasps of consternation around her and felt the satisfaction of knowing what other spectators did not. At last the parachute pulled out of its pack and Harriet smiled. But instead of a blossoming of white silk, the parachute stayed closed, trailing limply on the ends of its shroud lines behind the plummeting body until it hit the ground.

There was an absolute, shocked silence, then members of the ground crew ran forward. Soon the smashed body was shielded from the eyes of the spectators. Around the perimeter of the field, the loudspeakers began to blare out a tune.

'God Save The King.'

Gradually some semblance of normality was re-established. The spectators wandered back towards their cars, talking in hushed voices. Harriet turned away and went back to the tea tent, feeling numb. Ivor Price had been married for a few weeks and his bride was with him on the tour.

'He always packed his own parachute,' Tom said, later. 'He used to lay out the chute on a field somewhere quiet, sort out the lines and tie a handkerchief round them near the top, under the canopy, to keep them in order, before he folded up the canopy. He must have done it hundreds of times. God knows why, but this time he forgot to untie the handkerchief.'

The next day when the tour moved on to Retford, Naomi Heron Maxwell jumped alone.

'How can she?' Harriet wondered, 'knowing what happened yesterday?'

'I suppose it's a bit like having to get back on a horse when you've been thrown. Do it sooner rather than later. Anyway, it's her livelihood – and the show must go on,' Tom said. Harriet resisted the impulse to say, *Why?* Increasingly she found herself questioning Tom's attitudes. The way he had shrugged off the fatal accident to a man who had been a friend was just one instance of the way he seemed to skate over the surface of life, never letting deep emotions affect him.

She supposed it was the same detachment that had always kept him from making any declarations to herself about his feelings. She longed to hear him say that he loved her but he never did, even in their most intimate moments.

'Naomi's very brave,' Tom said now, and Harriet felt a spurt of jealousy. 'There's something I've always wondered about,' she said, to divert him from the subject of the lady parachutist, whose courage she couldn't match. 'When you took your nephew Edward flying, his mother was almost hysterical. James Allingham said afterwards that she'd seen

366

someone she cared for killed in a flying accident. Do you know the background?'

'It wasn't just the flying,' Tom said. 'Laura's always been a bit inclined to drama – my mother says it's the cumulative effect of her war experiences. The story, as I understand it, is that when she was a young girl she was desperately in love with a man who didn't return her feelings. Of course this in itself made him irresistible and, as young girls do, she therefore elected him The Great Love Of Her Life. He reinforced this impression by dying tragically in battle, which permanently enshrined him. She never had the chance to discover his foibles, alas.'

'Tom, you're a cynic,' said Harriet uneasily.

'I have reason to be, where women are concerned,' Tom told her. 'Maybe I'll tell you about it some day . . . but not now. Anyway,' he resumed briskly, 'to continue the saga of Laura and James: she'd acquired a husband by this time but he was a cavalry officer and promptly sustained fatal injuries too, so she promoted him to Great Love Number Two.

'No sooner had she dried her widow's tears when she fell madly in love with a dashing French airman whom she met at a medal ceremony. They had nine days of overheated romance before *he* got himself killed in an aerobatics display – his safety harness gave way and dropped him out of an inverted Spad onto a hard airfield. Which just goes to show the importance of checking your equipment thoroughly before you try anything flamboyant. Take Ivor's accident: it was bloody sickening that it happened, but it was his own error. Unfortunately, Laura was watching her particular aviator at the time of his death and it rather put her off the concept of aerobatics as entertainment, which isn't entirely surprising in the circumstances. But it's tough on Edward, who wants to fly. And it's tough on his father, too. James was a damned good pilot, but to keep Laura happy he's had to give it up entirely.'

'But don't you feel sorry for Laura? All that loving and losing,' Harriet said sadly.

'Maybe. But she doesn't have to give James such a hard

time for it. Laura's all right most of the time,' said Tom, 'but there are moments when she can be a real pain in the neck!'

Tom, for whom flying was the most important thing in life, felt only sympathy for James who had been deprived of it. Harriet, who had recently seen a man killed by a fall from an aeroplane, felt only sympathy for Laura.

On 14th June at Maidenhead, Harriet handed a jam doughnut on a plate to a slender hand with coral-tipped fingers and heard a voice she recognized from somewhere.

'Why, it's Harriet, isn't it? Tom's friend? Do you remember me?'

Harriet looked up and saw Diana Somerville, and at her shoulder, Gavin Draycott.

'Yes, I remember,' Harriet said, becoming acutely conscious that her hands were work-roughened and her face sallow with tiredness. Under the over-large apron, her cotton dress had faded in patches because she had pinned it out on a makeshift washing line in the field beside some display site and had been too busy to retrieve it before the end of a day's bleaching in the sun. Her hair was strained back from her face with a ribbon which didn't match the dress, and an escaped tendril drooped lankly over one eye.

Diana, in contrast, was perfectly coiffed, cool and elegant in a flowered voile dress with a peplum flaring out from her narrow waist.

'How are you? And how is Tom?' Diana asked, while Gavin sorted out the money for their tea. Harriet muttered that they were both very well.

'I haven't seen Tom since last autumn when you arrived at my flat to stay and then changed your minds. It was all a bit hasty. Nobody told me what was going on.'

'I'm sorry,' Harriet said. Behind Diana, the queue was already growing restless. 'I suppose Tom thought I'd explained and I thought he'd explained. We had the offer of accommodation from a relation of mine instead.'

'Oh. Well, it's so nice to see you again. We'll go and

have a word with Tom in a minute. I gather he's doing the loudspeaker announcements today.' Diana picked up her teacup and saucer and prepared to move on, but added, 'I expect we'll see you later, Harriet.'

Gavin and Harriet exchanged glances. It was only a moment of eye contact, but it was long enough and cold enough to make Harriet realize that he still resented the way she had snubbed him at Welcome Farm, and the possibility that Diana and Gavin might still be there when she emerged from the tea tent overshadowed the rest of Harriet's day. She hoped fervently that they would have grown bored and gone back to London, but when at last the staff of the tent had finished clearing up the debris of the day's catering, and she went in search of Tom, she found him standing beside one of the Tiger Moths, deep in conversation with the visitors.

'Hullo, Harriet. I've just given Diana a joy ride in the Moth.'

'That's nice. Did you enjoy it?' Harriet asked Diana, with forced conviviality.

'I simply adored it. It's no use, Tom, after such a thrill I shall simply *have* to learn to fly.'

Tom looked pleased, but Harriet noticed that Gavin seemed distinctly put out and guessed that he felt threatened by the parading of another man's skill in an area which his fiancée admired. If that was true, it echoed her own reaction.

Since her first flight with Tom last autumn, Harriet had been treated to further flying. She had overcome the early tendency to be sick, but she knew that he was disappointed by her failure to share his enthusiasm for what he considered to be one of life's richest experiences.

'I've heard Cobham's has had some accidents,' Gavin said.

'Only because someone was careless,' said Tom, on the defensive. 'An Avro that crashed at Harrogate, for instance, tried a spin from too low an altitude. Another time a plane ground-looped on landing and hit some cars and a tent. I hear the spectators thought that was all part of the show,' he added, 'and gave it a round of applause. Then there were a couple of incidents in Ireland, but they were in 1932, before my time with the show.'

'What about two weeks ago in Cheshire?' said Gavin. The question was followed by a silence, until Diana came to the rescue, effervescing determinedly – like a glass of her favourite champagne, Harriet thought sourly.

'Oh, as Tom says, flying can be dangerous if you don't take care. It's hardly on a par with ballroom dancing, is it? Anyway, the whole show is so frightfully good. Tell us more, Tom. Those formation flights in the red planes – what were they?'

'Avro 504Ks,' Tom supplied, thankful for the distraction.

'And the parachute drop . . . and that plane that flew over upside down! And the one that burst the balloons tied to those posts with spikes on the tips of its wings . . . I nearly died of excitement! As for the wing walking . . . words fail me.'

'It *is* good, isn't it?' Harriet interposed. Gavin switched his attention from Diana, which such an air of boredom and dislike that she found herself adding, 'I've always rather wanted to have a go at that.'

'Have you?' said Tom, eager and incredulous. 'Have you really?'

'Yes,' said Harriet, wondering what had possessed her to make such a claim.

'Why on earth didn't you say so?'

'I didn't think there was much chance of it,' Harriet told him, regretting her rashness more with every moment.

'Nothing easier. We could do it now. I'll clear it with Johnnie.'

He sprinted off across the field. Gavin eyed Harriet with evident disbelief.

'I wouldn't have thought wing walking was your style.'

'There are plenty of things you don't know about me,' Harriet said. The three of them waited in an uneasy silence until Tom came back with a white overall and a pair of tennis shoes. 'I couldn't find Johnnie, but we'll go ahead anyway,' he said. 'Here, I borrowed these clothes and shoes from Naomi. And some extra socks in case the shoes are too big. You'll have to wear them to get a decent grip on the wing surface.'

Harriet pulled the overalls on. Inside them, the skirt of her dress was bunched up round her hips, making her feel even more plain and lumpen beside slender Diana. As she tied the laces of the shoes with clumsy fingers, her brain was insistently replaying the image of a body falling through the air and hitting the ground. She turned to Tom to say, *I've changed my mind.* But he looked so eager and happy that the words wouldn't come.

'Getting cold feet?' Gavin said softly.

There was no help for it. She would have to live up to her declaration.

'I'll give you the signal when to go out and come back,' Tom said before he switched on the engine of the Moth. It did not seem to have occurred to him that there could be any risk in what Harriet was about to try. She nodded and climbed into the rear cockpit. At a signal from Tom, Gavin swung the propeller.

'Contact!'

As the plane took off it occurred to Harriet that the numb, unreal sensation she was experiencing was probably the same feeling that gripped a condemned prisoner about to die – the realization that what was about to happen was inevitable and there was no point in panicking about it. Already in contrast to her previous flights she was without safety harness . . . hadn't Laura Allingham's aviator died from a lack of safety harness? She shut her mind to the thought. The Moth climbed to a hundred feet and levelled out. Tom turned for a moment and gestured with his spread hand towards the starboard wingtip.

Harriet hauled herself to her feet. Above the sheltering rim of the cockpit, the slipstream from the engine was more powerful than she had anticipated, buffeting at her body so that she had to brace herself to keep standing. Almost her heart failed her until a glimpse of Diana and Gavin's upturned faces below lent her courage. Common sense might instruct her to admit she was too scared to go on and face their derision and Tom's disappointment, but pride balked at the prospect. She took hold of the rear landing wires with her right hand and clambered out of the cockpit, forcing her bent body and legs forward against the wind.

Turning her back to the cockpit she inched her way along the wing, changing one cautious hand-grip for another on the struts. Once she was clear of the slipstream from the propeller she felt a little more secure. She clambered around the inboard struts and lowered herself into a sitting position on the leading edge of the wing with her legs dangling down. Tom grinned and gave her a 'thumbs up' sign.

'Hang on,' he mouthed at her before putting the plane into a steep banking turn and then a dive. They skimmed over the airfield at about fifty feet before Tom gestured again. Clinging to the spars, Harriet shuffled her way back to the safety of the cockpit.

As she lowered herself into her seat, her legs began to tremble. She sat shaking, hardly believing what she had done.

By the time they landed, she was beginning to recover. Tom jumped down from the lower wing and held out his hands to her. She came into his arms and he swept her towards him and hugged her, then kissed her with more conviction than he had ever done.

'Well done!' he said, his eyes sparkling with pride. 'Now you're a real barnstormer!'

Harriet wondered wearily whether the winning of his approval had been worth the cost. She supposed it had – so long as she never had to do it again.

Tom was in trouble. Johnnie Johnson was furious rather than impressed by what he called a foolhardy stunt with an inexperienced amateur.

'We don't need any more deaths,' he said. 'It's bad enough getting people to forget about what happened to Ivor.

Tom, I'm supposed to report you to Alan Cobham if you and your lady friend cause us any trouble, and that I shall have to do.'

The dressing-down dented Tom's satisfaction a little but, even so, Harriet basked in his approval. That night in their hotel room he said the long-awaited words; though being Tom he diluted them.

'I must be crazy, but I've got a funny feeling I might love you.'

Because she wanted so much to believe him, she did.

At the end of June the Cobham Circus prepared to divide itself into two teams with separate itineraries to cram more shows into the flying season. The number one team had a Handley Page Clive Astra as its leading attraction and was known as the Astra Tour. The second team, the Ferry tour, was led in its fly-pasts by an Airspeed Ferry, a three-engined biplane which had been specially designed and built in Portsmouth for Alan Cobham by a company of which he was a director.

Harriet and Tom went with the Ferry team.

'What's next?' Harriet was taking a brief respite from the tea tent and had joined Tom on the edge of the field, where his task of the day was selling programmes. Tom consulted one of them before answering her question.

'Actually, it's an extra. A chap called Collins has turned up from Cambridge. He's offered to show us some glider aerobatics. There he goes now.'

Harriet shaded her eyes and watched an Avro towing a glider heavenwards. By now she was expert at identifying the height of an aeroplane and knew that it was at roughly two thousand feet that the glider released the tow wire. It fell towards the ground as the Avro banked and turned, leaving the glider spiralling on a thermal.

Harriet thought idly, as she watched the display that followed, that it was astonishing what could be done in a plane with no engine. Beside her, Tom murmured the names of the various manoeuvres. 'The man's a ruddy marvel,' he sighed with frank admiration. 'Watch this one – it's his *pièce de résistance*. It's an inverted loop, known as a bunt, which is tricky enough in any machine, let alone a glider. Of course the machine's been specially stressed to do this kind of thing. By the way, it was with a bunt that Laura Allingham's dashing Frenchman met his end,' he recalled casually.

Harriet shuddered and reached for his hand as the glider passed over the heads of the crowd on its back, with a peculiar whistling sound.

'It's so quiet, it's almost sinister,' she said. But as the aeroplane came out of the loop, still inverted, there was a sharp cracking sound and the starboard wing broke away from the fuselage.

The glider spun into the ground. Afterwards, Harriet found that her fingernails had dug so deeply into the back of Tom's hand that they had drawn blood.

24

Louella was sorting through the contents of her wardrobe, thinking ahead for autumn. In the dressing room next to her bedroom she took out various garments from the vast mahogany wardrobe and examined them briefly before either returning them to the hanging rail or passing them to her maid, who stood with an armful of discarded dresses folded over her arm.

'You can have this one as well, Alice. Or if you've no use for it, perhaps you can sell it.'

The tea gown was one of her own designs and had been made up at her factory: an electric blue dress shimmering with sequins. Being a 'Louella Ramsay' creation, it hung beautifully; but in practice she had found its weight too irritating for its flattering effect to be adequate compensation. In any case, so many of the clothes she designed were too grand for the restricted social life she led nowadays.

She was still invited out to the homes of Hector's old business associates, but on the few occasions when she accepted, she didn't enjoy herself. Her pride recoiled from the well-meaning efforts of hostesses to pair her off with an unsuitable partner, as if *any* man would do. Worst of all, she suspected that people like Helen Moffat still whispered behind her back about Stuart Armitage.

The liaison with Stuart now seemed like a bad dream or an episode from a previous life. The memories and the regrets had been pushed into the background by Michael Pritchard. At least the heartache of knowing Michael had produced that one good outcome, Louella told herself. She had come to terms with the fact that she and Michael could never be together, and as he had hoped and requested, they had stayed friends. It had required an effort on her part, but in the weeks that followed his admission they had gone on taking weekend walks together and sharing meals in country inns, and gradually the ache of longing for him had dwindled to a bearable pang of sadness.

After all, she was used to dealing with disappointments.

The most serious problem that he presented for her now was that he worked for Rupert Brownlowe. If she ruined Rupert, the manager's job would go down with the business. She couldn't do that to Michael . . . so for the time being her vendetta against Rupert was in abeyance. But now that it looked like being permanent, she had more cause than ever to rue her childlessness, and he remained the focus of her need to blame someone.

Louella took a hanger from the wardrobe and considered the fate of a black two-piece costume, the one she had worn at Hector's funeral. She couldn't grieve for ever, she decided. No more black. The widow's mourning outfit joined the garments on Alice's receptive arm.

'Well, that's cleared a bit of room for next season's new designs, anyway,' she announced. The next dress on the rail was one that she must have worn once or twice at most, but Harriet had borrowed it while she'd stayed in London and it had suited her far better than it ever suited her aunt.

Louella had a vague intention of giving the dress to Harriet – but first she would have to find her. Travelling round the country with the National Aviation Day team, that young lady was hard to keep track of.

Downstairs in the hall, the doorbell pealed.

'Everett can get it,' said Louella. 'You take those dresses away and sort them out, Alice.'

'Yes, madam. And thank you ever so much for all these lovely things, madam.' The maid carried the clothes out of the room and Louella was alone when Everett knocked at the door.

'A lady to see you, madam. I've put her in the drawing room.' He consulted a calling card held between his fingers.

'It's a Mrs Stuart Armitage, madam. She says you know her.'

Stuart's wife stood in the drawing room, looking out of the window at the broad green of Blackheath. She turned quickly as Louella came into the room, but there was nothing in her gentle features to suggest anger and Louella, who had braced herself for accusations of adultery, drew in a long breath of relief.

'Forgive me for calling on you without an appointment. I hope you remember me. I came with Helen Moffat last year, collecting for Doctor Barnardo's Homes.'

'I remember,' said Louella, wondering how the poisonous tittle-tattle of Helen's circle had apparently missed the ears of this woman. She made an effort. 'When we last met, you were expecting a child. How is your baby?'

'He was stillborn,' said Anne Armitage quietly.

The simple statement caught Louella off guard.

'Oh, I am so sorry,' she said inadequately. 'It must have been so very awful for you . . .'

'It was a blow.' The visitor's brown eyes met Louella's directly. 'People don't seem to understand how badly you can miss a child that was never alive outside you.'

'I might,' said Louella. 'I lost a baby too . . . it was twenty years ago but it still hurts.' She swallowed. 'His name was Danny. If he'd lived his proper life instead of just an hour, I expect he'd have been taller than me by now.'

'Mine was a boy as well. I was going to call him Guy. I knew he'd be a boy,' said Anne. 'We'd had such conversations beforehand, him and me . . . but he was born with the cord round his neck.'

'Oh, my dear.' Without any conscious intention, Louella found herself hugging Anne Armitage, the wronged wife of her erstwhile lover. When they stepped away from each other, there were tears on the cheeks of both women.

Half an hour later, over a pot of tea and the sandwiches brought in by Alice that neither of them could eat, Anne revealed the reason for her visit.

'I became more involved with the work of the Barnardo's Homes after the collection last year, and this made me aware of the background from which some of these orphans come. And then I realized how many families in this great city of ours are living in desperate want. I do try not to play Lady Bountiful, but I visit, and take things that I see are lacking. There's an enormous need . . . and I wondered if by any chance you could find the time to join me occasionally? It may be presumptuous of me,' Anne added apologetically, 'but I had the feeling, when we met, that you were a woman who could identify with the problems of these people, as someone like Helen Moffat could never do. She *plays* at charity. I thought you could genuinely feel it. And when you said you were brought up in Bethnal Green . . .'

'I would be honoured to help you,' said Louella.

Afterwards she told herself that she must be insane. She had agreed to an activity that would bring her into regular contact with the very woman she ought to be avoiding. What if Anne were to discover what Louella's relationship with Stuart had been? But overriding that fear was a growing delight at having come across someone with whom, for once, she felt a real affinity. In all her years as Mrs Ramsay of Medlar House, she had never taken to any other woman so quickly, or liked her so much, as Anne Armitage.

It was at Lytham on the sixth of September that Alan Cobham's reaction to Tom and Harriet's wing-walking escapade caught up with them.

'You're fired,' said Johnnie Johnson to Tom, at the end of the day's display. He passed over a letter. Numbly, Tom looked down at the terse paragraph and scrawled signature.

'I'm sorry, but the boss's decision is final. He says he warned you when we took the girl on that you'd both be out at the first hint of trouble.' Johnnie tried to soften the blow. 'If it's any consolation, there's only a little over three weeks left of the tour and, between ourselves, I doubt if there'll be another one next year – not under Cobham, anyway. He reckons the days of the flying circuses are numbered. The public's getting jaded. He's thinking of selling out.'

'Can't I stay on till the end of the season?' asked Tom.

'I'm afraid not.' Johnnie's response was sympathetic, but uncompromising.

'What shall we do?' Harriet asked, when Tom told her.

'Go to Maple Grange, I suppose, until I get a better idea. Anyway, I think it's time you met my mother.'

Harriet and Tom stood in the porch at the Grange. Harriet had uncomfortable recollections of the last time she had been here, and as Tom jerked at the iron handle which operated the bell, she was hoping that the same maid would not reappear. But when the heavy mahogany door swung open, it was a man in the dark suit of a butler who stood there.

'Hullo, Docker. I'm back. Is my mother at home?'

'Not just at the moment, sir. She's in Godalming at a committee meeting about the Surrey Fund.'

'Well, you can take these up to my room,' said Tom, nudging Harriet's little suitcase and his own with his foot.

'Yes, sir.' The butler stooped to pick up the cases. 'We read about it in the paper, sir, it was a shocking tragedy, wasn't it? Those poor young girls . . . I bet they never thought when they bought their tickets that they'd be laid out in the mortuary before nightfall.'

'What poor girls?' Tom said.

'The girls in the crash, sir.'

'Docker, what are you talking about?'

'Don't tell me you don't know, sir? I thought that was why you've come home. There's been a terrible accident at Blackpool.'

'Blackpool?' Tom cut in. 'The Cobham show was at Blackpool yesterday.'

'That's right, sir. Mid-air collision. A Wessex and an Avro, so the paper says. One young girl in the Avro thrown out, fell among the crowd, and then the plane crashed on a house and killed the other passenger. Sisters they were. Their poor mother, that's what I say. And the pilot was killed, too, of course.'

Tom cleared his throat. 'What was his name?'

'The Avro pilot? Captain Hugh Stewart, I think it said. And the pilot of the Wessex was a fellow named Carruthers, only he managed to get down safely. The Avro hit him from below according to the report, and was cut in two. I've got the paper in the kitchen, sir, if you want to see it.'

Tom put his hand to his eyes for a moment. 'So Hugh's dead, too. Three crashes in a season,' he said flatly. 'Cobham's luck's run out and no mistake.'

Harriet said nothing. She was ashamed of her first, instinctive reaction, which was to be thankful that she had escaped from the Flying Circus in time to be spared the witnessing of this latest tragedy . . . and of her second reaction, which was relief that for the time being at least, the victim of the next fatal accident would not be Tom.

'So you're back.' Rupert Brownlowe's greeting to his stepson was less than effusive. 'For how long?' he added suspiciously.

'I haven't decided yet. May I introduce you to Harriet Griffin?'

'How d'you do?' Rupert took hold of Harriet's shyly extended hand and shook it in a perfunctory way. 'Griffin? The name sounds familiar. Do I know you?'

'You knew her father,' said Tom. 'He used to work for you.'

Rupert concentrated. 'Griffin . . . good Lord, the groom! Cocky sort of fellow. Threatened me with violence in my own kitchen, I seem to remember.' He frowned at Harriet. 'Well, you're a good-looking young woman. I trust you're not going to come to blows with me? What's she here for?' he asked Tom.

'Harriet is my companion,' Tom said calmly.

'Companion? What does that mean?'

Harriet darted an agonized glance at Tom, who merely looked amused. It was at this point that Marion Brownlowe came into the room.

'Tom, Docker said you were back. And with a friend. How nice.'

Marion's social graces made no problem at all of Harriet's status. When Rupert persisted with his questions she patted him kindly on the hand and told him not to worry, she'd explain it all later.

'I like your mother,' Harriet said to Tom later, as they changed for dinner in his room. 'She was very nice to me, considering what she must have thought.'

'Oh, Mother's a real lady,' said Tom. 'Besides, she's used to me turning up here with all sorts of strange people,' he added, leaving Harriet to wish that he hadn't. She unwrapped her black lace tea gown. It had spent months in tissue paper at the bottom of her suitcase, but it was all she had and, as such, would have to do.

An awareness of being crumpled and smelling musty added to her worries about whether she could pass muster with the Brownlowes after months on the road with the Flying Circus, where meals were taken hurriedly and late, among a crew of people who had no time to worry about the niceties of passing the port.

'I don't know why you're so fussed about it,' Tom said unhelpfully. 'Mother never interferes with my friendships. And Rupert is going to dislike any friend of mine on principle.'

Whatever Marion had said privately to Rupert about her son's friend, by the time the family assembled for dinner, she had succeeded in persuading him to accept Harriet's presence at Maple Grange without further questioning. Even so, Harriet found the occasion a strain.

'It's so nice that you've come just now,' Marion said, at the end of the evening. 'Laura and James and Caroline are coming down tomorrow to stay for a few days.'

When Harriet had last seen Laura Allingham, more than a year ago, Laura had been dispensing with her services.

The prospect of meeting her former employer again only added to her tension.

Louella was late. She had waited too long for Anne Armitage to collect her. Instead, a message had come that Anne had a migraine and that for the first time, Louella would have to make the trip alone.

She had crossed the river by the foot tunnel from Greenwich and walked to her destination. She knew the way; since Anne Armitage's visit to her house, the two of them had come to this place together on several occasions. But now she was wishing that she had hired a car to take her into Poplar . . . or developed a migraine of her own. In Anne's company she had felt confident and useful. Alone, she was only conscious of feeling vulnerable.

The Jarvises were what Anne had called 'friends' ever since they had been brought to her attention by a doctor who had treated two of the children for rickets. Probably Helen Moffat would have called them 'the worthy poor'. They had eyed Louella with suspicion when she was first introduced to them, distrusting her unmistakeably well-to-do appearance. She had learned her lesson. Today her coat had been borrowed from her cook and she had left her pearls in her jewel case at home, but even so, she felt very conspicuous as she walked along the narrow street towards the house where the Jarvis family lived.

The houses were terraced, built fifty years or so before out of cheap bricks whose surface was flaking badly. There would be yellow stains on the peeling wallpaper inside, Louella knew, and a smell of dampness in the small rooms, warring with the odours of cabbage and bad drains. The stains and smells of her own childhood.

In some of the houses, preparation of the evening meal would already have begun, the long, slow stewing of the cheapest cuts of meat and the bruised vegetables sold for a song in the market as the stallholders cleared their wares away at the end of the day. She'd stood in line for such bargains herself on the days when her mother couldn't; the days when Bert Wilkins' random beatings had left Agnes too battered and shaky to cope with mundane chores.

She could remember playing hopscotch barefoot in a street like this, where the children suspended their game to stare at her now.

Louella tried to shrug the memories away. Bert Wilkins of the drunken rages and the punishing fists was dead long ago, if his son Jem was to be believed. Her mother, Agnes, was dead too . . . poor, frightened Agnes, who'd fallen into a second marriage because she didn't know how to live alone, and had ended up worse off than the most poverty-stricken of widows: victim of a sadistic monster who'd raped her . . . and who, in his worst moments, had inflicted the same treatment on her children.

The women standing in doorways, arms folded, watched her with a sullen curiosity as she walked by. She supposed that despite her past in Bethnal Green and today's borrowed coat, they could tell that she didn't belong, and never had. Coming from the Essex countryside, from a different, cleaner kind of poverty, she had been shocked by the slum to which her stepfather had brought them. It was Jem, her half-brother, who had grown up a true child of the London streets, ragged and cunning.

She had almost forgotten about Jem, and now she wondered where he was and what he was doing. The fact that she did not know made her feel faintly insecure.

The Jarvis family had cockroaches.

'They comes out at night,' said Enid Jarvis. She gestured around the room hopelessly. 'I try to keep 'em off the kids. Me and Bill, we have the little 'uns in bed with us. And I try to keep the place clean, I really do. But those bloody bugs, they comes out of the cracks at night and drops off the ceiling.'

'Mrs Armitage told me. I've brought some powder,' Louella said, fishing in the bag which was another of the props supplied by a reluctant cook. 'You sprinkle it where they run and it discourages them.' Already she was aware that she hadn't brought enough.

'Thanks very much.' Enid took the packet of powder from her and studied the instructions printed on it, brow creased, before setting the gift down carefully on the mantelpiece. Louella guessed that she couldn't read.

'Fancy a cuppa tea?' Without waiting for an answer Enid bent under the mantelpiece to transfer the kettle to the centre of the hotplate. She was eight months pregnant with her fifth child, living in two rooms on the ground floor of a crumbling house with no electricity, no gas and no running water. The kitchen in which they were standing stank of fish and when she moved a cooking pot to one side to make room for the kettle a stronger waft of the smell rose from it.

'Cod's 'ead,' said Enid. 'I come by it down the market. I'll be making fishcakes later.' She hesitated, then added doggedly, 'You'd be welcome to stay, Mrs Ramsay.'

Louella recognized the heroism behind the offer. Bill Jarvis was on the dole, payable every Thursday. By Monday the money was usually exhausted. Today was Friday and the cod's head would have been part of yesterday's spending spree down at the market to compensate for three days of semi-starvation. If she stayed there would be that much less for the hungry children and for their gaunt, stubbornly proud parents. She also knew that Enid had seen her instinctive recoil from the smell and that to refuse would be to compound the insult.

'I wish I could. It smells delicious,' she said carefully. 'But I'm afraid I already have a supper appointment.' At Medlar House there would be steak tournedos. What if she brought steak, another time? But Anne had made her aware of how fine was the balance between welcome help and resentable charity. 'I would love to stay another time.'

'Oh well, if you're sure you can't . . .' Enid lifted the lid on the pot and prodded at the contents.

'Mrs Armitage sent some clothes,' Louella said, putting her bag down on the table. 'She says a cousin's children have outgrown them so if you can use them you'd be doing her a favour.'

'Bless 'er. She's a good sort, is Mrs Armitage.' Enid threw

two teaspoonfuls of tea from a battered tin caddy into the brown teapot on the edge of the stove and added boiling water, stirring the contents vigorously.

The cries of the children in the street were faint in the background as Louella sipped her dark brown tea. The room grew shadowy with twilight. Enid moved to the window. ' 'Ere's the lamplighter.' She pushed up the bottom half of the sash and leaned out. 'Phyllis, you bring the little 'uns in now.'

Louella knew Phyllis, the oldest Jarvis child, aged eight. Every day after school she was sent into the street with responsibility for her siblings. Every night when the lamplighter came round her mother called her in and she would deliver up the younger children. At eight, Phyllis sometimes behaved like a wise little old woman despite her plaits and the gap-toothed smile of a child. As she appeared, manoeuvring a pram through the doorway, now came the moment that Louella had been waiting for.

'Just you behave yerselves and Mrs Ramsay'll tell you a story while I dish up yer grub.'

Phyllis sat down cross-legged on the rag rug in front of the stove and gazed up at the visitor. Two smaller Jarvis children leaned against Louella's thighs, eyes bright with anticipation under unkempt fringes, as Enid transferred the youngest from the pram to her lap.

'Can it be 'ansel an' Gretel?' asked Phyllis.

'You had that last time.'

'I'd like it again.'

As Louella recited the familiar lines, the baby fell asleep in the crook of her arm, lulled by her voice. She wondered for an insane moment whether Enid would part with the baby, for money, and knew in the same heartbeat that it was no use even asking.

Although Harriet had been dreading the arrival of Laura and James Allingham, her welcome from Caroline was so wholehearted that it smoothed over the difficult moment. Caroline's new nanny, who might have been defensive of her position, was blessedly untouched by jealousy and Harriet spent a happy day with the little girl in the garden at Maple Grange.

Tom, who had disappeared after breakfast 'on business', reappeared in time for supper.

'I've been to see Diana,' he told Harriet. 'She's still engaged to that Draycott idiot,' he added, on such a sour note that Harriet wondered with a pang whether he was still in love with Diana.

'Anyway, she's going to try to get me some work,' said Tom. 'It was through a contact of hers with a chap called Tilston at the Airspeed company in Portsmouth that I got on to the Cobham team. Tilston founded the company with Nevil Shute Norway and they built the Ferry for Cobham's show. Now Diana thinks she might be able to wangle me a job at Airspeed.'

'As a pilot?' asked Harriet, heart sinking.

'No, as an engineer, worst luck, but needs must when the devil drives.' Tom, resigning himself for the time being to a flightless career, did not notice Harriet's small tremor of relief.

Over supper, Rupert cross-questioned his son-in-law James about his political activities and James parried his comments with restraint, while Laura noticeably chewed at her lip and exchanged expressive glances with Marion. Harriet sat silent at her place, grateful that nobody was paying her any attention, until the lull between the clearing of the dessert course and the bringing in of the cheeseboard, when James turned to her, suddenly.

'What about you, Harriet? What will you do now that you've left the Cobham team?'

'I take it you won't be a nanny again, anyway,' Laura put in, with an artificial brightness which suggested that Harriet had better not harbour any such ambitions.

'I don't know,' Harriet said. 'I suppose I might be a stenographer. I did the training last year and I worked for a solicitor for a little while afterwards, only I had to leave when the Cobham tour started again in the spring.'

'Really?' said James kindly. 'Well, if you think of taking that up again, I may be able to help. And Tom? Any plans yet?'

'I'm hoping for an interview with Airspeed in Portsmouth.'

'Have you ever been to Portsmouth, Harriet?' asked Laura. Harriet shook her head, and Laura continued, 'How do you think you'll like living in a naval port?'

'She won't be coming with me anyway,' said Tom.

'It's the most sensible thing,' Tom explained afterwards. 'You go to Croydon. You'll have your friend Vera there for company, and you might even get your old job with that solicitor back. It won't be for ever,' he soothed, belatedly aware of the shuttered expression behind which Harriet's world was disintegrating. 'I'll go on putting out feelers for flying work, maybe some more mail-plane flying from Croydon if I'm lucky. But in the meantime I'll be working all hours at Airspeed – assuming I get a job, that is – and you'd only be lonely if you come with me.'

'I'll be lonely without you,' said Harriet in a small voice, but Tom pretended not to hear what she'd said.

His decision confirmed her fear that whatever his feelings might be towards Diana, his love for herself had run out . . . if it had ever existed.

No ties, no regrets, no expectations. That way, when it's over, nobody gets hurt, he had said at the beginning. It wasn't true. Harriet was getting hurt, and she didn't know how to bear it.

Because she didn't know what else to do, Harriet obeyed Tom's instructions and returned to Croydon. But when she called at the flower shop, it was only to be told that Vera no longer worked there.

'She's married now. I'll give you her address, if you want it,' said the florist, and scrawled the information down on a scrap of paper.

'Cheer up, it may never 'appen,' he said as she was leaving.

'It already has,' said Harriet.

By the time she reached the address she had been given, it was already twilight. Vera opened the front door of the neat little house in a back street not far from the florist's and stood silhouetted against the light. The door opened directly into a small sitting room and behind her the wireless was playing dance music.

'Harriet?' she said. 'Is it really you?'

'Yes, it's me.'

'Well, don't just stand there, come on in and let's give you a proper hug!' She caught hold of Harriet's hand and pulled her in over the doorstep before delivering the promised embrace.

'Fine friend you turned out to be!' Vera scolded, when the first breathless welcomings were over. 'Didn't even come to my wedding!'

'I didn't know about it,' Harriet said.

'Well, it wasn't exactly easy to let you know, was it? Travelling around from pillar to post and hardly even a postcard. I'd written you off,' Vera said, with a broad smile that belied her words. 'Hang on, I'll put the kettle on.' Crossing to the kitchen door she paused by the sideboard to turn down the volume on the radio. 'Sorry, it's a bit loud. I have it on all day, I'm a real addict of dance music. Well, better make the most of it, I suppose, I won't have much time for dancing once the little 'un's born.' She patted her stomach.

'Vera, you don't mean you're going to have a baby?'

'Too right I am! Fred didn't waste much time once he'd got the ring on my finger. Come into the kitchen, it's cosier in there. And I've just made a cake. You want feeding up a bit, by the look of you.'

Within five minutes, Harriet had a cup of tea in one hand and a plate of cake in the other. In ten minutes, she had a roof over her head.

'You can stay here, we've got a spare room. It's tiny, like

all the rest of the house, as you can see. But it's got a bed in it, which is the main thing! I'm afraid I'd have to charge you a bit of rent, though,' Vera added apologetically. 'Fred *would* have me give up working once we were married, and he's even more determined about it now there's going to be a youngster; but it's a struggle to make ends meet sometimes, and we'd been thinking we ought to let the room to help pay off what we owe on the furniture.'

Harriet unpacked her suitcase thankfully in the small room that Vera had shown her. As she took out the tea gown, Vera whistled.

'My, I bet you look a real treat in that! You'll have all the boys after you when you go dancing. But I forgot, you've got a young man already, haven't you?'

'I don't know,' said Harriet. When she explained about Tom and Portsmouth, Vera was properly indignant.

'Left you in the lurch, has he? Cold as yesterday's roast dinner, by the sound of him. Good riddance if he *has* gone, if you ask me. But oh, Harriet, you have been a bit of a silly girl, haven't you? These young gentlemen . . .'

Finding a job with which to pay her rent was Harriet's next problem. When she called at the office where she had previously worked, a smart young woman with a supercilious smile was seated behind the typewriter, attacking the keys with daunting efficiency, and the solicitor told her that there was no vacancy for her. She turned to go, but he called her back.

'You weren't very fast, but you were careful and conscientious,' he told her. He scribbled down a few more addresses of law firms in the area for her to try and supplied a letter of testimonial. By the afternoon of her second day back in Croydon she had found herself a job.

'Well, for someone who's just fallen on her feet you do look down in the dumps,' Vera told her that evening. 'What's up? Is it that Tom of yours? I told you, you're better off without him.'

'Yes, I know it.' But knowing what was good for her didn't make it any more palatable to Harriet. She missed

Tom terribly. The mere act of going to bed alone in her narrow bed in Vera's house, instead of in some anonymous hotel bedroom with Tom's arm thrown casually across her shoulders, made her feel achingly desolate, and the faint sounds of Vera and Fred from the room next door compounded her loneliness. It was bad enough when they made love. It was worse when they talked softly and laughed together.

Tom had promised to write but she couldn't be sure that he would.

25

Will Griffin had sat up all night with a cow whose calf was taking a long time to be born. It was her first, and she lowed plaintively at each convulsion of her sides, her wide, distressed eyes rolling sideways towards the farmer. Will stood beside her and made soft soothing noises, one hand laid reassuringly against her damp neck until, an hour before dawn, the newborn calf lay in the golden straw of the barn. It was a heifer, Will discovered, with a flicker of relief. This one could join the milking herd and wouldn't have to go early to market for butchering.

He stretched his arms above his head to ease his aching back, smiling with satisfaction. After all his years as a dairy farmer he still found it moving and miraculous to watch a cow giving birth. The heifer had finished licking the calf's body dry and now she prodded with her nose, nudging it up on to its shaky legs. A minute later the baby was upright, eyelids still glued together but already feeding hungrily from its mother's udder, and Will was free to go indoors.

In the kitchen he made himself a cup of tea and sat in the Windsor chair beside the kitchen range, drinking it slowly. The first faint dawn light was showing outside the window as he dragged his weary body upstairs to snatch half an hour's sleep before the relentlessly recurring task of morning milking.

Jem Wilkins had earned a packet, roadbuilding on the A3, but he'd spent it as fast as he'd earned it, on alcohol and girls, or on the card games with which the road gang kept themselves amused at nights. He'd got into a fight over marked cards and which woman belonged to which man for the night, and the fight had led to a death.

Jem didn't see it as his fault – he'd just pulled a knife faster than his opponent – but he wasn't sure the law would agree with him, so he'd decided it would be wise to make himself scarce for a while. Being at a loose end, he flipped a coin to decide which of the women in his past to look up first – Louella, his half-sister, source of lucrative commissions, or Kitty, his abandoned common-law wife.

The coin came down tails, which meant Kitty. He had a vague recollection of having blotted his copybook at Welcome Farm, not least with his sudden departure, but he wasn't much bothered by the prospect of what Will Griffin might have to say about that.

The trees along the lane that led towards Starling Cottages were vivid with autumn colour. He'd forgotten how clean the air smelled in the country, and how soothing the sound of birdsong could be. When he came in sight of the cottages, he had a pang of something that might even have been homesickness . . . he'd drawn the building once, trying to reproduce the texture of the stonework and the warm russet flush of the tiles on the roof. What had happened to that sketchbook? He'd probably left it behind when he stormed out.

He noticed as he came closer that the little place looked smarter than when he'd last seen it. The oak door had been oiled and the window frames had a fresh coat of paint. There were new curtains at the window and flowers in a pot on the sill. Kitty must have turned into a proper little housekeeper. She'd even holystoned the doorstep.

At that moment he was feeling quite drawn towards the memories he had of Kitty. She'd irritated the hell out of him sometimes with her frightened-mouse imitations, but she'd been a comforting armful on a cold night, and not such a bad cook either. And she'd taken the blows he'd handed out with a surprising courage for someone so thin and scared-looking. He could have done worse. He thought it might be time to reclaim her, along with his sketchbook.

He knocked at the door and waited with pleasurable anticipation.

'Jem! What're you doing here?'

Kitty's reaction was a mixture of surprise and anger. Whatever kind of welcome he'd expected, it wasn't this.

'Thought I'd see how you were getting on.' Jem looked past her into the little room. It was neat and comfortable and there was a fire burning in the grate. Jem had slept rough most nights for the past few months, rolled in a blanket inside one of the pottery pipes that were laid for drainage under the new road surface. He felt the lure of the fire, coupled with an awareness that Kitty had filled out and grown up while he was away. She might even be described as pretty, now, and the traces of refinement that had attracted him to her in the first place had reappeared. It was interesting, too, that she wasn't frightened of him any more.

'Aren't you going to invite me in?' He stepped forward, and found the door rammed against his foot.

'No, I'm not,' said Kitty, from behind it.

Jem resisted the closing door. Kitty shoved. For a moment her left hand was curled round the side of the door. There was a thin gold ring on the third finger. It took him a moment to work out the significance of that. By the time he'd done so, the door was closed in his face and, behind it, he heard the sliding of bolts.

Jem hammered on the oiled wood. No answer. He hammered again.

'Kitty? Open the bleedin' door, will you?'

Silence. He bent to the letter box.

'Married, are you? Who was it took you on, then? Not that one-armed cripple?'

'Go away, Jem, or I'll have your eye out with a broom handle.'

Kitty's voice sounded remarkably strong. Jem considered breaking the door down and teaching her a lesson, but what would that get him, apart from a few minutes' satisfaction and more police after him? He recognized a lost situation.

'Don't kid yourself you've seen the last of me,' he told the closed door before he turned away.

Walking back towards the crossroads, he heard the sound of a tractor on the far side of the hedge. As he drew level with the field gate he stopped to look in at the chocolate-brown stripes of newly turned soil and felt another pang of regret that he'd walked away from Welcome Farm and the tasks associated with farming.

It had been hard physical work, the same as any work that came to a man of his background was hard, but there'd been a satisfaction in transforming a field of wheat stubble into that dark, ribbed expanse ready for sowing. And then, so quickly, the new shoots had come up, turning the land green again, and that had been satisfying too . . . except that the crop and the land that generated it had belonged to someone else.

His mouth twisting sardonically, Jem shut off the moment of nostalgia like a tap. He was a townie, born and bred. For the likes of him, farming was a mug's game and farm labouring was one degree better than slavery. He straightened his shoulders and walked on quickly down the lane.

Will Griffin had been in a daze, driving the tractor mechanically until, turning the Ford at the end of a furrow, he caught sight of the watcher at the gate. He shook his head to clear away the fuddled sensation that was the result of virtually no sleep last night and today's five hours on the tractor. The afternoon sun was in his eyes and he couldn't be sure of the identity of the man, but there was something vaguely familiar about that figure in the distance – the way he leaned his arms along the top bar of the gate, and that dark hair, the red scarf knotted at his neck.

Jem Wilkins? It couldn't be. Already the man was out of sight. But as Will drove on down the field, the nagging sense of unease stayed with him, making it even harder to concentrate on the task in hand.

*　　　*　　　*

The London train stopped at Farnham station. Glancing idly out of the carriage window at the platform, Jem was in time to see a familiar figure reaching for the handle of a compartment further down the train.

'Rupert Brownlowe . . . wonder where he's going?'

Since he had nothing better to do, Jem decided to find out.

Rupert didn't get off the train at Guildford. He travelled on to London and at Waterloo, he took a cab. Jem, sifting quickly through his remaining cash, climbed into the one behind it.

'Follow that geezer in front, will you?'

The cab took Brownlowe to a street in Greenwich.

'Carry on round the corner,' Jem instructed his driver. 'Stop here.' He paid off the driver hastily and sprinted back to the corner of the road, in time to see his quarry disappearing into a house along the street. Strolling past it, Jem made a note of the number on the door and sat down on the pavement with his back leaned against a lamp-post to await Brownlowe's reappearance.

'Waiting for Maudie, are you?' A middle-aged man with sallow skin and a balding head had materialized silently from the shadow of a neighbouring doorway.

'No, I'm waiting for a friend of mine,' said Jem.

'But he's at Maudie's? Number Twenty-three?'

'What if he is?' Jem said, cautiously.

'Regular of hers, is he?'

'What's it to you?'

'I keep an eye on Maudie,' said the man. 'Some of her customers can be a bit dodgy sometimes. I seem to remember seeing your friend here before, though. He's a bit old to give her any trouble, but it's as well to be on the safe side. Not going in yourself, are you?'

'No,' said Jem. He uncrossed his legs and rose to his feet in one easy movement. 'Matter of fact, I don't think I'll bother waiting for my mate. I've got better things to do.'

So Rupert Brownlowe patronized a knocking-shop. 'Randy old sod,' Jem muttered to himself as he strolled away. He made for Blackheath, wondering what use Louella could make of this gem of information.

'Madam's not at home.'

Everett had a long memory for faces, especially faces that spelled trouble, and in the course of their occasional past encounters, Jem Wilkins' features had impressed him as particularly high in trouble potential. Jem scowled at the black-coated figure blocking the front doorway at Medlar House.

'When's she likely to be back?'

'I'm afraid I couldn't say.'

'Well, can you give her a message? No, on second thoughts, I'll write,' Jem said, remembering that at present he had no address through which Louella could contact him. He wasn't about to hand over news that could be worth cash to the butler. 'Tell her I called,' he said over his shoulder, as he ran down the steps. 'The name's Wilkins. Tell her I'll be in touch.'

'The less contact Madam has with the likes of him, the better,' Everett decided, and when Louella came home an hour later from Poplar, he neglected to mention Jem's visit.

Jem's next move was a mistake: he went back to Bethnal Green, intending to resurrect some old contacts and call in a few old debts, and he compounded the mistake by revisiting his former home. He only strolled down the street past the house, but it was enough. Edie Perkins was still nursing resentment – and a long, livid scar on her midriff – from the scalding soup that Jem had tipped over her on the day he'd learnt about his mother's death. When she glanced out of the window and saw him in the street, she recognized an opportunity for revenge.

Edie wanted Jem punished, but she didn't want him to know it was her he had to thank for it – she knew too much about his long memory and his ways of dealing with his enemies. So she ran round to the Crown and Cushion to have a word with Kitty's Uncle George, who didn't share that knowledge.

George reported Jem's presence in the area to the police.

Arrested for the theft of the overnight stash from the pub, Jem admitted in court that he had taken the money – but only for the girl he loved, to save her being cheated by her uncle. He hadn't benefited from the cash himself. As for the girl, she'd used him to make her escape, then deserted him. He'd been pretty cut up about it at the time. His frank confession of culpability appealed to the magistrates, as did the plight of a young man in love, led astray by a scheming woman. The six months' sentence they handed down was correspondingly light.

Jem's humble thanks to the bench was not entirely a sham. It was better than being fingered for that murder on the A3, he reckoned, and it would get him three meals a day and a roof over his head through the winter, even if the bed was a hard one and there were bars on the window.

'Harriet, you're an orphan, aren't you?'

Coming in from work to be met by Vera's enquiry, Harriet remembered just in time that she had told her friend in Kew Gardens, more than a year ago, that her parents were dead.

'Yes,' she said cautiously. 'Why?'

'I suppose they can't have meant you, then. Funny, though, he said something about her being with Cobham.'

'Who did?'

'The man in the radio announcement. They put it out a few minutes ago, at the end of the news. *Harriet Griffin, last heard of in September of 1934, thought to be travelling with Cobham's National Aviation Day team* . . . I started to write it down,' said Vera, 'only my pencil broke. But if you're an orphan, it can't have meant you.'

'What did it say?' demanded Harriet.

'It said would Harriet Griffin go to some hospital in Guildford, where her father, Will Griffin, is dangerously ill.'

*   *   *

397

'I'm Will Griffin's daughter. There was a message on the radio for me to come.' Harriet was still breathless after running up the hill from Guildford station.

'Oh, you're the one they didn't know how to find,' said the woman at the reception desk. She sounded hostile, and her eyes were cold.

'How is he?' Harriet said. 'I only heard he was ill.'

'He's very poorly indeed. He had an accident with a tractor.'

'But he's going to be all right?'

'That I couldn't say. He's got a punctured lung. Your mother's here,' the nurse told her. 'Perhaps she can give you more details.'

Daisy sat alone on a hard chair in a corridor, her hands linked in her lap. She looked older, Harriet thought: small and sad, and wan with worry. There were grey streaks in her copper-coloured hair that hadn't been there before.

'Hullo, Mum.'

'Oh, Harriet!' Daisy rose from her chair and spread her arms wide and Harriet came into them, to be cried over like the prodigal daughter that she was.

'He was turning the tractor at the edge of a field,' Daisy explained when the tearful reconciliations were over. 'He must have got a bit too close to the drainage ditch and one of the back wheels went over the edge. The tractor toppled on its back, and Will was under it. I don't understand how it could have happened – he's normally so careful. Except that he'd been up all night seeing to a calving. If Rob hadn't come past from school just after it happened and gone for help, it might have been too late.'

'The nurse said he'd got a punctured lung?'

'And smashed ribs and a crushed leg. It's been touch and go whether they'd amputate the leg. Matter of fact, it's been touch and go whether he'd live at all,' Daisy said starkly. 'But the doctors who operated say they think he'll survive now. So I'm sitting here with my fingers crossed . . . Heaven knows what's happening at home, but Kitty said they'd cope and not to worry. Oh, Harriet, what an awful time for you to come back! I can't even be properly glad to see you, because of the reason you're here.' Daisy wept quietly into her handkerchief while Harriet sat beside her and patted her shoulder and swallowed her own tendency to be weepy because she was afraid that if she once started, she would never stop.

'How did you know to come?' Daisy asked at last, resorting to Harriet's handkerchief to mop up the last of her tears.

'Someone said they'd heard it on the radio – that my father was dangerously ill.'

'I hope you didn't mind me telling them he was your father,' said Daisy. 'Things were so muddled, I couldn't think straight. And I don't know if they'd have put out the message if I hadn't said you were his daughter. You *are* his daughter, you know,' she added, after a moment. 'In everything except the first little bit – and that's the least important, it seems to me! He's always loved you and cared for you as if you were his own.'

'I know,' said Harriet. 'I've been so stupid about it. I suppose the shock of finding out about . . . "the first little bit" knocked me sideways – it seemed as if there was no bottom to what I'd been standing on, if you see what I mean. Then by the time I started to come to my senses I'd gone too far, and said too much, and been too awful, to know how to come back. And it got harder the longer I left it.'

'Well, you're back now, anyway,' said Daisy, with a tremulous smile.

'Can I see him?'

'He's asleep now. A bit later on. Oh, it'll be such a lovely surprise for him when he wakes up!'

An hour passed and then another. Daisy's eyelids drooped. Harriet sat on in the hospital corridor with her mother's sleeping head heavy on her collarbone, her own eyes wide open, offering silent thanks to whatever deity might be responsible for the fact that Will was alive and that she hadn't come too late to make amends.

*　　*　　*

On the hatstand in the narrow hallway of Fred and Vera's house in Croydon was a shelf with a tray in Benares brassware on which Vera had told her new lodger that she would put any letters for her.

So far in Harriet's residence there had been no letters, though she had looked every morning on her way out to work, in the hope that Tom might have kept his promise to write to her.

Today the postman had come late. Vera, picking up the letter addressed to Harriet from the doormat and seeing the Portsmouth postmark, had sniffed and said, 'About time too, my lad,' before laying it on the tray; but in the evening flurry of discovering that her friend wasn't an orphan after all, and helping her in her dash for home and hospital, Vera had forgotten to draw Harriet's attention to the letter.

'And what with all the panic, the poor girl never left me any forwarding address. Oh, well,' Vera remarked to Fred, when she noticed it still lying on its tray, 'she'll just have to have it when she comes back.'

Once Will was off the critical list at the hospital, Daisy turned her attention to how the family and the farm would get on during what was bound to be a long convalescence. She found to her astonishment that the situation had already been sorted out.

'I'm taking time off school,' Rob said. 'Jackie wanted to as well, but I wouldn't let him. He's at the grammar with me, these days,' he added to Harriet, who was standing silently in the background. 'You missed all the family excitement last year, when he got a scholarship as well.'

It had cost Will and Daisy some sleepless nights to decide, nearly three years ago, that since Rob had passed the scholarship examination he should take up the chance of attending the grammar school in Farnham, even though it meant postponing the time when he could be a full-time helper at Welcome Farm. When Jackie, too, won a scholarship, there had been no agonizing over what to do for the best. Jackie had always been what Rob called 'the family brainbox', and there was no question of denying the younger boy what had been granted to the older one.

'There wasn't much point in him falling behind in class and messing up his chances when he's only just started at the grammar,' Rob told his mother. 'Anyway, I'm the one with the muscles.'

'But you shouldn't be missing your lessons either,' Daisy worried, though she suspected that if it wasn't for the unhappy circumstances of Will's accident, Rob would have been glad of an excuse to escape from school. He had never complained, but she'd had the impression that he felt out of place among the grammar boys and found it hard to keep up with the schoolwork, unlike Jackie, who had taken to the academic life as if to the manner born. 'Maybe we could hire a manager, just for a while,' she suggested, trying not to think of what that would cost.

'That'd be silly.' Rob dismissed the suggestion briskly. 'I know the stock, I know the work – I've not been watching Dad all these years for nothing. And I'm no swot like Jackie, I'm nowhere near the top of the class anyway, so a few weeks off won't make much difference to me. Billy's been doing the work of two able-bodied men, he's been splendid, and Kitty's been a perfect brick as well. You know how petrified she's always been of the cows, but she's rallied round and learned to use the milking machine. And now Harriet can help her, can't you, Harry? Assuming that you're prepared to stick around for a bit,' he remarked pointedly.

Harriet flushed. Daisy's welcome had been unreserved, but the boys' reaction to the arrival of their sister had been distinctly cool so far. 'Of course I'll stay, for as long as I'm needed,' she said.

'And Allie says she's prepared to come and stay for a while, Mum, to keep the house in order and all of us properly fed and clothed, so you can spend all the time that you want at the hospital, with Dad,' Rob finished. 'So you see, we'll manage fine.'

* * *

401

Precipitated back into the daily routines of the farm with a vengeance, Harriet had little time in which to wonder what was happening in her other life. She supposed her employer would have found another typist. Vera and Fred would probably have taken a new lodger. Tom . . . ?

She didn't want to think about Tom.

After two weeks of fending for himself, Stanley Briggs took to coming along to the farm for his evening meal, on the grounds that if Allie was cooking for seven, she might as well be cooking for eight. He would return home by way of the Red Lion, and then report the prevailing gossip to his wife on the following evening.

'I hear that young toff Gavin Draycott's taken a knock,' he said, one night at the kitchen table in the farmhouse. 'His lady love's given him the elbow, so they say.'

Harriet looked up quickly. Stanley speared a chunk of beef with his fork and rotated it in the sea of gravy on his plate, then popped it into his mouth and chewed with agonizing thoroughness before he continued.

'He was engaged to some girl in London – rich girl, too, she was. His family were over the moon. But she's given him the push. There was a notice in the nobs' paper to say, *"The wedding will not now take place."* '

His voice imitated the precision of a *Times* announcement. He prodded at another lump of beef. 'Wasn't Draycott after young Harriet, a few years back?'

Harriet didn't answer and Allie, with a rare moment of insight, recognized that the subject was a sensitive one. Since Harriet's return she had been cold towards the absentee, who in her opinion had behaved like a spoilt young madam and upset Will and Daisy for no good reason, but now she remembered Harriet's misery at the time of Gavin Draycott's defection and her sympathy was engaged. Standing behind her husband at the table, she dolloped a strategic second helping of beef stew on his plate as a distraction. It did the trick.

Lying awake in her room at midnight, Harriet told herself

that Diana Somerville must have thrown Gavin over because there was someone else in her life. Logically, what simpler explanation could there be than that the 'someone' was Tom? It had been bound to happen. After all, he had never really loved herself. And he'd never stopped loving Diana . . . who was rich and well dressed and pretty in a blonde and fragile way – like a china doll. She was also silly and snobbish and vain. Well, if that was the kind of woman that Tom Searle liked, he was welcome to her and she didn't care a bit!

Except that he had been funny and silly and serious, unreasonable, unpredictable and, just occasionally, achingly tender. It was those moments of tenderness that had kept her with him in spite of all the other persistent, jarring signs that he didn't love her.

Harriet stared at the ceiling while the hot, angry tears slid sideways over her cheeks and trickled into her ears. She told herself savagely that she had been silly to get involved with Tom, silly to get involved with Gavin, silly in just about everything she'd done in the past two years. And now was the time to pay for her mistakes.

Christmas was looming and Rupert Brownlowe felt even less enthusiastic about the prospect than he had done in previous years. The truth was that the season was damned expensive. So far as possible, he had cut back on the festivities and the charitable donations that seemed to be expected from someone of his social standing. He knew that in the process he had earned himself a reputation in the area as a bit of a Scrooge. Even so, there remained an obligatory core of expenditure: the Christmas Boxes for the staff, and the presents for his family.

Rupert totted them up grimly: his daughter Laura, James and their two children. His son Oliver, Oliver's wife Claire and their big, boisterous sons, who would expect train sets and Meccano sets and heaven knows what else. Marion. Tom. He knew Marion would be happy enough with a token bottle of perfume – she was a good woman and understood that money was tight without his having to go into embarrassing details about it. But he really begrudged Tom a present.

What was Tom doing nowadays? They hadn't seen him since his unexpected arrival at Maple Grange in the autumn, with the red-headed girl in tow. She'd been a good-looker, Rupert recalled, and surprisingly well mannered considering her background: Will Griffin's daughter.

Thinking about his former groom reminded Rupert of the chestnut colt in his stables. Starbright had spent the summer running loose in the paddock with his dam, but now he was in for the winter, eating his head off and growing more wilful by the minute. Rupert had hired a succession of lads from the village for general stable duties, but they all found Starbright a handful.

It was high time the colt commenced his formal training. He should be handled, bridled and backed ready for breaking in, but who was to do it? Not Rupert, elderly and arthritic. He'd had hopes that perhaps Tom . . . ? But Tom had gone off flying.

Will Griffin's daughter, Laura had mentioned, came from a place called Welcome Farm, just over the border into Hampshire. Rupert wondered whether Griffin had retained his old magic with horses and, if so, whether he might be persuaded to take on Starbright's education? He might even be prepared to do it on the cheap, Rupert told himself hopefully. For old time's sake.

'You'll have to go round the side, to the kitchen door. It's too much of a performance to open this one.'

Standing on the front doorstep at Welcome Farm, Rupert was taken aback by the brisk instruction issuing from the letter box. He was not accustomed to being directed to kitchen doors – he'd have trouble remembering what his own kitchen door looked like. His complexion darkening, he stumped round the corner of the house, to be met by a dumpy countrywoman with a dour expression, topped by a permed frizz of hair that some inept village hairdresser had presumably copied – badly – out of a women's magazine.

Rupert scowled at her. 'I'd like a word with Will Griffin. Kindly tell him that Mr Brownlowe is here to see him.'

'I can't. He's not here,' said the woman. She did not volunteer any further information about the whereabouts of the owner of Welcome Farm. Nor did she invite him into the house despite the December drizzle settling on the crown of his hat.

'Are you Mrs Griffin?' Rupert demanded.

'No. I'm the daily.'

'Ah.' Now Rupert remembered that at the end of the Great War, Will had married a widow who already had a child. Hadn't she been a housemaid at the Grange before the war? His memory was full of holes nowadays, but he seemed to recall some vague unpleasantness over that housemaid. Still, it had all been so long ago. What was her name? Some flower or other. Marigold? Primrose? Daisy? That was it, *Daisy*. And she'd been a pretty little thing, who could never in a month of Sundays have aged into this unprepossessing female.

'Is Daisy Griffin here?'

'No, she's at the hospital.'

'Harriet Griffin, then.'

'She's at the hospital too. There's Rob, if you must 'ave a Griffin,' said the daily. 'He's in the stables over the yard.'

As Rupert crossed the farmyard, a boy emerged from the stable block. Rupert's patchy memory gave him a moment of clarity. This dark-haired lad of about fourteen or fifteen had Will Griffin's wiry frame and alert eyes.

'You'll be Rob Griffin. The woman at the house told me you'd be able to help me, as your father's not at home at present.'

'I might. Depends what you want.'

Rupert told himself ruefully that Will Griffin's lad had also inherited his father's lack of respect for his social betters. He controlled his temper.

'I want someone to take on a colt. Rising two. Been left

405

to run wild. Needs bringing in hand. I haven't the time myself. Your father used to work for me before the Great War,' he said. 'The name's Brownlowe. Perhaps you can tell him that I called.'

'My dad's in hospital,' said Rob Griffin. 'He had an accident with a tractor. He won't be handling your horse, or anyone else's, for a long time.'

'Oh.' Disappointed, Rupert started to turn away.

'I might do it, though. I mostly see to the horses,' Rob told him, 'even when Dad's here.'

'Starbright's a thoroughbred – and he's a handful,' said Rupert dubiously.

'Nothing I can't handle.'

'Well . . .' Rupert gave the lad an appraising stare. 'Are you as good as your father?' he demanded.

Rob returned the stare uncompromisingly. 'He reckons I am.'

'All right.' Rupert made a snap decision. 'I'll get the colt sent over.'

'We haven't discussed the money. Full livery plus schooling fees,' Rob reminded him.

Within two minutes, Rupert had to accept that he had been wrong about getting the job done cheaply for old time's sake. Whatever concessions Will Griffin might have made, his son drove a hard bargain.

26

In December, at the end of an afternoon spent with the Jarvis family in Bethnal Green, Anne invited Louella home to tea.

The suggestion took Louella by surprise. Her first instinctive liking for Anne had been confirmed on further acquaintance, but so far their contact had been limited to the Bethnal Green visits, after which they usually went their separate ways and Louella had checked her own impulse to try to deepen the friendship. However much she would like Anne as a friend, she was held back by the memory of her past relationship with Stuart Armitage.

Now her first reaction to the invitation was, 'Will your husband be there?'

'No,' said Anne. 'I can understand why you might prefer not to meet him, in the circumstances, but there's no need to feel awkward. Stuart explained the situation to me.'

'You don't mind?' Louella's eyes widened. Surely Anne's placid manner was totally at odds with what she had just said? Could any wife be so untroubled by the knowledge of her husband's affair?

'Of course not. Once Stuart had decided to leave Graham's firm, how could you let him go on seeing to your investments? After all, Graham had dealt with them on your husband's behalf for years and it would have been so hurtful for him if you'd transferred your business. I thought it was rather decent of you to show such loyalty to Graham. It's one of the things I already liked about you, before we got to know each other.'

Louella's pulse rate slowed again as her panic subsided. Stuart's 'explanation' of why he had lost control of her investments was like everything else about him, as plausible as it was dishonest. *Poor Anne*, she thought. But perhaps Anne was better off not knowing what kind of a man she had married.

'I must confess I have a selfish reason for inviting you today,' Anne continued. 'You see, my baby was born a year ago. It would have been his birthday. I want to share it with someone who understands. Stuart simply won't talk about it – I suppose it hurt him too much, losing his son. But oh, I do feel so desperate, sometimes, just to *mention* Guy. If I don't, it's as if he wasn't real . . . and he *was*. Do you see what I mean?'

Louella did see.

'So you'll come?'

'Yes. Of course I'll come,' said Louella.

Sitting beside Anne in a cab driving towards Greenwich, Louella's fear that this might result in an encounter with Stuart was equalled by her curiosity. She had never seen his house. The cab drew up in a quiet street of Georgian terraced houses near the park and she could see the domed building of the Observatory, perched on the hill overlooking the river.

Inside the hall, Anne handed her coat to a quietly spoken maidservant and asked for tea to be brought to the drawing room. Louella followed her hostess into a pretty room where a fire burned brightly in the black-leaded grate under a marble chimneypiece. Tall windows, framed by flowered linen curtains, gave on to the street at one end of the room and, at the other, a well-tended walled garden. The winter daylight was fading, but beyond the wall, glimpsed through a wrought-iron gate, Louella could see a footpath edging the grey expanse of the river.

The Armitage house was a little like the one in which Stuart and Louella had enjoyed their afternoon assignations; except that in the property hired by Louella, the furniture and fittings had been merely adequate. In this peaceful room there was evidence everywhere of a caring and tasteful owner. In the past, Stuart had seemed dogged by money worries, but it was clear that he was prospering nowadays – river views and Chippendale chairs didn't come cheap.

But after all, Louella reminded herself reluctantly, *the man of the house specializes in rich widows*.

Sitting on the elegant sofa beside Anne, sipping tea from a Minton tea service patterned with oriental birds, it was hard for the visitor to relax. She had an ever-present apprehension that Stuart might suddenly appear in the doorway. Anne seemed unaware of Louella's tension as she talked softly and sadly about her dead baby and her regret that she had no photograph of him.

'They took him away so soon. I wanted to hold him for a while but they wouldn't let me. Sometimes when I close my eyes I can imagine cradling him in my arms, and it feels as real as if I had really done it. Oh, I do miss him so . . .'

'I know,' said Louella gently. She covered the other woman's hand with hers. Her own reactions to losing first Robert, then Danny, then Hector, had been to lock her emotions away behind a stony exterior, trusting no-one to understand her grief; but, oddly, she found that she could empathize with Anne Armitage's need to talk out her sorrow.

The farewell hug that Anne gave her visitor in the hall afterwards was wholehearted and Louella returned it with equal warmth. But as the cab pulled away from the kerb, her main reaction was one of relief that there had been no confrontation with Stuart under the eyes of his unsuspecting wife.

Rupert Brownlowe's colt Starbright arrived at Welcome Farm in a horse box, attended by a gloomy middle-aged man who told Rob and Harriet by way of introduction that the Griffins were welcome to him.

'Old Brownlowe's pride and joy he may be, but he's a holy terror,' the man said feelingly. 'I've had to take my life in my hands some mornings, just to get his hay net into the stall.'

From inside the horse box a series of thuds underlined Starbright's impatience with his restricted surroundings.

'Hark at him – he'll kick a hole in the side of the box if we don't get him unloaded sharpish,' said the groom.

Rob headed for the back of the box to unbolt and lower the tailgate. Inside the right-hand compartment a tall chestnut colt danced a brisk fandango at the end of his halter rope, nostrils flaring and eyes swivelling backwards as the ramp went down.

Rupert Brownlowe's groom eyed the horse nervously. 'I'll let him loose and you two can get him into the stable between you. No, tell you what,' he amended the suggestion, 'maybe it's better if I leave it all to you. You might as well know what you've let yourselves in for.'

Rob shrugged and walked round to the door in the side of the box. 'You wait here. Better let him get used to me first,' he told Harriet.

The groom fished in the breast pocket of his jacket for a tin of tobacco and a packet of cigarette papers.

'Fancy a smoke?' he asked Harriet, propping his spine against the side of the box. She shook her head. He shook out a ration of tobacco onto one of the papers, rolled himself a thin, wilting tube, licked the glued edge of the paper, then found a box of matches in a hip pocket and lit the cigarette, drawing the smoke deeply into his lungs. From inside the box, Rob's quiet voice could be faintly heard, saying something indistinct to the colt.

'Praying for his life, is he?' said the groom, grinning. 'If you ask me, he'll be needing all the prayers he can think up with that one.'

Harriet ignored the comment. Another minute passed, then a chestnut rump emerged and the colt backed steadily down the wooden ramp, foot by delicate foot. As Starbright's head came into sight with Rob's hand on the halter rope under his jaw, Rob was still talking steadily. Ears pricked, the horse reached ground level, backed a few paces more, turned and let himself be led calmly towards the stable block. The groom dropped the stub of his cigarette and it burned away on the ground at his feet as he stared, open-mouthed, after the boy and the horse.

'Blimey,' was all he said.

* * *

'Rob, I was so proud of you,' Harriet told her brother impulsively, as they watched the horse box receding down the lane. 'Mum, you should have seen him,' she added, as Daisy joined them in the yard. 'Talk about taming the savage beast! That groom of Rupert Brownlowe's was so impressed, he could hardly believe his eyes.'

'It went well, didn't it,' Rob conceded. 'Better than I expected, actually. It won't last, of course. Starbright's quite capable of giving trouble – anyone can see that. He's been left to develop bad habits. Still, at least we've got off to a good start and the groom'll take a favourable report back to Maple Grange. And the money'll come in useful.'

'Well, I can't deny that. But I wish it didn't have to be from Rupert Brownlowe,' Daisy said with a sigh. 'The less I have to do with him, the better I like it! And Rob, I'm not sure it was wise to take a young horse on. How are you going to manage him on top of all the other farm work, especially once you're back at school?'

'I won't be going back to school,' Rob told her simply. His mother's mouth opened and shut, soundlessly. 'There's no point,' Rob continued. 'Face the facts. Dad's never going to be a hundred per cent fit again, and if we're going to keep the farm on it'll be up to me to take over whatever he can't manage. I'll be fourteen in January. After that I can leave officially anyway and they're hardly going to make a fuss about a few more weeks, the way things are.'

'But we always meant you to stay on and take your school certificate,' Daisy protested. 'And maybe even your higher certificate. It'd be a crying shame not to, after you got the scholarship and all. And I thought you wanted to, because the maths would help you later with learning to fly.'

It was the first time that she had ever openly acknowledged such a possibility to her elder son, and she had only done so now as a desperate tool of persuasion. But Rob didn't bite the carrot.

'Things have changed,' was all he said, doggedly.

Watching his face, Harriet was struck by how much he

411

looked and sounded like his father. Will's face tended to wear the same deceptively calm expression when he was announcing an unshakeable decision. Daisy recognized it too, and although she went on voicing her doubts over the wisdom of Rob's choice, in her heart she already knew that she was beaten.

For the time that Allie Briggs 'lived in' at Welcome Farm, she had been using the parlour as a bedroom. When her husband came out of hospital, just before Christmas of 1935, Daisy decided that Allie's full-time help at the farm was no longer necessary; besides, the parlour would now be needed for Will who, with his mangled leg still healing, could not manage the stairs.

'So you've got your missus back, then,' Stanley's friends at the Red Lion commented, grinning broadly. 'That'll be a relief to you, eh? You must've been missing her, what with the winter nights being so cold and all.'

Stanley bore the nudges and winks good-humouredly. He *was* glad to have Allie home again, though in reality he had missed her housekeeping efforts, long taken for granted, more than he had minded having the bed to himself at night. On the other hand, when cooking for the Griffins Allie had felt she had something to prove and the meals he had shared at Welcome Farm had been noticeably better than the dinners she dished up at home.

Allie had liked living at Welcome Farm. Sometimes, stirring a casserole on the kitchen range or replacing the willow-patterned dinner plates in their rack at the back of the pine sideboard, she'd been able to pretend to herself that she was a farmer's wife, mistress of the house. Her own home seemed smaller and shabbier on her return, and Stanley's sloppy habits grated on her more than they had done before. So in the first few days after her reversion to the status of part-time help and charlady, Allie was in a bad mood, not least out of envy for what she could see of the Griffins' comparatively lavish preparations for Christmas.

On Christmas Eve, while she was washing up the dishes

from the midday meal at the farm before setting off for home, she heard a car drive into the farmyard. Because of her mood, she deliberately ignored the knocks at the door which followed, scouring stubbornly at the last of the saucepans in the basinful of soapy water in the sink. Finally the visitor lost patience and lifted the latch.

'Yes? What do you want?' said Allie, unwelcomingly.

'I want to talk to Harriet. Where is she?'

'She'll be upstairs in her room,' Allie said. 'I'll fetch her down.' She reached for the kitchen towel behind the door to dry her hands. 'Who shall I say is calling?'

'Oh, you needn't bother to announce me. I'll go on up,' said the newcomer, striding past her. Allie gaped. By the time she had gathered her wits enough to protest at the invasion, he was running up the stairs. Allie shrugged her shoulders and returned to her saucepans, reasoning that there was no point in worrying about the proprieties where Harry was concerned – she'd gone off the rails long ago.

Harriet had taken to lying down for half an hour after dinner, because in her time away from the farm her body had lost the habit of late nights, early mornings and hard labour in between, and she was finding it hard to readapt. Dozing on her bed, she had heard the car engine and wondered vaguely who might be calling. The sound of footsteps coming up the attic stairs shook her fully awake.

She had taken off her grubby working clothes before she lay down, to save the sheets, and was wearing only her underwear. Hastily pushing back the bedclothes she snatched up her dressing gown from the foot of the bed. She was still slipping her arms into the sleeves when the door opened.

Harriet had been expecting her mother, or Allie. Instead she found herself face to face with Tom Searle.

'I wrote,' Tom said accusingly. 'I wrote to you at Vera's. Several times. You didn't reply.'

'I didn't know. Your letters must have arrived after I left. Vera didn't send them on.'

'How could she?' said Tom. 'You didn't give her any

forwarding address. Anyway, when you didn't answer my first letter, I wrote again. When you didn't answer the second, or the third, I was worried. I thought you might be ill. Or dead . . . So I went to Croydon to find out what the hell was going on. Vera told me you'd gone home, but she didn't know where home was. Fortunately, I did.' His gaze travelled from her flushed face down to her hands, which were ineffectively trying to hold the edges of the dressing gown closed over her half-clothed figure.

'Well?' he demanded belligerently. 'Aren't you pleased to see me? Don't I get a kiss?'

'Oh, Tom . . .' Harriet's control dissolved.

A moment later his arms were round her and his mouth was finding her lips, then her neck and her shoulder inside the slipping dressing gown. She swayed against him. Tom nudged the door closed with his foot, half-pushing and half-lifting her towards the bed.

'Christ,' he said hoarsely. 'I've missed you!'

His lovemaking was quick and ungentle, as if punishing her for making him worry. Harriet was swamped by her own hunger and his urgency. When it was over she lay on her back, still not quite able to believe that he was here after the long, agonized weeks of believing that he might never be with her again. The beginnings of happiness crept into her as she watched him sit up in bed and reach for his scattered clothes. She touched a hand to his naked back.

'Don't get up yet. Lie down here beside me for a bit longer.'

'Better not,' Tom said prosaically. 'Anyone might walk in – and I have a feeling this is not the kind of behaviour your family would approve of. Anyway, I have to be going.'

'Going?' Harriet repeated, her momentary happiness already evaporating. 'Going where?'

'Back to Maple Grange. I'm there for Christmas. I only came to make sure you were all right,' Tom told her. He pulled his clothes on quickly and Harriet watched him stony-faced. In his arms, for a short while she had forgotten how abruptly he could switch from physical intimacy to this utter detachment. Now, sick with disappointment, she recognized that nothing had changed.

'When Allie said who'd turned up to see you, I was afraid you were going to go off with him again,' said Daisy, later, in the milking shed. Harriet didn't answer at first. Instead, she dipped a rag into the bucket of disinfectant beside her and bent to wipe down a cow's udders, her red hair falling forward to hide her face. She was attaching the suction cups of the milking machine by the time she answered.

'No fear of that. I wouldn't run off and leave you in the lurch, not while Dad's still getting over his accident. And anyway, Tom said it'd be better to keep things the way they are for the time being.'

'The way they are . . . ?' Daisy probed.

'I'm needed here, and he'll be going back to Portsmouth to work as soon as Christmas is over.' Harriet tried not to let it show in her voice how much she was minding that Tom hadn't even invited her to Maple Grange for the short time that he would be there. Having casually reasserted his claim on her body, she thought bitterly, he was satisfied. And now he was ready to abandon her all over again.

'He isn't going to marry you, is he?' Daisy said.

Harriet straightened up to meet her mother's concerned gaze. 'No. I don't think he is,' she admitted bleakly. 'Not now, not ever.'

A few days after Christmas, Laura arrived at Welcome Farm.

'Oh, Miss Laura, how lovely to see you!' Daisy was torn between welcome and chagrin that she had no proper place in which to entertain her visitor. 'I can't ask you into the parlour,' she confessed, 'because Will's in there, and he's in bed, asleep. He had an accident, you see—'

'I know,' Laura reassured her. 'I heard about it. I thought I'd come along and ask how you're managing.'

'Oh, we're doing very well, considering,' Daisy said. 'Harriet's home, you know.'

'Yes, so Tom said. We came down to Maple Grange for

Christmas,' Laura explained. 'And Tom mentioned he'd popped over to see Harriet, that's how we knew about your husband's accident.' She accepted the offer of a cup of tea in the kitchen, though she didn't really want one, and controlled her impatience while Daisy scurried about unearthing best china when earthenware would have done. When the tea had been poured and the essentials of hospitality dealt with, Laura asked for more details of the situation at Welcome Farm.

It was absurd, she supposed, to go on being concerned about the wellbeing of Daisy, so many years after the mistress-maid relationship had ceased; but the news about Will Griffin, as relayed laconically by Tom, had been alarming. To her relief, she gathered that Daisy wasn't just putting on a brave front. The Griffins were genuinely coping.

'One good thing about it was, at least it brought Harriet home,' said Daisy. 'That makes up for a lot, for Will and me.'

Laura leaned forward across the kitchen table and lowered her voice slightly. 'Daisy, how *is* Harriet? Tom didn't say much, and I didn't like to ask, but I have the impression he's rather left her high and dry.'

'You could say that,' said Daisy succinctly.

'I'm very sorry. It was what I was afraid of when I first saw the signs of attraction between them.' Laura sighed. 'For Tom, it's always been a case of, *I must have my freedom.* He thinks that as long as he explains that at the outset of an entanglement, any disappointment the poor girl may feel later is not his responsibility. Unfortunately I don't have any influence on him at all and neither does his mother. He goes his own sweet way. Is Harriet *very* upset?'

'She doesn't talk about it,' Daisy said. 'Miss Laura, can I ask you something? We heard that Mr Searle used to be engaged to a young lady in London, but that then she got engaged to someone else instead. Now we've heard that her new engagement's off. Do you happen to know . . . has Mr Searle made it up with her again?'

'I don't know,' said Laura. 'If he has, he certainly hasn't

mentioned it to me. Do you want me to make enquiries?'

'Oh, no. It's not that important.' Daisy changed the subject. 'Did you and Mr Allingham have a good Christmas?'

'Not really,' Laura said frankly. 'James hates these visits, and I don't blame him. Pa is *so* tactless. You may not know that James stood as a Labour Party candidate for one of the northern constituencies in November's general election. He worked very hard canvassing and making speeches, and so did I, but although he polled a very respectable number of votes, he didn't get elected. It was more or less the outcome we'd expected, but it was very disappointing all the same, after all that work.

'Of course, Pa couldn't stay off the subject, he had to keep rubbing it in that Labour had lost, and in the end James went back to London yesterday, though we were supposed to be staying until tomorrow. I'd have gone too, if it wasn't for poor Marion – she'd have been very upset if I'd had an open break with Pa and stormed off with the children. So we've been grimly papering over the cracks . . . but thank goodness, we'll be going home tomorrow. Anyway,' Laura concluded, rising from the table and reaching for her gloves, 'I must go. It's been so good to see you, Daisy. Do give my best wishes to your husband, and to Harriet, of course. Oh, and James asked me to tell Harriet that if she wants a stenographer's job later, when things have settled down at the farm, she's to be sure to come and see him about it.'

Daisy duly reported Laura's visit to her family. 'It's a shame Mr James didn't get elected,' she said. 'He'd have made a good Member of Parliament. I felt so embarrassed when Miss Laura told me about it, because I'd hardly noticed there was an election going on, what with all the other things on our minds. Still, the National government got back in, so I don't suppose there'll be any changes.' As an afterthought she relayed James Allingham's message to Harriet.

'That was nice of him, wasn't it, to offer you a job? Though of course it's out of the question now.'

She didn't tell her daughter what Laura had said about Tom Searle, and Harriet didn't ask. After the brief exchange in the milking shed, Harriet had not mentioned Tom again.

The team of Rob, Jackie, Kitty, and Billy had done their best, reinforced by the return of Harriet, to keep the milk production of Welcome Farm at its normal level in the aftermath of Will's accident, but there had been a short period when inevitably they had failed and the milk churns which the dairy lorry collected from the stand by the gate had been less than the usual number. In the New Year, a letter from the dairy manager informed the workforce at Welcome Farm that the shortfall had been made up, and would continue to be made up, elsewhere.

'Damn,' said Will. He sat in the Windsor chair beside the kitchen range, crutches propped against the arms of the chair on either side, frowning down at the letter in his hand.

'What is it, love?' asked Daisy, from the breakfast table.

'The dairy. They've cut our quota.'

'Oh, no,' Daisy said, dismayed.

'Not by a lot,' Will hastened to reassure her. 'A couple of churns a day, that's all. But it's a nuisance. I don't want to sell any cows and I don't want to pour away milk. I wonder . . . I've thought, sometimes, that one of these days we might set up our own little milk round.'

'A milk round?' Daisy echoed. 'What would the dairy think of that?'

'It'd have to be in one of the remoter areas that they don't cover already, so they don't take umbrage over it.'

Later, in the feed store, Daisy repeated Will's idea to Kitty while she turned the handle on the machine for grinding up cattlecake.

'The trouble is, it couldn't be a very big round or as Will says, we'd be treading on the toes of the dairy and taking the risk that they might refuse our milk altogether. Allie says there are houses in the lanes outside Bentley village where the dairy won't deliver because it wouldn't be worth their while that far out on such a small scale. It would use up our surplus, though . . . but Will can't do the round, not with his bad leg. And Rob's got enough to do, what with taking over almost all of Will's work and having that colt to school on top of it.'

'Billy could do it,' said Kitty, after a moment's thought. 'He could take a couple of churns in the trap, with Joseph. Joseph goes all right for Billy. And he could have measuring ladles hung on the side of the churns to serve out the milk,' she went on, warming to the idea.

'What about taking the money, though?' Daisy asked.

'Billy can count all right.'

'I meant, one-handed,' said Daisy. 'How would he manage, giving out change and all?'

Kitty considered the problem. 'We could build a little shelf on the side of the cart,' she suggested, 'with a money bin under it. That way he could lay out the coins on the shelf to sort out the change, and then scoop the money into the bin.'

Rob and Billy added the shelf to the cart that evening and the next morning Jackie cycled round the icy lanes to announce the new venture to the residents of the outlying cottages that Will had identified from Allie's reports. At the beginning of the following week, the Griffins' milk round made a start.

Kitty had her doubts about the wisdom of the idea when she saw Joseph standing harnessed to the cart in the grey light of morning, the frosty air vapourizing the breath from his nostrils. Perched up on the seat of the trap, Billy was wrapped in two coats, a balaclava, a scarf and woolly gloves, and Daisy had found an old blanket to wrap round his legs, but still it looked like a cold and lonely task to Kitty, who felt any physical discomfort to her husband more acutely than she would have felt it to herself.

'But he loves it,' she told Daisy at the end of the day. It was obvious that the milk round suited Billy. In spite of the bulky layers of extra clothing his step was jaunty and his eyes bright as he came back to Starling Cottages. Nor did his enthusiasm wane in the days that followed. He enjoyed meeting the customers, the scraps of gossip on doorsteps and the friendly offers of cups of tea. He liked the homeward journey with the churns satisfyingly empty and, afterwards, the tallying of the day's sales with the money in the bin and the orderly recording of the totals in neat rows of figures in a ledger. He felt more useful and more respected than he had done for years. Altogether, Kitty recognized happily, it had given him a new dignity.

Allie Briggs came into the farmhouse on a morning in January with a black armband sewn around one sleeve of her coat.

'Not somebody close to you, I hope?' Daisy asked her, cautiously. Seen through the kitchen window as she cycled across the yard, Allie hadn't looked particularly woebegone – her red face had signalled nothing beyond the coldness of the morning and the usual breathless flush that went with a late arrival and a tale of the wind being against her.

Allie shook her head. 'Bless you, no. It's for the king.'

'The king?' Daisy echoed.

'Haven't you heard? He's dead, poor thing. And only a few months after his jubilee. Still, he didn't seem too well when all that was going on, so the papers told us.'

Daisy hadn't listened to the radio lately, partly because she hadn't had the heart to play her usual dance music what with Will being laid up and partly because there had been too much to do. As for the newspapers, there was even less likelihood of a spare moment to sit down with those, and she took them straight through to the invalid, who was several days behind in keeping up with them. As a result, the household was out of touch with national events. Now she heard from Allie that the nation was in mourning.

'Still, we'll have King Edward now. Edward the Eighth – that's what he'll be known as, though he's David to his friends. And that's all to the good, isn't it, a young king? I won't say King George didn't understand our problems, but he was a bit of a stick-in-the-mud, God rest his soul. Not like his son, dancing and going to the races and mixing with the people . . . But he's got his serious side, too. They say he's even been to see the unemployed miners in Wales and shown he really knows what they're going through. That got up the noses of some of the government,' said Allie with relish. 'Still, now he's king he'll be able to get the nation sorted out, won't he?'

'It'll be quite a job,' said Daisy.

After Tom's Christmas visit, Harriet heard nothing more from him in the weeks that followed. When she wasn't being depressed about it, she was hating him for the way he was treating her. She remembered with shame the way she'd fallen into his arms when he'd appeared at the farm, and how casually he'd taken her and then left her again; but still she couldn't cure herself of the spasm of disappointment that recurred every time the postman came and went without bringing a letter from him.

She had sent Vera a Christmas card and in the New Year, her friend sent a reply.

I hope everything is well with you. I have worried a lot about you, and was glad to get the news that your Dad wasn't as bad as it sounded on the radio. Also it's good to have your address. Your young man turned up here in December. He seemed very upset when he found you had gone home. He said he knew where that was, but he left so quickly that we didn't get a chance to ask him for the address then.

Fred and I are very well, though I get quite tired now, as the baby is due in March. We are hoping you will be godmother. Come and see us when you get the chance.

Your Tom had sent several letters before he came here. I was keeping them to send on to you, but he took them away with him.

Harriet groaned with frustration. So now she would never know what Tom had written. She told herself that it didn't matter anyway. Probably the next news of him would be a newspaper report to say that he was married to Diana Somerville.

One of the few bright spots in Harriet's life was that her father was getting better. The doctors had said he was unlikely to walk again without crutches, but they had reckoned without Will's dogged determination. Under his direction, Rob and Billy constructed an exercise frame at one end of the hay barn, consisting of twin rails on upright poles, waist high and a few feet apart. Every day Will heaved himself out of his chair and propelled himself on crutches to the barn, where he would abandon the crutches and haul his body up and down the frame. At first his arms took most of the weight, but gradually his legs grew stronger until he was able to free one hand for a few uncertain steps, then the other. Finally he could walk along the frame, still with a noticeable limp but unsupported.

On the morning in March that he achieved this feat, the family was summoned to witness the miracle. Allie Briggs, cycling up to the farmhouse two hours later than usual because she'd had to go to the dentist in Farnham, was startled to hear the sound of cheering and a steady, metallic clanging coming from the barn. Inside, she found Daisy hugging Will, Rob and Harriet dancing a wild polka and Jackie sitting cross-legged in the hay, drumming furiously on an upturned metal feed bucket with an old gardening fork. When she realized what the commotion was about, Allie joined in the polka.

27

Daisy had postponed telling her sister-in-law about Will's accident, because Louella would undoubtedly want to *do something*, and that something would probably consist of offering money to hire extra workers for the farm. Such assistance might relieve the pressure in the short term, but Daisy knew that in the long term it would only add to Will's problems to know that his debt to Louella was being increased. It was a big enough worry to him at the best of times.

Once Will was on his feet again, Daisy supposed there was a moral obligation to let Louella know about the accident. After all, she *did* own a share in the farm, and she would be furiously indignant if she wasn't told and then found out later from other sources. So Daisy wrote a chatty letter, dropping the news about Will's narrow escape from death into a paragraph which included Harriet's return, Rob's decision to leave school and Jackie's achievement in coming second in his form at the grammar in his first term.

Louella, who was not a successful businesswoman for nothing, homed in immediately on the most important aspect of Daisy's communication and came down from London on the day she received the letter, to see for herself that all was well at Welcome Farm. She found that on the whole, it was.

'But I'm horrified to hear that Rob's given up his education,' she scolded Daisy. 'How could you and Will encourage him to do that? I know you wouldn't let me pay school fees for the boys, but I did think that once Rob had passed the scholarship examination, you'd let him take advantage of what his brain had won for him.'

'We didn't encourage him,' Daisy objected, feeling a little

windswept in the face of her sister-in-law's vehemence. 'He chose for himself and there was nothing his father or I could say to dissuade him.'

'For heaven's sake, Daisy, he's only fourteen!'

'Fourteen is old enough to know your own mind, when you're a boy like Rob,' said Daisy. 'You haven't seen him lately, have you, Louella? Well, he's out with the tractor, but he'll be in for his dinner, so you can talk to him then about how much better it would be for him to go back to school. If you can convince him, Will and I won't stand in his way. In fact, we'd be grateful to you!'

Rob came in for dinner and Louella took him into the parlour to have a private talk. Five minutes later, Rob was placidly eating his lamb casserole at the kitchen table while outside in the hall, Louella, a little pink-cheeked and tight-lipped, was having to concede to Daisy that she had been right. Rob had made his decision and that was that.

'But what about Harriet?' she said. Daisy sighed.

'Ah, Harriet. She's made it up with Will – I can't tell you how glad I am about that . . . and her coming back when she did was an absolute godsend. But she's not happy, Louella. It's partly to do with that wretched flier she's got herself involved with. He does seem to be an awful cad – or at the very least a totally selfish young man.' Daisy's tone sharpened. Suddenly, she was on the attack. 'Come to think of it, it was you who started it all.'

'Me? What did I do?' Louella protested.

'You showed her a different way of life. You made her discontented. What with London and pretty clothes and all that kind of excitement, how could she settle to life on a farm?'

'All I did was invite her to stay occasionally,' said Louella. 'After all, I *am* her aunt.'

'If she hadn't gone to you in London and had her expectations raised, she might have stayed here and found herself a nice young man and got married. But with all that *"better yourself"* nonsense you were always feeding her, she was ready to be knocked sideways by Gavin Draycott, and that led to the nannying job with Miss Laura, which threw her into Tom Searle's company. And look where *that's* got her,' Daisy finished, running out of breath.

'Of course you're worried about Harriet. Any mother would be.' Louella gripped her hands together to control the sharp response which had been her instinctive reaction. 'But Daisy, I wish you would admit that she's not cut out to spend her life on the farm. She's bright and pretty and adventurous. She'd be wasted as some stolid farmer's wife, knee high in cattlecake and poultry feathers. Not that I'm including you among those ranks!' she added hastily. 'But Will *is* exceptional, Daisy, you must accept that! The chances of Harriet finding herself someone like him, if she stays here, are very small. And she does deserve someone exceptional. All I was trying to do was to give her a wider choice.'

'I'm sure you meant well.' Daisy's indignation evaporated as suddenly as it had begun. 'But oh, Lou, I just wish that a wider choice hadn't turned out to mean Tom Searle, that's all.'

On a fine day in April, Jem Wilkins was released from prison. In the street outside the iron-studded gate, he stood in the spring sunlight, considering his next move.

His stay in prison had been tedious but useful, in that he'd learned a few new skills and made some new contacts – but that was no thanks to Kitty's uncle, George Crowley. Jem decided to go along to the Crown and Cushion later, after hours, and demonstrate to Uncle George the folly he had committed in taking on Jem Wilkins. But in view of his intentions, it would be wise not to be seen in the area by daylight – after all, he'd just spent six months in clink for making that particular mistake.

How to pass the intervening hours? On his last day of freedom, Jem recalled, he'd followed Rupert Brownlowe to a house in Blackheath, home of a prostitute called Maudie. He decided to pay her a visit.

Maudie's minder materialized outside as Jem lifted the

knocker on her door. 'Maudie expecting you, is she?'

'Don't you ever change your patter?' Jem asked, with an easy smile to defuse the jibe. 'No, she's not – I didn't have a chance to send a message but I'm hoping she'll see me all the same. I was here last autumn with Rupert Brownlowe, remember? The old geezer who's a regular of hers.'

The man's features relaxed. 'Thought I knew you from somewhere. All right, you can go ahead.'

The woman who opened the door in answer to Jem's knock was probably in her late forties. She'd have been pretty once, he guessed, and she was still attractive in a faded way, small-boned, brown-haired, tidily turned out in a navy blue tailored dress that suited her colouring. Recovering from his first surprise, Jem supposed it wasn't Rupert Brownlowe's style to use a tart who looked like a tart.

'This one's a friend of Brownlowe's, Maudie,' said the minder. 'Got time for him, have you?'

'Rupert's friend?' The woman stared at Jem, her eyebrows lifting in disbelief. 'No offence, but you don't look like the sort of company he'd keep.'

'I never said I was. I work for him now and again,' Jem told her.

'Have you brought a message? Is he coming to see me?'

'Not that I know of. I'm here on my own account. The thing is, I'm in town and I'm at a loose end, don't know a soul . . . and I'll say one thing for the guvnor, he's got good taste. So I thought I'd look you up. I've got money,' Jem said. He gave her a warmer version of the disingenuous smile that he'd used earlier on her minder, and waited.

Maudie looked at him hard. 'What'd he think if he knew?'

'He'd be bloody furious. Only I won't tell him if you won't,' said Jem frankly.

The corners of Maudie's mouth lifted. 'You've got a nerve, I'll say that for you.' She stood aside. 'Come in. We'll talk about it.'

Jem waited until she'd closed the street door before he reached for her, purposefully. 'It wasn't talking I had in mind.'

'Not so fast.' She pushed him away, but the rejection was discernibly half-hearted. 'You can't afford me,' she teased.

Jem grinned and renewed the attack. 'Do us a discount, then, love? You wouldn't regret it.'

'Well . . .' Maudie deliberated. There was a pause. Her brown eyes met Jem's hazel gaze, speculatively. 'Oh, all right, then. It'll make a change. I don't get many young ones, these days,' she said.

Jem had told Maudie that he hadn't come for conversation. But it was surprising how much a woman would tell you without meaning to, he reflected, once you'd got her on her back and made her good and comfortable. Drowsy and smiling, her brown hair on Jem's shoulder in the plainly furnished bedroom upstairs, she told him a lot about Rupert Brownlowe: about their first meeting more than twenty years ago, soon after his wife had died; his offer to set her up in a little house with a small regular payment, how he'd tacitly let it be known that he didn't much mind what she did in between times, so long as she always made him welcome when he was in London.

'But I don't see much of him these days. Well, he's getting on. I think he comes more out of habit now. Not that he expects much when he *does* come,' she said. 'Just a bit of a cuddle and some sympathy. Poor old thing, he's got a lot of money worries.'

'Has he?' Jem said. 'Serious worries, are they?'

His tone hadn't achieved quite the right casual note.

'I shouldn't be talking about him like this,' Maudie realized. 'Time you were going,' she decided briskly.

'How about one more for luck?' Jem wheedled. It was getting dark outside, but there were still at least three hours before it would be advisable to head for the Crown and Cushion. He shelved the information-gathering side of his visit and concentrated instead on killing time.

'How much?' Jem said in the hall, several hours later. He started to pull out his scuffed wallet but, as he'd anticipated,

427

Maudie shook her head. She smiled ruefully up at him, hugging her wrapper against her thin body.

'Forget it. I told you, you couldn't afford me. Have this one for free.'

'Thanks.' Jem replaced his wallet. There was no need for her to know it had been almost empty anyway, he decided. What the eye didn't see, the heart didn't grieve over.

'Maybe I'll see you again, one of these days?' Maudie said. An element of hope crept into her voice.

'You can count on it,' said Jem, who had no intention of coming back.

George Crowley was replacing the last of the glass tankards on the high shelf above the bar at the Crown and Cushion when someone rapped on the etched glass panel of the door.

'We're closed,' he said. The knocking was repeated.

'Are you deaf? I said we're closed.'

'Open up,' said a voice. 'Police!' A fusillade of knocks followed.

Scowling, George plodded towards the door. 'All right, all right, I'm coming. No need to break the glass.'

He slid back the top bolt and then the one at the bottom. Before he had time to straighten up the door crashed open, pushing him off balance. He sprawled on the scuffed wooden floorboards and gaped up at the man who stood over him.

''Ere, you ain't a copper!' he gasped.

'My, ain't we observant? Lesson number one, don't believe everything you hear through a locked door,' said the intruder. He knelt deliberately on George's chest, took hold of his flailing arms by the wrists and pinned them to the floor. 'Quieten down, will you.' His knees were accurately positioned to deliver maximum discomfort to his fallen victim.

George gave up the struggle and lay still, his ambitions limited, for the time being, to being allowed to breathe.

At last his assailant relaxed his grip and stood up. 'All right. You can get up now . . . but don't try anything,' he warned, taking something from his pocket.

George scrambled to his feet, snarling, and made a lunge. The other man sidestepped neatly, swaying his body out of reach. With a click, six inches of shining blade sprang from the haft in his hand.

'We can either have a nice, quiet talk or I can slit your throat. Which is it to be? Smart decision,' he added, as George's hands dropped to his sides. The man gestured with the jack-knife towards a table near the bar. 'Sit down.'

'I know you,' George discovered. 'You're Jem Wilkins, the geezer that went off with Kitty.'

'That's right. And you're the grass who told the coppers I was around. Not very friendly of you, was it? That's what I want to talk about. Pour us a drink before we start. Whisky. I reckon you owe me one, I've just had a dry six months. And have one yerself.'

Hands shaking, George splashed amber liquid into two glasses. Jem Wilkins downed his in one gulp. 'Now you.' He watched while the publican swallowed the contents of his glass, then pushed the bottle towards him across the table. 'Have another one.' He covered his glass with his left hand, his right hand still holding the knife. 'No, just you.'

For half an hour George drank one whisky after another, sitting at his own table in the public bar of the Crown and Cushion. The first bottle, empty, was replaced by another one from the store behind the bar. Bleary-eyed, he looked at it and shook his head.

'No . . . no more,' he pleaded. 'I'm s-sozzled already.'

Implacably, the man on the other side of the table poured another drink, filling the glass. He nudged it towards George.

'Go on.'

'No. Can't. I'll be sick.'

'Drink it.' Suddenly the knife blade was under his nose. George drank the whisky.

'That'll do. Now get up. We're going upstairs.'

It took George Crowley a long time to drag himself across the bar. The room tilted crazily around him as he cannoned into tables and chairs on the way. He clung to the newel post at the foot of the stairs, his legs buckling, sweat pouring down his face, and vomited the contents of his stomach onto the dirty carpet. Jem Wilkins stood aside, waiting till he had finished retching.

'Up.'

The thirteen stairs seemed to go on for ever. Reaching the galleried landing at the top, George reeled against the bannister as his enemy slid past him.

'What're-you-gonna-do?' The words came out slurred, almost incomprehensible.

'Stand up straight when you talk to me,' snapped Jem Wilkins.

George made an effort. He let go of the railing and straightened his sagging body, focusing on the glinting knife blade. Suddenly it darted towards him, aimed between his eyes. Gasping, he ducked away, lurching backwards into the stairwell.

Jem watched without emotion as George Crowley fell down the stairs. At the bottom, his body lay still, piled in an untidy heap against the newel post, head tilted at an unnatural angle. Jem make his leisurely way down, stepping carefully over the third step where the carpet was soggy with vomit. He squatted briefly beside his victim, checking that there was no pulse in the limp wrist; not that there was any doubt from the way the bloodshot eyes stared upwards, but Jem was meticulous when it came to killing.

He rinsed and stowed away one of the two glasses beside the half-empty whisky bottle, left the other one on the table and bolted the street door top and bottom before leaving by the sash window out of the scullery, as he had done on the night Kitty had fled from the Crown and Cushion. Tomorrow someone would find a drunken publican with a broken neck and they'd call it an accident. Who'd care anyway? Nobody had cared when his own mother died and he doubted whether George Crowley would be mourned, any more than Agnes.

Louella had failed in her renewed attempt to persuade her nephew Rob to go back to school.

'It's my business, not yours,' he'd told her, steadily, and

he hadn't wavered in his decision even when she'd reminded him about his ambition of flying lessons.

'There's more important things to consider now,' he'd said. 'I'll think about the flying later – I'm too young anyway. If you don't want to help me when the time comes because I won't do what you want now, then that's up to you.'

Rob was as stubborn as a mule . . . but she had been more successful when it came to her niece. Daisy and Will had acknowledged that Harriet, having once left the farm, was never going to settle properly into her old routines, and now that Will was well on the way to recovery she could be spared, at a pinch. Daisy had a quiet word with Harriet and reported sadly to Will that his daughter had jumped at the opportunity of accompanying Aunt Louella back to London.

'We can't keep her, love,' Will said.

'I know,' agreed Daisy, trying not to sniffle. There had been plenty of partings in her life, but they never seemed to get any easier. Will patted her hand without speaking. When Daisy glanced at him sideways she saw a muscle in the side of his cheek twitching and guessed that underneath the stoical façade he was as upset about Harriet's going as she was. The thought was oddly consoling.

Harriet said goodbye to her father privately while Louella's chauffeur, hired with the car for the day, was loading her hastily packed suitcase into the boot.

'Keep on getting better, Dad. I'll be back to see you soon.'

'When you're ready. We'll be here,' said Will, smiling faintly. Harriet hugged him, burying her face against his shoulder in the old, moth-holed woollen jumper as she had done when she was small and needed consolation for some fall or misdeed. He hugged her back.

'I'll miss you. I do love you, you know that, don't you, Dad?' Harriet's voice was muffled, but Will heard her.

'Yes, love,' he reassured her gently. 'I know.'

'Madam is not at home,' Everett informed Jem Wilkins, without regret.

Jem allowed himself to visualize Everett with a broken neck and staring eyes like George Crowley, before he replied. 'That's what you said this morning. You said she'd be back this evening.'

'I said she *might* be back this evening. Madam had expressed that intention. I cannot answer for the possibility that Madam might have changed her mind,' said the butler, not bothering to conceal his pleasure in disappointing the caller. Jem decided a broken neck was too good for Everett and played with the idea of slicing off his nose and ramming it between his teeth. Something about his expression conveyed the depth of his animosity and Everett erased the smile from his features.

'If you would care to come back later, sir—?'

'I wouldn't,' Jem told him curtly. 'I'll wait. Out here or indoors – it's up to you.'

He turned his back and sat down on the top step of the short flight that led up to the front door of Medlar House. Eyeing the sight gloomily, Everett weighed up the alternatives. He could order the caller off the premises altogether, but he had an inkling that he would prove unco-operative. He could leave him sitting on the step, but his continued presence would be embarrassing and bound to set the neighbours talking. Or he could let him in. It was a risk . . . there was no knowing what this ruffian might get up to if admitted into Medlar House, but it seemed the best of a bad bunch of choices. After all, whatever her reasons, Madam had always seen him when he'd called in the past.

'You'd better come in,' he said reluctantly. He led Jem to the study, which seemed the safest place to leave him since the drawing room was so full of tempting, liftable trinkets like the vitrine full of silver vinaigrettes and snuffboxes. As he turned to leave the room he heard a car engine, and hurrying to the window he saw a taxi pull up in the street outside. A woman stepped out and ran up the steps. A moment later, the doorbell pealed.

'Wait here,' Everett hissed, his brow furrowed. He left Jem standing in the middle of the study and hurried to the front door. On the doorstep stood Anne Armitage, her face pale.

'I've come to see Mrs Ramsay.'

'I'm so sorry, but Madam isn't here at present.'

'Damn! I *must* see her,' the visitor said. 'When will she be back?'

Everett struggled to overcome his shock at hearing a blasphemous word from the lips of Madam's genteel friend. 'I imagine she won't be long.'

'Then I'll wait.'

'Well . . . I can't *promise* that Madam will be back soon,' Everett amended, mindful of Jem Wilkins already in the study. 'Perhaps it would be better if you came back another time?'

'No, I'll wait.' Mrs Armitage marched past the butler into the hall.

After a helpless moment he shrugged his shoulders and led her to the drawing room. 'Would you like some tea, madam?'

'No, thank you.' The reply was curt, deepening the butler's sense of unease. To his relief he heard the arrival of another car outside and scurried back to the front door. Louella swept in, Harriet in tow, and handed him her hat and gloves.

'Help the man with the suitcase, will you, Everett? And then some tea.' She was already on her way towards the stairs when his urgently hissed '*Madam*' stopped her. Everett followed her down the hall, hands flapping uncharacteristically.

'That man Wilkins is in the study, madam, he *wouldn't* go away. And Mrs Armitage is in the drawing room. She wouldn't go away either.'

Louella put her hand to her forehead and closed her eyes for a moment. 'All right,' she said. 'I'll see Anne first. You'd better bring the tea in to us, Everett. Harriet, do me an enormous favour and keep Jem Wilkins occupied for a while, will you?'

Harriet's eyes widened with alarm, but it was too late.

Louella had already disappeared into the drawing room and Everett was heading for the swing door to the kitchen regions. She drew a long breath to steady her nerves and prepared to face Jem Wilkins, whom she had last seen more than eighteen months ago, glaring at her from the far side of a hastily closed gate, at the end of an undignified struggle in a wheatfield at Welcome Farm.

In the drawing room, Louella was expecting a friendly encounter with Anne, where the only tension would be her own, caused by the knowledge that her sinister half-brother was in the next room with her niece; with whom, as she remembered too late, he had admitted he was not on the best of terms. But Anne's expression as she turned to greet her hostess banished all thoughts of Harriet and Jem from Louella's mind.

'Louella. I have something to ask you.' Anne was very pale and very straight-backed, her face unsmiling. 'Is it true that you have had an affair with my husband?'

The directness of the question robbed Louella of breath for a moment. She stopped dead, staring at her friend, the colour draining from her own features.

'There's no need to answer, is there?' Anne said in a low voice, in which the very absence of emotion was frightening. 'Your face tells me all I need to know.'

'Anne . . .' Louella gestured helplessly. 'I don't know what to say.'

'Is there anything you *can* usefully say in the circumstances?'

'Who told you? Was it Stuart?'

'No. I heard it from Helen Moffat. You can imagine how she enjoyed letting me into the secret,' said Anne, her mouth twisting with distaste at the memory. 'And *then* I asked Stuart . . . who wriggled frightfully, like a worm on the hook, before he admitted that you had indulged in what he called a passing fling, of no importance.'

'Oh, Anne . . .' whispered Louella, wracked with shame. 'I hoped and prayed you'd never know. It was before I met you. You were in Dorset, an invalid, he told me. He said you weren't . . . he said you didn't . . .'

'I can imagine what he said.' Anne's chin lifted. 'He's always been that way, even when we were first married. Clients, acquaintances, even tarts. I pretended not to know. It was too awful, too humiliating even to talk about. When I had my accident, I was actually *glad*, because it meant I could get away from him. Then he came crawling to Dorset, begging my forgiveness, swearing he'd reformed, and my parents kept saying, give him another chance . . . and then I got pregnant and I made myself believe him. But I should have known he hadn't changed – he'd just got better at disguise.'

She made a gesture with one hand in front of her face, as if brushing away something distasteful. 'Well, it's over now.' Her white flame of indignation had burned itself out and now she drooped with tiredness. 'I just wish it hadn't been with you, Louella. The others I could have borne, but not you. I'd counted you as my friend.'

'And I you. Can't we go on?' pleaded Louella. 'Can't you forgive me? It was before I knew you or I would never have done it.' The excuses tumbled out. 'Try to understand. My husband was dead. I was so lonely . . . and he was so persuasive.'

'I know very well how persuasive my husband can be. Who is better qualified to know?' Anne told her quietly. 'Yes, I can understand it, Louella, and I can forgive you. I do forgive you. But you must see that I cannot go on knowing you. In any case, I'm going away. I'm leaving Stuart.'

'Where will you go?'

'Back to Dorset. Goodbye, Louella.' Anne held out her gloved hand and Louella took it numbly. 'I wish you luck with your life, and better men than Stuart to share it with you. You needn't see me out.'

Louella stood alone in the drawing room. The front door opened and closed and she heard light footsteps hurrying down the stone steps outside and away down the street. She was still standing there, unmoving, when Rose carried a redundant tea tray into the room.

Jem Wilkins, who had been waiting in the study for Louella, was confronted instead with Harriet Griffin. Surprise and delight crossed his face, to be replaced by a defensive half-smile as he remembered the circumstances of their last meeting.

'Well, this *is* a surprise. Not that I'm complaining,' he said warily.

'I am,' said Harriet. 'I have no desire whatsoever to talk to you, now or ever again! But my aunt is otherwise engaged for a few minutes and has asked me to . . .' Her colour heightened, '. . . to keep you occupied until she is able to see you herself.'

'Mmm,' said Jem. 'So how *are* you going to keep me occupied?' He seated himself on a corner of Louella's desk. His self-confidence had returned and, with it, the sparkle in his eyes as he gazed at Harriet. She forced herself to stand still, controlling the instinct to bolt from the room.

Jem hadn't changed much in the intervening year-and-a-half, she recognized bitterly. He was as lean and dark and sexually arrogant as ever. His mouth smiled that old crooked smile, his hazel eyes seemed to burn into her and she, who'd grown up a lot and lived a lot, seen men die and taken a lover since that day in the wheatfield, found that in spite of all her hard-won worldliness, he still had the power to shake her to the core.

28

'Well, I don't know what all that was about.' In the kitchen below stairs, Rose dumped an untouched tea tray on the table and helped herself to a biscuit. 'But the visitor's taken herself off without being seen out and now Madam's standing in the middle of the drawing room looking like Lot's wife.'

'Whose wife?' queried Everett.

'Lot's wife,' Rose said. She risked a bit of cheek. 'Don't you know your Bible? The one that saw something she shouldn't and got turned into a pillar of salt. All stiff and pale she was – Madam, I mean – and not a peep out of her. She just waved me away.'

'Maybe I'd better go up,' Everett said dubiously.

'If I was you, I'd wait till she rings,' Rose advised. 'She'll do that soon enough if she wants you. I got the feeling she was proper cut up about something, and she wouldn't trust herself to say so much as a word to me because if she did, she'd scream or burst into tears or something. And you know how Madam hates anyone to catch her showing she's got feelings like a normal human being.'

Louella stayed in the drawing room for five minutes after Anne's departure, forcing herself back to calmness. She would think about what had happened later in the privacy of her bedroom. Maybe then she could find some way to repair the broken friendship? For the moment, such considerations were a luxury because there was another visitor to be dealt with: Jem.

The study door was open. Her half-brother was seated in the chair – *her* chair – behind the desk, sifting idly through a folder of papers which lay on top of the blotting pad. Harriet stood by the window with her back to him, staring out at nothing in particular. As Louella approached her across the Tabriz carpet, a floorboard creaked.

Without turning round, Harriet hissed, 'Don't you *dare* touch me!'

'That's not a very respectful way to talk to your aunt,' Jem commented. He closed the file of papers, not at all abashed at being caught prying among them, and rose to his feet in a leisurely way. 'Hullo, Lou. It's been quite a while . . . I'd like to do the gallant thing and say you don't look a day older, but to be honest, you're looking a bit peaky at the moment.'

'Aunt Louella,' muttered Harriet, crimson with embarrassment. 'I didn't realize . . . I wasn't talking to you.'

'Naturally not,' said Louella dryly. 'Harriet, I expect you'd like to go to your room and unpack. Jem and I have things to discuss.'

Harriet walked towards the door, head held high, avoiding Jem's eyes. But he moved quickly and was somehow in the doorway before her.

'Don't touch you? Not now I won't,' he said softly. 'But one day, when you want me to . . . when you come to me and say, *Please, Jem* . . . And you will. You will,' he repeated, smiling down at her. 'You know it, don't you? I can wait.'

With a sharp intake of breath, Harriet slid between him and the door frame and bolted towards the stairs.

'What was all that about?' Louella said, as she closed the door. 'Are you bothering my niece?'

'Didn't you just hear me promise her I wouldn't?' protested Jem, with an air of injured innocence.

'You've got a nerve, Jem.'

'Course I have. That's the secret of my success.'

'What do you want?' Louella wasn't in the mood for parrying. 'I haven't seen you for months.'

'I've been busy,' said Jem. 'But I'm here now because I've come by some information that might be useful to you.

Matter of fact, I came by it last autumn, but you were out the last time I called. I meant to come again but I got distracted . . . In a hurry, are you, Lou?' Having registered Louella's impatience, he inserted a deliberate pause before he proceeded. 'What I've got to say concerns your favourite enemy, Rupert Brownlowe – or have you lost interest in hounding him to his grave?'

'No, but I've suspended it for the time being.'

'Never thought you'd give up on that vendetta, Lou.'

'The situation's complicated,' said Louella irritably, thinking of Michael Pritchard. 'I haven't given up, merely postponed.'

'So do you want to hear what I've got, or not?'

Louella sighed. 'You may as well tell me. I daresay it'll come in useful, sooner or later.'

Jem told her, succinctly, about Maudie. 'And what I reckon is, his missus doesn't know about it. Could cause a lot of trouble in the Brownlowe nest if someone was to blow the gaff. Want me to do it for you?'

'No. I'll deal with it myself.'

Louella was experiencing a tangle of reactions, all of them unfavourable towards Jem. He'd come at a bad moment, without warning. He'd sat at her desk as if it was his own, he'd swaggered across her carpet to be offensive to her niece. True, he'd just supplied Louella with a weapon with which to damage Rupert Brownlowe . . . but she hated him for it.

In her own way, Louella had standards. For twenty years, ever mindful of her childless status which she attributed to Brownlowe, she had done what she could, at intervals, to hurt the owner of Maple Grange. And all of it had been illegal. But still she recoiled from using the secret that Jem had just handed her. Just for a moment, in the telling, his gloating expression had reminded her of Helen Moffat relaying a particularly salacious piece of gossip. *No!* Louella told herself with disgust. To use such methods against an enemy would be to debase herself to their level.

'Thank you for the trouble you've taken,' she said. A nagging headache was making itself felt in the region between her eyebrows and it was becoming increasingly difficult to think coherently. She wanted Jem out of her house before he detected such a weakness.

'No doubt you'll want paying for it?'

'A man's got to earn a crust somehow,' Jem said, with a shrug. 'So's a woman, I suppose . . . unless she makes a lucky marriage.'

Tight-lipped, Louella jerked the top left-hand drawer of her desk open and took out a metal cashbox. She counted out a bundle of notes and, precisely because she was so angry with Jem, the folded wad she passed over was a generous one. He stowed it in the breast pocket of his jacket, then touched a hand to his brow with his usual lopsided smile.

'Grateful thanks, m'lady. You're getting soft, Lou . . . I know my own way out. Be seeing you.'

After he'd gone, she realized that once again he'd left without giving her an address where she might contact him. She didn't delude herself that he had gone for good – she only wished it was that simple! Here was just another problem to add to her load: how was she to get rid of Jem? He'd been useful at the start but he'd got cleverer as he got older and now, she had to admit, he was way out of her control.

By eight o'clock that evening, Louella's headache had settled down into the kind that lasts all night and into the next morning. Manners and family feeling dictated that her niece should not be left to eat alone on the first evening of this visit, but the headache finally drove Louella to bed, where in the darkness she could consider the consequences of today's interview with Anne Armitage.

Harriet accepted the alternative of a tray in her room with relief. She had the memory of an encounter of her own to deal with. The verbal exchange with Jem Wilkins had taken place in the safety of the study at Medlar House, with Aunt Louella in the next room and a basement full of servants who could be summoned at the tug of a bell rope.

It *should* have been far less unsettling than the kiss he'd extracted from her at Starling Cottages or the inglorious tussle in the wheatfield, yet it had left her feeling angry and threatened.

Was he right? Was something deep inside her drawn to him, in spite of every conscious reaction? It was as if the first time she'd seen him, in the congregation at Hector's funeral, he'd lodged a tiny dart in her, with an invisible thread attached to it that stretched between them. Mostly she didn't know it was there; but every time Jem came across her again he gave it a tug, and every time it dragged her inexorably closer.

By midday on the following day, Louella was feeling better. She'd written a letter to Anne, expressing her sadness over what had happened and her hope that something might survive of a friendship she valued enormously. She'd added a question about what was to happen with regard to the Bethnal Green visits. Since they had been at Anne's initiative, must Louella give them up too?

It was an excuse to re-establish a contact that Anne's parting words had been meant to sever permanently. It might work. At least she'd have tried. With the letter sealed and sent to the post, she turned her attention to Harriet.

'We must think what's to be done with you,' she said at lunch, when Rose had set down two plates of chicken soup and padded silently away. 'I don't mean just for this visit, I mean with your life. You are twenty years old. You have cut loose from family ties. I know you went home after Will's accident, and all credit to you for doing that, but it was only temporary, wasn't it?'

'I suppose so.' Harriet stirred at her soup, making no move to eat it.

'Have you made any plans? You aren't committed to that young man from the Flying Circus?'

'No,' said Harriet, more sharply than she had intended. She softened her voice. 'I don't have any choice in the matter. He's not in the least committed to me! It was a

441

mistake I made, that's all, at a difficult time when I couldn't think what else to do.'

'You know you could always have come to me, whatever trouble you found yourself in,' Louella reproached her.

'Do I? Sometimes we haven't got on too well. That was why I was back at the farm last year before I went with Tom – because we quarrelled and you hit me.'

'I know,' Louella said. 'I regret that enormously, Harriet. I can only say in my own defence that it was a difficult time for me, too. You must know yourself what havoc a bad man can wreak in one's life,' she explained ruefully.

'Yes. I know. Aunt Louella, I don't want to seem ungrateful. That incident was one small thing, when you've always been so kind and generous to me . . . but that's why it upset me so badly – because everything else that I'd been sure of had been overturned and then you as well. I've got over all that now, but there's something I want to ask you, about Rob and Jackie. You're good to them too, with presents and so on, but it's only me you invite. Why?'

'Because . . .' Louella considered the question. 'Your brothers are my nephews and of course I'm fond of them. But you've always been more than that to me, ever since you were small.'

'Mum says you looked after me when I was a baby, while she worked at the Arsenal.'

'Yes, I did,' said Louella. 'It was a happy time for me. Daisy worked long hours, so it was me that did everything for you and watched you grow and learn, and cut your first teeth and take your first steps. It was as if you were my own little girl. When Daisy got married to Will and stopped working and wanted you back, it seemed as great a loss as my own baby dying, all over again.'

Harriet put her spoon down and stared at her aunt. 'You had a baby?' she said. 'I never knew.'

'I don't suppose anyone thought to tell you. He was born, he lived for an hour or so and then he died. People don't seem to count it as a proper bereavement when a baby dies so soon. Most people don't, anyway,' Louella said, with a painful recollection of the bond she'd shared with Anne Armitage.

'I'm so sorry, Aunty Lou.' Unconsciously, Harriet had used the old, childish form of her aunt's name. 'You've had so many awful things happen to you.'

'Fate deals us a hand and all we can do is cope with it as best we can. But it did hurt. I nearly couldn't bear it,' Louella admitted. 'Robert was dead and with his child gone too, there seemed to be nothing left to live for. And my Danny was the second baby I'd lost – the first I miscarried in 1914, soon after Daisy found she'd fallen pregnant with you. So when she talked about getting rid of you, it upset me terribly.'

'What did you say?' Harriet broke in sharply. Louella realized she had let slip what was meant to be a secret between herself and Daisy. She had a brief struggle with her conscience, and won.

'Your mother was in a lot of trouble. It wasn't going to be easy, bringing up an illegitimate baby. Your father, your *real* father, was dead, killed at First Ypres. So when she realized she was pregnant, she went to a woman in Guildford who specialized in solving that sort of problem. She asked me to go with her. It was me that talked her out of it at the last minute, when this dreadful old woman had rolled up her sleeves all ready to do the deed. It's because of me that you were born at all,' said Louella urgently. *'That's* why I care about you more than your brothers. *That's* why I want to give you a better chance in life. I married well, I've a successful business, but I've nobody to pass it on to. It can be yours if you'll live here with me and take it over when the time comes. Everything. That's what I've always wanted, for you to be my heir, for you to benefit from what I've fought for, for you to be the child I never had . . .'

She broke off. Harriet's white face and harrowed expression told her that she had gone too far, too fast.

When Jem ran down the steps from the front door of Louella's house in Blackheath, he did so with apparent purpose; but once he was out of sight of the long windows he stopped. In truth he had no idea where to go next.

In Bethnal Green, George Crowley must have been found by now, if only by frustrated customers breaking down the pub door. The obvious assumption would be that his death had been accidental. All the same it would not be a good idea for Jem to be seen in the vicinity for quite some time, in case his release from prison and George's fatal fall should strike someone, somewhere, as an interesting coincidence. In any case, he felt no inclination to linger in the area. His time amid the green spaces of the Hampshire countryside had spoiled him for the dirt and squalor of his old habitat.

Realistically, a return to work at Welcome Farm was no longer a possibility. A pity, that. He still had moments of missing the farm. Jem's mouth twisted in a self-mocking grin as he acknowledged that he even missed the pungent smell of the midden behind the stables, the mud-streaked flank of a dairy Shorthorn under his cheek in the milking shed on a wet winter's morning, or the ache of physical exhaustion after a day spent forking hay into a cart under a blinding sun. He supposed he could get the same labour elsewhere – but not on the generous wage that Louella had provided, and not with Will Griffin for an employer.

He'd actually *liked* Will. And the liking had been returned. He'd been valued, not only for putting his back into a day's work, but also for the companionship: the meals eaten together out in the fields; the shared silences; the moments of exasperation when an overworked machine broke down and the satisfaction when between them they'd got it mended.

Friendship. It wasn't an emotion with which he was familiar and it would probably have cost him something, sooner or later. He'd accused Louella of getting soft; but he was a fine one to talk, he scolded himself. It was a good thing he'd got away from the farm.

To hell with sentiment. What did he want? Louella's money in his pocket should take care of the bare essentials for a while. There wasn't a lot else that he *really* wanted –

apart from Harriet Griffin, on her back and begging for more. That was something that he didn't despair of achieving, but it would need patience and it would require him to be in the right places at the right times. Harriet was at Medlar House now, but presumably she'd be back at Welcome Farm sooner or later. And apart from that consideration, it rankled to think of Kitty being happy with some other man when once she'd belonged so thoroughly to Jem Wilkins.

Maybe he should spoil it for Kitty.

He decided to catch a train down to Farnham and look around the district for work.

The letter from Vera to Harriet had been delivered to Welcome Farm and sent on to Medlar House. It announced that Vera and Fred were now the proud parents of a son, Frederick Junior, born on 28th March: 'He was a big baby, nearly nine pounds – it was like giving birth to an elephant! But he's lovely and healthy, especially his lungs! You're going to be godmother, remember? Please come and see us soon.'

Harriet was glad of an excuse to go to Croydon and get away from Aunt Louella for a while. She didn't know how to tell her aunt, without being unkind about it, that she didn't want the rôle that had been planned for her. She didn't want to be the heiress to Medlar House, its antiques and its servants and everything that went with the position. She didn't want to control a factory of seamstresses making ready-to-wear fashions. Most of all, she didn't want to be the child that Louella had never had. She wanted to be Harriet Griffin, free to make her own mistakes, however enormous, and choose her own future, whatever that might be.

Frederick Junior lived up to his mother's claim about the strength of his lungs.

'Come in! Sorry about the din.' Opening the door in response to Harriet's knock, Vera stood in the doorway with a scarlet, wailing infant clasped against her shoulder.

'Freddie's just had a feed and he's full of wind. Sit down and give us a minute or two to settle him.'

Harriet sat in a chair on one side of the kitchen range while, in the other, Vera propped the struggling bundle that was Freddie into a sitting position and tilted him forward against the heel of one hand, rubbing vigorously at his back with the other. In due course her efforts were rewarded by a loud burp. Vera cradled him on her lap and the small, furious face relaxed into sleepy satisfaction.

'You look so expert,' said Harriet admiringly.

'A week or two of this and it feels like for ever,' Vera told her, with feeling.

'But you're glad you had him?'

'I suppose so . . . when I'm not too tired to be glad about anything. I never realized how much of your life a new baby swallows up,' Vera said. 'You think they mostly sleep when they're this tiny, but not a bit of it! And by the time they do finally drop off, they've created so much work that you're always running to catch up with yourself. Still, I shouldn't complain. He's healthy, that's the main thing.'

'How does Fred like being a father?' Harriet asked.

'Oh, Fred thinks he's wonderful; but then, Fred isn't the one that has to feed him all hours of the day and night and deal with all that washing! He just comes in from work and hangs over the cot for a few minutes playing the proud father. Expects his dinner to be ready same as usual, mind. But that's what it's like being married,' said Vera. 'Once the novelty's worn off, it's like being in domestic service, only there's no days off and no pay. Maybe I should have tried being a mistress, like you and that Tom of yours,' she jested.

'You don't mean that,' said Harriet.

'No, course I don't. Only kidding. Seen anything of Tom, have you?'

'No. Well, he came to the farm at Christmas, but he only stayed an hour. He hasn't even written to me since.'

'Hasn't he? Cheeky blighter. He's written to Fred, though,' said Vera.

'*Fred?*' Harriet echoed. 'Whatever for?'

'Oh, it's a silly thing. When he came here looking for you and you'd gone, he seemed a bit down about it. Fred was just on his way out to a meeting of a group he's got involved with, and he said Tom could go along too, just to give him something to do with himself. Well, they were gone for hours and hours. I gave Fred a proper talking-to about it later – not that he paid much attention. Anyway, Tom only went along out of curiosity and expected to find it all a bit of a laugh, only when he got there he was dead impressed and he said what he'd heard made a lot of sense, and he was going to get more involved with it when he got back to Portsmouth. He asked was there a group in Portsmouth? And Fred said there was bound to be, there's groups everywhere.' Vera glanced down at the baby on her lap.

'His nibs here's dozed off – must be in honour of your visit, he's on his best behaviour. Put the kettle on, Harriet, and let's have a cuppa while we've got a bit of peace and quiet.'

Harriet reached obediently for the kettle on the side of the stove and moved it on to the hob, averting her face so that Vera wouldn't see that she was feeling sick with resentment. Tom, who hadn't had time to write to her, had written to Fred. Tom had spent a bare hour with her at Christmas and 'hours and hours' with Fred at some meeting in Croydon. Tom had told her that he would be working too hard in Portsmouth for it to be practical for her to join him there, but he could find time to 'get more involved' with some organisation or other.

'Groups of what?' she asked stiffly.

'Communist Party,' Vera told her. 'I must say I was surprised at how serious he seemed to take it. I mean, he's one of the toffs, isn't he? And they're the opposite. But I suppose he's not exactly a *typical* toff. He said he was sick of watching his class lording it over the rest and thinking that just because they were born with money it made them better than people like Fred and me. He said Fred had more brains than quite a few toffs he could think of, like his

447

stepfather – or a nitwit called Gavin something-or-other that his old fiancée'd got herself engaged to. Dinah, was that her name?'

'Diana. Diana Somerville. Well, that explains it,' said Harriet, and her resentment grew.

'The Griffin boy seems to be doing a good job on Starbright,' Rupert Brownlowe told his wife at supper one evening. He'd visited Welcome Farm that afternoon and been treated to a show of the chestnut colt being cantered in circles on a lunge rein and driven in a bridle on long reins. Starbright had taken his lessons calmly and even submitted to having a saddle dropped on to his back and the girth done up loosely. Rob had said that in another week or two he'd be backed and then ridden.

'The horse is going well. And he's certainly good-looking. If young Griffin can make his manners match his conformation, he should be a prizewinner at next year's county show. I think that venture may turn out to be a success,' said Rupert with satisfaction, leaning back in his chair to reach for the brandy decanter on the sideboard behind him.

It was a comfort to think of *something* he'd handled being a success. Admittedly, the lawn-mower factory was doing better than it had done before that widow's timely injection of capital. Michael Pritchard had insisted on paying a designer for restyling the mowers as well as new machinery for making them, an outlay which Rupert had resisted so determinedly that Pritchard had actually threatened to leave. Rupert had then had to back down, but he had hated doing it.

So far, the increased sales of the new model had justified the expense – and no doubt Pritchard was crowing about it inwardly, though he never said anything. But it would only need a small slump in demand to push the factory back to the brink of bankruptcy, and the loan would have to be repaid one day.

It wasn't a *gentleman's* occupation, Rupert told himself, this borrowing and budgeting and worrying about last month's sales figures. He'd far rather be a horse breeder, an activity for which he had a flair. Now that he'd found a good breaker-in of horses in young Rob Griffin, he should really set about rebuilding the Maple Grange reputation for producing fine hunters . . . *before it's too late*, an inner voice completed the sentence.

'I think I'll get Leonora served again by the same stallion that sired Starbright,' he said to Marion. 'Then when Starbright starts taking prizes I'll be in a good position to capitalize on his pedigree.'

'Are you sure that's wise?' said Marion. 'You were saying yesterday that you weren't happy with Martin – that he's lazy and slipshod. You said it's almost impossible to come by a fit, reliable groom nowadays because all the young men go off to the factories instead of into service. And if Leonora's to have another foal, you'll need someone reliable. Shouldn't you be making sure you can find a decent groom before you risk any more money on stud fees?'

Rupert scowled into his brandy glass, his moment of enthusiasm punctured. Marion had such an irritating habit of being *right*, damn her.

While Harriet was away in Croydon, the postman delivered a reply to the letter that Louella had sent to Anne Armitage. Anne wrote that she also regretted the loss of a friend, but after careful reflection she had to confirm that in the circumstances it was impossible to continue knowing one another. In any case, she was about to leave London to return to her parents' home. She had found a lady to take over the welfare visits to the families in Bethnal Green and this lady preferred to choose her own colleagues for the work. Anne thanked Louella for her interest in the slum families and wished her well for the future.

It was a polite but unshakeable rebuff. Louella tore up the letter and tried not to think about the Jarvis children listening to her stories while the baby lay warm and sleepy in the crook of her arm, an experience now forfeited for ever. To fend off the desolation that this prompted, she telephoned the Brownlowe lawn-mower factory in Guildford and asked to speak to Michael Pritchard.

'Louella? How nice to hear from you,' came his voice. 'I suppose it's been months since I saw you. We've been so busy here, installing the new machinery and finding extra outlets for the mowers . . . but I think you'd be pleased with what we've achieved.'

'I'm sure you're doing a wonderful job,' said Louella dispiritedly.

'Are you all right? You sound a bit down.'

'To tell the truth, I am a bit, Michael. Yes, it has been months. Tomorrow's Saturday, and even a dedicated manager like you must have *some* leisure time. I suppose there's no chance of you coming here to lunch and cheering me up?'

Since the day that Michael had told Louella why he could not marry her, they had met infrequently. The traces of baffled desire were still there between them, under the companionship, and when they parted it always took days for Louella to settle down again. She supposed it was the same for Michael and they had tacitly let the gaps between meetings lengthen. But today, hurt by Anne's letter and Harriet's too-eager departure for Croydon, she felt a longing for his company that was almost uncontrollable and it showed in her voice.

There was a pause. Then he said, 'All right. That would be very pleasant.'

Louella put the telephone down and ran to the kitchen to consult with Cook over the menu for tomorrow's lunch. Everett, polishing silver in the butler's pantry, saw her face as she went by and noticed that Madam looked happier today than she had done for several days.

'Thank God for that.' It was a reflection not entirely prompted by affection for his employer. For the staff at Medlar House, whenever Louella was miserable, there was hell to pay.

*   *   *

'I had the devil of a job persuading Mr Brownlowe to accept the new design for the mowers,' Michael told Louella, over lunch. 'He hates to see any changes that he hasn't initiated himself. But it really was essential to give our machines a more modern appearance! They hadn't changed since about 1910, and though it was a very good machine in its day, it had definitely *had* its day . . . but I'm boring you,' he finished abruptly.

'Not at all,' Louella murmured, though his remark had been only too accurate. The fate of Rupert Brownlowe's lawn-mower factory interested her only in that its bankruptcy and closure had to be postponed because Michael's fate was tied up with it. She made an effort. 'I mean, I can just imagine how tiresome it must be to work for someone who wants everything his own way, when you know that his way is strangling the business.' An idea occurred to her and she leaned forward across the table. 'Michael, have you ever considered working for someone else?'

'Oh yes,' Michael admitted straightaway. 'In fact, I reached such a pitch of frustration that I told Brownlowe that if he couldn't respect my judgement, maybe he should look for another manager. So then he caved in and let me have my way over the design, but I could see how much he resented doing it – since when I've had a nasty feeling that he'll pay me back for it at the first opportunity he gets, and maybe it would be wise to find myself a bolt hole before that happens! But I've been too busy seeing the changes through to do anything concrete about finding another employer.'

'I can think of a bolt hole,' said Louella. 'Though it would also be very hard work! But there'd be no question of this particular employer doubting your acumen as a manager,' she confirmed.

'Who do you have in mind?'

'Me,' said Louella. She saw his face stiffen and hurried on. 'Let me explain before you dismiss the idea out of hand. This isn't an attempt to patronize you or a casual suggestion to rescue you from an unsatisfactory job. I really do need a manager for my business. You know roughly what I do: "Louella Ramsay Fashions." Smart ready-to-wear for department stores at a price that's affordable to office girls and housewives who need to look good for a special occasion but can't afford couture.

'I've reached the point where the name sells itself and, frankly, I'd rather take a back seat now. I'd want to go on approving the designs of course, and perhaps organizing the seasonal shows or talking to the store buyers – I've built up contacts over the years and it would be a shame to let that go to waste. But the day-to-day running . . . the hiring and firing, the cost-controlling of manufacture and all the things you do so well—'

'*No*,' said Michael. He reached across the table and covered her hand with his own to soften the refusal. 'Thank you for the offer, Louella, but no. I don't want to work for you. I want to go on being your friend, and that isn't best achieved by becoming your employee. I'm too proud – and you're too autocratic,' he stated baldly. 'I admire you for that – but if I was on the receiving end, we'd be at each other's throats in no time.'

Louella slumped in her seat a little, accepting defeat. Michael's hand was still covering hers, and she turned her own palm upwards to keep hold of it. 'You're probably right,' she admitted. 'It was just an idea.'

The hand tightened on her fingers for a moment, comfortingly. 'Dear Louella,' he said, then with a determined change of subject, 'It's a beautiful day. What shall we do this afternoon?'

'Well, there *is* something I'd like to do . . . or rather, that I need to do, but I'll find it hard. I'd very much like your company to help me – only I'm afraid that it might bore you.'

'You never bore me, Lou.' It wasn't often that he used the familiar shortening of her name and for a moment Louella felt such anguish for what might have been between them that she wanted to howl.

'What do you have in mind?' he asked gently.

'There's a grave I want to see.'

In twenty years she had not been to her baby's grave, though once a year she paid a sum of money to the cemetery keeper's wife to keep it tidy. She couldn't explain why she now felt this need to visit it, unless her recent loss of access to the Jarvis baby had got mixed up with the old grief and the pilgrimage to the grave could be a mourning for both of them. It took her a while to find the small mound in the cemetery, with its plain headstone which gave only Danny's name and the year that had seen his brief taste of life. She stood looking down at the carved letters on the grey stone, and found that she was crying and that Michael's arms were round her for comfort. But like every other source of comfort in her life, it couldn't last.

29

'Do you mind if I take the motor this afternoon, dear? I need to do a little shopping in Farnham.'

For Marion the request was just a formality. Rupert, as the man of the house, liked to be deferred to as having a higher claim to the Landau, but as he couldn't drive and relied on her to chauffeur him when he did need to go somewhere, in practice he seldom objected to her plans.

The Austin Landau had been the Maple Grange car since before the Great War. The chauffeur, Aldridge, had 'gone for a soldier' in 1914 and when Laura Brownlowe had learnt to drive, Rupert had thankfully dispensed with the services, and the wage requirements, of Aldridge's replacement. But after the war Laura had inconsiderately married young James Allingham and gone to live in Kew, meeting her father's plaintive comments about how such a departure would leave him stranded with the tart observation that if he missed her services behind the wheel, he could always learn to drive himself.

Rupert had conducted furtive experiments inside the garage, from which he had gained the impression that he was too old to learn the co-ordination of wheel, levers and pedals required to steer the heavy old car at speed along the narrow lanes of Seale, let alone the broad highway of the Hog's Back. So the Landau gathered cobwebs while Rupert rode his elderly gelding Plumbago to visit those acquaintances who still maintained a stables to receive such visitors, or he hired a taxicab when he had to catch a train. But Plumbago had eventually dropped dead in the paddock from sheer old age and Rupert had been delighted to learn that the talents of his chosen second wife Marion included that of driving a motor car.

At that stage, he had not anticipated that a lady so emancipated would want to use the motor on her own errands too.

'*Must* you see to your bits and pieces today? It isn't very convenient. I wanted to go over to Welcome Farm and take another look at Starbright's progress.'

'So, I'll take you to the farm,' Marion proposed briskly, 'and leave you there for an hour or two while I run my errands. Then I'll collect you again and have you home in time for tea.'

It was a perfectly practical solution. He couldn't deny that. So why, as his wife drove away from the farmyard, did he feel like a small boy dropped at a playground to amuse himself while the adults got on with the *important* business of life?

Kitty was pegging out a sheet on the washing line behind Starling Cottages when a shadow on the expanse of white cotton alerted her to the presence of an intruder. She spun round.

'Jem! What're you doing here?'

'I *might* have been pining for a sight of you, Kitty my love.'

'Garn! You're after something. What is it? Let's not waste time beating about the bush.'

'*I'm* in no hurry. From where I'm standing, the view's fine.' His wicked grin hadn't changed. Head tilted to one side, he let his hazel eyes travel over her. 'You've filled out a bit,' he observed. 'Suits you. You used to be all bones.'

He took a step forward and passed a deliberate arm around her waist, hooking her towards him. 'Got a kiss for me, then?'

'Get off, Jem, leave me alone!' Kitty hissed, rigid, her arms doubled up between his chest and her own. Jem's mouth twisted against hers for a moment before he released her, as authoritatively as he had taken hold of her.

'Saving it all for your husband, are you? You always were a prissy little thing. But you made me promises, remember? *"I'll always love you, Jem . . ."* That's what you used to moan of a night, when we were first together.'

'You've no business to lay a finger on me!' Hot-cheeked, Kitty tugged her dress straight. 'You're a fine one to twit me with broken promises! You were the one that walked out – and you left me in a right state when you did. I was pregnant, Jem, but you hit me and kicked me so bad that last night, I lost the baby. I reckon that cancelled out any promises I made when I was a silly girl, taken in by your tricks.'

'A baby, was there?' Jem's mocking expression altered, just for a moment. Then he shrugged. 'Wasn't the first – and it won't be the last if I have any say in the matter. Well, Kitty, so you've been married a while. Any more signs of little 'uns on the way? Or is your cripple a bit lacking in that department too?'

Kitty was silent. How had he picked so easily on the one bar to her contentment with Billy? Now that the two of them were settled, with a nice little home and employment on the farm and with Billy's steadily expanding milk round as well, she would have loved a baby to lie kicking and cooing on the rag rug in front of the fire. But there'd been no luck, and she didn't know if it was because her old lover's parting bout of violence had damaged her insides for ever or if Billy was, as Jem had so uncomfortably expressed it, 'lacking in that department'.

'Where is he, by the way?' Jem asked, glancing around.

'He's out doing his milk round,' Kitty said. 'We don't want you round here, Jem, and neither do the Griffins. So why don't you go back where you came from?'

'Aren't you going to offer me a friendly cup of tea?'

'No, I'm not!'

'Or an hour or two in bed, for old time's sake?' Jem advanced again and Kitty backed away.

'I'll scream,' she said.

'I might like that. You always were a bit too quiet,' said

Jem, his gaze suddenly so intent that a shiver of fear ran down Kitty's spine. To her relief she heard the sound of a horse's hooves and the creaking of cartwheels in the lane. She fled towards the back door, darted through the house and clung to the front door frame, heart pounding wildly. In the lane, Joseph and the pony trap stood still and Billy was climbing down from the bench seat.

Jem hadn't followed her into the house. She scurried back to the kitchen, slammed and bolted the back door. When she peered out through the window at the little back garden, her visitor could be seen in the distance, loping away across the field beyond.

'Hullo, love.' Billy came into the kitchen, carrying the money box she'd designed for him, unhooked from the side of the cart.

'You're early,' said Kitty, instinctively trying to hide her agitation.

'We made good time today,' Billy said. 'Old Mrs Hatcher usually keeps me gassing for a good ten minutes but for once she was out, so I left her jug on the step, covered over. Joseph missed the peppermint she usually gives him, though.' Belatedly, he recognized some sign of tension in her face. 'What's up, love?'

'Nothing's up. I just thought I'd have a bit more time to get my chores done before you wanted your tea.' In the space of a few seconds Kitty had reached the decision that led to the lie. There was no sense in telling Billy what had happened, any more than it would have been wise to mention Jem's previous visit.

He would be worried, he would be angry. He might even go in search of her tormentor; and that wouldn't make her feel any safer, it would merely add to her fears.

Once, Billy had squared up to a drunken Jem, fuelled by anger at the beating she was getting. But in a cold-blooded confrontation she knew that her husband would be no match for a seasoned street-fighter like Jem. And she didn't want him hurt.

* * *

Marion climbed out of the Landau in one of the twisting lanes which led from Bentley towards Welcome Farm, and stared with exasperation at a distinctly flat front tyre.

There was a spare wheel strapped to the back of the car, but Marion's emancipation only extended so far. Twenty years ago she'd have rolled up her sleeves and set to, but nowadays much of her physical strength had deserted her, and with it her confidence when it came to mechanical matters. The prospect of struggling with a jack and the tight-screwed nuts which held the damaged wheel in place filled her with dismay.

Rupert would be furious if he had to wait. And when Rupert was furious he sulked. Rupert was a *champion* sulker.

'Having trouble?'

The man had stepped out, soft-footed, from among the fringe of trees. He was in his twenties, slim and sallow, faintly gipsyish in appearance, with a peaked cap pulled down to shadow his face. Black hair under the hat. Workaday clothes. A more nervous lady might have been alarmed, but Marion turned to him with relief.

'A puncture. Do you know how to deal with such things? I don't, though I'm ashamed to admit it,' she said.

'Let's have a look.' He squatted beside the flat tyre and his fingers tested the nuts. 'No problem,' he told her, rising again. 'Tools in the box on the running board, are they? You sit down on the grass, lady – or in the car if you'd rather. This won't take long.'

'I'll watch, if you don't mind. I ought to remind myself how to deal with punctures. How lucky for me that you happened to be here,' said Marion. He had the toolbox unstrapped and open already, selecting the right implements with deft fingers. He removed his hat and jacket and tossed them on to the grass verge.

The problem of the car solved, Marion was able to pay attention to a vague impression that his face looked familiar.

'Haven't we met before?'

The man glanced up from fitting the jack into position under the chassis of the car. 'Could be,' he said.

Marion concentrated, scanning her memory. 'I know! It was you that brought our mare Leonora back to us after she was stolen, a few years ago.'

'That's right,' he said. 'You'll be the lady up at the big house near Seale?'

'I'm Mrs Brownlowe, yes.'

'How's the mare doing these days? I seem to remember she was due to drop a foal any day.'

'Yes. She did. A lovely colt. Two years old, now. He's being broken in and schooled at a farm along the road here.'

'Welcome Farm? Will Griffin's place?' guessed the man, his voice oddly eager.

'It's his son who's handling Starbright,' Marion said.

'Rob? Why not his father?'

'I've heard Mr Griffin is a first-class horseman – or was, but he had a serious accident with a tractor last year and he's not fully recovered yet. I gather you know him?'

'Not now. I used to, one time. Used to work for him,' the man said.

'And where do you work now?'

'Nowhere. I'm looking for a place.'

'What did you do for Will Griffin?' Marion asked.

'All sorts. Farmhand.'

'Did that include handling horses?'

'Horses, cows, chickens, all the livestock on the farm.' He had lifted the damaged wheel clear and now he lugged the spare round to fit it into place.

'Do you like working with horses? Because if you do, it's possible I might know of a job for you,' said Marion. 'My husband needs someone to look after Leonora. We have a groom but he's not entirely satisfactory. And there's general maintenance work on the house and the outbuildings which he doesn't deal with very enthusiastically. I know my husband's thinking of replacing him. Have you any experience of that kind of work?'

'I can do all sorts.'

'I don't suppose you can drive?' Marion asked hopefully.

'I can do all sorts,' the man repeated. 'Want me to show you?'

Will's lessons with the farm Austin had been some time ago, but Jem Wilkins' air of confidence disguised any fumblings. When he ground the gears Marion accepted without question his casual remark about an unfamiliar make of car. The wheel replaced, he drove her to Welcome Farm.

'He's perfect,' Marion told Rupert in an undertone. Her proposed new employee sat waiting in the driver's seat of the Landau, hands resting on the wheel, face impassive.

Rupert glanced towards him doubtfully. 'Well . . . I don't know. I've seen him before somewhere.'

'He's the one who found Leonora.'

'Mmm.' All Rupert could remember was over-tipping the man at the time. But at least he'd shown proper respect and gratitude in receiving the money, a characteristic which had been distinctly lacking in the behaviour of the groom Martin lately.

'He seems very capable with cars,' said Marion. 'He could drive you about as well. And do odd jobs, carpentering, painting and things like that, on top of seeing to Leonora. And he wouldn't want any more wages than you're already paying Martin. He seems like a real bargain to me.'

It was a line of persuasion that always worked with Rupert.

'Did you see the man in the motor that collected Rupert Brownlowe?' Rob asked Daisy when he came into the farmhouse after Rupert had gone.

'No. Why?'

'I only caught a glimpse of him through the window as they drove away,' said Rob. 'And he was wearing a hat. But he looked a bit like Jem Wilkins.'

Daisy dropped a plate.

'I don't suppose it could have been him,' Rob reassured her, as he helped her to sweep up the shattered pieces of what had luckily only been one of the everyday plates and not part of Daisy's treasured willow pattern service. 'He'd never have the nerve to show his face round here again.'

Daisy wasn't so sure. Jem had never been short of nerve.

After two days with Vera, Fred and the baby, Harriet was ready to return to Blackheath. The little house had seemed cramped enough before the advent of Freddie Junior. Now it was crammed – and although Vera moved Freddie's crib out of the small back bedroom into his parents' room in honour of Harriet's arrival, the mere interposing of a thin partition wall between her and Freddie's middle-of-the-night proclamations of hunger was not enough to preserve her sleep. And the heavy eyes and surly manner of the baby's father as he ate his breakfast on the second morning hinted that the move hadn't been popular with him either. Guessing by Vera's harassed expression that what Fred was too polite to say to herself was being conveyed out of earshot to his wife, Harriet made her excuses and left, promising to return when Freddie's christening date had been set.

Back at Medlar House she was dismayed to find that in the two short days she had been away, Tom Searle had come in search of her.

'He'd been to Welcome Farm and they sent him here. He seemed rather annoyed when I told him that you were in Croydon,' said Louella. 'And as I didn't know when you'd be back he left a telephone number for you to contact him. "*If and when she comes back*," was how he put it. I couldn't make up my mind whether his behaviour meant that he really cares about you and was disappointed not to find you here, or that he has very bad manners,' she added.

'Probably the bad manners,' Harriet said. 'Almost certainly, I should say, considering that he hasn't cared enough to contact me since Christmas. And then he has the nerve to be annoyed that I'm not sitting here on a shelf waiting for him, like a doll! I wonder what he wants?' She took the piece of paper on which Louella had written Tom's contact number. 'Do you know where this is?'

'A flat in Park Lane. He said you'd know it – it belongs to someone called Diana Somerville.'

Because Tom Searle had left her in limbo for so long, and because he was now staying with his old flame, Harriet forced herself to wait another day before she telephoned him. When the operator put her through, the voice that answered was Diana's, as she had grimly anticipated.

'May I speak to Tom?'

'May I ask who is calling?'

'It's Harriet Griffin.'

'Oh, yes. I remember you. The one who impressed us all so frightfully with that wing-walking exploit,' said Diana, her cool voice indicating that she had not been impressed in the least. 'Tom's about somewhere, I'll call him.'

Harriet waited. She distinctly heard the distant voice drawling, 'Tom, it's your little rustic.'

Tom's voice came down the line.

'Harry! Where are you?'

'I'm at Aunt Louella's.'

'Well, you weren't three days ago when I came looking for you. You're devilish hard to pin down. Why can't you stay in one place where a fellow can find you?'

'I might,' said Harriet, 'if a fellow gave any indication that he might *want* to find me occasionally.'

There was a pause. Then Tom said, 'Oh damn. You're sulking because I haven't been in touch.'

'I'm not sulking. Just surprised that you should resurface after such a long silence and still expect me to be in the same place.'

'It hasn't been that long . . . oh, I suppose it *has*. Listen, Harry, I thought you knew me. I'm not steady, I'm not predictable, I won't dance regular attendance on you like some of the men you may meet. But I do care about you, even when I'm not there. And when I start missing you, I come back. As it happens, I started missing you, and I came looking for you, and when you weren't there I missed you even more. So, have *you* missed me at all?'

It wasn't fair, Harriet thought. She'd thought she was clear of all this, but he only had to switch on that warm, personal voice and she was longing to see him again.

It wasn't until after she'd agreed to meet him the next day, and replaced the receiver, that she remembered to wonder why, if it was herself that he cared for so much, he was staying with Diana Somerville.

'Diana's a friend. That's all. Anything else between us was over long ago.' In a teashop in Blackheath, Tom took Harriet's hand and turned it over to trace a forefinger across her palm.

'This is a working hand. I can tell you've been back at the farm . . . Listen, Harriet, I've got my old job back with the mail plane company, based in Croydon. I start next week. I'll need to find somewhere to rent. You can come and live with me, if you like.'

Tom's usual line. Not '*I want you to come*', but '*If you like . . .*'

So that when he got tired of the arrangement he could leave her again, without any inconvenient stirrings of conscience. '*I didn't make you come here. It was what you wanted.*'

Was it? Harriet thought about it. Last Christmas she'd been missing him so badly that she would probably have come running at the slightest lifting of his finger. Now?

'You turn up after weeks and months with no word,' she said, playing for time, 'and expect me to drop everything and fly into your arms—'

Tom surveyed her calmly. 'You're one of the few girls I've ever come across who can still look attractive when losing your temper,' he commented. 'I suppose it goes with your hair. I remember you telling me off the first time we met, when I landed the Moth among your father's cows. It really impressed me, then. I can't say you've gone on impressing me to the same extent,' he added, deliberately stoking her indignation, 'but even so, I enjoy your company enough to want you with me in Croydon.'

'On the old basis, naturally? Tom Searle's philosophy?' Harriet quoted it sarcastically. 'No ties, no regrets . . .'

'Naturally,' Tom told her, unperturbed. 'I'm crass and inconsiderate, you should know that by now, and I'm not likely to change, so you'll have to take me or leave me as I am. Well? Which is it to be?'

The choices, Harriet realized, were between life with Tom, which was insecure, frustrating, maddening and against all the social conventions; but which yielded occasional patches of pure delight – until the inevitable moment when she got hurt all over again; or life at Welcome Farm without him, which consisted of hard work, boredom and the perpetual awareness of an unfulfilled hunger; or life in London with Aunt Louella, as official heiress to Medlar House, the Ramsay money and 'Louella Ramsay Fashions', as if she were Louella's own child.

The last opportunity was one that most girls in her position would probably jump at. But she wasn't most girls, and she wasn't Louella's child either. Marvellous opportunity or not, she couldn't quite swallow the thought of living her life to suit Louella's ideals and not her own. Because that was what it would come to.

Tom and too much freedom? Or Aunt Louella and too much control?

'Well?' said Tom again, across the table. 'What's your answer?'

'All right. I'll come to Croydon.'

Billy Marshall was having a patch of bad luck with the milk round. First it was something in the milk that tainted the flavour, leading to a litany of complaints from his regular customers.

'Dunno what it was, but it didn't half make the tea taste funny. And the milk wasn't the usual colour. Will Griffin been feeding those cows of his on something different, has he?'

Billy reported back to Daisy at the farm and together they

drained the dregs of the churn and then scrubbed it out with extra care.

'There *might* have been something mixed in with the milk,' he told Kitty that night. 'It certainly did taste a bit odd, and we found traces of something that Daisy thought could be powdered leaves from some kind of dried herb, like she uses for her medicines. But she couldn't tell what it might be, or how it could have got into the churn. Now she's worried sick that the dairy churns will have had the same problem.'

'Suppose it was poisonous?' Kitty said, after a moment. 'Who tasted it? You or Daisy?'

Billy paled. 'Both of us. Oh Lord . . . and if it was, what about the customers?' But the tainted milk had no ill effects that night. All next day, Daisy waited for bad news from the dairy and Billy braced himself for reports of illness among his customers, but nothing happened. The complaints about an odd taste were not repeated. The mystery remained unsolved.

A week later the normally placid Joseph, who could be relied on to crop grass peaceably while Billy served the customers, galloped off without warning, dragging the cart bouncing and banging behind him and eventually tipped the day's milk supply for the round into the hedge.

'Lord knows what started him off. Could have been a horsefly, I suppose, but he doesn't normally get that fussed,' Billy said, perplexed. He'd had to delay his round until afternoon milking was over to replace the lost milk; his customers were duly annoyed at being let down, and for the first time Billy was getting an unfriendly reception on their doorsteps.

'They must have known it wasn't your fault,' Kitty consoled him that evening.

'Oh, yes. But still . . . Mrs Hoggart had scones half-made, and Mrs Bray had the village fête committee to tea and only half a jug of yesterday's milk to go round. You can't blame them for being upset.'

It was on the third week, when a wheel of the cart was

found to be loose at the start of the round, that Will pointed out that these events always seemed to take place on a Wednesday.

'Could be someone's getting at you – someone with one day of the week free on which to do it,' he suggested, as he and Rob struggled to re-fix the wheel in a hurry so as not to reinforce the reputation for unreliability that Billy and the Welcome Farm milk round were beginning to get.

Billy told Kitty what Will had said. 'And he's right, these things have been happening to a pattern. But who could possibly be working that kind of mischief?'

Kitty didn't answer, but privately she wondered where Jem Wilkins had gone after he'd left Starling Cottages, and what he was currently doing with himself of a Wednesday.

30

'Come in, quick. The baby's just woken up and he's bawling his head off – takes after his dad, he's that impatient when it comes to wanting his dinner on time!'

On a morning at the end of September, Vera led Harriet into the kitchen, scooped up six-month-old Freddie from his crib in the corner, hitched up her blouse and planted a nipple in his mouth to shut off his strident wails before she gave a proper greeting.

'My, you're a stranger! Must be five or six weeks since you were here last. What are you doing with yourself these days?'

'Nothing much,' Harriet admitted. 'I tried to get some typing work after we came back to Croydon but there didn't seem to be any jobs going. Tom said when we first came that it didn't matter because he'd get his half-yearly allowance in July, but we've already spent so much of it that I don't know if it's going to last us until the New Year. And now that autumn is well and truly here, we'll be having to pay more for electricity and coal.'

'Doesn't he earn anything with that job of his?' Vera asked. 'I thought he was flying again on the mail planes?'

'Yes, but he seems to spend most of that as fast as he gets it. He's used to good wine and smart restaurants, and he's *not* used to economizing. And he keeps buying me clothes and bits of jewellery so that I won't disgrace him when we go out, which is very generous of him, I suppose, only it makes me feel a bit like a dressed doll.' Harriet sighed. 'I wish I could earn my own keep. I hate having to ask him for money to pay the rent or for the laundry and so on. It's demeaning, somehow.'

'Dunno why,' Vera commented. 'Men are supposed to be the providers, aren't they?'

'It'd be different if we were married,' Harriet said unhappily.

'Well, if you're not, that's his nibs' fault, not yours! You do the shopping and cooking and housework, don't you, same as if you were his wife? What's he think you do it *with*? Magic? Put the kettle on, Harriet, and let's have a cuppa tea.'

When the tea was made and poured, both women sat down in the twin Windsor chairs on either side of the stove to catch up with news.

'If Tom's still with the mail planes, then I suppose that leaves you on your own a lot?' Vera asked, shifting a greedily sucking Freddie to her other side.

'Sometimes, if the weather's bad and he can't fly back across the Channel when he's supposed to. But I expected that. I've learned not to worry when he doesn't appear.'

'So what *is* the problem? You looked like a wet weekend when I opened the door,' Vera said. 'The first thing I thought was, *Hullo, she's in trouble.*'

'It's this war in Spain,' Harriet told her. 'Does Fred talk about it too?'

'He never stops,' said Vera, with disgust.

'So do you understand what it's all about?'

'I ought to, the way Fred gives me lectures at the tea table! Mind you, he only sees one side of it . . . but the way he tells it, there was a new government elected by the Spanish people in February, the Popular Front – a sort of workers' government – and the Spanish army didn't like that, so in July they came out in rebellion against it. And now there's a real war going on, with the army and the supporters of the old government fighting the new army of the new government – which of course doesn't have much training or weapons, being a scratch force of volunteers. And Fred goes on about how wicked it is of that man called Franco, who's the Spanish army leader, to try to overthrow a democratically elected government, and how everyone in the world who believes in freedom ought to stand up and be counted.'

'That's what Tom says. And I'm so afraid that by "Stand up and be counted" he means actually go and fight.'

'Oh, I shouldn't think so. Spain's a long way off. And there's a big difference between saying something *ought* to be done and actually doing it. Fred talks a lot about the international brotherhood of the workers, but it's mostly hot air. 'Sides, if he went, he'd miss Freddie and me so much he'd be back before we noticed he'd gone,' Vera said comfortably.

'But Tom's so restless. I think he's well and truly bored with the mail planes. And with me,' Harriet confessed. 'He's been very critical lately. And his old girlfriend has just got herself engaged again, which seems to have made him even more edgy. As far as I can make out, she gets a new fiancé about once a year, like other girls might choose a new coat. Tom *says* he doesn't care one bit what she does with herself, but I keep wondering whether he's ever really got over her.'

'Harriet Griffin, you've no business to be thinking like that,' Vera scolded. 'Why should he be pining after someone else when he's got you? Haven't you got any pride in yourself? If you think you're worth nothing, the man'll think you're worth nothing,' she added. 'I have to give my Fred a good fright now and again, pick a quarrel and keep him at arm's length for a day or two, just so's he won't get smug.'

That was the trouble with Vera's opinion, it was given from the point of view of a woman who was sure of being loved. Harriet had no such confidence.

'I'm worried about Harriet,' Vera said that evening, as she dished up her husband's dinner at the stove. 'She looked so down-in-the-mouth today. She doesn't know from one day to the next if that Tom of hers is going to stay with her or be off on one of his jaunts, which is a shocking way to treat a woman – that's assuming you're fond of her, which I'm not entirely convinced he is,' she added darkly.

'Oh, I don't know.' Fred wanted to eat, not listen to a

lecture on the shortcomings of another man. 'Tom's a decent enough chap.'

'Well, if you think so you must know him better than I do,' Vera said. But from that observation an idea came. 'Fred, why don't you have a word with him, man to man? Tell him he's making her unhappy. Tell him she wants a bit of cuddling and cosseting, not to be made to feel like she's walking a tightrope all the time.'

Because it was the easiest way to get his dinner finished in peace, Fred agreed reluctantly to talk to Tom. But somehow, when the two of them got together, the subject of Harriet never cropped up. They had too many other interests in common. Finding that they were in agreement about the moral rights and wrongs of the Spanish war, they moved on to Fascism in general and the behaviour of the English Fascist leader Mosley in particular. Within a week Vera was regretting her well-meaning attempt to influence the course of Harriet's relationship.

'Your Tom's trying to persuade my Fred to join the counter-demonstration against the Fascists in East London on Sunday,' she told Harriet on her next visit.

'I know,' said Harriet. 'Tom's asked me to go along too.'

Vera stared. 'You're not serious? And you've actually agreed?'

'Yes, why not? It's just a way of showing that there are some people who don't agree with the Fascists and their behaviour.'

'But the Blackshirts are planning to march through Stepney, right into the heart of the Jewish community, which is about as deliberate a way to pick a fight as you can think of, and of course the Communists and the dockers are spoiling to give them one! Fred and Tom are like two silly boys wanting to join in a playground scrap,' Vera said severely. 'But those Fascists are nasty pieces of work and there's real violence at these mob clashes – there was a man killed demonstrating against them at a rally at Wembley a while back, didn't you hear about that? Fell down from the roof and of course the Mosleyites claimed it was a mystery

470

how he came to fall, but it don't seem much of a mystery to me! And if it isn't the Fascists, it'll be the police – mounted baton charges and I don't know what else. I'm surprised at you letting Tom talk you into going along with him. What on earth are you doing it for?'

Harriet was silent. She was still smarting from Vera's last scolding. *Haven't you got any pride in yourself?* had cut her to the quick and, yes, she was shamed by her own compliance. How could she explain to Vera now, without incurring further scorn, that she was ready to go to the anti-Fascist demonstration even if it meant danger, because at least she and Tom would be sharing that danger. He so seldom seemed to want to share anything else with her nowadays.

On Sunday, 4th October, Oswald Mosley, formerly of the Conservative Party and now leader of the British Fascist movement, proposed to stage a rally of his organization in East London. As Vera had said, it was a deliberate invitation to a fight and as far as the Communist Party was concerned, they were going to get one.

It was still dark at five in the morning, when Tom and Harriet walked through the streets from their lodgings to Fred and Vera's house.

'Come in, comrades.' Lately Fred had taken to calling his friends by this name. To Harriet and to Vera, pulling an expressive face behind him, the term seemed faintly ludicrous.

'Fancy a cuppa?' Vera offered.

Tom shook his head. 'No thanks, no time. What's the plan, Fred?'

'Well, according to the advance publicity for the rally, Mosley's mob is planning to assemble in Royal Mint Street then march up Leman Street past Gardner's Corner and along Commercial Road.' Fred and Tom went into a huddle over a map spread out on the table. 'They'll be aiming to pass through Stepney and on to Bethnal Green. So where will they go after Commercial Road? Our local comrades reckon either the Highway or Cable Street. The Highway's down by the docks so it wouldn't be such an impressive route for them – it could be seen as sneaking in the back way. The cops won't want them in Cable Street because it's too narrow and there are too many side streets and alleys to police effectively. But Mosley won't want to be diverted off his chosen route because that could seem like bowing to pressure . . . so the likelihood is he'll go for Cable Street. If so, the dockers and the locals will turn out to support us in stopping his lot from getting through. In the first instance, we've been asked to rally at Gardner's Corner. Got yer marbles?'

'Yes, I bought some yesterday.' Tom patted his trouser pocket, setting up a clinking of glass.

'Right, then. We'd better be off.' Fred pulled his cap down over his eyes in a businesslike way and turned up the collar of his jacket. He and Tom exuded a kind of guilty excitement – like two boys about to go scrumping, Harriet thought; afraid they might be caught but unable to resist the adventure anyway.

'So long, love. See you later,' Fred said to his wife.

'Mind you do! You've got a family to take care of, don't forget.'

Fred tried to kiss Vera goodbye, but she jerked her head back, turning her face away so that the kiss landed on empty air. Harriet had been about to ask what was the point of the marbles, but was distracted by the realization that behind her disapproving manner Vera was genuinely upset by this parting and worried for Fred's safety. For the first time she herself felt a thrill of fear.

At the corner a van waited with the engine running. The back was already half full of hunched bodies. Harriet climbed in and seated herself awkwardly with her knees drawn up to her chin, aware of a dirty floor and the smell of not particularly clean humanity. Like Tom, she had put on her oldest clothes. 'In case we get dragged down the street. No sense in spoiling good togs,' he had advised her prosaically. Now he was wedged in beside her, his pocketful of marbles pressed uncomfortably against the hip of her old woollen slacks which were leftovers of her farming days.

In Hampshire they'd be ploughing now ready to sow the wheat, she remembered, and generally getting ready for the winter. There would be rooks circling over the newly stirred plough and smoke curling upwards from the fires lit to burn the hedge cuttings as the hedgers did their work. Bonfire smoke was an essential element of autumn mornings in the country, a different, cleaner smoke than that which blackened the brickwork of the London streets towards which they were heading now.

The doors slammed shut. The van bumped and swayed and an anonymous elbow dug into Harriet's side as they rounded the corner of the road. Nobody spoke as they set off for Aldgate, where they were to rendezvous with the main body of the opposition to the Fascists' march. As the sky paled gradually beyond the small, dirty windows in the back door of the van, Harriet glanced sideways towards Tom. His earlier air of excitement had gone and in profile, his features were set and cold. She wanted the touch of his hand, for reassurance, but he was too remote from her to supply it.

Afterwards, the events of what became known as the 'Battle of Cable Street' were a blur in Harriet's memory. From the moment that the van's occupants piled out into a street already seething with bodies, she was jostled and shoved; hanging on to Tom's coat sleeve or threading anxiously after his brown jacket, she was terrified of being separated from him and stranded.

'Mosley's Blackshirts are arriving from all over London in coach loads. There's a bunch of our boys posted at all the later staging-posts of their route in case they manage to get past the main resistance. *They shall not pass*,' said Tom. It was the slogan of the day, she had heard it chanted by other voices.

'Make way. Message from headquarters!' A motor-cyclist steered his machine among the demonstrators. Somewhere ahead his message was delivered and a whispered instruction ran through the surging mass, which quickened its pace in response. A burst of cheering came from a side street and standing on tiptoe Harriet saw a band of men in khaki uniform marching in the centre of the road. The crowd parted to let them through.

The cheering intensified. Harriet felt a pricking of tears because these men were veterans of the Great War and there was something at once noble and pathetic about their proudly raised heads and thrown-back shoulders and the medals glittering on their chests.

Tom was conferring with a fellow-demonstrator.

'They're a Jewish servicemen's contingent of the British Legion,' he reported back to Harriet. 'The police *have* to let them through. This is their own borough. They fought the bloodiest war in history for democracy, and for the right to march like this.' Then a wave seemed to run through the veterans and the crowd on either side, melding them together in a surging mass. Somewhere ahead the march had hit a block.

'Police,' said Tom. He craned above the crowd. 'Mounted and foot. They're fighting over the banner – our own police! Christ, they've got it off the standard-bearers . . . they're ripping it to shreds!'

Fred materialized at Harriet's elbow. 'Come on, Tom, can't let the bastards get away with that!' The two men slipped away through the crowd, leaving Harriet breathless and bewildered. From somewhere ahead, the noise intensified: shouting and screaming, the raucous blast of whistles and the neighing and plunging of the police mounts. Hemmed about by human bodies, a bay horse reared up, forelegs striking at the air, then a hand on its bridle hauled it down. As its rider flailed desperately with his baton, the bay seemed to lurch sideways. The rider was tipped from the saddle and swallowed by the crowd as Harriet watched, aghast.

'Good, they've got the marbles out,' said a voice beside her. Horrified, she saw other mounts go down. *Oh, the poor horses!* was her instinctive reaction. Suddenly Tom was at her side again.

'Come on,' he said, catching hold of her hand. 'The police are bringing in reinforcements. They must have every foot and mounted man in London out today. Time to make ourselves scarce.'

'Where's Fred?' she asked. Tom jerked his head.

'Back there. Come *on*!'

For a moment, the crowd thinned. A path seemed to clear itself and Harriet saw a body on the ground, amid a circle of stooping figures. The face of the fallen man was unrecognizable behind a bright mask of blood, but the green jacket and sprawled brown worsted trousers were familiar.

'It's Fred!' Even as the realization came to Harriet, the men surrounding the injured party were being hauled aside by other men, a sea of dark blue and silver-topped helmets.

'They're arresting that lot and they'll take us too if we don't get out of here,' Tom said.

'But Fred's hurt. We can't leave him,' she protested.

'No sense in staying.'

As Tom dragged her away, Harriet turned her head and saw Fred being dragged in the opposite direction between two policemen. His head hung forward between his shoulders, his arms were wrenched up behind his back. The toes of his shoes scraped along the ground. He seemed barely conscious.

The clashes of the day were over. In Stepney the makeshift barricades were being cleared away and the broken glass swept up. Mosley's supporters had been forced to abandon their rally and the counter-demonstrators assessed their injuries and exchanged tales of triumph. Those who had been arrested were being traced to the various police stations and bailed out by their friends.

At eight o'clock that night, Fred was brought home by a fellow Communist Party member.

'I've to appear before the magistrate in the morning,' he

told Vera, ruefully. 'Sorry, love. Bound to mean a fine at best.'

'You stupid lummox.' But Vera was too relieved to have him home alive, and too shocked by the expanse of white bandage over his face, to be properly angry with him for getting himself arrested. Most of the blood had been mopped away, though there were still dried deposits in the creases round his eyes. Determinedly prosaic, she fetched a bowl of warm water and a flannel.

By the time Tom and Harriet arrived at nine o'clock, Fred was asleep in the iron bedstead in the front bedroom, his forehead dramatically swathed in rather more bandage than the police surgeon had been prepared to bestow. To calm herself down, Vera had been polishing the scuffed toes of his shoes, but the sight of Harriet and Tom revived her anger.

'You've got a nerve, turning up at this hour.'

'Is Fred back?' Harriet asked. 'Is he all right? We saw him being taken away by the police.'

'Yes, he's back. An hour ago. Bill Butcher paid his bail. And yes, he's all right if you don't count the bruises and a sprained wrist and a cut on his forehead that'll take a fortnight to heal. But it's no thanks to you that he's alive at all.' The words were aimed at Tom. 'I've heard what happened,' Vera continued, her voice gathering strength. 'How *could* you just walk off and leave him when he'd been bashed about like that? And you didn't even come and tell me he was in the police station. You *knew* I'd be waiting. You *knew* I'd be worried.'

'I was otherwise occupied.' Tom had taken Harriet on a confused tour of battle hot spots where they found on arrival that the action had moved on. Frustrated and tired, he'd eventually had time to remember Fred's plight. By now he was feeling guilty about abandoning his friend and, because he was on the defensive, he switched unwisely to the attack. 'If you were so worried about him, why weren't you there with him?'

'I've got little Freddie to think about, that's why,' Vera

retorted. 'I can't go parading about making trouble when I've a baby needs looking after.'

'That's your problem,' said Tom. 'Or your excuse.'

Vera turned a heated, furious face towards Harriet, who was hovering unhappily in the background.

'Harriet, you'll always be welcome here. But come on your own in future, will you?'

She slammed the front door in their faces.

'Bloody woman,' muttered Tom. He hunched his shoulders and stuck his hands in his pockets. 'She's got no idea. When you're in a battle situation, personal loyalties have to give way to the broader plan of campaign. Fred would understand that. There was no point in both of us getting arrested at that point, it would simply have reduced the numbers available to go on resisting the Fascists.'

Privately, Harriet agreed with Vera that personal loyalties should come first. If they didn't, you weren't much of a friend. She wondered whether Tom would have interceded if *she* had been the one dangling half-conscious between the two policemen, or if he would have consulted 'the broader plan of campaign.'

'Loyalty' was a difficult word to live up to, Harriet discovered in the weeks that followed. Who had the prior claim on hers: Tom, her lover; or Vera, her friend? Tom had shrugged off the altercation on the doorstep and didn't want to talk about it, to Harriet or to anyone. He was still attending Communist Party meetings, and said that Fred was back in circulation and being perfectly sensible about what had happened.

Even so, Tom was barred from Vera's house.

'The wife's still a bit miffed about things,' Fred told him, looking shifty. 'Better leave her to simmer for a while.'

The outcome of Harriet's agonizings about where her loyalty should lie was that while Tom remained unwelcome at Vera's, she felt unable to go there herself. It was a costly decision. She missed Vera badly; but Tom, if he noticed her sacrifice at all, didn't comment on it.

*   *   *

As she picked the letter up from the doormat, Harriet knew instinctively that it must be from Diana Somerville. It was addressed to Tom in violet ink, and the envelope was scented with violets. She felt a pang of jealousy that was like a physical pain.

'Diana's invited us to a party tonight,' Tom said, scanning the printed card.

'Oh,' said Harriet, without enthusiasm. Tom detected a note of censure in the single word.

'I think we should go. I haven't seen Diana for ages and she's one of my best friends. She's a lot of fun.'

'I'm sure she must be,' Harriet said.

Tom sighed. 'What's the matter with you, Harry? Why do you have to take offence at every remotely approving thing I say about her?'

Harriet didn't answer, but inwardly she cried, *Because you never say approving things about me.*

She desperately needed such reassurances. It had always been there at the heart of her relationship with Tom: the feeling of something being not right between them. From that night when she had first taken down the sheet that divided his bed from hers in a cheap hotel on the Cobham tour, she'd had to live with the conviction that he didn't care for her enough. And increasingly she'd kept fretting about it, like an itch that you can't help scratching even though you know it will only make things worse.

Every tender moment between them was followed by a statement or action from Tom that seemed designed to reaffirm his independence. The result, ironically, was to make Harriet very dependent indeed. She could hear herself nagging, clinging, questioning, and she hated herself for it.

One day he would leave her again – perhaps for Diana, perhaps simply because he wanted his freedom back – and her instincts warned her that this time it would probably be for good. And then what would she be? A discarded lover, like something out of the newspaper scandals that Allie Briggs used to report with relish back at the farm. A girl who was 'No better than she should be', and who had got 'No more than she deserved.'

'Will you come to this party?' Tom said.

'I don't know. I don't particularly want to.'

'Well, I intend to go, so you can please yourself.'

Harriet contemplated the alternatives of an evening with Tom at Diana Somerville's party, overhearing herself pointed out by his snobbish acquaintances as 'Tom's little rustic', or an evening spent alone in their shabby rented flat, imagining him having fun without her. She supposed the party was the lesser of the two evils. And at least it would give Aunt Louella's black lace dress another rare outing.

Diana's party was being held in a large room on the first floor of a hotel in Park Lane. The room had been hired for the occasion, Tom told Harriet in the cab on the way, because her society friends were apt to get a bit rowdy when they'd drunk too much champagne.

'And you've seen her flat, haven't you? She chose everything herself, designing interiors is one of her talents. All that beautiful Art Deco furniture and glass is worth a fortune, she wouldn't want it smashed up.'

'Why invite friends who are liable to get drunk and break things?' Harriet asked, pointedly.

'It's just high spirits. These things happen at parties. Oh, for heaven's sake, Harry, don't be such a spoilsport.'

'Tom, my love, you may congratulate me. Gavin and I are engaged again.'

Tom looked blank. 'I thought I saw an announcement in *The Times* a couple of months ago, and I could have sworn the name of the lucky man was ''Bernard''.'

'Oh, *Bernard*. A sweet man, but he wouldn't do. Too much of a lapdog, darling. A girl likes a little dominance in her life.'

'Well, you won't get it from Draycott,' muttered Tom.

Diana looked arch. 'You'd be susprised. Gavin has his moments . . . Actually, he can be quite thrilling when he's angry with me. Who knows, we may even tie the knot one of these days. And at least he's come up with a bigger sapphire this time round.'

She flourished her ringed hand in front of Tom's face, then laughed at his dour expression. 'Don't look so happy for me, darling.'

'I don't know how you can even contemplate marrying that moron,' complained Tom. He seemed to have forgotten Harriet's existence for the moment.

'Well, *you* wouldn't marry me, Tom – it's against your religion or something – so I suppose I have to settle down with *someone*,' flashed Diana, looking up at him through artificially darkened eyelashes. 'I'll be an old maid soon if I don't. Anyway, come and say hullo.' She tucked her arm through his and marched him away towards a part of the room where Gavin's fair head could be seen among the party-goers.

Harriet, ignored, wondered whether she was supposed to trail after them and decided that to do so would be too humiliating for words. Instead she looked around for somewhere to sit where she could be inconspicuous, and sank down thankfully on a chair tucked behind a large potted palm.

A circling waiter proffered a tray of glasses and she accepted one, sipping moodily at the champagne. At least it gave her something to do with her hands. When the glass was empty the waiter returned and replaced it with another.

The noise level in the room escalated. Diana darted around being vivacious in a sleeveless dress of gold satin, with a plunging V-neckline. It fitted closely down to the knee, where it exploded into a froth of gauze. Her high-heeled ankle-strapped sandals matched the dress and gold earrings swung from her lobes beneath her shining cap of cropped hair, their movement accentuating every turn of her head on the long neck around which Harriet was currently feeling a powerful longing to wrap her fingers.

'I shouldn't have come,' she told herself, feeling sick with jealousy and wishing that her black dress was less sophisticated and more dazzling. Tom was following Diana round like a pet poodle, his eyes never leaving her face. It looked like being a long evening. The waiter glided by and Harriet reached for her third glass of champagne.

'Oh, do look!'

Diana knelt up on the sofa beneath the window, elbows on the sill. Outside in the darkness of the late October evening, the street was full of lights and moving figures. Mounted police. The sight of the horses reminded Harriet horribly of the events of the Fascist rally nearly a month ago. She swallowed the contents of her glass and then choked on the fizzy liquid.

'What's going on out there?' Tom asked, standing behind Diana.

'The Jarrow marchers,' she said, not turning her head. 'I'd forgotten they were arriving today. Do look, Gavin!' But on the padded leather of the sofa beside her, Gavin could not be bothered to turn his head. He dragged at a cigarette in an ivory holder and concentrated on blowing smoke rings.

'Aren't they quaint?' Diana addressed her remark to the room in general. 'Those tough little men. How far have they marched? Three hundred miles? Goodness, it must have worn out their shoes!'

Harriet said, 'It probably *has* worn out their shoes. Which is something they can ill afford.'

Her voice had carried surprisingly clearly across the room.

'Then shouldn't somebody have told them that it would have been more sensible to stay at home and use the shoe-leather money for something else, if they're so hard up?' Diana turned away from the scene outside. She sank on to the sofa beside Gavin and laughed, earrings swinging.

Harriet had the distinct impression that with that light retort, her rival had just crossed swords with her. 'They're not doing it for fun,' she said, hating Diana for her mocking tone, hazily aware that Tom was staring at her and that her own speech was blurred. She recognized, too late, that the champagne had made her belligerent and tried to sound reasonable instead. 'They're trying to draw attention to the fact that they've got no work and no hope of work since the shipyards closed.'

'My heart bleeds for them,' drawled Diana, and led the ripple of laughter that ran round the room.

'Those men have worked all their lives,' Harriet said, 'and now they have nothing. There was talk of a new shipyard being built that would have saved them, but then the government decided against it. So their hopes were dashed all over again. And their pride. How can they support their families?'

'Forgive me for my ignorance,' Diana said, 'but isn't there something called the dole?'

'Oh, yes. The barest minimum. It wouldn't keep you in champagne for half a day!' Harriet retorted. 'How would you like it if you were in their situation?' she demanded tightly.

'Oh my, do we *have* to get so serious?' Diana tilted her head to one side and smiled at Harriet, her blue eyes very cold. 'I suppose you can identify with people like that because you're from their sort of background, but I'm not, thank goodness. I mean, I'm frightfully sorry for the unemployed and all that, but this is supposed to be a party; so can we leave the deserving poor out of it for this evening?'

'You stuck-up bitch. You're not worth half of any one of those men,' said Harriet. By now she was the focus of a distinctly hostile attention from the rest of the guests, but she was too angry to care.

'Tom's Little Rustic is being bolshie,' said Diana, into the silence which had followed Harriet's last only-too-audible remark. 'Don't be such a bore, whatever-your-name-is. Tom, tell her not to be a bore.'

Tom took Harriet by the arm and propelled her towards the door. 'Come on,' he said grimly. 'Time to go home.'

'You sided with her!' Harriet said, when they were back at the flat. She had been seething all through the silent cab ride, unable to vent her indignation because even in her

482

current state she remembered that it wasn't done to argue in front of a taxi driver. Not that it was 'done', she supposed, to call your hostess a 'stuck-up bitch'. But she *had* been provoked.

'I didn't side with anyone,' claimed Tom.

'Well, you certainly didn't stick up for me. Or for those poor men on the march. That horrible Diana was laughing at them and making fun of them, and you just stood by and let her do it. I thought you were supposed to be a Communist!'

'I am,' said Tom. 'But Diana's crowd aren't. And there's a time and a place for everything. Grow up, Harriet. What's the point in rubbing people up the wrong way and picking arguments just for the sake of it? I'm not going to fall out with an old friend over a little thing like that.'

'No, you'd rather fall out with *me*! You wouldn't want to annoy your precious Diana or her crowd for "a little thing" like a principle; or to stand up for me when I'm being insulted. Oh, I forgot,' Harriet spluttered furiously, 'Leaving people in the lurch is one of your specialities, isn't it? Peter Morris, Vera's Fred, the Jarrow marchers . . . I'm in good company.'

Tom stared at her, his face that had been flushed and defensive turned pale. 'You think I'm a coward? Is that what you're saying?'

Harriet didn't answer. She knew the viciousness of what she'd just said, but she was too blazingly angry to care. At the party, he'd frogmarched her out of the room in front of Diana's friends, letting all of them smirk at her humiliation, adding to the pile of times when he had patronized her and made her feel insecure. Now, she wanted to hit him. Instead, they faced each other across a distance of three feet, fists clenched, while the silence answered his question.

Eventually Tom gave her a queer, oblique smile and shook his head. 'That's it, then,' was all he said.

A cold draught came into the room as the door of the flat swung to behind him.

Once, at Welcome Farm, Harriet had seen two of the farmyard cats having a squabble. A tabby and a rather raffish ginger, they'd confronted one another, eyes challenging, until finally, the tabby had walked away and in the shamed lines of its body there had been no doubt which of the two had lost the confrontation.

Harriet sat down, legs shaking, laughing a little hysterically at the idea of Tom as a farmyard tabby, beaten by Harriet, the ginger. Yes, she had won that argument. But gradually the effects of the champagne ebbed and with them her defiant mood evaporated, to be replaced by a realization of just what she had done.

Ever since Vienna, Tom had lived with a question mark over his courage and with her hasty words she had rubbed salt in the wound. Was that unforgivable? When he came back, she thought tiredly, she'd apologize; she'd grovel if she had to, she'd make it all right somehow.

All night, she lay awake in the double bed, straining her ears for the sound of the key turning in the front door, rehearsing what she'd say and do to repair the damage when he came back. But Tom didn't come back. In the morning the postman brought a battered envelope. The note inside had been scribbled in pencil on a blank endpaper torn out from a book.

I have gone to the war in Spain. I've been thinking about it for weeks – you were the only reason I didn't go before. There's a group setting out tonight for Paris and from there we'll be going to the border and crossing on foot over the Pyrenees. Sorry there wasn't time to tell you in person – but I don't suppose, the way things are between us at present, that we could have a rational discussion about it anyway. Maybe this will at least show you I'm not a coward. I'll write when I can. Wish me luck with dodging the bullets. Tom.

PS Could you tell my mother where I've gone?

Vera was hanging out washing on the line in her tiny back yard, singing with more energy than tunefulness as she pegged out nappies and baby vests.

Early one morning, just as the sun was rising,
I heard a maiden singing in the valley below:
Oh, don't deceive me, oh, never leave me.
How could you use a poor maiden so?

It was her favourite song from her schooldays, and she was putting heart and soul into the more emotional passages when an odd, snorting sound came from behind her. When she turned, peg bag in hand, there was Harriet framed in the back doorway.

Harriet had knocked in vain and then tried the door. Finding it unlocked, she had ventured inside and then, following the sound of Vera singing, had walked on through the house to the back. Waiting for her arrival to be noticed, she had been listening to the words of the song: *Remember the vows that you made to your Mary. Remember the bower where you vowed to be true?*

Tom had never vowed to be true.

Vera's first reaction was gladness at the sight of her friend, which was checked by the memory of the Cable Street protest and the estrangement that had followed it. Then both considerations gave way to concern, because Harriet's shoulders were shaking and although she had shielded her face with her hands, it became apparent to Vera that behind them, she was crying fit to burst.

'What will you do now?' asked Vera in the kitchen, looking up from Tom's note. Harriet, calmer, but still looking distinctly bedraggled, shrugged dispiritedly.

'Go home, I suppose. I've no money, or at any rate, what little I have will run out soon. I've told the landlady that Tom's just gone away for a few days to visit his family, but I think she's guessed that isn't true.'

'Mmm.' Only the most myopic of landladies, Vera

thought, could fail to recognize in Harriet's shattered features the marks of a woman who had been abandoned. She shook her head sadly. 'Oh, Harriet . . . I did warn you. These young gentlemen . . . Well, I suppose there's no point in me saying, *I told you so.*'

'Why not?' said Harriet bitterly. 'Everyone else will. I may as well get used to it.'

31

On the fifth of November, Rupert Brownlowe was in a good mood at the breakfast table. Yesterday, Starbright had been sold, and even considering what he'd had to pay the Griffin lad for schooling the animal, Rupert could consider that he'd made a profit. Leonora was in foal again to the same stallion that had sired Starbright. He was beginning to feel like a horse-breeder again.

If nothing else, it took his mind off his other money worries – not that the lawn-mower factory was doing too badly nowadays. Sales were up, as his manager Pritchard had promised they would be once investment was made in new design and new machinery. But there was still the matter of that loan from the rich widow to be repaid. Fortunately, she didn't seem to be in any hurry for her money.

Pritchard, when asked, had said rather dourly that she hadn't been near the factory for a while, so Rupert's initial fear that she'd want to meddle had proved unfounded. The profits were starting to trickle through and in time, if his luck held, he'd be able to clear the debt.

On the far side of the table, Marion had finished her breakfast and was starting on her mail. As Rupert watched her slide the ivory blade of her letter knife under the flap of an envelope, he was reminded of a small problem which, unless he tackled it soon, might well become a larger one.

Yesterday, while handing over the cheque for Starbright, the colt's new owner had made a highly gratifying comment about the Brownlowe reputation for turning out quality horses. He'd followed it up with a casual comment about a good little brood mare for sale. 'She's in one of my stalls now – the owner said I could have her here for a few days and see what I thought. I'm sorely tempted – she's a nice looker and sweet-natured. But I don't have your expertise; I'd be a fool to go in for breeding,' the man had said wistfully. 'Want to take a look, while you're here?'

Rupert, with the cheque for Starbright safe in his wallet and the glow of praise in his ears, wanted to be seen as the successful breeder he had once been. He had agreed to 'take a look'.

One thing had led to another. He'd bought the mare.

Now the glow had faded and he was uncomfortably aware that he hadn't consulted Marion; not that he *should* have to consult his wife when it came to such a purchase – a man should be master in his own house. But Marion had a way of making her feelings known, and for the sake of his domestic comfort it was best to give her at least the illusion of having some say in financial decisions.

The mare was to be delivered this morning. Time was running out. He cleared his throat.

'I've been thinking – that is, I've *decided* that it would be a good idea to get another brood mare, as Starbright was such a successful experiment.'

Marion looked up with the half-read letter in her hand. 'Do you think you should, dear? With winter coming on?'

'Why not? She's a good mare at a fair price,' said Rupert.

'But can we afford the winter feed? After all, we don't have the home farm now.'

For the sake of Rupert's pride Marion wasn't supposed to know about his money problems, but it had been impossible to hide from her the fact that he'd had to sell off most of the home farm land last year. The income from that injection of cash was what paid the Maple Grange bills now, but it meant that every bag of oats or bale of hay had to be expensively bought in, not to mention the vet's bills and the blacksmith's bills and, in due course, schooling for the offspring of *two* brood mares.

'Perhaps you should wait until spring to buy any more horses.'

'I can't. I've done it. She'll be here this morning,' Rupert

488

admitted. He switched to the attack. 'And surely it makes sense to keep that Wilkins fellow you made me hire fully occupied, now Starbright's gone. Otherwise I'll have to sack him, won't I, and get rid of Leonora as well?'

'Well . . . what's done's done, I suppose.' Marion abandoned economic considerations for the time being. The prospect of Rupert without his horses to occupy him was even more daunting than the expense of acquiring another animal. She returned to her letter.

'This is from Laura. They're all well,' she reported. On the far side of the table, Rupert's face darkened, the last of his good mood gone. Laura didn't write often, but it was an ongoing source of pain to him that when she did, the letters were to her stepmother and not to her father.

'. . . She writes about the Jarrow Crusade – you know, the marchers from that northern town which has lost its shipbuilding industry? She and James went to greet them when they reached London, three days ago.'

'Jarrow? Isn't that the town your Surrey Fund people tried to help? And they were most rudely rejected, as I recall.'

'Well, I suppose you can see the point – they didn't want charity, they wanted work. This march was to remind the government, and the whole country, about what's happening to their town.'

'We've all got our problems. Surely the nation's sick and tired of hunger marches,' Rupert commented sourly. 'Apart from the pie-in-the-sky socialists, of course, who tell us we've got to nanny every inadequate who can't earn a living, from the cradle to the grave.'

The remark would have stung Laura into bitter argument. Marion let it go without comment. Rupert scowled as he hacked the top off his boiled egg. He couldn't even get a decent quarrel at his own breakfast table any more.

Breakfast over, Marion took her calm expression and her letter down the corridor. In the morning room, she closed the door carefully behind her before giving vent to a silent scream.

Sylvia, the first Mrs Brownlowe, had chosen the room's contents and its heavily floral blue-green wallpaper. Rupert had let it be known, when showing his replacement bride the home that would be hers, that he didn't like changes. Marion had not been sure at the time whether this attitude arose from parsimony or sentiment and, many years later, she was still not sure. Rupert never spoke about his dead first wife, but the morning room, like the rest of the house, remained very much as it had been in her time.

In her more fanciful moments Marion could picture the graceful figure of Sylvia, in the cream-coloured dress and pearls from her portrait over the dining-room fireplace, sitting at the tall secretaire, answering her letters. She seemed a friendly enough spirit and at times her faint smile, as imagined by her successor, was tellingly rueful.

'Oh, Sylvia Brownlowe, however did you *tolerate* the man?'

These days it was getting more and more difficult for Marion to put up with Rupert's attitudes, so much in contrast to her own. But what could she do? She was married, for better or for worse. She had known something of his character and beliefs before the wedding, but at the time it had seemed a case of 'any port in a storm'. And it wasn't such a bad port, she reminded herself with a pang of conscience. She had a home at Maple Grange which, though it brought its share of financial worries, was a lot better than anything she could have afforded on the meagre remains of a dead war hero's estate. And it had been a home for Tom, too . . . although her other hope, that Rupert would provide a firm hand and fatherly guidance for her wild boy had proved unfounded.

She sighed and lowered the polished lid of the secretaire. To shake off her despondent mood, she would answer Laura's letter about the Jarrow marchers: '*It was very moving, seeing them coming along the Edgware Road in the rain, with mackintosh capes round their shoulders and cloth caps on their heads, soaking wet of course, but with the drums and mouth-organ music to maintain their spirits and keep them in step. I know people make fun of those old paintings like* The Dignity of Labour, *but that's what they had.* Dignity. *But because of the weather being so awful, not many people had bothered to turn out to welcome them, and it was too cold and wet to raise much of a cheer. That seemed so sad, after they'd walked all that way . . .'*

''Scuse me, mum. There's a young lady at the front door to see you.'

Absorbed in the letter, Marion had failed to notice the soft knock and timid entry of the maid. She turned from the desk.

'Who is she, Susan?'

'Oh Lord, I never asked. I'm ever so sorry, mum.'

Susan had started at the Grange as a scullery maid before the Great War, but lately her duties had become more varied, a reflection of Rupert's cut-back policy on staff. Her employer was apt to bark impatiently over her omissions of procedure, with the result that she made even more mistakes out of fright than she would have done if allowed time to find her feet.

'That's all right, Susan,' Marion said soothingly. 'It doesn't matter. Just show her in.'

The visitor who followed Susan into the room was the girl that Marion had once described euphemistically to Rupert as Tom's 'friend'. It had been a way of not confronting him with the declining moral standards of the young, but Marion had no illusions about the relationship between her son and Harriet Griffin. At the time she had been rather uncomfortable about Tom's brazen introduction of his *petite amie* into Maple Grange, but her impressions of Harriet had been favourable and she had done her best on that occasion to put the girl at ease.

Harriet Griffin was far from at ease now. Under the tousle of red hair, inadequately tied back with a black ribbon, her pale face was scrubbed clean of the cosmetics which she had worn on her previous visit. Her eyes were pink-rimmed and she looked as if she hadn't slept for days.

'Tom asked me to come,' she said flatly.

'How nice to see you.' Marion tried to hide her disappointment that her wayward son had not seen fit to visit his mother himself.

'He said I should tell you . . . but I don't know how to . . .'

'Well, whatever it is you have to tell me, come in and tell me in comfort,' Marion said, gesturing towards the sofa. But Harriet declined to sit down and instead, stood in front of the fireplace, twisting her hands together.

'Tom left me a letter, and said I should tell you . . . Oh, perhaps you'd better read it for yourself.' Harriet thrust a crumpled sheet of paper towards her hostess. Marion was still reading the contents when Rupert came into the room.

'The mare's arrived. They're unloading her now. D'you want to come out and look at her?'

'Oh, Rupert. Tom's gone to Spain!'

Rupert, excited by the arrival of his new purchase, took a few seconds to recognize that the news his wife was conveying was bad news. Once he had taken in her anguished expression, he didn't know what to do about it. Emotional women always flummoxed him.

'Spain? What the dickens did he do that for?'

'He's gone to fight,' said Marion, groping for her pocket handkerchief.

'We're not at war, are we? I haven't seen today's papers yet.'

'*We're* not. It's the civil war. He's gone to join the POUM,' Harriet said, from beside the fireplace. For the first time, Rupert registered her presence.

'Who are you? Oh, yes. Tom's fancy piece,' he said, rather proud at remembering. 'What was that you said?'

'He's joining the POUM. The *Partido Obrero de Unificación Marxista*,' Harriet recited, with a painful recollection of Vera's crowded little front room and Fred and Tom poring over the newspapers. *Learning the lingo*, Fred had called it. She'd tried to please Tom by picking up the jargon herself, and had only succeeded in irritating him because her memory for the unfamiliar words was better than his.

'And what's that when it's at home?' Rupert demanded peevishly.

'It's the anti-Stalinist Communist party. Fighting against the Fascists.'

'Communists? Oh, good grief! Stupid boy. Bally foreigners, they're always squabbling. Best thing is to leave them to it. If it isn't the Spanish it's the Italians and the Abyssinians. Or the Japanese in China. Everywhere you look they're chucking artillery at one another. You'd better write to Tom,' Rupert advised his wife, with an air of having solved the problem, 'and tell him to come home.'

As usual, the sight of Rupert being obtuse restored Marion's common sense. She blew her nose determinedly then put away her handkerchief and tackled the practicalities; first of which was the situation of the girl to whom Rupert had referred as 'Tom's fancy piece'.

'What about you? What arrangements has he made for you while he's away?'

'I don't think he made any.'

'So . . . do you need money?' Marion asked gently. Harriet hesitated.

'Hang on, Marion,' Rupert broke in. 'We don't owe the girl anything. If Tom's made promises, that's his affair. Damnit, he has his allowance.'

'Rupert, do be quiet,' Marion said, with tired exasperation. She turned back to Harriet. 'I do want to help,' she offered.

But already Harriet was shaking her head. 'Thank you for asking,' she said proudly, 'but no. I don't need anything. My family will take care of me. I'm on my way there now. I only came to tell you where Tom's gone, because he asked me to in his letter.'

'Then at least you must let our chauffeur run you home,' said Marion.

'I can't spare him now,' Rupert objected. 'I need him to help get the new mare settled in.'

Marion drew in a long breath and expelled it before she trusted herself to reply.

'This is more important, Rupert. Miss Griffin *must* be driven home. I insist.'

In the stable yard, Jem waited with the new mare. She seemed a docile enough animal, he'd noted with relief, unbothered by a horse-box journey which would have had the more highly strung Leonora or Starbright wild-eyed and ready to give trouble. And old Brownlowe was as pleased as punch with his new acquisition, panting to show her off to his wife. But when Rupert came out he was alone, and patently disgruntled about something.

'You'd better put the mare away for now,' he said. 'And as soon as you've done that, get the motor out and bring it round to the front of the house.'

Jem did as he'd been told. A few minutes later, having changed hastily into his chauffeur's jacket, he drew the Landau up on the gravel sweep in front of the house. Marion Brownlowe emerged from the porch, followed by a tall, slim girl with red hair.

Marion was still trying to cope with the news that her son had gone to fight a foreign war, so she missed the moment of shocked recognition between Jem and Harriet.

'Load Miss Griffin's suitcase, will you, Wilkins? I must just have a word with my husband.'

A moment later, Harriet was alone with Jem.

'Hullo, Miss Griffin.' As he stooped to take the handle of the brown leather case she stepped back, instinctively. When he straightened up again he smiled at her, the lazy, impudent smile which had always made her so uncomfortable in the days when he'd worked at Welcome Farm.

'How've you been?' he enquired.

'All right, thank you,' Harriet told him primly. Behind the newly controlled mask of indifference she was wondering how and why Jem came to be working for Rupert Brownlowe and, more importantly, what his presence in the area might mean for her.

'What brings you back to these parts?' Jem's question echoed her own thoughts.

'I don't want to talk about it.' The last thing she wanted was for Jem to know the details of her current situation. Letting Jem know *anything* seemed to have its dangers.

Marion came back, saying with a wry expression that Rupert seemed to have disappeared for now. She held out her hands to Harriet, who allowed herself, awkwardly, to be drawn towards the other woman and briefly hugged.

'I don't know how to say this . . . we hardly know one another,' Marion said, releasing her. 'Tom's my son and I love him dearly but that doesn't mean I'm blind to his faults. This must be a very difficult time for you. Please, if I can help in any way, let me know. Don't let's be strangers.'

'Thank you. You're very kind,' Harriet murmured, conscious that Jem must have overheard those words.

His eyes had met hers above Marion's head and for a moment his dark brows had lifted. He opened the rear passenger door of the car.

'Where to, Miss Griffin?'

'Welcome Farm. I believe you know the way,' said Harriet.

Jem drove. Harriet, sitting in the back of the Landau with the glass screen between them, watched the back of his head and wondered if he remembered their last encounter in Louella Ramsay's study.

Don't touch you? Not now I won't. But one day, when you want me to . . .

She shouldn't have got into the car with him. She should have thought of a reason, any reason, why not to. But with Marion so determined to observe the decencies and Rupert so obviously keen to be rid of her, it had been impossible, somehow, not to fall in with what had been suggested. And why should it be so disturbing? When Jem had worked for her father, she had let him get under her skin and on one occasion, she admitted to herself, she had very nearly let him go too far. But that had been months, years ago. Now he worked for the Brownlowes, and surely there was no reason to be afraid of him.

Except that what really frightened her about Jem was something in herself; some suppressed part of her own nature responded to him. Without its promptings, there would be no danger at all from Jem Wilkins.

On the village green at Bentley, children were dragging wood towards a giant stack in the centre of the green. Harriet had forgotten about Bonfire Night. She turned to watch them through the rear window until they were out of sight, glad of the distraction. But when the village houses gave way to open road and the Landau turned off on to the country lanes, that led towards Welcome Farm, her mind veered back to the problem of Jem. She'd run away before from the chaos that he always made of her life, and had ended up with Tom Searle – and what a mistake that had been, she told herself bitterly. Now Jem had appeared again, his dangerous attraction undiminished. Where was there left to run?

In the farmyard, the Landau came to a halt. There was no sign of activity from the farmhouse, but the back door stood open as usual.

Jem opened the passenger door and his hand cupped Harriet's elbow to steady her as she stepped down. It might have been the automatic gesture of any chauffeur, but his fingers seemed to scorch through the material of her coat.

'Here we are, then,' he said. 'I'll get your suitcase out.'

'Thank you,' said Harriet, and waited for him to retrieve her case from the boot before she ventured into the house. She expected him to put it down and go.

Instead, he lingered. 'Will you be going to the bonfire celebrations in Bentley tonight?'

'I don't know.'

'I would if I thought you'd be there,' Jem said deliberately. 'Will you?'

His hazel eyes were very dark under the shadow of his peaked cap. Not at all like Tom's clear blue gaze . . . but Tom was in Spain. Tom had left her, and might never come back. He'd gone off to play the hero, and in doing so he'd proved yet again how little Harriet counted in his life. He'd left her destitute, with no choice but to crawl home with the tattered shreds of her reputation. And now what was her future supposed to be? Weeks or months or even years of waiting for news of him which might never come, or might come in the form of some sparse report to say that he was dead.

It was too much, Harriet told herself, and all the resentment she'd been trying to keep in check flooded over her. Tom wasn't the only man in the world. Jem still wanted her. At least somebody did.

'All right,' she said.

'Till tonight, then.' He nodded briefly, in acknowledgement of an agreement entered into, and drove away, leaving Harriet shaking with a mixture of apprehension, shame and a shocked excitement about what she'd just done.

'The Prodigal Daughter's back again,' Allie Briggs reported to Stanley, when she came home from her half-day at Welcome Farm. 'And the Griffins are killing the fatted calf, as usual. That girl's spoilt silly.'

It wasn't entirely accurate to describe Daisy and Will as 'killing the fatted calf', but Harriet was accepted quietly back into her place at Welcome Farm. As an explanation of her return, she only said without elaboration that Tom Searle had gone abroad for a while. Daisy said afterwards to Will that there was more to it than Harriet seemed ready to disclose at present, but that no doubt she'd tell them all about it when she was ready to.

'How do you feel about Bonfire Night?' Daisy asked, late in the afternoon. 'There's going to be a fire and a guy on the village green, and I'm supposed to be helping with the food. But it's all ready, Allie and I did it this morning. I could just send it down to the village and somebody else can serve it up.'

'Why should you do that?' Harriet said.

'Well, I don't like to leave you, your first night back.'

'Can't I come too?'

'Are you sure you want to, love?' Daisy said, surprised.

'Why not?'

'I just thought you might like to get settled in at home before you go out and about. You know what it's like with village life. People are bound to be curious, seeing you back . . .'

'If they're going to be nosy, I may as well get it over with,' said Harriet, wondering what Daisy's reaction would be – or Kitty Marshall's, for that matter – if they knew that Jem Wilkins was the reason for her wanting to go to the bonfire celebration. Harriet wasn't entirely sure herself, yet, what she intended to do when she saw Jem again; but she thought he might have ideas of his own, and she was in a reckless enough mood to fit in with them.

As the sun set behind the trees which fringed the back lawn at Maple Grange, a squirrel sat on the bare stone terrace outside the drawing room. From his seat beside the fire, the owner of the house eyed it sourly and as the squirrel stared back, its bright-eyed arrogance seemed to embody all the dissatisfactions of the day for Rupert.

It was a long time since he had shot a squirrel. He put his newspaper aside and stumped off towards the gun room, but by the time he had unlocked a glass-fronted gun case, selected a shotgun from the dozen in the rack, loaded it and returned to the terrace, the squirrel had gone. Frustrated, he decided to check on the wellbeing of his latest acquisition instead. He headed for the stables, wincing at the twinges from his arthritic hip.

Yes, he was getting old. Too old to ride, too old to shoot, too old even to be a man for Maudie in Greenwich; his last few visits there had been shaming experiences, though they had brought him comfort at the time. Still, Maudie was a good woman, she'd give what you wanted without question. Not like his wife, Marion, who'd promised to honour and obey him. Yesterday, she'd commandeered the car with only the least pretence of deferring to him, as if she was the one in charge. Probably that had accounted for Wilkins' surly, almost sneering manner this morning.

Damnit, Wilkins could not be permitted to sneer. He must

be put in his place; but to achieve that he must first be caught out in some inadequacy or misdemeanour.

Gun still tucked under his arm, Rupert stopped to collect his walking stick from the back porch before he headed for the stable yard. There, in neighbouring stalls, fetlock-deep in clean golden straw, the new mare and Leonora were pulling hay peacefully from well-filled racks hung on the whitewashed walls. There was nothing to complain about.

It was getting dark. As Rupert emerged from the stable block, Wilkins ran down the flight of stone steps from the groom's quarters overhead. He was wearing his chauffeur's jacket and had combed his hair, Rupert noted sourly. Unaware of his employer's presence, he was humming softly under his breath.

'Where do you think you're going, Wilkins?'

Jem stopped dead. After a pause, he said, 'It's Guy Fawkes Night, sir. I thought I'd go to one of the village celebrations.'

'It's not your afternoon off.'

'I thought that just this once, sir . . .'

'I don't pay you to take time off *just this once*,' said Rupert.

This time the pause was longer. Then Jem said, 'This is important to me, sir. It's a personal matter.'

'Personal matter be damned! What makes you think you're entitled to have personal matters in the hours that you are supposed to be working for me? Keep your *personal* matters for the proper time.'

Rupert had found the excuse he wanted to take Wilkins down a peg or two. Unwisely, he overdid it, jabbing the ferruled point of his stick into Jem's chest to emphasize what he was saying. There was a blur of movement and something struck him hard in the face; when his vision cleared he was on his back on the cobbles with a salty stickiness oozing from his stinging lips and trickling down his chin. The two pieces of his stick, snapped neatly in half, landed on his chest.

'You *hit* me . . .' Rupert said, stupidly, struggling to a sitting position. Blood dripped onto the front of his jacket.

'That's right,' said Jem. Something silver-bright glinted in his hand. 'To teach you not to poke me with that stick of yours. And if you get up, I'll teach you *another* lesson.'

'I wouldn't do that if I were you.'

Jem spun round. Stevenson, the gardener, peered at him along the barrel of Rupert's gun. Eyes narrowed, Jem took a step towards the older man. There was a click as Stevenson cocked the trigger of the shotgun.

'You wouldn't shoot,' Jem said.

'I wouldn't count on that. I was in the Great War, sonny, and I haven't forgotten how to fire a gun. It wouldn't bother me, particularly, to put a bullet in you. I've killed a few in my time.'

'So've I,' said Jem softly, and the knife in his hand sketched a little circle, anti-clockwise, in the air.

'I reckon you have,' Stevenson told him. 'And that's why I'll shoot you if I have to.' He gestured with the gun. 'Throw down that knife. And get into the grain store.'

There was a long moment in which Jem calculated the odds. Then reluctantly, he obeyed, his violent mood ebbing away.

Later, locked securely into the grain store amid the feed bins, while he waited for the police to arrive, he had ample time to regret his rashness. It had been a satisfying moment, bloodying Brownlowe's nose . . . but his boss was one of the breed that populated the benches at the magistrates' court. The jack-knife was a residue of Jem's old street-fighting days; carried in his pocket out of habit, it had come to hand automatically, but it hadn't been such a bright idea to bring it out. He suspected there'd be a longish prison sentence to pay for that moment of indulgence. And with Harriet Griffin waiting for him at the Bentley bonfire, the impending loss of his liberty was particularly galling.

Daisy had been right about village interest in her daughter's reappearance. Harriet had braved the stares and the whispered comments and it had all been for nothing. Jem hadn't put in an appearance.

Why was she surprised? Harriet scolded herself. The humiliation was all the harder to bear because of the degree to which she'd been looking forward, guiltily, to seeing him. But it seemed that rich or poor, dark or fair, privileged scions of the gentry like Tom and Gavin, or smart survivors like Jem – men were all the same: you couldn't trust them.

With Marion as his reluctant companion, Rupert went to court to give evidence against his former groom. The case was dealt with rapidly: Jem proffered no excuse for his behaviour, other than a loss of temper. It emerged that the miscreant had a previous conviction on his record, with an unexpired binding-over to keep the peace. The sentence took account of this.

'Only two years in prison,' Rupert complained to Marion as they walked down the front steps of the courthouse. He pressed two tentative fingers against the side of his neck, aware of the throbbing that signalled his blood pressure had soared again. Marion said nothing. On the one hand, she was feeling sorry for Jem Wilkins. Two years was a long time out of a young man's life, a prison sentence could tell against you till your dying day, and besides, if the truth be told, there had been many occasions when she had shared his impulse to hit Rupert herself. On the other hand, she had been shocked by the revelation that a knife had been involved and blamed herself for being the one who had persuaded her husband to hire a man with such a capacity for violence.

Early in December the British newspapers began to take notice of what the press abroad had been gossiping about for months: that the new king Edward the Eighth was having an affair with an American divorcee. Worse, she had still been married to her second husband when he'd met her and was now in the unsavoury process of divorcing him. Worst of all, the king wanted to marry her.

Before the death of King George the Fifth, his son had been a notorious flirt and the list of the world's most eligible bachelor's love affairs was common knowledge. But what had been acceptable and even traditional conduct for a Prince of Wales was not to be condoned in a ruling monarch, and Wallis Simpson, the lady in question, was not an acceptable Queen of England. The nation would not tolerate it.

Fleet Street had ignored the situation for a long time, under a tacit gentlemen's agreement that the behaviour of the monarchy was not a suitable subject for sordid press speculation, but now the story was out and the rights and wrongs of the king's situation were discussed in every home and every public house in the land. Edward had his sympathizers, but not enough of them. After days of argument and counter-argument with his Cabinet, the king announced that if he couldn't marry Mrs Simpson, he was 'ready to go'.

It was the last card of a desperate man and he lost the game. On the tenth of November the Prime Minister read the king's abdication announcement to the House of Commons: *'I, Edward the Eighth, of Great Britain, Ireland and the British Dominions beyond the Seas, King Emperor of India, do hereby declare my irrevocable determination to renounce the Throne for Myself and for My descendants, and My desire that effect should be given to this instrument of Abdication immediately.'*

In the evening, Edward broadcast a radio speech. 'At long last I am able to say a few words of my own,' began the ex-king, but in the seventy seconds of the announcement there was only enough time to sound sad, dignified and generous in defeat, not to defend his decision adequately. He could no longer bear the heavy burdens of his rôle, he said, without the help and support of the woman he loved. His younger brother would become King George the Sixth and he commended him to his subjects.

'. . . God bless you,' concluded Edward bleakly, 'and God save the King.'

The Griffins had gathered round Jackie's wireless to listen to the broadcast. 'Poor man,' said Daisy, into the silence that followed the closing sentence. 'How awful to have to make such a choice. He must really love her, to be ready to give up his throne for her.'

The photographs of Wallis Simpson stared out of the newspapers, sharp-featured, severe, neither young nor pretty. Across the nation women wondered what special quality in Wallis had inspired such devotion in her Edward that he would renounce the crown for her sake.

Lucky her was the unspoken thought in Harriet's mind.

'More fool him,' was the opinion voiced by Allie Briggs.

Tom Searle had written to Harriet. She wasn't sure by what means his letter had reached England – it seemed odd to get mail from a war zone – but he wrote that he was in Aragon. The walk across the Pyrenees had been hard and some of the less fit members of the party had been left behind. It was cold where they were, the food wasn't up to much and the soldiers were mostly raw conscripts, astonishingly ill-equipped. Living out in rough trenches scraped out of the stony hillside, it was a luxury to have so much as a blanket and a decent pair of boots. The weapons with which they had been issued were out of the Ark, but fortunately there had been very little in the way of fighting, so far, beyond an occasional desultory exchange of rifle fire with the opposing troops on the other side of the valley.

I've spent most of today teaching the men of my unit how to fire their rifles. It's ludicrous to think that I'm the most experienced of us in that field, just on the basis of Officers' Training Corps at Winchester and shooting pheasants in the school holidays! I'd be glad of one of Rupert's decent guns here, instead of the rubbish we've been issued. It's downright dangerous to fire some of these old things.

The political situation seems very confused. It's hard to make sense of it – the newspapers at home probably tell you more about what's happening than we are able to find out here. The bunch I'm with seem decent enough – my Spanish is progressing by leaps and bounds – but they're always squabbling among themselves about the best way to defeat the Fascists. There's no doubt about right being on our side, but the army's on the opposing side and that's a distinctly sobering thought.

I've heard that units have been formed of volunteers from various countries, calling themselves the 'International Brigades'. They helped out with the defence of Madrid in November. I wish I'd known about them before I left England – I probably should have joined them in the first place, rather than teaming up with this local contingent. But there wasn't much information available at home because of the government's non-interventionist policy. It's actually illegal, officially, to have come here at all, hence the walk over the Pyrenees instead of just hopping on a train! I wonder what will happen to me when – if – I get back. I suppose I might even be hauled up before the magistrates for doing the forbidden. Better cross that bridge when I come to it . . .

In several closely-written sheets, Tom hadn't said anything about missing Harriet, or of *wanting* to come home. He finished by asking her, again, to pass the news in the letter on to his mother.

Marion, contacted by telephone, came over to Welcome Farm in the Landau. Harriet, steeling herself to see Jem, was disappointed to realize that Marion had driven herself.

'Is your chauffeur unwell?'

'He's no longer working for us,' said Marion. 'As a matter of fact, there was . . . an *unpleasantness* between him and my husband in November – it must have been the same day that you came to Maple Grange, now I come to think of it.'

'An unpleasantness?' echoed Harriet.

'A dispute of some kind. I think Rupert caught Wilkins sneaking off somewhere when he wasn't supposed to,' said Marion, too absorbed in trying to remember what Rupert had told her at the time to notice Harriet's reaction. 'Anyway, I'm sorry to say that Wilkins attacked Rupert, knocked him down and threatened him with a knife. Of course, in such circumstances the police had to be called. And when he went before the magistrates, it seems he had an earlier conviction for something or other, so they gave him rather a long sentence on account of it.'

'How long?'

'Two years, I think. I can't remember. We had an awful job finding someone else to help with the horses,' Marion went on, 'but there's a lad from the village now. He isn't very quick – Rupert says he's half-witted. But beggars can't be choosers. At least his wages are low. And I can drive, so there's no need for a chauffeur – it's an unnecessary expense.' She sighed, thinking about all the other 'unnecessary' expenses which had once seemed essentials in the eternally shrinking budget of Rupert's household. Then she returned to the matter in hand. 'You said you'd had a letter?'

Harriet handed over the pages of Tom's letter, thinking that Jem Wilkins' incarceration in prison somewhere meant that at least she was safe from him now. Or safe from herself? It came to the same thing. But from what Marion said, it seemed that at least he had *tried* – and tried very hard – to keep their rendezvous on Bonfire Night. It was an oddly consoling thought.

Part 5

1938–1939

32

In April 1938, James Allingham wrote to Harriet at Welcome Farm.

> *My wife's stepmother tells us that you are back with your family. I seem to remember that you have some experience of secretarial work for a solicitor and I am writing to ask whether you might be interested in helping in a similar capacity with something that we are undertaking now. It may be that you are needed at home, in which case I quite understand, but if you would like to discuss the position that I have in mind, please telephone me to arrange a meeting.*

Harriet showed the letter to her mother.

'What do you think?'

'Do you want to go?'

'I don't know. Perhaps. It depends on what kind of job he means. But I won't go if you can't spare me.'

Daisy considered the question in silence. She had told herself, when Harriet came home at the end of 1936, that maybe she had finally got the thirst for adventure out of her bones and would settle down to life as a farmer's daughter, the life that her upbringing had intended her for . . . but somewhere inside her, a part of Daisy had always known that Harriet wouldn't stay. She had been lost to the farm long ago, seduced away by Louella Ramsay's lifestyle, which Daisy scathingly thought of to herself as 'London glitter'.

Louella hadn't won Harriet entirely, but what she had taught her niece *had* made her chafe against country life, like a bird in an undersized coop. There was no help for it, Harriet would have to follow her reshaped destiny. They'd had her back for eighteen precious months. Now it was time to bless her and let her go.

'I won't say you're not needed,' said Daisy, 'but I won't say you can't be spared, either. You'd better go.'

'Do you think Dad will agree?'

At least Harriet was calling Will 'Dad' again as a matter of habit, almost as if the discovery that he wasn't her real father had never happened. Daisy said, 'He'd never want to stand in your way, love. You go and see what Mr Allingham wants. We can manage.'

The doorbell of James Allingham's office in Kew was controlled by a brass knob set into the wall beside the big front door of the Georgian building. Harriet pulled the knob and heard the bell inside jangling away. She waited, and the door swung back to reveal an unexpected figure.

'Hullo, Miss Griffin. Do you remember me?'

Yes, Harriet remembered Peter Morris, whom she had last seen nearly four years ago in Vienna, when he was sitting propped up in bed with the marks of a recent savage beating on his face. The marks were long faded, though there was a slight kink in the bridge of a previously straight nose that might be a legacy from that incident. He looked older than the engaging young man of her Vienna memories, gaunt and tired, with lines around his mouth and dark shadows under his eyes. She supposed she must look older, too.

'James said you might be joining us,' he said, as he led her down a wide, stone-flagged hallway.

'I don't know what he has in mind, yet. He just said some kind of secretarial work.' She also remembered how much she had liked Peter, and she was relieved to be able to hide that memory by talking shop.

'There's more to it than that.'

The office which opened off the corridor was high-ceilinged and lined with books and filing cabinets, with a huge pedestal desk in the middle of the room. The surface of the desk was littered with files and papers, as were the tops of the filing cabinets. The general impression was of a barely controlled tide of paperwork.

'Will you sit down? I expect Laura or James will be back in a minute.' Peter stooped to remove a further stack of papers from a chair. There being no room on the desk to put the papers, he laid them on the floor beside the desk.

'As you can see,' he said apologetically, 'assistance with filing is one of the many things that we need.'

'Is it some very complicated case?' Harriet asked. The solicitor's office in Croydon where she had worked had had its share of paperwork, but nothing on this scale.

'No. Not exactly. This is nothing to do with the law firm, or with James's work for the Labour Party. I suppose I should start to fill you in on the background, Miss Griffin . . . or may I call you Harriet? You may remember that when you were in Vienna in 1934 the Nazis were beginning to have an influence? In particular on the way the Jews were being treated?'

'Yes, I remember.' Kirsten Reinhardt, pale and silent, had sat at supper with a gash on her forehead caused by a stone flung by a Nazi supporter. Later, in the Michaelerplatz, Harriet had seen an old man taunted and manhandled by a jeering gang of thugs and Peter Morris, who stood beside her now, had intervened in that ugly little incident, walking steadily into the beating which he must have known was coming.

There are some things you can't walk away from, he had said. She had respected him for that line at the time and she remembered it now.

'It's got worse,' he told her. 'Ever since the *Anschluss* last month – when Hitler marched his troops over the border and occupied Austria. I was there in Vienna that day. Masses of people stood in the streets and shouted *Sieg Heil*! They welcomed Hitler as a liberator, not an invader. They said that he was only reclaiming land that was wrongly ceded from Germany after the war. I don't know about that. What I do know is that the Nazis are all-powerful now and terrible things are being done, barbaric things. Do you know about the Nuremburg Laws?'

Harriet shook her head. 'Not really. I think I've heard them mentioned, or maybe I saw something in a newspaper.'

'In September of the year you were in Vienna, 1935, legislation was passed in Germany that effectively outlawed the Jews. They weren't allowed German citizenship and they couldn't intermarry with Gentiles. They were excluded from holding many jobs – teaching, the civil service, acting, journalism, farming . . . More and more. They couldn't buy food in non-Jewish shops. Not even medicine, or milk for a baby. And as for their own shops, the non-Jews were told to boycott them. I can't begin to describe the impact on their lives – it was a systematic dismantling of their livelihood. They've had to wear yellow stars pinned to their clothes to mark them out. Their children are taken out of the schools they used to attend, and shunned by the friends they used to play with. They aren't even allowed to sit on the park benches that are reserved for *proper* German citizens. And there are signs posted up everywhere to encourage hatred and cruelty: *Jews not admitted. Jews not welcome here.*

'I was in Vienna reporting for my newspaper. I was supposed to write something about tourism – a nice little series of travel articles. I sent home a report about what was happening and the editor wouldn't print it. He said it wasn't the sort of thing that would interest his readers,' Peter concluded bitterly, his voice shaking with suppressed emotion. He made a gesture with his hand in front of his face, as if brushing something away. 'I'm sorry. That still disgusts me.'

From the doorway, James Allingham's quiet voice filled the gap.

'Since the Nuremburg Laws were introduced there have been further laws passed which have worsened the situation. People are being arrested, beaten up, taken away to camps. And on top of the official persecution, because they're unprotected by the authorities they're a sitting target for any thug or looter. As a result, any members of the Jewish population who *can* manage to leave Nazi-controlled territory are doing so. But it's difficult – they have to find other countries that are willing to take them in. Peter is in touch with refugees in Vienna and various people around this country, including Laura and myself, are trying to find sponsors for as many as possible. Which is why I wrote to you: accurate records must be kept of what we do and, as you can see, there's a lot of paperwork involved,' said James. 'Will you help us?'

'. . . So I said yes, I would,' Harriet told her friend Vera, later in the day. Still dazed by the sudden change in her fortunes, she had taken the chance to travel to Croydon before going home. 'It'll mean living in London – Mr Allingham says he'll arrange board and lodging for me.'

'When do you start?' Vera asked, raising her voice because at her feet Freddie was pushing a small wooden truck about with appropriate noises and the conversation had to compete with this background.

'Straightaway. I'm just going home to get some things packed and I'll be back tomorrow. There's an awful lot to do,' Harriet added apprehensively. 'I hope I can manage it all right. I'm not a very *fast* typist, and it's such important work. All those desperate people. It's like trying to catch a flood in a thimble, Mr Allingham says, but you have to do what you can, even when it's not the beginnings of enough. Some of the refugees are children, coming without their parents. They're the ones that Peter Morris is especially concerned with.'

'Without their parents?' Vera echoed, incredulously.

'Yes. It takes so long to get a visa to come, you see, and there are so many waiting . . . and it's easier to get permission for the children alone, apparently. So some parents agree for them to be sent by themselves, to be more or less adopted by an English family.'

'Well, it seems unnatural to me,' said Vera. 'I can't imagine ever doing a thing like that. I mean, I don't think

I could bear to send Freddie away to a foreign land to live with strangers. Suppose I never got him back?'

'According to Peter, the parents are so afraid of what may happen to their children if they *don't* get them out of the country, that they accept the risk of never seeing them again.'

'I still don't see how they can do it.' Vera had lifted a startled Freddie onto her knee and was hugging him to her. Freddie, unaware of what had prompted this demonstration of maternal affection, struggled furiously to get down and, reluctantly, Vera returned him to his truck on the floor.

'His father made that,' she told Harriet, with pride. 'He's good with his hands, is my Fred. Hope the nipper takes after him – in that way, anyway. I won't complain if he leaves out the political stuff.'

'Is Fred still in the Communist Party?' Harriet asked.

'Oh, yes. And still having pangs of conscience about not going off to Spain with your Tom.'

'He's not *my* Tom,' said Harriet sharply. 'Not any more. He went, and that was that.'

'I thought he still wrote to you?'

'Oh, yes. Now and again.'

'You must be worried sick about him.'

But was she? Harriet asked herself. Mostly, nowadays, her time with Tom seemed like a vaguely remembered dream. He wrote spasmodically, usually just when she'd given up expecting ever to hear from him again, and this bothered her, stirring up memories that were better left to lie, reviving a reluctant concern for his safety. The sparely worded contents of the letters were so chilling. So much was left out.

Last spring he had written that he had transferred from the *Partido Obrero de Unificación Marxista* to the British contingent of the International Brigades. Later, in the summer, the English newspapers reported that the POUM had been outlawed by the populist government it had supported, and one of its leaders murdered by Soviet agents. Tom's next letter had arrived in August, and told of involvement in a battle at Brunete in July. There had been terrible casualties from high-level aerial bombing. He had been drinking foul water scooped out of puddles on the hillside and had suffered a dose of dysentery. He'd nearly died but was better now.

At Christmas, unexpectedly, he'd sent a parcel containing a long-toothed tortoiseshell comb and she'd found herself sitting upstairs in her bedroom with the gift in her hands, crying.

'The last letter was months ago. I can only suppose he's still alive,' she told Vera.

'He is. Leastways, he was the other day when he wrote to Fred,' Vera said.

'Really? Does he do that often?'

'Oh, hardly ever.' Vera became aware, a little too late, that she had dropped a brick. Her friend's flushed cheeks and pursed lips suggested that if Tom Searle was in sufficiently good health to write to Fred, he should also have written to herself.

'So . . . what did he say?' Harriet asked, after a short struggle with her pride.

'I dunno. The letter came today, just as Fred was going off to work. He left it out on the hall stand, I think. Tell you what, I'll open it now, seeing as you're here. Fred won't mind.' Vera fetched the letter and slid a knife blade under the flap. 'Oh, there's a photograph.'

Harriet studied the photograph that Vera passed her. From underneath a rakishly tilted beret, Tom's face stared unsmiling at the camera. He wore an open-necked shirt, jodhpurs and high leather boots. His left arm was encased in a sling and the sight of it brought back a flood of memories about the days in Vienna: his injured hand and his injured pride, and the kiss on a train that had been the beginning of their time together.

'He says he's been slightly wounded – a sniper got him when he was out doing a reconnaissance,' Vera said, reading the letter. 'The worst bit was having the bullet dug out without any anaesthetic. *Sounds nasty* . . . but the good bit was being sent down to the town to recover. The area's been hit hard by the war, there's a lot of hardship and food shortages. At the camp they did a whip-round to send some tins of food to town with the convalescents. His came in very handy because – Oh!' Vera's voice broke off sharply.

Harriet looked up. 'What is it?'

'Nothing,' Vera mumbled, pink-cheeked. 'Just some of the rubbish men say to one another. You know.'

'Let me see,' said Harriet, holding out her hand.

'I don't know if I should. I don't think I was supposed to be reading this, let alone you, Harriet.'

'Give it to me, Vera,' Harriet said grimly.

The local population is starving. It's amazing how far you can get with a tin of potted meat and a few cigarettes. O'Brien and I went down to the market place and negotiated with a couple of the girls we met for an hour of 'rest and recuperation', if you understand what I mean! Mine was a pretty little armful: black hair, dark eyes and a sad face. She told me her husband had gone on a paseo. That's the local term for being taken out and executed – I suppose he got on the wrong side of some faction or other. This lot are always quarrelling among themselves and the war gets used as an excuse to settle all sorts of local vendettas. Poor girl! I felt a bit guilty about if afterwards, taking advantage of her hunger like that. But like O'Brien said, we weren't the first and we wouldn't be the last . . .

Harriet looked up. She passed the rest of the letter back unread.

'He seems to be adapting to the local conditions very well,' was all she said.

Back at Welcome Farm Harriet found a letter from Tom waiting for her. She supposed that he must have sent it on the same day as he wrote to Fred. There was a similar photograph of him in his beret, sling holding his wounded arm across his chest, with the difference that in this shot he was smiling.

Unusually, amid the sketchy news about conditions in the war zone he wrote that he was missing her. Perhaps, Harriet thought, her stomach churning with anger and revulsion, his moments of 'rest and recuperation' had reminded him of his discarded lover at home. She tore the letter and the photograph across and threw the shreds in the fire, jabbing viciously at them with the poker as they burned, and told herself that learning about Tom's black-eyed Spanish girl had been the final, unforgivable straw.

At James Allingham's office, Harriet began to deal with the mountains of paperwork relating to the Jewish refugees that Peter and his colleagues in Austria were bringing to England. Peter had gone when she returned to Kew from Welcome Farm, and she learned that he was on his way back to Vienna to organize visas for another batch of the children who were his special concern.

It was Laura Allingham's job, with Harriet's assistance, to find sponsors for Peter's refugees.

'Before any of them can obtain a visa, a sponsor in this country has to be found,' Laura explained on the first day, as she gave Harriet a bewilderingly rapid tour of the cubbyhole of an office with its overflowing trays of paperwork. 'That sponsor must be prepared to employ them at a living wage, or in the case of the unaccompanied children to guarantee their keep for however long they might need to stay, and to provide fifty pounds with which to cover the cost of repatriation at some future stage, when the crisis in their country is over and it's safe for them to return.'

'Do you think there's any chance of that?' Harriet asked.

'I don't know. *Something* must happen. Nazi Germany is just too frightening and terrible to be allowed to go on doing what it's doing. After the Great War the League of Nations was started in the hope that countries could put diplomatic and moral pressure on one another and stop this kind of thing from going on, but it's getting nowhere with its protests to that man Hitler. James says another war is inevitable. After his last trip to Germany he came home and joined the Royal Air Force Volunteer Reserve . . .'

She bit her lip, looking grave. 'As you may know, I belong to the Peace Pledge Union. I worked very hard campaigning before that Peace Day we had. And of course when the Peace Ballot was taken in 1935 to see whether people wanted disarmament, ten million said they did. I thought that was a triumph at the time. Now I'm not so sure. I really do believe that a war like the last one is never the answer, all the wrong people suffer instead of the ones who are causing it; but when I look at what's happening in Germany I just don't know what *is* the answer. Well, anyway,' she added briskly, 'one thing at a time, and what I'm supposed to be doing now is showing you what we do in this office.

'I write articles, and give talks, and try to persuade people to come forward as sponsors or to offer jobs. Mostly the jobs are for domestic work. The refugees will agree to do anything, just to get out; it's a bit difficult, sometimes, when some woman who's obviously had her own servants and hasn't the first idea how to scrub pots and pans arrives over here to take up work as a kitchen maid. *Needs must when the Devil drives*; I suppose. At least they'll be safer than they were at home.'

'How did you start doing this work?' Harriet asked.

'Oh, Peter found that in Vienna people kept approaching him to ask if he could help. And as he said, you can't just turn your back on it. So he contacted James and we said we'd do what we could. It's been eating up our lives ever since. There's so much need and we can do so little,' Laura added sadly. 'I have to keep reminding myself what my stepmother Marion's friends in Farnham say: *Every little helps*. Not that we're the only ones, there are others doing the same – one lovely pair of sisters I've met travel frequently to Germany and Austria on the excuse that they're opera fans. In fact they really are, and have been making regular trips abroad to attend opera for years, so of course the authorities don't suspect what they're up to nowadays.

'They take a lot of risks to smuggle out jewellery and so on for their refugees so they'll have something to get by on when they arrive here. It's terribly dangerous. Peter does the same sort of thing, he's been known to shepherd a train-load of children across the border into France with ten or twelve gold watches strapped up his arms. Heaven knows what would happen to him if he was caught, because the rule is that they're only allowed to bring out five marks apiece and whatever they can carry in one item of hand luggage. He says a little girl on one of the early trips was found to have a diamond bracelet fastened under the sleeve of her dress – her mother must have put it there in hopes that it wouldn't be found. But it was hurting her because it was so sharp and she must have rubbed at it, poor thing. So then it was spotted and the guards simply ripped it off and then dragged her off the train and nobody knows what became of her. Since then Peter's taken on the job of carrying anything he finds has been sent with the children, because it's better than letting them take the risk. And there always has to be another adult on the overseas part of the trip, to take charge of the children if he gets arrested.'

Harriet shivered. She could imagine only too clearly the scene that Laura had just described: the small, terrified child assaulted and shouted at and bundled away from her companions by brutal strangers, while Peter Morris watched and raged helplessly, unable to intervene because so many other children depended on him. She supposed it was experiences like that which had carved the new lines around his mouth.

Harriet's first task was to familiarize herself with the contents of the heaped files in the office. Each refugee had a file, often a pathetic little collection of letters pleading their cause, stated in the barest terms for fear that the material would fall into the wrong hands; or notes brought into the office by Peter on his trips to London, which included harrowing scraps about the loss of homes and possessions, precious family heirlooms stolen or 'bought' by the Nazis at derisory prices, or family members taken away to a concentration camp.

Once the applicant had reached England, Harriet would be required to add a note of the date on which they arrived, together with the details of whoever had sponsored them. The stack of files completed in this way was pathetically small when seen against the mound of those still waiting. Occasionally Laura or James would come into the office, tight-lipped, and call for a file to be found and marked 'inactive', indicating that the refugee had lost contact with their would-be helper. 'Which probably means,' James explained flatly, 'that they're on a train to some god-awful camp. So we were too late to help that one.'

At Welcome Farm, the Griffins couldn't ignore the growing storm clouds over Europe. In Spain, the war was going the way of the Fascists, reinforced as they were by Italian and German airpower. At home the unemployment situation of the early half of the decade now seemed a thing of the past. Across Britain, factories and dockyards were building aeroplanes, weapons, tanks and warships.

'*Arming for peace*, they call it,' said Allie Briggs in August. As usual, she knew more about what was in the newspapers than anyone else and was more interested in reading them than in preparing the parlour for the impending arrival of Marion Brownlowe.

Months ago, Marion had come to the farm intending to see Harriet, but arrived just after Harriet had left for London and James Allingham's office. Marion had stayed to form a tentative friendship with Daisy Griffin, who was not her social equal but a transparently good woman for all that, and the visits had continued. The two women had at least one powerful common interest: their troublesome offspring. Marion's Tom and Daisy's Harriet had combined to cause their respective mothers much private worry.

'Allie, do hurry up with that dusting,' Daisy said. 'It's

almost time for you to go and I wanted some help with hanging out sheets.'

'Coming,' Allie called mendaciously, on her hands and knees in the parlour. She turned over another page of the newspaper she was reading. 'Oh, that's interesting. I'll leave that for your Jackie.'

Daisy was too distracted by household matters to pay much attention to Allie's last remark. Later she was to regret that lapse, because Allie did leave a page, torn from a daily paper, for Jackie to read when he came back from school. It was a notice to the effect that the Royal Air Force was recruiting large numbers of boys as apprentice fitters, engineers and trainee aircrew.

Without mentioning it to his parents, Jackie made enquiries and informed his stunned mother that he intended to apply.

'I always thought that if either of them went, it would be Rob,' Daisy told Will sadly, when the worst had happened and Jackie told them that he had been accepted for air force training. 'He's the one that was so mad about aeroplanes. Not Jackie. Oh dear! We'll just have to hope that he'll become a fitter or something and not have to do any flying.'

But Jackie demolished even that hope by announcing, bright-eyed with excitement, that he had performed so well in his initial tests that he had distinct hopes of qualifying as an air navigator in a bomber crew.

Rob didn't say anything when he heard the news. Always a realist, he had abandoned his flying ambitions on the day his father had had his accident with the tractor. Somebody would have to take over the heaviest of the farmwork or the Griffins would not be able to carry on at Welcome Farm, and he was the obvious candidate. He had shouldered the burden and the disappointment like the steady young man that he had become, and mostly he bore it cheerfully. But all the same, it hurt to see his younger brother was now to have the opportunity that he had lost.

*   *   *

That same August, Czechoslovakia was in the news – a nation of whose whereabouts and origins Daisy Griffin, like most other Britons, had only the sketchiest idea.

'It's near Austria – used to be part of the old Austro-Hungarian Empire till the Treaty of Versailles scrapped all that and created a new state,' Will said, when she asked him about it. With a butterfly mind that collected odd scraps of information, Will could usually be relied on to know something about whatever area of current events puzzled Daisy.

'So what's all the fuss about now?' she asked.

'Well, the new nation never really settled down and accepted its new form. It's an odd mix of nationalities – Slovaks, Hungarians, Germans, Czechs – and they don't get on. The Hungarians want to redraw the boundaries on their border all over again – in their favour, naturally. The Slovaks don't feel particularly loyal to the new government; the Sudetanland Germans are a minority but they reckon they're badly treated by everyone else and want their independence; and now Hitler's using that as an excuse to go in and take back the Sudetanland. Some people might think he's entitled to.'

'Do you?'

'I don't know what the rights and wrongs of it are. I do know that Hitler's got a nasty habit of using troops instead of diplomacy, and he's already used the same excuse with Austria. What worries me is that he won't know when to stop.'

In the complex network of international pacts and treaties, Britain, France and Russia had some responsibility for protecting Czechoslovakia. The Prime Minister, Neville Chamberlain, flew twice to discuss the situation with Herr Hitler, first at Berchtesgaden, then at Godesberg, and came back with plans to pacify the Germans. Pressure was put on the Czech government by its supposed allies to be 'reasonable' and make some concessions for the sake of peace, but there was a general fear that war could not be averted.

For weeks, with memories of the last war still painfully clear, the British public waited tensely to discover whether they were to do battle all over again, this time in defence of an obscure little country which nobody could pronounce. In London, walking from her lodgings to the office in Kew, Harriet would pass workmen putting up steel air-raid shelters or digging trenches in the parks, and she would read the notices instructing her to have her regulation-issue gas mask fitted at the distribution centre.

At the end of September Chamberlain flew again to Germany, this time to Munich, for intense negotiations not only with Hitler, but with Italy's dictator Mussolini as well. When he came back, landing at Heston airport, it was with a piece of paper which, he told the waiting crowd, ensured 'Peace in our time.'

'It won't last,' was Will Griffin's sober judgement. And whatever Chamberlain might say to a public giddy with relief that war had been averted, the mushrooming provision of trenches and shelters, the dispensing of gas masks and emergency instructions, the recruitment and training of Air Raid Wardens and all the frantic preparations for war on the home front went on; as did the work of the armament factories.

Late on an October evening, a small group of people waited at Liverpool Street station for the train from Harwich.

'Peter is due to arrive today with a group of children,' James had told Harriet that morning. 'Their sponsors will be collecting them from the station this evening. Can you go along and help get them paired off with the appropriate families?'

The train was a little late and Harriet, armed with a fistful of lists, had time to identify the various sponsors by name. With the traditional reserve of the English middle classes they had been waiting independently, in silence. Now, as a result of her intervention, they clustered together and began, cautiously, to talk to each other.

'What's yours?' she overheard one elderly woman say

to the fair-haired younger woman standing next to her.

'Oh, a girl. Her name's Freida. I asked for a girl. Much less trouble. And I have a daughter of my own, you see. This Freida can be a playmate for her – she doesn't have many friends. What about you?'

'I said I'd take a boy. I didn't think about him being trouble. I hope I did the right thing.' The elderly woman sounded worried. 'It's all a bit of a lucky dip, isn't it? All we get to see beforehand is the photograph and those few lines about their age and their background and so on. It isn't much to choose from.'

The train pulled in with a rush of steam, and Peter stepped down from the first carriage behind the engine. After him shuffled a subdued crocodile of children, each carrying a small suitcase or bag and, in some cases, a much-loved favourite toy to ease the heartache of parting from their families. The oldest, a tall, thin boy, Harriet estimated to be about thirteen. The youngest, a girl, looked barely four or five. The waiting adults pressed forward, peering at the labels attached to the lapels of the children's coats.

'This one's mine!' said the blonde woman, laying claim to a brown-haired girl who might have been about ten years old. 'Hullo, dear. How was your journey? I know you're going to get on beautifully with my Betty – she can't wait to meet her new sister.'

Freida looked blank. Harriet wondered how much German the woman or her daughter could speak to bridge the gap and suspected the answer was not much. The other children were being similarly identified and, one by one, after she had ticked them off on her list, they were led away.

'There's a problem,' said Peter, at the end of an hour.

Harriet had cramp in the hand that clutched the pencil with which she was making notes. Her head ached, her feet hurt and she was longing to sit down. She looked past Peter along the platform. A small girl stood under the light outside the Waiting Room, beside a small brown leather suitcase. She was perhaps five years old, dressed in what her parents had probably thought was a suitably English outfit; a tweed coat with a velvet collar, thick ribbed stockings, patent leather shoes and a tam-o'-shanter with an enormous tartan bobble, from beneath which emerged two small, stiff plaits of black hair. She clutched a toy dog to her chest with both arms.

'A family in Hampstead was supposed to be taking her, but they haven't arrived to collect her.' Peter beckoned to the child, who picked up the suitcase and trudged along the platform towards them. To carry the case was just within her strength. *Five marks apiece and whatever they can carry in one item of hand luggage*, Harriet remembered. That was all that the children were permitted to take out of Nazi-controlled Austria. It didn't seem much with which to make a new life.

The girl dumped the case beside Harriet, set the toy dog down on it, and made a stiff, formal curtsey.

'I am called Gilda,' she recited carefully. 'I thank you for your kindness.'

'Gilda?' Harriet echoed. There was something faintly familiar about the child's face.

'Gilda Reinhardt,' Peter said. 'My Uncle Jurgen and Aunt Kirsten's little girl. I think you saw her once, when she was a baby.'

Now the familiarity was explained. Harriet remembered Kirsten's face on the day when they had first met. Gilda had the same dark eyes, huge in a pale face and, just now, the same look of strained apprehension.

'They asked me to bring her, this time. Before, they didn't want to let her go. But things have got very bad in Vienna, now. Kirsten's father was taken away last month,' Peter said flatly. 'I had to do some urgent cabling to find someone to sponsor her, and then queue at the various departments for three days solid to get her papers stamped. We only just made it in time. And now these damned people haven't shown. I don't know if my last message went astray, or if they changed their minds; or what.' He rubbed his face with his hands. 'What on earth am I going to do with her? Any ideas? I'm sorry. I will try to think of something. But I'm so darned tired . . .'

'I don't know . . . or maybe . . . We could take her to Blackheath,' Harriet suggested. 'My aunt has a house there. We can contact these people in Hampstead in the morning.'

'So *please* would you take her in, Louella, just for tonight? We can't think of anything else to do with her.'

In the hall at Medlar House, to which she had been summoned by a startled Everett, Louella looked at the small girl and the small girl stared back.

'What's her name?'

'Gilda.'

Louella sat down on the stairs. 'Come here,' she said. Gilda stood rooted to the ground, her face crumpled with resistance.

'*Muttie* . . .' she whispered. '*Ich meuchte meine muttie.*'

'Tell her,' said Louella, 'that her mother can't come to her just now; but that until she can, I will love her and look after her as if I was her mother.'

'It's only till tomorrow, Aunt Louella,' said Harriet.

'To hell with that,' said Louella. 'Gilda? Don't be afraid, darling. I won't hurt you. Come here?' she repeated. 'Come and be cuddled.'

Harriet's eyes widened. Louella's voice had taken on an unfamiliar gentleness. She held out her arms and rather to everybody's surprise, Gilda went into them.

33

'It's all worked out beautifully,' Harriet told Laura Allingham, a week later. 'My aunt adores children; it's always been a tragedy for her that she never had any of her own. And she's got stacks of money. I can't think why it never occurred to me before to approach her to join your list of sponsors.'

'What happened to the people from Hampstead, the ones who never turned up?'

'They told Peter that they never received the last cable, the one that confirmed Gilda would come to them. I don't think they were too sorry at not having to take her – they were rather panicking at having made such a rushed decision. Peter says he'll work on them while he's here and see if he can't persuade them to consider another child.'

'Well done, anyway, Harriet. You've done wonders since you came – far better than I expected. I must admit,' Laura said frankly, 'that when James told me he intended to ask you to join us, I thought you were far too young and irresponsible for such a serious business. You've proved me wrong.'

'I did get the impression when I came that you weren't very keen to have me working here,' Harriet said.

Laura smiled ruefully, remembering a time in the Great War when she had been Harriet's age and struggling against the apparently universal attitude that she herself was too young and irresponsible to be of any use. As a VAD nurse she'd succeeded in overturning that opinion – and found herself in situations that only her stubborn pride and a deep well of hitherto-unsuspected courage had carried her through. 'I've been wrong a lot of times in my life,' she said.

'What puzzles me is why, with you so strongly against it, Mr Allingham did employ me?'

'Oh, that was Peter Morris's doing,' said Laura. 'He asked for you specially.'

'I wonder why?' said Harriet.

'My dear,' Laura told her, lightly, 'I daresay it was the age-old reason.'

Harriet found Laura's suggestion uncomfortable to contemplate. But what if she was right and Peter Morris was attracted to her? In Vienna he'd certainly seemed to like her . . . but that had been such a fleeting encounter. In any case, four years later, Harriet was not the same person. She'd grown hard and disillusioned, and her instinctive response to any man who showed an interest in her was to hold him at a distance. In her eighteen months at home after Tom Searle's departure for Spain, a number of young men in Hampshire had had cause to testify that however warm and alluring the red-headed Griffin girl might seem at first sight, beneath the surface she was pure granite.

Laura must be mistaken. Peter Morris had mostly been away since she'd started working in the office, but when he *was* around he'd shown no signs of having any special interest in her. Apart from practical exchanges to do with the welfare of the children in his care, he'd hardly looked at her, come to think of it.

Yes, Harriet decided. *Laura was definitely wrong.*

In any case, there was soon no time to think of personal matters. In Paris a young German-Jewish refugee had shot and killed a diplomat at the German Embassy. It was said that the boy had carried out the assassination in revenge for the deportation of his father to Poland, and as a general protest against what was being done to the Jews. The Nazi response was to unleash a wave of destructive and murderous violence against the helpless Jewish population in the territories it controlled. The orgy of arson and killing, rape and looting, lasted for a week and its first night, 9th November, became known afterwards as *Kristallnacht* – the night of broken glass.

From Vienna, in the aftermath of that week, came a flood of desperate letters.

In Spain, the tide was running out for the Republican government. At the beginning of October their Premier, Juan Negrín, had made a broadcast saying that the Spanish people must come to an understanding with one another. Did the Nationalists desire to carry on the war until the country was destroyed? He made it clear that he wanted to negotiate.

Britain's Neville Chamberlain offered himself as a mediator. 'He's all puffed up with pride over Checkers-whatever-it-is,' Allie Briggs commented to Daisy at Welcome Farm, as usual reading the paper when she should have been doing something else. 'And thinks he can solve all the world's problems with a few bits of paper.'

'Well, good luck to him. *Somebody's* got to stop that awful fighting,' Daisy said. But the Fascist leader, Franco, scenting victory, declared that he would accept nothing less than unconditional surrender.

The Russians, too, were tired of the never-ending Spanish war. So far, they had supported the Popular government. Now they contemplated a friendship with Germany, or at least a diplomatic understanding. Their rôle had been to support the International Brigades and now they suggested that the Brigades should be withdrawn.

Premier Negrín was prepared to let them go. They were largely made up of Spaniards by now anyway. He suggested that the League of Nations should supervise the withdrawal of the Brigades.

Tom Searle was in action with the Fifteenth Battalion at Ebro when the decision was taken. The offensive along the Ebro River had been launched on the twenty-fourth of July, with Republican troops wading thigh-deep across the river. At first it had been a successful advance, but

Franco's Nationalist troops counter-attacked and their German-supplied artillery caused heavy casualties. On the twenty-second of September Tom's unit took part in their last engagement. Afterwards, what was left of them learned that they were to go home.

How did he feel? *Too tired to care*, was probably his most coherent immediate response. Long ago he'd lost his illusions about the war he was involved in; the fine principles of freedom and justice and democracy that had brought him to Spain had now gone to the wall. He'd only stayed because he was stubborn, or perhaps because he was too busy surviving to work out any positive strategy for extricating himself from the mess he was in. Now he had no choice.

The Spaniards of the Popular Front did their best to show some gratitude and make the going of the Brigades a memorable event. There was a farewell parade in Barcelona in November. The Premier was there and the fiery woman politician, Dolores Ibarruri, the one they called '*La Pasionara*', whose speeches had stirred so many people to such gallantry – *and such folly*, Tom thought dourly, as he stood in the parade. He and his companions had echoed her '*No pasaran*' so proudly in the so-called 'Battle of Cable Street', that little tussle against Mosley's Brown Shirts that he was now able to compare, in battle terms, with the real thing.

Wasn't it *La Pasionara* who had said, too, that it was better to die on your feet than to live on your knees? It was a fine sentiment, but he'd *seen* men die on their feet. They fell down soon enough, and rotted where they lay.

But when this woman stood up and addressed the assembly, against his will he was won over again by her words. First she spoke to the women of Barcelona, urging them to tell their children, in days to come, of the Crusaders for Freedom who had come 'over seas and over mountains, crossing frontiers bristling with bayonets, and watched for by ravening dogs thirsty to tear their flesh.' Later, she turned to the men of the Brigades, the gaunt and scruffy survivors

530

of an adventure that must have seemed a Crusade when it started.

'You can go proudly. You are history. You are legend . . . We shall not forget you, and when the olive tree of peace puts forth its leaves again, mingled with the laurels of the Spanish Republic's victory – come back!'

Just for a while, Tom Searle felt like a Crusader again. Later, he heard that even while they stood on parade, the Ebro battle was ending with the retreat of the Popular Army.

'Tom's come home. He asks after you.'

It was Marion Brownlowe's voice on the telephone. Harriet stood in James Allingham's office and tried to work out what the news meant to her. On Marion's behalf she could feel glad that a mother's long trial of endurance was over. For herself, she discovered, she felt nothing.

'Will you speak to him? He's here with me now.'

A moment later she heard Tom's voice.

'Hullo, Harry! I could mouth all sorts of platitudes about "long-time-no-see" and all that. But this telephone call is devilishly expensive. I want to see you. Are you free for supper tonight?'

'I suppose so.'

Tom laughed. 'Well, you don't need to sound so enthusiastic!'

He took her to a small restaurant near the river. He had probably chosen it for its romantic ambience. He was more smartly dressed than she had expected, in a suit and tie. Harriet, in one of Aunt Louella's creations from bygone days – now shiny in patches and distinctly outdated, sat opposite him and watched his altered face as he spoke about his experiences in Spain.

He turned everything into a joke, she realized. Even death. That was his style. She let him talk and even found it amusing sometimes. He drank a little too much wine. Finally he reached round the candlestick in the centre of the table and tried to take her hand.

'Don't,' said Harriet quietly, withdrawing from his reach.

531

'So that's it,' said Tom, after a pause. 'I'm not the blue-eyed boy any more, am I? Is there someone else?'

'No,' said Harriet.

'What about that character Morris? Laura told me he's around.'

'I work with him, yes. But there's nothing between us.'

'Then why—?' Tom suddenly checked himself. 'All right, I left you in the lurch. You have a right to resent that. But I'm back now. I'll make it up to you. Hang it all, Harriet, I've been through some bad times, and one of the things that helped me through them was the thought of you. That's why I kept writing to you – so you wouldn't forget me.'

Harriet was silent, still watching his face.

'Will you marry me?' said Tom, unexpectedly.

'I thought you weren't the marrying kind.'

'Maybe I've changed. So what about it?'

'I can't, Tom,' said Harriet softly.

'Why not? I've learned a lot since I went away. I've had some of the rough edges knocked off me. I've learnt the value of things I took for granted before. You're one of them. Can you believe that?'

Yes, she could believe that. She still liked him, in spite of herself. He could still make her smile. No doubt if she let him he could still drag a response from her with his kisses, and the expert touch of his hands – kept in practice, she reminded herself wryly, by attentions to sad, black-haired señoras. But she had lately begun to recognize that what she wanted from a man was the kind of steady support, the quiet, steadfast loving, that Will Griffin gave to Daisy. And Tom, for all his charm, was still someone who needed to joke about death. It wasn't enough.

Tom seemed downcast for a bit when he realized that her resolve was not to be shaken. Then he shrugged his shoulders and finished the wine.

'It's probably just as well. Deep down, I suppose I'm really *not* the marrying kind.' He changed the subject. 'Mother tells me that my old flame Diana Somerville broke up yet again with *your* old flame, the picturesque but vacuous Gavin . . . and that thanks to a breathless series of broken engagements since then, she's once more on the market. Perhaps I'll look her up.'

'How did you get on with Tom? Is he still the same old charmer?' Laura asked next day, in the office.

In the background, Peter Morris was making notes on a file. He glanced up briefly and down again before Harriet answered.

'Oh, yes, the same old charmer.'

'He had a word with me yesterday when he arrived. So, am I right in thinking that congratulations might be in order?' Laura asked. 'I can't think of anyone I'd rather have for a stepsister-in-law, Harriet.'

'Sorry, but no,' said Harriet, flushing. 'I mean, thank you for what you said, Laura, but Tom and I aren't . . . we won't be . . .'

'Don't say that dilettante devil has changed his mind,' Laura exclaimed, embarrassed. 'He told me very decidedly yesterday that he was going to ask you last night.'

'So he did,' Harriet said. 'But I said no.'

'Oh,' said Laura. There was a short pause before she added, with a forced laugh, 'Well, that must have come as a bit of a shock to him. Still, I daresay he deserves it. You don't think you'll change your mind?'

'No,' said Harriet. 'I won't change my mind.'

On the far side of the room, Peter Morris had closed his file. His eyes rested on her for a moment, his expression difficult to interpret, then he said, 'I'm sorry to interrupt your conversation, ladies, but can we get back to work?'

At least, Harriet noted, *that* remark must have taught Laura the error of her impression that Peter Morris had some interest in herself.

In the nursery on the top floor of Medlar House, Gilda and Louella were playing with Noah's Ark. The toy had been bought by Hector Ramsay, around the turn of the century, for the son who was later posted 'missing' at Loos. It had been a favourite, first with John Ramsay and later with Harriet Griffin when she'd lived in the house as a small girl during the last year of the Great War. As a consequence the paint was faded and the assorted pairs of animals were battered by use. Now it was a regular part of Gilda's daily lessons in English.

Louella sat on the Indian carpet beside the Ark, from which she had removed the lid so that the animals could be fitted into its interior, two by two. Gilda knelt beside her.

'Now we put in the horses,' said Louella.

'Now we put in the horses,' Gilda repeated, leaning over the boat with a carved wooden animal in each hand.

'Now we put in the elephants.'

'Now we put in the e-le-phants,' the little girl said, carefully. She picked up a hippopotamus and frowned at it. 'No. That's wrong!' She found an elephant at the second attempt, beamed with satisfaction and looked for its twin.

'Now we put in the lions. Have you ever seen a real lion?' asked Louella. Gilda shook her head.

'No, but I seen horses.' Her English was progressing fast.

'Then we shall go to Regent's Park this afternoon and see the animals at the zoo.'

'*Zoo?*' Puzzled, Gilda pursed her lips to rehearse the word and then laughed at the sound. 'Like Everett zoos the cat from the milk jug?'

'No, that's *shoo*. A zoo is a place where animals are kept, special animals that would usually live far away in strange countries,' Louella said, trying to find words to explain the concept in a way that Gilda would understand. 'So some are brought here to England and kept in the zoo so that people can go and see them.'

'Excuse me, madam.' Alice had come into the room unnoticed. 'There's a lady here to see you.'

'Who is she?' Louella asked, exasperated by the interruption.

Alice hesitated. 'I couldn't catch the name, madam. She's foreign.'

'Oh, all right. I'd better see her, I suppose. I won't be

long, Gilda. You finish putting the animals into the Ark with Alice and then we'll go to the zoo and see the lions and elephants.'

In the drawing room a stranger stood by the window, looking out over the green. A slight, serious woman, her dark hair severely parted over a pale face. She turned to face Louella.

'How can I help you? I'm afraid I haven't much time,' Louella said, thinking of Gilda waiting upstairs for the promised outing. The woman took a step towards her and held out her hand.

'Good afternoon. I am Kirsten Reinhardt. I have come for my little girl.'

'I have a distant relative in America,' Kirsten explained. 'I wrote many letters and eventually this person agreed to sponsor us. So then we applied to the United States embassy for a visa. Now we have a number on the waiting list – that means we will get a visa in the end, we only have to wait our turn. And with that number, we are permitted to come to England, because the English authorities know they do not have to take us in for ever,' she elaborated, with a touch of bitterness.

Like every other refugee in the desperate queues, she had been forced to humble herself and plead her case before a stony bureaucracy. As James had told Harriet, none of Germany's neighbours wanted to recognize the seriousness of the Jews' situation because that would impose a moral obligation to accept a flood of immigrants. Kirsten had been lucky and now she was safe; but so many of her frightened neighbours who had flocked to the various embassies had been turned away.

The Reinhardts had disembarked at Harwich early that morning and travelled to London by train. They'd asked Laura and James Allingham to let them stay until they could find suitable lodgings, and to provide the guarantees for their keep that had been a further requirement for their visas.

'My husband Jurgen has taken our luggage to Kew. I came

straight here in a taxicab from the station. Harriet Griffin wrote to say you had given Gilda a home, that you have been very kind to her and she is happy, for which I thank you with all my heart. But now we are here,' said Kirsten.

Louella stood silent and stunned. She had thought Gilda was hers for ever, a child on whom she could bestow all the wasted maternal instincts she had suppressed for so long. Now this pale, correct young woman was here to smash the illusion. Gilda would go away in a taxi to Kew and, sooner or later, across the sea to America.

You can't take her away from me. I won't let her go!

But Kirsten Reinhardt was the real mother, with all the rights and entitlements that nature had denied to Louella Ramsay, and in the end there was no help for it. Gilda had to be given back.

34

'I'm so sorry, Aunt Louella, I really am.' Harriet, sitting in Louella's elegant drawing room, wished herself anywhere else at that moment. She could hardly bear to look at her aunt, who seemed to have aged ten years overnight. 'If I'd known what was going to happen, I'd never have brought Gilda here.'

'You weren't to know. It's my luck. Anything I get attached to, I'm fated to lose. How does that poem go? "*I never loved a tree or flower but 'twas the first to fade away*". At least Gilda isn't dead. She's happily united with her parents, who have been lucky enough to get to safety. They can't help it that their gain is my loss.'

Harriet looked down at her hands. There was something she had to ask, and she was dreading it.

'I don't suppose you'd consider taking another child . . . ?'

'No!'

It was the answer she had been expecting, but the force behind her aunt's exclamation took Harriet by surprise. Louella had stood up and was pacing up and down in front of the fireplace: three steps each way, then an abrupt turn.

'I couldn't bear it, if I had to go through all this again. I couldn't bear it.'

'Hardly any of the children's parents do manage to rejoin them,' Harriet said, making one last attempt on behalf of the unknown children on the list in her coat pocket.

'*No*. And you've no right to ask.'

When Harriet had gone, Louella gave way to her own weariness and collapsed onto the sofa. Rose found her there an hour later, when she came in to close the shutters over the long windows.

'Are you feeling all right, madam?'

'Perfectly, thank you, Rose,' Louella lied. 'Just a bit tired.'

'Cook asked me to find out what you fancied for supper, madam.'

'I don't want any supper.'

'Oh, madam, you must eat.' Rose's forehead creased with concern. 'You hardly touched your lunch. And it was the same yesterday. You're getting ever so thin.'

'Stop nannying me, Rose.'

'. . . But it's true, she's not eating enough,' Rose told Cook in the kitchen. 'I think it's on account of missing that little girl. Fair broke her heart, it did, when Gilda went away. Madam was ever so attached to her.'

In the drawing room Louella levered herself up off the sofa, then put a hand to her lower back and grimaced. It was here again, that sharp, nagging pain, like a corkscrew being turned in her spinal column. She'd had it for weeks now, intermittently, but it was getting more regular and more noticeable. She'd meant to ask her doctor about it, but her days had been so filled with the delightful business of getting to know Gilda that she'd postponed such a mundane activity. She'd lost some weight, too – not that it had seemed a cause for complaint at first, but lately it was getting ridiculous. Rose was right. She did look thin. She would telephone from the study.

She had reached the door of the drawing room when she found she could go no further. Clinging to the edge of the table that stood beside the door, she managed to tug at the bell-pull which hung there. A few moments later, Everett arrived and at the sight of her his normally urbane expression echoed Rose's earlier concern.

'Madam? Are you unwell?'

'I seem to be,' said Louella faintly. 'Send for the doctor, will you, Everett?'

Dr Saunders took her temperature and her blood pressure, pulled down her lower eyelids, told her to stick out her tongue and then proceeded to poke her back and stomach in a most painful way.

'I think it might be best if you went into hospital, Mrs Ramsay.'

'Hospital? What for? I daresay I've just eaten something that disagrees with me.'

'I think not. According to your maid, whom I spoke to just now, you've hardly eaten anything for days. Loss of appetite, severe weight loss over a very short period, back pain, general malaise . . . it's probably nothing, but I think we should have a little exploratory operation, just to be on the safe side.'

When Louella drifted back to consciousness the surgeon who had operated on her was standing beside her bed; a short, round-shouldered Scotsman with watery green eyes. Every visible inch of him was freckled; there were even freckles on the pink dome of his skull, glimpsed among the sparse strands of ginger hair. Earlier, as the ether had begun to take effect, his face had hovered above her and under the anaesthetic she dreamt that he had turned into a leopard – a rather benign, apologetic leopard in a jungle that was as bright and crude as a child's drawing.

'Well, Mr Maclean, what ghastly discoveries did you make on slicing me open?'

He had described the proposed operation, beforehand, as 'Just a wee investigation, nothing drastic, Mrs Ramsay.' But there was no lightness in his reply.

'We found cancer of the body of the pancreas.'

Cancer. Her first husband's mother had died of cancer. Louella had a chilling recall of the old woman's long decline into helplessness, the dogged endurance of months of unremitting pain. But surely, she reminded herself, rallying her courage, medicine had made advances since those days before the Great War?

'So what's the treatment?' she asked. 'Another operation?'

Mr Maclean didn't answer. As the silence lengthened,

Louella guessed what it was that he didn't want to tell her.

'I take it there *is* no treatment. It's incurable, isn't it?'

'By this stage . . .' He spread his hands.

'But I only began to feel unwell a few weeks ago. It didn't seem serious.'

'Unfortunately, that's the nature of this particular version of the disease. We don't really know much about it. The symptoms manifest themselves very late, by which time . . .' His voice tailed away again.

'How long have I got?'

'It's difficult to say.' Maclean's eyes were still avoiding Louella's. It was the part of his job that he hated most, this telling of bad news.

'You must have *some* idea. I need to know,' Louella said sharply. 'I have responsibilities. Come on. Make an informed guess. I won't hold you to it if you're slightly out. A year? Six months? A fortnight?'

'Two months,' the surgeon said, tiredly. 'Perhaps three.'

Louella discharged herself from hospital as soon as she was able to stand.

'I wouldn't advise it,' said the ward sister.

'If I'm going to die,' Louella told her, 'I may as well do so on my own premises, away from the smell of boiled cabbage and disinfectant.'

The sister pursed her lips. 'You'll need full-time nursing care,' she warned.

'I'll hire a private nurse,' Louella said, and went home to Blackheath.

Everett, alerted of her impending arrival by a telephone call from the hospital, was watching out of the drawing-room window for the taxi. As Louella emerged from the black cab, he hurried down the steps to meet her.

'Madam, may I say how good it is to have you home again.'

'Liar,' said Louella, tartly. 'I've no doubt the staff have been making hay ever since I went into hospital. Don't worry,' she added, with the ghost of a smile. 'On this occasion I shan't be checking the levels in the decanters.'

'*Madam,*' Everett protested, pained. Louella moved past him towards the three stone steps which led up to the front door. As she did so she seemed to stumble, putting a hand out for the iron railing and not quite reaching it.

Instinctively, Everett caught hold of her arm and then put his other hand under her elbow to support her, with the fleeting realization that this was the first time, in all his years as Mrs Ramsay's butler, that he had made any physical contact with her. It seemed a presumption and he half expected her to shrug him off, with one of the imperious gestures that had always put him in his place before. Instead, her other hand clung to his arm as if she was drowning.

It was only a few seconds before she regained her balance; but in that time Everett registered that in the two weeks she had been away, Madam's flesh had peeled from her. She had been thin before, but now her frame was almost skeletal. The hand that gripped his forearm was like a claw and all the bones of her face seemed sharper under a shrunken skin. Suddenly he felt sick with foreboding.

'Shall I tell Rose to bring you some tea, Madam?' he asked her in the hall.

'Later,' said Louella. She went into the study and Everett heard the key turn in the door.

'Michael?'

'Louella?' At the other end of the telephone line, Michael Pritchard's pleasure was unmistakeable. 'How lovely to hear from you.'

'Will you come and see me? Tonight?'

'Tonight?' he echoed, surprised. 'It's rather late. I'm not sure if the trains—'

'At this moment,' Louella said, 'I need a friend rather badly. I wouldn't ask if it wasn't important.'

There was a silence, then he said, 'I'm on my way.'

It was almost midnight when Michael Pritchard rang the doorbell at Medlar House.

'Madam has retired to bed,' said Everett, when he opened the door. 'But she left instructions that you should be shown up to her room as soon as you arrived.'

Michael hesitated. It was more than a year since he had told Louella that they had no future together, but the old, pointless longing was still there and he felt an instinctive backing away from the thought of seeing her in bed, so total an embodiment of everything he wanted and could never have.

'It *is* awfully late. Perhaps I should just go to a hotel and call again tomorrow?' he said, trying not to think about the trouble that might arise from his non-appearance at the Brownlowe factory in the morning.

'I think you should go up, sir,' said Everett. Michael wanted to ask what this urgent summons was all about – if anyone was in the know, it would be Everett – but the butler was already leading the way towards the stairs.

In the high-ceilinged bedroom Louella lay propped against the pillows of her four-poster, a vividly coloured Indian shawl wrapped around her shoulders over a nightdress of ivory satin. She gestured towards a chair at the side of the bed.

'Hullo, Michael. Thank you for coming.'

Michael stood rooted to the spot. He was barely aware of the quiet withdrawal of Everett from the room because he was so taken aback by the sight of her, normally so commanding a presence, now so pallid and so painfully thin. Louella without her inner light. Even the black hair, released from its chignon, was devoid of its usual sheen.

'Yes, I do look frightful. I've been ill,' she said. 'Do sit down, Michael, for heaven's sake,' she added, with a flicker of her old energy.

Michael subsided into the chair, his eyes fixed on her face.

Louella smiled. 'It's so good to see you,' she said, more gently. 'I'm sorry to drag you here at this ungodly hour but I need to ask you a very big favour. Some time ago, I suggested that you should take over the day-to-day running of my business. At the time you said you wouldn't because I was too autocratic. Now I want to ask you to reconsider your decision, because the main obstacle will be removed. It's a good little business, with a good workforce. I don't want it to go down because I can't go on giving it my attention. My niece Harriet should be able to take over as the owner in time, but it'll need the services of a good manager until she's ready. You can name your salary.'

Michael cleared his throat. 'Can I ask why you're giving it up? You say you've been ill.'

Louella's eyes met his. 'I still am. As a matter of fact,' she said quietly, 'I'm going to die quite soon. Would you mind awfully holding my hand, Michael? Just for a bit? I'm feeling rather sorry for myself just now, and I could do with some consolation.'

Hours after Louella had fallen asleep, Michael sat on beside her, still holding her hand, his face stiff, his eyes staring blankly at the wall beyond the bed. At first his mind had refused to accept what it had learned. Now that it had, he was the one in need of 'consolation'.

The next day, Louella dealt with outstanding business.

'Stay and help me please, Michael. There are letters to write and so on.'

'Don't you have a secretary at your dressmaking business who can take care of that?'

'I'd rather have you. Please, Michael. What are friends for?'

'I'd better telephone the Brownlowe factory,' Michael decided, 'and tell them I won't be in for the rest of the week.'

By the time he returned to the bedroom there were papers spread out all over the counterpane of the four-poster and Louella was taking a paper-knife to a stack of unopened letters.'

'Let me do that,' Michael said.

'I'm not a complete invalid yet!' But she relinquished the knife without further argument. He passed the letters over, one at a time, and took notes rapidly at her dictation. For a sick woman, he thought ruefully, her brain was razor sharp. By the end of the morning he was recognizing that he had been right, previously, to refuse the job she had offered him as her manager. She *was* too autocratic. Then, looking up from his notepad, he saw her eyes resting on him and was reminded all over again of how much he loved her, and how much he was soon to lose.

Dr Saunders had recommended a nurse and Louella engaged her on the strength of this and on her references. But when Nurse Cotton arrived, Louella disliked her on sight – her bulk, her busyness, her moustache, her cheap cologne. Within a day the patient felt like screaming at the woman's habit of referring to her by a collective noun.

'How are we feeling this morning? It's time for our injection. Now, now, Mrs R, we mustn't get excited . . .'

'I have so little time left in which to get excited,' Louella retorted waspishly. 'Can't I be allowed to make the most of it?'

She thought of sending the nurse packing and hiring another, then discovered that she hadn't got the energy. Nurse Cotton became part of the household. All too soon there were other things that Louella wanted to scream about.

'Should I inform your family and friends of your illness, madam, now that you are back from the hospital?'

'No thank you, Everett. They would feel obliged to make visits to enquire after my health, and I don't feel in the mood for visitors. Sitting there wondering what to say. So tedious. Do go away, nurse.'

Nurse Cotton had come in with the box which held the materials for the patient's morphine dose. She set it down on the table beside the bed and began to sort out swabs of cotton wool. Everett took her arrival as a signal to leave the room.

'Oh, damn, I wanted to talk to him,' said Louella. 'Call him back.'

Ignoring her, Nurse Cotton tilted surgical spirit from a

bottle on to a swab and lifted Louella's arm. 'I'll just get this done, then we can call him.'

'No. Don't give me that injection yet. Once you have, I shan't be able to think clearly.'

The nurse scrubbed deftly at the spot on Louella's arm where she proposed to inject the dose. She inserted the needle into the morphine ampoule and drew back the plunger on the syringe, sucking the cloudy liquid up into the glass cylinder.

'Did you hear me, nurse? I want to talk to Everett.'

'In a minute.' Nurse Cotton advanced on her patient with the needle in her hand.

'*Now*.' With all her strength, Louella struck sideways at the syringe, knocking it from the nurse's hand. It flew across the room and shattered against the skirting board. Nurse Cotton said a rude word.

'*Everett*,' repeated Louella, faint but insistent by now.

'How are you feeling, madam?' said Everett, when a sulky Nurse Cotton brought him into the bedroom a few minutes later.

'I believe the phrase is "As well as can be expected." Dying is such a boring process. Quite apart from the discomfort,' Louella whispered. The struggle to get her own way had exhausted her. 'Go away, nurse. I want to talk privately.'

Nurse Cotton grimaced expressively at Everett and left the room. Louella waved the butler towards the bedside chair. She tried to concentrate on what had seemed important a few minutes ago but was now competing with the more strident clamourings of her body. The morphine injections were spaced to keep pain at a bearable level – but only just – and she had needed the contents of the broken syringe rather badly.

'Everett, you have been with me for a long time. I think we have come to respect one another.'

'Oh, yes, madam.'

'You know me. Perhaps better than any other living person.'

When he thought about it, Everett realized the statement was probably true.

'I'm not a patient woman, Everett. I never have been.'

'No, madam,' the butler agreed.

'This waiting for Death to come and fetch me is a difficult thing to bear. I would rather go to meet him instead, on my own terms. Can you understand that?'

Everett hesitated, unsure what was expected of him.

Louella's voice took on an edge of urgency. 'I've tried to think of ways. But I'm too weak. I've waited too long, I can't do it on my own. That fool Cotton could help me – increase the morphine dose so that it finishes me off. But she won't. Hardly surprising. She doesn't owe me anything . . . not loyalty, not affection.' Louella closed her eyes for a moment because the effort of talking so much was intensifying the pain.

'She'd be in trouble, madam, if she did give you too much at a time,' Everett pointed out.

'Who'd know? I'm dying anyway. Today, next week, what's the difference? Will you help me, Everett? An injection, one or two of those ampoules that damned nurse keeps in the box. Or something I can drink down. Rat poison, anything. If it hurts for a bit I won't mind. At least it'd be quicker than this.'

The butler looked down at his linked hands, his face pink and uneasy. 'I can't, madam,' he said at last. 'I'd do anything else for you. Anything in my power. But not that. I just *can't*.'

'All right,' he heard her say resignedly. 'It was a lot to ask. Send in that stupid Cotton with her magic box, will you? No, one more thing. You remember that young man who comes here sometimes – the one you don't approve of? Dark-haired, scruffy, rather sinister?'

'I know the one you mean,' Everett agreed cautiously.

'I want to see him. Arrange it, will you?'

'Yes, madam. I'll do my best to find him.' As the butler stood up, the light from the window glittered for a moment on an unaccustomed moisture in the hollows under his eyes. Louella watched him plod towards the door.

'Everett,' she murmured ironically, too low for him to hear, 'I do believe I've made you cry. I never knew you cared.'

Louella's request that Jem should be contacted was easier said than done. Everett sent a letter to the address Madam had written to in the past, left messages in various places and even took himself down to the seedy area on the other side of the river where the man was supposed to live. Nobody admitted to knowing where Jem might be, though a few muttered that if they did, they'd got a score or two to settle with him themselves.

'The word is out there's someone wants to see you urgently, Wilkins,' said one of Jem's fellow prisoners in the exercise yard. 'A woman name of Ramsay. I heard it from a geezer who came in yesterday.'

Jem shrugged. 'She'll have to wait, won't she?' he said. His date of release was just a week away. 'For the time being, I'm not at liberty to answer her summons.'

'Out you go, then, Wilkins. And don't let's see you back.'

'Oh, officer . . . that's a hardhearted thing to say, when I've enjoyed my stay so much. I'm going to miss the old place. And I'd have thought you were going to miss me, too.'

'Very funny, Wilkins.'

The iron-studded door in the prison wall swung open. Jem stepped through, heard it locked and bolted behind him. He stood in the street outside, considering what to do next. There was always Louella's summons. But first, there was something more important to see to, some unfinished business.

He caught the train down to Bentley and walked through the lanes towards the farm. Harriet Griffin. He'd brought her to the boil last time he saw her, he knew it. She'd been ready to give in to him, and if he'd turned up at the bonfire

547

as arranged, that's what she would have done that very night, in some shed or stable. But that bastard Rupert Brownlowe had ruined everything. As a result, Jem had had to postpone the moment of taking Harriet for two years. From his memory of the time he'd kissed her at Starling Cottages and the way she'd caught fire in his arms, just for a moment or two, in the wheatfield, she'd be worth the wait.

'Harriet isn't here,' said Allie Briggs, planted foursquare in the kitchen doorway at Welcome Farm.

'Where is she?'

'London, I think.'

Jem swore.

'That's hardly the language to use in front of a lady,' Allie told him tartly.

'Where in London? Do you have an address?'

'No, I don't. And if I did, I wouldn't give it to you,' said Allie. 'I wouldn't help you to any woman, let alone our Harriet. Not after the way you treated poor Kitty.'

'Where's Will Griffin?'

'Away at a farm sale. Him and Mrs Griffin. All day, I shouldn't wonder,' said Allie. 'If you want to speak to him you'll have to come back tomorrow.'

Yes, it was all Rupert Brownlowe's fault. Jem felt a need to do something swift and very damaging to pay him back. He went down to the Red Lion at Bentley and along with his pint of beer, cadged a sheet of writing paper, an envelope and a stamp from the landlady.

'*Dear Mrs Brownlowe,*' he wrote. '*I think you should ask your husband what he does at Number 23, Hatton Street, Greenwich, with a woman called Maudie.*'

He signed it, '*A well-wisher.*'

He'd had the information for years and Louella had shown no inclination to use it. He could try to blackmail old Brownlowe, but that was a bit risky, so soon after this latest prison stretch. No, what he was doing would be enough for now. It would humiliate the old bastard and sour his domestic arrangements.

He posted the letter in the pillar box near the pub. Tomorrow he'd come back to extract Harriet's address from her parents, somehow. Or maybe, he corrected himself, he'd have to do that next week. Buying the beer had reminded him that his finances were at rock bottom. The first priority must be to earn some money.

Marion read the letter at the breakfast table, then passed it to Rupert. 'An anonymous letter. Do you know what it's all about?'

Rupert didn't answer. After his first sight of the contents, he let the letter flutter to the floor. He leaned forward, both hands gripping the edge of the table, knuckles white.

'Rupert?' Marion was beginning to be alarmed by his expression and the hoarse, whistling intake of his breath. His eyes goggled back at her from a complexion patched with red and white, the veins in his forehead standing out. His mouth worked but no sound came. Gradually, as he tilted further forward, the tablecloth that he was clutching began to slide, bringing the whole paraphernalia of breakfast crockery crashing to the floor.

'A massive stroke. Doctor Hawkins said Rupert's blood pressure has been causing him concern for some time. He said the shock of reading the letter must have precipitated the crisis. It's all my fault,' Marion told Laura that evening, when her stepdaughter had arrived in haste by train from London. 'Whoever sent that letter obviously did so with the intention of causing trouble. I should have known better than to ask Rupert for an explanation. Your poor father. Now he's in bed and paralysed all down one side of his body. He can't talk. He can't even sit up, and there's no knowing how long he'll be like that, or even if he'll recover at all.'

'You mustn't blame yourself, Marion,' Laura told her. 'Of course it's not your fault. Pa's always been an irascible sort, it's probably only your calming influence that's kept him from bursting a blood vessel long before now. What was in the letter that set him off?'

'Something about asking a woman what your father does with her in London.'

'Oh.' Laura pulled a face. 'Sounds rather improper . . . but I wouldn't have thought Pa had it in him to do anything too naughty nowadays. What *exactly* did it say?'

Marion concentrated, closing her eyes. 'That I should ask my husband what he gets up to with someone called Maudie at 23, Hatton Gardens . . . no, it was Hatton *Street*, Greenwich,' she recited. 'That was it.'

'Do you know what it means?' Laura asked.

'No,' Marion said. 'I asked Rupert, but by then he was having his attack . . .'

'Perhaps, as we can't ask Pa, we should ask this Maudie.'

Maudie's minder, leaning against his lamp-post with his coat collar turned up against the mid-November chill, was intrigued by the sight of the two women marching along Hatton Street. One was about Maudie's age, one somewhat younger, both recognizable from their garb as ladies. Eyeing them curiously, he was taken aback when they stopped at Number Twenty-three and tugged at the bell-pull. By the time he arrived to investigate, Maudie had appeared at the door and after a brief exchange of words with the two women, had allowed them to walk past her.

'You all right, Maudie?' he asked.

'I dunno. I don't think they're going to bash me up, though. If I need you I'll scream.'

She shut the door.

'These last few visits he hasn't wanted much,' she told Marion, when she knew what had prompted the visit. The questioning which followed turned out to be a surprisingly civilized process. Rupert's wife didn't seem a bad sort at all; not outraged or jealous or pointing the finger of blame.

'He hadn't been for a while and when he did turn up again, he seemed a bit lost, poor soul. Didn't want what you'd expect, he just wanted to be tucked up in bed like he was a little boy. I gave him my lucky teddy bear to cuddle.' She pointed to a threadbare stuffed toy propped up against the water carafe on the cane bedside table. 'Then I read to him from an old story book he'd brought with him: Beatrix Potter's *Tale of Tom Kitten*. He went off to sleep, sucking his thumb. An hour or two later I woke him up and he paid me and toddled off home. That's all. Sounds a bit silly, doesn't it? I felt sorry for him, really.

'Mind you,' she added, facing Marion squarely, 'it's not my normal line of work, no use pretending it is. And I won't try to kid you that's all there's ever been between him and me. We go back a long way, Rupert and me, I've known him even before the Great War. He was quite a young man then and as virile as any of them. And first off, his wife wasn't the physical sort, and then she was dead. But it's not been like that between us for a long time. More like friends really, and then more like I was his nanny or something. Come to think of it, he even calls me "Nana" sometimes . . .'

'I see,' said Marion, quietly.

'Don't suppose he'll be coming any more, now you know about our little arrangement.'

'I don't think he can,' Marion said. 'Not that I'd want to deny him his bit of comfort, but you see, he's had a stroke and he's paralysed and can't really say what he wants. And he wouldn't be able to get here, even if he wanted to.'

'Poor old Rupert,' said Maudie.

Marion took her purse out of her bag and extracted some folded banknotes. 'Here,' she said. 'I think he'd want you to have this. A kind of parting present. I'm sorry it's not much, but we are a little financially embarrassed at present, what with his illness and everything.'

Beside her, Laura was staring, open-mouthed. Marion ignored her stepdaughter's consternation.

Maudie took the notes uncertainly. 'Well, thank you,' she said, holding them gingerly between her fingers. 'You're a proper lady,' she added. 'I'm sure I don't know why Rupert came to me, with a wife like you at home.'

'I expect he had his reasons,' said Marion. 'Thank you for being kind to him,' she added, at the door.

'Why on earth did you give her that money?' Laura exploded, at the end of the street. 'That awful woman!'

'I didn't think she was so awful. She seemed rather a generous soul, really. Poor Rupert. I'm glad she gave him what he wanted. I suppose I have rather shut him out. Anyway, it's all done with now,' she sighed. 'But I wonder who sent that letter and why?'

Michael Pritchard had resigned from his job as manager of the lawn-mower factory. It was just another nail in the coffin, as far as Marion was concerned. A sick, helpless husband with a guilty secret, a ruined business with no manager, no money . . . and hard on the heels of the visit to Greenwich, she discovered that Rupert was even more heavily in debt than she had realized. To finance the updating at the factory, he'd mortgaged the house . . . and the woman from whom he'd borrowed the money had now written to call in the debt.

'Who is this Louella Ramsay?' she asked the foreman at the factory, when she had read the letter.

'A widow who lives in Blackheath. She'd been here a few times.'

'What kind of woman is she?'

'I can't really say, Mrs Brownlowe. Pritchard, our manager, seemed to get on with her.'

Marion squared her shoulders. She was forming the resolution that she must go to London and see the unknown Mrs Ramsay; throw herself and Rupert on her mercy. If the loan was called in, they would be homeless.

It was disconcerting to hear that the person to whom she had to make her appeal was seriously ill. The butler, looming large in the doorway of the smart Georgian house, seemed disinclined even to take a message up to his mistress.

'Please . . . I must see her, if it's at all possible. It's terribly important,' Marion pleaded.

'Well . . .' Something desperate in her face moved Everett in spite of himself. 'Madam is having her injection at present. When she's comfortable again, I'll ask her if she feels up to seeing you.'

Marion waited in the drawing room, offering silent prayers to any saint that might be inclined to pay attention, that they would intercede on her behalf and move the owner of the house to give her a hearing. At last Everett reappeared.

'It will have to be very quick. And you must say nothing to excite her, or I shall have to ask you to leave immediately.'

These days Louella after her morphine injection was hard to excite. She was able, however, to summon up a flicker of curiosity as to why Marion Brownlowe had come to see her. Probably it was on account of the letter about the loan that Michael had sent on her instructions. Shouldn't Brownlowe have come himself to discuss the matter?

It would have afforded her a sweet moment of revenge to have him begging her for money, even all these years after the cruel interview at his house so long ago that had launched her hatred of him. And even in her current state she might have savoured it. Instead here was Marion Brownlowe, a decent woman, telling her in a halting voice about Rupert's stroke, his desperate condition and, if Louella insisted on the immediate repayment of her money, their impending homelessness.

'He's in a wheelchair. He can't walk or talk or feed himself,' Marion said. 'If we have to move out of Maple Grange now I don't know where we'll go or how we'll live.'

'What do you propose I should do about it?' whispered the wasted voice of the sick woman in the four-poster bed.

'I was hoping you might defer the repayment for a bit longer. Give me a chance to work something out . . . see what I can sell . . .'

'From what I've heard there's not much left to sell.'

Marion bowed her head, conscious that her appeal had failed. She rose to go, shoulders slumped in defeat.

'Goodbye. I will think about what you have told me,' said Mrs Ramsay.

Marion went home to Rupert, who could not be told where she had been today because in his impotent state it would only upset him further. She lay awake all night trying to think of ways and means to fend off the loss of Maple Grange. Could Laura and James help? Could Tom be asked to lend his modest little fortune? No, how could she beg of relatives? And none of them were rich enough, anyway, to part lightly with the sum that Rupert owed to Mrs Ramsay.

In the morning an envelope was delivered. Opened, it proved to contain the contract for the loan. Across it in red ink was stamped the single word, *Cancelled*.

A month after Louella had first sent Everett in search of Jem, the doorbell at Medlar House pealed and when the butler opened the door, the man he had been trying to locate stood on the doorstep.

In that month, Louella had gone downhill. Nowadays Nurse Cotton sat in a corner of the room all day, knitting stolidly at squares of wool which would one day become a patchwork bedspread. At night, either Rose or Alice would stand in. The household was waiting.

In the hall, Everett explained to Jem that Madam was seriously ill, his natural distrust of the visitor warring with his awareness that his mistress had asked every day if Wilkins had been traced yet.

When Jem was ushered into the room he saw at once that 'seriously' had been an understatement. He was surprised to find how much he minded the discovery.

'Hullo, Lou.'

'Jem.' There was a momentary flicker of animation in Louella's dark-rimmed eyes. The butler hovered uncertainly in the background.

'You can go now, Everett. And you, Rose. I want a word in private with Mr Wilkins.'

It was more than she had said for days.

'You can come back in an hour. Not before. Promise me, Everett.'

He wanted to ask why, but it went against all his training and the habit of years. As a butler he took orders unquestioningly; suppressing his misgivings when necessary, because what his employer wanted, it was his duty to provide. He had broken the habit only once, when Mrs Ramsay had asked him to help her to die and he had refused. That had been hard enough.

Still he hesitated. At the back of his mind he already knew why she wanted to be left alone with Jem Wilkins.

'Everett, I would like to say goodbye in private to my brother.'

For a moment the shock that Everett felt was recorded on his face, then he replaced it with his normal bland expression.

'Yes, madam.'

'D'you know, that's the first time you've ever acknowledged me in front of a witness,' said Jem, after the manservant had gone. 'Up till now you've always behaved like I was some kind of garbage which that Everett character of yours had accidentally brought in on his boots. What's got into you, Lou?'

'I expect I'm tired of pretence,' said Louella, in her faint but still animated voice. 'And besides, you deserve some kind of acknowledgement, in return for what you are about to do for me.'

'Oh yes? And what's that?'

'Take a pillow and smother me. Give me the *coup de grâce*.'

Jem stood looking down at her.

'Why should I? What have you ever done for me? I mean, that was really for me and not just to fit in with your schemes?'

'Nothing. I'm not asking because I deserve your help, Jem, I'm asking because I need it. Think how superior it would make you feel, to grant me this last wish.'

Everett came up the stairs from the staff quarters when he heard Jem walking down from Madam's bedroom.

'She said don't go in for an hour,' Jem reminded him.

'Is she all right?'

'That's a daft question, isn't it? For a woman as far gone

555

as she is?' Jem's tone was mocking, but his expression was strained.

'Perhaps I'd better take a look . . .' Everett hazarded.

The visitor shrugged. 'Please yourself. She said an hour. Lou always did like her own way. Even in her condition, I wouldn't put it past her to throw the water jug at you if you disturb her before she said you could. Well, I'm off. See you some time.'

He pushed past the butler and disappeared.

Against every instinct, Everett waited for the full hour before he climbed the stairs to Mrs Ramsay's bedroom. When he did, he found what he expected.

'A little sooner than I thought,' said the doctor, as he signed the death certificate. 'Still, it's just as well. A merciful release.'

'I guessed what she intended that Wilkins character to do, and I didn't stop it,' Everett confessed to Rose afterwards, below stairs. 'I mean, I don't know exactly how he saw her off without leaving signs, but I just know in my bones that he did it. Do you think that makes me an accessory to murder?'

'I think,' said Rose, 'the way Madam was feeling, she might say it makes you a friend.'

35

The threshing machine was painted a dull shade of pink, with the name of its makers, 'Ransome', stencilled on the wooden side in large black lettering. It arrived at Welcome Farm in February, towed by a tractor belching black smoke, and was manoeuvred into position beside the wheatstraw rick in the field behind the house.

'I was expecting you yesterday. Where were you?' asked Will Griffin of the driver of the tractor.

'Sorry,' the man said, climbing down from the high seat. 'The last job took longer than I thought. We're short-handed, you see – matter of fact, there's just me and Arthur – he'll be along on his bike any minute. The other two of my team are off sick with the influenza. I hope you've got plenty of workers who can give a hand.'

'I haven't,' said Will, dismayed. 'There's just Rob and me and Billy.'

The threshing contractor surveyed the workforce gloomily. Already he had taken in that Will, limping forward to open the field gate, was less than fully fit. Now he saw that Billy, too, was disabled.

'Well, we'll just have to do the best we can,' he observed without emotion. 'Mind you, I can only stay the one day, same as you booked me for. I've got a list of customers as long as your arm waiting. Seems like everyone's run short of wheat and straw at the same time this year.'

Already Will knew that they wouldn't finish the rick in one day. Not with just the two threshing men and the small contingent from Welcome Farm. *And Billy and me, we just add up to one able-bodied man between us*, he told himself despairingly. After today, he'd have to join the tail end of the queue again for the thresher's time. Would such wheat as they could deal with today see him through the waiting time?

Burgess, the owner of the threshing combine, had decided that the most efficient disposition of the less-than-satisfactory workforce would be to have Will on the tractor; himself and Rob tossing the wheatsheaves from the rick to the top of the thresher; Arthur in charge of the baler operations; and Billy on top of the thresher, cutting the twine from the sheaves and shaking them out to feed into the long, narrow gap between the rotating beater bars of the machine and the concave cage that covered them.

Early on it became obvious that Billy wasn't fast enough for his share of the operation. He had to hold each sheaf clamped between his knees to cut the twine, then transfer the baler knife from his belt to his one hand to slice upwards through the twine. The effort of holding the sheaf firmly while he did so was exhausting. Sometimes he could be seen sawing rather than slicing at the twine.

Will had never thought the day would dawn when he'd be glad to see Jem Wilkins again.

Jem came through the gate and sauntered up to the steam-driven tractor. The noise of the tractor, the thrumming of the drive belt that ran between it and the threshing machine, and the clanking and rattling of the revolving drum in the thresher made communication almost impossible.

Will craned down from the tractor. 'What do you want?'

Jem cupped his hands over his mouth. 'I've come about Harriet.'

'She isn't here,' Will bellowed in response.

'I know that. Where is she?'

'I can't go into that now. You can see we're busy – and short-handed.' Will gestured towards the stack of wheat straw and the vast, pink-painted wooden bulk of the thresher.

'Where is she?' repeated Jem.

Will shut off the engine. In the sudden silence Rob and Burgess, who had stopped tossing bundles of wheat from the top of the rick to Billy on the thresher, turned mutely enquiring faces towards the tractor.

'Look,' said Will, exasperated and resigned. 'You certainly picked your moment. We're threshing, for God's sake. I've only got the machine booked for a day and two of the crew are off sick.'

'I'll help,' Jem said. 'A day's work in exchange for your daughter's address.'

Will hesitated. Any other time, he'd have told Wilkins what he could do with such an offer, but at this moment a day's work from an able-bodied young man like Jem would be a godsend. 'I can't do that,' he said, reluctantly. 'How do I know she'd want to talk to you?'

'Let her decide that for herself. Just tell me where I can find her,' said Jem.

'This is hopeless,' said Will. 'We're threshing. Come back another day and we'll talk.'

'No. Tell me now.'

'Look,' said Will, with something like desperation. 'The best I can offer is to contact her tonight and tell her you're looking for her. Then if she agrees to talk to you, I'll put you in touch. Will that do? For a day's work,' he remembered to add.

For answer, Jem peeled off his jacket. 'Where d'you want me? Throwing up the wheat or on top of the thresher?'

'On the thresher,' said Will, postponing all moral considerations for a later occasion. 'You cut the bales and pass them to Billy, he can shake them out.'

'Oh, Christ,' said Jem audibly, as he climbed the wooden ladder on the side of the threshing machine to join Billy on top. 'Nobody warned me I'd be working with a cripple.'

Jem was in a foul mood. The long-anticipated meeting with Harriet Griffin seemed to get endlessly postponed and, on top of that, he was still feeling churned up inside about Louella. She was dead, with the help from him that she'd wanted, and she had thanked him in advance for that help with a touching show of sisterly regard. For the few minutes before he'd done what she asked, they'd had quite a friendly

conversation, with none of the mistress-and-servant over-
tones that she'd adopted in previous interviews. It was
long overdue, but now there wouldn't be any more of it,
not to mention the drying-up of the occasional well-paid
commissions she'd put his way in the past.

That wasn't the main point, though. It was that she'd been
his last living relation and now there was nobody. It was a
thought to make him feel bad inside and long ago, Jem had
learned that when he felt bad, the best antidote was to make
someone else feel worse.

Billy knew he wasn't as quick as a man with two hands, but
he'd been doing his best. Now he was spared one half of an
exhausting job, but in return he had to deal with having Jem
beside him – Jem, who was young and fit and contemptuous,
and who sliced the twine and passed the sheaves at a pace
that left Billy fumbling desperately. Inevitably, instead of
shaking the armfuls of straw out evenly, he would drop
an armful from time to time, and the narrow gap between
the beater bars on the drum and the cage became clogged.
Then his tormentor would signal to Will to stop the tractor
and take up an exaggeratedly patient stance while Billy
struggled to clear the stoppage. All too often, it involved
stopping the tractor and removing the cage to get at the
drum.

At midday Daisy brought out tea, and bread and cheese
in a covered basket for the workers and, reluctantly, Will
suspended operations.

'How's it going?' she said. Jem jumped down from the
top of the thresher, landed with the agility of a cat and
strolled towards the food basket. Daisy raised her eyebrows
at Will.

'He turned up,' Will told her, 'and said he'd help. And
we're that short-handed that I wasn't going to argue.'

'Do you think you'll get finished in time?'

'I doubt it. But we've got a better chance with an extra
hand.'

'The drum's jammed again.' Jem arrived beside them.

560

Ignoring Daisy, he addressed only Will. 'I was about to signal you to switch off anyway.'

Behind him, Billy climbed down the wooden ladder fixed to the side of the threshing machine. Jem jerked his thumb back towards Billy.

'The cripple's a liability. He can't shake the straw out fast enough and he drops it more often than he spreads it right. Of course with that narrow slit between the cage and the drum it jams. It'd be easier to work if we left the cage off all the time.'

'That cage is on for safety reasons,' Will said.

Jem shrugged. 'Suit yourself. You're the one with the problem. I'm only saying that's one way to solve it.' He helped himself to tea and food from the basket and took it away to eat at a distance.

Jem finished his dinner first and climbed back up on top of the Ransome machine. Out of sight of the rest of the crew below, he bent and quickly removed the guard cage, lifting it clear just as Billy joined him again.

'Have you got it freed up yet?'

'Just about.' Quickly, Jem cleared the jammed stalks of straw from the beater bars. He grinned at Billy. 'Well, that's done it – for a few minutes until you muck it up again, that is.'

Billy didn't answer.

'I reckon we should leave the guard off,' Jem said. 'We can work quicker that way.'

'Will said not to. He said it's there for safety.'

'What Will can't see won't hurt him. It'll be all right if we're careful. Or are you scared?'

Silently, Billy took up his place. Jem interpreted that as his assent to working without the guard. Below them on either side, Will was climbing on to the tractor and the others back to their positions on the rick and beside the baler.

'How's Kitty, by the way?' Jem asked. 'I must say I admire your stamina – a one-armed little runt like you taking on a goer like her . . . leastways, as I remember, she couldn't get enough of it. Took all my energy to keep her satisfied. Pass me that knife, will you?'

Billy swallowed. He avoided Jem's taunting stare, but his grip tightened on the curved baler knife that he held.

Jem, who missed very little, saw the involuntary reaction and laughed softly. 'Fancy taking me on with the knife, do you? You poor little sod, you wouldn't stand a chance. You'd be dead in a minute, as dead as that old dog of yours . . .'

That remark brought Billy's head up. He faced Jem, breathing quickly. 'What did you say about my dog?'

Will switched on the tractor and the long canvas drive belt started to revolve on its pins. Behind Jem, the drum of the thresher rolled, gathering speed as the motion of the drive belt quickened.

'Your dead dog?' Jem's voice was inaudible, drowned out by the noise of the tractor, but Billy could read his lips well enough. 'Where'd you bury her, Marshall? Must've been quite a job for a cripple, even to scoop out a shallow grave for a scrawny scrap of a thing like that.'

'How'd you know about Sally?' asked Billy, his face distorted with emotion.

'How d'you think I know?'

Jem, still trying to forget about Louella and lost opportunities, strung up tight because after all the long months of anticipation he still had no idea when he would be seeing Harriet, had gone too far and offered one taunt too many. Tried beyond endurance, Billy lunged at him with the baler knife. Jem laughed and easily swayed out of reach of the blade; but in doing so, he stepped backwards and lost his balance.

Billy stared and cried out and then ran to the edge of the thresher, gesturing frantically for Will to turn off the tractor. But it was too late. The threshing drum spun on relentlessly and by the time it finally came to a halt, it had battered the life out of Jem Wilkins.

*   *   *

It was after Louella's funeral that Harriet heard from her parents about the death of Jem Wilkins.

'The funny thing is, he was looking for you,' Will told her, as they walked back to Medlar House. 'I said if he'd do a day's work for me on the thresher, I'd contact you and ask if you wanted to see him. I'm sorry, love. I know I shouldn't have done such a thing – why would you want to talk to that man? But I was desperate for an extra hand and I just used whatever leverage I could to get him to help. If I hadn't,' he added sadly, 'I suppose he'd still be alive today – or if he hadn't taken the cage off the beater drum. There'll have to be an inquest, of course.'

Harriet was silent, stunned by the news that Jem was dead. She'd hardly thought about him in the past two years and when she had it was with a sense of relief that fate had saved her from making yet another awful mistake with another awful man. Even so, the finality of knowing that he was gone for good left her with a feeling of having had something wrenched from inside her. It might have been a cancerous growth, but at this moment the sudden, violent removal was hurting like hell.

Louella was buried in the same grave as her husband, Hector Ramsay, and at Daisy's suggestion her name was to be added to his memorial stone: '*And Louella Ramsay, his beloved wife, 1894–1939.*'

At Medlar House, Louella's staff, red-eyed but as efficient as ever, served sherry and fruitcake prior to the reading of the will. Harriet was still thinking about Jem and at first the words from Louella's solicitor went over her head. Then she realized that everyone was looking at her.

There had been bequests to the staff, in token of long and faithful service. There was a present of some jewellery to Gilda Reinhardt, 'For when she grows up', as Louella had expressed it in the codicil. Money gifts for Jackie and Rob, Daisy and Will. A pair of pearl and sapphire earrings for a woman called Anne Armitage, 'With my sincerest love and regret.' A picture of herself in a silver frame for

Michael Pritchard, who left the room in clumsy haste at this announcement, visibly dashing tears from his cheeks.

The bulk of her estate, the house, the dress factory, the money, she left to her niece Harriet, 'In the hope that she will use it more wisely and well than I ever did.'

'She asked me to be her manager,' said Michael Pritchard afterwards. 'Or rather, *your* manager, until you find your feet. Of course, if you'd rather appoint someone else . . . ?'

'No, not at all. I'll be very glad of your help,' said Harriet. 'The thing is, though, I don't really want any of it. Not if it means I have to stop the work I'm doing now.'

'Louella said you were helping to bring Jewish refugees out of Germany and Austria,' said Michael. 'She told me she thought you might use some of the money to sponsor refugees yourself.'

'Of course!' said Harriet. 'I hadn't realized . . . I must get back to the office straightaway and tell Peter.'

She didn't even notice, in her haste to convey the good news, that she had spoken instinctively of telling Peter Morris first and not James or Laura, who nominally ran the show.

The thresher was painted pink. On its wood-planked side, painted in black letters, was the word 'Ransome'.

Billy heard the steady thrumming of the engine which spun the threshing drum around. He saw Jem's mocking expression change as he stepped backwards, lost his balance and fell. Poor Billy relived his own realization of what was happening, saw the beater bars rotating viciously, savaging the flesh of the fallen man's body as it danced helplessly on the spinning surface . . .

'It's all right,' said Kitty. Her arms cradled him. Her cheek was laid against his. Billy, struggling back towards being awake, felt the chill of sweat cooling all over his shaking body.

'I had a nightmare.'

'I know,' said Kitty. 'It's all right,' she repeated.

'I dreamt about Jem.'

'He's dead.'

'I killed him,' Billy said. 'Or as good as. It was my fault.'

'I know.'

'I went for him. I didn't hit him, but I meant to. If he hadn't fallen over onto the drum . . .'

'I know,' said Kitty. 'You talk in your sleep.' There was a silence. Then she said, 'It doesn't matter. It's all right. He can't hurt us any more.'

In the months that had passed since Aunt Louella's death, being rich Miss Griffin hadn't changed Harriet's life much. Because of the long hours at the office in Kew, she still kept her lodgings nearby. Louella's money would sponsor two more children to come to England from Vienna. Harriet wanted it to be more but Peter pointed out that money alone couldn't buy the safety of the refugees. They had to have visas, and the quota imposed by the British government was almost exhausted.

'I can't bear it,' Harriet said, after she and Peter had talked to various government officials in a vain attempt to have the quota relaxed. Now, downcast by failure, they were driving back to Kew in a car borrowed from James for the occasion. 'I feel so helpless,' she admitted.

'So do I, sometimes,' Peter said. 'Tell you what, let's not go straight home. It's a lovely afternoon, let's make the most of it for once and drive out into the country for a bit.'

'Shouldn't we be getting back? There'll be work to do,' Harriet sounded doubtful.

'If there is, I'll stay on late this evening. That way we won't waste this sunshine.'

They crossed the river at Hammersmith and drove down towards Guildford. In time the suburbs gave way to open countryside and Peter turned the car off the main road.

'If the gods are kind, we ought at this moment to come across a charming little country teashop,' he said. Instead, at that moment there was a bang and a hiss and the car began to wobble in its course.

'Damn!' exclaimed Peter. 'Flat tyre.'

They climbed out of the borrowed car and surveyed the deflated wheel. Peter rummaged around in the boot and produced a tool kit. 'I suppose I'd better change the wheel,' he said. 'Stand aside if you please, young lady.'

'Why should you assume,' Harriet demanded, half-joking, 'that you're the only one capable of changing a wheel?'

Peter grinned. 'Are you telling me that you are?'

'Of course.' Harriet spoke with confidence. In her farming days, she had helped Will maintain the Welcome Farm vehicles and machinery.

'Then by all means, go ahead,' said Peter. He sat down on the grass verge at the side of the road and prepared to enjoy the spectacle.

More than a little daunted by the situation in which she had landed herself, Harriet searched among the tools in the kit for a spanner to remove the wheel nuts. Too late she discovered that it was a long time since she'd helped to change a wheel, that her memory of the procedure was sketchy and that in any case, though she had watched on numerous occasions, Will had always seen to the heavier aspects of the job.

To add to her problems, she had dressed in her most ladylike Louella Ramsay creation to impress the officials. The figure-skimming dress which had failed to soften their obdurate hearts was not much good for roadside repairs either.

Fifteen heated minutes later she was still wrestling with a spanner, trying to loosen the last of the nuts which held the wheel in place. Whoever had tightened this one, she told herself with gritted teeth, must have had the biceps of an ape. She was far from being a fragile female; she could hump hay bales about with the best of them. But she couldn't shift this accursed nut. She felt hot and cross and humiliated.

'A longer-handled spanner would give you more leverage. Here.' She looked up, frowning, into the afternoon sunlight. Peter Morris stooped over the box at her feet and selected an alternative tool. When she took it, his hands closed on either side of hers on the handle. His warm breath touched against her face as the nut that had defeated her gave way sweetly to their combined strength. He helped her to tug the wheel free and lay it down beside the car, then lifted the replacement wheel into place.

'Shall I . . . ?'

'Yes, you do it. I admit it, you're the expert and I'm just an incompetent woman.' Trust a man, Harriet thought waspishly, to come along when you are in the middle of something difficult and make it all seem so infuriatingly easy. She stood back and watched him as he squatted on his heels beside the car. Still rattled, she found herself noticing the hairs on the backs of his tanned arms and the tension of the muscles under the rolled-back sleeves of his shirt. His dark hair curled at the back of his neck.

She'd been here before, at this moment of heightened awareness of a man . . . and on those previous occasions it had ended in disaster. Dismayed, she backed away.

'There. All finished.' Peter tossed the spanner into the toolbox and stood up.

'Thank you,' Harriet muttered.

'What's the matter? You aren't offended because I made some remarks implying that women are no good at practical tasks, are you? If you are, I'm sorry, I was only teasing.'

'No, I'm not offended. Not really. Besides, you were right. I wasn't doing it properly. Men know about things like using a longer-handled spanner, women don't. I don't, anyway.' Harriet was talking too fast and her voice sounded strange and breathless to her own ears. She was trying to shut out the knowledge of Peter's nearness, which suddenly seemed very dangerous. She hurried on. 'I'm not a total dunce, but I admit that there are some areas where I can't compete with a man. Maybe it's because nobody ever expects a woman to be mechanically minded. Maybe if men didn't rush in so fast to put us right we'd get things sorted out for ourselves eventually . . .'

'Harriet,' said Peter, quietly. 'Shut up.'

Harriet was so startled that she did as she was told. She tried to turn away, but Peter took hold of her arms just above the elbows and held her facing him.

'That's better. Now, what are we going to do about this?' he asked.

'About what?' said Harriet feebly.

'You know.'

Harriet looked up into his brown eyes and accepted that she knew.

'I've wanted to do this for a long time,' Peter told her, some time later, when he had paused in the kissing of Harriet for long enough to allow for some conversation. 'At first in Vienna, but you went before I summoned the nerve to try it. Then I heard you were with that other man, Laura's stepbrother. And after I met you again last year I had the impression that these days you're not really interested in men, or not in me, at any rate. You're always so brisk and businesslike.'

'I didn't think you were interested in *me*,' Harriet countered. Her heart was thudding and she couldn't decide whether this was because she was frightened by what was happening to her or deliriously happy, but it felt like the latter. True, allowing yourself to fall in love was a recipe for disaster, but at this moment it seemed worth it.

In the days that followed they had snatched moments together and thought that nobody noticed. It was Laura who punctured that delusion.

'So you and Peter have finally realized what everyone around you has known for months,' she said. 'I must say it's a great relief to the bystanders!'

Kitty Marshall was expecting a baby. Daisy, normally so sensitive to such things, was taken by surprise when Kitty told her. In the years that Kitty and Billy had been married, their ongoing childlessness had become a subject that you didn't talk about. Daisy, who'd had experience of Louella's private anguish, knew better than to ask if Kitty was thinking

568

of a family, and even Allie Briggs had given up asking awkward questions. Now here was Kitty growing rounder by the day and visibly thriving on it, like a plant that's grown in too much shade and has been newly moved into the sunshine.

Billy glowed about it too. He seemed to have grown an inch taller, Daisy told Will. 'I wonder what happened? I mean, I know it's none of my business, but after all this time, for them to have suddenly hit lucky . . . I wonder what's changed?'

Kitty could have told her. Somehow the death of Jem Wilkins had freed Billy of a burden. Perhaps, having witnessed her anguish when Jem left her, he had unconsciously thought that she could never care for him to the same extent. Perhaps he had believed himself to be only a makeshift husband. But on the night that he confessed his involvement in Jem's death to her, Kitty had been able to convince him that she really loved him and that Jem, the spectre of his nightmare, did not matter to her at all. The baby was the seal on their happiness.

The Marshalls' patch of sunlight was not typical of the mood of the nation. The false optimism created by Chamberlain's piece of paper, brought back from Munich, had disappeared and in its place was a grim foreboding. There would be a war with Germany, that much was clear. The only question was, when?

Peter told Harriet, 'I've already decided that I won't be a part of it. Not as a fighting man, anyway. I'm a member of the Society of Friends, you see. A Quaker. I've taken something called a "Peace Testimony". That means I've vowed not to take up arms against any of my fellow men, no matter what the provocation. I'll be a Conscientious Objector.'

It was the first time that Peter had talked about his faith and it left Harriet uncertain how to react. Like any other girl of her background she'd had a Christian upbringing. She had gone to church, sung the hymns and said the prayers without really thinking about what she was doing. For Peter it was different.

'I agree that war is dreadful,' Harriet said. 'But surely sometimes there's no choice? Look at what the Nazis are doing in Vienna, to the people who are your friends?'

'Yes, it's terrible. It has to be resisted. But for me, there has to be some other way of resisting than flocking to take part in wholesale battles that involve the slaughter of thousands of innocents.

'Look at the Great War. Millions were killed – millions of mothers' sons. Germans, Russians, French and Belgians, troops of all the nations involved . . . how many of them were truly the enemy? How many were just ordinary folk like you and me, sucked into something they didn't choose and couldn't control? James and I have talked about this. He was a flying ace, you know, with medals for bravery. But he told me that if he'd had the nerve he would have been a Conschie himself.'

But in the face of Nazi aggression, Harriet wanted to point out, *last year James had joined the Air Force Volunteer Reserve*.

'Would you stop loving me if I did declare myself a Conscientious Objector?' Peter asked. 'If people pointed at me in the street and called me a coward?'

'No,' said Harriet. 'I don't think I could ever stop loving you. And I know you're not a coward.'

Etched in her mind for ever was that image of him in Vienna, walking into danger.

Now Peter was going back to Austria.

'This could be the last trip, the way things are going,' he said.

This was what loving somebody cost you, Harriet reminded herself: this sharp pain that tore at your heart.

'Take me with you,' she said.

'No. It's too dangerous.'

The situation in Vienna was desperate for the Jews. Daily the people who were still waiting for visas disappeared, to concentration camps or into hiding. The details of the

570

children on Peter's list now had a special urgency: 'Father arrested last month; nothing is known of his fate. Mother ill. Grandparents who are caring for this child are in daily fear that they will be taken to a concentration camp.'

Some of Peter's contacts had been arrested. It was thought that his credentials as a foreign journalist would make him safe, but for how long could that be relied on? Strutting, confident in their power, the Nazis were careless of international opinion and, increasingly, they did what they wanted in Europe.

'I don't care about the danger,' Harriet told Peter.

'I do,' he said. 'Try to understand, darling. By myself I can take risks: I couldn't bear to take those same risks with your safety.' After days of arguing, on the eve of his departure he produced his trump card. 'In any case, it's too late now for you to get a visa.'

Defeated, Harriet went to the station to see him off. They were early and waited together on the platform.

'What are you thinking?' Peter asked her, holding her left hand between both his own.

'I was looking at all these other women around us, hurrying to meet trains or take journeys . . . Wondering whether it'll be the same for them soon as it is for me now: saying goodbye to someone they love and praying he'll come back,' Harriet said with a catch in her voice.

'I'll come back,' said Peter. 'I'll come back,' he repeated. 'And until I do . . . I've been thinking this left hand of yours is a bit bare. Would you wear this for me?'

He dug into his trouser pocket and produced a ring: a gold ring with a small, sparkling diamond set in the centre of the shank. 'It's nothing much,' he said.

Harriet let him slip the ring on the third finger of her left hand. It was too big and she closed her fingers to stop it slipping off.

'I've done this wrong,' said Peter. 'I ought to have had a measurement, or taken you with me or something.'

'It doesn't matter. I can have it made smaller. It's a lovely ring,' said Harriet. He bent his head to kiss her, but briefly

571

because the train had come in. Now they were jostled apart by other travellers.

When the train had gone Harriet walked back to the house in Blackheath which she still thought of as belonging to Aunt Louella, though it was hers now. Just for tonight she could not bear to be alone in the shabby lodgings in Kew, near the office. Everett and Rose, Cook and Alice, still ran the house as if Louella had only slipped out for afternoon tea and would be back soon. For her sake they would keep her niece company.

When Harriet woke up next morning in the little bedroom at the top of the house which had been hers when she was small, she heard birdsong from the apple trees in the walled garden outside. It reminded her of being at home at Welcome Farm, and of a song that she had learned at school, gathered round the piano in the hall: '*And the larks they sang melodious at the dawning of the day . . .*'

Lying under the bedclothes she sang the words softly to herself, surprised by how much she remembered. How did it finish?

And if ever I return again,
And if ever I return again,
And if ever I return again,
I will make you my bride . . .

That morning was the last day of August. Next day Nazi troops invaded Poland. It was one act of aggression too many and two days later, Britain was at war with Germany.

'What news is there of Peter?' Harriet demanded at the office. His ring was still on her finger, held on by a twist of thread to make it fit tighter.

'None, yet,' said Laura.

'Surely they'll let him go? A foreign journalist?'

'Nothing is sure.'

After three days, Harriet couldn't bear to wait in London,

where an air raid siren had sounded just as Chamberlain finished his broadcast to the nation, announcing the declaration of war. Laura was almost frantic with worry herself, not just over Peter's situation but also because at any time James might be called up for the Air Force Reserve, and because their son Edward, away at boarding school, would reach an age for fighting if the war didn't end soon. It was, moreover, a blow for the Peace Pledge Union, on whose behalf she had campaigned tirelessly until Peter's activities with the Kinder Transport movement had distracted her. But partly because Harriet's listless misery moved her to pity and partly in an attempt to remove herself from the grim realities, Laura offered to drive her young friend down to see her parents at Welcome Farm.

'Terrible times we live in,' was Allie Briggs' greeting. 'Just when you think the world's learned some sense we're back in the same old mess again. And it couldn't have come at a worse time – Kitty and Billy were so happy about their little 'un that's on the way. But that's happiness for you: here today, gone tomorrow.'

Daisy was in the kitchen as usual, making rabbit-pie for dinner. If the world were to end tomorrow, Harriet thought with a gush of nostalgia that almost choked her, Daisy would still be in the kitchen, making rabbit-pie.

'Hullo, Mum. Where's Dad?'

'Out with the horses.'

Will was in the stable block, grooming Charlotte, one of the two matched Shires that made up his ploughing team. Harriet stood inside the doorway at the end of the block and watched him as, unaware of an audience, he brushed steadily at the mare's neck and chest, the brush tracing the direction of the hair as it spiralled. He was being careful, as he was in everything he did, smiling his lopsided smile which showed up the scar on his chin where the tractor had once thrown up a flint that cut him.

She'd been four or five years old then, and she could still remember him walking into the farmhouse with the blood flowing from the cut, and her own frightened reaction. He'd picked up one of Daisy's laundered tea towels and staunched the blood with one hand, and with his free arm he'd gathered up the little girl and hugged her. 'Don't worry, puss, it's only a bit of blood.'

And sitting astride his hip, held in the circle of that reassuring arm, Harriet had felt safe again – the same way she felt, she realized, when Peter Morris held her.

Will glanced up and saw her. He didn't stop what he was doing, but his smile included her. She moved to stand beside him.

'Hullo, Dad,' she said. When he had finished brushing Charlotte she reached up and kissed his cheek above the scarred chin. 'I just wanted to say I love you, and thanks for being my father.'

'What's this, then?' Sharp eyed, Will had spotted her ring. He captured her hand and held it up for closer scrutiny. 'Does this mean what these things used to mean when I was your age?'

'Yes. I'm engaged to be married, to someone I love very much.'

'Have I met this young man of yours?'

'Not yet. I was going to bring him down, but he had to go away. Oh, Dad . . .' Suddenly Harriet's control broke and she was crying. 'He's in Austria. And now we're at war and he may never get out. I might never see him again.'

But Peter, having made an eleventh-hour border crossing from Austria into Germany and thence into Holland, had successfully scrounged a passage on a Dutch boat sailing for Harwich and at that moment was queuing at Waterloo for a ticket to Bentley in Hampshire. There, according to James Allingham, he would find a place called Welcome Farm and a girl named Harriet Griffin.

THE END

A DISTANT DREAM
by Margaret Graham

It is 1920 and Caithleen Healy, as beautiful and spirited as her Irish homeland, dreams of fighting back against the Black and Tans, and of avenging her mother's brutal death. Unsure how best to serve Ireland's cause, Caithleen turns to her childhood sweetheart, Mick O'Brian, who shows her the way: she must strike up a friendship with an English Auxiliary and distract him from the work of the Volunteers. But the young soldier Caithleen must betray is a decent man. Ben Williams believes her tender words, and all too soon Caithleen finds herself believing them too.

Determined to escape the Troubles, Ben leaves Ireland and heads for Australia. And soon Caithleen follows him, fleeing her home to help save Mick O'Brian's life. But her hopes for a happy future are shortlived, for both Mick and Ben, each believing himself to have been betrayed by her, abandon Caithleen.

In the dust and heat of the Australian gold mines, Caithleen becomes Kate, turning her back on Ireland and forging a new life for herself. Yet the echoes of past treachery resound still. For as the years go by, and Kate begins to prosper, the figure of Mick O'Brian, as embittered and impulsive as ever, returns to make her pay once more the price of betrayal.

'Margaret Graham has a sure and delicate touch'
Good Housekeeping

A Bantam Paperback
0 553 40818 6

A SELECTION OF FINE NOVELS
AVAILABLE FROM BANTAM BOOKS

50329 4	**DANGER ZONES**	*Sally Beauman*	£5.99
40727 9	**LOVERS AND LIARS**	*Sally Beauman*	£5.99
40803 8	**SACRED AND PROFANE**	*Marcelle Bernstein*	£5.99
40497 0	**CHANGE OF HEART**	*Charlotte Bingham*	£4.99
40890 9	**DEBUTANTES**	*Charlotte Bingham*	£5.99
40296 X	**IN SUNSHINE OR IN SHADOW**	*Charlotte Bingham*	£4.99
40496 2	**NANNY**	*Charlotte Bingham*	£4.99
40171 8	**STARDUST**	*Charlotte Bingham*	£4.99
40163 7	**THE BUSINESS**	*Charlotte Bingham*	£5.99
40895 X	**THE NIGHTINGALE SINGS**	*Charlotte Bingham*	£5.99
17635 8	**TO HEAR A NIGHTINGALE**	*Charlotte Bingham*	£5.99
40072 X	**MAGGIE JORDAN**	*Emma Blair*	£4.99
40298 6	**SCARLET RIBBONS**	*Emma Blair*	£4.99
40615 9	**PASSIONATE TIMES**	*Emma Blair*	£4.99
40614 0	**THE DAFFODIL SEA**	*Emma Blair*	£4.99
40373 7	**THE SWEETEST THING**	*Emma Blair*	£4.99
40996 4	**GOING HOME TO LIVERPOOL**	*June Francis*	£4.99
40820 8	**LILY'S WAR**	*June Francis*	£4.99
40818 6	**A DISTANT DREAM**	*Margaret Graham*	£5.99
40817 8	**LOOK WITHIN YOUR HEART**	*Margaret Graham*	£5.99
40730 9	**LOVERS**	*Judith Krantz*	£5.99
40731 7	**SPRING COLLECTION**	*Judith Krantz*	£5.99
40206 4	**FAST FRIENDS**	*Jill Mansell*	£4.99
40612 4	**OPEN HOUSE**	*Jill Mansell*	£4.99
40938 7	**TWO'S COMPANY**	*Jill Mansell*	£5.99
40947 6	**FOREIGN AFFAIRS**	*Patricia Scanlan*	£4.99
40945 X	**FINISHING TOUCHES**	*Patricia Scanlan*	£5.99
40482 2	**A WOMAN OF PLEASURE**	*Arabella Seymour*	£4.99
40483 0	**SINS OF THE MOTHER**	*Arabella Seymour*	£4.99